# Worldwide Praise

*"John Patric.*

*... This writing is what being brave is all about.*
*It brings up the kinds of things that are usually kept so private that you think*
*you're the only one who experiences them."*
– Gay Times, London

*"'Barely Legal' is a great potpourri ... and the coverboy is gorgeous!"*
– Ian Young, Torso magazine

*"A huge collection of highly erotic, short and steamy one-handed tales.*
*Perfect bedtime reading, though you probably won't get much sleep!*
*Prepare to be shocked! Highly recommended!"*
– Vulcan magazine

*"Tantalizing tales of porn stars, hustlers, and other lost boys ... John Patrick*
*set the pace with 'Angel!'"*
– The Weekly News, Miami

*" ... Some readers may find some of the scenes too explicit; others will enjoy*
*the sudden, graphic sensations each page brings. Each of these Romans clef*
*is written with sustained intensity. 'Angel' offers a strange, often poetic*
*vision of sexual obsession. I recommend it to you."*
– Nouveau Midwest

*"Self-absorbed, sexually-addicted bombshell Stacy flounced onto the scene*
*in 'Angel' and here he is again, engaged in further, distinctly 'non-literary'*
*adventures ... lots of action!"*
— Prinz Eisenherz Book Review, Germany

*"'Angel' is mouthwatering and enticing..."*
– Rouge Magazine, London

*"'Superstars' is a fast read ... if you'd like a nice round of fireworks before*
*the Fourth, read this aloud at your next church picnic ..."*
— Welcomat, Philadelphia

*"For those who share Mr. Patrick's appreciation for cute young men,*
*'Legends' is a delightfully readable book ... I am a fan of John Patrick's ...*
*His writing is clear and straight-forward and should be better known in the*
*gay community."*
– Ian Young, Torso Magazine

In the still of the night,
As darkness descends,

An unrelenting desire fills the soul.

# BOYS
# OF THE
# NIGHT

## A New Collection of Erotic Tales Edited By

## JOHN PATRICK

STARbooks Press
Herndon, VA

First Edition Published in the U.S. in September 1996
Second Edition Published in the U.S. in September 2006
Library of Congress Card Catalogue No. 95-07244
ISBN No. 1-877978-82-5

# Contents

# Editor's Note

AS NIGHT FELL ...

"Then, there was sex. It was never spoken of during daylight hours, but as night fell, the stars and the flashlights came out, and we stripped naked in our summer sleeping bags and took turns. It was manual, it was mutual masturbation, partners were interchangeable, and the events amounted to meaningless, mindless rounds of primitive gratification. It seemed almost an out-of-body experience, ephemeral as a mirage, when recollected the next morning in full daylight.

"I often ask myself which came first, the tendencies to desire homoerotic activities or the seduction of one uncommitted boy by another?

"For me, the egg of desire for the same sex came first, but for the others it's hard to tell. Two of these boys are now practicing homosexuals. One is heterosexual. I have lost touch with the others."

– Christopher Shyer, "Not Like Other Boys"

\* \* \*

" ... Quickly you go into thick velvet night the waiting world barring from me your most exquisite beauty."

– Christopher Maynard

# Introduction: Deep into the Night

"Back when man was stumbling around the dusty savannas figuring out the best way to surprise woolly mammoths, he found his experience divided sharply between night and day," James Ireland Baker says in Time Out magazine. "In the light he was a naked animal, prey to those greater than him; but once darkness fell he became a god. Under the star-pierced sky with flaming torches smearing his vision and armies of drummers hammering out a relentless beat, he ingested sacred roots and berries, abandoned the taboos of waking life, welcomed the spirits to his table, and joined his sisters and brothers in the dance."

And no matter how times change, some things remain the same.

For instance, John Rechy, in Sexual Outlaw, describes a typical night in Los Angeles' Griffith Park, circa 1976: "Jim gets out of his car, climbs the short path, and enters the sex-charged silence along the trees. As always, he moves to where there are no others at first–along the rim of a path leading to a cave of leaves. He enters it. Two men are fucking.

"Jim moves through thickening mist, past darkening shadows of hunters. Sexsighs waft the woody area. No one stops now to another's approach, no one even pauses in the acts. This is their underground among crushed leaves. Hunters' expert eyes will soon penetrate the rapidly falling dark, finding each other. Without a word, bodies move in a silent symphony.

Jim is contained now in a cluster of hands, mouths, cocks.

"Entering his car to drive out of the park, he sees two men in cutoffs leading two young handcuffed outlaws to an unmarked cop car.

"At that moment Jim knows his hunt will continue deep into the night."

One special night over a decade later, Sean Frye found himself in a back alley somewhere in West Hollywood. Here's his report:

New Year's Eve, 1988: 2:00 A.M. ... Trying desperately to look casual, and yet hurrying so as not to be seen, I saunter down the steep incline of a dark, wet driveway into a dimly lit subterranean parking lot. Quietly, I stand in the corner alongside the trash bin–how appropriate.

Crunch, crunch goes whatever it is beneath the size twelve Cochran tip Paratrooper's boots that slink down the driveway behind me. In contrast to his well-worn, butch attire, the boy in the boots looks quite the little prince actually, very collegiate cherry. However, he's got that unmistakable, tiny "tweak" that betrays a very long, hard seventy-two hours of drugs and sex– ah yes, the little prince is on a binge, just like me.

Crunch, crunch, crunch. Someone follows.

"As if!" I think to myself, sizing-up the Mr. Gucci-loafered Troll Daddy stumbling down the driveway after the two of us. Don't ya hate when that

happens? Just when you're ready to go in for the kill. Sheesh, can't he find another forest to wander through? "Go away" I try indicating to Daddy with my eyes. The college boy seems receptive to his presence, though–visibly cold from too much lurking. He is obviously seeking an indoor affair. Oh well, I'm sure Troll Daddy has a nice condo somewhere between here and Numbers–a warm place to play.

"What's your name?" boy asks Daddy enthusiastically.

"Steve," says Daddy.

"No way, that's my name", the boy exclaims with misplaced excitement over this "coincidence."

Oh please.

"And you ..." Daddy asks, focuses on me with his tired eyes, "what's your name?"

"Steve," I hiss at him. "Let's keep it simple."

Back at Troll-nando's Hideaway the three of us reenact Caligula on Daddy's colossal sheepskin that is placed strategically in front of his fireplace. Pictures of Daddy with President Reagan, and, better yet, with Nancy, decorate his opulent mantle piece–in much the same way our "host" decorated her bathroom in Bel Air, to be sure. The fire roars. Between trips to his mirrored wet bar for an occasional nip of Bushmills whiskey and amyl nitrate, and increasingly more frequent trips to his guest bathroom (drugs maybe? "Stay-Hard" ointment, more than likely), Daddy tries his best to service and please us.

Our "host" for the evening really goes ravenous, rolling over for anything like the dog in heat that he is. Without even the slightest appetite for anyone or anything, I go through the lurid motions, topping off every orifice offered me.

What the fuck am I doing here?

My thoughts float elsewhere. Ima Sumac howls in the distance from Daddy's ten-thousand-dollar stereo system. I mindlessly plow into the twisted, naked bodies before me ...

Another ten years pass, and across the American continent, sex hunter Chris Leslie, publisher of Dirty magazine, had never been to what is popularly known as "the Rambles," in Central Park, so he decided to finally check out this mainstay of public night sex. "Unfortunately," Chris says, "we decided to go there by our lonesome, without a friend to help us find it! Dumb, dumb, dumb. We were told that it was near Seventy-Ninth Street, on the West Side of Central Park. With only that information, we set out to find it. We wandered around in the dark for an hour before we even saw another person–and in this case, it was three cute homeboys drinking and playing in a playground. At first we thought that we had struck gold–cute rough boys in the Ramble!–but it turned out that they weren't cruising.

"So after not finding anything we went out to the street and saw a bunch of queens-in-training hanging out; one yelled at us that he thought we were cute. We knew we were getting close.

"We sat down on a bench to rest, and a drug-dealer type also sitting on a bench started checking us out; after he fucked us in a secluded part of the park that was not the Ramble with a red condom, we asked him if he knew where we should go. He gave us a look that said he should have been more than enough for us and told us he didn't know exactly but it was 'over there.'

"Right.

"So after walking around some more, this cute black guy roller-blading on the main road 'let' us quietly suck his dick under a bridge. We say quietly because there was a bunch of homeless people sleeping there and he didn't want to disturb them. It took him forever to cum and when he did it was just a few drops; we suppose he just roller-blades around all night and gets sucked off until he collapses from exhaustion. But in a moment of passion he said, 'Yeah, suck that fuckin' big black dick you stupid white faggot,' which amused us because despite his skin color he was whiter than us (and despite our proclivity to suck dick, he was a bigger fag, too).

"So while we were sucking dick we saw a lot of police patrols, and we knew we were even getting closer since we had been all over the park and that was the only place police were patrolling.

"We then saw an older man carrying a Gap bag, and knowing that older men carrying Gap bags is almost as good as men walking their dogs as an indicator of sex areas, we followed him. He took us down a few trails and over a bridge and then all of a sudden we saw a sign that said 'The Ramble.'

"Yes, girl, there's a sign! But we'll be dammed if we can tell you how to find it. Ask your friends or, if all else fails, you can do what we did: suck dick until you get there.

"But we're not really sure if it was worth all the effort; there were a lot of gay men there to be sure but they were all friends and their intentions seemed to be more to socialize than to get busy. But a few guys were there who were cute and into it–we suppose as the weather gets warmer, there will be a lot more action there. We also have heard that the place is busy there during the day, but it's kind of hard to find somewhere to go when you actually meet someone."

Finding somewhere to go is no problem for most of today's Boys of the Night, be they Club Kids, boys out for fun, or hustlers. The cruising scene in today's clubs is described most succinctly by Matthew Rettenmund in this excerpt from his best-seller, Boy Culture:

... Joe flailing with abandon, looking like an old man's fever dream, a juicy little Monster in rubber and boots and a dick-sock. The lights are flashing mechanically, an intricate engine-like panel of hot young sprockets

dancing with the same precise electricity. Their desire is their lubricant; their limbs are their gears. Raves at Boykultur have a way of turning into orgies.

Joe is always the center of attention. Why not? He's extremely young and looks it, he's a natural blonde with a head full of teeth, and he has all the membership credentials for a fun date: He's got the head of hair, the pout, the beads, the biceps, the corn-fed ass, the rhythm, the inviting eyes. Except at a particularly hot rave, Joe is no hotter than the next little boy; they all look the same to their older peers who have graduated from being club kids into being the studs who make the club kids' hearts flutter.

So Joe does what he has to, to keep himself the center of attention. He smiles extra-wide. He winks. He exposes more of himself than is legal. He will give head to a man in a back room within plain sight of everyone just to stay popular.

Joe sees a guy looking at him–no major deal, except the guy has something about him that makes Joe look twice. The stranger is staring openly, gazing at Joe with an astonishing urge. He is taller than Joe, broader, with big, strong, generic arms. He is built to last, has dark, curly hair, and probably shaves his chest, which is partially exposed, a simple sterling silver cross beaming from a pierced nipple on the beginnings of an assembly-line pec. He is "swarthy." My grandmother would call him "an ethnic." Joe would call him a god.

God smiles menacingly at Joe, shaking His head to the music to emphasize how fierce He would be with Joe if given the chance. He moves His hips from his position flattened against the wall, communicating the thrusts He would use to demolish Joe, to pin him to the bed like a pretty little butterfly, caught, its wings forced apart, nailed into a monstrous child's glass display case.

Joe breaks from his friends and dances over to God and fondles His nipple-cross lasciviously. "It's nice," he says blandly. "I like it."

"I bet you do."

A half hour later, they are in God's car. It's parked beside the bar, so the ponderous rumbling of techno is heard through the wall.

"Today," Baker notes in Time Out, "despite such advances as gene therapy and on-line services, we still have a need for pagan communion. More than ever do we feel compelled to escape our workaday lives and enter the warm cocoon of nighttime ritual. And though the tribal signifiers have changed over the years–masks and drums traded up for coke spoons, multiple piercings and tent-like canvas pants–the same spirits remain in possession of the night.

"After dark, New York's clubs make the city like no other place on earth. If your stamina and wallet are equal to the experience, you can visit three or four different worlds every night."

One of the most popular such places at the moment is Bump! at Palladium, where gay party promoter Marc Berkley holds sway.

"I've slept with maybe 10 percent of the people in this room," Berkley declares, perhaps proving Henry Kissinger's theory that power is the ultimate aphrodisiac. Berkley, 42, is arguably the single most significant force in contemporary queer nightlife. And his career, which started when he was hired by a club as a publicist, has lasted nearly 15 years.

"Marc!" shouts a shirtless, sun-kissed porn star with a black eye, stopping Berkley to explain the origin of his shiner: an altercation at the Black Party.

"I had a three-way with him," Berkley says cheerfully as we leave the star behind.

Berkley's carnal confessions won't do much to change his reputation as a sleaze merchant. He was one of the first promoters to incorporate backroom sex into a mainstream club (Lick It! at Limelight). "I do promote sex," he says. "I promote safe sex, because that is a big part of the gay community, but one of the false rumors about me is that I sleep with everybody, like with my go-go boys. I've had sex with some of them, sure, just like co-workers anywhere sometimes do. But if you're paying a go-go boy a hundred dollar a shift just to sleep with him, you're pretty desperate." He laughs. "I'd rather buy somebody for a hundred dollars."

Buying somebody is, of course, a part of nightlife that cannot be denied. Here again, the scene really hasn't changed all that much. In Basketball Diaries, Jim Carroll recalls night cruising in the Manhattan of 1965:

"If there were, say, a book like 'The Pervert's Guide To New York City,' the bathroom at Grand Central Terminal should, without any doubts, figure in it. The bathrooms in the subways themselves are bad enough, but at least you've got the Transit fuzz popping in and out of them often enough so the pervies are uptight to directly take a grab at you, but not so at old Grand Central, where anything might go. I was catching a train up to Rye, N.Y. tonight to visit old neighborhood chum Willie at, I'd say, just after five-thirty p.m. Man, all those business cats just lined up along the piss machines (there must be forty machines, whatever the hell you call them, that's right, urinals, lined next to each other) and then along with them the usual seedy dudes, hustlers, etc. and all these eyes peeking down at the guy next to me who's peeking down at me along with the guy on my other side and jacking off like madmen, forty arms like pistons pumping back and forth at incredible rates. Not a bit of class in the entire place, just a bunch of office worker closet queens getting off their rocks before they miss the 5:50. Any of those Westchester housewives that ain't had too much lately can come down here and find out why. But the peeky-boo scene is old hat and that goes on in any john, it's just that here you suddenly feel a hand moving across your leg and grabbing your fucking cock. No raised eyebrows about it from anyone, fuck, I'm beginning to think I'm the only person in the place that came down just for normal body functions. I jumped back in the middle of pissing while this stately chap grabbed me and I wound up spraying all over the Brooks

Brothers number the guy is wearing. I had to move down to another whatever they are to finish it off. Same bit. This cat next to me now I thought for a second was going to pull out a pair of binoculars. It's true, guys even sucking dick down there right in front of other cases if the 'attendant' isn't looking. Shit, what am I gonna do, complain to this 'attendant' about what's happening. He looks like he might pull my jeans down and bugger me on the spot. Besides, rarely these days do I complain about anything.

"The businessmen are the worst, no doubt. And they all have a thing about checking out the young guys. I've seen cats who are probably vice-presidents of toothpaste firms or shit fighting over the piss machine next to me. This form of flattery will get them nowhere with me. Spades too, they dig getting next to the spades and tuning in on a little black stuff. Don't ever let your kiddie go pee-pee in that joint by himself, and if you do and he comes back up the stairs smiling, I suggest you have a little chat with the boy."

When Jim was about nine he and his friend Kenny would spend a lot of time hanging around the cellar of their apartment house, mostly tossing a ball back and forth or listening to the radio. "The superintendent of the place, Buddy, was a jolly dude who was the laziest bastard on earth but who, when bugged enough, would and could fix anything any tenant had a bitch over. He's an on and off drunk who is totally on lately, so his job seems hanging on pretty thin wire. He digs us though, and let us hang around like the older cats who would play big card games in the boiler room. It was a seedy and dark, smelly place now that I think about it. I guess that's why I dug it. I know these other guys, in fact, that hung around in an old busted down news truck for about two years without once realizing what a boring idea it was.

"This particular day in mind something really strange happened. Kenny and I were flopping around as usual, watching the card game when one of the older guys' younger sisters, Sharron, who was about thirteen and a little funny looking with a lot of make-up, and her friend Lou-Lou, dropped in. After Kevin and I moved into the bigger room, they followed us, watching us play baby baseball for awhile and suggested that we go into the radio room and check it out. We got in there and they immediately suggest that we play a little game that was unfamiliar to both Kenny and me, 'Doctor.' We said great, how's it go? 'Well,' Lou-Lou piped in, 'the game is, in this case, Nurses ... Now you and Kenny take off your pants and Sharron and I give you an examination.' Total mystery to both of us but we follow nurse's orders and drop our little jeans. Kevin peeked over at me and I peeked over at him and realizing our young pricks were more or less the same size we gave cool smiles. The two girls gave cool smiles too, in fact, they immediately whipped off their dresses to even things out, and they literally did 'even things out' cause I knew girls were different than boys in that sense and that's what was ..."

In Winston Leyland's new anthology Partings at Dawn, the Japanese author Hiruma Hisao demonstrates that no matter where you go, the traditional sex-for-hire transaction with a boy of the night stays pretty much the same:

The man was a member of the Self-Defense forces. He'd felt restless and irritable late that night and had rushed out of his barracks. He came to the same part of town he'd gone to just once before and bought a boy. Anyone would do, though in fact he'd chosen a quiet, gentle-looking kid. The man chose one of the hotels the bar-manager suggested: it was one of the lowest even among that class of place, its walls reeking with the smell of semen.

As soon as they got into the room, the man said, "I'll pay in advance," and handed the boy a ten thousand yen note. He didn't have much money, though he was already well into his thirties. The boy made no effort to hide his disappointment as he took the money. Why should he? A guy couldn't feel much enthusiasm for his work when he knew he was only going to get the minimum amount. And the man had taken him out for the night, so this ten thousand yen would be his whole day's wages. The man didn't look like the sort of rich customer who'd give a nice tip afterwards, either. No, there was nothing more discouraging than to know in advance just what your reward would be–and, in this case, such a poor reward.

The kid had sex with the man, doing just the minimum. He let him touch his body, minimally. He pleasured him, minimally. You couldn't expect super service for ten thousand yen, after all. That was just cold common sense in this world of the selling-bars. Even as they were going at it on the bed, the boy was trying to think of some excuse to leave and go back to, the bar. Same as always. The man didn't really care much about the sex. He just couldn't stand being alone in his room any longer. He hadn't expected much from the boy. It had been the same with the first one. That one had stunned the man his constant harping on "money, money." The man had stopped coming to this part of town after that.

After they'd had sex, the man flopped down on the bed. He felt no emotion, no pleasure. The kid made no particular effort to clean up the mess they'd made of the bed, and asked coolly if he could take a shower. "It's nothing but business to them," the man thought angrily, but he closed his eyes and nodded yes. While the kid was gone, he took a yukata and wiped the semen from his body. Now for some sleep. The thought made him feel a bit more relaxed. When the boy came out of the bathroom, a towel around his hips, he went and sat on the sofa instead of coming back to the bed. He started to smoke, with the look of someone who'd just finished a task of some sort. He was thinking about how he could free himself of this man.

"So, what kind of work do you do?" he asked in a bored way.

The man saw no point in lying. "I'm in the Self-Defense Forces."

"Oh yeah?" And here the boy really looked at the man for the first time. He seemed to show some interest. The boy liked to talk. And not pillow-talk

either, but the kind of serious topics that didn't match the occasion at all well. It's a fairly common trait m boys of his age, who are all eager to deal with the world in words. The "intellectual" seems very attractive to them at that stage. And they itch to show off their own intellectuality (half-baked, to be sure) when they have the chance. They want to voice their opinions, to show they're "different from all the others." They want to blow their own horns a bit, so as to be noticed. And It seemed that this urge was much stronger than usual in this particular boy. Naturally enough, too, his curiosity about the unknown was just as strong. The boy went on asking the man various questions. The man didn't really feel much like talking. But when it came to questions about his work, he didn't mind so much, and gave casual, careless answers. The boy's questions ranged from the sensational to the ideological, all jumbled together higgledy-piggledy. It was only natural, since he was just saying whatever popped into his head. "Is it true there're lots of guys who like this kind of stuff in the Self-Defense Forces?"

"Yeah, I suppose it is. There's nothing but guys in there, after all."

"And is the Emperor, like, absolute to you guys?"

"Right. I'm ready to lay down my life at any moment on His Majesty's orders. Or on the orders of my superior officers. If there was a coup d'etat I'd be ready to kill the Prime Minister himself."

In the middle of this dialogue, the man motioned the boy to come back to bed. The boy did as he was told, but he kept right on talking. (There was a reason for this: he hoped to ward off sleep by continuing to talk, and so find a chance to escape.) When the man had answered a question, the boy would aggressively offer his own opinion on the matter. Feeling more and more sure of himself, the boy failed to notice the effect this was having on the other. The end result was that the man got furious, and the boy was half-strangled into silence.

The boy didn't say a thing after that; he clammed right up. Then, around four in the morning, he asked the man to let him leave. He had to get back home before his parents woke up–that was his lame excuse. "Shut your gob and stay till the fuckin' morning!" the man shouted.

"So, he's lonesome. He's afraid to be left alone," thought the boy. Nevertheless, about an hour later when he was sure the man was sound asleep, the boy slipped from the bed, put on his clothes and snuck out of the hotel. He knew all too well how desolate and angry the man would be when he awoke, alone, in the morning; but he didn't care: he just wanted to get out. He was still oppressed by the fear that had gripped him as the man gripped his neck. "If he'd squeezed a little harder, I'd be dead now. The guy's a master of killing-techniques, that's for sure." This thought revived the boy's terror. How could he ever go to sleep here? And the sight of the man snoring there beside him made him angry as well. He hated him so much he felt he couldn't stand to spend another second with him. And so he left, even though he knew there might be problems later with the bar. All he wanted to do was go back to the bar, relax, and chat with the others. Then,

too, there was the hope of earning a little more in what remained of the night.

The kid had been knocked down and out by a thing called violence, by a thing called power. That's all there was to it: no need for further explanation. But if the reader wants a nice moral lesson from all this, it might be that sex became impossible for him in that situation of real humiliation–even though it was to experience precisely that that he had come to this part of town in the first place. You see, don't you? Even as he did this kind of work–this much-despised, limp-wristed "faggot" work–he still had something of the "male's" cheap pride. (No, not cheap, really. For if it were, why would he feel so down and out?) How could anyone be expected to enjoy taking it up the ass while being so totally humiliated, shamed even to the point of death? No, that wasn't an experience open to anyone who was not a born masochist, or a guy of the most tough-hearted courage.

And yet if the man's member had not shriveled, if the boy had been raped by brute force (though it seems a bit odd to speak of a man being "raped") ...

The thought of this quite natural sequel to the events of that night remained with the boy, as a kind of yearning. And if the boy had been raped, perhaps this narrative would have turned into something more interesting. If it had happened, perhaps the boy would have turned out quite differently.

And, to add just one more point, we should note that the boy made tremendous efforts after that to cure the vice of argumentativeness, of talking back, of saying more than was needful in hotel rooms. After all, it wasn't to engage in such talk that the customers went to the trouble of buying the boys. And it was a negative factor for the boys as well: it was only the sweet words of love that could be reduced to hard cash. Besides, the boy had begun to feel that "intellect" was something to be ashamed of. For no matter how big you talked, no matter how plausible the opinions you expressed, you could always be silenced by someone else's violence. It was simple, direct, and instantly effective, like twisting a baby's wrist. Faced with the truth of man's primitive violence, he was powerless to say a word. "The pen is mightier than the sword." Yeah, we've all heard that saying. But the "pen" had must be a reference to something else. All you men out there, you know what I mean, don't you? As the boy has thought back on what happened, it's all come to seem quite meaningless. It remains inside him, an unresolved problem that he can't get a handle on, even now.

Keith Ridgway describes a typical nighttime encounter in Ireland (in the book Quare Fellas): "He walked down towards the river, not really paying too much attention to where he was going, for the moment at least. He wanted to walk off his meal a little before going back to the public toilets. He decided he would turn down the quays to where the rent boys usually hung around. He just wanted to have a look, perhaps make some eye contact.

"There were only two there that he could see, both leaning against the river wall, facing the street. He slowed his walk down to a stroll as he approached the first of them, a young man in his early twenties with very short hair and a thin moustache. He wore a track-suit top and jeans and was smoking. Their eyes met, briefly.

"The second one was younger, about sixteen or seventeen. He had shoulder-length dark hair and wore a full track-suit. He was quite pretty and smiled easily. 'Ya wouldn't have a cigarette, would ya?' he asked. 'Yeah.'

"'Thanks very much.' He lit it for him and their hands touched. 'That's great, thanks. I was dying. Bleedin' freezin' isn't it?'

"'It is a bit, yeah.'

"'Are you doin' business then?'

"'What do you do?'

"'Anythin' ya want basically, y'know, fifteen quid.' He paused for a reaction. When he didn't get one he added: 'Ya can fuck me for twenty-five. With a condom, like.'

"'Where?'

"'Have you got a place?'

"'No, I don't.'

"'Well we can go to the toilets then.'

"'No, it's too dangerous.'

"The boy looked at him and smiled gently. 'Sure it's added excitement,' he said. They both laughed quietly. 'Isn't that what it's all about?'

"'It probably is. I'll leave it for tonight. I'll see you around.'

"'Alright. Would you have any odds at all?'

"He gave him five pounds because he liked him, and they parted with smiles and a friendly wave, each thinking himself a little richer. He continued on and crossed the next bridge, turning to walk up the way he had come, but on the opposite side of the river. They were building here, huge cranes looming up out of the dark. He looked at them and wondered if they would be all right in the storm. He tried to work out whether, if they fell, they would be tall enough to bridge the river. He thought they probably would. Squash a rent boy.

"He looked across the water just in time to see his friend get into a car. He waited to see if the car would come around his way, but it disappeared down the river, heading towards the sea, making him feel foolish."

Speaking of feeling foolish, Jaime Manrique recalls a memorable night out during a recent trip to Colombia: "We entered one of the barrios populares, one of Barranquilla's poorer neighborhoods. The taxi stopped in front of a house at the corner of an unpaved street. I paid the driver, and we stood in front of a house with its door and windows shut. From inside the house I could hear salsa music playing. The street was dark, and next to the bar was an empty lot full of smelly garbage. "Ramon rang the bell. The door was opened a crack, and when he was recognized we were let in to an empty

room, where two bouncers who looked like heavyweight boxers checked us for weapons. The one checking me put his hand inside my underwear. Ramon made orgasmic sounds as he was searched. When the men were satisfied that we didn't carry weapons, we are admitted. We crossed a series of dim rooms, where men gathered around tables drinking or making out. Then we entered the patio, where the jukebox was playing salsa music. High walls surrounded the patio so that the neighbors could not look in. Multicolored papier-mâché lamps provided the suggestive illumination. The floor was inlaid with tiles in Arabian designs, and in the center of the dance floor there was a lighted Moorish fountain. The tables for the customers were placed against the walls of the corridors, and in the back of the patio, under guava trees, tame parrots and macaws pirouetted about. A profusion of red and yellow hibiscus, the kind that opens for the night and dies at dawn, and bougainvillea in bloom, created a camavalesque garden. We sat at a table, and a barefoot waiter in shorts and wearing a guayabera approached us. Ramon asked for a bottle of rum and Coca-Colas.

"... A young man was doing salsa moves on the dance floor. He wore tight ripped jeans, sneakers, and a T-shirt draped over his muscular torso. With the exception of the people engaged in conversation, everyone was staring at him. The salsero was performing for all of us, so that we could admire his great body and his dancing, but he never, not once, looked up. He danced always looking at his crotch. When the record changed, the dancer joined his friends at a table, and another one replaced him. He, too, danced alone, totally absorbed in the intricacies of his steps. 'Do they always dance by themselves?' I asked.

"'Mostly by themselves,' said Ramon. 'Though sometimes there are two people on the floor, but far apart, with their back to each other.'

"'Why is that?"

"'Darling, have you forgotten?' Ramon said. 'Real men don't dance together. These are working-class boys; they aren't gay.'

"'So why are they here?'

"'For money, carino. These boys are not homos. They just do it for money. They dance to advertise their talents and their baskets. If you like what you see, you go to their tables, buy them a drink, and negotiate a price for the night.'

"'Is this a hustlers' bar?'

"'If you want to be that precise, yes. I prefer. to think about it this way: they have what I want, and I am willing to pay for it. No, people don't come here looking for love, if that's what you're thinking about.'"

But nowadays, if you're looking for love, or just some sex, no matter where in the world you happen to be, you have to look a little harder for it, and you usually find it after dark. In Island People, Coleman Dowell's hero Christopher found a stud standing under a streetlamp: " ... He saw Victor Ramos, standing with one leg encircling a fire hydrant, light from a distant

streetlamp picking his bones clean. He was ostentatiously waiting for a bus; a sign around his neck could not have proclaimed it more clearly, especially to cruising police cars, than did his stance which, despite its leg-looped casualness, wore transience in every line as does a bird's on a telephone wire, with awareness of the hazards of high tension. The image that reached Christopher's brain was multiple, a straticulate cross section of an emotion, spheroidal by virtue of its two poles, ultimately static (it was Christopher who circled the emotion, its restless satellite) because both poles were named 'delivery boy': a delivery boy; a dark gold young man of ideal beauty, a skull; a statue of phallic symbolism (the hydrant between the legs) both lewd and desexed by antiquity, like a temple carving; a person hunted, without explanation, as Christopher had just been; the embodiment of the type through whom Christopher could restore his superiority and toward whom he could, therefore, be benevolent: a delivery boy. Miss Gold (the cat) was spending the night with Christopher's housekeeper, the practice when he went out for the evening. Fear slept. He caught the boy's eye, unsmiling, the game too serious for that. Then, apparently forgetting the exchange, he paused and took a cigarette case from the pocket of his dinner jacket, extracted a cigarette, tapped it on the case (recalling, he saw the movement as calculated to draw attention to the case, which was platinum with a jeweled monogram and a concealed lighter which did not work), and futilely flicked the lighter with the exact degree of impatience to seem to remain entirely private: no drop of self-amusement, with which the knowingly observed indicate the basic good humor of their natures. Back bent over the lighter, Christopher watched with a resurgence of foreboding a shadow advance on the pavement and cover his shoes and mount his ankles like dark secret water. When a lighter snapped under his nose he jumped without pretense at the flame leaping in the dark hand. He drew on the cigarette, loathing its staleness (he carried the case for others, in all senses, and had last filled it in the fall), and expelled a cloud of flat smoke before he again looked at the other's face, finding deep shadow in which two hazy luminosities seemed no more committal nor unbenevolent than a moon divided into twins by capriciously unfocused binoculars.

"It was soon clear that, by lighting Christopher's cigarette, the other had exhausted his part in the pickup, or the part he was willing to play. It was equally plain, because he did not move away, or speak, that he knew there was more to come, and the quality of his waiting bespoke experience at such encounters, which depressed Christopher in some undefined way. Reliving the night, depression took the form of Then and Now, for two reasons: the unresolved and the all-too-plain. He had always kept a special reserve of dislike for those relentless trackers of the virgin experience. Seeing himself among them, he could not find the courage of hypocrisy to make the distinction between their purely physical intent and his own. Chilled by hindsight, the most he could do for himself was to press on, knowing that the door to that room was now permanently ajar and that, sooner or later, he

would have to go back to it, and enter, and take inventory. He moved, the boy following, until the light was on the other's face. Watching him closely, Christopher said, 'Yo estoy muy agradecido,' and ease settled over him at the expected reaction: the quick reappraisal of his clothes, skin color, and hair (the latter a repeated mystery until Victor explained about 'good' and 'bad' hair) by eyes in which a certain deference had been replaced by a like amount of familiarity dimly tinged with tentative contempt. To exorcise the contempt while retaining enough of the familiarity, which was a kind of trust, to make the rest possible: this was the delicate task, differing from case to case, which Christopher felt lifted the moment above the potentially sordid.

"'Here is the end to pretenses.' When he had thrown himself on the sofa he had flung his arms up and back, clasping his hands over his head, resting them against the unprotected surface of a painting. Christopher had thought of the hands sticky with food on the white-lit street of the Chirico; it had been a corner of his fury. Victor opened his hands, palms backward as though to smear the painting, then brought them slowly down to rest, equal partners, precisely sharing, on the perfect hemisphere that swelled at his crotch. His curved palms rode the swell, tightened only enough to reveal how thoroughly his manhood filled his big hands.

"'Now,' he said, and Christopher felt his heart jolted by fear. There was a vacancy between him and Victor that was like the space between quotation marks set in the air; he expected the space to be momentarily filled by the words of the dream that he had not understood and yet understood. 'Quiere que te lo ponga en el roto?' Frantically he felt certain, he had to be certain, that if Victor looked at him, really looked at him, he would be able to read in his eyes without error his mistake about Christopher. There had been what could be called flirtation between them, there had been sexual nuances, but in a sense that Christopher had always known was Lawrentian: that male antagonism has a sexual base, and the more submerged, the more sexual, but
…

"Victor's sigh, loud and disgusted, saved him from what for all he knew might have been some overtness. With relief he saw that Victor's hands were moving, moving away, and then lay at his sides. As though demonstrating the wide possibilities of drama within the 'Now,' he said it again, 'Now.' He proceeded onward without the frightening pauses. 'You ever had a fren' like me, Chris?' His enunciation retreated before his earnestness, consonants dropping by the way. 'Like' was 'l',' or as Christopher saw it, inevitably, 'lie.'

"'You ever had a fren' li' me? I mean, no money exchain hans, liddle loan between fren's, but no pay for talkin'?'

"'No.' He hoped Victor would not say, 'Well, could you?' for the answer–what was the answer?"

Editors at *Drummer* magazine are never at a loss for answers. They say one of the best bets in Manhattan is a place called Hands On: "Around 2 a.m. on Friday nights a good number of the horny men who've spent the night cruising for cock at the Lure head over the Hands On party at the Maze on Tenth Avenue. The late night sex session begins at midnight and usually keeps going heavy until six a.m. Many of the club's patrons take advantage of the clothes check. The group sex here is plentiful and uninhibited. Everyone seems to be having a very good time. Hands On also sponsors Everhard sex parties which require an invitation to get in."

Another popular spot is J's Hangout: "This place stays open after the bars close at 4 a.m. Because this is one of the only after hours gay hangouts, it attracts guys from all different communities. Gay men of all shapes, sizes, ethnicities, ages, and appearances end up here. The common thread seems to be that no one wanted to go home at 4 a.m. They do not sell liquor here, but you may check liquor at the bar.

"Make sure you check your wallet, as there are pickpockets here like at most establishments of this nature. The bathroom ends up seeing the most action, even though employees with flashlights do come in to clear it out regularly."

And speaking of checking your wallet, at the tubs you can check everything at the door. The late, famed writer T.R. Witomski once said, "The tubs are gay life as a classless society; sexual performance is all that matters. Good looks matter less than one might suppose.

" ... Also, there is a certain lessening of standards at the baths: after all, you're not taking any of these people home with you. Tub sex doesn't involve the caring or trust–or the tensions–of relationship sex; it's free from all the qualities that make us human.

" ... The gay baths are dominated by male sexuality. The way gay men behave with each other, a rather crude sexual abruptness, is probably the same way that straight men would act with women if they thought they could get away with it, if they thought women would accept it. There is almost always a pretense of some sort in heterosexuality; straights pretend that their one-night-stands are not one-night-stands. Gay men do not. It is only in male homosexuality that the masculine view of sex is ascendant."

Best of all, T.R. says, most gay bath houses are windowless, almost timeless. "The world does not enter this exclusiveness. The 'private club-ness' makes the rituals all the more exciting: they are forbidden to ordinary people. At the tubs it is always just after midnight."

Just perfect, for all of us boys of the night.

# Sunglasses after Dark

## *John Patrick*

"Hey, how's it going?" He approached my convertible, peering over his dark sunglasses. He was wearing wrinkled khakis that fit snugly at the crotch and a white T-shirt. His longish dark hair was slightly tousled. He had an impish smile. He looked around anxiously and asked where I wanted to go.

I wanted to go to my hotel, with him, if he was willing.

He agreed, for fifty.

As he slid in next to me, I sensed fifty could well be a bargain.

But the sunglasses after dark bothered me.

"Moon too bright?" I asked as I pressed the accelerator.

"What?"

"Your glasses. Moon too bright?"

"Oh, my shades," he said, pulling them off, examining them. "They're new. From France. A guy I know bought 'em for me."

"Cool."

"Yeah," he said, putting them back on, "cool."

A quick thrill surged through me as his hand fell to my thigh. He was unusually friendly for a street hustler, and I didn't want to think about what else he could be. Something about the leer now on his face as he stroked my swelling cock didn't seem to fit, but I was past noticing subtleties.

I had no business out on the street at this hour. I'd had a massage (with a complimentary blowjob) and had a great blowjob and a swift fuck by a kid from Kentucky I met at the Bus Stop bar earlier. Still, I couldn't sleep. And I knew that the boys come out when the Copa begins to close down, so there I was on Route One, cruising. I hadn't found anything of interest and was on my way back to the hotel when I saw this boy ambling along.

"Were you at the Copa?" I asked.

"Shit no," he said, squeezing the shaft of my cock. "I was just out for a stroll."

"Out for a stroll at this hour?"

"Couldn't sleep. Too hot to sleep."

"I can see that." Too hot indeed. He had left my cock and had taken his own out. It was belly-up and beautiful. He noticed where my eyes were and his grin grew as he pried his dick down away from his flat, hairless belly and let it slap back up with an incredible thud.

"Like it?" he asked.

I reached over, stroked it. "Love it."

"The guy that bought me the shades loves it too. He took pictures of it he liked it so much. He says I should make movies."

"He took pictures?"

"Yeah, and now he says he's gonna get a video camera so he can videotape it."

Just the thought made me hard; in fact, I'd never been harder. He said his name was Tommy. I suddenly realized I'd never known a Tommy.

"You got a big dick," he sighed, running his hand along my thigh.

"Never had any complaints."

"Maybe you'd like to pose for him."

I chuckled. "Me? I'm hardly chicken."

"Doesn't matter. He doesn't shoot all of you, just the dick."

"Just the dick?"

"Yeah, just the dick."

Now I was really afraid of what might happen tonight. There was, after all, a full moon. "Let me think about it."

"He lives right over there," he pointed to the right, "off Las Olas."

I'd never had my dick photographed. Once I took Polaroids of it while one of my lovers was sucking it, but nothing like this.

His hand moved back to my bulge. He pulled down the zipper, drew out my erection.

"Oh yeah, Meyer'd love this one." He stroked it. "He loves uncut dicks. He says he'll pay me more if I can get some big uncut ones and here one is."

"He pays you to find cock?"

"Yeah," he said, absorbed in his close examination of my engorged, throbbing tool.

It made a lot of sense, having a boy like this out looking for cock for you.

"What did you wanna do?" he asked.

"What?"

"Tonight. What did you want to do with me?"

I gulp. "I really hadn't thought about it."

"Well, whatever, if you pose for Meyer, I'll go with you for forty. How's that sound?"

I could never resist a $10 discount on a $50 piece of merchandise. "Sounds okay. How long will it take?"

"Not long. I just left there so I'm sure he's still up. He usually stays up for awhile in case I find somebody interesting," he went on, stroking my cock, "and I sure found him a good one tonight."

"Thank you."

"You'll thank me before the night's over, I'll tell you that."

I looked at the clock embedded in the dash. It was four a.m. I hadn't been up this late in years. By all rights, I should've been in my hotel room

sleeping, but there I was, wide awake, crossing the Intra-coastal heading down Las Olas.

The moon grew bright; it hung in the sky clear and close by, surrounded by stars. The dry leaves of the palm trees rustled over our heads as we drove along. Pre-cum oozing from my cock glistened in the moonlight. Tommy wiped it away with his thumb, went on stroking.

We pulled into the driveway of a rambling house nestled in high trees and hanging on the edge of the waterway. On the mail box it said, "Rothstein."

Meyer's large master bedroom was furnished all in white, with white curtains, and a fabulous bed with a firm mattress and a door onto the garden.

Tommy went to the bathroom and Meyer sat on the bed with me, fussing with his camera. I suddenly felt sad. An aging Lothario initiating young males into the secrets of sex, using his camera to entrap them. Nothing new under the sun. But who was this man actually, with a name straight out of a Mafia movie? Where did he get the money that let him buy homes like this in the Isles and spend his time photographing cocks?

"Are you retired?" I asked.

"Oh, no. I work all the time," he shot back and his muscles tensed.

"I mean, were you ever employed? Did you ever work in an office from nine to five?"

"Oh, I tried banking, but it is such a vulgar occupation. All that focus on money, making a buck off every little transaction. The focus of life should be love."

His gaze fell upon Tommy as the boy emerged from the bathroom, a towel wrapped around his waist. There was love in his eyes for Tommy.

Tommy stood before me and I pulled away the towel. He arched his back a little. His nicely cut cock moved closer to my face. I leaned forward and kissed the bullet-shaped knob. The cock twitched slightly. I began licking the head, letting my tongue circle slowly around the crown. The cock began to harden. I slipped the knob in my mouth. My own cock began to stretch and grow again. I did some deep-throating on Tommy's erection, sliding my face forward as much as I could, filling my mouth with it, nudging my lips into his pubic hair before pulling back. A couple of times I slipped him out of my mouth so that Meyer's camera could catch the glistening, seven-inch rod in all it's glory. Then, without much warning, the kid was coming, his legs spasming slightly as his jism splashed on my chest. Meyer zoomed in for a close-up of the puddle. Tommy dropped to his knees on the floor and unzipped my trousers. I stood up and he took my place on the edge of the bed. His mouth went to my cock and, playing to the camera, he began to suck it. He spent considerable time nibbling the foreskin to Meyer's direction. Soon, my hips bucking and jerking, cum was shooting out of my cock. Meyer captured on film a puny puddle on Tommy's cheek. After all, I came twice today (or was it yesterday by now?).

Our photo session was accompanied by the droning of the air-conditioning, as if there were a giant bug buzzing in the room with us. The sound was regularly punctuated by the ringing of the telephone. The answering machine would record young voices, offering up their cocks. Meyer was busy in his retirement.

I stepped away from Tommy to see that finally Meyer was naked. I hadn't even noticed he had removed his clothes, so busy was I watching Tommy suck my cock.

Meyer was a robust 60-year-old man, a bit on the stocky side, with a gray growth of hair on his chest and on his lower belly, below which hung his half-hardened penis. His scrotum sagged and looked shriveled, as though worn out, and I was overwhelmed with pity. He grabbed Tommy's hand. "Stroke me," he begged.

Tommy licked the tip of his penis. Then he opened his mouth and let him in. Meyer choked him and, with each wrong move, made Tommy retch. I sensed Meyer's excitement coming dangerously to a head. Tommy moved away from his groin and lay on the bed on his stomach. Meyer got on top of him and began to force his penis into him, but he was impatient, shoving it into him in a horrible rush. He managed to get it in and puffed away, working at it like a hydraulic piston.

I sensed he wanted to hold it but couldn't. He cried out and with one spasmodic burst he spurted into Tommy. He then still went on pumping feebly for a few strokes, perhaps as a vague way of apologizing for his haste.

"Oh Tommy," he whispered and kissed him on the shoulder. He lifted himself away and, without looking at me, went to the bathroom.

Tommy turned his head. He smiled. "Next?"

"Not now. Can we go back to my hotel?"

"Sure," Tommy said.

"So, you have a lover?" Tommy asked as we crossed the causeway.

"I did. I gave him an education in sex. It was thorough training. It lasted almost four years."

"And then?"

"I got to be too old for him. I lost my air of freshness. After all those nights of fucking it was no wonder," I said bitterly, recalling those wonderfully long nights of fucking. "The first few weeks, maybe months, after he left, I thought I'd go crazy. It was like losing an arm or a leg, or half of myself," I went on. "You remind me of him. You're not like him in appearance, but you move the same way, the same smile, the same mouth."

He moved closer to me and brought his hand to my groin again.

"Where do you live?" he asked.

I told him about my house on the Gulf coast, where there is nothing but an empty beach, seagulls, pelicans and the sunsets are glorious.

"No boys?" he asked, his hand finally stroking again.

"Not like here. I have to come here to find boys."

"You come here often?"

"Not nearly enough." It seems to be the story of my life, never enough.

The room was icy cold, the air conditioning rattling softly at full blast. I turned it down and Tommy went to the bathroom.

I stripped and got in bed. Tommy came out of the bathroom naked, except for his sunglasses. I laughed. "Moon too bright?"

"My eyes hurt. I think I burned 'em at the beach today."

"Why didn't you wear your sunglasses?"

"I didn't have them. That's why Meyer bought them for me."

"Of course," I said.

Tommy carefully set his newly prized sunglasses on the nightstand and stretched out on the bed on his stomach, complaining that he had a sunburn. I smeared his back with lotion, then worked down to his buttocks, still moist from his shower. They were perhaps the nicest mounds I'd seen in many years.

I worked my fingers in, applying more and more lotion. I was sure Meyer had hurt him and I didn't want to do that. Still, it was such an inviting ass and he had asked me to fuck him at Meyer's. "Hurt?" I asked.

He shook his head and hugged the pillows. I set the lotion on the table after wiping some on my belligerent organ sticking out. I got on the bed, straddling him.

My blood was pounding until it rushed to my head. It pounded in time to my pumping. I fucked him slowly at first, then ferociously, forcing him to give up any memory of what Meyer had just done to him.

Suddenly I stopped and rolled him over. I wanted to make love to him, to face him while I fucked him. I parted his legs and entered him again. Now our faces were pressed together and our fingers became entwined. Our shoulders, chests, abdomens smacked together as I fucked him. The bed made a terrible racket and I couldn't stop myself from thinking about the thousands of bodies that had left their imprints on it. And all the men who had done this to Tommy.

I didn't come; I couldn't. But eventually I tired and withdrew. "Hold me," he asked, suddenly more a child than a lover. When I put my arms around him he cuddled up to me, gently, almost meekly. I held him in my embrace and wished he really was my lover, but only for an instant.

# Up All Night

## *John Patrick*

It began as a windless storm, so far as blizzards go, its real danger the delivery of a massive snow. Twenty inches of it had fallen in six hours in Nebraska. In certain parts of the Midwest phone lines had been down since the preceding day. Motorists were cautioned not to drive. The storm gathered momentum as it traveled east. I watched the sky descend. In Manhattan, wind gusts were reported up to sixty miles per hour. Television broadcasters were advising elderly people to stay at home. Tuning in at random, hearing this, I began to worry about Chance. I hadn't heard from him since he was about to board his flight in Los Angeles. He had a tendency to get lost, but I knew he would be on the move, moving, if not in a straight line, moving, nonetheless, doggedly, with purpose.

He was flying in to attend my party. He was my gift to Larry on the occasion of his 40th birthday. And Chance's rent was due. He needed the money. Yes, Chance would keep moving.

When the phone rang after midnight I jumped at it. The call, fulfilling all the odds, arrived collect.

"Chance? My God, where are you?"

"Logan?"

"What?"

"Some place named 'Logan.'"

"Logan, Chance, is the airport in Boston. Logan. Are you at the Boston airport?"

"I guess. If you say so."

I chuckled. He always believed everything I said. "Good. How are you, Chance?"

"Fuck, man, it's been a long day, but everyone's been so nice, especially them flight attendants."

"I'm sure."

"But I'm sleepy. They're putting us up for the night."

"Good."

"I invited the flight attendant, the cute one with the nice smile, to share my room."

"That's nice. Does he know who you are?"

"No. My ticket has my real name on it."

His real name was Hungarian and unpronounceable. I named him Chance Wayne after the gigolo in Tennessee Williams' play "Sweet Bird of Youth." He bore a startling resemblance to Paul Newman in the movie version of the play.

"Shit, man, everyone has been so nice, John."

"Good."

But, beyond the physical, Chance bore no resemblance to the brainy Newman. In fact, Chance was what you might call dumb, but he could fuck like nobody's business. "Young, dumb, full-of-cum," was what they said in porn circles about Chance. In the world of sex-for-hire, intellect is held to be effete, essentially feminine and suspect, the porn director/writer Sonny Gilbert told me once. "Better a blank slate," he laughed, "clean and unpolluted, than a mind."

It's odd how it worked out: Chance's gift from God was an incredibly long, thick penis, plus he had the ability to get it hard and keep it hard. I had experienced it first hand and told Sonny about him. Sonny invited me to Hollywood to attend Chance's first shoot. I sat in back seat of the big white Cadillac Fleetwood Sonny was driving. On the way to the warehouse Sonny uses as a studio, Sonny asked Chance what he thought of the script.

"Give him time, he just got through the first sentence," Kris said. Then he and the other porn veteran in the car, Eric, started laughing.

I whispered to Chance, who was sitting next to me, his thigh tight against mine, "Tell him you hate it. Tell him to change it."

Chance nodded and pushed the script into the front seat. "I hate it," he said. "Change it."

"Change it?" Sonny said, hardly able to contain his astonishment. "Like what kind of changes?"

"Maybe like smaller words and bigger letters," Kris said.

Everybody roared with laughter at that one and Sonny, shaking his head, turned up the stereo. Suddenly the car became a floating disco, with Kris and Eric shaking their heads in time to Donna Summer doing "They Work Hard For the Money."

But Chance wasn't getting into the merriment. To him, this was serious business, his first porn flick, and he was nervous. Not nervous enough to be unable to function, however, and when Kris and Eric saw his hard-on, well, Sonny had all he could do to keep them off of it until he got the cameras rolling.

The result, as they say, is porn history. From then on, Chance Wayne was billed as the biggest cock in gay porn.

\* \* \* \* \*

Larry arrived late. He had attended another party in his honor in Wall Street and traffic was very slow in the heavy snow. I knew the minute I saw him things would not go well. He was drunk.

Chance, on the other hand, had been sipping orange juice all night, smiling benignly while the other guests tried to cop a feel. Once my friends discovered Chance loved the attention, they were all over him. By the time Larry arrived, one guest was licking Chance's cock through his chinos. As Larry entered my apartment, I pulled the insatiable one off Chance and

called the visiting stud to attention. Of course, his cock was nearly at full attention by this time, and Larry was delighted with his present. I knew, however, that after the first drink at my place, Larry would pass out. To prevent his embarrassment before our friends, after I poured him a glass of champagne, I ushered him and Chance into the guest bedroom.

I awoke with a start. Someone had crawled into bed with me and was rubbing my cock. It was Chance, and he was rubbing my cock! My cock! I couldn't believe it. "What's wrong?" I asked.

"Fucker passed out."

"He was feeling no pain when he got here. I'm worried about his drinking–"

"I'm worried about this–" He yanked on my limp prick. "You haven't done anything with me in so long."

It was true. I hadn't had the urge for him in months. After the first couple of times, my fascination with him wore off and I needed new challenges. Still, whenever I was with someone else, I compared them to him. I knuckled my eyes. "I'm tired, that's all."

"I never thought I'd hear you say that. Shit, man, you let me fuck you all night in the beginning."

"I'm older now. Besides, you're the only one I know who can fuck all night."

"And tonight I'm so fuckin' horny. Feel it …"

He put my hand on his swollen prick. I always liked the feel of it. The silky smoothness, the healthy pink hue, the hardness, the hugeness. I remembered the first time I put it in my mouth, just the head and a couple inches of shaft. It tasted so good, I paid him for the entire night and he took that to mean I wanted him to fuck me all night. Just before dawn, I was begging for mercy. Chance was pleased that I was pleased.

I lowered my head to his lap and took the head of it in my mouth. Precum had formed and I licked it off, then began sucking in earnest. It tasted just as delicious as it had in the beginning. Suddenly it didn't seem to matter how many others had sucked it, either on a movie set or elsewhere. It was here now, in my bedroom, begging me to take it.

"Oh yeah," he groaned as three inches of shaft slid in. "Suck it." He was always ready.

What a cock. I licked it, then kissed it, nibbled on it. And there was no pressure with Chance. He just stood there, like a tree, while you adored it, adored this incredible manhood.

"I really want to fuck your ass," he growled.

"Okay," I moaned, coming off his prick and kissing the tip of it, as if saying goodbye temporarily.

I got on my hands and knees on the bed. It was the way I liked to start with him. It made it easier. I felt a delicious sticky heat as he prepared me with lube, then pressure as he started to penetrate. My ass ring stretched

wider and wider, finally accommodating the girth of his knob. He began rubbing his belly as he slid up into me, inch after thick, throbbing inch of hard dick penetrating to the center of my being.

When his ass was pressed tightly against my hips, he pulled me back against him and began nuzzling my neck. His five o'clock shadow tickled my skin, and his lips were hot against my shoulders. I looked down, watching his hands slide slowly up my belly to my chest. He grazed my stiff tits, then zeroed in on them, pinching and pulling, making my ass channel contract around his thrusting shaft.

I began to buck and squirm, riding up and down on his incredible hard-on, savoring the raunchy sexual rushes that began to rock me. He was breathing heavily, his arms tight around me, his heart pounding against my back, his massive prick reaming my channel from end to end. His balls banged against my thighs as he increased his speed, his belly slapping rhythmically against my ass cheeks. He was riding dangerously close to the edge, his balls drawn up tight at the base of his shaft.

"I'm close," the stud gasped, his lips brushing my ear.

"I'm closer," I said, craning my head around to him. "Kiss me while I come." Our lips touched, and my tongue shot into his mouth just as my jism began shooting onto the pillows. The stud never stopped pumping that famous cock into me and my asshole clenched. Now his cock flexed, and soon he was filling me. He kept fucking, shoving me to the mattress, pinning me beneath his sculpted bulk.

We lay still, catching our breath.

"You missed me," he said flatly, as if reading my mind.

He hugged me to him. He was warm, sweating. His cock was still packed up my ass, and it was getting hard again. He started rotating his hips, slowly growing inside of me.

"Oh, shit," I moaned.

# Just Another Night in Finsbury Park

## *Ian Young*

Darkness comes on quickly in the autumn evenings, and Finsbury Park–even in daytime the greyest of London districts–succumbs passively to a chilly gloom. Deserted streets become more depressing under the hard, magnesium glare of silver lamps jutting from concrete pillars, too high for vandals to bother with.

London is a conglomeration of villages that have been absorbed over centuries by the spreading city. Each has its own High Street and its own small park. Some of these districts are green and picturesque, but Finsbury Park is not one of them. Tucked into a neglected pocket of North-East London, it's a grey, dusty, ugly district of looming Victorian and Edwardian row houses made over into flats, of oil shops and repair garages struggling to survive, of boarded-up factories and crumbling brickworks, and a few scraggly paradise bushes poking out of the dirt of neglected gardens.

At its centre, gathering rubbish and wind-blown newspapers, a grimy brick and stone tube station of indeterminate age squats under a jumble of rusting bridges, like some enormous, collapsed machine. Twice a day it stirs itself to life, wheezing and clanging in the crush of shuffling rush hour crowds, and then emptying, leaving its musty passageways and gloomy tunnels as desolate and lifeless as before.

On the side streets off the Holloway Road, at random intervals among the tall stone houses, identical rectangular patches of grass appear, provided by the local council with a bench and one–only one–bush apiece. At the edges of these utilitarian parks, the walls of the remaining buildings show the paint and plaster outlines of what once were houses: for the little parks are the last of the war-time bomb-sites, playgrounds now for quiet, Indian children, watched over by their sari-clad grandmothers.

This is the London that Thatcherism passed by–and left even more broken and depressed. It's not the worst London has to offer, by any means: it hasn't sunk to the despair that wafts like a bad smell through the crime-infested filth of Brixton. It's just a grey area, a pocket for dreary weather, with an odd, unsettling quietness about it. Some of the abandoned buildings have been taken over by squatters–young, homeless, unemployed. A few storefront groceries run by Rastamen keep erratic hours selling take-out patties and bags of flour. Sikhs and Chinese stay open a little later than everyone else. By nine o'clock, no-one is on the streets, and most of the house-lights are out. Only the sweeping headlights and the swish of cars on their way to other places keep the district from appearing completely deserted.

John Patrick

The boarding house I lived in was the last of a line of crumbling, wedding-cake gothic piles on Turle Road. Before the bombing it had been in the middle of a row called Finsbury Mansions, but a couple of direct hits had demolished the end of the street. Part of the empty space was now a hideous secondary school, sardonically named after George Orwell. The rest served as the local cricket pitch. Some evenings, shadowy figures would linger there for a while after dark, running through the thick shadows (there are no lights) and sometimes calling to one another, determined to finish their game before rain or total darkness sends them home.

That fall the evenings were especially cold and damp, and I would bundle up in my old tweed overcoat and brown wool scarf for my nine o'clock walk down High Street and through the twisting back roads, with a packet of shrimp chips in my pocket and–if it was a Friday night–(what luxury!) a precious, thinly rolled joint.

It wasn't raining when I set out, but a cool wind was springing up, blowing papers and discarded wrappers through the weeds in the boarding house garden. Fugitive newspaper pages clung to the rose-bushes by the wall like crude veils. In the autumn cold I hunched against the damp English wind that gives half the population chest complaints by middle age. My friend the black and white cat wasn't at his usual window-sill perch tonight: probably inside, sensible and warm.

I headed for a little row of shops on one of the twisting back streets. The street lamps there are older, and more friendly, than the penitentiary-style lights above the main road. The shops were shut of course, most of their windows dusty and unrevealing, or lit by a single bare, low-watt bulb. Heath's Tools had a front window full of second-hand engines, belt-drives and odd-looking gears. A faded cardboard sign, left over from the Sixties by the look of it, incongruously promised "Fun in the Sun" on Majorca. I cupped my hand, pressed my nose against the glass and peered inside. Metal desks and wooden swivel chairs were piled one on another, and off to one side, a battered looking garden gnome presided, arms akimbo. At the back, a table was piled high with papers and tins. The sky began to spit rain.

The chemist's shop was the only one of the row, on either side of the street, with a properly illuminated window. Fluorescent lights threw a flickering glow onto tubes of toothpaste and stacked boxes of paper towels. A poster showed a well-groomed young couple, each smiling into the other's face while running along a beach, bizarrely dressed in a selection of trusses, supports and elastic knee and elbow bandages. I thought of collaging it with "Fun in the Sun," perhaps adding a tank or two, and some picturesque beggars.

The raindrops began to get bigger and I smelled the distinctive, musty odor of rain on dusty cement. I ducked into the doorway of an Indian grocery; its windows were piled high with sacks of rice, dented tins of curried ochra and faded sample packets of custard powder and Ovaltine. From a window above the shop across the road, a light revealed a room with

beige walls and a painting of a country cottage of the sort used for the tops of biscuit tins. No one seemed to be in the room. I leaned back against the door-jamb of the grocery and took the slightly bent joint out of my pocket. I was about to light it when I heard someone whistling.

The tune was familiar, a haunting, slightly melancholy dance that scurvy, syphilitic old Henry VIII had expropriated along with the monasteries, and passed off as his own. "Greensleeves"–and the metal-cleated footsteps that came with it–told me who it was even before I spotted him from my shadowy doorway.

"Andy."

"Fuck, why'ncha frighten the life out o'me!"

"Sorry. Here, come in out of the rain and smoke a joint with me."

"Yeah, right on man. What a pissy night, i'n' it."

Andy was a fellow boarder in the lodging house we called "the mansion." He was an intriguing fellow, a bit secretive, usually friendly, but moody and unpredictable. He was a skinhead, and I had never seen him go out in anything but regulation skinhead garb: jeans held up by black braces, work-shirt or T-shirt, work-socks and one of his half-dozen pairs of Doc Martens, to which he added a trade-mark touch of his own: metal cleats–"the better to kick your fuckin' head in wiv." In fact, Andy was remarkably gentle by nature, until the rare occasions when some real or imagined indignity to himself or another triggered his violent temper and he erupted in a reckless storm of fists, boots, blood and fury. He worked at odd jobs, mostly on building sites and dishing up food in cafeterias. Like most skinheads, he took pride in being scrupulously clean.

Andy was tall, like me. His lean body and strong hands contrasted with luminous, long-lashed green eyes, full lips and prominent cheekbones. He had a sneering smile that seemed cheeky, mischievous and appealing. With those he liked (the rest he preferred to ignore) he adopted a quiet, conspiratorial manner that assumed an immediate intimacy. He was tremendously sexy.

He joined me in the shop doorway and turned down the collar of his leather jacket. "Sid came round today," he said, dragging on the joint. "We went for a ride in his car, out to his place. Ever been out there?"

"I have indeed," I said, as he blew the smoke into the street. "Nice house he has. Epping, isn't it?"

"Yeah, Epping, near the forest."

"I don't know why he keeps it so gloomy though. The dining room and the front room look as though he never goes into them. I don't think he ever opens the curtains either. Bit creepy. He's a funny bloke."

Sid Brown was a fortyish Jewish stockbroker who'd gone into early retirement so he could write and live an openly gay life. Somehow, he hadn't gotten around to doing much of either and instead had become something of a recluse, puttering about semi-detached in a housing estate at the edge of the Forest and occasionally venturing into central London with enough money to

pick up a rent-boy, which is how he'd met Andy, who was always willing to supplement his wages with the right customer.

Sid had become an occasional, welcome visitor to the mansion–nervous, funny, a little seedy, and alternately miserly or generous, as the mood struck him. He always wore a Gay Is Good badge pinned to his suit-jacket, and smoked constantly, usually letting the ash tumble off his lapels onto his wool cardigan.

"He's got some great old boxes in that place," Andy said. Antique boxes were one of his odd interests. "You know what he said to me?" he asked, unscrewing a roach-clip that looked like a bullet. "I think he's a bit lonely out there all on his own. He asked me if I wanted to move in with him–you know, into the house in Epping like. Asked me a couple of weeks ago."

Andy looked straight into my eyes, nodding slightly, nodding, nodding, as he did whenever he wanted to be sure you were paying attention.

"Permanently?!" I said, stupidly, raising my voice a bit.

"Yeah of course!" He sounded a bit indignant. "He says I could do a bit of gardening for him and help out around the house like. Says I can type up his manuscripts for him and ... we might go into business together."

"What sort of business?" I asked, as a picture of Andy with a tea-towel in his hand flitted through my mind. That would be a change! We were huddling together against the shop door now, Andy in his jeans and black leather and me in my overcoat, sharing the last of the joint. It was very strong grass and we were both getting a nice buzz.

"This is good grass, man. From the Rastas?"

I nodded.

"Financial Advice," he said with a leer that turned into a grin. I'd forgotten his chipped front tooth. "Or maybe he just wants to pimp me to wealthy gents. Anyway, it'll get me out of the mansion, won't it. Your room's alright but mine's fucking cold. And too bloody noisy right next to the loo." He turned suddenly toward me and ran his fingers up my lapels, looking me straight in the face. "Here, d'you think I'm too old to do it for money?" I could see his breath, and feel it, warm against my mouth.

"You're in your prime, my darling!"

"Fuck off."

"No, seriously. If you want to do it, do it. You're good-looking, you can get all the tricks you want. Just remember though, pal, unless you're planning to do yourself in soon, there is a future to be thought of."

"Yeah, well. That's what I mean." He took a sudden look around the street as if he'd heard someone coming. "I'm sick of it round here. There's nuffing for me, nuffing at all. I like old Sid. It'll be all right, moving in with him. I mean, I didn't say I would. Said I'd think about it. He was a bit pissed off I think."

"Well, you don't want to look too eager, do you."

"Well, that's it, i'n' it."

"Did he go down on one knee when he proposed to you?"

"Fuck off or you'll get my knee in your balls. Epping's a bit boring but I expect I'll get used to it. Not that this place is so fuckin' exciting."

"Oh, I don't know," I said. "Look, the rain's eased up. We can walk down to the Laundromat and see if Mrs. Singh's cleaning the machines. She might favor us with a song. See, always something to do."

"Ha. Ha.'

We were both nicely buzzed by this point. I noticed Andy was wearing his tight jeans, ripped in one knee and nicely outlining the bulge at his crotch. He was leaning against the shop window with his head back and his eyes closed, hands in his jacket pockets, one boot-heel hooked on the window ledge. He looked great. I leaned against him with my thighs around his and clasped my hands around the back of his neck; short, sharp hairs pricked my palms.

"Kiss me you fool," he said, his eyes still shut.

His mouth felt warm and his tongue scraped against my teeth. He kept his tongue in my mouth for a long time before he broke away. "Shit,'' he said, and looked around. "I'm getting cold."

"Let's go home then."

"We'll go home and fuck."

Well, I thought, lucky me.

The mansion always looked odd standing at the end of the street where the row came to a sudden stop, a ragged wall showing the traces of what were once stairways in an adjoining house. As we came near, Andy broke away and ran ahead of me onto the uncut grass, jumping high in the air and swinging his latch-key on a string over his head, not making a sound. On the back of his black leather jacket he'd painted a white A in a circle and SKINS RULE underneath. His small bottom looked good in his tight fitting jeans. Sid wasn't the only one who wanted to get into that arse. Andy would never let him—or anyone else.

The house looked dark from the outside but the kitchen light was on in the back, as always. "Cup of tea Andy?"

"Yeah, get warmed up. 'Be down in a minute."

It was bright in the kitchen. Electric wires and disconnected pipes hung from the ceiling and a roll of new linoleum stood in one corner, ready to replace the cracked Victorian floor tiles that had worn thin, exposing the blackened wood underneath. The window over the table looked out onto a ramshackle porch that had once been a greenhouse. Now it was full of old furniture, rolled-up carpets, broken bicycles and stacks of gritty flower-pots.

I put the kettle on and looked at the clock. Too late for the news. Then I saw the note pinned to the television.

It was from Russell, our landlord.

Lads–Gone over to gay painting show at Pink Triangle. Yes I'm come over all artistic all of a sudden! Frozen meat pies in the fridge, help yourselves.

John Patrick

Did you hear, Sid's decided to go to Australia–Sydney. Sidney in Sydney. To live with his sister, his Mum's very ill. Says he's sick of living on his own. He's put his house up for sale and all his furniture, silly bugger so I don't suppose he'll be coming back. I'm going to buy that hall-stand. Says he's got to go next week. Shall we give him a party?

Harry owes ‚5 on the rent from last week. The back toilet is plugged up again. Be good I know you will!–Russell

The kettle shrieked as I took the cups off the hooks. Andy came downstairs, without his coat and shirt now, just in his jeans, braces and boots, but with his glasses on. The round, old-fashioned National Health specs gave him an strangely scholarly look. His bare chest was smooth and white, at odds somehow with his brown neck and big hands. One shoulder had a tattoo I liked, a Robertson's Marmalade golliwog, waving. Andy was whistling to himself, not "Greensleeves" this time, but the Stones' "Just Another Night."

He broke off suddenly. "You'll come and see us–out in Epping–won't you? We'll all have tea in the drawing room. Lah di dah!"

"Of course," I said. "If it all works out." I folded Russell's note and stuck it under the radio, trying not to think too hard.

Would it have been possible? I imagined solitary, neurotic old Sid, dithering about in a cloud of cigarette ash and suspicion, and horny, twenty-year old Andy, with his ornamental boxes and violent fits, the two of them settling into domestic bliss together among the suburban families ... Pretty bloody unlikely. On the other hand, you never know.

I looked out the window. The back garden beyond the greenhouse was nothing but blackness. The last cricket players had gone home; the rest of the boarders were asleep, or nowhere in sight. Only the two of us up and about now, just me and Andy, under the kitchen light. Outside, the wind was springing up again, and the greenhouse windows were rattling.

"Yeah. If it works out," Andy answered. "I really like the forest, all the green trees. I like that funny wet smell the earth gets."

He carried the cups–no saucers–over to the arborite table. "Yeah, I'm getting too old for it, man. Gotta settle down. Gotta get fuckin' organized." Then, without a pause: "You think old Sid would rent you a room?"

And suddenly he was looking right at me again with those clear green eyes of his.

"I don't suppose so."

He was quiet for a moment. He swallowed a mouthful of tea and leaned back to tip the chair on its back legs, hooked his thumbs in his braces and flashed his grin at me. "Let's go to your room," he said, "it's nicer than mine." He took his glasses off and laid them gently on the table. "Is this the new tea?"

"Yes. From Russell's Mum," I reminded him. "Expensive!"

"The best, eh!" he laughed, and I laughed with him. "Right on! Only the fuckin best!"

And we headed upstairs with our half-drunk tea as the damp English wind rattled the loose panes in the greenhouse door.

# Night Watcher

## *Louis Abreu*

I'm just sitting here in my studio apartment with my feet propped against the window watching the activity on Hillside Avenue, a residential street in Washington Heights, the nosebleed part of Manhattan. It's ten o'clock on a Wednesday night and the summer heat has formed a light layer of perspiration on my body. The jazz from the stereo fills my apartment.

As usual, the kids outside are playing basketball. One of the kids misses a shot; the ball careens off a building and hits a car. The alarm goes off–the shrill, screaming kind and the kids scatter into the nearby buildings. I'm thinking to myself, It's too fucking hot for that shit! They should be home fucking each other! They are fucking cute enough, damn it.

A couple of minutes later, the light of the apartment across from my studio goes on. Who do I see? None other than two of the kids that just hit that car. They're kinda cute. One is white, with long blonde hair in a pony tail. He is about five-nine, and his cute shorts and T-shirt tell me he's not from around here. The other is a Latin guy, five-ten, with a smooth swimmer's body–he probably got it that way playing basketball on the corner of Hillside and Bogardus.

I can see from my window that they are still breathing heavily from all the excitement. The white boy takes off his T-shirt and jeans. As the Latin boy walks out of my field of vision, the blonde boy sits on the couch, which faces the window. After a while the Latin boy comes back with two tall glasses of dark liquid (probably iced tea or cola).

As they drink, they touch each other's cocks and massage their chests. They're moving fast, and I wonder if this is something they do all the time. The blonde then puts his drink on the coffee table and starts to kiss his companion's nipples. The Latin boy puts his drink on the coffee table, too, and without regard for his companion, he takes off the boy's underwear to set free a fat, white dick. He puts it into his mouth.

The blonde lies back and enjoys the mouth of that hot Latin guy. Without taking his dick from the Latin boy's mouth, he gets up, lays the boy on the couch, and begins to fuck his face. The Latin boy puts his hands on the blonde's ass and begins to massage it, taking one of his fingers and putting it up his hole. While the Latin boy gets his face fucked, he takes off his bikini with his free hand. He then takes out a condom from under the couch, puts it on his dick, and goes back for some lube. He gently removes the blonde boy from his face and sits him I down on his cock.

The blonde boy moves himself up and down on the boy's stiff dick, slowly at first. When the blonde gets comfortable with the boy's length, he starts to move faster.

John Patrick

I start stroking my cock; looking at these boys was making it drip. The blonde boy is in complete control as he moves up and down on the Latin boy's cock. He then throws his head back as the Latin boy strokes his cock. Within a few moments, the blonde lets his load spill all over the Latin's chest and torso. Damn, he should not have done that. It makes me feel this extreme rush all over my body, and I come right then and there.

The blonde is still moving up and down on the Latin boy's cock while he is spreading the hot liquid across his chest. That must turn him on, because I see his mouth contorting; he's moaning, probably really loud. Now the Latin obviously has come, because the blonde gets up and takes the condom off of his companion, flings it to the side, and lies in his arms. They look so cute together.

After my orgasm, the mixture of the summer air and the cum on my body makes me want to go to bed. I turn off the stereo, clean myself with a towel, take off my jeans and head towards bed.

But I can't get my mind off those boys. My eyes are wide open, and there is no way I am going to sleep. I am too horny, and it's too hot. I put my jeans back on and head toward the bathroom.

The bathroom light blinds me, and I run my fingers through my hair. Bad hair day, I think, putting on a baseball cap. I leave the bathroom and search for a T-shirt. I can' t find one, so I just put on my light brown leather jacket, grab my keys and head towards Fort Tryon Park.

The journey down Hillside (or "Hellside," as I say when I have to walk that damned hill) is a bitch cause it is so fuckin' hot. However, as I walk into the park a cool breeze hits me and I stop my bitching. Fort Tryon Park was built on a hill, but despite all the energy it takes to get to the top, it's great for cruising. I forget that taking the elevator at the 190th / Overlook Terrace train station is my best bet, so I climb the park stairs. My dick is doing all the thinking.

I finally get to the gazebo, which is halfway up the mountain. I walk in, and this troll tells me that the cops have just been there and took a couple of guys down to the three-four (the local precinct) for indecent exposure. Anyway, I decide to go to the top and get away before he thinks I want something from him. This, of course, means more climbing.

Upstairs, the action is pretty hot, considering the pigs have just raided the joint. I see a cute little white guy (unusual in these parts) standing by himself. He's about five-six, blonde, clean cut–just the way I like them. I walk right up to him. He's kinda shocked or scared. "Calm down," I say. "I'm not gonna hurt you."

He relaxes. "What brings you here?"

"My hard dick and the hot air."

"Hmm ... That's inspiring. Don't go near that Puerto Rican guy. He's out for money."

"Don't worry. I have my eyes set on you," I assure him.

"Let's go back to your place."

"I live down in Chelsea," he says.

"Then I guess it' s my place. But I gotta warn you, my air conditioner is broken."

"We'll just have hot, sweaty sex!"

As we head down the hill to the street, I tell him that taking the elevator at the train station would be much cooler and less tiring.

When we get to the apartment, I slam the door, grab the boy and start kissing him. I'm neither taller nor stronger than he, but I wrap his legs around my waist and carry him to the bed while I have my lips planted firmly against his. We kiss and dry hump each other for awhile, then took off each other's clothes. Finally, we are naked.

The street light bathes his beautiful, buff, white skin. We kneel on the bed, kissing and touching each other. I grab him by the neck, throw him down, and shove my tongue down his throat. I kiss his neck and lower myself to his chest. Then I go down on his cock as he slowly moves to cop mine. He lays me down on the bed, and with my dick still in his mouth, he gets on top of me in the sixty-nine position. He takes his dick out of my mouth and puts his balls in its place.

As he sucks, I am touching his ass, first around the rim and then poking the hole lightly. I take his balls out of my mouth and lick his pecker. He lets out a moan. I poke his hole faster with my tongue and licking around his hole. I am about to come, so I pull him away from my dick.

"Why did you stop?" he asks.

"Because I don't want to cum just yet," I say, turning him towards me and kissing him. I pull out a condom and lube from under my pillow and he immediately grabs them and puts them on me. He kneels in front of me with his knees by my pelvis, then lubes my dick and lubes himself.

The boy sits down on me, and with quick thrusts I start fucking him. He's breathing hard, which turns me on. With every thrust, I feel myself coming close to orgasm. We are sweating like animals, and as he moves faster and faster on my stiff hard dick, I am moaning louder and louder, and finally come.

I withdraw my still-hard cock and reach under my pillow for another condom. This time, I put it on him and lube him up.

I have to move fast because I don't want to lose my hard-on. The boy knows immediately what to do. With my back to the bed, he grabs my legs, puts them on his shoulders and puts his tip slowly inside me. He's facing me, and as he fucks me the drops of sweat from his forehead start landing on my face and neck. The pillows are absorbing the sweat from my head. The aroma is driving me crazy.

I am breathing fast, and he grabs my dick and starts stroking it. I know where this is going. He's pumping my ass and stroking my dick. He's driving his cock into me like crazy, and I am close to coming a second time. He's breathing hard and moaning loudly, and I start my moaning fits as well. The juice inside of me is ready to explode. With one final yell, he unloads

his cream inside of me. At the same time I erupt and the cum flies all over my chest, head, and bed. Some kids just know what they are doing!

We lie in each other's arms and fall asleep.

It's an hour or so later. He has awakened and I offer him something to eat. He politely declines and says he has to go home because his parents were expecting him from night school. I'm beginning to like this kid. We exchange numbers, and I offer to walk him to the train station.

As we leave the building, another alarm goes off–the same shrill, screaming kind–and we laugh and make a show of covering our ears.

*– This story has been adapted from text originally appearing in Dirty magazine.*

# Barrio Boy

## *Michael Bates*

Our ship was to be in Valparaiso, Chile only two days, and I was determined to make the most of what little free time I had. Not long after the end of the work day I was shaved, showered and dressed in a moderately tight pair of Levi's topped with a light shirt partly unbuttoned at the chest. The climate at this time of year is much like San Diego; warm and pleasant when you're wearing the right clothes. I opted to leave my wallet, with credit cards and other important stuff, on the ship; buttoning a single ID card in a shirt pocket, and stuffing a wad of bills into my front pants pocket. I also added the insurance of folding two or three five and ten thousand peso notes into small, individual squares and secreting them in places like my watch pocket, deep in the bottom of a back pocket, and one inside a shoe. I might be wandering the streets and alleyways of Valparaiso late into the night, and there was no telling what I might encounter. I had heard of occasional petty thievery in this city and didn't think I might actually get attacked, but you could never be too sure. Even if I got out-and-out rolled, there was a good chance at least one of my cached bills would be overlooked; giving me the means to at least get back to the ship. It was my own urban survival preparation, which I'd used in many cities around the world, although never utilized, thank goodness.

My first instinct was to go to Villa del Mar. It is the tourist Mecca of Chile, and again reminded me of San Diego with its flowering, tree-lined streets, neatly landscaped gardens and grounds, a plethora of hotels, motels and pensions, long sandy beaches facing the Pacific, and attractions such as a casino, botanical gardens and an amusement park. On a previous visit I had had an interesting encounter with a vaquero boy who drove one of the many horse carriages near the seaside for the tourists. I strolled through that area on the off chance he might be there this year, but there seemed fewer of them now, perhaps because it was later in the year, and he was not among them. Just as well. I was looking for more than just a quick turn-on in the back of a carriage. I wanted a companion for the evening, or better yet, for my entire, albeit short, stay there. Most of all I wanted to feel the heartbeat, literally and figuratively, of the Chilean male which is so deftly hidden beneath a seeming staunch layer of machismo. There had to be a lot of frustrated young men out there, hiding their true feelings and desires; ready to burst free with love and sex with the first unthreatened, anonymous opportunity. I was in a country where this was still a forbidden love, with laws still on the

books prohibiting it. The populace of queer men, of which there had to be a great number, remained secretive, closeted. The seeds of a gay scene had only begun growing in the larger urban areas, but it was still mostly an unspoken love. I could very well have been in the States in the forties or fifties. It was challenging, provocative.

Things didn't really start happening here until rather late–eleven o'clock onward–so there was still plenty of time to kill. I wandered up and down Avenida de Villa, eyeing the young men in the mercantile shops, the boys bagging groceries at the super Mercado, and countless tanned tourists browsing the shops. There was some eye contact here and there and an occasional smile; sometimes encouraging me to pursue, but I just wandered onward, enjoying the enticing looks and variety of bodies like window shopping at a candy store. One can never tire, or get fat, from simply looking and smelling all the delightful varieties.

In an out-of-the-way alleyway, I found a tiny restaurant that served Italian food with a Chilean flair and treated myself to a serving of lasagna smothered in chopped tomatoes and parsley with, yes, fresh, hot chilies on the side. The green salad was loaded with tomatoes as well, as they were in season now, and deliciously vine ripened; blood red and brimming with juice. A half bottle of Chilean red wine, Santa Emiliano, topped off the meal. The only thing that made it incomplete was the lack of a companion to share it with. If I met someone in due time, I thought, I would return to this very restaurant. It was quiet and unobtrusive; perfect for intimate conversation without looking too "romantic."

I relaxed and took my time, and then resumed my strolling about the streets of Villa. After sunset I found myself in Plaza de Villa, a place I'd heard had possibilities for cruising. It took up an entire block and was a maze of walkways through gardens and shade trees with a showering fountain highlighting the center. Most of the benches were occupied; some by vagrants, others by couples and singles. No interesting prospects now, though. I sat on a vacant bench and watched the incessant flow of strollers through the park. I'd heard this place was frequented by hustlers and wondered if any would be out this early. Would they approach me if I looked "ready," or would they try to look ready themselves and wait to be approached?

Gradually, the volume of casual strollers thinned, and more and more of the benches became vacant. My attention was drawn to a group of young people joking and laughing, gathered by a nearby bench. The conversation was all in Spanish, of course, so I had no idea what was being said. There were four or five guys and two girls and they had the air of familiarity that says they were at home here and with each other. Was this the nightly, pre-business meeting of the park's hustlers? Were they sizing up who was where on the benches and in the shadows and dividing up the territory? One or two of them glanced my way a few times. I looked back and exchanged smiles. Friendly enough, they seemed.

After a while one of them sauntered over my way. He looked in his mid-thirties and had a page-boy hair cut and remnants of a pock-marked face. His shoulders were broad, and he was obviously in good shape.

"Que pasa?"

"Nada," I said, with a shrug of the shoulders. That was as much Spanish as we were able to exchange, for he came back with a long diatribe in that language which was totally indecipherable to me. I gave him a puzzled look and instinctively pulled out my pocket dictionary, but before I could begin to look up even the first word, he threw back his head with a big laugh and returned to the group. I then heard a chuckle erupt in the group as he no doubt told them I was a non-Spanish speaking tourista.

Moments later, one of the others left the group and approached me. He looked younger than the first, probably in his late twenties. His black hair hung straight and long over his ears and down to the base of his neck. He had a pug nose and small, beady eyes. His build went with the face: short, stout, compact. He looked like someone weaned on the streets, if I was any judge.

"Hello," he said, tentatively, with a somewhat high voice, almost sounding like a girl.

"Buenos noches."

"Oh, you speak Spanish?" he said, smiling.

"Only a little," I replied meekly. "Your English is good."

"Thank you. What is your name?"

"Mike. Miguel."

"I am Fernando. Come meet my friends." He nodded toward the animated group.

This must be it, I thought. They decide what I'm interested in, and then one of them makes a move. Well, Fernando looked just fine to me. I imagined he must have a hot, stout cock just like the rest of him. A little tingle went through my groin at the thought of it.

The group fell silent when we approached. Fernando and the first guy exchanged a few words, then he turned to me and said something in Spanish followed by "Miguel." Shifting to English, he told me their names. One of the girls, Maria, smiled and said, "Fernando learned some English in primary school so now he thinks he's interpreter for the U.N.!" They all laughed. "Miguel, we want buy, how you say, whiskey? Can you help us. We need only hundred pesos more." She held out a handful of peso coins.

"Sure," I said, digging into my pocket. I felt the huge wad of notes as I pulled out the coin, and wondered what they would think or do if they knew I had that much money. They were obviously scraping. As soon as I handed her the coin, she gave the money to the older guy who went off in the direction of the few shops still remaining open. They joked some more amongst themselves until he returned with a bottle of cheap gin. Someone already had a half jug of orange juice and it took only moments to pour the gin, nearly all of it, into the jug. It was shaken up and then passed around.

The strong, raw alcohol dispelled any fears that I could catch any germs from sharing the same jug with these strangers; it would easily kill anything, including us if we drank enough of it, I supposed. I was already feeling light headed from the wine I'd had earlier, so took only very small sips when the jug came my way.

There was more joking and laughing, and with the conversation mostly in Spanish I had no idea what was being said. One thing became obvious: these were not hustlers. They were just some people out for a good time together. I was touched that they had invited me to join them, but this wasn't quite the way I wished to spend the evening. It was now near midnight, and if I was going to find something, this was the time to do it. So I thanked my new friends for the drink and bid them good night, sauntering into the shadows and across the plaza. I hailed the first taxi I came across and asked him to take me back to Valparaiso.

I had heard that Plaza Victoria was another possible cruising spot, and often frequented by hustlers. I asked the cab driver to drop me a block from the park. The streets here were still bustling with traffic and pedestrians, and there were still many more shops open here than had been in Villa.

This plaza was smaller than the other, and obviously much older. There was no fountain in the center, but bigger bushes scattered about, and a small structure in one corner that looked like a rest room. There was no lighting here, and it was very dark. The only light was ambiently provided by the adjoining street lights. Were those figures I saw lurking in the shadows, I wondered, as I sauntered casually along the cobbled walkway. Was that someone standing next to the rest rooms? Someone sitting on a bench stood as I approached. I slowed. He looked me up and down. It was difficult to make out his face in the darkness, but he seemed rather young and not very well dressed. Was he a beggar about to ask for money? I was prepared to give him the brush-off.

"Bueno noches," he said softly, almost in a whisper.

"Buenos noches."

Then he said something in Spanish, softly again. I didn't detect any words for money, and it didn't sound like a plea for anything.

"No comprendo," was all I could reply.

He nodded and smiled and looked me up and down again. I could see his face better now, and he indeed looked young, early twenties I guessed.

He looked momentarily toward the rest rooms, and back again. Was he getting at something, or was it my imagination? He asked my name.

"Miguel," I replied.

"Arnaldo."

He asked nothing more. If he was a hustler, he sure wasn't putting on the hustle. I could still feel the lingering effects of the alcohol, and was thirsty. It was well past midnight now, and I could probably eat something too.

"Comida? Hambre?" I asked.

"Si," he said, shrugging his shoulders.

"Donde?" Where, I asked.

He began walking, and I followed. Across from the plaza stood a small cafe. There were only two or three tables and they were all taken, but he led me up a set of steep wooden stairs to a sort of inside balcony where another half dozen tables stood. All were full except one. The place was packed at this late hour. As we squeezed past the tables toward the vacant one, it seemed that the din of conversation ebbed a bit, and several of the patrons stared at us momentarily. Was it because I was so obviously a tourista, or did they know that this guy was a hustler (was he a hustler?), or was it because of the unkempt clothes he wore? The bright lights of the cafe showed them to be frayed and threadbare. He wore a brown, oversized sweater over a grimy T-shirt and slacks that looked a few sizes too large. They were drawn tight at the waist by an old leather belt, and the legs hung straight down like two stovepipes. His shoes were cracked and splitting, with the sole of one pulling loose from the top.

His warm smile and excitement at the prospect of eating more than made up for his rather unkempt attire, though. Arnaldo had olive-brown skin, and doey, brown eyes. His cheeks were the slightest bit rounded; not chubby, but just ever so slightly round.

"Algo," I said, as the waitress handed him the menu. Anything.

He ordered chicken and I asked for the same; beer and ice water as well.

The food came quickly, as though they were used to feeding huge crowds at this hour. The plates were heaped with home fried potatoes and a quarter of a chicken topped with two fried eggs. Arnaldo dug in with gusto. I sipped my beer and watched him devour the food on his plate. He had medium-sized hands with well proportioned fingers. There were signs of calluses and the nails were cut short and showed some dirt, as though they were used to manual labor.

Before all the food was gone he carefully laid aside a drumstick and small heap of the potatoes. Looking from my untouched plate to me he said, "No hambre?"

I smiled. "No. No comer. Bebida," I said, holding my beer up.

"Salud!" He lifted his beer in a toast. "Por favor ... ? he said, looking again at my plate.

"Si!" I handed across the plate, and he immediately went to work on it. It looked like he hadn't eaten for days.

He ate only about half the chicken and then called to the waitress and exchanged a few words. Moments later she returned with a small take-out box and he slid the remainder of the food into it.

We sipped our beer and water and looked back and forth at each other.

"Amigo," he said.

"Amigo." I knew it had to be well after two in the morning, and I felt tired. I still had no idea if this guy was hustling me or what. He had not asked for anything or even broached the subject of sex. I wasn't even sure I

was ready for it if he did. I just wanted to go to sleep. It was nice having a companion to share a meal with and talk to, or at least try communicating with; our fluency of each other's languages left a lot to be desired. Whether he intended anything or not, I thought, I needed to get some sleep, and it was too late to go all the way back to the ship. "Dormir?" I said, sleep. "You, me, dormir?"

"Donde?" Where?

"'Otel."

"Donde?"

I shrugged my shoulders, "Cerca." Near.

We left the cafe and I led the way. There was supposed to be a place called the Reina Victoria near Plaza Sotomayor which was cheap and clean. It wasn't a long walk. I thought how nice it would be to take a good shower, and wash off all the grime of the city. Judging from his appearance I guessed it had been some time since Arnaldo had had a good wash himself. We walked purposefully through the narrow, darkened streets, and I was glad there were two of us at this lonely hour. It looked like the perfect place for a mugging.

The sign for the Reina Victoria was not lit, and there was a large paper, with Spanish written on it, pasted to the door. Arnaldo read it. "Cerrado." Closed. He turned to me, and I shrugged. Then he brightened and motioned for me to follow. We turned the corner and he stopped at a tall, unmarked door. He rang the bell, and we could hear it echo deep within the establishment. We waited several minutes. He rang the bell again.

A light came on and the door opened a few inches revealing a wrinkled old woman's face. She exchanged whispers with Arnaldo and then opened the door to admit us. We ascended a flight of marble stairs behind the old woman. She was short and wore a robe. Obviously she had been sleeping. The wooden floors creaked as we made our way into a small room with a desk which served as an office.

She spoke no English, so I used my dictionary to find the right words. A room with two beds cost ten dollars a night. She took us to see the room. It was quite large, with a high ceiling and two medium-sized beds. There was a table and chairs and a bureau and wardrobe, all looking old and antique-like, but very beat up. The bathroom was across the foyer from the room. It was shared by other occupants, but was large with a huge free standing tub and shower. I wasn't thrilled by the shared bath, but who could complain at ten bucks a night. The room looked clean, albeit very aged. I paid for two nights and filled out the little registration slip.

Arnaldo seemed delighted with getting the room, and immediately headed for the bathroom to take a shower. I still had no idea what I might be getting into. Here I was alone in a cheap hotel room with a complete stranger who I'd met only briefly in a park in the middle of the night. Was I out of my mind? Had he somehow set this all up with the idea of ripping me off? I was unduly suspicious, although there was no reason to be, except to protect

myself from the unexpected. I wanted to give him the benefit of the doubt, but at the same time I needed to use caution. I folded a few ten thousand peso notes and slipped them far under the mattress. If he tried to take my money, he would only get what was in my clothes, not thinking there could be any in the room. When he returned, I took my turn in the shower, taking my pants and money with me. There was a decided lack of hot water, but the warm summer weather didn't make it unbearable.

Arnaldo was in one of the beds when I returned; only his smooth, olive-brown shoulders and arms showed above the sheets. His black hair was damp and mussed from being toweled dry. A clean, soapy aroma pervaded the room. His eyes were closed, but I knew he wasn't asleep. I feasted my gaze upon his round cheeks and relaxed face. I wondered if I should make a suggestion, make a move. But he had never referred to doing anything; never hinted or asked or gestured. Perhaps he was just a poor, hungry young man in need of a friend. I turned out the light, slipped out of my pants, rolled them up, money and all, and tucked them under my pillow. If he had plans of taking my money and slipping out while I slept, he couldn't do so without first waking me, I thought. Then I slid under the sheets of my own bed.

"Miguel?" his voice came softly from the darkness.

"Si?"

"Amigo?"

"Si."

I heard his sheets rustle and the floor creak. Then he was next to my bed, and without another word, simply slipped under the sheets next to me. He was wearing only a very brief pair of shorts. His cool, silky skin slid against me, and I took him in my arms with a firm embrace. He let out a sigh. I was naked and my cock instantly came alive with the feel of this young, smooth body next to me. Our legs entwined, and I felt his own cock stirring within the confines of his shorts. As though reading my thoughts he reached down and slipped them down and off, and I felt his half-hard dick flop against my thigh. Whether he just wanted to be next to someone, or more, I don't know. We were both very tired, and it just felt so exquisite having our clean, naked bodies in contact; legs and arms intertwined into one. Our dicks were aroused by it all, but the sex act did not follow. If it were going to happen, there would be plenty of time for it in the morning. For now we both fell into a dreamy, peaceful sleep.

\* \* \* \* \*

There is nothing quite so wonderful as waking with someone in your arms, and it's ever so intriguing when that person is a stranger; an innocent face and flawless, naked body sleeping peacefully, trustfully in your arms. You, too, are a stranger, and you, too, are naked and trusting.

I awakened at dawn and felt the rhythmic breathing, wisps of breath caressing my face with each brief exhale. The sheet was a twisted maze

entangling our feet and ankles, leaving us naked and exposed on top of the bed. A brown arm rested dead across my waist, contrasting against my whiter skin. My eyes roamed freely about this body of Adonis. Oh, how much those grubby, ill-fitting clothes, the dark of night, and my own mild alcoholic stupor had hidden from view! He was truly handsome; a mature young man in the prime of life. He had the slightest fuzz of brown hair on his arms, but was otherwise totally hairless down to his ankles where again there appeared more light brown fuzz. Of course he had generous darker patches under the arms and around his penis, but not overly so. The dark brown rosettes of his nipples were large as half-dollars. His dick lay limp across a thick brown thigh. It was uncut with the head hidden far inside the dark, wrinkled tube of skin. To one who is circumcised, this is always a special sight, offering a sense of uniqueness and mystery to this most prized member.

The feel of his smooth skin, caress of his breath, and feast of his beauty to my eyes was enough to keep me content even if no sex were to follow. My eyes closed again and I dozed.

The room was flooded with bright light from the outside when I awakened again. It had to be late morning. Arnaldo's eyes were open, and he was looking downward. In his hand was my cock, standing hard and stiff in his fist. He looked up and smiled when he saw I was awake. His own cock had come alive and the pink head had pushed out beyond the foreskin which was now pulled back, stretched taut around it. Without words we explored each other; caressing, feeling, stroking. I have always preferred sex in the early morning. I have always preferred it in light rather than darkness, and better yet in natural daylight. I want to see the body, the organ, the juices, not just feel them in closed-eye darkness. A sculpture is meant to be seen just as much as it is to be touched and caressed. And so we came to appreciate each other's sex story in the morning light. Arnaldo did not lead at all, yet he was not totally passive. He simply participated. He seemed comfortable with whatever transpired, which was simple enough; more exploratory and naively uncomplicated, like two pubescent youths exploring their sexuality. It was safe and sensuous, wonderfully sensuous, and I wanted it to last forever. But we were both extremely aroused, and it wasn't long before our explorations resulted in the final zenith. What a great way to start the day!

We found a cafe in the neighborhood and enjoyed a breakfast of eggs and ground meat, rough cut slices of bread, and beer. The place had an ancient bar with hunting trophies and knickknacks hanging dusty on the walls behind it. The creaky wooden floors, high ceiling, and mismatched furniture was so typical of Chilean establishments. The only other patrons were a couple of cronies drinking beer and watching a televised soccer game.

With the help of my dictionary, drawing on napkins and plenty of sign language, I told Arnaldo that I wanted to buy him some new clothes. He smiled and nodded eagerly. He led me to a mini-bus and we rode to the

outskirts of town where an outside market was located. It was a shoulder-to-shoulder jumble of merchants selling everything from dishware to underwear, radios to tennis shoes. We strolled among the stands, stopping to look at a shirt or some pants. Arnaldo seemed concerned over the prices, and I assured him it was no problem. "Algo," I said. Anything. This was far better than had we gone to some big department store in the city. He picked out a pair of jeans and tried them on. They fit snugly and properly, unlike the slacks he wore. We bought some shirts and socks and several pairs of the tight, sexy briefs he liked to wear. The shoes caused him some consternation. He wanted a pair of high tops, and looked at the cheapest ones he saw, but I was drawn to a more expensive pair, a name brand. "Mucho dinero," he said. Too much money. I shook my head and insisted he try them on. You get what you pay for with shoes, I thought. These would last much longer than any of the others. He beamed when they were fitted and laced up, and we left the old ones with the merchant to dispose of.

It took the two of us to carry all the bags and packages back to the pension. We looked like two tourist shoppers. On the way, I pondered again if Arnaldo was really a hustler or if this was something that was happening on its own. He still had asked for nothing, even when he could see I wanted to spend money on him and that I had a considerable amount to spend. He almost seemed concerned that I was spending too much! Perhaps it was his technique. Perhaps he sensed that if he asked for money I would be hesitant about giving it to him. If so, he was right. It felt good to give to someone in need, without being begged for it. Had he simply asked me for a sum of money after our night together, I would have paid him and been finished with it; a deal closed, payment for services rendered. But by simply being my "friend," my companion, he was getting much more. I was in need of the warmth and friendship; virile, youthful sexuality, and he was in need of some very basic things for survival–food and clothing. Granted I was indeed "buying" his companionship, and he was "selling" it, and we both knew it, I suppose, but it was unspoken, and we were doing what felt best to both of us, so what did it matter?

I sat on the bed and watched Arnaldo shed his tattered clothes so he could try on his new ones, piece by piece. He stood unabashedly naked in front of me removing them from their packages and cutting off the labels. The skin-tight briefs slid over his flaccid cock and firm butt, confining his youthful sex in a neat, compact package. I checked out the fit by running my finger under the elastic, sliding it around and stretching it outward. It touched the tip of his cock once or twice and then I kneaded it a couple of times, and it began growing instantly. "Mmm, muy bueno," I said, referring to the fit, of course. He smiled and reached for the remainder of the clothes to don. He walked and strutted and turned in front of me, showing them off, and eyeing himself in the cracked mirror on the wardrobe. "Muy bueno!" he said. "Gracias, Miguel."

He picked up his discarded old clothes and folded them and placed them inside one of the shopping bags. The leftover chicken from the night before was still in its container on the table, and he put that in the bag as well. Then he turned to me. "Vamos," he said.

"Donde?" Where?

"Mi casa. Mi familia." My house, my family.

"Tu casa?" Your house?

"Si!"

The shared mini-cab cost only a few pesos, and took us far out of Valparaiso. It went up into the steep foothills behind the city, winding and turning this way and that up the steep road to the summit overlooking the harbor. It descended into a valley on the far side, and the number of houses grew sparse. The paved road turned to gravel. "Parada!" called Arnaldo. Stop!

The taxi ground to a halt, letting us out, and then U-turned back toward town. The sound of the departing car left us in silence except for a rustling breeze, the far off barking of a dog and occasional call of a rooster. From the hectic bustle of the city, we were suddenly in the country. Such a contrast. A dirt path led off the road and I followed Arnaldo.

From the tall grass bordering it emerged a half-naked youngster, perhaps four or five years old. He greeted Arnaldo and stared at me a moment before running on ahead of us shouting in Spanish. Further ahead, another, smaller path branched from the one we were on and led up a steep incline. As we reached the top of this, it leveled on a clearing where a number of dwellings were built. I call them dwellings because they were far from being proper houses. They were more like shacks, built of plywood and corrugated tin; no two looking exactly alike. The ground around them was uneven, bare earth, trampled smooth by endless foot traffic, no doubt.

There were not many people about, but those who saw us stopped what they were doing, stared, and waved a greeting to Arnaldo. He led me to the largest of the structures. It had a cement floor and a doorway with no door. The first sight I saw, just inside the door, was a young girl and boy on the floor. They looked surprised and the girl was rearranging her disheveled dress. The boy, not much older than Arnaldo, looked up with a guilty grin on his face. "Hermano," Arnaldo said, gesturing to the boy. Brother. I guessed that the girl must be his girlfriend, possibly even a cousin, and we had caught them in some naughty play. I chuckled at his brother's grin and both he and the girl smiled guiltily. He stood and shook my hand, and then hurried out. Meanwhile several people had gathered at the open doorway and shutterless window openings (there was no glass, just big square openings) staring in at us. Arnaldo's brother returned carrying a chair and placed it down for me to sit. The girlfriend eyed Arnaldo's new clothes and commented something. Everyone laughed. A boy stepped inside and held his hand out to shake mine. "Hermano," said Arnaldo. Another brother. This one looked a little older than him. Arnaldo handed him the bag with his old clothes, and the boy

immediately took it to the far side of the room, and, without a thought to all the people staring into the room, began undressing and putting on the old clothes. They looked new compared to what he had been wearing. As a matter of fact, no one was wearing anything much better that what Arnaldo had worn when I had first met him. These people were obviously poor. Besides the chair in which I sat, and a solitary table, the only other furnishings in the room were two bunk beds and a double mattress on the bare cement floor. I guessed that at least five or six people must sleep in this room. The beds were unmade and each had a jumble of thread-worn blankets on it. There were miscellaneous pieces of clothing, all looking very tattered, drooping from the beds and heaped on the floor. A small heard of flies flew in endless loops in the middle of the room.

I wondered what they thought of this gringo tourista that Arnaldo had met and brought back with him. Even though I was wearing only jeans and a T-shirt, I still felt extravagantly dressed and almost wealthy in front of them. There was an awkward silence for a few moments, and then the younger brother made an attempt at speaking with me. His English wasn't much better than my Spanish, but we managed to communicate. I was able to get across that I was American and worked on a ship and that Arnaldo had been showing me around Valparaiso. As I spoke I wondered just how much they knew; if they suspected just how their brother came across all these new clothes and in exactly what way he had "shown me around" in Valparaiso.

There was another long silence as we ran out of words. Seeing there were a number of children, I dug in my pocket and produced some peso coins. With them I began an impromptu magic show. I also had a rope and handkerchief, and with these it worked into a mini-performance. More people gathered outside, looking in, until there was quite a little crowd. Someone even came up with an old pair of scissors when I asked if there were any. They were terribly dull, and it made the act all the more humorous when I did a cut and restored rope routine.

Afterwards Arnaldo beamed and slapped me on the back. He was genuinely surprised that I did magic, and I think a little relieved that I had been able to do something to justify our visit to his family. Otherwise it would have looked as though we had come simply to view their squalor and show off how much better dressed we were. That's how it felt to me, anyway.

As everyone dispersed, Arnaldo pulled at my arm and led me outside to an older woman, short, chubby, with matted hair and grimy dress. "Madre," he said. Mother. I bowed slightly and took her hand. "Buenos dias."

She whispered something to her son, and he led us around to the back of the dwelling. The few children who followed were vehemently shooed away by Arnaldo. Then he turned to me.

"Por favor, Miguel," he said. "Dinero? Dinero por comida?" Money. Money for food. It was the first time since I had met him that he had asked for money, asked for anything.

"Por madre?" I asked. "Cuanto?" How much?

"Por madre. Por familia," he said, and shrugged his shoulders. "Cinco mil?" Five thousand pesos–about twelve dollars. Not much to feed a whole family.

I pulled out some notes and handed them, folded, to his mother. She beamed, clutching them, "Gracias, senor, muchas gracias." Even the fifteen thousand I had given her would not go very far with that brood. I learned later that Arnaldo had twelve brothers and sisters, and no doubt there were twice that many cousins and in-laws living with them as well.

The afternoon was waning, and it was time to go. I looked forward to spending the evening with Arnaldo: sharing a meal together, enjoying some wine, strolling about Valparaiso, and of course ending up at the pension. Our ship would be leaving early the next day, so this would be the last chance to savor the beauty of this young Chilean; his smile, smooth skin and willing body.

Some of the young children accompanied us down to the road, including Arnaldo's older brother, the one wearing Arnaldo's old clothes. I gave them some peso coins and patted them on the head as each said good-bye. At the main road it was just the brother and us waiting for a mini-bus or taxi. When one finally arrived, I realized his brother had not come along to say good-bye. He wanted to come with us! Before I could even question what he was going to do, he was in the car and away we went. I looked at Arnaldo with a questioning look, but he acted as though it was the most natural thing in the world for his brother to be coming along. As the car leaned and curved along the winding road descending into Valparaiso, I asked Arnaldo where his brother was going, thinking perhaps he was just getting a free ride into town. He was going with us, he said, and instantly my idea of spending an evening alone with Arnaldo went out the window. Would he want to go to the hotel and spend the night with us as well? So much for a last intimate night together.

The car dropped us in town and we began walking without any apparent destination. I asked Arnaldo what he wanted to do, but he just shrugged his shoulders. His brother followed in silence. He spoke virtually no English. I wanted desperately to talk with Arnaldo, to tell him how much I wanted to spend this last night alone with him. Most likely his brother had no idea about our "friendship," and if he were to stay with us at the pension, it would most certainly turn out to be a dull and frustrating night. But the brother was with us, and he was part of Arnaldo's family, so there wasn't much else I could do except hope that things would work out.

I wondered what we could do. Go to a movie? Just walk around? I know, I thought. I asked if either of them played pool, billiards. Yes, they said. And so it was that Arnaldo led us to a neighborhood pool room. It was located in the basement of an aging building, and had only about four or five tables; all in a pretty dilapidated state.

Neither Arnaldo nor his brother were very experienced players, and with the language difference, it made for quite a challenging time for all of us. It was a dark, dingy sort of place, with a lazy proprietor half snoozing behind the small counter in the corner. We had a good time in spite of the fact that the table was not very level and most of the balls had chips and gouges in them.

It was after dark when we finished, and I asked Arnaldo and his brother if they were hungry. The answer was no, but I decided to take them to a cafe for a drink, at least. Along with our Cokes, they ended up ordering some sandwiches, and Arnaldo's brother ate not only his own, but half of Arnaldo's and mine (I wasn't really hungry at that point). I kept trying to think of a diplomatic way, and in Spanish, to tell Arnaldo that I didn't want his brother hanging around with us all night, but just didn't know how to go about it.

Once again on the sidewalk, we began again strolling the streets of the city. Finally at a corner we stopped. As though he had read my mind, Arnaldo began saying something about his brother wanting to go to a night club. He wanted to go and dance and meet some girls, but didn't have any money. Whether he was asking for some or not, I didn't care. I pressed several peso notes into his brother's hand and said it was for him to have a good evening with, and also to catch a mini-bus back home for the night. His brother opened up with a wide grin, and without hesitation thanked me and headed off down the street. Arnaldo was smiling too, so it had all worked out well.

We walked around some more, and even took a bus to Vina del Mar for one last look before heading back in the direction of the pension. On our return, since neither of us had eaten much, we stopped at a cafe where we had some sandwiches made to take out, and I also managed to find a nice bottle of Santa Emilino Cabernet. We took the whole lot back to the room and ate in splendor. It may not have been the most elegant meal, but with a fine bottle of wine and a fine looking young man such as Arnaldo it was divine. I savored every moment of it.

Knowing I had to get up and leave very early to get back to the ship, we showered and went to bed early. It was so wonderful to intertwine the arms and legs of our cool bodies once again, and caress this handsome young Chilean. Not only had I met someone genuinely warm and giving in so many ways, but now I felt I knew him better having met his family.

It was difficult to tear myself away at dawn. Arnaldo was wide awake to say good-bye although I insisted he go back to sleep when I left. The room was paid for, so he might as well enjoy it.

With my day pack slung over my shoulder, I slipped quietly out the door with the vision of Arnaldo, his brown, half naked torso barely visible in the weak morning light. It is a memory I have carried across the sea all the way

John Patrick

back to America and it will still be there when we return next year. I hope Arnaldo is.

# Angel of Mercy

## *Kevin Bantan*

The knock on the door meant that it could be only one person, given the dreadful weather. Sure enough, there was Rud, beaming, dressed for an evening out in white jeans a size too small for him. "Well, are you ready to party, girlfriend?" He swept past me into the living room.

"Are you crazy, Rud? There's freezing rain out there," I said, pointing in case he'd forgotten where 'out there' was. "The sidewalks and streets are as slick as your bottom used to be many, many years ago."

"Watch it, Tim. I didn't come all the way downstairs to be verbally abused."

"Sixteen whole steps. Are you serious about going out?"

"Of course."

"But the freezing rain."

"No, dear, sleazing rain. Only the hardcore sex seekers will be out tonight. It's a guaranteed score."

"More like the most hard-up. Have you gone off your Ritalin again?"

"You know very well I don't take that stuff, Miss Sniper Fire. Besides, unlike you, my libido never gets tired and my ego always needs to be stroked."

"Your head's gonna get stroked bad when you fall on the ice." With a flourish he pulled from his pocket something that looked like dozens of tiny ice picks strung together. "Voila!"

"What is that? It looks like something a serial killer would use during working hours."

"These, my dear, are cleats, which I shall wear to tame the nastiest of Mother Nature's tricks in the course of getting my own. And, I have another set that you can wear."

"No, thanks. I'm going to stay in and intact."

"Suit yourself. But I assure you that I'll be having a lot more fun tonight."

"I'll try to remember to be envious. Good luck"

"Won't need it. I'm assured of success. Ta ta," he said as he swept back through the doorway.

"And don't forget to take your Ritalin," I said, closing the door.

"Bitch!" shot through the wood loud and clear.

Rudyard and I somehow managed to be friends, as opposite as our personalities were from one another. Our tastes in men were, too. So there were never any sexual feelings between us or competition for the same guy. And he was no doubt right about finding a sex partner. Only the horniest would be out in the bars or in the parks. I was feeling horny, too, but not

desperate enough to risk a broken neck, ice picks on my feet or not. There are lines each of us draws, and one of mine was drawn around my apartment for the evening. I'd content myself with watching something inane on TV.

I went to the kitchen and poured a snifter of brandy, as insurance against any chill that my flannel shirt, sweater, cords and boots couldn't ward off. I settled into my comfortable old sofa, which has a depression in it that fits my bottom exactly, even if the bottom isn't quite as smooth as a newborn's. But not bad at all for a twenty-something guy. It turned out that the show wasn't even inane, it was simply boring. A spin off of a popular sitcom, it was badly in need of a laugh track, because I was sure that most of the other people watching weren't laughing either. I switched channels, but disappointment followed me up the dial. I decided to put on a porn video. None of the titles got my juices flowing, so I just inserted one with Joe Simmons, hoping that he would do his typical magic, but then I walked away absentmindedly.

After refilling my snifter, I went to the window facing the street, which was covered with a shiny horizontal icicle. Being on the first floor of this older building, I would look out to see the heads of pedestrians bobbing past. I didn't expect to see anyone tonight, but it was force of habit to look anyway.

So I was surprised by the form coming down the street on the opposite sidewalk. From the size and shape of the overcoat, I figured it was male. As it approached the streetlight, I was certain. It was a young man clutching the lapels of his coat closed with a leather-gloved hand and desperately trying to keep his balance by taking short, halting steps, but he was teetering. Then I saw arms flail and legs swoop out from under him, causing him to land hard on the icy concrete. I cringed in sympathetic pain. Immediately my Clara Barton instinct kicked in and made me do a stupid thing. I ran out of my apartment, down the hall and onto the front stoop. I went airborne and missed the four steps, which surely would have smashed my coccyx, among other things, paralyzing me for life. The cleated rubber on the soles of the boots acted as a minor braking device, serving only to pitch me forward. And there I was, sliding across the narrow residential street on my belly, unencumbered by the laws of physics. That is, until I hit the curb.

"Are you okay?" I managed to ask the prone figure next to me, when my breath returned. He turned his head to look at me, somewhat dazed. State of mind was of no consequence. I was staring into the most beautiful face I had probably ever seen in my entire life. His black eyes were flanked by long, curling lashes. The small, lean, ovular face was covered with soft brown skin made shiny by the rain and the glow from the nearby street lamp. The lips, while not as full as I would have expected, were slicked with a sensuality that made me want to kiss them. Bad. The lips moved. "Uh, I think nothing's broken. More stunned than anything, I guess. But soon to be hurting somewhere, when the shock of the fall wears off."

"Here, let me help you." Now remember, this is from someone lying in the gutter on his belly. The foolish statement elicited a laugh from him,

revealing gorgeous, even white teeth. "Yeah, I guess that was kind of stupid. Well, why don't we help each other. I live behind me, which is how I ended up here. I usually don't frequent gutters, although sometimes my mouth does."

"No shit?" We laughed together. With difficulty, he stuck out a tightly-gloved, soft leather hand. "My name's Dorian." Adorable Dorian.

"I'm Tim." We set about trying to right ourselves against the slickness made worse by the fact that the rain was heavier now and not freezing immediately. Once upright, we held onto each other, both afraid to move. His body was slim. It felt firm. Imitating the streetlamp was not a working plan, because we were getting soaked. "Let's coast."

"Do we have a choice?"

"Yeah, we could fall again." I wanted him to fall into my arms, but not until we got inside the apartment.

We made it to the opposite curb, bumping to a stop and almost ending up pitching onto our faces. Gingerly, we made it onto the sidewalk, only to be confronted by the steps. Now what? "Maybe if we tried to take them in our socks, we might get more traction." Even as I was speaking it, it sounded stupid, but I was determined to get Dorian's beauty into my apartment, whether anything came of it or not. He evidently couldn't come up with a stupider plan, because he shrugged his compact shoulders. So we sat on the bottom step and doffed our footwear. Surprisingly, it worked. Maybe the heat of our soles helped, but we got inside, in any event. We were shivering from the cold and the fact that we were wet to our skins. No meteorologist has ever explained to my satisfaction how it can be 23 degrees out and still rain.

Once inside the apartment, we began to take off the saturated clothing. It would have been enjoyable watching Dorian strip, if I weren't shaking like a leaf. Realizing that we'd need to put something on to try to warm up, I went to the bedroom to get a couple of my heavy robes, turning up the heat on the way. I finished undressing and donned a long, thick black terrycloth robe. It's companion, a white one, I gave to Dorian, who was down to white bikini briefs, hugging his arms to his sleek brown body. He accepted my offer of a brandy and I padded off to get it. When I returned, he was sitting on the sofa, a look of amusement in his eyes. He accepted the snifter and said, "If I were a film reviewer, I'd give you both thumbs up for your discriminating choice of movie fare." Confused, I turned toward the TV to see, to my horror, Joe's big dick plugging the snowy white ass of a very tanned blonde boy. Dorian laughed at the stricken look on my face. "Relax, Tim. You're with a friend." He reached up, took my hand and pulled me down next to him. The remnants of my embarrassment disappeared when he raised his snifter and said, "To us." The glasses tinkled as we sealed the toast and sipped. The room was suddenly much warmer. The brief chill had been banished, thanks to my sofa mate.

"This is damn good brandy."

"Thanks. It's only Christian Brothers, but I like it. Besides, it's not a budget buster like some other brands I could name."

"It's just fine. And it was fortuitous that one of us was prudent tonight."

"Yeah, a friend tried to coax me to go out with him, but I thought it was crazy. Him, too, for that matter. Why were you out?"

"Family get together at my sister's. I went there before it started to rain. In fact, I didn't even listen to an updated forecast. I thought that it was just going to snow a little bit."

"Surprise."

"Tell me. Nothing's moving, except for the fools, who have to prove how macho they are by wrecking their cars. So, it was walk or go crazy being around three little hellions for the rest of the night. Actually, I did make it more than half-way home before the tumble."

"Speaking of which, are you hurting anywhere?"

"My kneecap doesn't feel great. And my elbow, but otherwise I'm okay. Thanks." I poured more brandy. It was doing its job and then some. "So is Joe Simmons your favorite?"

"One of them. He's supposed to be a nice guy in real life, so I guess that wins him extra points in the sexiness department, too. You?"

Dorian shrugged. "No one in particular. Well, maybe Dino Phillips. He does make my heart skip a beat or two."

"Does your family know? I mean about you. You said you were at a family shindig."

"It is the subject never discussed, but, yes, they know. Not talking about it helps them to deny it. Does that sound vaguely familiar?"

"Too familiar. Are you warm enough?"

He looked at me with a mischievous grin, batting his long lashes. "Not as warm as I'd like to be." With that we leaned into each other and pressed our lips together. "Mmm, that's a start." It certainly was. My original appraisal of the ripe mounds guarding his mouth had been underestimating. They were positively incandescent. He wrapped an arm around me and pulled me back to his luscious lips. As our snifters found the top of the coffee table, our tongues found havens in each other's mouth. I wrapped my arms around Dorian's slim body, excited by it, despite its thick, protective layer of terrycloth. Well, hey, I hadn't expected any companionship to begin with, so this was all gravy.

As we continued to probe mouths sweetened by the liquor, my robe began to tent with my burgeoning erection the center pole. I reached into Dorian's crotch and found that he had slipped off his bikini and he, too, was camping out, and on such a lousy night. I loosened the tie on the robe and parted the cotton to gain unfettered access to him. It was long and narrow, like his body. At the same time, he was tunneling under my robe to check me out. He moaned when he hit pay dirt. It was nice to be appreciated. As if by instinct, we stopped kissing and looked at each other.

"It's down the hall."

"I'm right behind you." He was, too, feeling my buns, which had been molded into hard hemispheres by hundreds of squats each week. "Can I stay right behind you forever," he asked.

"That might be arranged, although you seem to be fickle. First you liked the front, now the rear."

He chuckled. "Okay, then, how about a split shift?"

"Yeah and then you'll want time and a half for overtime."

"And why do I think you'll pay it?"

"Because you're gorgeous and I will." We were in the bedroom now. Our robes were open, and we embraced. Like mine, Dorian's torso was smooth and tantalizingly silky. Our hard-ons were trapped between us against the ridges of our abdominal muscles, creating a wonderful feeling of togetherness, a brotherhood of two men hot for each other. He stopped kissing me to nuzzle my neck.

"I guess the perfect host would show his guest to the bed," I said.

"The host has been perfect so far. I have no doubt that his good manners will continue."

"This way." We doffed our robes and I turned down the bedcovers. We jumped in. The sheets were definitely colder than we were. We pulled up the covers and snuggled against each other. "This is fun," Dorian said in a whisper.

"Yeah, it sure is. Of course almost anything beats slipping and sliding and being soaking wet."

"But few things, if any, beat this."

"I couldn't agree more." We began to kiss again, allowing our free hands to explore the contours of the other's anatomy. I, myself, was quite pleased with the body lying next to me. He was as lean and hard as I'd first surmised. His ass cheeks were high and firm, conjuring a delightful fantasy. I can honestly say that I would have been content to kiss him all night until we each came. And considering that neither knew what the other liked to do in bed, we could be hopelessly incompatible in bed. We hadn't been thus far, though, so there was always hope. I really wanted to get to the secret place in the cleft between his mounds, while he was playing with my right nipple. Not a sneak attack, but a casual stroll to the entrance of his honey pot. If he didn't like it, I could live with it, but I hoped that he would acquiesce.

My finger sauntered down his smooth back into the hairless valley, where it found the differently textured, slightly wrinkled skin. I probed. It responded. It opened just enough for me to stimulate Dorian. He liked it evidently, because he pressed his ass against the would-be invader. Without lubrication, I wouldn't be able to go farther. I removed the finger and he caught a hold of my wrist. He brought my hand to his face and left my lips long enough to put the digit into his mouth to coat it with saliva. "Please be gentle."

"There's no way in the world I want to hurt you."

"I believe you."

"Just stop me if it feels uncomfortable." He put the finger into my mouth to wet it further, removed it and replaced it with his tongue. I found his opening again and slowly began to slide it inside him. He met the intrusion and facilitated its entry. Before long, it had slipped into him as far as it would go. I stroked his smooth inner surface, hoping to arouse him into wanting something else there.

Still snugly in him, Dorian came out of my mouth. "I know what you want, Tim, and I'm willing to try, but frankly I don't know if I can take what you've got."

I knew what he meant. The curse of being well-hung reared its ugly head again. I knew too well the fear engendered in a number of guys I had dated over the years. Most flat out refused. Others cried in pain. I didn't want to hurt this beautiful male animal, but I couldn't assure him that I wouldn't. "But if I'm fool enough to try to walk three miles over a sheet of ice, how much more foolish can it be to try this?" He reached down and stroked me lightly.

"You're sure you want to find out?"

"Nothing ventured, nothing pained."

"Which is exactly what I don't want you to feel."

"You're sweet, Tim, but it seems inevitable. Let's at least try." I took the bottle of very expensive lube from the nightstand drawer. Dorian threw back the bedcovers, took the bottle from my hand and pushed me onto my back. "I get the feeling that you like to be in charge, but let me do the work this first time, okay?"

"You're the boss. It's your body. You call the shots."

He squirted the slippery, viscous fluid onto his fingers and began to coat my shaft with it. "Where in the world did you ever get a cock this big, Tim?"

"I don't know. I've never seen any of my male relatives naked. Well, nor my female ones, either. But they don't count, I guess."

He let out a low laugh, melodic in its delivery. "You know, if we believed the old myth, I should be the one with this."

"Well, let me point out that your equipment is far from inconsiderable."

"String bean."

"String bean?"

"That's what I call it. It's long and lean like me. Does yours have a name?"

"Nope. How about Dorian's pet?"

"We'll see."

"We certainly hope so." He finished the paint job, having used the better part of the bottle from the way my cock glistened in the light. He spent a few more moments slicking himself and recapped the bottle. The excess on his fingers he smeared on the ripples of my belly. Then he kneed his way up to straddle my crotch. Holding my shaft, he raised up all the way and then lowered himself and made contact. "Wish me luck."

"All the luck in the world." He took a deep breath and sank onto me, pausing momentarily to breathe deeply again and lowered himself farther. Within a minute he had impaled himself on me. I was amazed. I guess he was, too, because he moaned, happily, "Wow!"' He set his hips in motion and began to ride me, while I teased his dark brown nubs, making them stand out in bold relief from his chest. It felt wonderful to manipulate him while he was returning the favor big time and seemingly effortlessly. "Oh, Timmy, I can't believe I have you inside me and that I can't get enough of it. It's positively bloating me and I'm loving it."

"You feel great, Dorian. I've never felt so good."

"You deserve it, my stud rescuer. I'm glad that I'm actually able to do it. Amazed, but glad."

"I'm getting close."

"Hallelujah."

"No, I mean it."

"So am I. I can't believe how it's stimulating my prostate. That's never happened before."

"I'm honored. I'm also going to come. Ahhhh!" He rode me for a few more short strokes before he, too, erupted onto my body, spewing enough of his seed to father a continent of children.

I crawled back into bed, having retrieved the snifters of amber delight and handed Dorian his. We toasted our new-found friendship. "What can I say, Timmy?"

"Just keep saying 'Timmy,' Dorian. It's been years since anyone's called me that. I like the sound of it, well, coming from your mouth."

"Good, and you can call me Dory. I know it sounds kind of fagoty, but how masculine does Dorian sound in the first place?"

"It sounds beautiful. Just how old String bean and what he's attached to looks."

"I thrive on flattery. How interested in him are you?"

"Interested enough to try and curious as to whether I can take him."

"You're a top, too, aren't you?"

I nodded. "Yeah. I've never wanted another guy's cock up my ass before, but then I've never met anything quite as beautiful as String bean."

"I have a feeling that he feels the same way about you."

"Don't you know for sure?"

"Well, he doesn't tell me everything. You know how boy cocks are. They have a mind of their own. Or is that a myth, too?"

"Having lived with one for twenty-some years, I'd have to say it's often sadly true. Are you hungry?"

"Actually I am for some reason. As if I've been doing heavy lifting with a barbell," he said, grabbing my rod. "But no crackers in bed, please."

"Better than that. I think I have some individual deep-dish pizzas in the freezer."

"That sounds suitably hearty after a hard night's work."

When we'd finished licking the grease from each other's lips, we returned to brandy and bed. I took a slug, uneasy about what the loss of my virginity would feel like. But I decided to be a brave little fuckee, considering the feat that Dorian had pulled off earlier. Anything less would be cowardice. There was an occasional tinkling on the bedroom window now. It sounded as if the rain might be changing to sleet. That would make the going outside a little easier, giving Dorian the opportunity for a quicker exit. Oh, well, I figured. You've already gotten much more than you expected this evening. Enjoy it while it lasts. Unless it hurts.

I was afraid that I was getting addicted to Dorian's lips. They were much fuller than I'd first thought and harder to part from. "You're sure about this, Timmy?"

"Of course not, but let's do it anyway." He was on all fours backwards and bent over to begin preparing me for String bean. He parted my cheeks and used his tongue to tease my opening. No one had ever touched me there. As an aggressively-butch top, I had never allowed it. But there I was enjoying his tongue darting into me, although not so mindlessly euphoric that I couldn't take his heavily-hanging ball sac into my hand for some playtime. Then I felt the tongue replaced by a wet finger as he began to go farther in. Then there were two of them. Then, unbelievably, three and I was living to tell about it. With the trio of digits buried and at rest, he decided to suck on his new pet for a while, but the feeling in my posterior was becoming seriously good now. "Dory, please put String bean in me. I'm ready for him. Please, I need it."

He came off me and said, "I love it when they beg."

"Don't get too smart, asshole. I've got you by the balls." I squeezed gently for effect. "Oh, shit, I forgot. Yes, dear, I'll be glad to accommodate you now. How was that?"

"Spoken under duress, but it'll do. Now will you please let String bean have his way with me?" He pivoted to a position behind me and I tossed him the bottle of lube. He went through the same routine with the slippery stuff, except that our preparation points were reversed this time. Fortunately he didn't draw out the process, so as to make me beg again. Still, my cock had become rock hard. I watched as he coated String bean, making it shiny, almost like a piece of patent leather. God, his penis was beautiful. He wiped himself on me again. "Hey, that's the second time you've done that."

"Don't 'hey' me. The once-perfect host forgot the towel again. He gets what he deserves."

"We'll see about that." And I didn't have to wait long. I felt the head push against my narrow opening and enter the tight channel, causing a sharp intake of breath.

"Hurt?"

"Yeah."

"At least you're man enough to say so. I'm going to make it hurt more temporarily. Try to keep breathing normally." It was impossible, when he pushed completely in. I thought that my diaphragm had collapsed. My eyelids were closed hard as if they could somehow absorb the pain. Then, wonder of wonders, the sharp pain began to ebb and I could feel String bean in possession of my lower tract, my rectal walls caressing him. "Fuck me, Dory."

He did with surprising gentleness. I experienced something akin to shame when I recalled how merciless I'd sometimes been when I was screwing someone. If nothing else, Dorian was teaching me a valuable lesson. "You feel great, Timmy."

"So does String bean. Really. It's hard to believe. Make String bean leave his come in me."

"He's well on his way, stud. You are one hot man, Timmy."

"And an angel of mercy."

"What?"

"Well, I rescued you from the tundra, didn't I?"

"Like a crippled guy with a rubber crutch."

"Wait a minute here. Before you said I was."

"Yes, wait a minute. Please." He put a finger to my lips to shush me, but my mouth swallowed it instead. He speeded up his movement and took my shaft in his other hand. After a few strokes, I gave it up, spurting helplessly in the air. He let go of me and closed his eyes and I experienced the feeling of someone coming in me for the first time. I wished that I hadn't shot yet. It would have felt much hotter. He collapsed on me, String bean slowly slipping out. He chuckled. "What?"

"It seems as if two tops can coexist in the same bed. I'll be damned."

"Can I be damned with you?"

We laughed.

The freezing rain continued for two more days before temperatures warmed up enough for the rain to banish its own icy grip from the city. In the meantime Dorian and I were housebound but by no means trapped. We used the time to nurture what has turned out to be a great relationship. I was glad for Mother Nature's intervention, and ever so thankful that I hadn't gone ice picking with Rudyard.

Oh, did I mention that despite, or more likely because of his prophylactic footwear, Rud fell and broke his wrist and cracked his knee cap within a block of the bar and his certain rendezvous with love? Poor dear. One of us had scored big time, but it wasn't the one at the beginning of the evening whom the casual observer would have predicted.

# Doing It

## *John Patrick*

Donny loved doing it – anytime, anywhere. He just loved sucking cock. He blew me in bed, of course. But, more often than not, in the living room, on the couch, on many a lazy afternoon. He sucked me off in the bathroom before work, the shower steaming up the mirror behind the closed door. He did it in the kitchen, catching me while I was standing by the sink, arms covered in bubbles, coffee warming on the stove. He did it in the car on the way to the beach, and on the way back as well. He did it in a dressing room at Neiman-Marcus, while I was trying on brand new jeans. He did it in the last row at the dirty picture show, watching straight porn in the dark. He did it in the john at our favorite restaurant. He did it on a mountaintop with a picnic of fruit and cheese and wine. He did it at my office while my boss was at a meeting. He did it in the john of a big Delta jet when we flew to New York. He did it in the gulf, as we floated on the waves. He did it in the thicket behind the dunes at the beach.

After six years of this, I was so used to getting my cock sucked three to four times a week, with a few fucks of his ass thrown in for good measure, that I was in a state of high anxiety for many months when it finally ended. He moved to San Francisco, hoping, I was sure, to improve his odds of obtaining more dick to suck. I was sorry to see him go. I've never met a more dedicated cocksucker than Donny. And he was terribly good at it, as you might expect, as if to prove the rule that practice makes perfect.

Even after he brought me off, he seldom let me go easily. I would drift back to consciousness thinking how wet I felt. I would lift my head to see his pretty face staring at my load on my chest and belly. He always seemed fascinated by my cum. He trailed his fingers through it, licking up some of it, then rubbing most of it into my stomach with a sly grin on his face, proud of what he'd done.

As he stroked my cock to renewed hardness, he kissed my navel and slurped downward. His tongue-tip lapped my cock, slowly encircling the now throbbing organ. Soon it was as if he was possessed. He used the same basic method: letting his lips sneak up on my nerve endings on a layer of hot spit and then ripping into my weakened defenses with his talented tongue. Now his suction went into overdrive as he worked his head steadily downward along my nine thick, uncut inches. Eventually he would move between my wide-spread legs and take his time bringing me off. He would suck my balls while he stroked my cock, then return his mouth to the action, teasing me unmercifully before finally letting me come.

A few months before we finally broke it off, we took a trip. The first night out, Donny stood before the mirror of the bar's john, arms raised. The rows of dirty incandescent bulbs lit him like a shrine. He slid his hands down his short, sublimely hunky body. He turned, sliding his right hand across his ass.

"It is gorgeous, isn't it?" he snickered.

"Best one I ever had," I admitted, toweling dry my hands.

He had blown me but not to orgasm. I had come twice already that day and knew he'd want it again once we returned to the hotel. We were visiting Philadelphia for the first time and spent most of the time in the hotel room, Donny over me, sucking. I wanted to see the Liberty Bell. He didn't care if he ever saw it, but the clubs were another story. He wanted to show off.

We walked slowly through the club. It was too cold, but less smoky than the bars we went to in Cleveland. The pulsating lights and noise merged into the drinks. They overwhelmed the senses to an almost desperate level. But Donny smiled, made eye contact. At the vaguest sign of interest, he'd stop. All it took was a raised eyebrow.

"Hi. Having fun?" a boy asked him.

Donny stopped. "Yeah–what's your name?"

"Andy." He extended his hand.

"May we join you?" Donny asked the kid, bringing an arm around my waist.

"Sure."

"So what do you do?" Donny asked.

"I work for Wal-Mart."

"Great," Donny said, somehow always feigning interest in whatever someone said they did. I had a hunch the kid may work at Wal-Mart during the day, probably sweeping up, but at night he sold it by the hour. Donny propped his elbows up on the table, pressed his leg against the kid's thigh, and did his best to look fascinated. They sat like that for a song or two. Andy didn't seem to want to talk; I was grateful. Donny's hand on Andy's thigh must have felt comforting. The music was too loud, a handy excuse to avoid the banter.

They decided to dance. Andy stood up. He had a hard-on. He began undulating his hips to the beat and soon his crotch was right in my face. I shifted in my chair. Donny bent over, shoved his ass into Andy's crotch. They laughed and moved off to dance.

When the song ended, they had their shirts off, wiping their sweat with them. I could see dark-haired Andy in all his glory. His stomach was hard and flat. It wasn't flat from endless sit-ups; it was the gentle flatness only youth ensured. You could look at his body and admire it, but it didn't demand the same respect as the chiseled muscularity of Donny. Blonde, blue-eyed Donny's body was a hymn to human form. But, although he appreciated it, it remained a commodity and a tool. He had stripped in straight clubs and had developed a perspective. It was plain: all workers had

a supply that filled a demand. Strippers peddled arousal to the lustful. Why not exploit his body while he could? His college degree would last longer.

Donny always worked up a good sheen as he danced, and a thirst. I had beers waiting for them. While they drank, I looked over at Andy. He was an object of beauty. A bit roughened. Charming on the surface, probably because he was a devious little thing at heart. He had a slightly malicious streak and I saw it.

"What do you want, John? Hmm?" he mocked cautiously. He thought I might be the sort who bit back.

Donny slipped his hand under my T-shirt. "Is your neck still bothering you, John?"

"You hurt your neck?" Andy asked, finishing his beer.

"Yeah, whiplash."

"Whiplash?"

Donny laughed. "Yeah, I hit him in the face with my dick."

"I'd like to have seen that," Andy said, watching us intently. Donny's other hand moved to my cock, engorged and throbbing. His touch was very light. I drew in a breath. "My neck is fine, Donny. Thank you."

He increased the pressure of his fingers and I shuddered.

"Good. I want you to feel relaxed when we go back to the hotel. You are beginning to feel a little better, aren't you?"

"Yes. You're really turning me on."

"I am?" His fingers squeezed my crotch. "Oh, you should see this," he said to Andy.

"How hard is he getting your cock, John? Let me see," Andy sneered sweetly, coming over to me. Now I had one young stud on one side, one on the other. Andy was terribly interested in the bulge Donny was rubbing. I suddenly felt self conscious, being examined so impersonally. Completely absorbed in their probing, they ignored my pleas to stop.

Andy looked back up at my face after a few excruciating minutes. "You don't mind if I pay you a little bit of attention now, do you?"

"No." I was almost panting now. Donny had worked the zipper of my pants down and his right hand kept on playing with the head of my cock persistently. He would tease, circling the head mercilessly without really touching it, then sliding over it gingerly until I could take no more. "Please, let's go," I begged Donny.

"Okay," he said, "but I gotta pee first."

He stood up; Andy stood up. Donny went to the john, Andy in hot pursuit. I waited a few moments, letting my hard-on calm down, and then followed them.

Sure enough, Donny was bending over, blowing Andy at the urinal. He stopped when I came in.

"That's sick," I said, "I'm getting out of here." And I ran back to our table where my fourth drink was waiting for me. I dove right into it. Donny followed and sat down like nothing had happened, but we kept sneaking

looks at each other, staring when we didn't think the other was looking. I felt edgy about what was going to happen when we returned to our hotel. Donny may have been unfaithful to me, but I never knew it. Now I had seen it!

Andy joined us, nervous about what was to happen next. I smiled at Donny. "You want to invite Andy to our place?" I asked him. After all, he had just had the boy's cock in his mouth. He must have wanted a new cock very badly.

"No, you invite him. It's up to you. I don't want a scene."

Whenever Donny had paid any attention to anyone in the past, I grew angry and often ruined the evening. I had no intention of ruining my first night in the city of brotherly love.

"C'mon," I said, taking Andy by the hand.

He smiled at Donny.

In the hotel room, I let Andy touch me where he wanted to. But it was Donny making me feel so weak, nearly six years later, still sucking all my breath away.

I leaned back on the bed and let Donny work. Most of the time my eyes were closed but when I opened them I couldn't help but see Andy now had all his clothes off and so did Donny. Andy got down on his knees on the floor and started sucking Donny while Donny sucked me. Then Andy got on the bed and started sharing my cock with Donny. Donny was soon on the bed over me, and started stroking my thighs, moving his hands up and down and pushing my legs apart as he did it. I reached out to his crotch and rubbed my hand over his penis, which felt fat and hard and was leaking. I started real slow, licking it up and down, and then sucking just the first inch or so in and out of my mouth while my hands bunched up his balls to hold it steady.

Suddenly, I had an urge to not only have two cocks at once, but I also wanted to see them doing it together. I pulled Andy up, onto his knees so that both their cocks were in my face. I sucked one, then the other, then both at once. Andy's was much longer than Donny's, but not as thick.

After all these years as a top, I wanted Andy in my ass. I rolled over, keeping Donny at my head, and lifted myself to Andy.

As Andy was pumping his cock into my ass, on the brink of orgasm, Donny whispered, "Wouldn't you love to see me get fucked by another guy?"

I nodded, but I continued sucking Donny's cock while Andy fucked me from behind. When Andy came, the sensation was indescribable–like being totally filled, totally satisfied.

After a while I took Donny's dick out of my mouth and said innocently, "I think Andy can work it up again, can't you?"

Andy shrugged agreeably. Donny lay down on his back next to me. Andy climbed on top and slowly licked Donny's throbbing cock, then mine. I gently pushed Andy's head down between my legs.

Watching Andy suck me drove Donny wild. He begged to have Andy in him. Andy obliged, sliding his thin prick into Donny without stopping. I soon was licking Andy's prick as it made its journey in and out.

For a moment that seemed like hours, we were suspended in time. Then the moment passed, and I was over Donny and he took the whole of my cock down his throat, sucking eagerly, his fingers kneading my balls. Andy pumped in and out of Donny's ass just the same as he had mine.

Donny was delirious. He pulled my cock from his mouth, stroked and squeezed the head, finally taking the pulsing meat back into his mouth just as I came.

I lay back and began stroking my spent cock, feasting on the sumptuous vision before me.

Feelings of lust coursed through me, along with a little bit of jealousy. The boys now became so involved in their sex, they forgot I even existed.

Before long, Donny was stroking himself to orgasm and Andy stepped up his attack on his ass. I had never seen Donny come as hard as he did at that moment. As their hard-ons withered and they returned to reality, both boys looked at me with a mixture of embarrassment and apology. They broke apart to lie on either side of me.

"That was so hot," I finally said.

They both let out a sigh of relief. After a while I reached down and took a cock in each hand, stroking and kneading them until they were again erect. Eventually I sat up and pushed their cocks closer together, rubbing the head of one up and down the other's shaft. I knelt and licked each of them, then took both inside my mouth, though I could only fit an inch or two. We were all breathing heavily.

While I had always expected I'd be a passive partner in this kind of triangle, I was, after about half an hour of petting and pawing, again orchestrating all the action. I knew the boys wanted to get it on with each other but were too inhibited to do so without my encouragement.

And encourage them I did. I told Andy to lie on his belly, then directed Donny's cock to his asshole. I lubricated the head and Andy's hole, then gently guided the cock inside. Andy moaned, spreading his ass cheeks as Donny sank it in inch by yielding inch. He began to fuck Andy, slowly at first, then faster, until Andy was on all fours, pushing against Donny's dick, silently begging for more. Donny pulled out and I took over. I entered him easily and thrust in and out of his asshole without missing a beat.

I thought I'd die of pleasure right then and there. I have always loved the sensation of fucking a boy, pounding him into the bed, dissolving all my tension. Now I had the added sensation of Donny entering me while I fucked Andy. Having the weight of two men on top of him, Andy collapsed to the bed. Donny was grunting, making animal sounds I'd never heard from him before, and Andy was sighing in ecstasy, having totally surrendered. I felt Donny's cock stiffen and I gripped it hard with my ass muscles. As he shot his load into me, spasms rocked my body. At the same time, Andy let out a

loud grunt that was almost a lion's roar, and the three of us shook together as one organism, holding onto each other in near desperation.

We collapsed in a sweaty, exhausted heap. After a while I got up went to the bathroom. In a few moments, Donny was there, standing next to me, rubbing my back, watching me pee.

When I was finished, I turned and took him into my arms. Although he told me how much he loved me, and would always be true to me, I somehow felt he had graduated that night. I had taken him out of town to experience life and he had. And I had joined in and loved every minute of it. But now what? Sadness overcame me, but it quickly dissipated when Donny dropped to his knees and began doing it again.

# Street Scene

## *Thom Nickels*

I'm usually up at 6 A.M. to attend to a handicapped friend of mine who lives eight blocks away. My usual ritual consists of making coffee and a few minutes of quiet contemplation in the pre-dawn hours when I look out my kitchen window. On this particular day I saw or heard nothing, which is odd because sound on my street really carries, even when you whisper on the street below. When I left my apartment at 6:40, there was no one outside either; it was just the cozy and idyllic tree-lined street I've known for five years.

When I headed back to my place later that morning, I noticed the neighborhood dog walker (an old man who walks dogs all day with his hunky straight assistant) standing on the corner talking to a number of policemen and ambulance personnel. He was pointing to the stairwell.

I didn't bother to take a look because I assumed there was an injured homeless person in there, or a passed-out drunk, since that's what one usually finds on the streets of Philadelphia these days. As the minutes unfolded, however, the scene on the street magnified: onlookers began to gather, as did policemen, detectives, reporters, and TV cameras. I even saw a newsman pan a camera towards my bay window, as strangers from all walks of life collected on my front steps, including some hunky boys who stopped to gawk.

I've learned how, through a study of human nature, to read signs in the way people look at something, especially men, when the visual object touches on the erotic. Something sexy in a female's nude body, placed stomach down and positioned in such a way that the dog walker assumed she was "a mannequin"–until the dogs recoiled in horror, that is–resonated in the body language and stares of the detectives and cops who kept glaring into the stairwell. Their looks remained fixed too long and communicated the fact that the body was not that of an ugly homeless person but something more "captivating." Indeed, it seemed that while I was sipping my coffee my neighbor Kimberly Earnest, a pretty girl with flaming red hair, was being raped and getting her head bashed against the bricks in the stairwell.

For a week or so after the murder, the activity on my block resembled a movie set. At night, TV lights and cameras blared; during the day, reporters stalked the area, interviewing passers-by or knocking on doors. Mourners left flowers, notes, religious pictures and other mementos so that the scene became a shrine. But the shrine also became a kind of erotic Mecca.

On the day Kimberly was killed, I raced outside after spotting a young man whose feet I had massaged in Philly's Judy Garland park one summer night. The poor boy–or boy/man, since he was not really a boy, but not yet

what you would call a man–lay passed out drunk on a park bench when I went over to him and began feeling his sneakers, eventually taking them off and exposing his bare feet to the elements. I then proceeded to give him a foot massage he was only dimly aware of. You can imagine my surprise when I saw him among the onlookers gazing at the stairwell and pondering the mystery of death. That's when I darted outside and asked him what leads the police had, if any.

In the daylight, I could see that he was really not a boy, though he was a sexy, tough type–a petite Irish, fey/macho, (and probably) big-dicked dude.

I had no trouble inviting him in for coffee, a smart move since once in my apartment he praised my bay windows for their excellent view of the stairwell. In my living room I was able to get a close-up view of his compact "little boy's" butt, his firm body, his tough, street fighter's persona.

"Yeah, I used to hustle when I was younger," he told me. "I don't do that now but I'm used to getting a little something, a few dollars, you know." By now he was sitting on my large sofa and I was positioned at his feet, slipping off one of his sneakers. "I'm a bike messenger now. I bike all over the city and I work for a real bastard–wow, that feels good."

I remembered seeing him years before, when he wasn't quite so tough, a little prettier even. "Maybe I had you back then. There's something familiar about you. Anyway, I've seen you around for years ..."

"I can't hustle like that now. They want really young kids. A lot has changed," he said.

I agreed, adding, "Yeah, can't you feel the whole world rushing towards some event, some large episode, like everything's on fast forward and none of us knows what's in store?"

The murder was making me maudlin even if the pandemonium associated with it was stirring up other juices: I was as horny as hell, and, from the bulge in his jeans, so was he.

He had a hard-on of considerable merit: thick and curved, a juicy specimen for one so petite. I began by sucking on his toes as he stretched out on my sofa in a blowjob prone pose. He was succulent looking, eager, and excited by the nearness of the media and maybe even the possibility of cameras panning my bay window as he orgasmed.

I brought out my glory hole prop, a big board the size of a large artist's canvass with a hole gorged out by constant stabbing with a knife and fork. The large board fit best in my bedroom braced against the side wall of my protruding closet corners and bedroom door. Some of my best tricks have stood against this board: teenage boys in X-large knit hats, married executives, UPS delivery men, twenty-something roller-bladers. The board works this way: the one getting major licks or a lubricated hand job sticks his cock through the hole, his hands clutching the sides of the board as he helps to hold it upright. For tall men I have to put pillows under the board so they don't have to crouch down. Smaller men and boys have an easier time of

things, although some of them have to tiptoe to stick their cock through comfortably.

Why a board? For one, it's an excellent way to give ordinary blowjobs a kinky public sex angle. Most guys adore it, especially if they're straight and like to imagine that a woman is on the other side.

Wow, the bike messenger's cock looked superb through the hole; it was so stiff it could have been a teenager's. Copious pre-cum flowed over my hand as he fucked the tight hole I made with my fist. His thrusts were worthy of the pedal power of the best bikers: in no time he shot huge gobs down the front of the board, zigzag rivers with many tributaries that added to the board's Jackson Pollack semen imprints of many potent ex-tricks.

Afterwards, I handed him a couple dollars, like he said, and he was off, a reporter accosting him as soon as he left my place. Outside, more hunky men and boys came to pay their respects, many of them in their twenties mourning a beautiful girl who might have been their girlfriend. I spotted many of them leaving flowers or kneeling on the ground. Especially memorable was a sexy youth who brought a drum and who sat cross-legged near the stairwell and banged out ritualistic sounds till late in the morning. I was about to go out and offer him a foot massage when he picked up his drum and walked away.

\* \* \* \* \*

On the afternoon of the murder, I was taken to the police station for questioning. Living near the stairwell, I could have been an important witness. The police wanted to question me about a certain heterosexual peeping tom who'd been canvassing the neighborhood for years. Though he couldn't be called handsome, he had a sexy, lean body and enormous feet. I first saw him one night on my way home from the bars, standing on a doorstep near the stairwell. Since I thought he was cruising, I stood on my own doorstep and did everything I knew to get him to come over: winking, nodding my head, pacing up and down my steps.

When there was no response, I started to walk over to him whereupon he took off like a frightened sparrow.

I realized he wasn't interested in guys when I saw him peer into a woman's apartment window later that week. There was a soft light on in the apartment and a woman's shadow could be seen through the lace curtains. He was on the doorstep where I'd first seen him, peering into the window, oblivious to who might be watching. After that I started to see him in the neighborhood all the time, going from window to window in a carefully orchestrated program of voyeurism. I told the cops I thought he was a benevolent sicko but the detective questioning me wasn't so sure.

On the way back from the station, a beefy, red-headed cop I had seen in the neighborhood asked me if I thought a hustler might have been the killer.

John Patrick

"A hustler? Don't hustlers usually interact with their own sex? Why would a hustler have anything to do with a woman jogger," I said, wondering if the cop was a homophobe.

But I was way off base. I wasn't thinking of the quality of Philadelphia hustlers these days, crack-addicted meatheads who'll do anything for a fix, who disappear into your bathroom to shoot up as soon as you invite them home.

There's lots of reasons why most Philadelphia hustlers these days are no good. First, a sizeable minority demand money before sex–"as security," they say–but this is always a portent because inevitably they want more money after the act. Most are also petty thieves. They take anything they can get their hands on. Snow shovels. Ladders. Bottles of cologne. But the crack-crazy ones are the worst; these guys are not interested in sex, and they care little about client "needs." They think they deserve $10 or $20 just because they go to your apartment, pull down their jeans and show you their cock– which they couldn't get hard if their life depended on it.

Some nice hustlers still exist, however, but they are a minority. Take Duane, for instance. He's a cute 23-year-old with a small loop earring in his left ear and light tattoos on his arms. Duane likes drugs, and he gets high, but he doesn't shoot or exchange needles. He's a kid who needs affection, a big brother or a sugar daddy figure. And yes, no matter how high he is, he always loves sex. I met him a year before the murder when he was walking around with a kerchief on his head, his succulent red lips reminding me of a cherub, his slim body the apex of boyishness. He could have passed for sixteen.

My boyfriend at the time agreed that we should try Daune and pay him $50. We brought him to my place where all three of us stripped down. Duane got on the bed with his legs spread far apart, his lips open to suck both of us if that's what we wanted. He was so cute, with his boy's hard-on and his chest nipples looking so perky. My lover and I also liked the look of his feet: his long toes had a creamlike delectability. When we sucked on them Duane's dick rotated and oozed boy sap.

Tense with pleasure, the little guy came in violent jerks as my lover and I worked on those toes. He became an epileptic during his orgasm, thrashing about as if he was getting ready to levitate off the bed.

Duane the murderer? Not a chance. Neither could it have been Dennis, the tall blonde with sparkling (but crack addicted) blue eyes, as handsome as a movie star. I met Dennis on Pine Street as he was trying to flag down traffic. He said he was from Florida (still had his Florida tan) and was desperate for cash. He said he needed a place to crash: he'd been dumped by his girlfriend. He went on to say he was used to getting $100 for sex. "No way," I said, "that's not my league. And you probably won't make that much in Philadelphia. There are too many five dollar-crack addicted hustlers here. Bring your price down and you may survive."

He commented on his scruffiness and his being on the road; this meant that he could go for much less. Yes, he'd do something for ten dollars, providing I fixed him a cup of coffee. So off we went. Dennis striped nude at my place, his dolphin-white body reminding me of Flipper and the Florida Everglades, his size eleven feet hanging over the edge of my bed, cock standing straight up but ultimately impotent because he'd ingested some drug. Drugs: yes, it always comes back to drugs–the killer of young men and their virile cocks.

"Hopeless but not totally lost," I remember thinking as I slipped my tongue between his toes. Soon he was so stress-free he fell asleep on my bed, a prime Jeffrey Dahmer target were I a crazy sort.

In the morning we said our farewells, and he headed back to the street–those blue eyes of his filled with such sadness. Months later, I spotted him on the street holding himself up near a pay phone. He looked like he was about to collapse and his eyes were the color of plums. "My mother just died," he told me, catching my curious glance, "My mother just died. Fuck the world!"

I could only tell him that I was sorry. I had to leave him there to work things out as I was on my way to work.

As we spoke, another hustler–a sheepishly dressed scumbag in woolen scarves and a knit hat pulled over his wide Peruvian nose–approached us for a five dollar sex/crack score.

\* \* \* \* \*

The pay phone at the end of my street is about two hundred feet from my stairwell and cannot be seen from my bay window. I can only see who is walking towards it, be it an old lady, old man, snotty Penn student or potential foot massage victim. I admit it's fun to dial the number when a hot guy walks towards the phone, or when a group of straight students passes–usually processions of hand-holding boys and girls. Often one of the guys will answer as the girls giggle in the background.

College students are anything but original these days. Most answer: "Dan's street pizza" or "Doc Watson's sex therapy clinic!", expecting to out-shock or out-"Saturday Night Live" what I'm about to say. But my offer of hot Columbian coffee and a stimulating foot massage always leaves them speechless. Most hang up right away. Most guys walking alone do not answer the phone, but some do. When a woman answers I hang up immediately.

My first call to the phone was a random dial: I'd seen no one on the street but just dialed 545-9060 on blind faith.

I got a boy of 20 who was waiting for a friend to pick him up, the friend being an older sugar daddy type crazy in love with him. We agreed to meet the next day when we both discovered that we went to the same high school and had the same history teacher. When I met him, I was amazed at what I

John Patrick

saw. He had beautiful Hawaiian-Italian features, wavy dark hair, perfect skin. I could not believe my luck as he asked me what I wanted to do to him.

I said: "Go into my bedroom, take off your clothes, and lie face up on my bed." He did as he was told. His body so handsome I wondered why he wasn't in California modeling or pursuing a movie career.

He stretched out on my bed, arms behind his head, cock erect, feet over the edge of the mattress. I massaged his fine legs, then hovered over him on all fours, smelling his nipples and glazing his chest with my tongue.

"You're really quite beautiful," I whispered, something I don't say often and really don't like to tell people, but this boy had to know. For a few minutes I just looked at him before nuzzling my face between his thighs, working down towards his feet where I began my stress-reduction technique: he wiggled his toes as my mouth slipped over each foot, my tongue gliding over the silky undersides. He uttered a soft "Yeah," as pre-cum oozed down the sides of his boner. In no time, he was jerking off, his left foot tense in my mouth as he lifted it up in the air. He yelped and moaned before he came and then he let out primal scream.

I never saw him again, although the pay phone yielded more surprises in those months before the murder. Once a skateboarding kid picked it up and said yes to my offer of a body massage. I told him where I was, answered the door, and saw a pasty-faced kid of about 18 in baggy pants, an over-sized hat pulled over his head. This surely was Philadelphia's finest, an authentic teen who couldn't wait to undress and get his cock sucked. He was so energized he didn't want to take off his clothes or go into the bedroom; he just unbuckled his pants and asked me to suck him on my sofa. He was going a mile a minute, bursting at the seams to come, grabbing hold of my neck and holding my head down to his crotch while I begged him to slow down and savor every minute. "You're moving too fast, partner. Can't you take off your clothes? Can I massage your feet? Can I see your chest?"

To all this he answered no ... until he saw my ass. Then it was, "I want to fuck you!"

He jumped behind me, his teen pecker rubbing against my butt as he tried to direct it with his hands and as I kept pushing it away.

"Calm down, what drug are you on?" I said. "What the hell is the hurry anyway?"

"Gotta cum, dude."

"Look, you need a condom for that. I don't fuck without a condom."

He was going faster than a train and still trying to ram it in me, teen pre-cum wetting my legs, his accelerated breath in my ears.

"Besides, I only fuck people I'm in relationships with," I said. "What do you think I am?"

"Oh, no, man, I want to fuck you. Open up. Let me get it in. You'll love it!"

Realizing it was hopeless, he threw himself on the sofa, legs spread wide, his right hand shaking his dick. I knelt down between his legs in a

gesture of goodwill and sniffed his balls and licked his cock shaft, but not going over the head, health fanatic that I am. I may want his pre-cum on my fingers and mustache but not in my mouth–I didn't know where this jackrabbit had been.

"Suck my balls," he ordered.

I did is I was told. He shot enormous gobs of sperm all over his chest and abdomen. His paste smelled like chalk and skateboard metal. It was all over too soon.

"Man, you are some dude," I said. "I could take seeing you every day, even with that hat."

"What's wrong with my hat?"

"You never take it off."

There was no time for me to come. He was up in a jiffy, buckling his baggy pants and fixing his chain, pulling at the sides of his knit hat and reaching for his skateboard. Then he was out the door, without so much as a good-bye.

\* \* \* \* \*

Eventually they arrested two suspects in the Kimberly Earnest murder. They published a 19-year-old blonde's picture in the papers. I recognized him immediately. I hadn't been looking for boys when I spotted him on Pine Street, walking with a confident bounce towards the pay phone. I studied his gestures and decided he might like what I had to offer, so I picked up the phone. Sure enough, he answered on the second ring. He had a craggy voice, like a black rap singer.

"Is this the blonde boy walking down from 21st?''

"Yeah, it's me. What's up?"

"Well, I saw you from my window and I think you're pretty cool. I'd like to know if you'd like a foot massage."

"Yeah I'd like a foot massage, but I have to go home first and shower up. I'm on my way home from work ... I live on 21st Street. Can I come by in about twenty minutes?" He said this as if it were the most normal thing in the world. I might have been selling encyclopedias.

I told him where I lived, half of me thinking he'd never show up because it all happened too fast. Usually guys who say they'll call later never do. In most cases, it's now or never. I also didn't like the sound of his voice. Something about it made me uneasy.

Four hours later, my door buzzer rang. By then I had given up on him and was on the phone making up with an ex-boyfriend, Polonsky. Polonsky was calling after a two-month separation and we were in the middle of a heavy discussion. He heard my buzzer and asked, "Who is that?"

I said, "I don't know," and pressed the enter-buzzer. I expected my best friend who lives several blocks away but instead I saw the blonde in a red

hunter's jacket. He was heading straight for my open apartment door with a wide grin on his face.

"Hey, remember me, I'm the guy from the pay phone–"

I panicked because I didn't want Polonsky to hear anything like this. "Look," I said, "you'll have to leave," and so I very quickly escorted him downstairs, my stomach turning the whole time because he was the most beautiful blonde boy I'd seen in a long time. He even had a dainty Adam's apple and long slender feet in new sneakers.

I thought I'd seen the last of him until that morning his picture was on the front page of The Philadelphia Inquirer. In the paper his face looked more twisted than it did in my apartment.

News reports said that she spotted the hooligans trying to break into a car with a wrench and crowbar. Earnest, who was from the Midwest, told both boys to "Cut it out!" as she whizzed past them – almost whizzed by I should say because the younger of the two men, the lithe 19-year-old blonde (who once answered the call I made to the pay phone booth at the end of my street), grabbed her by the wrist and punched her in the face.

A struggle erupted, during which Kimberly – an athletic girl nearly five-ten with red hair and a statuesque physique (she was wearing a skimpy black tank top during her run) – slugged the blonde pretty hard. Police say the boy was upset because she was getting the best of him so he slugged her in the face with the wrench and knocked her out.

At this point the story varies, depending on who you talk to, and which of the two confessions from the boys you want to believe. One report says that the older, dark-haired boy (a beefy, big-boned, unattractive motorcycle type) drove the stolen car around town while the blonde raped Kimberly in the back seat. Another report had the blonde undressing Kimberly in the car but not doing anything till the driver came to a stairwell where they dumped her. At the stairwell, which is across the street from my apartment, the blonde got out of the car and dragged the unconscious, bleeding girl jogger over a wrought iron fence. The girl's weight was crushing, however, so both boys threw the body on the stairwell steps, where the blonde then proceeded to pull down his pants, strangle and rape the early morning jogger.

The blonde told police that he stopped fucking Kimberly because he was too nervous to ejaculate. That's not hard to imagine, since she was already dead, the result, police said, of her head being bashed against the brick wall of the stairwell. In other words, the sight of her caved-in face with blood and guts pouring out all over the place made the blonde lose his hard-on.

"It was not a pretty sight," a detective told me later. "And it's a horrible way to die."

I read and re-read the story of his arrest: how he was from a nearby suburb but had moved into Center City to stay at the apartment of his friend, who lived over a garage. The two of them, the news report stated, went joyriding early every morning, riding through town in a beaten-up Bonneville Pontiac, harassing or mugging whoever caught their eye. I could

have been one of those people because I'm up every day walking the streets of the city at 6:30 A.M. I imagined what might have happened if I hadn't been on the phone making up with Polonsky, and had decided to let him stay. Would he have sliced my head open after I sucked his toes? Would he have stolen the signed Warhol serigraph? Or the original Audubon lithographs? Would he have dragged me over to the stairwell?

As I watched the mourners come and go across the street, and as I attended city memorial services for the slain victim and even wrote an op-ed piece on the murder for The Philadelphia Daily News, I couldn't believe that I had the murderer in my own house, and that I'd met him in such a simple fashion: through a simple call to a corner pay phone. Somehow I also felt that had I let him in nothing would have happened to me. Some things you just know and this was one of those things.

I caught myself fantasizing about the killer the way the twenty-something student males stood at the stairwell, making Kimberly their mythical girlfriend. I remembered the boy's dainty Adam's apple and the way his hair curled on the back of his head.

I imagined myself fucking him in a punishing fashion, the same way he'll be buggered in prison till his pink asshole is ripped open by the desperate power tools of men who might then sling him over chairs or pin him to bunk beds in cells full of sweat and sperm.

The pay phone has not been the same since the murder. It has been four months. The veil of paranoia and suspicion is everywhere. Once I called and thought I was making some headway with a college student, a poor lonely, repressed thing. He perked up at the mention of a foot massage–a novel idea, yes, and safe from every AIDS education standpoint. But then the ghost of Kimberly kicked in.

"Well, you know, there was a murder here not long ago. How do I know you're not some sicko?"

"Look, this is a civilized massage. I'm no thug with a crowbar."

"But I only have your word. I don't know that for sure."

"What is for sure, when you think about it?"

# The Runaways

## *Leo Cardini*

"School buses," Ramon says, standing there naked in front of me, his semi-hard, down-curving dick just inches from my face. I'm about to take it into my mouth again and suck on it until it reaches the nine rock-hard inches I know it's capable of when I pause to look up at him, admiring how beautifully tight-muscled, lean and all-over tan he is, an Incan god towering above me as he scans the rural Vermont countryside, one hand shading his eyes from the bright, July sun, the other resting lightly on my shoulder.

I return my attention to Ramon's irresistible Peruvian dick, repositioning my knees on the thin Indian bedspread we'd spread out in the middle of this grassy field up in the hills a mile or so behind Goddard College, where I go to school. It's mid-afternoon now. We've been here since dawn, when we shed our tee shirts and cutoffs (we traveled barefoot), meditated in the gentle warmth of the rising sun, and then ate the potent mushrooms Ramon got from a fellow classmate at Tufts, where he goes to college.

Since then, we've been communing with nature, romping through the grassy fields, quietly passing through needle-carpeted pine forests serene as cathedrals, and standing in awe of cliffside panoramas that extend for miles in every direction across the gently rolling Green Mountains.

And the sex! Twice already. Sex between us is always good. I suppose that's why we snatch every opportunity we can to make love to each other–on beaches, behind barns, atop Boston townhouses, and once, in a drugstore phone booth. Really! But never has it been so prolonged or intense as today.

The mesmerizing, mushroom-induced aura that surrounds his dark, thick-shafted cock pulls me closer with open mouth. His piss slit produces a pearl of pre-cum, a gift I delicately lift off his over-sized cock head with the tip of my tongue and swallow.

"Lots of them," he says as he looks in the direction of the seldom-used dirt road passing by us about twenty yards away.

But I've forgotten what he's talking about, so before I finally take his cock into my mouth once again, I ask, "Lots of what?"

"School buses," he repeats, like it's obvious.

Now, you're probably thinking that as compelling as a heavily-veined, half-hard cock can be, especially one as big as Ramon's, wouldn't I be at least slightly curious to know about these school buses–like whether they're matter-of-fact real, or a drug-induced hallucination? Well, you have to understand that at this particular point in time–of Stonewall and Woodstock–Goddard College was so strongly counter-cultural, and everyone so into doing their own thing, you got so nothing surprised you. From the sight of a

classmate with a heavy stack of books under one arm walking into the library dressed in nothing but a loincloth, to the complaints of farmers five miles away that a heavily-amplified rock concert was disturbing their cows; and from the naked dish crews in the cafeteria, to course offerings such as "Grokking The Beethoven String Quartets," you got to expect the unexpected.

Maybe Ramon does see school buses. Maybe it's an acid flashback. Whatever.

So I wrap my lips around his dick, closing my eyes and gripping my own cock as I sink into the indescribable pleasure of feeling his fleshy, semi-soft member filling my mouth, anticipating its gradual growth until it's once more hard enough for me to deep-throat.

"I can see five so far, and they keep on coming."

Okay, okay. Since he's not going to let go of this bus thing, I reluctantly dismount his cock and stand up beside him.

Along the twisting road that emerges from behind a cluster of trees comes a school bus, followed by another. And another. And another.

This seemingly endless caravan snakes it way along the road. Each bus is yellow, of course, but that's just the backdrop for a psychedelic spattering of peace signs, flowers, mandalas, and messages of universal love.

Ramon slips his arm around my waist and we stand there watching this bizarre procession approach, like we'd just be transported into the middle of some zany Beatles flick.

When maybe a dozen of them have come into sight, and they're as close to us as the road gets, the first one stops. The rest follow suit and a brown-haired, bell-bottomed hippie jumps out of the first one, shakes the stray shoulder-length hair off his face and smiles as he flashes us a peace sign.

Ramon returns the greeting and heads for him. Telling of the differences between us, I hurriedly slip on my cutoffs first and then run to catch up with Ramon, hoping no one will much notice how uptight I can be.

As we approach the first bus, I see it's filled with wide-eyed flower children passively staring out at us.

"Hey guys," this hippie says to us, "I think like we're lost. You know how to get to Goddard College?"

As Ramon gives directions, I'm distracted by this shirtless adolescent looking out of one of the windows. He arrests my attention and somewhere in my mind violins well up in the background, isolating the moment and filling it with romantic significance. He has long, lustrous black hair held in place by a red bandanna headband knotted in the back. He can't be very old– late teens, maybe?–judging from his face that has all the prettiness and delicacy of youth, with expressive eyebrows, long eyelashes, and dark-ringed, deep set black eyes that look up at you seductively from the slight tilt of his head, and lips as full and come-kiss-me pouty as Mick Jagger's.

Our eyes meet. He smiles. I smile back, madly in love-at-first-sight with him. Our instant mutual interest couldn't be more obvious and he gets up to leave the bus.

By now Ramon's offered for us to go back with the buses and show them the way. You see, he has to be back on campus soon anyhow, since he and some hippie he picked up hitchhiking the other day are driving up to Maine for a week-long bliss-in with some yogi or another. I can never keep their names straight.

Ramon's always going off to events like this. And being an astrologer, he always manages to find several fellow star-gazers to rap with, as well as a nighttime partner or two. I know no one like Ramon for being able to move with such ease from first greetings to impassioned sex.

My bus buddy, barefoot and in cutoffs, approaches and quickly gets the gist of the conversation.

"You don't have to go back, do you?" he asks me.

"No."

"Far out. Let me get my knapsack."

And with that he saunters back into the bus.

Ramon and I walk back to the bedspread. He gathers up his clothes and we kiss good-bye.

When will he be back?

"Next week. The week after. It all depends."

I don't ask what it depends on. That would be an uptight thing to do. And when you travel with the counter-culture, anything can happen. A new acquaintance, word of a great rock concert, an invite to crash with some back-to-the-earthers living in the woods, exchanging horoscope readings for food and a blanket; all of these are possible, so when he'll be back all depends.

That's the way Ramon comes in and out of my life. I never know when he'll turn up, and as we kiss good-bye, I feel that familiar twinge in my chest when I realize the role I'm playing is just that. I pretend I'm as comfortable as Ramon is in going with the flow. But the uncool, unvarnished truth is, I want a lover. I want someone who is always there, someone who'll share the good and the bad, someone I can be "we" with. And although I would like it to be Ramon, I would never risk our relationship by letting him know.

He turns and walks away, passing the kid who's now heading towards me with knapsack in tow. They smile and nod at each other, but don't say a word.

"You guys were having sex, weren't you?" the kid asks when he reaches me, throwing his knapsack down and rummaging through it.

"Yeah."

"Will you have sex with me?"

"Sure."

He pulls out a joint, lights it and the two of us pass it back and forth as we watch the buses slowly disappear.

I say, "Ten minutes ago there must've been about a dozen buses ..."

"Fourteen."

"Okay, fourteen. And now you'd never know they were here."

("Just like Ramon," I think to myself.)

"Yeah. Heavy," he says, slipping off his cutoffs. He bends over to pull his feet through the leg holes, and when he stands up again, he reveals a dramatically oversized cock; fat, pale and smooth. It hangs down heavily between his legs, looking several sizes too large for his lean, sleek-muscled body.

All I can do is gape at it.

"I know," he says smiling. "It's pretty big, isn't it?"

And with show-off pride he grabs his dick and gives it a shake. Then he reaches for my cutoffs and quickly undoes them, getting down on his knees in front of me to help me slip my feet through. My own cock springs out in front of his face, already well on its way to the eight and a half inches of up curving hard-on it's capable of.

He stares with hungry appreciation.

"I hope you don't mind," he says, looking up at me, "but I have this thing about sucking cock."

"Oh?"

"Yeah. It's like I can't get enough of it!"

"I know the feeling."

"Far out. Then we can sixty-nine."

"Cool."

We get down onto the blanket in mutual suck off position. I take hold of his neatly-cut, big-headed cock and examine it close up from several angles. I don't think I've even seen such a light-skinned cock shaft. It's practically white and stands out in dramatic contrast to his thick bush of black pubic hair and his reddish, deeply-furrowed ball sac that encases two enormous nuts clinging close to the base of his dick.

He, too, is engaged in rapt cock examination. The touch of his inquisitive fingers quickly excite me to full erection.

"Oh boy," he says, half to himself, as he admires my cock. "Far fucking out!"

He wraps his warm lips around my dick, tongues my piss slit, and then goes down on me. I follow suit, burying my head in his crotch and losing myself in the inexpressible pleasure of sucking and being sucked, naked and tripping under the warm midday sun.

\* \* \* \* \*


It's now around four in the morning. Keith–my horse dick friend from the busses–and I are in Johnny T's Jive-Ass a Go-Go, an illegally-operated bar in the basement of Goddard's Community Center. The Center itself is a renovated barn built into the side of a hill, one of the original buildings of the large farm that now forms the nucleus of Goddard College. It is indeed

spacious, housing the Haybarn Theatre on the upper level, the Cafeteria and lounge on the main level, and Johnny T's in the windowless lower level, with one side below ground level, and the other several steps down from the lounge.

In previous incarnations it was a rathskeller and a coffeehouse. But now it's Johnny T's, a dive with ancient wooden booths enclosing tables covered with red-and-white plaid plastic tablecloths in need of a good scrubbing. Votive candles–one to a booth–provide most of the illumination. It's run by one of the students, the Reverend Jim Dodge, a dollar-by-the-mail minister of the First Church of Cybernetics.

Keith and I are drinking mugs of cheap burgundy, since all the wineglasses were destroyed the night before during a rowdy round of toasts that got out of control. Even now, in the dim candlelight, you can spot the occasional gleam of a piece of glass that escaped the haphazard cleanup afterwards.

Keith wasn't kidding when he said he likes to suck cock. And he's clearly had lots of experience, especially for someone his age. Although I don't know his exact age, I do know that until he ran away from home several months ago he was a high school senior.

He has this habit of staring straight into your eyes when he's sucking on your cock, which he told me later is something he really grooves on. So although we began by sixty-nining, he soon managed to get me raised up on my elbows with my legs spread apart, looking down at him as he sucked on my dick while returning my gaze. Sometimes I'd squint up at the sun, concentrating on the sensation of his tight lips working their way up and down my dick. Then I'd look down at him again and there he'd be, his eyes staring right into mine again. I wonder; what does he feel that he's so eager to be observed with his mouth full of cock?

We trekked back to my dorm room around dinnertime. The buses had completely filled the parking lot, spilling over into Pritchard's field, looking like a modern-day covered-wagon roundup. Word of mouth travels quickly at Goddard, so by the time we reached the cafeteria, everyone knew of our visitors, an on-the-road commune from the West Coat, that had saved up enough money to buy a fleet of used school buses and travel across the country. They asked to spend the night before moving on. The Goddard Community, by informal consensus, voted yes and quickly-made plans for a rock concert outside of Kilpatrick dorm, complete with acid punch and all the grass you could ever want to smoke.

By midnight, everyone was high on something or another and most had stripped off their clothes to dance naked in the moonlight. So no one noticed when Keith blew me in the bushes behind the dorm.

And now, here we are, post-concert, sitting in Johnny T's. The Reverend Jim's not there because he left for the concert hours ago, leaving behind a hastily-scrawled sign at the bar announcing, "Serve Yourself–And Don't Forget to Pay Up."

John Patrick

For all our time together, I still don't know much about Keith except that he's running away from home, but then in this kaleidoscopic counter-culture, it seems like everyone's a runaway from something; society's expectations, the draft, commitment of any sort. Though I know I'm supposed to think dropping out is really cool, I have to admit that deep down inside me there's this feeling that you really ought to graduate from high school first, and then drop out.

I know he wants to be an actor. He says he ran away from home after he saw the Living Theatre. It seems his parents grounded him when they discovered that not only did he sneak out against their wishes to see a performance of "Paradise Now," but when the actors stripped off their clothes and encouraged the audience to do the same, he was the only one to do so, jumping up on the stage and joining in their bacchic celebration of human sexuality.

But that's all I know about him. I would like to ask questions, but one unspoken rule of the counter-culture is you never go too far into anyone's past without invitation.

We sit across from each other, our hands clasped across the table. One moment we're discussing Abbie Hoffman's Revolution For the Hell of It, and the next the Stonewall riots. Then a mischievous smile animates Keith's face as he asks me, "You ever been blown in an illegally-operated bar?"

I search for a clever answer, but before I can come up with one, Keith disappears under the table. Soon he has my cutoffs down to my ankles.

The only other people in Johnny T's–four of them–are seated at a far booth, intensely interpreting the Tarot cards spread out on their table, and the place is so shadowy I'm sure it's not easy to make out what's going on at our booth.

Keith pushes my knees apart, grabs my balls, and deep throats my dick, getting me hard in no time. I lean back against the bench, press my hands against the side of the table, and concentrate on the exquisite sensations of Keith's tight-lipped blowjob, distancing me from Johnny T's as it seems to fade into the background.

Then I spot tall, lanky Carl Dewey descending the steps leading down into the bar. The sight of him pulls me back into the present, the inevitable surge of lust that always wells up inside me whenever I see him mingling with the sharp, slippery pleasure of Keith's expert job of deep throating me. The combination of the two as they merge into one sensual tidal wave is mind bending.

I don't know Carl very well, in part because he lives on Northwood, Goddard's satellite campus, six buildings on the other side of the library, about a ten-minute walk through the woods. I know he's gay, though I forget how I ever found this out. And it's rumored he sometimes has threesomes with Paul Rose, the drama teacher, and Paul's wife, which makes me regard him as the epitome of cool. Far too cool, I imagine, to ever be as interested in me as I am in him.

He's one of those guys who never seems to say much. Whenever he's in the Community Center, he's always the listener, always the observer, an amused half-smile on his, narrow, oddly handsome face.

As Keith's tight warm lips ride up and down my stiff cock, I watch Carl stop at the bottom of the stairs, shaking his long blonde hair out of his face and allowing his intense, deep blue eyes to adjust to the dark as he looks around. Loose Levi's ride low on his hips, and a brown suede vest reveals the fine features of his tightly-muscled chest, the patch of blonde hair between his pecs narrowing to a thin path that descends to his navel and then continues downwards until it disappears behind his beltless Levi's to territory I've often contemplated during nighttime jack off sessions.

He goes behind the bar, pulls a beer out of the bin, and deposits some change into the till. He looks around again, spots me and saunters over.

I try my best to appear laid back and in control. Still, I wonder what he's going to think when he discovers there's this runaway high school kid under the table sucking on my cock?

It doesn't take me long to find out, since as soon as he slides into the bench opposite me with a "Hey, man," he discovers an unexpected obstruction under the table. He lifts up the portion of tablecloth hanging down in front of him and sticks his head under.

In the few seconds it takes him to check out what's going on, I anxiously hope for his approval, and then criticize myself for wanting it in the first place.

When he sits up again, a slow, conspiratorial smile spreads across his face.

"Far out! Sure wish someone would suck me off."

"You would?"

He looks at me with an uncharacteristically wide grin as he eagerly nods his head up and down.

"Sure. Got any grass?"

Keith pokes his head up and says, "I do. Back in the dorm."

\* \* \* \* \*

So five minutes later we're in my room, and Carl's seated at my desk skillfully rolling a joint while Keith browses through my record albums–ultimately selecting the Stones' Sticky Fingers–and I busy myself lighting the dozen or so candles around the room.

Carl moves over to this real comfortable bamboo chair next to my bed that's shaped like an over-sized coolie hat nestled in a black metal frame. He holds up the completed joint, examines his work in the flickering candlelight, and then hands it to Keith, who lights it, inhales and passes it on to me. I take a toke and pass back to Carl and light the final candle.

Then I lie on my bed, tucking the pillow under my right armpit so I can lean on my side.

John Patrick

I watch Carl take a huge, chest-expanding toke as he slumps down into the chair with his legs wide apart, one fully extended, the other bent at the knee.

Keith steps up in front of him just inside the triangle of his legs, takes the joint from him, inhales and then hands it back to me again.

As the joint passes around between us, Keith begins to shed his clothes as if it were the most natural thing in the world to do, tossing each one across the room and into the corner where his knapsack's rested since we came down from the hills.

When he's totally naked he stands there facing Carl and wraps his fist around his cock, his long, pale cock shaft arcing heavily downwards as it spills out of his hand.

"Someday I'm going to be an actor," he says to Carl.

Carl looks up at him silently with raised eyebrows.

"Yeah, I'm going to join up with the Living Theatre and travel all over the country with them."

"Heavy," Carl says as Keith continues to hold his cock on display while swaying to the music.

The grass and the music and the candlelight wash over us. We're in that hazy time before dawn when all the drugs you've had that day and all the hours of sleep you've missed transport you into an unreal corner of existence where cause and effect become unglued and any inhibitions you might still have slip away.

I dig my free hand into my cutoffs as I watch Carl stare at Keith's huge cock, contemplating what I would see and what I would feel if I could see Keith through Carl's eyes.

"Here. Stand up," Keith says to him.

Carl turns and looks at me. He smiles and then turns back to Keith who digs his hands under Carl's armpits and helps him to his feet.

Keith slips off Carl's vest. It drops to the floor. I greedily take in this cock-hardening profile view of Carl's torso, his tight, flat stomach, his firm, hard-nubbed, nipple-crested pecs, and the graceful contour of his back as it ascends and broadens.

Next, Keith unbuttons and unzips Carl's jeans. He lowers them just below the hips and they fall of their own accord to Carl's ankles, revealing white, loose-fitting B.V.D's that have lost their elasticity and sag way below his navel, suggesting a substantial burden inside.

Keith gets down on his knees, sniffs Carl's crotch and then matter-of-factly pulls Carl's briefs down to his ankles.

My God! It turns out he has a cock to rival Keith's. Long and thick, it arcs outwards, gravitating towards the floor. Behind it rests a low-hanging ball sac encasing two huge nuts.

Keith stares and says, "Far out! Do you know you're hung like a fucking horse?"

"Yeah," he says with a laugh.

Keith helps him slip his feet out his Levi's and briefs and then says, "Here. Sit down again. Yeah. Now, spread your legs and relax."

Carl slumps ass forward in the chair with his legs wide apart as before, one bent at the knee, the other extended straight out. Keith lovingly fondles Carl's cock and balls as he examines them.

Carl tilts his head backwards and closes his eyes.

"Mmm," he purrs in response to Keith's attentions.

By now I've unbuttoned and unzipped myself and I'm stroking my cock, perfectly satisfied watching them.

Keith looks over at me, holding Carl's stiffening cock on display and says, "Look at the size of it!"

"Yeah," I say, my voice thick with lustful admiration as I watch Keith go down on it, quickly sucking Carl into full erection with those powerful suck strokes he's so good at.

Carl's cock swells to a good nine inches. Unlike Keith's, and you can witness the contrast since Keith's now stroking his own down-curving dick with one hand while playing with Carl's nuts with the other, Carl's stands up rigid and rock hard, ruggedly textured with huge veins that run riot all along his fat, slightly brown cock shaft.

Spit shiny, it gleams in the candlelight as Keith abandons it to lick Carl's pliable, big nut ball sac, sucking one ball in, then the other. As he gently tugs on this mouthful, Carl's cock repeatedly twitches upwards in grateful response.

Side one of Sticky Fingers comes to an end and I get up to turn the record over, peeling off my shirt first. But before I can pass by him, Carl reaches out and grabs me by the wrist

I stop, slightly surprised, uncertain exactly what he wants of me.

With pleading, puppy-dog eyes and a nervous smile, he pulls me closer. He tilts his head up towards me and purses his lips. I lean over and kiss him. As his moist, expressive lips press against mine, I close my eyes and feel like I'm falling into him. Our tongues spar and then he suddenly sucks mine deep into his mouth. Overwhelmed and caught off guard, I have to grip the back of the chair to keep my balance as I bend over closer to him.

And all this time, there's Keith down below. He's abandoned Carl's nuts, busy sucking him off again with loud slurping sounds as if to make a bid for our attention.

When our lips finally part again, Carl says in a low, hoarse voice, "Take your shorts off, huh?"

Which I do. I stand there naked with hard-on. I watch his eyes as they stare at my up curving dick. Again I want to be his eyes and experience what he sees and what he feels as he examines my cock. I give it a voluntary twitch, which, he acknowledges with a hardly-audible "ah!" as he reaches into my crotch and cups my balls. At the warm support of his palm, his fingers curling up at the back of my ball sac, my cock now twitches involuntarily out of control.

Keith is still blowing him, his right hand busy stroking up and down his own cock as his eyes follow in close-up profile the showoff performance my cock is putting on, and the rapt audience it has in Carl, who stares with open mouth.

Then, as if it's happening in slow motion, Carl leans forward and goes down on me. I watch my dick disappear down his throat, overwhelmed by the electric sensations that travel along my cock shaft. He closes his eyes, looking absolutely blissful, and slowly sucks up and down my dick. Every time he has just my cock head in his mouth, he pauses to give me a thorough tonguing under my piss slit.

Keith dismounts Carl to watch him suck me off. When Carl finally opens his eyes again, his lips halting on me midshaft, he looks over at Keith. He slides his lips off my cock and pushes it over to Keith, who eagerly takes over sucking me off while Carl looks on.

Eventually, Carl moves in again and begins to lick my balls. Then bit by bit he takes over the base of my cock, gradually tonguing up my cock shaft, proving a progressive obstruction to Keith's cock sucking efforts until Keith finally yields all my cock to Carl, who instantly deep throats me while Keith does the same to him.

A prolonged, repetitive moan escapes me, mingling with the slurpy sounds of the cock sucking below that I stand there looking down on, hardly believing the remarkable reality of this big dick threesome with a runaway kid who stepped off a psychedelic school bus and into my life, and cool, hip Carl, who I'd always considered way out of my league. As if the sensation Carl's lips on my cock isn't enough to convince me this is really happening, I place my hands on the back of their bobbing heads. Carl responds by running one hand along my ass, slipping it into my ass crack and fingering my butt hole.

I don't know how long we remain like this–Keith sucking Carl sucking me. Eventually, however, Carl's muffled, cock-stifled "ohhs" announce he's close to coming.

Keith accelerates his suck strokes, rapidly bringing Carl to the edge of orgasm. Carl dismounts my cock and flings himself back into the chair, his body rigid with his approaching climax.

"Oh!" he goes. "Oh! Fuck!"

And then he comes with a loud, primal "Ahhh!" He throws his head back, violently tossing it from side to side as his entire body spasms with each fresh spurt of cum down Keith's throat. The force of his orgasm surprises me since it's in such contrast to his usual laid back manner.

When he's done, he further surprises me by going down on my cock again, energetically sucking me off with a technique to rival Keith's. In no time I feel the cum ready to blast out of me.

"Oh shit!" I yell.

Carl dismounts me and my cock jerks upwards, swollen and gleaming with spit.

"Shoot it, man!" Carl orders with surprising intensity, "Shoot it all over my fucking face!"

Keith takes this opportunity to quickly get up off his knees, grab my dick and expertly coax the cum out of it, aiming it at Carl. Spurt after spurt of creamy white jism gushes out, landing all over Carl's face. He closes his eyes and opens his mouth, issuing a prolonged, guttural "Ohh!" as Keith directs the final squirts of my cum into his mouth.

When I've shot my load, feeling so drained I can hardly stand up, Carl opens his eye and desperately demands of Keith, "You too! All over me!"

Keith grabs his own dick and with just a few quick strokes he gets his cum flowing, aiming it at Carl's mouth, announcing each new gusher with a strained, staccato "Ah!" His supply is as bountiful as mine, though his squirts are less forceful, much of it missing Carl's mouth and landing on his chin, accumulating there until it begins to drip down into his crotch.

When Keith's fully depleted his supply of cum, he stands there, cock in hand, and snakes his free arm around my waist.

Carl dips his fingers in the cum on his face, licks some off with his tongue and then holds his fingers up to my mouth. I suck on his index finger, tasting the salty mingle of Keith's and my cum. Keith leans over and takes another of Carl's fingers into his mouth. But not content with such a small allotment of cum, he leans over and begins licking it off Carl's face.

"Oh, man!" Carl says, closing his eyes and looking absolutely blissful. "Far fucking out!"

How can I resist joining Keith, licking off a cheekful and then moving down into Carl's crotch to lap up the drippings from his chin, and then the final ooze of his own cum that escaped Keith's throat, stubbornly nestled in his piss slit?

When no cum remains, we take a few moments to recover and then Carl rolls another joint. We sit there in the nude silently passing it around until we're so fucking stoned, sleep finally overtakes us.

\* \* \* \* \*

The next day I wake up around noon to find Carl gone and Keith fast asleep beside me.

In my mind, I play back to the events of the preceding day. As unreal as life at Goddard often seems, I consider the possibility of hallucination. But there's the small blue plastic box on my desk that contained Ramon's mushrooms. And there's Carl's briefs still on the floor. And I reach for Keith's cock and I can feel it fat and pliable in my hand, and so irresistible, I lower my face into his crotch, and begin sucking on it.

\* \* \* \* \*

John Patrick

In just four days, the habit of having Keith around has taken root like a dangerous addiction. The signs of his presence are all around my room, from his knapsack in the corner, to his stash of drugs and drug paraphernalia in my top bureau drawer, to the dirty clothes he leaves wherever they fall when he sheds them.

I get used to waking up with him lying next to me. And he's so accustomed to the way I reach for his cock, fondling it fist and then taking it into my mouth, that by the fourth morning he hardly wakens. He mumbles a vague "Huh? Oh," and falls asleep again for several more minutes. This, I think, is what it's like to have a lover, and I savor these moments, knowing they won't last.

I tell myself not to get too attached. He'll drift out of my life as easily as he drifted into it. So, when several days later I walk into my room and there's Keith and Ramon lying on my bed naked together, kissing while locked in a tight embrace, I know the inevitable has finally come to pass, and I feel a very uncool stab of jealously.

But the two of them look up at me with beaming smiles, clearly glad I'm there.

"Hey, man," Ramon says, disentangling himself from Keith to jump out of bed, his big stiff cock bouncing out of control as he steps over to me, and taking me in his arms with a powerful show of sincere affection.

He explains how now that he's all blissed out, he's heading back for Boston.

"And guess what?" Keith asks enthusiastically. "I'm going with him. The Living Theatre's in Cambridge. Maybe they'll let me join up with them. Wouldn't that be cool?"

"Yeah," I say, trying my best to make it sound sincere. Truth is, I am indeed happy for him. It's just that I really want a lover. So much so, that the silly illusion that the two of us actually were lovers is going to be difficult to give up.

"Anyhow ..." Ramon says.

He and Keith exchange knowing smiles and then, like they'd rehearsed it, they slip their arms around me, pulling me into a tight embrace as they meet me in a threesome, tongue-teasing kiss.

Soon they have my clothes off and Keith's down on his knees sucking me off while Ramon carefully slides his Vaselined cock up my ass. I lean my head against his left shoulder and we kiss as he runs his hands across my chest and toys with my nipples.

While Ramon settles into a relaxed butt fucking rhythm, Keith dismounts my cock, stares at it twitching in front of his face, begging him to continue, and then looks up at me to say, "I'm sure gonna miss this, man."

Then he resumes sucking me off, fondling my balls with one hand while working on his own cock with the other. I melt into the moment, ecstatically sandwiched between blowjob and buttfuck.

Five minutes later I explode in Keith's mouth. Ramon now has his hands on my hips to steady himself and he shoots his load up my ass. At the same time, Keith jacks off his usual overabundance of cum, much of it landing hot and sticky on my legs and feet.

And another half an hour after that, they're gone.

\* \* \* \* \*

I need to wallow in my sadness and sort things out. I truck on down to Mae's General Store and buy a bottle of Gallo burgundy. I return to Kilpatrick, sit on the back steps just outside my room and drink it right out of the bottle as I watch a mix of students and faculty offspring play Tarzan on the rope swing that's suspended on the tall oak tree just outside my window.

The back door swings open and out steps Carl. He sits down beside me.

"How ya doin', man?" he asks.

"Not bad. Want some?"

"Cool."

He takes the bottle of wine and gulps down a big, hearty swing, wiping his lips with the back of his hand when he's done.

"You look really bummed out," he observes.

"Yeah."

"Where's Keith?"

I explain about him and Ramon.

"So he's left already?"

"Yeah. Why, were you looking for him?"

"No."

And then he slowly adds, "Actually, I was looking for you."

"Oh?"

"The other night. You really blew my mind."

"I did?"

"Yeah. That was a really hot scene. And you ... you've always seemed so ... distant. So ... unapproachable."

I turn my head to look at him.

"That's what I always thought about you."

His eyes meet mine.

"Hmmm. I brought some grass with me. Wanna get stoned? Sorta make up for lost time?"

I smile. He smiles. And as we get up and step into the dorm, I think getting over Keith isn't going to be so difficult after all.

# The Way Home

## *John Patrick*

On our way home from the club it's late and Larry stops to pick up a hitchhiker, something he has never done. My face is pinched shut, and I don't move when Larry gets out to help the boy, who stumbles with his duffle bag. Once we are rolling again, I turn around and recognize the boy. He'd been in the club. I had even seen Larry talking to him. Was this pre-arranged? No, I don't want to think such a thing, yet I can't help it.

Larry introduces himself. The boy says his name is Lloyd. I turn away and stare out the windshield, furious with Larry. "Where you headed?" Larry asks.

"To St. Petersburg. A guy at the club said there was a park there where I could meet somebody."

A park cruiser, or, worse yet, a park hustler. I fold my arms and keep staring out the window. How, I ask myself, could Larry have done this to me? To us?

Over my snort Larry says, "I like that club. You never know what'll happen."

Lloyd leans forward and taps the back of Larry's seat. "I like parties at people's houses best," he says. "I went to one a couple of days ago where a fellow took apart a refrigerator in ten minutes. Ten fuckin' minutes! Nobody thought he could do it. He won two hundred bucks!"

"That's a good one," Larry says.

Lloyd taps the seat again. "I got my own two hundred before the night was over."

"I'll bet," Larry says.

"I've been to lots of parties," I break in before Larry agrees to spending two hundred bucks. "I went to one where the guys swapped underwear. Now, that was fun. And when I was up north visiting my parents I went to one where we set off fireworks in the snow. Neighbors called the police to report UFOs."

"Haw," Lloyd says. "I'll remember that."

"I went to one," Larry begins, trying to invent, "where somebody wanted to go sailing, but there wasn't any lake around. Behind the house was this little valley, so we ran a hose out there and tried to block off the ends of the yard with bags of cement." As usual, Larry was boring even himself. Finally he changed the story. "Then there was this time when I was at a party and one of the guys won the lottery. "

"How much did he win?" Lloyd asks. "I won twenty-five bucks one time."

"Thirteen million," Larry and I say together, as if with one voice. I continue, suddenly amused by this whole charade, "I've heard this story before."

"He bought a house," Larry says.

"And a Mercedes," I say. "Two, in fact."

"Nice cars, Mercedes." Lloyd nods. "This here is a Jaguar, right?"

"Right," Larry says.

"But he was an asshole," I break in before Larry tells the kid how much the car cost him. "He didn't deserve all that money." Glaring at Larry, I add, "Some people just don't deserve their luck."

"Got that right," Lloyd says emphatically.

I say to Larry, "Wasn't that the same party where you guys ran the chicken up the flagpole?"

Lloyd guffaws.

"No," Larry chuckles. "That was a chicken hawk, remember?"

Lloyd says, "Hey, you two aren't chicken hawks, are you?"

"Us?" I say. "No, we like 'em with pubic hair."

"You got pubic hair, don't you Lloyd?" Larry asks.

"Not much, but some."

That gets Larry laughing even harder and rather than get off the exit ramp to St. Petersburg, he zooms past.

I usually point those things out but I figure Larry knows what he is doing: He is taking Lloyd home with us.

Coming out of the shadows to sit beside Larry on the bed, I kiss him gently on the cheek. "Well, where is little Lloyd?"

"He's still in the guest bedroom. I don't know if he'll join us."

"Maybe we'll have to join him."

"I've never seen you like this, Carl."

Since we've been home, I've changed my mind. I won't fight it. I'll just be like they say the girl should be when she's being raped, just enjoy it. "I've never seen you like this." I stroke his hard-on. "Not in a long, long time."

"Long, that's what you want, isn't it? That's what I haven't been able to give you. Not strong, not long, not anything."

"You've been sick. I understand that."

"You haven't been lonely though, have you?"

"Let's not start that again." I want to shut it off, so I go down on him. I don't need any more talk of my boss, Stanley, who has, while Larry has been in the hospital, become my lover. Stanley is ten years older than Larry, and he's had many lovers and lots of experience. He doesn't have Larry's long prick, but he gives better head and adores my cock. He also eats my ass out better than Larry ever did. And his cock is thicker than Larry's and feels great when he's pumping me.

"Is it over? Is it really over?" Larry asks.

I can't answer. My mouth is full of cock. Anyway, I don't know if it's over or not. I never know from one day to the next whether Stanley will take me to lunch or not. It always happens on our lunch hour. We can walk to his apartment from the office and he has little sandwiches prepared, not that he's ever eaten them, he is too busy, but I do. I eat every damn sandwich on the serving plate and have at least two vodkas while I am at it. All while Stanley busies himself between my thighs.

"Does he blow you first?" Larry asks, holding my head steady. "Does he suck your cock before he fucks you, or does he just stick it in?"

He has asked this countless times. I didn't answer then and I don't intend to answer now. Larry really doesn't go in for much sucking; he'd rather be sucked, which used to be fine with me–until I met Stanley. If Larry hadn't come looking for me last week, he'd never known about Stanley. He followed us to the apartment building, was waiting for me when I came out. He could tell what had been going on. I denied it, but he could tell.

I keep sucking, nibbling, stroking Larry's long, thin cock. It seems as if my stud has fully recovered and is dangerously close to coming. I pull off of it because I know he is interested in Lloyd. Picking up Lloyd seems to have revived him. "Lloyd'll love that long dick," I say, and slowly make my way out of Larry's bedroom and down the hall.

Lloyd emerges from the shower a vision of teenage perfection. Nude, he could barely pass for 18, and he does have pubic hair, in a dark, cute patch above a dark, cute, nicely cut dick. I drop to my knees before him and kiss his cock.

"Don't waste any time, do you?" he says, toweling the hair on top of his head. He needs a haircut badly.

I let the cock drop from my lips and look up into his dark brown eyes. "We've wasted enough time already."

Larry soon joins us, stands beside Lloyd, runs his hands across Lloyd's perfect pecs. Lloyd bends over, starts sucking Larry. Larry closes his eyes.

In a few moments, Larry's hard again and pulls Lloyd off his cock. He kisses Lloyd, hard, deep. I've never seen Larry kissing anybody else. I don't know that I like it.

I'm still sucking Lloyd. He has a hard little pecker; it's been throbbing like crazy since Larry entered the room. Larry's fingers are toying with Lloyd's ass. I know what's coming; I go right on sucking. Larry grabs me by my long blonde hair and yanks me over onto his cock, slick with Lloyd's saliva. I've never sucked Larry after some guy's been there ahead of me.

Lloyd bends over, lets Larry start finger-fucking him. Larry's so excited he starts face-fucking me. I gag. He pulls his cock out and whips my face with it, as if to show me he's okay now, back to normal, if you call this normal.

Larry opens the drawer of the nightstand and applies a lubed rubber to his erection. I want it so bad I can taste it, but Larry's cock is aimed at Lloyd's hot little ass.

John Patrick

I watch Larry sinking his nine-incher into Lloyd's young, upturned ass. Lloyd reaches behind him, spreading the cheeks. Larry is in him totally in seconds. This kid is a real pro, I see. And, besides, he loves it. He loves the way Larry is fucking him.

I'm still on my knees, stupidly watching the fucking of this whore by my lover of two years, close-up. In my face he's giving it to this piece of scum. I stroke my cock; I hate it but it is turning me on, this scene. I come just as Lloyd does. Now it's all up the Larry. He pulls out, pushes Lloyd towards the bed.

Lloyd is on his back in no time, opening up wide, wide for my lover! Larry, his faintly handsome face contorted in pleasure, slings Lloyd's lightly furred little legs over his shoulders and plunges in. He goes crazy now, fucking Lloyd like he used to fuck me–in the beginning. Fucking me like Stanley does now during our lunch hour. Suddenly, I feel very thirsty.

I can hear Larry groaning, then silence. Deadly silence.

Larry finds me in the kitchen, sitting on a stool at the breakfast bar. I've finished one drink, pour another.

"Don't have much patience, do you? Or maybe it's trust you don't have."

"Nobody could have more trust than me," I say, taking a long swallow.

"Yeah, sure. I'm the one who doesn't trust. That's it, isn't it?"

"You never wanted to believe me, that there was nothing to it. That Stanley doesn't mean shit to me."

"Hell," he says, "every day I believe in you all over again. See, I'm not the one who comes home smelling of vodka and all fucked-out."

"Meaning?"

"Meaning, if you clear things up, you can go on."

"Okay."

"So, is that what you're doing? Clearing up?"

I shake my head. The longing to hold him rips through me like a gale-force wind, but I look at my feet as I rise from the stool and try to steady himself. "No," I say, "not me. I'm clearing out."

# No Stranger to the Dark

## *John Patrick*

*"People of your appearance and merit never pay anything ..."*
*– Voltaire*

His pants are tight and sleek, the black leather jacket classic. He walks as if he is familiar with the night.

The closer he comes, the more I am sure he is no stranger to the dark.

But I am not afraid. I am looking for a really hot stud tonight. I am looking for someone to take my hand and drag me out of this club and into the alley and fuck me senseless.

He steps so close that I'm forced against the mirror. The glass is as cold as his eyes. He dances without touching me. Next to me, around me, through me.

He is stunning. And he can't take his eyes off me!

As I follow him across the bar, guys stare after him as we pass. It is his look, heated and sharp; it is his walk, strong and determined; it is his eyes, noncommittal and challenging, that causes men to turn their heads, to dream all kinds of sordid fantasies.

As we leave the bar, my eyes shift from the men's wistful looks to the dark god's impressive arms. He has swung his leather jacket over his shoulder and his biceps bulge noticeably.

And then, in a breath, we are in the alley.

He pushes me against the dirty building. Rough brick scrapes against my back. I like it. My tank top does little to protect me from the cold, from the harshness of the grimy wall. His focus is direct. His hands grasp my arms with firm intention. His gaze burns with this intensity. He desires me even more than I desire him.

He bites my neck. He fondles my pecs and my nipples tighten in response. Oh please. Yes, please. His tough face is hard with desire. His no-nonsense demeanor entrances me.

"Listen, you little shit," he whispers in my ear. "I'm going to fuck you right here against the wall. And you aren't gonna make a sound. I'll fuck you against this wall and if you make one sound, I'll walk. I'll walk and I won't look back. Not once."

His tone is rough, almost mean. Yes, take me. I can be quiet. I'm so hot for his prick that I can barely stand. His lips are warm against my ear. His breath is steady. He pushes his body against mine. I have no place to go but further into the wall.

John Patrick

All I can think about is the sensation of his big dick plunging into me. I hope my back is scratched. I want to look in the mirror tomorrow morning and see the marks that he's left.

He unzips my little white shorts, lets them fall to the ground. His face is twisted into a snarl, and he grasps my nipples between his thick fingers. He twists them and the hurt feels good. I moan. I squirm. He is such a stud. So tough. I love it.

My fingers reach to his crotch. He allows me to rub him there, to feel the hugeness of the bulge, then he abruptly pushes my hand away. He turns me around, bends me over, my hands flat against the brick.

He lets me reach around, to feel his cock, now sheathed in lubed latex. I strain to look behind me as well, in the shadows, to see the cock, the cock that will fill me. I get a scant peek as he lines it up. It isn't the biggest one I've ever seen but it still looks monstrous, moist and gleaming in the moonlight.

I start to cry out and he puts a hand over my mouth. I remember that he told me to be quiet. I bite his hand as he jams his sex into me. Tears begin to flow down my cheeks.

My stud has it all the way in. Now he starts to fuck. I haven't had it in such a long time, it feels strange. I claw the brick every time it plops out and he has to shove it back in again. I reach down, begin to jack off. I want to come, but I'll wait for him. Even if it takes all night–which, of course, it doesn't. He comes almost immediately, pulls out. I'm still beating my meat.

I open my eyes. I can barely breathe. My heart beats furiously. I feel shaken and drugged. I stop beating my meat. What's the fucking use?

He zips up, then pulls a business card from his back pocket. He says, "Give me a call sometime."

My allure has obviously faded. He has had my ass. He is moving on, to something bigger, something better. And I, decidedly, am going home–alone.

I open the car door, slide into the seat. I am still tingling with heat. What a fuck. My ass aches like it hasn't ached in months. Suddenly, there he is, standing next to the car. He bends down. He wants me again, it's written all over his handsome face.

"You're so fuckin' beautiful." His voice has a marked urgency to it.

He traces his fingers across my lips and he lightly presses them into my mouth. He is strangely timid now as he gently forces his fingertip between my lips

"So sweet," he whispers, prying into the dampness, running his finger against my tongue.

I ache with desire for him, tortured by the dull ache of my ass. But now, more than anything, I want to suck his cock.

He gets in the car next to me, starts playing with my tits. I want him to pull my nipples, to suck them until they are raw. He pinches the sensitive skin. He tugs the nipple between his teeth.

I reach for him blindly, eager to lift his tightly-stretched T-shirt. The shirt that has teased me, and every other guy in the bar, all night. I want to see the nipples. I want to savor their beauty, suck on them.

I pull at his shirt, but he grabs my hand, not letting me touch him, not letting me feast on him.

"Drive," he commands.

"Oh yeah?" I say, tough.

"Yeah," he says, his strong arms pushing my hands away.

He says, "Mind if I take a shower?"

"No. Help yourself."

He closes the door.

I undress, go to the bathroom. He's standing in the tub, the water trickling over him.

"I want to bathe you."

"What?" he asks.

"I want to bathe you."

He chuckles. I step into the tub. He notices I have a hard-on, but then he turns his head toward the wall. He says nothing, turns. "Never had anybody do this before," he says.

"Well, it's about time," I say.

I go up and down the spine several times, from the small of the back to the base of the neck, then move to the massive shoulders and soap each arm in turn. Although the limbs are relaxed, I feel bulging knots of muscle. His forearms are covered with dark hairs. I work back towards the deep hairy armpits. I lather up my hands and massage his ass. Though on the big side, his buttocks have a pleasing shape and I go over and over their roundness. I get on my knees and bring my mouth to his asshole. I stick my tongue in. He moans. I push them apart and shove my tongue in further. I could fuck his asshole for hours, but quickly move on, down the hairy, solid legs. Then he turns towards me. I raise my head and see his swelling balls, his taut cock, straight above my eyes. Now, in close-up, I see it is a beautiful cock, one of the prettiest I've ever seen.

I get up. He doesn't move. I take the soap between my hands again and begin to clean his broad, solid, moderately hairy chest. I begin to move slowly down over his distended stomach, surrounded by powerful abdominal muscles. It takes some time to cover the whole surface. His navel stands out, a small white ball outlined by the rounded mass.

I kneel down to massage his abdomen. I skirt round the genital area slowly, quite gently, towards the inside of the thighs. His penis now seems incredibly large. It throbs, teasing me. I resist the incredible temptation to touch it, continuing to stroke his thighs. He is now leaning back against the wall, his arms spread, with both hands pressed against the tiles, his stomach

jutting forward. He is groaning. I feel he is going to come before I even touch him.

The steam froths around us, but I can see he has his eyes closed. He is waiting for me. He will wait as long as I want to make the pleasure last. I move my hand over his balls, back up to their base near the anus. His cock stands up again, more violently. I hold it in my other hand, squeeze it, begin slowly pulling it up and down.

I close my eyes. The only sounds are of the water trickling over us and of his cock sliding under my fingers. I first nibble on the head, then stuff my mouth with it. I love it. I love this cock more than any I can remember. My sucking is expert now; everything I've ever learned I apply to this. I put my hands on his thighs, holding him.

"Oh ... oh ..."

I pull it from my mouth and the cum spurts out in bursts, splashing my face. When he's finished, he kneels down as well, and licks the sperm from my face.

I open my eyes to see him staring at me with his washed-out blue eyes, the eyelids still heavy as if under the effect of a drug. "You're beautiful," he says. I'm beginning to think those are the only words he knows, which is all right, I suppose.

And then he kisses me, pulling me into his arms. It is a kiss like you only see in the movies. It leaves me breathless.

He steps out of the tub, dries himself, then leaves me alone.

I lean back against the tiles and finally bring myself off.

I go into the bedroom. He is dressed, walking out of the room. Without even saying goodbye.

"Shit," I say, picking up a pillow and tossing it across the room as he closes the door behind him. "You prick! Fuck you."

\* \* \* \* \*

I dial the number on the card. He said, "Give me a call sometime," but that was before he was here, had taken everything, including my heart, and walked out on me.

I don't know what to expect. According to his card, his name is Barry. I never imagined his name would be Barry. I don't know what I anticipated but somehow not Barry.

On the phone I play it cool. It is nice to sit in the safety of my bedroom and play a role, coast along breezily on the possibilities, amazing Big Barry with how clever I can be, as if I were an expert with studs like him, as if I were an expert with any man. Finally, he agrees to meet me for dinner, at Ruby's, a gay club with a little restaurant.

Now, waiting for Barry at the bar, I am plagued with insecurities. What if we have nothing in common, nothing to say? To end up just staring at our food?

My rocky relationship with Paul begins to look surprisingly good. I remember the better days, when we would sit in this same cozy restaurant and whisper to each other, without pressures, without the fear of rejection. But Paul was a lousy fuck. I wonder if Paul misses me, my fucks. Poor Paul, who would be as anxious as I to be fucked by Barry. That was the problem: we both wanted the same thing.

"Taking a bus is a bitch." Barry's arrival catches my attention. He throws his arm around my shoulder in a gesture of intimacy.

We order dinner, then Barry wants to dance. We go to the dance floor in the back. His dancing is hypnotic. It is impossible to watch him and not think of lying under him, naked, in a king-sized bed, or beneath him on a hardwood floor, or even slammed against those damn bricks. He lunges, he thrusts his hips, he pushes his arms. His eyes, quick-shifting and dangerous, seem to be laughing at me.

He is hot, ready. Serious pleasure is oozing all over him, oozing all over me. I'm going to get it tonight, I think, my cock wet with desire. I imagine him, above me, his legs spread, filling my mouth, then my ass.

"I think we should call it a night," Barry says suddenly. He pulls me from the dance floor. "I've had a long day."

Disappointment swirls around me. What does he mean, "call it a night?" I fret like a kid whose candy has been taken away. He has danced with me like we are going to fuck again, he has smiled like sex is a certain conclusion.

He throws his arm around me, then he escorts me through the dining room and to my car. I am quiet, have nothing to say.

"Can I call you?" Barry asks as he hugs me. He touches his warm lips to mine. I think of grabbing his dirty blonde hair, of smashing my lips to his, of pushing him against my car hood and ramming my face between his legs.

I kiss him back, gently. My tongue lightly touches his. "Yes, I'd like that," I murmur and climb into the car.

I don't want to go home. I know exactly what will greet me there–a darkened room, an empty bed.

"Can I give you a ride?" I ask.

He smiles. I realize I have no idea where he lives, but he has taken a bus to Ruby's.


He knows what I want. It is written all over my face.

"Shall we go to my place for some coffee?" I suggest, heading home.

Barry hesitates, runs his fingers through his silky hair. "Sure," he says.

Who am I kidding? I don't drink coffee, never have. I don't even have any in the apartment.

I melt with the touch of his fingers on my neck.

"I want you on top of me, like before," I say, my cock already leaking pre-cum.

"You liked that?" Barry asks teasingly. "You liked being fucked in an alley?"

Oh he's a hot pepper, this one.

"No, I just liked being fucked by you."

In my bedroom, I scramble toward him. I have no shame now, not with this stud. I rip open his shirt, I don't care. I squeeze his pert nipples.

Thinking of the night before, of sucking that big cock, I suck his nipple into my mouth. I want it, like before, and I don't care. I can smell sex. I smell sex all over him. He oozes sex from every pore. God!

He pushes me off, gently. He looks away. "I did a client on the way over," he says. "I didn't have time to shower."

A client? He did a client? What is this? Now everything falls into place, sort of. But he hasn't asked me to pay. "I don't care." I reach for his cock.

"Are you crazy?" he asks.

My voice is reckless, my body aches. He sells it and he's giving it to me for free. This has never happened before.

"Yeah," I say. "Crazy for you."

He holds my hand over his cock. "Could we sleep together and not have sex?" he asks.

I am not certain if this is a statement or a dare. It doesn't matter.

"Sure." I stop what I am doing. "Okay, no sex."

In his world, these things are always negotiable, I think impetuously. I can hear the subtle beat of my heart, dull yet insistent, in my ears. No sex. No big deal.

He flails himself across my bed. "I'm fuckin' exhausted," he groans as he works his boots off with his foot.

I stand over him, staring at him. He is so beautiful, I marvel that he could be tired. But he's a working boy.

I go to the bathroom to rinse my face, brush my teeth, then return to the bedroom. He's already asleep, tight jeans and all.

I give him a slight shove, partly to make room for myself, partly to stir him. He doesn't respond, so I sit wide awake and watch the stud of my dreams sleep blissfully.

He looks surprisingly open and vulnerable as he sleeps. I run my hand gently through his hair, across his cheek, and am unexpectedly consumed with a sense of caring, of intimacy. I kiss his forehead lightly.

My thoughts drift. A cold sensation passes through me. I think of Paul and our sexual adventures seem suddenly dismal and empty. It was moments like this–first of brutality, then enveloped in the steam of the shower, and then the tenderness of his kiss–that I really want.

Paul was always a quickie before we went to sleep, like a sleeping potion.

But here is a man I could fall in love with–totally. I am amazed at the look of contentment on his face. I have a thousand questions, but they can all wait until he's ready to tell me. The idea that he's a prostitute fascinates me. I encircle him in my arms and drift into sleep.

I awaken to see Barry, smiling, over me. He is naked now and he kisses me. His tender touch arouses me. His caress is mesmerizing.

There is nothing in the world for me now but Barry. He kisses my hair, my cheeks, my neck, and we start to soar. I am swept into him, captive to his explosive masculinity.

I press my lips to his neck. He moans softly as I lovingly taste his freshly-showered skin. Little bites, gentle licks–I kiss my way down his neck, across his shoulder, to his tits.

I encircle a nipple and take it into my mouth. His succulent flesh is firm yet pliable and I roll it carefully with my tongue.

"So sweet," he says.

My fingers pluck and pull the other thick nipple.

"Oh, yes," he murmurs. "You're so beautiful."

I work my way to the cock, glorious this morning, bigger than ever. I begin sucking. He fucks my face, then rolls off me, lets me get between his thighs. I take my sweet time, sucking, licking his balls. I have never loved a cock as much as I love this one.

He grabs my hair as he shudders. "Don't stop," he cries.

And I won't. I will make him come. I will take my time, but I will please him beyond all reason.

# The Gift of Night

## *John Patrick*

It was unseasonably cold and it was raining. Martin kept his hands stuffed into his pockets, and his denim jacket buttoned up as far as the few buttons allowed. The body was shaped under the cloth, showing perfect, harmonious young male musculature.

Martin had kept wishing for night to fall throughout the day. He had no luck anywhere in town at the usual places. And only now he saw his luck was about to change. He had been sent the gift of night.

His pace was slow, persistent, like the rain, and he arrived at last. How he had longed to be at this place all day! The house stood there alone, a single lamp in the window, as if the man inside was expecting Martin. He had never been inside this fine house, but he had been told by many who had it was a "safe place."

His pace quickened as he opened the gate, climbed onto the porch, and went to the front door. He shivered as he knocked on the huge oaken door.

Music was playing. Classical music. Martin knocked again, harder this time.

All around the house were flowering shrubs. Martin admired the lushness of the setting of a grand house lost in its loneliness at the very end of Country Club Drive.

He had endured a long train ride and walked so far to get here, he should have been tired, but he was strangely energized by the thought of meeting the man who lived here. He had heard the man paid well, for services rendered.

He knocked again. His fingers were stiff and he shoved them back into his pants. Through the ripped lining of his pockets, he touched his silken thighs, and his fingers moved to his cock. He wore no underwear and he squeezed the hugeness he found there, extraordinary in its size even when soft. The man inside will love this, Martin reasoned. He felt suddenly happy, and knocked again, this time using his fist.

Now the porch light came on, the door was unlocked. It opened slightly.

"Who's there?"

"Martin," the boy said, in a hushed, humble voice.

"Do I know you?"

"I'm a friend of Billy's."

Now the door opened all the way and Martin saw the man, the man known in town as "the weirdo," but the man Martin and the other boys of the night knew simply as "Doc." Doc wasn't a real doctor, at least the boys didn't think so, but he had anything you needed to make you feel good.

"Well," Doc said, smiling, "any friend of Billy's–"

Doc closed the door behind Martin and clicked on the overhead light in the foyer of the grand house. He peered through his wire-rim reading glasses at the boy before him, as if inspecting him. He was, Doc decided, no threat to him. He snapped out of his gaze and said in a honeyed voice: "Won't you come in?"

"I'm soaked," Martin said, shaking the moisture from his arms.

"Oh, so you are."

Doc led Martin to the maid's quarters behind the kitchen. The woman who worked for Doc no longer stayed the night. And since it was the weekend, she wouldn't be back until Monday morning.

"Why don't you go in the bathroom there and I'll get one of my robes from upstairs for you."

"Can I take a hot bath?" Martin asked, his eyes wide at the splendor of the bathroom.

"Of course," Doc said. "Make yourself at home."

By the time Doc returned to the downstairs bathroom, Martin was soaking in the tub.

Doc tapped lightly on the door. "Are you decent?" Doc asked, his voice full of mischief.

"Sure am," Martin answered with a giggle. He had been examining the bottles of bath potions lined up next to the tub, and began pouring some of the honeysuckle into the water.

Doc stepped into the bathroom with a burgundy velour robe over his arm. His raw laugh at seeing Martin in the tub, bubble bath in his hair, cut through the air.

Startled, Martin looked up.

Doc was about to laugh again, but he couldn't. A blast of thunder shook the house. The lights flickered.

Above the sounds, the strong smell of honeysuckle took over. Doc kicked Martin's soaked clothes over into a corner and leaned against the sink. He fluffed the robe. It was an old robe, one of his favorites, but he had outgrown it. He had worn it when he was lean and worked as a dental surgeon in Manhattan, until his wealthy father finally died and left him his house–and free to pursue research and writing.

Doc hung the robe on the hook on the back of the door. "There," he said to Martin. "When you're ready."

Martin said nothing. He leaned back, luxuriating in the warmth.

Doc, dressed now in his own robe, stepped out of the bathroom, but left the door open.

In the living room, Doc touched his forehead; it seemed on fire. His whole body seemed to burn, burn with desire. He poured a cognac and sat in his favorite chair. He sipped his drink while he listened to Bach, and waited.

To Doc, the boy seemed sweet, alive, and, above all, carnal. He was, after all, an acquaintance of Billy's. Billy. Beautiful, filthy Billy. Billy who

never stole anything from you except your heart. Doc had been good to Billy. And now Billy was paying him back.

To Martin everything that seemed impossible, faraway, was now real. The sumptuousness of the living room, with its antiques, the stereo system, the wall of books, overwhelmed him. He had been in rich men's living rooms before but none quite like this. And then there was Doc. He seemed kindly, ever-smiling, as if amused by everything, and especially now by his gift of the night.

Doc sipped his cognac and feasted his eyes on the boy sitting across from him, bundled in his old robe.

"Just get to town?" Doc asked finally.

"Yeah. 'Bout a week ago."

"You ran away from home?"

"I guess you could say that. Not much of home, though. They were just my foster parents. They couldn't have cared less."

"And you met Billy the first night you were here, right?"

The boy nodded. "Afternoon. It was in the afternoon."

"At the bus station?"

The boy nodded again.

"Good Billy. He works that station like a trouper. You staying with him?"

"Till I find a place."

Doc had heard this story many times. "I'm surprised Billy didn't call me."

"I guess he thought I should just come out here. Let you see me." With that, Martin lifted his leg and the robe dropped open, exposing his genitals.

"My god," Doc hissed. The fever to his brow returned.

Without a word, Martin slipped out of the robe.

"Mmm, I like it," Doc said.

Martin smiled and did a turn, displaying his ass to Doc. Aware of Doc's eyes on his body, Martin walked to the sideboard and poured himself a cognac. When he returned to the center of the living room, Doc told him to bend over the back of an easy chair.

"I'll do nasty things to you," Doc warned.

Martin quivered as he wondered what Doc intended. He glanced quickly at the revealed cock Doc was stroking.

At the easy chair, Martin bent over the back of it, exposing his magnificent ass to Doc's eyes.

"Perfection," Doc said, but he wanted to inspect the front more closely and turned the boy around.

Martin swayed his hips as Doc leaned forward to take the large knob of the cock in his mouth.

"That's it," Martin said. "Suck it."

Doc took more and more of the shaft. His lips spread around the thickness of it.

"Relax your throat," Martin said. He coaxed Doc, "Just relax your throat and take it."

Almost all of the cock vanished into Doc's mouth. Doc felt the tip pushing at the back of his throat. His face was filled with Martin's cock, his mind numbed by it. He gagged; he recovered; he went on with it.

Martin rose to lean against the chair and be sucked. Doc fondled Martin's ass as he continued to suck the cock.

Doc was enthralled by it now, swept away with pleasure as he moved his rounded lips back and forth on Martin's big cock, the tool that the boy used to pleasure his tricks.

Martin fondled Doc's head, thrusting with his pelvis, fucking Doc's mouth. Doc worked his fingers into Martin's ass as Martin pistoned his cock in and out of Doc's willing mouth.

Martin started coming. The event was cataclysmic for both of them. He groaned and shook and shuddered, and Doc had to back off a bit in order to avoid being hurt by the slamming cock.

But Doc kept the cock in his mouth, sucking it, loving every inch of it.

Yielding to Martin's persistence, Doc led the way upstairs.

Martin moved into Doc's arms and Doc kissed him, the kiss wet, hot, demanding. Doc's hands slid down Martin's back to come to rest on Martin's buttocks.

Martin made a halfhearted protest. Of course it was no use. He was aroused by Doc's hands, aroused by the way Doc's strong hands clutched and squeezed his ass. He was always such a pushover when he had a man's hands on his ass.

Doc's fingertips lightly stroked his cock. Martin closed his eyes, shuddering with delight as Doc gently rubbed the swelling tool in Martin's crack. Martin arched his pelvis forward.

Doc spoke in a throaty voice. "You're hot, baby."

"For you, Doc."

"Show me."

Martin's hands trembled as he opened his ass with his fingers.

Doc gazed down at it, at the pink, hairless groove.

Doc applied some lube to it. When it was wet and glistening, Doc said, "I love your ass."

Martin groaned and gave him more, opening his legs, stretching the crack even farther apart. With his neck bent, he gazed back at himself and watched Doc's finger as it played with his butt hole.

A cry of pleasure escaped Martin's lips as he felt the fingers slide easily into his wet opening. He squirmed on Doc's hand.

Doc said, "You're so tight."

Martin's heart pounded. "Fuck me."

Doc let the boy up and Martin got on his back, his knees up, his feet on Doc's shoulders. Doc's fingers moved inside Martin's ass as he leaned over to taste his mouth. Martin shivered. Bending lower, Doc sought out the big

dick. Only one lamp was on, but it was enough to show everything: the pink tube of flesh, the stream of glistening pre-cum, Doc's fingers sliding in and out of Martin's ass. Martin put his hands on Doc's head, and Doc lowered his mouth to the pink cock. He blew his warm breath against the skin, and Martin moaned in response. Doc ran his tongue over the underside of Martin's cock and Martin gasped again. His tongue teasing, sliding up and down on it. Doc eased his fingers out of the hole and licked them, then rubbed his nose into the wet, now ready asshole.

Martin groaned and flung his knees wider. Doc lapped the ass, then put his fingers back inside and began moving them slowly in and out. He took Martin's cock in his mouth and felt it swelling as he sucked it softly, his fingers continually sliding in and out, in and out. Then his tongue moved down to the opening. Martin whimpered and humped upward as if to grab Doc's tongue with his ass. Doc began slurping, not caring about the noise he made, his face wet, breathing on the wet ass, the tip of his tongue flapping against it. Doc got into position and Martin squirmed and pushed upward as Doc entered him. Soon Doc was all the way in and Martin was bucking up and down and up again. With his fingers, Doc pulled at the big cock and suddenly Martin jerked and started coming, his ass contracting on Doc's erection, gripping it, Martin crying out as Doc fucked him.

"Oh, God! I came while you were fucking me. That never happens to me."

"I'm flattered."

Martin hugged Doc to him. "Fuck me." And that is what Doc did, long into the night.

Sunday, it finally stopped raining and the sun was bright. Doc was up early, washing Martin's clothes. Then, in white T-shirts and shorts and white sneakers, Doc led Martin down one bike path after another, until at the end of two hours the sweat dripped off their bodies. They returned to the house to shower separately.

Afterward, as Doc stood in the kitchen preparing a snack for them, Martin came up behind him and kissed his neck.

They were in their robes again. Martin pressed his cock against Doc's buttocks.

Doc turned and took the boy in his arms. He said, "I had a nice view all afternoon."

"What do you mean?"

"I had to work to keep up to you, trying to catch that butt in those old jeans."

Martin blushed. He felt Doc's fingers stroking his buttocks, and pulled away.

Doc said, "Do you want mustard on this?"

"No, I want jelly on your ass."

Doc was amused. "I think that would be a bit sticky."

John Patrick

"Blueberry jam, if you have it."

"You're not serious?"

"Raspberry is good, too, but I'd rather have blueberry."

Doc chuckled. "I think we're getting into uncharted territory." He went to the cupboard and withdrew a jar of strawberry jam. "This is the only jam I have."

The food no longer seemed important. Doc's heart was thumping as Martin slipped off his robe and spread the jam on his erection.

Doc was immediately aroused by the sight of Martin's cock looking so sweet. Martin loved the way Doc looked at him, the heat in Doc's eyes.

Doc began by caressing Martin's thighs. Martin soon had the older man on his knees, licking the jam, then sucking the cock.

"Tasty," Doc said. "It's good ... eh, jam." Doc thought it was all too crazy–but it amused him.

Martin had Doc remove his robe and bend over. He began to paint him. Dollops of jam all over his ass. And in the crack. Martin began smearing it slowly over Doc's asshole. Doc looked behind him and watched Martin's fingertip paint the opening. Martin pushed his forefinger inside the tight ring of Doc's anus, then replaced it with his thumb. He put the jar down and slid the other hand around front to stroke Doc's cock. Doc groaned as Martin began licking his ass.

When Doc's buttocks were cleaned of jam, Martin spread them to open the crack. Doc's asshole appeared open and wet, a deep-red, strawberried pucker.

Doc trembled as he felt Martin's warm breath in the crack of his ass.

Martin moved in, gently kissing the closed little hole, licking at the jam. A jolt of lust rushed through his body as he felt the knot of Doc's anus with his tongue. He felt the ring contract. Martin spread his buttocks farther apart, gripping the sticky cheeks. His lips against the opening, his teeth nibbled and bit at Doc's anus.

Doc groaned again, arching his back, his body trembling.

"Relax," Martin said.

Doc did his best, his head hanging as he waited for Martin's next move.

Martin's tongue worked again, his mouth pressed against the opening, his tongue pushing at the ring of muscle.

Doc moaned, his dangling sex swaying from side to side as he was bent forward.

Martin licked away all the jam, bathing Doc's asshole, now wedging his tongue inside, deeper and deeper, his tongue like a wriggling serpent in Doc's ass, his tongue swirling in the sticky opening.

Doc moaned as he felt it, his eyes closed, his body tense as he focused all his attention on what was happening to him.

Finally Martin withdrew his tongue and rose. "Don't move," he said, going to the bathroom.

Doc waited, bent forward, his legs apart. No one had ever worked his ass like this. Young Martin made him feel like a novice.

When Martin returned, Doc glanced over his shoulder and saw the kid furiously stroking his cock. Doc was both afraid and eager for it. He prayed he could take it. He wanted it. Martin's tongue had opened his ass wide, and now he craved to have it filled.

Martin wasted no time. He moved in behind Doc to steady him with his hands, placed the tip of his cock at the opening, and then worked it slowly into the ring of muscle.

Doc's body tensed, then gradually relaxed under Martin's coaxing.

"Nothing to be afraid of, man. You're doing fine."

Doc's anus grabbed at the sliding cock. Martin moved with small wiggling motions of his hips as he took him.

"Oh, shit," Doc moaned.

Martin shoved it all the way in and then slowly out again.

Then Martin grasped Doc's hips securely as he increased the length of the strokes. He bent over Doc's back.

"How's that?"

Doc groaned.

Martin's free hand found Doc's cock and rubbed it as he continued moving his cock in and out.

Doc came, his cock exploding, his legs shaking as Martin fucked away.

After Doc caught his breath, he said, "Don't run away from me."

"Oh, don't worry about that. I'm not goin' anywhere."

"Good. You're different."

"Different than what?"

"The others. My last few, anyway."

"I'm glad," Martin said.

"Oh, baby, fuck me," Doc begged. And that is exactly what young Martin did, long into the night.

# Mounting Mikey – A Cherry Tale

## *William Cozad*

I spotted him on the meat rack, which meant he was hustling. Not my usual place to get tricks. I don't even remember the last time I picked up a hustler. Nothing against them, everybody's gotta make a living, and they provide a service. Problem was that these boys were focused on the money instead of the sex, and they were in a hurry. At least that was my experience. Not to mention that some couldn't get it up, and if they could, they couldn't get it off. So my preference was for tricks who just wanted to have some fun.

Sometimes you see a guy who makes you hot to trot. Like a sweaty construction worker, a soldier in uniform, a college jock, even a punk. Whatever triggers your fantasy.

I had never been into the grunge look until I saw the boy on the meat rack. Long blonde hair, beard stubble. Emerald green eyes. Wearing jeans with torn knees, a wrinkled red and black plaid flannel shirt and black combat boots. He was tall, slim, around nineteen. He was a beauty, all right. When our eyes met he smiled. He had nice teeth, sensuous lips.

"What's up?" he said.

"Just out for a stroll," I answered.

He shifted his weight to show his basket more prominently. It looked packed. "See anything you like?" he asked.

"Yeah. Depends–" I started.

"Depends on what?"

"How much?" I blurted out.

"Not a cop, are you?"

"Nope. Just a normal cocksucker."

"Yeah, right. Well, I don't usually do this. But I lost my job." Between gigs, I'd heard that one before. Like he needed money for the rent when he spent the night with different johns and lived out of a locker at the bus station. I'd been around the block.

"What do you do?" I asked.

"Uh, well, I was a bike messenger but got laid off. Had to sell my bike. I'm busted."

I shook my head. "I mean, in bed."

"I dunno. Tell the truth, this is my first time doing this. I had a fight with this chick and she split. Guys told me that you could make some bread, you know, selling my body."

Now that I thought about it, this was the first time I'd seen him on the street. I was kind of jaded. I'd been burned before by hustlers. Now I remember the last cutie pie who looked like a cherub. I should have known better, in a bookstore arcade. I gave him twenty bucks upfront. Chomped on

his prick, which couldn't get hard if his life depended on it. Then he pulled out and turned sideways, faking an orgasm, and bolted out of the booth. Not a drop of cum spilled by him. Like I should just keep walking now. But I couldn't. I was hooked on his sexy grunge look. I'd seen those messenger bikers weaving between cars at lightning speed with their butts up in the air like jockeys.

"What's your name?" I asked.

"Mikey." I hadn't heard that name since the brat in the cereal commercial on TV was so popular. Mikey hated everything.

"How much?"

"Depends. I'd really like enough so I can get something to eat. I'm hungry, that's why I'm out here."

Hmm. He could eat free at the mission. But it wasn't open now.

I decided to make an investment, take a chance. He looked kind of innocent. That could be real misleading if the pix in the papers that showed baby-faced boys who offed gay men meant anything. What I'd do is buy him a cheap meal. If he split, no big deal. If he went with me, I could deduct it from his fee. Figure twenty was the going rate, despite hustlers who bragged about two hundred dollar scores. From experience I knew they lowered their prices the later it got, down to ten, even for just a place to crash for the night.

So I took Mikey to the burger joint down the alley from my digs. He was hungry alright. He devoured a burger, fries and washed it down with a large cola. He looked sexy eating, especially dipping those fries in ketchup and sort of sucking on them before he swallowed them.

"Feel better?" I asked.

"Yeah," he said, chewing.

"Still wanna mess around?"

"Sure. You're a nice guy. I like you. Don't gotta pay me nothing. I was starving."

What kind of scam was this? Maybe he was a thief. I had my doubts now. "Hey, you can go. I mean if you're looking for big bucks. I enjoyed your company." What the hell, now I was talking myself out of it. Even though Mikey made me hot.

"It's cool. Besides, I'm horny."

Those were the magic words.

I escorted him to my apartment building a couple of blocks away. I didn't take many guys home with me. Leery, I'd had sex in other guy's cars most recently, guys I'd met in bars who just wanted to get their rocks off with little talk and no involvement.

Inside my studio Mikey sat on the couch with his legs spread invitingly. He even rubbed his crotch.

"Like music?" I asked.

"Of course."

I flipped on the radio to a rock music station.

"Fucking Nirvana. They were my favorite. Till Kurt Cobain did a number on himself. People even say I look like him."

I had no idea what he was talking about. Swinging into action, I kneeled between his splayed legs. I kneaded his denim crotch bulge.

"Oh, yeah, take it out and suck on it," he said.

He was in terrible heat, and I unzipped his jeans and sniffed his white cotton briefs that had piss- and cum-stains on them. He lifted his ass up in the air while I tugged down his jeans and briefs. Out flopped his soft, fat, uncut dick. it was smooth and white, looked like a sausage. I wondered if it could get hard. I hoped he wasn't like the last punk I'd picked up in the arcade who couldn't get it hard.

"Suck on it, man. Get it hard," he commanded.

Holding his cock by the lace curtains, I nibbled on the foreskin. His shaft became engorged, with the glans poking out of the foreskin. Oh, Jesus, I had a monster on my hands. Hard, his cock was a fat eight-inch beauty with a slimy, bloated crown and veiny shaft. His heaving balls were big, too.

"Eat it. Eat my big dick," he said.

Tasting the smegma, I gobbled up his cock down to the blonde pubes and I choked a bit.

"Oh, fuck yeah. That feels good. I'm so fucking horny," he moaned.

Holding the rubbery stiff prick, I darted my tongue into the slit and lapped up the bubbling pre-cum.

Letting go of his throbbing dick, I lapped at his balls. "Yeah, suck my nuts. I love that."

With difficulty I managed to get both of his cum-laden balls in my mouth and hum on them.

"Get on my dick, cocksucker. I'm gonna fucking blow. It's coming!" I managed to get my mouth on his exploding cock just in time to get the full force of his orgasm, feeling the jism gush into my mouth, then spit it out.

When I let go of his cock it deflated, the rosy glans retracted into the prepuce. My own cock was raging in my pants. I had to whip off a load to get some relief.

"Let me look at you naked, Mikey. Take off your clothes. I need to get off bad," I begged.

When Mikey stood up and stripped off his grunge drag, leaving on just his combat boots, I was blown away. His body was gorgeous, much more so than I expected, like a marble statue.

"Hot stuff, huh?" he grinned.

I nodded, beating off.

"Why don't you get undressed?" he suggested.

My mature body didn't compare to his adolescent beauty, but I was no slob either. I shed my clothes.

"Oh, yeah, you got hair. Wish I had some," he said, running his hands across my chest.

"You're perfect the way you are." Suddenly I decided the couch was cramped quarters for our session. So I pulled down the Murphy bed. Mikey didn't take off his boots and I didn't ask him to. He looked hot, naked in them. I pulled back the covers and he sprawled out on the sheet.

My cock stayed stiff, just from looking at the long-haired blonde beauty.

Excited by his smooth, hard body, I gave him a tongue bath. When I licked the hair in his pits he squirmed. I lapped at the salty skin on his chest. I tweaked and sucked his pink nipples till they became erect. Crouching between his legs, I licked his satiny smooth thighs. He surprised me when he reached down and grabbed my boner. I didn't expect any reciprocation, figuring him to be strictly trade. He squeezed my dick and tugged on it with his hot hand.

"Got a big dick, man," he said.

I had to shove his hand off or I'd shoot pronto. I wanted to make it last longer. Lord knows when I'd ever get my grubby meat hooks on a wet dream grunge punk like Mikey again.

Straddling his chest, I jacked my cock in his face. "Suck it, Mikey. Take a few slides on it."

"Oh, wow, man. Can't suck your dick, ain't no queer."

Anger welled up inside me. I'd pleasured him and gotten him off. All he could do was take, not give.

"What kind of hustler are you?" I lashed out.

"I told you, this is my first time. I'm no hustler."

"Roll over," I barked.

"Whatcha doing?" I rolled him over onto his belly.

"I wanna look at that butt of yours while I beat my meat."

If his natural cock was a work of art, his bubble butt was a masterpiece. Just looking at it made my cock ooze.

Mikey peeked over his shoulder. His green eyes were cloudy.

"God, look at that cock! You wanna buttfuck me, doncha?" he asked. "You'd pay to fuck it, wouldn't you?"

I didn't expect that. Of course I wanted to, but I was content to jack off. I'd never rape a guy, that wasn't my style. But I sure wanted a piece of his macho butt. Spreading his alabaster cheeks, I looked at his small, pink pucker.

"Yeah, I'd pay a lot for that."

"How much?"

"Virgin?"

"You know it," he grinned.

I looked at the asshole again, winking at me. "How's a hundred sound."

"Okay."

Was this all an act after all? Or was I about to get a piece of cherry boy butt? I never in my life had a virgin that I knew of. At least I could imagine it was cherry. Somehow I knew once I started I'd know for sure.

Diving into his crack, I wanted to taste his butt first. It was hot and tangy.

"Oh, yeah, eat out my ass. Get it ready to fuck."

Mounting Mikey with a mammoth boner, I slapped it against his tender ass cheeks. Intimidated by it, he buried his face in the pillow.

Slowly I nudged my cock head into his spit-soaked butt hole, stretching his ass-ring.

"Oh, shit, it hurts," he whined.

I stayed still, feeling his ass lips expand around my cock. His hole was on fire and tight as a vise. I started to prod his hole slow and deep.

"Oh, shit," he groaned.

God, maybe he was cherry. I figured the pain must have eventually turned to pleasure though because Mikey began moving his ass around and bucking back.

"Shit! Fuck me. Fuck my cherry butt, man," he begged. Pouring on the coal, I rammed his ass hard and fast. "Harder! Fuck me harder."

His hole liked my cock as much as I liked it. I pumped it, feeling every nook and cranny. Grabbing his hair, I prodded his ass for all I was worth. "Pull my fucking hair. I dig that. Tear it out, I don't care. Just keep screwing me."

Mikey likes it! Mikey loves it!

I tried to make the fuck last, but the cum was churning in my balls. It just rushed up my shaft and blasted wads deep into the boy's deflowered butt hole.

Sweaty and panting, I collapsed on top of him. Lost in passion, I just chewed on his stringy hair.

Soon my cock softened and plopped out. I rolled off him, and he rolled over onto his back, sporting a giant boner.

"Look what I got for you, man." His voice was husky. "No extra charge, man."

My jaws were tired, but I wouldn't deny him another suck job.

In a sudden maneuver, Mikey was between my legs, lifting them up in the air.

"What the hell!" I screamed.

"Gonna fuck your hairy butt, man."

"Think you're big enough?" I teased.

"You're about to find out," he shot back. "You turn me on, man."

"Use spit. It needs lube," I said.

Mikey drooled spit down onto my crack. His monster cock oozed precum. He looked like a blonde god in combat boots.

I wanted to protest, to tell him I didn't get fucked, to prolong the agony, even piss him off and make him rape my butt. But there was no time for games.

When he crammed his big cock up my ass I let out a bloodcurdling yell which startled him, but didn't stop him.

John Patrick

With his long blonde locks covering his face like a sheepdog, the punk sawed in and out of my ass. I'd had my share of dicks up the ass, but couldn't remember a bigger one that was like a crowbar.

His big, smooth balls slapped against my hairy ass cheeks as he cornholed me, gripping my thighs.

"I'm fuckin' you in your ass, man. Like it, doncha? Like my big cock up your ass," he panted.

"Oh, yeah. You're a total stud."

Although it was only minutes, it seemed forever as he mercilessly rammed my asshole, making mush out of my guts. I managed to wrap my legs around him while he humped me.

"Oh, fuck. Oh, Mikey, God, I can feel it coming! God, it's so big and hard. Oh, your hot cum squirting into my hole."

The punk collapsed on top of me, with his damp hair cascading on my body. His cock slid out. He scooted up on my chest and presented me with his prick.

"Clean it off, man."

I licked his cock until the head retracted into the hood. Then he rolled off me.

"You can stay the night," I invited.

"Thanks, but I gotta hit the road. Gonna hitchhike down south for a job interview tomorrow."

Mikey took his clothes into the bathroom. I went to my jeans and found two twenties. Then I went to the secret stash and found three more twenties. That was all the money I had to my name.

He came out of the bathroom dressed and smelling of my cologne. He took the bills out of my hand and examined them. "Hey, thanks," he said, slipping the bills into his back pocket.

"You earned it. Every penny."

He smiled and even hugged me before he split. And that was the last I saw of Mikey.

# The Ski Bum

## *Jarred Goodall*

"Good morning." A long-haired blonde boy in rather ratty ski attire sank into the lift chair beside him. "Nice day, right?"

"Yes," Calley said. "Beautiful." And it was. Bright March sunlight glinting on fresh packed powder, as the lift swept them upwards towards the mountain domain of pine and spruce, bare rocks and splinter-blue sky. "This is the kind of day that makes duffers like me think they're experts."

"I suppose." The boy looked glum. Calley caught the unmistakable smell of hangover in the white breath-plume hanging about the youngster's face.

"Not a good morning?"

The boy shook his head. "I feel awful. I don't know why I'm out here today at all. I got piss drunk last night – I'm so ashamed of myself."

Calley laughed. "Sounds like you should have stayed in bed."

"That would've been worse." A slight shiver, and Calley wondered if the boy was dressed warmly enough, especially for the mountain top. "Besides, I came here to ski and I'm gonna ski."

"Brave man."

"Just stupid. I'd actually connected last night, with this older woman, and I blew it."

"Where you staying?"

"Like in what ski lodge?"

"Wherever."

"Wherever is the word. I can't afford a ski lodge. Hell, I can't even afford a hostel. I slept in the van last night, and let me tell you it was cold. There was ice on my eyebrows when I woke up. Thank God I wasn't puking."

Youth and its tortures! More energy than it knew what to do with, less sense than was needed to control it. To Calley, already in his thirties, alien– and attractive. "I take it you're broke."

The boy nodded twice, three times. "You could say that."

"Well, you probably won't regret missing lunch."

"Please, mister, don't talk about food."

"I'm not Mister, I'm Bob Calley."

"Hubie Kozinski, hi." The boy said it as though names were unimportant. "The only thing tradeable for value I have right now is this week's ski ticket. It's still got another day to go. Peggy-Ann bought it for me. That's one connection I didn't fuck up."

"Peggy Ann?"

Hubie dug with the tip of his ski pole at a piece of ice lodged beside his toe-release. "I spotted her on one of the intermediate runs, having trouble. She's wearing real expensive clothes and dragging all this costly equipment but it isn't doing her any good. I'm no expert but I'm better than her and I help her out–you know, choosing the easy way down and picking her up when she falls. Peggy-Ann was real grateful and, well, I moved in. She bought me this ticket the next day."

"Sounds like good duty."

Again the triple, emphatic slow nods. "Only she had to go back to Minneapolis a couple of days ago. How does your wife like it out here, Mr. Calley?"

"I don't have a wife."

Hubie turned his head quickly and studied him for a moment. "You're a very wise and profound man, do you know that?"

The boy had grey eyes, verging on green, a straight nose, no trace of beard growth yet, a rather square jaw. Calley could see how Peggy-Ann, if Peggy-Ann had money to burn, would have been happy to stake Hubie Kozinski to a one-week ski ticket, plus food and probably drinks and entertainment, in exchange for on-slope chaperoning and in-bed insertions of six-plus inches of tumescent boy-flesh with terminal splash-downs of heady liquor.

The thought gave Calley the beginnings of a hard-on, and hard-ons, even semi-hard-ons, are not comfortable to support sitting on a ski lift with the whole genital area confined in stretch-tight ski togs. Hubie, hung-over or not, was definitely good looking. Hubie was definitely his type, his preferred age. Hubie was sexually opportunistic, sexually active, maybe even over-active. Hubie Kozinski was going to be food for many a jerk-off fantasy, no doubt about it.

When they parted at the top of the mountain, Calley pressed a twenty-dollar bill into Hubie's hand. "One of these hours you'll suddenly find you're feeling terrific and you've got a gigantic appetite. You'll need this. Good luck, and good hunting ... for a more comfortable bed."

"Thanks, man–I mean Mr. Calley. If there's anything I can do for you, I mean ever, just ..."

His semi-hard-on persisted, despite a couple of energetic runs. Something had to be done about it or the whole morning would be ruined. He chose a little south-facing outcrop of granite just off one of the less used trails, and there, free of his skis, he lay down in the sun, brought out his cock and, staring up into the clear Colorado sky, went to work ridding himself of the tension that Hubie Kozinski had unexpectedly brought into his life.

Masturbation as an art had started for him back when he was an unhappy, not very popular boy of thirteen. One day he was sitting, as usual alone, at the beach when almost in front of his toes two boys of about his age started wrestling. One was dark-haired and muscular, the other lean and

blonde; both were very good-looking. The dark-haired boy was on top of the blonde, demanding surrender. The blonde just giggled. Another demand and another refusal. The dark-haired boy had a full, muscular ass which he started pretend-humping down onto the blonde boy's hips. "You my fuck-boy now!", he panted, which got the expected response, "Shit I am!" Then, "Say you're my fuck-boy or I'll spit," followed by, "No way," and then, to Calley's amazement, the dark-haired boy dribbled a stringer of spittle down onto the blonde boy's chin, whereupon the blonde boy spat upwards at the other's wildly ducking face. At last they tired of the game and got up, laughing, and chased each other into the water, and Calley staggered to his feet and somehow made it back into the woods where he fumbled himself through the first masturbatory experience in his life.

After that something seemed to turn him on every day: the scene in the showers following gym class at school with the boys parading around in the nude flipping their towels and sometimes their cocks at each other; bicycling past a farm boy driving a tractor with the sleeves of his work-shirt rolled up and his forearms running with dirty sweat; having a near collision in the school halls with a good-looking senior who called him by his last name and told him to watch it; a museum trip in the school bus when one of the appealing smaller boys sat the whole way on his lap.

As Calley entered the long tunnel of puberty and adolescence, masturbation was about the only thing that kept him sane. He was soon averaging five times a day. He would come home from school and shut himself up in his room and pull out his growing cock and rub it off to at least three wet climaxes, showing up at the dinner table a little haggard and hollow-jawed (his mother put it down to "growing pains"). After the dishes had been washed and put away, he would return to his room to fight the battle of homework vs. cock (the latter usually won) before it was time for him to strip for bed, pee, do his teeth, all in preparation for a final jerk-off under the covers before going to sleep. Sometimes he would wake up in the middle of the night, often after some sexy dream, and flood the ripped T-shirt he kept tucked under the mattress for that purpose; almost always he managed to get in one more "shuddergasm," as the boys at school used to call it, before his alarm clock radio clicked on to wake-up music at 6:30.

High school, college, business school. Calley got better and better at pleasing that tyrannical penis of his–caressing and petting it not as often as during his explosive puberty but with greater and greater skill, feeding it the most imaginative and exquisitely erotic stories and images. Perhaps, aside from fear of discovery, that was why, even by now at the age of thirty-one, as a small but successful businessman, he had never made love to anything else.

The high Colorado sun warmed his jacket, warmed his face. There was the distant sound of skiers swooshing down the nearby trail. He knew just what he wanted to do, but when he conjured up the image of Hubie, the sound of the boy's light adolescent voice, the intensity of his response

amazed him. He had actually told Hubie on the lift–feeling somehow bold, feeling lucky, perhaps because it was such radiant weather and he just knew today was going to be one of those good days on the slopes, and perhaps because Hubie looked so ashamed of himself and little-boy unhappy–that if nothing turned up for the boy by late afternoon, Calley's car was down at the back Sugar Creek parking area and he would be there around four-fifteen getting ready to go home.

The orgasm worked. His cock subsided afterwards into submission and he tucked it away and skied, if anything, better for the rest of the day.

At four o'clock he set off down the back trails, pleasantly tired, wondering if the boy would be at the bottom waiting for him. Probably not: a good-looking, enterprising youngster like that ought to be able to find an all-night date for himself on a day such as this. And, sure enough, when he reached the Sugar Creek parking lot there was no sign of Hubie Kozinski.

Damn! Youth could never be pinned down. Youth was totally unreliable. Youth had its own priorities quite independent of a thirty-one-year-old virgin's concerns. That the offer had been quite open was of little comfort. Calley stowed his skis and poles on the ski rack atop his car and backed carefully out of his parking place. He now faced a last supper in the chalet restaurant and an evening alone reading by his bedroom fire before he had to head back to Denver and his work in the morning.

And then, as he was pulling out of the parking area, a more-or-less-skiing bundle of humanity hurtled over a fringing snow bank and collapsed in a heap almost in front of his wheels.

"Gee, Mr. Calley, I shouted and shouted, but I guess you didn't hear me back there on the trail, huh?"

Whatever his skiing ability, Hubie Kozinski had obviously recovered from his night of alcoholic over-indulgence and was now the picture of vigorous young health. As he took off his skis he explained that he'd had no luck up on the mountain.

"No Peggy-Anns, no grateful older women?"

"Man, it was all married couples–or college girls with dates they came with." They were talking over the car, now, racking Hubie's skis beside his own. "One little boy that had fallen and I picked up crying told me I stank out of my mouth–that was pretty early in the morning, but you were right, Mr. Calley, 'long about noon I was starved. I used up fifteen dollars and seventy-five cents of your money on pizza and Coke and ice-cream, so I owe you four twenty-five–and just a whole lot more if you were really serious about putting me up tonight–are you?"

"Well, my room in the chalet's got only one bed." Calley found his heart thumping harder than it had all day, after even his most exhausting runs.

"Man, that's no problem!" Hubie's handsome face broke into a big grin as he ducked down and climbed into the passenger's seat. "I'm used to sleeping with guys as well as girls–aren't you? I mean, I got three brothers and for years we only had two double beds up in our attic room, and in the

winter when it was cold you were glad to have company–and sometimes in the summer, too."

Jesus, what did the boy mean by that?

Hubie saw the confusion on Calley's face and laughed. "Like I was the youngest and if I had a bad dream or something I could snuggle up to a brother and feel safe."

In his room at the chalet, Calley got a nice blaze roaring and sparking in the fireplace while Hubie showered and blow-dried his hair. Calley poured himself a Scotch highball. When the boy finally came out, bath towel tied around his waist and reeking of Calley's after-shave, anti-perspirant and cologne, Calley couldn't repress a little gasp: Hubie in his now near-nakedness was everything his erotic imaging had ever desired: strong shoulders, full chest covered with the leanest of flesh, narrow waist and, below the towel, muscular legs, nicely shaped, lightly dusted with rather blonde hair.

"It's all yours," the boy said, gesturing toward the bathroom, then, noticing the fire, "Aw, look at this!" He dropped down and stretched out on the deep pile carpet facing the hearth and stared through the fire screen into the flames, chin resting in one palm. "This has just got to be ... hell, I don't know, Mr. Calley ..."

Calley tore his eyes away from the nicely rounded rump stretching tight a dampened towel and showered, trying to fight down, not very successfully, a new erection. He dried off, put on his bathrobe and stepped out into the bedroom. "I'd offer you a drink," he told Hubie, "except ..."

"Definitely not interested. This has just got to be the most luxurious place I've ever seen, no shit."

"Better than Peggy Anne's?"

"Aw, that was a dump in comparison. Jesus, Mr. Calley, I'm just so fucking grateful ..."

Calley joined the boy on the carpet. The smell of wood smoke and the boy's perfumed body had blood singing in his ears, drowning out the sounds of the fire. Almost without thinking, now that his erection was hidden, pressed into the carpet, he reached over and dropped a hand on Hubie's shoulder, expecting some kind of rejection, or at least negative response, but Hubie just lay there looking into the fire, immobile, as though he'd been expecting the move. Suddenly Calley chickened out. He took his hand away. Hubie turned his head, rested a cheek on his forearm and said, very seriously, "It's okay, Mr. Calley."

Panic. Calley's heart threatened to jump clean out of his throat. "What ... do you mean?"

"It's okay, that's all." Hubie's green-grey eyes met his – serious, almost cat-like, and unconcerned. "Go ahead. I'm cool."

"You mean ... ?"

A smile crossed Hubie's lips, the kind of friendly, embarrassed smile you have around a mischievous but lovable little child. "Sure," he said. "I'm here, aren't I?" and he rolled over on his back and parted the towel.

Sweet Jesus! Calley found himself staring, drop-jawed and bug-eyed, at a large, full but not erect, circumcised penis lying athwart one hip. There it was, after all these years–a cock, a big adolescent boy's cock, practically under his nose, ostensibly on offer. He must be dreaming. This couldn't be happening. He would wake up in a few minutes and find himself alone in the bed on the other side of the room, his brain having just delivered itself of one more not-quite-wet erotic dream.

Hubie touched the purple tip of his penis with a couple of finger-tips, stirred it a bit. "Go ahead, take it," he said lazily. "Like I said, I'm cool."

Panic. This was no dream. This was actually happening. Calley shuddered and staggered over to the big armchair on the other side of the room.

Hubie sat up and faced him hugging his knees. "What is it?" he said. The light from the fire behind made a kind of halo in the boy's fluffed-out hair. "Have I got you psyched out wrong? You only go for women, right?"

"It's not that," Calley mumbled.

"You probably think I'm some kind of scum-bag ..."

Calley closed his eyes. "No." He shook his head. "It's just ... like taking advantage ..."

"Me of you or you of me?"

Calley blinked. What a ridiculous question. "Come on," he said, annoyed.

Hubie stared at him for almost half a minute. Then he got up and with a wooden face started pulling on his clothes.

Calley had been looking forward to buying Hubie the biggest sirloin steak the chalet restaurant had to offer, garnished with platefuls of French fries and, as encore, some sort of fancy but ample ice-cream dessert dripping with syrups and fruits of the boy's own choice. Instead Hubie ordered spaghetti, the cheapest thing on the menu, and sucked it down rapidly, the flailing ends splattering sauce all over his face and jacket. Calley realized he'd made some kind of terrible mistake back there in his room. He'd thought at the time he'd done the boy a favor, let him off the hook, but that didn't seem to be the case. He had to find out what was wrong. He didn't look forward to spending the whole evening with a teenage grouse and sleeping beside his resentful body.

"There," Hubie said, spaghetti finished, spoon and fork crossed on the empty plate. "That'll keep me going. And it didn't cost you too much, did it?"

"Is that what's worrying you?"

"Why shouldn't it?"

"You like girls, don't you?"

"Of course I like girls. What's that got to do with anything?"

"A whole lot, I'd think."

"Look, Mr. Calley, there's not much a kid like me can do for a man that's got everything."

"Do? You don't have to do anything."

"So just having me around is worth all this?" He waved his hand to indicate the chalet, the restaurant, perhaps Calley's room as well. "Come off it. I don't believe you. I always pay my way. I'm not one of these guys that takes advantage of other people's kindness without trying to give something back in return."

"And this, my 'kindness', is worth ... doing that?"

They stared across the candle-lit table at each other and not for the first time Calley realized how little he knew about young people–and how accepting he himself had become of the luxuries that went with his earnings, luxuries that must be mightily impressive to a poor boy just starting out along his road through manhood.

"'Doing that'! What's this 'doing that'? Jesus, you old people got more hang-ups about making out than the Pope's got sins!" Hubie sat back with just the suggestion of a smile coming to his lips.

"You really ... wouldn't have minded?"

Hubie shook his head. "I figured I was getting the better deal, if you really want to know."

"Oh." Calley took a big swallow–and decided to take a chance. "There's something else, Hubie."

"I'm listening."

"I've never done anything like ..." Calley paused, wondering just how to put it.

"Like what was going down in your room–almost?"

Calley nodded.

"'Cause you didn't want it, right? 'Cause you only go for women, right?"

"I wanted it. And I don't desire women. I've never had a women, either."

"Sincere?"

"Yup."

"You've wanted cock – just cock – all these years?"

Calley sank a little farther down in his chair and nodded again.

"And you've never made out with any guy in your whole life?"

"That's right."

"So now, when it's just about over ..."

"Over–my life?"

"Naw, I didn't mean that." Hubie was recovering his pleasant grin. "But, gosh, you've sure put it off a long time."

"I guess I've always been too much of a coward."

Hubie reached across the table and closed his fingers around one of Calley's wrists. "But it doesn't take any courage at all. My brothers showed me how nice it was when I was just a little kid. Didn't you have any big brothers?"

Calley shook his head.

"Now, that's a real shame. Let's go back to your room, and if you let me big brother you a little, just to get you started, you can buy me that steak for breakfast, agreed?"

Hubie withdrew his hand and spat into it and put it out for Calley to take. Calley reached for the hand, but Hubie said, "Nuh uh, you spit too. Otherwise it doesn't count."

Calley spat, took Hubie's hand, feeling both squeamish and aroused by the warm, slippery clasp, and wondered how he was going to slip away from their table without the erection in his pants broadcasting to the whole multitude of après-skiers and the well-scrubbed young waiters serving them the intensity of his feelings for the handsome but badly dressed youth he was with and the shape of events soon to come.

Calley sat on the side of his bed, naked. Hubie stood like some erotic statue in front of him, equally naked, offering Calley his cock.

"Go on, Mr. Calley. It'll stiffen up soon as you start to work on it. Give it a few strokes–yeah, that's right, that feels real nice, and don't forget about my nuts–they like it, too. Just get to know everything good. We don't have to go too fast–unless you want to, of course."

It was a magnificent penis, the most beautiful penis in the whole world, and it was starting to smell less of the cologne sprinkled on it a couple of hours earlier and more of itself. Calley couldn't imagine anything more wonderful than what he was being allowed to do now. He ran his fingers up and down the rubbery shaft, lifted the cock-head to look underneath at the rumple of loose skin bifurcated by the tiny ridgelet that would be the epicenter, he was sure, of all Hubie's good sex feelings, as it was in his own.

"One thing that's real nice," Hubie was saying as his fingers came into Calley's hair, "is when you lick it, lick it all over, especially around the head and on the loose skin. That feels just mind-blowing good ... ."

Calley closed his eyes and moistened his lips and pressed them against the underside of Hubie's cock while its soft head snuggled up against his nostrils. Yes, Hubie's cock was definitely beginning to take on its own natural, sexy scent. With his tongue he began to tickle the frenulum and found the corpora cavernosa, the two erectile bodies inside, expanding, beginning to stiffen.

"Aah, that's nice," Hubie breathed. "Man, nobody'd ever know you never done this before."

Calley kept on licking, making excursion up and down, now, around the back, over the tip, moistening everything, making it slippery, making it glint in the subdued bedroom light. He could smell the pubic hair, feel the boy's

smooth, hairless abdomen pressing against his forehead. He dropped his mouth to Hubie's ball sack and licked the crumpled skin, getting more, now, of the scent of Hubie's cleft from cock-root to asshole and beyond, an ecstatically arousing smell of adolescent male sexiness.

But it was the cock which drew him back, that wonderful teenage cock, now quite stiff, that experienced cock which had weathered the storms of puberty and adolescence so much better than Calley's had and thrown its sperm far and wide, certainly into numerous women and probably over sibling knuckles and bellies and down the throats of grateful men. Calley worked upwards again and captured its tip between his lips and began to suck. For how many years had he dreamed of this? He'd tried it out on his fingers, a hammer handle, a carrot, a cucumber.

Hubie's cock was a lot thicker than a carrot and warmer than a cucumber, and it smelled a lot better, even covered with his own spit. He increased the vacuum and let the shaft slide in, perhaps half way, allowing his tongue to caress the little frenulum as the cock traveled in. Hubie's fingers in his hair tensed and tightened.

"You give head like an expert," the boy breathed. "That's better than most women know how to do ... ."

In and out, back and forth went Hubie's cock, sliding beautifully between Calley's pouting lips. He heard Hubie's breathing sharpen, become irregular, air suck between teenage teeth. And now the tip began to expand as blood rushed into it, inflating it like a balloon, stretching tight the super-tender skin. The fingers in his hair tightened and held his head steady.

"Uh, Mr. Calley, if you don't want to take a load, you better cool it ..."

But that is just what Calley did want to do, wasn't going to let Hubie prevent him from doing. He wanted that squirt of sperm, wanted it more than anything he'd ever wanted in his whole life, wanted to feel it spilling into the back of his mouth, taste it, savor it, treasure it.

And now there was something else that was just as remarkable: his own cock, untouched, for his hands were grasping both cheeks of Hubie's buttocks, his own cock was rising all by itself towards a beautiful cum. All he had to do was keep on sucking, bringing Hubie closer and closer to the brink, and if he was very lucky ... .

He tightened his grip on Hubie's ass, the tips of both middle fingers digging almost by accident into the boy's anal ring, and kept on sucking, moving his head.

"Okay, Mr. Calley, if that's what you want ..." The boy started thrusting with his hips, strongly controlling with his hands in Calley's hair the depth and speed of penetration he wanted. Calley felt the hands tremble, the boy's whole body tremble, heard a kind of throaty gasp from above him as the cock one final time shoved home.

Miraculously, both penises let go then, Calley's jetting outwards and upwards into space and decorating the blonde hair on Hubie's legs with gobs

of dense, white semen, Hubie's discharging against Calley's palate, puddling deep in Calley's throat.

They took a break, Calley in the armchair he'd dragged up to before the fireplace, Hubie on the floor leaning against his knees, sipping a Coke, accepting Calley's hand that fondly stroked his shoulder, smoothed his bright hair. It was only now that Calley began to realize what a truly seismic event had occurred, how somehow not only had the earth stood still for magic minutes but his future was irrevocably altered, set careening off its conservative course, that, in effect, he was a new man, reborn but in a very different way from those poor souls who "find Jesus" through some kind of mortification of the flesh.

They had thrown a couple of logs on the fire, turned off all the lights. Once again Hubie's head seemed to radiate a kind of St. Elmo's fire, the flicker of flame playing also over the boy's bare shoulders, touching like jewel-light the tip of one ear. They didn't talk, didn't need to talk. For long minutes they just enjoyed the comfort of each other's touch, the snap of pine logs expending themselves behind the fire screen.

Hubie finished his Coke, stirred. Calley could see the boy was hard again, or almost hard. He got lazily to his feet and put out a hand for Calley to clasp. "Well, Tiger, how about round two?"

They made for the bed. Hubie lay down on his back and patted his stomach in invitation. Calley lay down on top of him and felt the boy's arms tighten around his back. "This is nice, too," Hubie said, and then they were kissing, running wet lips all over each other's faces. Calley could smell, taste the Coke on Hubie's lips and also something peculiar to the boy's own mouth. It was said that dogs and cats could unerringly recognize humans by the smell of their breaths; Calley was sure the scent of the lips which were clasping his own was Hubie's own and not shared by any other boy.

It was over, for Calley, all to quickly. The writhing of their bodies, the flow of pre-lube from Calley's cock, the incomprehensible wonderfulness of being clasped in Hubie's arms and kissed by Hubie's lips sent him sky-rocketing into orgasm almost before they had started.

"Oh, Jesus, I'm sorry," Calley gasped, as soon as he got his breath back.

"That's okay, no sweat," Hubie said, patting his back.

"But I left you ... ."

"Don't worry about me, Tiger. This is your night."

Calley mopped up, then rolled off onto his back and pulled Hubie's head over so it was resting his chest as the boy curled his long body beside him.

"Time for a sleep break, huh?" Hubie murmured and draped a comfortable arm over Calley's stomach. He nuzzled his cheek in against Calley's right nipple.

Three more times that night Calley woke up with a hard-on, sought and found Hubie's penis and either stroked or sucked it into consciousness.

Hubie always came awake befuddled but good-natured and responded to just about everything Calley wanted to do. Once he even took Calley's cock into his mouth and sucked on it for a whole ecstatic minute–"just to let you know now nice it feels although this is something I never really do".

When dawn lightened the window at last, Calley couldn't help staring at Hubie's sleeping head turned toward him on the other pillow, hair crossing one cheek, lips slightly parted to reveal the tips of a couple of strong white teeth. Most people are ugly in sleep: not Hubie. The boy's breath was even pleasant, although early-morning strong. There was a tiny wet place on the pillow where his sleeping lips had leaked. All night long Hubie had slept with the quiet of the young.

Hubie did get the promised steak at breakfast, although it was a skinny brother to what had been on offer the night before. When Hubie went back to the buffet to take on more fuel for the coming day he was gone a long time. Calley got up for another cup of coffee and spotted the boy talking animatedly with a well-dressed girl, obviously putting on the make.

His first reaction was jealousy, a sharp stab to the stomach. Then he shook his head and began to laugh. Of course. Their lives were parting, Hubie's and his. This was what the kid was put together for, whatever excursions the boy might make in the direction of hospitality. Besides, for Hubie it was a matter of survival, wasn't it?

He left a note for Hubie at the table and went back to his room and began to pack. There was a knock on his door and a rather sheepish Hubie came in and looked around as though he'd lost something.

"She looks nice," Calley said.

"Huh? Oh, yeah. Paula." He spotted his scarf lying on the dresser table.

"Well ..." It was suddenly heart-breaking to say good-bye. "It's been real."

Hubie's head nodded up and down, slowly, three times. "It sure has, Mr. Calley ..." Obviously Hubie's thoughts were elsewhere. God almighty, couldn't the boy show more feeling, even if what had happened last night wasn't the earthquake for him it had been for Calley?

Hubie stretched the scarf around his neck, then looked at Calley, his eyes suddenly coming into focus again. He smiled, a big, generous smile, and put out a hand. "So long, Tiger," he said. "You're on your way. And it looks like so am I."

# Rock Hard

## *John Patrick*

"My name is Rock." He looked at me expectantly.

"Like in Plymouth Rock?" I asked.

"Like what?"

"Plymouth Rock. It's a place."

"Is it somewhere funny?"

"You might say so, sure."

"Why?"

"Well, because Plymouth Rock is funny."

"Plymouth Rock is?"

"Funny. Yes. Have you ever been there?"

"No."

"Well," I said, as if I'd proved a point. "You should go someday. You'd see."

He stared at the drink I had just bought him.

"Of course, the most famous rock is the Rock of Gibaltar. You've seen its picture. In 'The Rock' commercials."

"In 'The Rock'?"

"You know. 'Own a piece of.' Insurance."

"Oh," he said, having lost all interest now. He seemed to be offended, as if I was making fun of his name. Which I guess I was. I could have said, "Like in Hudson," but sometimes I like to test these studs with a bit of geography.

I continued, "But what they've done to Plymouth Rock is funny. You see, they've built a cage around it. It's so people won't deface it, you know, with their names and dates. They've built this big cage 'round this tiny little rock. Kids have to stand up on their toes to look at it through the cage." I laughed, but Rock looked hard put to respond appropriately. I cleared my throat and said, "So, you just get into town?"

"Yeah. Just got in." He took a long swallow of his bourbon.

Now I focused all of my attention on the sad story of Rock. Rock was, after all, his stage name. He was going to be dancing at this bar starting on Friday night. He apparently had used up all of the available johns in Fort Lauderdale and now found himself in Tampa.

I tugged at his "F**k Me" T-shirt. "Take it off," I insisted.

He hesitated.

"Go ahead," I begged, "it's allowed."

He took off his T-shirt. His chest was as magnificent as I had presumed it would be. I ran my nails across his shoulders, down his back. He shivered

with pleasure. My nails pressed deeper into his deeply tanned flesh as I moved my thigh against his.

"So," I whispered in his ear, "is that what you want?"

"What?"

"What it says on your T-shirt."

He looked down at the lettering. "If that's what you want."

At my condo by the sea, he was relaxed with me, until the moment I was above him, ready to enter him. I stroked his thighs until he looked up at me.

"I want you so bad," I whispered hoarsely. We both moaned softly as I pushed the head of my cock gently inside of him. He tensed his body; I waited. Then Rock relaxed and his hips began to move, pulling me into him. When I was deep inside of him, I lay still on top of him. Our bodies relaxed, fitting into each other. I didn't move until he did. I stroked him just a little slower than his motion demanded; his body demanded more. His cock wasn't long but it was thick, nicely cut. He also lived up to his name: his cock was rock-hard. I sucked it for a few moments when we arrived, but it was his ass I was paying for.

I felt his orgasm building long before he came. As he began to come, his hands clawed at my back and pulled me deep into him. Once he pulled my hair so hard I cried out with him. As his orgasm began to ebb, I followed it with my own, pulling out so I could made a puddle of cum to join his on his chest.

"Oh, John." It sounded so nice the way he sighed my name. His fingertips slid down my back and pushed at my ass, forcing me back into his ass.

His body felt so good. I kissed him deep and slow. He moved for me, gave me everything a boy can give to a lover, and I was excited. At the moment when it became unbearable for me to go on any longer I pulled out gently.

I lay facedown on the bed with my head resting on his cum-soaked belly. His hands played with my hair. His fingertips ran across my shoulders, arousing the surface of my skin. I wished I could just stay in that moment in time.

We lay together without speaking for a while. "I have to go to the bathroom," I said.

"Me, too."

In the bathroom, he came into my arms and kissed me deeply. He squeezed my cock. "You ready for more?"

I answered by bending down to kiss his nearly hairless chest. I began licking his skin. He tasted like cocoa butter, mixed with sweat. My tongue worked in broad, moist strokes across his breastbone, then tickled his navel.

He moaned for me to continue. He slumped toward me, and I felt his cock, again rock-hard. I studied his face: round and golden and yearning, as beautiful as any sight I had ever seen. His eyes were closed, his face tight

with bliss and a growing need for release again. Rubbing his extraordinary chest, I kissed him.

His lips were hotter than any I had ever experienced. Even I was beginning to grow hungry for another orgasm. I rubbed and squeezed his cock.

When he did pull his mouth away from mine, it was to whisper, more breathlessly than ever, "Suck it again, please."

There was a dancing light in his pale green eyes, and he smiled at me as my own excitement grew more and more obvious. I began lapping and kissing and sucking his miraculous organ. No wonder he got the job dancing at Big Bill's. Bill loved nothing more than a hard cock. I imagined that earlier in the day Bill had enjoyed this one in his little office.

I sank to my knees, eye-level with his cock. His balls hung down loosely, and I cupped them in my hands. I licked the scrotum, enjoying the contrast between the silky skin and wiry copper curls. He clasped his hands tightly to my shoulders and moaned, tipping his pelvis forward and bracing his legs. I stroked him, happy to feel the hardness. I held him tightly as I sucked and a deeper need had just begun to build in me. Careful not to bring him to orgasm, I licked and sucked his cock and balls. First I sucked the glans alone, then I took his shaft deep into my throat. With more and more speed and enthusiasm I kept sucking, kissing, and nursing. As I nuzzled and nipped, sucked and smooched, I could hear him moaning, "Oh yeah, suck me."

I held his thigh with my right hand while I jerked myself with my left. Soon my knees became weak. My need was to have this cock up my ass.

"I want you in me now," I said. He smiled and led me back to the bedroom.

I kissed him on the cheek, then on the lips. He quickly grew aroused again; my whole body tingled. I had never been with anyone as sexual. We kissed deeply and strongly, Rock running his fingers through my hair and pulling me even closer to him. I gently traced the contours of his torso with my fingers and felt myself smile.

Rock kissed my nose, and then went back to my mouth. Our arms were wrapped around each other; I pressed my body to his more tightly. He grabbed my ass in his broad hands, pulling me even closer. I felt his flesh stir against me.

As he sucked my nipple, he reached his hand down to my cock. He smiled when his fingers found it nearly erect.

I could see that he was ready, too: his cock stood up proudly, the head blushing a deep red as he rolled me onto my stomach and mounted me.

In one instant I felt his hands on my hips. In the next, his prick probing against my asshole. And then he was in. I bucked back against him. He stroked forward even more forcefully.

I wished I could have admitted to him how wonderful it all was for me. His hard prick was a welcome presence, filling me. His pelvis slapped firmly

against my hairy, lush ass and all I could do was whimper. The tempo of my sounds matched his thrusts, speeding up as they did. Joy pulsed through me, screaming for release.

We finished together. Just as my tension broke into orgasm, I heard him yell and felt his pulsing gush. He continued milking his cock deep within me, and I loved every second of it.

Afterward, he lay next to me, panting and flushed. I clung to him, exhausted and energized. I was ecstatic and speechless, changed in some way I couldn't define.

While still affectionate, his voice conveyed some kind of distance as well. This bothered me, especially after the closeness hot sex brings. But then it always bothered me, especially when I brought a trick home with me.

I wished to somehow prolong the intimacy we had shared, or reinstate it. Finally I cuddled closer against him and said, "Where are you staying?"

"Nowhere," he said. "I left my shit at Big Bill's. I didn't have time to get a place."

His look was now a bit sad, but he brightened considerably when I said, "Well, why don't you stay here?"

# All Night Long

## *Andrew Richardson*

"I'm not really a proper rent boy," Dave said as he breezed into my apartment. I must admit, I was quite nervous about having phoned for sex–it was the first time I had done it–I was feeling so horny but just couldn't be bothered to make the trip into town to find a good-looking boy.

When I saw his advertisement, something just clicked; "Dave, pumped iron body, very well endowed. Young, versatile, dark hair and horny."

It was simple and direct–just as I wanted my sex.

He was a little shorter than I had imagined, with a mop of jet black hair and a little stubble–adding to an overall look of toughness. Either he wore very thick pullovers, or his chest was even nicer than I had hoped. When he took his coat off, seeing he had only a T-shirt on, I was delighted. His pert nipples stood out hard under the white cotton of the shirt, and he comfortably walked over to my sofa to sling his coat down.

The fabric of his Levi's cut into his fine backside, and looked well worn to that really comfortable stage. As he turned to me, I could see just how well hung this guy was–the bulge was incredible. I couldn't believe that I would definitely have his cock in my mouth without all the hassle of a bar and so on.

He continued. "No, I've got a regular job. I'm just a horny bastard. I love fucking. I love getting home from work knowing there might be a message on the phone for me to go right back out again to have sex, without having to bother with chatting and all that."

Fair comment; a man after my own heart. "Glad I was the first on the list." I said, obviously impressed with my purchase.

"Oh you weren't," he replied. What? He can't have been somewhere else already! "There were a few messages. I just liked the sound of your voice. And I'm pleased I came. Now let's get a look at you."

He walked right up to me and slowly around me as I stood stock still. His eyes scrutinizing my face, my neck, my body. I felt like he'd missed the point–that I should be doing this to him. That I should be watching his cock start erecting in his jeans.

"Not bad. Not fucking bad at all," he said. "Glad I came." Standing behind me, Dave got a handful of my ass and breathed into my neck, "You're fucking gorgeous. Now let me show you what you've just bought." As he said this, Dave pushed his groin onto my left leg–then gently took hold of my hand and guided it along an alarmingly long length.

He grinned and stepped back. "Get your fucking clothes off," I said. By the time we got upstairs, he was half naked and I got my cock out and ready for him. I was behind him. His shirt was half way down the stairs. His naked

back was broad and smooth. He was frantically pulling at his belt and the fastening of his jeans. "Christ I want to fuck you." I said.

In the hallway upstairs, he left his belt hanging open, with a couple of buttons unfastened. His immense cock was pushing down his left leg and swelling the denim out. A soft line of hair trailed from his belly button to the bush of pubes I could just see on the V of his opened jeans. The fly of his white brief shorts had parted to give me a glimpse of his prick-flesh.

Dave got his mouth onto my erection and worked the foreskin down with his lips. His tongue spiraled around my head and shaft and slicked it with thick spit. I was pleased, my cock was a decent length itself, and he was obviously enjoying himself. As he took each of my balls into his mouth, my cock slid over his forehead and hair. He was really pulling my balls hard in his mouth and rubbing my exposed head with his fingers. I could have ejaculated into his black curls right then–but Dave released my plums from his mouth, and with surprising politeness asked me if I'd like to suck him off.

As I stepped out of my jeans, which had been around my ankles, I said, "All night long, if I could." Then I ripped his jeans down. His erection was straining underneath the white boxer shorts–it's massive size swollen with sex, and pointing downwards, tenting the fabric. His swelled head was forcing itself out of the tight fitting leg hole, and it was such a turn on. I was just about to tear his shorts off, when Dave stuck his fingers into the fly of his underwear. He fished for the thick shaft and drew it up from alongside his leg. The cock hung before me and my asshole throbbed for it.

"Sure. I'm fucking staying all night if I get a cock like yours to chew on."

I was thrilled at his willingness to stay–and delighted he that he liked my prick too.

"You're welcome to stay if I get this prick," I replied and saw him smile as his truly enormous member swayed in front of me. I gazed at the hole in the end, and clenched my hands around the shaft. As I squeezed and squeezed, Dave groaned deeper and deeper. His end stretched and shone as it became engorged with blood. His big hands held my head firmly and he moved my face forwards.

"Fucking lick my piss hole! Now!" he commanded, and I flicked my tongue over his end–getting a taste of the salty lubricating cum just bubbling to the top. Then I opened my mouth wide, slid my hands down the shaft and got his prick deep into my mouth. "Oh, oh, my God. Oh, yeah," Dave was slowly rocking his pelvis and nudging his cock to the back of my throat. His hands were like clamps over my ears but I was hardly listening to the rush of blood that they amplified.

I was running my fingertips over his powerful thighs. Down to his calves, up the backs of his legs, over the cotton shorts, kneading his buttocks. It was a temptation to tear the shorts down and feel his ass flesh, but I knew I had plenty of time to taste his asshole later on. With one hand,

Dave was now gently applying pressure to the back of my head, encouraging me to take his full length in my mouth. His fingers went through my hair, "Oh yes," he was saying, "Oh yes, your mouth on my cock. I want to feel my cock going down your throat and my balls on your face."

As he stood there before me, jeans around his ankles, with his cock in my mouth, his shorts were fitting so tightly that each testicle was pulled snugly up to his cock base. Dave was groaning with pleasure and really began to force his prick forward. I looked up to see his sexual gratification; up along the flat, firm stomach, the bulging chest mounds and dark nipples, and the thick biceps held forward to grip my head.

I carefully relaxed my throat and stretched my neck out. Then, just as I went to squeeze his buttocks, he shoved forward and got his whole monster length into my head. Then Dave got his other hand down his shorts and started to frig his asshole while my face was pressed onto his groin.

Dave was nearly suffocating me. His pubic hair was in my eyes as he bent his knees and leaned forward. As he eagerly fingered himself my head was like a skull on a pole–his arm wrapped around it and holding me in place–his sharp, jerky thrusts rammed cock further down my throat than I'd ever had it. Momentarily, I was worried he wanted to keep me like this.

Suddenly and in a flash, he drew his prick out of my throat, whipped his boxer shorts off and had his ass in my face. I inhaled deeply and was relieved to draw breath. His fingers had loosened the hole up already and I stuck my face onto the crack, my tongue into his dark, moist hole. Dave was groaning. I slid my fingers up him, two, three. Then two from my other hand. I stretched my fingers apart and rimmed the pink flesh of his soft and damp rectum. As my mouth worked on his ass hole, my hands were busy masturbating his fabulous and slick cock.

Then I got into a rhythm of jerking him off whilst fingering his ass and licking the hairy flesh between his balls and his slit. When he was truly relaxed, Dave pushed down onto my hand, almost sitting on it. "Oh, get that fucker up me. Harder. Harder. Push it, ooh, push it." Frantically spitting on the back of my hand and wrist, I kept my fingers together tight and forced it up into his tight passage. I was slowly rubbing his huge cock with my other hand, and as he tensed, then relaxed again, my knuckles passed the tough sphincter of his ass–the tight skin of the crack stretching and giving under the pressure–and I slid my hand in up to my wrist. He gasped.

Gently, I pulled down a little, and then forward. My own cock was as hard as a rock watching Dave's blissful face and the sweat gather on his brow. After a couple of seconds, his ass relaxed again and I worked my fist fucking hand in and out, in and out.

Dave knelt forward into the doggy position and I rubbed my own shaft over his torso. Slowly and carefully, I got my hand more and more lubricated. As I shoved it in and pulled it out faster and faster, Dave's hole gaped wider and wider. After a while, I could pull my hand out, softly taste the tender flesh of his ass and then slide my delving fingers in again. I

cocked my leg up onto his back and drooled over his buttocks and balls, as I rubbed my prick along his body.

We were both panting and groaning as our cocks got more and more worked-up. The juices were shimmering over his bum cheeks and slid down his inner thighs. "Oh yeah, get that arm up my fucking innards," he was gasping and I felt the warmth of his rectum squeeze over my arm. The hairs of my skin were slicked down as the tightly stretched lips of his crack smoothed over them.

I was desperate to feel some of that hot gut around my cock head and shaft, and tenderly drew my fist out of the succulent bum hole. Dave knelt up and faced me. He embraced me tightly, squeezing our cocks together as we kissed and groped the other's buttocks. He leaned onto me and guided me to lie back on the hallway carpet. My prick was almost glued to my stomach it was so furiously hard. He slowly took it into his mouth and carefully nipped the tip, encouraging a glob of semen onto his tongue and into his mouth. Dave suddenly eased his whole face down onto my prick and pressed his stubbly chin onto my scrotum.

I was watching my cock going in and out of his gorgeous face, and got closer and closer to a climax. He didn't stop ravishing my cock, it felt raw and hot, almost painful but too exquisite to hurt. "Ugh, oh, I'll fucking ... ah ... fucking shoot in a ... ah."

Dave held my foreskin peeled right down and lashed his rough tongue over my cock head. Within seconds, I couldn't hold back any more and saw a jet of my white creamy cum spurt into his mouth. Then more, and more. My pelvis rammed up and down. Dave's tongue, teeth and lips were smeared with thick spunk which he swallowed eagerly.

Before my raw prick was even recovered, Dave straddled me and had got his arse cheeks separated over my cock. With one hand, he held my member up, with his other hand he separated his pucker. Then lowered himself down onto me. For a brief second, I felt my cock going slightly softer–it was almost a relief–but as soon as the moist ringer was pressing it's soft flesh onto my prick, I was solid again.

"Let me do all the work now," he said, and he sat up and down on my shaft. I rested back and ran my hands over Dave's solid thighs as they controlled his rhythmic motions. "Oh, I can feel your cock deep inside me." he panted.

"Your ass feels great," I muttered. "Ah, ooh yeah, ride me man."

I began playing with Dave's cock as he glided up and down. His length was like a hard rubber truncheon in my hand; as I squeezed hard and rubbed my hands over the swollen, bulbous head, Dave speeded his movements up a little.

The skin of his chest glistened as more sweat built up in the fever. Our groans got louder–my cock felt like it had split in half but I knew I couldn't stop until I'd blown another load of cum up Dave's backside.

He sat right down onto my cock, his eyes fixed onto mine. "Fuck me now and fuck me hard." Dave crouched up onto his feet, keeping a firm ass-grip on my cock and I brought my knees up to allow me to ram into him.

My piston cock got faster and faster. Dave's face was a picture of pleasure and slight grimace as the nerves in his rectum were constantly being fucked. Keeping myself steady with my hands stretched back and my feet apart, I frantically rocked my groin in and out of the bum hole slurping on my cock. The rhythm got faster. The panting louder. The sweat thicker and the orgasm closer. Staring deep into his eyes, Dave did not once look away. Between grunts, he was whispering "Fuck me fuck me fuck me."

His balls slapped against my wet pubic hair as I screwed him upwards. Then, still looking into me, Dave grinned. He was rubbing his exposed cock glans and my thrusts were going faster and faster. "Oh, oh, urh, oh."

A stream of semen ejaculated over my chest. I rammed a tremendous orgasm into his arse. Another spurt came from his cock and splattered over my face. His eyes were piercing mine. My cock slid out of his hole and up his back, smothering his crack with my paste. Dave released a final jism into the air and over my head.

He collapsed forward and licked his seed from my face. Then we lay together holding onto each other–steadying the nerves. Occasionally, Dave licked my ear. "No," I said to him with great affection, "you certainly are not a proper rent boy."

# My Night Caller

## *John Patrick*

*"Of my 66 years, 61 of them have found me a member of the brotherhood; I came out, at least to myself, at the age of five.*

*In the '30s and '40s, I was lucky enough to have fun with cousins my age. In the '50s, I had my first romance with a faculty colleague. In the '60s, I came out to the area and tried the baths.*

*In the '70s I was lucky enough to be visited by my night caller, a former student. In the '80s, I had my second romance. This decade is still forming!"*
– Ralph in Tacoma

Joey came in the night. And came and came and came. He could never get enough. After a while, neither could I. I hadn't believed it was possible that two months after I saw Joey graduate from high school with honors he was earning credits toward a masters degree on my front porch.

I had closely followed Joey's progress (and the incredible undulating of his hips) over the two years he was at the Unionville school where I taught mathematics. Joey had a keen mind and math was his favorite subject; he became my favorite pupil. But as much as I admired him and the awesome sight of his hunky young body poured into jeans too small for him, he was off limits to me, being underage and, even worse, my student. However, the images of him, naked before me, warmed many a cold night.

Which brings me to the warm night in July when, unable to sleep, I had gone out onto the front porch and was sitting quietly in the dark with my feet up trying to identify the sounds I was hearing from the yard. Suddenly, there was a sound I knew quite well: "Pssst–Teach." Joey was forever sharing confidences with me, whispering the latest gossip about his girlfriends. He had so many relationships I had trouble keeping up. But, Joey, apparently, never had any trouble keeping it up. "I'm always up," he'd kid me, his eyes falling to his crotch.

"All boys your age are up."

"Not as up as me," he would chuckle and then be off to meet one of the lucky young ladies who, I was sure, were feeling first-hand how up he really was.

Now I was saying, "What's up?"

This got Joey chuckling. As he ambled up onto the porch he said, "Not much these days, Teach."

"Oh?"

He dropped down in the chair across from me and spread his legs invitingly in front of him. I couldn't help it–I just kept staring at the humongous bulge at his crotch. "Looks like you're up right now."

His eyes fell to his crotch and then back up at me. "That's the problem. I'm up all the time but I can't get anything."

"You? You can't get anything?" Dirty blonde hair, baby blue eyes, the face of an angel. He couldn't get anything?

"That was all a lie, Teach. I let everybody think that. People will believe anything if you tell them enough times, you know?"

"A lie? You aren't always up?"

"No," he chuckled, "I'm always up all right. The part about putting it in 'em. I've never put it in any of 'em. None!"

"I'm relieved to hear that."

"What?" he asked, leaning toward me.

"Oh, the diseases you could get from those pussies–you could die from 'em."

"But what a way to go, eh? Fuckin' die of fuckin'!"

"Why are you telling me this now? Did you decide you needed to confess to someone?"

"Yeah, I guess. I'd go see a priest but I'm not Catholic."

"Well, you've come to the right place. You can confess anything you want to me, you know that. In fact, I might be able to help you out of your predicament."

The word "predicament" (and the way I said it, emphasizing just the right syllable) got Joey laughing again. "Yeah, did all right."

"See, you can laugh about it. If we laugh at our troubles, they tend to disappear."

"Sometimes I wish this would disappear," he said, slamming his fist down on his crotch.

"You're just highly sexed, with no way to vent it. You aren't really attracted to those girls and all the boys you know who are gay are dreadful sissies."

"How did you know?"

"I'm not 'Teach' for nothing."

It was decided. We would do something about Joey's predicament. I asked him to stand up and unzip his pants. "Out here?"

"It's after midnight. Everybody's asleep and besides, that's why I have all those trees in the yard."

He needed no more encouragement. Down went the zipper, out came the cock. It was hard all right, jutting up at a rakish angle and sort of waving to the left.

"The girls don't know what they're missing," I said, sitting up straight. "Now, bring it over here and let me examine it more closely."

He smiled and stepped before me, the stupendous thing in my face. I examined it as closely as I could in the dark and dabbed the pre-cum with the tip of my finger. "You are up in more ways than one."

"Yeah, I've been up but what about you?"

"Me?"

"Yeah, you. I've known it from the first day of class."

"Known what?"

"That you liked me a little too much."

"I don't think anyone could like you too much. I mean, there's so much to like." With that I finally took the throbbing penis in my hand and began stroking it. "So very much."

"Do you like it?"

"I love it."

"Why don't you kiss it then?"

"I'm afraid if I got started I wouldn't want to stop."

"C'mon, kiss it."

I was right. I didn't want to stop with a kiss. Although I did try. I kissed it all over, trying to prolong it, make up my mind. I kissed the ball sac, almost every sweaty inch of it, before going back to the gleaming phallus again. I pulled back and it bobbed before my eyes, tantalizing me.

"What's wrong?"

"I just want to look at it. It is a very nice cock, Joey."

"Don't stop kissing it. That felt so good."

When someone pays me a compliment, I feel I must pay them one. "It's easy to be good when you have something good to work with."

"You really do like it?"

It was a foolish question that deserved no answer except the one I gave him: totally engulfing the cock in my mouth with one giant gulp. This shocked him and he put his hands on the top of my head, steadying me as I began to suck. I realized this was the first time he had ever touched me. His hands felt warm, firm. After making a few preliminary passes back and forth on the rigid shaft, I could feel he was in the mood to control things. He started thrusting his hips and as he held my head I let him fuck my mouth with it. The orgasm came upon him quite suddenly and at first he was going to withdraw the cock but I held his buttocks. I wanted it all.

It was a scene that was destined to be repeated many nights that summer, before Joey went away to college. And on his return visits home, he would make my porch one of his first stops ... but always–and only–at night.

This story, originally published in our anthology *Insatiable/Unforgettable*, introduced Joey. The tale that follows is narrated by Joey and shows us another side of him.

# Night Visitors

## *John Patrick*

At Louis's I drank a gin and tonic and felt at home, soaking myself once again in the air of worldly well-being that emanated from his beautiful home. Unobtrusive warmth, an extensive wine cellar, well-deployed lights, hundreds of videos, porn and otherwise, books on all the bookshelves, and pretty duck-egg blue towels with his monogram in the bathrooms. At one point, I could have moved right in. Now I was in my first year at Ohio State and home for the holidays. I stopped in one night to say hello.

Anyway, after an idle hour or so, in which we talked about the past, I began to feel the pangs of nostalgia and desire. I grew hard as Louis recalled the first time he sucked my cock, when I was very young and very precocious, eager for any attention I could get.

Louis saw I was getting turned on and moved from his armchair to a spot next to me on the over-stuffed couch. As usual, his hand covered the bulge in my jeans. "I see you're still a horny little devil."

"Always horny, and no pussy. It's awful."

"No pussy at Ohio State?"

"Oh, lots. But I've been hitting the books–hard."

"Hard it is, Joey. Very hard."

It wasn't long before my jeans had been removed and Louis was on the floor, between my thighs, sucking. He was the best cocksucker in Unionville, outside of my math teacher. The "Teach," as I called him, was the best, but I think I made him nervous–too close to home. Louis, on the other hand, was never nervous. He had family money and his own investments and didn't seem to care what people thought. I was walking home from school one day when he kept driving past me. I knew what he wanted.

And now he wanted the same thing, and I was happy to give it to him. My orgasm was awesome.

"Oh God," he kept moaning between swallows. He always told me nobody had a load as heavy as mine. I was beginning to wonder just how true that was.

Wiping some cum from his chin, he decided we needed something to eat.

"Why don't we eat out?" I suggested.

"People will stare."

"Well, let them."

"I don't like being stared at. I would like to be ignored."

"I don't mind being stared at."

"I know. You're young and pretty."

"Well, what's wrong with that?"

"Nothing, if you're young and pretty," he said, standing up.

I obediently followed him into his lovely French country kitchen. Louis seemed to be pleased to have me in for dinner; he felt like cooking, so we had "something quick," spaghetti. I stood aghast as he tipped wine and garlic recklessly into the sauce, and splashed tomato puree on his oversized Polo sweat-shirt. I chuckled thinking how life would be if I didn't have to worry about dry cleaner's bills and grocery bills.

"I just love the smells and the mixtures," he cooed as he started to strain the spaghetti through an enormous stainless sieve. I remembered my mother's old red plastic colander, and how delighted she would be to have one like this. I decided it would be the perfect Christmas gift.

We sat in the spacious dining room, and Louis opened a bottle of rare red wine from his wine cellar. The spaghetti was most delicious, and when we had finished it we took the dishes into the kitchen. I started to clean them and Louis said, "Stop that. We're going out."

"Out?"

"Yes, it's Thursday and Marty dances on Thursdays."

"Marty?"

"Oh, you just have to see him," Louis said, looking at his watch. "Come on, I can't spend a whole evening in. Especially if you're here." He put his arm around my waist.

"I really should be getting home."

"Hey, you're a college boy now. No curfews for you."

"I dunno."

"Come on, I want to show you off. Anyway, you are my chance with Marty."

In the car, it seemed Louis was exhilarated, as though we were setting out on a great gay adventure, which perhaps we were. I wondered, as I watched him sideways steering his big black Sedan deVille with his inimitable, ostentatious grace, whether the night would end as he told me his nights with his young lover Bob had: Louis watching, sometimes even photographing, the boy he called "the new boy" with the "old boy," namely young Bob. On rare occasions, Louis said he had involved himself with the boys, but mostly, he watched.

Louis described Marty as a real stunner. "You know, I suppose it is odd, compared with the old days." He paused, smiling at his own reflection in the glass as a car passed us. "I used to like everything I saw, just about, because I couldn't have it ... and now I scarcely like anything that I see."

I'd never set foot in a gay bar but I had heard about them, that they were life in excess–dirty, exaggerated life–and I felt a strange elation as we parked the car under a streetlight near the entrance to Jack's Club.

We walked down a dark, mirrored hallway with doors on both sides. At the end was a high-ceilinged, shadowed room like a cave. A few older men murmured and elbowed each other there, jostling for a view. When a few caught sight of us, they snickered.

Louis waved to a few guys but was busy guiding me to a table near a little carpeted stage at the far end of the bar. He pointed Marty out to me. The dancer was tall, muscular, not much older than me. Marty was between sets and was chatting up the customers dressed only in a G-string. He acknowledged Louis (no one forgets a big tipper) and soon he was coming over to join us. I saw that everything Marty did seemed to make a noise: all his actions were larger and more physical than other guy's. I wondered if that was because he was a dancer, or whether he was a dancer because of that.

Louis introduced me as "an old friend" and sent Marty for drinks.

"God, look at that ass," said Louis as Marty stood at the bar.

"He's hot," I said, but he had what I considered a false bravado that turned me off.

"He is, isn't he?" he said. "You wouldn't mind if we invited the big stud home?"

"Hell, no," I said, perhaps a bit too quickly.

The music changed and we were ostensibly watching another dancer, but both of us had eyes only for Marty. He stood between us, an arm around each of our shoulders. Eventually he saw where my eyes had settled (on his abundant crotch) and he pulled me close. Presently he exposed himself to me.

I found myself almost liking Marty, so touched had I been by his justified pride in his endowment. I shall never forget the way it lay there with its huge head peeking out from the minimal foreskin. I reached down and squeezed the shaft. "Later," Marty said with a wink, pushing my hand away.

Suddenly, he had both hands on my shoulders, giving me a mini-back rub. I remembered how warm and comforting it was when Louis used to put his arm around me on a cold night. I felt acutely lonely: no one had touched me in months; and now this boy was making a play for me, thanks to Louis's generosity. I grew hard, thrilled by the sensation of the darkness and glamour of the night, and the strangeness of being with Louis and this young stud. Nothing so strange is ever really unbearable. Marty danced off to get ready for his set.

"Well?" Louis asked.

"Well what?"

"You want him?"

"I dunno," I said, sipping my beer.

"Your problem is," Louis said, "that you only like the idea of it. You just like the idea of Marty's cock."

I assured him I did not simply like the idea of it; I liked the reality of it enormously, it was just I had never had much chance to show just how much I liked it.

This got him laughing. "Yeah, I wasn't the one who was peeking. I was too embarrassed."

As the minutes passed I was amazed by the easy familiarity with which everyone treated Louis. He was evidently a well-established fact. I gathered he had been coming here for some time. Tall, dark and sexy, Marty looked very predatory. I enjoyed gazing with admiration at the dangerous curves of his body as he did what passed for a strip: just taking off his jeans to reveal a different G-string.

"What would you like to do with that?" Louis asked.

"Oh, I dunno," I said, but I was casting my mind over them–things like sucking that dick, nibbling on those nipples, applying my tongue to his asshole, discovering the power of his load.

Louis grew strangely silent at this point, no doubt thinking back. A great wave of nostalgia came over me as well, nostalgia for the nights I spent with Louis in his splendid bedroom, or in his car, or in every room of his house. Louis never asked me to touch his cock; he always jacked off while he sucked me, but I knew he had a nice one and I would have done almost anything he asked, but he never did.

As Marty danced, Louis looked at me, his breath quick, intoxicated, his bald head shiny with sweat.

The blonde dancer joined Marty for a few months. Slowly the blonde caressed him with his tongue while we watched, and when I looked again at Louis I could see he was smiling. "How do you like that?" he whispered, and I heard muffled shouts from the front of the bar.

In sex there are new rules, sometimes no rules; the body takes charge, and my own hunger seemed to explode. In front of me was all this simulated sex in slow motion, and a warm hand was slipping into my crotch to stroke my hard-on in the dim, coppery light. Then the blonde rose up from Marty and left the stud to finish, flash the men at the bar, and then approach them. I admired his confidence. The sexual fantasy being a prostitute, not just going to one, had always tantalized me. I had never asked any of the men who had sucked me off for any money. Some just gave me money; some bought me things.

I got up to go to the bathroom. There, a tall, distinguished looking man approached me. He offered me a hundred dollars. And I was flattered, in an odd way. Could I, really, take money as Marty did? I could pay Marty for sex, that I knew. Yet I felt embarrassed about my body, anxiety about my performance, fear of rejection. And it bothered me that for Marty it would be just work.

As I approached the table, Marty was getting unnervingly amorous with Louis. I was relieved when Louis suggested we leave.

At Louis's house, Marty went to the bathroom; Louis fixed brandies. I walked over to the bar in the far corner of his living room.

I began examining the gold ornaments on the Christmas tree that stood tall next to the bar, and said, "I think I should go."

"What?"

"Well, I don't know if I'm up to this tonight."

"Up? But you're always up. You know what?" He looked closely at my face. "I wanna give you a Christmas present for letting me suck your cock again. This is it."

"All the same, I like to create a good impression."

"You do create a good impression," said Louis, warmly, and patted my head.

"I've had a long day–"

"And it's not over yet. Here he comes."

Marty came into the room. Rather it seemed he barged into the room. He went over to the sofa and plopped down on it.

"Make yourself at home," Louis laughed.

"Looks as if he has." I sat beside Marty on the sofa.

"Mind if I light up?" Marty asked to no one in particular, pulling a joint out of his shirt pocket.

Louis disdained drugs and he looked at Marty carefully. Still, he said nothing, simply took his place in the armchair across from us and sipped his brandy.

The two brandies Louis had carefully placed on the coffee table in front us sat unattended while I took a toke and began to feel quite elated, thinking what Louis would do while I discovered all about Marty.

Marty helped himself to the brandy, gulping it.

I took another toke and handed the joint back to Marty. Louis smiled nostalgically through the smoke. "Do you remember Bob?" he asked.

"Oh, yes." I remembered the photos he had showed me. I would have done something with Bob.

"How that one loved pot. I finally had to let him go."

"It was a shame."

"Pot don't hurt nothin'," Marty said, taking a last drag on the joint.

"Obviously it hasn't hurt you."

Marty nodded and placed a hand on my knee. I put my hand over his and squeezed it. He finished his brandy and turned his full attention to me.

I settled myself more comfortably, but I began trembling. I wanted Marty so much. I had never wanted anyone as much. Marty put his arm around me and said, "Now, where were we?"

"What?"

"We were gettin' along pretty good in the car, as I recall."

It was true. We sat together in the back seat and my nervous hands explored his body intimately. "Louis's back seat has been the start of a lot of things."

"You two dudes carry on like this all the time? I've never seen you in Jack's before."

"No, it was my first time. But, no, I've been Louis's private stock–till now. We have lots of great memories, don't we Louis?"

Louis stood over us, fully in command of the situation, like a director on a movie shoot. "You can't live without memories, and Joey's given me some great ones." He patted my head. "Joey of the Beautiful Cock," Louis went on. "You never forget that cock after you've seen it."

Marty snickered again, nervously. Perhaps he wondered whether his own cock might possibly someday be called memorable, too; that we would be here discussing him on some other Christmas. I moved into his embrace, and Marty panted, "Okay, you gonna let me see that beautiful cock?"

"If you'll let me see yours–again."

"Okay," he said, grinning.

As I fumbled with the buttons of Marty's 50ls, he leaned back and closed his eyes. Louis came round behind the sofa and perched on the back of it, watching intently as I peeled back the fabric to reveal the huge, nearly hard dick. It was a beautiful cock. Darker, longer and much thicker than mine. The foreskin disappeared along the shaft and he thrust it towards my mouth. I was still trembling. I didn't know if I wanted to do this or not, but Louis, the director, made up my mind for me: he clamped his hand on the back of my head and shoved. Marty's erection bounced off my cheek and slammed into my eye. I reached up and held the shaft. I began by kissing it, finally working my way to the head. Marty took my head in his hands and guided me.

"You ain't trained this one, Louis?"

"No, he's strictly trade."

"Till tonight, man. Till tonight."

Louis kept shoving me and my face got buried in the stud's crotch. My mouth was forced onto the head of the dick.

They held me and Louis said, "Fuck his face, Marty. I want this one to know what it means to get his face fucked."

At that, Marty let go with all the pent-up frustration accumulated on the drive home. Just when I thought my aching jaw couldn't take any more, Marty's dick was jerked from my mouth.

"Now, get outta those jeans!" came Marty's command.

I stood and as I unbuttoned my jeans, my nose started to itch. And then tickle. And with a growing sense of dread, I realized there was a sneeze knocking on my head begging to come out. I couldn't help it: I sneezed. My cock went limp. Marty came around in front of me, a wicked little smile lifting the corners of his mouth, a glint in his narrow hazel eyes.

I stared helplessly up at him, and his smile broadened. He took my cock in his hand and, squeezing it just a little too hard so the sensation shot through me, snickered. "You allergic to me?"

"No, no," I stammered.

"I won't hurt you," he continued. "But if I do, you'll love it anyhow."

He tipped his head to one side, considering me. "How long do you think you could stand it?" He had the same maddening little smile. "Kiss me, little one," he said.

I turned my head to him, his mouth closing over mine, and I tried to put wordlessly into the kiss that I was desperate–desperate–grateful to be here, to be taken by him wherever he wanted me to go. There was a peculiar intimacy to the moment, to the kiss that went on and on, his tongue rolling into me, over me, familiar with every surface of my inner mouth. He kissed me as if he had me on a hook, as if he were reeling me in, as if he could draw me right out of myself and into him.

I let my head go back, let my eyes close, let the heat of the kiss take me over. And in my surrender to the stud, the heat rolled slowly through me. My erection grew in his hand.

He let go of me and laughed. "My poor hungry baby," he said, brushing the side of my face with his open hand.

Louis handed me my brandy and then led us into the bedroom. I set the brandy on the nightstand and lay naked on the bed and started trembling again when Marty climbed over me. He sensed my hesitation and growled across at me, shaking his cock. Louis joined us and soon I was straining against his hands holding me down.

Marty jammed two fingers into my ass. I hissed and thrust my hips up so hard I felt his knuckles. I guess he took that upward thrust was his signal and he gently eased his fingers deeper inside me, twisting, then fucking. Louis leaned forward, urging him onward, while he pumped my now fully hard cock.

"Oh, god, oh Jesus," I cried. My body convulsed, my ass muscles grabbing at his fingers. My orgasm brought out a sweet gush of cum, and Marty quickly pulled free. He eagerly put his own hand out to catch some and brought it up his mouth to taste. Then Marty rubbed the cum all over my body, into my chest and stomach, massaging it into my legs and feet. God knows there was enough.

I was out of it, leaning back, my body covered in cum and sweat, my breath coming in lusty gasps. Louis went back to working my cock and I bucked and writhed in continued reflex, working out all my pent-up desire.

Marty leaned back, grabbed the brandy snifter that he had left on the floor and poured some of it into his hand and splashed it on my face. The next move was to splash some on my cock. "That oughta cool you off, sweet boy."

"Oh, Marty, that was so hot ..." Louis's voice was hoarse, his face flushed.

Marty's eyes bored into me for a moment, taking in my quickly rejuvenated prick, lingering on my exhausted face. Slowly and with great drama, he spread my legs wide. "No one's ever gotten a piece of that hot ass, right?"

I nodded. I thought it was over, but I should have known better. Louis held me down and I began whimpering when I felt Marty's fingers again.

I lay back, panting heavily, and raised my head in time to see his thick black head of hair lower toward my cock that now stood straight up. He kept fucking me with his fingers while he brushed his stubbly cheek up the shaft of my prick. He forced my rock-hard cock down with one hand so that it snapped back up, slapping my stomach. It was again so hard it hurt.

Suddenly, Marty rolled me over on my stomach. Louis lifted me up so that my little round ass was pressed up against Marty's huge erection. He pushed it against the outer part of my asshole, rubbing and probing. Then, without warning, he eased the head into me. I bit my lip. As he continued to press it into me, it felt so good I thought I would explode again. I reached between my legs to grab my own cock, jacking off. He kept still a few seconds, getting my tight hole used to the invasion. My eyes were watering, tearing up from the pain, my teeth grinding. I pushed my ass further toward him and soon he gave a last push of his hips. Working his way out until just the tip was barely in my ass, the stud shoved himself all the way in again and began fucking me with incredible stamina.

Louis stood next to the bed, jacking off, his eyes feasting on the sight of my ass being invaded.

"Oh, I'm gonna shoot," Marty cried suddenly.

"No, I want to see it. Please!"

This made Marty stop and Louis flipped me over just in time.

Marty stroked his cock and his cream was luscious, shooting like mad. I thought it would never end. I scrambled over to him and went back to sucking on it. Soon I felt Louis's fingers on my ass. My ass was sore and yet starving for more. It wasn't long before Louis mounted me and I felt that thick cock pulse and burst as he buried himself all the way up me and shot his load. Marty's cock slipped from my mouth as the sensations jolted me.

Marty grabbed my hair, forcing my mouth back down to his cock. "You ain't done here, yet." His hands stayed in my hair, forcing me down harder to deep-throat his incomparable cock. Each time his dick bashed the back of my throat, his grip in my hair tightened even more.

Louis went to the bathroom and Marty pulled away. He climbed on the bed and I groaned as he parted the cheeks of my ass and just slammed his cock into me. He fucked me for a few moments and then decided he wanted it another way. He maneuvered my body so that I was on top.

My own cock was hard again now. He grabbed my hips and drew me closer. I spread my legs until they wrapped around him and I was straddling his cock.

He snickered. "Oh, yeah, you like it so much."

"Yes, yes," I murmured, then kissed him.

His hands stayed on my hips, forcing me down. I reached between my legs to grab his dick and hold it steady. Slowly, I lowered myself onto the swollen purple head and was quickly reminded by the dull pain of how much bigger Marty was than Louis. As I began to take the shaft into me, he thrust instead, tightening his grip on my hips and pulling them down at the same time. I took all of it at once. He began raising and lowering my body, making me ride his cock. I wrapped my arms around his neck, bobbing in his lap, my eyes tearing. I flung my head back, moaning, "Oh, Marty!" I flung myself down onto it harder and harder, bouncing off his lap. He grabbed my cock, now hard and ready, squeezing it. It didn't take long; I shot another load that hit him in the face.

Snickering again, he pulled me off his throbbing prick, then forced my face down so that he came all over my cheek, my hair, in my eyes and on my mouth and neck. It was everywhere; I had to admit his load was at least the equal of mine. He squeezed the last of it out, wiping it into my hair.

Louis was back, handing us moist towels. I wiped myself off a bit but didn't really want to clean it all away. Marty bounced off the bed and bounded into the bathroom. Louis joined me in bed and held me as we listened to the water running in the shower.

"Well?" Louis asked, dabbing the cum from my hair.

"Well what?" I grinned.

"Was that a Christmas present or what?"

"How much did it cost you?"

"Oh, it was a bargain. He wanted you even more than you wanted him."

"Oh, I doubt that," I said, snuggling into the comforting crook of Louis's arm and promptly falling into a deep, satisfied slumber.

# Wait Till Dark

## *Ken Anderson*

*"Only connect."*
*– E. M. Forster*

Ray opened a drawer, shut it, opened another to collect the utensils. He'd been living with his aunt only two days and hadn't learned exactly where things were. Pru picked up the lid to one of the pots on the stove, and swirls of steam uncurled from the beans, filling the room with their bland, starchy smell. It was Sunday, June 21, his twenty-first birthday, and she had baked a surprise–a German chocolate cake. She also had bought him a black umbrella.

"We'll do better next year," she promised, her eyes a watery brown. "But you didn't have an umbrella, and I know you'll need it, going to school and all."

Ray could see the family resemblance, but it was like seeing his mother's features in a pudgier, more anxious face. Her hair was bluish grey and curled into such mousy little knots that she looked as if she were trying to pin up her thoughts. Everything about her eyes, including the bags, was beginning to sag sadly, and she had penciled her eyebrows at such an odd slant that she managed, he thought, only to emphasize her age. To Ray, she looked like an old clown.

Ray's parents had divorced too early for him to remember his father, who moved to Atlanta, but Mr. Barton, who owned the grocery in Xenobia, had stepped in, by chance, as a sort of makeshift dad. Since twelve, Ray worked in the store and, since fifteen, drove the delivery truck. When Ray was seventeen, Mr. Barton–or Nunks as Ray called him–let him take the truck home after work and use it as his own. When it was time for Ray to go to college, Nunks let him use it even to commute in the evenings to a small yet costly Episcopal school about thirty miles to the south. There, though he was good in English, Ray had become a business major, but since his father was a lawyer, had fantasized about eventually becoming one. He was tired of both working and going to school, of course, but held out hope that one day, with a decent degree and a lucrative job, he'd find some time to enjoy himself like other people.

After his mother's death, Ray decided to move in with his aunt, his only living relative, in Hobbes, a quaint college town nestled in the rolling foothills–or ankle bones, as locals liked to joke–of the Smokies. The town was also known for what bordered it to the north–the Harz House, a large estate in the style of an early Renaissance chateau. In fact, the main gate to the property was only a few blocks from his aunt's little picket one. On one of their visits to Hobbes, his mother had pointed out a subtle dip in the

countryside, and since he remembered where to look, Ray caught a faint glimpse of the place from the train the other day.

Pru was a retired teacher who had taught social science in high school and later part time at the college, but who now occupied herself with church work and the garden club, really a social group. When she retired, she gave up her car, but the campus was within walking distance, and Ray could also catch a bus at the corner. Most of his credits had been accepted, and living with his aunt, he would have just enough money to finish. He had about a year and a half to go.

Standing at the stove, Pru stirred the beans, then asked, "What did your mother do with that cradle with those storks and babies on it?"

Cherubic babies and bespectacled storks danced among the fluffy, pillow-like clouds in Ray's thoughts, a vague vision that tried to focus, then blurred.

"I don't have the slightest, Aunt Pru."

Ray reached napkins from the pantry, then glasses from a cabinet and filled them with ice. They were plastic, ringed with bright pastels, and he wondered what his aunt, as reserved as she was, was doing with something so summery and festive.

"I wish you'd saved the Christmas-tree stand and that box of ornaments, especially that precious, little nativity scene."

The kitchen was a small, square, ordinary room perfectly in line, Ray thought, with his image of his aunt, that is, old and depressing. To him, the dingy walls somehow reflected the work that had gone into thousands of solitary meals. The color itself was enough to dampen his spirit, a gloomy hospital-green. The chairs were comfortable, everything was within reach, and the refrigerator hummed contentedly, yet a ripe, stuffy smell hung in the air despite Pru's fastidiousness. Out the back door were modest vegetable and herb gardens, and through the window over the sink he could see, silhouetted against a rosy evening, the ancient pecan tree at the back of the yard.

Absently, Pru stared out the window, then coming to, turned off the burner.

"Christmas with you and your mother was always so much fun," she stressed. "I looked forward to it all year."

When he had arrived Friday afternoon, one of the first artifacts she showed him was a photograph album. She pored over several pictures of the family and friends on outings and special occasions, pictures of his grandparents, her brother (his uncle), and her husband (his other uncle), all dead. The brother had never married, and Pru and her husband, he knew, couldn't have children, but she lingered over one photograph much longer than the others, a tilted, yellowing snapshot of a Christmas gathering when Ray, she claimed, was only two.

"The last Christmas with all of you together," she sighed, staring at it enviously.

Ray's father was the tall, dark stranger in the photo, a moody, athletic-looking man with lush, handsome eyes. Ray's coloring was of a lighter hue, however, and he figured he favored his mother, who, according to Pru, was known, when young, for her wholesome looks.

At a glance, Ray did look like the nice guy, the all-American boy. He had a sweet, emotionally honest face, and there was an innocent, unguarded air about him that at times had made his mother and Pru, even Mr. Barton, quietly ponder the sad, yet inevitable fallibility of life. His eyes were direct, excited–hazel eyes flecked with green around the deep pupil. Only when his illusory father was mentioned did he sometimes, smiling, stare ahead stoically. Yet the father's departure was an unintended slight, he knew – a chance cut healed, he believed, through time.

"Think I'll take a walk after supper," he said, setting the glasses on the table. "I need the exercise."

He hadn't played sports in college, only in high school, and the most exercise he got was an occasional jog, but his body was naturally lean and sinewy, well defined.

"Maybe over to the Harz House–get a load of it up close."

"Well, wish you wouldn't."

"Why not?"

"The land's posted."

"I'm sure they don't patrol the place, Aunt Pru."

"Might."

Silence. Pru began spooning up the rice and white beans.

"Some German count or the other owns it," she began. "Oh, he doesn't call himself that–this is America–but he has a title. Family made its fortune in railroads and such. His father turned the place into a vineyard. French grapes on local stock. A winter residence, they call it. He's here now, though. Here a lot lately."

"A real count, huh?" Ray grunted. "Don't think a little walk in the woods would hurt."

His hazel eyes narrowed to a puzzled squint, and the more Pru talked, the more he was stirred to know.

"Well, it's something I don't like to talk about," she began again, doddering. "A boy, a college student, disappeared up there a couple of years ago."

"In the woods?"

Ray reached a pitcher of iced tea and a saucer of lemon wedges from the refrigerator. Pru set the bowls on the table, then brought the butter dish.

"Yes and no," she hesitated. "Last seen–round here, anyway–going through the gate. Course, he worked up there, helping restore a room or something."

The mention of restoring a room reminded Ray of his own, the guest room at the back of Pru's house, a prim retreat where he, as a child, had slept during visits. One of his conditions of the move was that he could redo the

place as his own. He, of course, didn't have the money to buy less fussy furniture, but at least he could remove a few things, and removing a few things was about all he'd accomplished in a couple of days.

The first items to be retired were the sallow doilies on everything–on the chest of drawers, the dresser, even the desk she'd had moved in for him. The small stuffed toy went, too, a soft, pink kitten propped on the bed. Pru had plain, white pillowcases he could use, instead of the embroidered ones, and, when she had grasped the drift of his taste, informed him that the skirt on the dresser was simply tacked on and could easily be peeled off. The skirt with its prissy ribbons looked like a demure petticoat.

A lot more time–in fact, most of Saturday–had gone into his final attempts at paring down the room. He took down the Victorian window treatments, leaving just the Venetian blinds, and, since the room was stuffy, stuck an old, ratty fan in a window. Instead of the picture of "The Hen and Her Chicks," he hung a big, blue Scout flag over his bed, and he took considerable care laying out just so his own spare items: his desk articles, a bottle of cologne, three jade figurines of a rabbit, fox, and duck. There wasn't much he could do about the flowery wallpaper, rows upon rows of faded pink azaleas. He'd just have to live with them. His bed looked like an arbor in a garden, he thought, a flesh-pink garden wilting into the walls.

He wasn't sure what to think of one odd item, though, a heavy, old-fashioned alarm clock sitting on a shelf of the headboard. The clock had a bell on top with clappers, and when he'd first noticed it, he immediately made sure the alarm was off. At least for a day or two, he wouldn't need it, and when he did, he'd set it somewhere across the room or under the bed.

The views, however, made the room worthwhile. To either side of the bed, a couple of windows faced the oleander and hydrangea between Pru's house and the next. But the better view was from the casement window near the northeast corner of the room. It opened onto the back yard and the old pecan tree and, beyond that, the delicate tablecloth of a field of Queen-Anne's lace. In the distance, somewhere among the hills, he knew, stood the manor.

"Maybe I could restore a room or something," Ray mused, his voice soft and melodious. "Gotta find a job."

"Hm?"

"Up at Harz," he explained. "What do you think happened?"

"To the boy?"

Pru slowly untied the loaf of Sunbeam bread on the counter, took out three slices, and arranged them on a plate.

"Strange things go on up there," she announced melodramatically.

"Such as?"

He smiled a quick, lovable smile, a smile full of sparkle.

"Pawties," she said in a word. "The man has peculiar friends."

Like Ray's mother, Pru had a way of speaking through her teeth in what was considered a refined, if curious, Southern accent, but when she said pawties, he burst out with a loud, genuine laugh that seized him completely.

"Come on, Aunt Pru. Don't be so droll. You're breaking me up."

"Well, I hear they're wild," she insisted, setting the bread on the table. "That's all."

He pulled up his chair, scraping the floor.

"You make 'em sound like a flock of vampires."

"Could be for all I know. 'A little boat should keep near shore,'" she added, quoting Franklin.

He'd taken all of his English courses, and the maxim recalled a stanza from Burns he'd had to memorize.

O life! how pleasant, in thy morning,
Young Fancy's rays the hills adorning!
Cold-pausing Caution's lesson scorning,
We frisk away,
Like schoolboys, at th' expected warning,
To joy and play.

"Chip, I think, was his name," Pru said, interrupting his thoughts. "Had some peculiar name like–Chip."

Ray smiled to himself at her use of the word peculiar.

"No, Boyd. No, Beau. Beau Doughty."

"Sit down, Aunt Pru."

"About your age. Even looked like you. You know, sort of slim," she said, taking a seat. "A towhead. But as far as behavior went, not like you at all. Can't imagine you playing a prank on anyone."

Some odd idea had hatched in Ray's head, but it was as if his mind were refusing to share it with him. The names Chip, Boyd, Beau had chipped away at some psychic shell, pecked at it from the inside until it had cracked and split open. But what was born? All he knew was that she didn't want him to stray onto the estate. Therefore, he would.

But he was amazed by his new rebelliousness, his desire to deceive her.

"What's the count's name?" he smirked.

"Bidencourt," she answered. "Delbert Bidencourt."

"Delbert!"

"Doesn't look like a Delbert," she remarked. "More like a Wolfgang or Conrad or Klaus."

Ray took it she meant her idea of German and pictured a plump geezer of military bearing.

"You've seen 'im," he concluded.

"Yes," she faltered. "In town. In the paper."

She looked worried.

"What were you going to say?" he asked.

"Oh, I don't know," she claimed. "You know how my mind wanders."

She bit one of her nails.

"Why Harz House?" he asked.

"The name? I don't know. Never thought about it. Why's anything called what it is? Why Ray? Why Pru?"

"Because you're so prudent," he quipped.

Ray gulped some beans.

"You must be hungry," Pru said. "I'll fix my chicken paprika next Sunday."

Ray waited till dark, then headed out.

"Going out like that?" Pru asked, meaning his outfit.

It was a sultry night with thunderstorms flashing on the horizon, and he was wearing only a pair of loose, pleated shorts, a soft, grey T-shirt, and a pair of scruffy tennis shoes. Yet even at his most casual, he still managed to look fresh and dapper.

"Think I'll stroll into town."

"Storm's coming up," she reminded him.

"I can hear thunder probably better than you, Aunt Pru," he remarked with a good-natured smile. "I'll be OK." Then brandishing it like a sword, he said, "I have a very big umbrella."

At the gate, he looked toward the lights of town, then in the other direction, toward the estate. He thought of how hard Pru must've worked over the years and of how good she always was to him. Still, he couldn't see how taking a walk could matter to her or anyone else for that matter.

He noticed a grey moth caught in a web between an azalea bush and the white picket fence. With the utmost care, he grasped a wing, freeing it, then watched it flutter toward the watchful eye of the ice-blue streetlight.

He ambled along the sidewalk, wielding the umbrella, clicking it against the pavement offbeat with his steps. The humidity was palpable, an invisible pool of lukewarm air. It reminded him of the whirlpool bath in high school when he'd sprained his ankle. The moist, sticky feeling also reminded him of the prime, yet agreeably weary way he'd feel after jogging. He was glad that he was wearing shorts, that he was finally out of the house.

Over the houses and blue-green trees came the dreamy staccato of a dog barking, the calls of children playing, strains of Tchaikovsky floating out a window from a radio. He noted the various political placards in the yards, ads with unfamiliar names like Burgess, Norman, Doakes, and for a second, as he rounded a corner, he thought he heard church music, but checking his watch, decided not. The houses were humble enough, like Pru's, he remarked, plain, yet cozy-looking. Even the ones with lights out looked like large, comfortable nests, mushroom-white in the dark.

And yet a vague, free-floating anxiety tinged the scene, like the dim haze in the air, as if somehow he'd been permanently cut off from everyone, from the various prosaic lives going on around him, as if, unseen in the dark,

glancing through the screened doors and curtained windows, he were somehow spying on people, like a Peeping Tom. In short, he felt like an outsider, and he guessed he was, pensively tapping the umbrella on the cracked concrete. The last time he and his mother had visited Pru, he was only–what? He couldn't remember. Pru had always visited them at Christmas.

Another reason he felt so detached, of course, was the loss of his mother, his one real link with the world. He hadn't expected her to die nor how he'd respond to losing her. Though he tried not to show it, he'd become emotionally unmoored, drifting about at the mercy of his urges and whims. In time, he hoped, he'd feel more at home with Pru.

He turned onto the drive to the estate, strolled around a turn-around with a circular flower bed in the middle–gardenias, azaleas, canna lilies–then approached the entrance, an imposing affair of stone lions and iron filigree. The gate was open. To the right stood a large, brick gatehouse with a tile roof.

He paused, then, seeing no lights, walked right up to a window and peered in, but the window was opaque, a polished jet-black. He felt as if he were peering into a tomb. What he didn't know was that a friendly old guard was standing directly on the other side of the window, staring back, and that, as Ray turned to leave, the guard picked up the phone.

Ray looked straight up, over the eaves of the gatehouse. A crescent moon, like lips, was smiling down on him. He glanced toward the northwest. Sheet lightning, like a giant short circuit, blinked quietly. He wandered to the middle of the road, to a spot under the wrought-iron arch. He was standing on a square stone with two deep holes for bolts. He stood the umbrella in one of them.

Square one, he thought.

He loitered awhile, gazing up the road to where it disappeared into the woods. Hundreds of fireflies floated like stars on a dark, green sea-water of gleaming rocks and leaves.

To-who, to who? called an owl. To-who, to who?

He didn't really know why he was there, why he was strolling on, poking the asphalt with the umbrella. He felt as if, following the thread of his instincts, he was simply killing time, playing some interesting game. He would see where he led himself. He would see where the road led. At the moment, it was following a ravine with a trickling stream and shiny black pools. The rub was that the woods were smoldering, rife with mosquitoes. Scratching his leg, he changed his mind. He wished he'd worn long pants.

On a crest of the road, a stag appeared, a ten-point buck, silhouetted against the sky. It froze, its head turned in his direction, then, without a sound, stepped into the trees.

When Ray reached the crest, he stopped and gazed into the woods. Patches of moonlight, blotches of shadows glided across the broken, jade-

green floor, quietly plating a branch here, obscuring a log there, shifting as the moon shifted, like a burglar, in and out of the clouds.

For a moment, the clouds parted, and Ray squinted at his watch: a few minutes after eleven. Later than he'd thought. But just as he set off again, he heard a car approaching from somewhere down to his right. The trees ahead of it lit up as it looped, ascending, but he could not see the car itself, as if only its headlights were visible.

He stumbled over a root into a ditch, breathing deeply. He crouched behind a tree to watch the car pass— a long, black Cadillac limousine with, like those at the gatehouse, perfectly opaque windows. Its somber appearance reminded him of the gleaming hearse at his mother's funeral.

It climbed the hill, then took a sharp left, vanishing, like the deer, among the trees. He could hear the receding rasp of the tires, then nothing.

He stood up, suddenly aware of the hush, then turned carefully, peering into the blind, confused depths of the dark. No fireflies. Not a sound. He could make out no more of the maze around him than he had, peering into the jet-black window of the gatehouse or the car. Apparently, the limo had taken the last of the light with it, the last noise.

Slowly, a step at a time, he found the road again, then, at a cautious pace, made his way to the crossroads where the car had turned, a triangular clearing, where, with a little light, he considered his choices. One road led to the north, one to the northwest, and the one the limo had taken, yet higher, toward the southwest. He figured the limo was headed toward the house and struck off in that direction. Yet at times, especially under thick foliage, he became disoriented, straying onto the grass, swinging the umbrella in front of himself like a cane.

"Wish I'd brought a flashlight," he muttered, wary of snakes.

A breeze swept past, a warm, pine-scented wave of air washing over him. Trees and bushes stirred. A limb snapped. Thunder rolled over the hills. Mist, like spirits, floated across the road. Far off, just audible over the wind, some animal—or was it baby?—was crying.

There was nothing that could really hurt him, he told himself, nothing big with fangs and claws. And he was quick, he knew. Agile, tough, sly. He could handle himself in a tight situation. He always had. He could handle himself in the woods. Besides, he smiled to himself, he had his trusty umbrella.

All he knew was that, uncertain as he was, the walk excited him. He wished he could relax more, though, enjoy himself more, become more in tune with himself, with the night. How great it must be, he thought, to prowl like a fox, to fly like an owl, to snatch what he liked from the dark.

He thought of the time he'd become lost on the scouting trip, the closest to nature he'd felt. At twilight, he found a comfortable perch in a hickory tree and tied himself in with wisteria. When night came, he could see nothing, nothing at all, not even a star, not even the moon, but his dreams smelled of wisteria, and when he woke in the morning, he knew he'd been

someplace deep and dark inside himself as well, a magical place pulsing with locust.

All at once, the clouds broke, and shafts of blue, like searchlights, combed the woods. Clutching the umbrella, he sprang into a jog–the spry, alert trot of a creature of the night, as he thought of it–emerging on the grounds around the mansion. To the left stood a group of greenhouses; in front, a stable; to the right, a wall. On the hill to the right loomed the dark, sepulchral house.

The Roman arch of the stable entrance gaped like a mouth. He steeled himself, then inched along the passage toward the splinters of light in a pair of huge, planked doors. The doors wouldn't give. Then one did, scraping the cobblestones, and he squeezed through, stepping into a muggy courtyard. He imagined the limo and other expensive automobiles gleaming in the dark behind the garage doors. Directly ahead lay an open passage, through which he arrived at a walled garden, a virtual moonlit paradise of roses.

Having come that far, he felt a sense of relief, as if he'd successfully completed some practice run for a longer hike. It was too late to go much farther, he thought. He'd give himself a rest, ride out the rain if he had to, then head back. And the storm, in fact, wasn't far behind, blowing up from the northwest, an immense black curtain rising on rain and wind. A skeletal play of lightning flashed across the sky. Thunder rumbled across the terraced landscape. Hundreds of rose bushes whispered in the wind, then, in a lull, fell silent.

He stood the umbrella against a bench in the passage, then, gazing at the garden, became aware of how wonderfully alone he was. He was enjoying his new sense of freedom. But he also felt, as in town, cut off from everything, from the full, rich life, he imagined, that buzzed in the house. The roses weren't his, he knew, and to pick even one was a crime. His mere presence was a crime. What kind of world was it, he smiled, in which he had to sneak into the garden?

He leaned against the wall, gazing toward the house. With the lights out, it looked abandoned. The wind whipped up, splattering the stones with the first few incredibly heavy raindrops.

Turning his head, he caught a glimpse of something in his peripheral vision, something at first indistinct, like a little, silvery window, then, in a flash of lightning, all too clear–a big, brass buckle. A tall, powerfully built man had materialized from the dark directly across the passage from him, had been leaning against a wall, too, watching him. But for how long?

With a start, Ray took in the boots, the jeans, the bare, sculpted chest, the flash-blue features of half a face. His father's eyes were fixed on him from thick, black brows, and though they weren't his father's eyes–they couldn't be, he knew–the thought, in the seconds that followed, never quite left him.

Thunder clapped, and a hoarse scream tore from Ray's throat, a reflex animal-sound. He turned to run, but the stranger's hands shot out like clamps, pinning him to the wall, where the man held him, staring at him.

Ray bucked against him, trying to kick him, to knee him in the groin, but the man slipped between his thighs so that Ray's struggle against him became a sort of rough, intimate dance. Ray held the iron arms holding his arms, their bodies pressed together at the belt buckle.

Then, in a spate of lightning, he saw the man's face, all at once, for what it was, its look not of anger nor cruelty, but of such irredeemable loss, such brutal longing that when the man released him, he at first hesitated, then, in his confusion, clutched him in a fierce embrace. The man who had frightened him was calming him, automatically folding him into his arms. "Oh, Beau, you're back!" the man whispered, his voice husky, deep, laced with the burnt-wood smell of some strong, rich alcohol. "I've missed you," the man sighed.

Ray's fear gave way to pure, inconsolable grief. He had no idea where it sprang from and, thus, could not control it, giving himself up to great, gulping sobs, grabbing and stroking the man's hair.

Gusts of rain swept the passage, bathing the cobblestones and bricks, the men, their clothes, hair, faces– the man's face streaming with rain, Ray's with rain and tears.

"I'm sorry, I'm sorry," the man murmured, his lips at Ray's ear, his breath like steam.

Ray went limp from exhaustion, almost passing out ... .

When the man had first grabbed him, he ripped Ray's shirt down the left, exposing his chest, the crease of the pectoral, and as Ray slumped backward, dipping his head into the dark, his pec caught fire. The man was mouthing it, and a visceral thrill flared through Ray's body.

From the bottom of the trance, as from a pool, Ray could see a raindrop hit the surface, flashing blue, concentric halos. He floated up. He emerged, clasped to the man's chest, rocked from side to side like a child.

Ray dreamed of a gold-inlaid, jewel-encrusted casket on a plush-lined bier in one of the garages at Harz House. A knight in red armor was prying it open with a crowbar, assisted by a tan blonde in a pair of surfer's shorts and a small, black mask. The boy was gleaming with suntan lotion, and when Ray tried to pull him away from the casket, the boy slipped from his grasp. When Ray tried to stop the knight, the knight stared at him through the visor, then struck him with the back of his gauntlet.

Ray sat up in bed, feeling his face, the flit of wings echoing in his mind. For a moment, he was convinced that his nose was broken, that his mouth was full of a thick, red glue.

"Damn," he blurted, shaking his head to clear it.

He reached the alarm clock and stared at it with incomprehension. The hands, the minutes, the hours meant nothing. He set it down, wondering if

the strange encounter in the stable had been a dream, too. He looked out the window at the rainy morning, at the lush, wet woods. He noticed the pile of damp clothes on the floor and, flinging back the covers, swung from bed. He bathed and shaved, then he slipped into khakis, a blue Lacoste, and penny loafers. Then he ambled to the kitchen.

"You must've stayed out late," Pru frowned, cracking eggs into the frying pan. "It's nearly noon." When he failed to answer, she asked, "Where'd you go?"

He decided for her sake, as well as his own, just to lie.

"Uh, nowhere really," he mumbled, pouring himself a cup of coffee. "Got caught in the rain."

"Going over to the college?"

Though he couldn't actually hear it in her tone, he felt that something subtly accusatory had prompted the question. If he didn't register immediately, in other words, he couldn't get in this quarter.

He gobbled down breakfast, and as he was leaving, Pru said, "Don't forget your umbrella, dear."

She gazed after him blankly, and all at once, he realized he'd lost it. He didn't know what to say.

"To be perfectly honest, Aunt Pru," he stammered, "I must've left it somewhere, but I think I know where it is."

Her face squinted on a hurt expression as he hurried out. He took a bus to campus and spent the first part of the afternoon in the Registrar's Office, enrolling, and in the Student Aid Office, filling out applications for scholarships and on-campus jobs.

"What about work at the Bidencourt place?" he asked openly.

There was a pregnant silence. Two secretaries glanced his way, then smirked at each other.

"You could," the counselor said, assuming a kind, yet arch tone of voice. "But Mr. Bidencourt likes to import most of his staff from New York and the West Coast."

Ray narrowed his eyes, thinking hard.

"Thinks locals don't have the proper, uh–"

"Sensibilities," Ray suggested.

"Yes," the counselor agreed. "The proper sensibilities."

Ray sipped a Coke in the student center, then idled in the library until he was to meet his adviser and sign up for classes, which had started. While there, he decided to see if there were a book on the Harz House. There was, and so far he'd figured out that Bidencourt was a direct, fifth generation descendant of one Stanislaus Bidencourt, who, in 1873, while hiking through the woods, had come upon the view and bought the land. Ray knew that from Harz House, a person could see Mount Sylvan. The house was named after the mountains in Germany where Stanislaus had been born.

Then he had the idea to research Beau's disappearance and found an index to the local paper. According to the one, discreet account, Charles B.

"Beau" Doughty, a senior at Hobbes College, had been reported missing while accompanying Delbert S. Bidencourt, owner of the local winery, to New York to attend an antique auction. Several witnesses placed Doughty with Bidencourt in New York, and the case, the article concluded, had been turned over to authorities there.

When Ray returned that evening, Pru could see that he didn't have the umbrella, but didn't mention it. He took another bath, then helped her set the table. They were having leftovers, white beans and rice. She said she wanted to be frugal. He said he didn't mind. Of course, there was plenty of birthday cake for dessert.

"The guy at financial aid said it's too late to get anything on campus," he commented, scooping up his last bite of the rich cake. "Don't think I should try up at Harz?"

"Well, no," she said, standing by the stove. "You need the job, I know. We could get by."

She set the lid on the pot of beans, then wiped the stove.

"It isn't that Beau Doughty business?" he asked.

"Well, yes," she admitted. "As a matter of fact."

Ray decided to risk a gambit.

"I hear that Beau was wild as squirrels, that Bidencourt was just trying to help him."

"True," she replied. "If Beau wasn't fighting with his father, he was playing pranks on his boss or a teacher or even the sheriff."

"The sheriff?" he asked, trying to smile.

"Beau had an old Dodge, and one night he drove it around with a dummy's arm sticking out the trunk."

Ray stared at the chocolate smears on his plate, the blue pattern of baskets and cornucopias around the rim.

"Sheriff threatened to lock him up," she added. "He'd been better off if he had wound up in reform school, I think. Not Hobbes College. I mean, better than wherever he is now. He even played a joke on the last bishop, Bishop Childs. Never could learn to accept–"

Ray perked up. His eyebrows arched, giving his face an expectant look as if, all at once, something about him were poised for flight.

"What?"

"I don't know," she paused. "Authority."

"What'd he do to the bishop?"

Again, she was wearing a drab, shapeless frock. When she sat, she tugged it to straighten it.

"Well, the bishop was getting old and having a little trouble remembering his message at times," she began, sitting up straight, clasping her hands meekly. "So he started typing it and basically reading it at the service. Not that the message was ever long."

She stared to her right, out the window, beyond the pecan tree. It was as if she had been rehearsing a sermon herself and could not look at Ray, a distraction.

"Well," she went on, "Beau sneaked into his office one day and retyped his sermon, substituting inappropriate words here and there, like immoral for immortal, so that before he realized it, the bishop, that Sunday, was talking about things like man's immoral soul. And: 'The Pharisees and the scribes have taken the skis of knowledge and have hidden them.' Instead of keys, of course. 'No greater dove,' and so forth."

Normally, despite himself, Ray would've burst out laughing.

"Well," she continued, "at first, we couldn't tell if we just couldn't follow the bishop or what. Perhaps he was waiting to give us the moral at the end. Then we decided that he was, in fact, senile and had better step down. Then he figured it out and apologized."

Ray sipped some tea, clinking the ice cubes.

"Let it suffice to say," she said, facing him at last, "the bishop soon retired."

Ray started to goad her for more, then decided to let the subject drop.

"Some laughed at the bishop," she concluded. "Some frowned on the sacrilege."

Ray knew that Pru was of the latter.

In a sudden sympathetic mood, she added, "But it's no wonder Beau disappeared, his father being no count and all–"

"In New York," Ray said, slipping in the detail.

"Hm?"

"Disappeared in New York."

"Well," she sighed. "If he is up there, no telling what's happened to him."

In Babylon, Ray thought.

"It was Mr. Doughty who asked the authorities to look into the matter," Pru explained. "Then he moved. Some say it was all just a trick to get Mr. Bidencourt to buy him off."

"You mean blackmail," Ray puzzled, squinting.

"From the word 'go,' Beau and Doughty fought like cats," she remarked. "Guess Doughty thought he'd get some cash for his trouble."

Finally, she dropped what Ray considered the most important crumb of information.

"Don't think Beau was in on it, though."

"The blackmail."

"He may have been wild, but he wasn't–"

"Bad."

Pru looked at Ray humbly, as if she had just revealed some incriminating evidence against herself, not Beau. Ray glanced down, absently folding his napkin, then straightening his place mat.

"Well," she decided, rising. "I'm turning in."

He knew that every evening she read before going to sleep. But it was early. He wondered if she were not feeling well.

"I'll clear the table," he said, sitting up, setting the lid on the sugar bowl.

"Just set the dishes in the sink," she said. "I'll get them in the morning." Touching his shoulder, she leaned to give him a pulpy kiss on the cheek. "Ouu," she sighed. "You always smell so good."

He knew she meant clean. As she left, fingering the doorjamb for support, he returned the butter dish and lemon wedges to the refrigerator, then collected the dishes and utensils.

When through in the kitchen, he went to his room and, having slept most of the morning, decided to get in bed, but stay up late, reading. At first, he browsed the college catalog and various brochures, then, fluffing the big feather pillows, settled in with E. M. Forster's Howards End, a book he'd begun for a sophomore English course, but never finished.

Around nine-thirty, he noticed the clock's ticking and wondered if it had actually grown louder. He got up and put the clock under some underclothes in the dresser, but while at the dresser, took a good look at himself in the mirror: his florid face, the shiny, pale-yellow hair dipping over his brow. He pushed it back, and his thoughts flew to the dark passage in the stable.

The stranger in him had caressed the stranger's face, had brushed his hair from his face, and the gesture at the mirror called up the image: the jaw rough with stubble, the deep dimple, like a thumb mark, pressed into the chin. He could even smell the man's sweaty, musky, private smell, like the smell of stacked hay, was conscious of even his body heat as a good, sure sensation.

The man had propped him gently against the wall, then sank to his knees in front of him. At first, he just knelt there, as if, bowed down, he were begging him for something or, head down, were praying to him. Then the prayer ended. He reached up and unfastened Ray's shorts, peeling them off his thighs. When Ray stepped out of them, the man tossed them onto the bench.

The man touched the inside of Ray's calf, and as Ray spread his legs, the mere proximity of the warm mouth gave him an erection. Freed from the shorts, his cock at first just hung there, head heavy. A callow bird just hatched from a shell could not have looked more vulnerable and solicitous. Then it lifted itself as if a string were tied to it, sliding into its length like a snake. It stood up and grew rock hard, so hard, in fact, it hurt, throbbing in sync with his pulse.

The man swallowed it deep into his throat, began sucking on it and soothing it, and Ray, lightheaded, leaned forward to brace himself on the man's back, a big, strong back all blue sheen and chrome in a flash of lightning.

The man placed Ray's hands in his hair, and Ray wrapped his hands in it, held on to big shocks of it, like reins, holding the man's head in place while he slowly, rhythmically slid into his face, dug deeper into his throat–a

thick, black mane of flowing hair glistening blue in the dark. The man sat up for a moment, working with his jeans, then sat back down, massaging his cock.

Then the control shifted. The man had showed him how he wanted him to make love to him, and now he was on his own. He kept reaching into the man's throat with his cock, shoving his cock head lower down his throat, lower and lower until the man's face was smashed into his pubic hair. He was trying to sink his cock head to the depth the man wanted, to choke him on it, if need be, to fill his need.

The man's left hand had been softly rubbing the back of Ray's thigh, but when it moved up, touching his bottom, Ray's mind clouded over. Some set of leather restraints had snapped inside him. Some long pent-up urge, like a horse, had broken free.

At first, he felt as if some wild animal had bitten him in the crotch and would not let go, gnawing and gouging, wallowing wet in his thighs. There was nothing Ray could do but give himself over to it, hang on to the man's hair while he stiffened and came, blinded, deaf, and dumb with desire. Then, as the orgasm subsided, he did not want it to stop, no, never, never, no. He wanted only to keep on standing over him as the man stroked himself, to keep holding on to the ropes of his tousled hair, to keep plumbing the depths of his throat's firm grip for more. The man arched, gagging on Ray's cock.

Long after they had come, the man kept stroking himself, kept pulling hard on Ray's cock with his mouth until he had wrung the last drop of semen from him. Then they waited, holding on to each other, attached face to groin.

When he slipped from the man's mouth, Ray just stood there, holding his crotch as if wounded. His legs were trembling, and his cock felt raw and swollen, burning with strange sensations at once both pleasant and sore.

The man watched Ray step into his shorts. Then he sighed heavily and rose to his feet. He zipped up and buttoned his jeans, then buckled the belt. The lightning grew dimmer, the thunder fainter. At moments, all that could be heard was the erratic splatter of a leaky gutter. Ray could feel his body literally cooling. Then the man stepped forward to give him one last surly kiss goodbye, and as he did, Ray could smell, laced with liquor, the damp, musky odor of his crotch on the man's face. Ray reached up to caress the man's face, to brush the hair from his face.

The face in Ray's mind focused to the face in the mirror. Ray threw himself into bed, but felt stifled, claustrophobic in the small, musty room. He became intuitively aware of the time, the second hand chipping away at midnight, the witching hour, and the closer it grew to midnight, the more he was drawn like metal to the powerful magnet of the sullen garage, the passionate, wind-swept garden. His body tightened, responsive, complaisant. Little pearls of sweat began to bead on his upper lip. Restless, he rose to turn on the fan, but when even that was not enough, pushed open the windows facing the woods.

John Patrick

In the woods last night, he'd depended on the sporadic lightning to keep him on the road, blue flashes of mica and grass, but he knew that in some deeper sense, he would have to put out all the lights before he could see his own. To see! it occurred to him. Not in the warped mirror hung on the wall, but the true one inside. To see, not with his eyes, but his heart. He would feel his way through the dark, the illuminating darkness of chance touch and wonder. The mute, terribly intense dark would be his light.

The umbrella was gone, but Ray waited near the garden for over an hour, tentatively scuffling around the passage, quietly gazing across the rows of roses. The ferric moonlight had drained them of their tint. The whites looked blue–the reds and yellows, black and grey and brown. They reminded him of the boutonnieres he'd pinned on his lapel, of the frail corsages he'd pinned on satin bodices for school dances. Across the walkways, across the acres of lawn stood the east wall with its espaliered plum trees and, in the middle, flagstone steps leading up into the dark. The prospect of taking those steps, by comparison, seemed infinitely more exciting than anything he had ever done in high school or college.

He glanced at the lights, like diamonds, at the house. In the calm, with lights, the house looked more like the fairy-tale chateau that it was. But slowly, one by one, the lights were going out. He could feel his face flush. Sweat trickled from his temples. Since the man hadn't shown, there was little he could do, he thought, but venture on.

He crossed the rose garden, climbed the flagstone steps, followed a gravel path into the labyrinth of a shrub garden. He was surrounded by banks of azaleas, dogwoods, and Japanese maples rhythmically thrilling with crickets, locusts, and frogs. At one point, above all the stridence, he could just barely make out the shrill, child-like cry he'd heard the night before. He faced that direction and, backing around a corner, bumped into a marble Pan. He jumped back, then brushed back his hair, glancing, through a break in the trees, at a rocket burst of falling stars.

When he stepped into the Italian Garden, he felt as if he had already reached the house. The tranquil pools, the statues of cherubs seemed an extension of it, an elaborate terrace. He took the steps to the drive and, hands in pockets, strolled past the entrance, gazing at the stonework and spires and near the top, perched on ledges, a troop of black gargoyles. What he didn't notice, of course, was that one had moved. A camera, disguised as a winged devil, was following him around the drive.

Through the air came the shrill cry, and Ray looked toward a small, white blur, like a ghost, near a circular pool in the middle of the lawn. A thin mist hung just inches above the lawn, and the little ghost seemed to be floating on it. At first, Ray could not figure out what it was. Then it slowly opened into a fan, and he realized that it was a white peacock. He watched it awhile, smiling to himself.

He looked to his left. At the east end of the house, the grounds sloped through Water Oaks toward a road, and as he was sidling and sliding down the hill, a light caught his attention, a faint, yellow square on the grass. He'd see what he could see, he thought glumly, then go.

He couldn't tell much from the small, high window, but at the back of the house, he saw an open door and a room which, for him, may as well have been from another world. He'd heard just enough about Mardi Gras to know that the walls were painted with scenes from one of the parades. White wicker sat around in groups, and orange-red Chinese lanterns hovered just under the ceiling. He felt guilty about leaning into the room, but once he'd set foot in it, he knew there was no turning back. What he didn't know was that, in an upper corner, a little, red light had blinked.

Next was a large room with ping-pong and card tables. Its size, the polished hardwood floors, the glossy, white, resonant walls–everything about the room brought home to him how small and isolated he felt.

He listened carefully, then tried the next door, entering, in the dark, what at first looked like a gleaming torture chamber. In the wall to the right was a door with a panel of frosted glass, and from the faint light filtering through, he finally could see that he was standing in a small, well-equipped gymnasium.

Next, he stepped into a shadowy locker room, a cold, tile room, like the gym, with dressing stalls down the center. How would he explain himself? he wondered. Or would someone simply shoot him and ask questions later?

But what was waiting for him behind the next door was so intriguing that he forgot his qualms. As far as he could tell, he had opened the door on the Void, an abyss even deeper and darker than the lush, wisteria-laden night in the woods, in his dreams. He could see nothing, hear nothing. Death must be like this, he thought. Or space–black, starless space. He could step into space. Warm, moist air flowed over him, and the dark took on the feel of a cavernous lake, a cosmic womb.

If no light could get in, he reasoned, no light could get out. He felt for a light switch, and when he flipped it, he found himself on the edge of a huge, indoor swimming pool. Potted palms sat here and there on the polished deck, loops of rope and rope ladders dangled from the wrought-iron railing, and at the deep end, wooden steps descended to a platform about waist-deep, he figured, in the heated water. His first impulse was to strip and slip in. The warm water, he knew, would be luxurious, soothing.

The next door, in contrast, opened on an ordinary hallway. He switched off the light, but left the door ajar, then eased down the hall toward a transverse hall, peeking around the corner. He sneaked down the hall to his left, tiptoeing to an open door, where he paused, catching a glimpse of a small, blue, well-lit bedroom. He could hear two young women whispering and snickering.

"Imagine getting a postcard from him after all this time," the first laughed.

"Imagine a movie star like Ronald Powers wanting some white trash like him," the other replied.

"Imagine Del-bert wanting him," the first said, making fun of the name. "He must be good."

"Damn good."

When Ray heard the bedsprings squeak, as if one had gotten up, he backed away.

"Want me to freshen yours?"

He slipped back to the intersection of the halls and noticed a stairwell to the left. From the end of the hall ahead came the clank and clink of pots and dishes. When he heard footsteps on the stairs, his pulse raced, and he hid around the corner, lingering just long enough to spy the polished black shoes and pleated grey of a service uniform. He ducked through a door marked "Vegetable Pantry." Shelves upon shelves of variously colored cans towered above him in the dark.

"A postcard," Ray puzzled. "After all this time."

When the footsteps receded, Ray peeked out, moving to the stairwell, then skipping up the steps.

On the first landing, Ray cracked the door, peering across a sunken, marble area. From the center rose a fountain wreathed in sago palms, Christmas ferns, and red geraniums, and from the trickling fountain rose, in turn, the shiny bronze of a frightened youth carried aloft by an eagle. A limestone arcade encircled the atrium, and through its arches, Ray could see marble statuary, imposing copies of Greek gods and goddesses, korai and ephebes. He let the door close softly.

"A postcard."

He scrambled up the steps to the next landing. He cracked the door, peered out, then stepped into the hall. On the table to the right stood a Majolica jug with two dozen white and yellow roses, some just budding, some in bloom. Straight ahead lay a long sitting room with a desk, armchairs, and portraits. To the left stretched a high, dimly lit hall with heraldic standards hanging from the ceiling. A thin, yellow rectangle of light stretched across the carpet outside the third door. Ray could just barely hear the murmur of voices and what sounded like an old, scratchy phonograph record.

The farther he'd gone, the more relaxed and sure of himself he'd become so that when he took the first step, then hesitated, then took the next, his tentative pace was more of a smooth wedding march than a stroll.

He could fit in here, he hoped. He didn't care how, tending lawns, picking grapes. He'd fallen in love with the place. He'd found his place and moaned with expectation.

To his left hung a huge tapestry, faded, even threadbare in spots: the scene of two savages locked in what looked like, to Ray, a solemn–or was it an amorous?–struggle. The nameplate at the bottom read, "Gilgamesh and Enkidu." What strange names, he thought.

The first door was closed.

Ray looked from the tapestry on the right, that of Akhilleus and Patroklos, to the one on the left, that of Jonathan and David.

The next door stood ajar, but with the lights out, all Ray could see was a dusky fireplace and book-lined walls.

Ahead were tapestries on a different subject, the one on the right entitled "The Signing of the Magna Charta," on the left, "The Drafting of the Constitution." At the end of the hall, on a marble-topped table, stood an alabaster bust of Schubert wreathed in palm.

At the third door, something chinked, and a small shadow darkened the threshold. A black Cairn terrier trotted into the hall. When it saw him, it stopped, head tilted, ears perked.

"Samantha," a man called.

"Sammy, where are you going?" a woman asked.

Ray paused, smiling, and the dog sauntered over, sniffing his cuff and wagging her tail. She had a glossy black coat streaked with grey and brown, and the silver tags on her collar jingled when she looked up, peering at him through bangs. Ray mussed her fluffy rump, then approached the door, and the dog trailed after.

Slowly, slowly, the room rotated into view, and at first, Ray saw a man in a tuxedo. He was slouched in a comfortable-looking, upholstered chair, holding a fragrant cigarette. For a second, Ray did not recognize him. The man was shaved, and his hair was slicked back, emphasizing his dark, olive complexion. Then, from the man's soulful expression, Ray did, and in the lamplight, he saw that the man was not that much older than he was–in his late twenties, not in his sixties as he'd been told nor in his forties as he'd believed the night before. He was the man who, in look and tone, as well as in the act itself, had made love to him in the garage, the man who was obviously the count.

Bidencourt crossed his legs at the ankles. He stared at the rug intensely, then glanced up, noticing Ray, but calmly as if he'd been patiently waiting for him, instinctively aware of his presence. He drew long and deep on the cigarette, then passed it to the woman.

Because of the taxidermy, the central impression of the room was that of frozen activity, so that when Ray, at last, confidently stepped across the threshold, he felt as if he'd somehow stepped from time. A bobcat crouched on a log in a corner. A turkey and a raccoon dawdled to either side of the hearth. Mounted bass and trout swam through the murky, lake-water green of the walls. The stuffed menagerie made the living, moving creatures in the room–the people and the terrier–seem oddly unreal.

With the fireplace wedged in a corner, the three armchairs faced each other in a loose triangle with a round, walnut table between each pair. Each pair of chair and table, as well, sat on its own small Oriental carpet lapping the next in a large trefoil. One table held a tray with a decanter of some dark liqueur, along with a little, etched liqueur glass; the second, an upright,

stuffed squirrel, an ashtray, and a box of matches; the one to the right of Bidencourt, a white silk scarf, a pair of white gloves, and a glass of the liqueur. Behind his chair, stood an RCA credenza Victrola playing, almost as background music, Bessie Smith's "Foolish Man Blues."

The couple with Bidencourt was facing him, not the door, and it was not until Bidencourt exhaled, then stood, that they–as the woman passed the cigarette–also noticed Ray.

"Oh, look," she laughed. "I've spilled maraschino on my gown."

She spoke with a strange–Ray presumed European–accent he couldn't place.

The other man rose, and the couple, setting down their glasses, seemed to assume that Ray was someone Bidencourt expected. The woman tried to flick the small, pink stain off her gown. The man handed her his handkerchief, and she dabbed the stain with it. The terrier, tail erect, minced over to Bidencourt to settle near his feet, and, for a moment, Ray just stood there, gaping.

"You're late," Bidencourt began perfunctorily.

At the sound of his voice, Ray could feel, in his blood, the heat of the chance rendezvous of the night before. It shot through his veins, like adrenaline, then subsided, leaving him tired, yet excited, his hand trembly.

Bidencourt's mess jacket accentuated his narrow waist. Three large buttons were fastened like brooches down the right, and a white vest, tie, and handkerchief set off the ensemble. Ray had never seen anyone so handsome, not even models in magazines.

The other man snubbed the cigarette out, and Bidencourt crossed to Ray, then took his hand, touching the knuckles.

"David, Isabella," Bidencourt said simply, "this is a very close friend."

"Ray," Ray blurted. "Ray Parker."

"Good to meet you," David said, gripping his hand, and Ray's face flexed to a ready, unreserved smile.

David looked in his forties. He had longish, greying hair parted down the middle and combed back on the sides. A receding hairline made his forehead seem larger than it was, and his modest hairstyle, together with a pair of circular, tortoise-shell glasses, gave him, despite the tuxedo, a somewhat stuffy air. A bright smile, however, broke through the staid appearance.

"Enchante," Isabella beamed, her eyes sparkling with mischief.

Isabella was undoubtedly the most beautiful woman that Ray had ever seen, a glamorous angel with half-sheared fleece for hair. She was not wearing lipstick, and her luminous skin, pearl-grey eyes, and blonde brows created a striking, overlit effect, as if Ray were seeing her through some marvelous, wintry glare. She, too, was dressed for some special occasion–in a tremendous, glittering-white, off-the-shoulder gown.

"I hope you have better luck with Del than we have." Touching Bidencourt's arm, she purred, "Not exactly the life of the party."

Ray broke into another broad grin. Her whiteness reminded him of the albino peacock–the pink stain, blood. If this were a dream, he told himself ingenuously, he never wanted to wake. Perhaps his life till last night was the dream.

"And this young mutt," Bidencourt announced, deadpan, "is Sammy. I think you've met."

Everyone glanced at Sammy, and she sprang to her feet, panting and waving her tail. For a small dog, she barked quite a loud, insistent bark.

"You forgot your umbrella," Bidencourt mentioned, his face hard, his eyes morose blue. "I put it away for you."

Then the new Ray spoke through the old Ray's mouth: "How's Beau?"

David and Isabella smirked, turning to Bidencourt. Sammy stood in the middle of the circle, looking from one to the other.

"Fine," Bidencourt said, his frown, all at once, replaced by a smile. "Heard from him the other day." Slipping his arm around Ray's shoulder, he added, "He's in California."

# A Hard Night in Georgia

## *Thomas C. Humphrey*

"I think we'll stop at Sheriff Blackmon's office. He's a friend of mine, and he asked me to report faggots messing with underage kids," Toby slurred drunkenly, wheeling my car around a corner.

"Underage my ass," I said.

John launched a looping right from the back seat that caught me on my eye socket and set off a Roman candle in my head. "Shut the fuck up, you shit packer," he growled.

"Let's do stop," I bluffed, rubbing my eye and fighting against the urge to knock the crap out of the stupid asshole. "The sheriff's a friend of mine, too."

"Naah. Maybe we'll come back," Toby said, gunning the car and heading out of town.

"Just let us out," Bill pleaded from the back seat.

I heard a couple of quick slaps and a loud groan from Bill, but I kept my eyes glued to the road, prepared to grab the keys and cut the ignition if Toby got too reckless. In the meantime, I frantically searched for a way out of this mess without Bill or me getting hurt too bad.

I had sensed trouble from the beginning, but the prospect of screwing one of these new hustlers blocked out all my caution. In my mid-twenties, I had been in the little Georgia country town not quite a year, and I had been amazed at how many kids were available for not much more than a six-pack of cheap beer, a bologna sandwich, and a pack of cigarettes. Bill had lived there longer than that, and he knew quite a few kids before I met him. He was too delicate and girlish to hold my interest sexually, and after he gave me one blow job, we had settled into a rather casual friendship, built mostly on our mutual lust for the young local kids.

A couple of times a week, at least, he would call me to say that he had kids at his apartment who wanted to party. I would grab some beer and head on over.

This particular night, I had called him, and Charles answered the phone. Charles was a real knockout kid, but he was so young he had scared me off. Not Bill. He had latched onto Charles and practically moved him in over the past several weeks. They were sleeping in the same bed every night, but Bill had complained to me that he couldn't get Charles to do more than let him blow him.

"Bill had to work late," Charles told me. "He said for you to come on over."

"Is anybody else there?" I asked.

"Yeah, a couple of guys," he said.

"Who?"

"Why don't you come find out?" he teased.

Charles had brought two or three of his friends over before and I had wound up in bed with them. His not telling me who was there stirred my hormones, so I soon arrived with a six-pack. For some reason, though, before I went inside, I stuffed my wallet and a new carton of cigarettes under the front seat.

As I headed for the kitchen, I saw two guys in Bill's bedroom, rifling through his jewelry box. They were new to me, and bigger and older and tougher looking than the crowd Bill and I had cultivated. Right away I sensed trouble.

The big round-faced blonde kid followed me into the kitchen. "We weren't doing nothing, okay?" he said. "You don't have to mention it to Bill."

"That's cool," I said, shoving a beer at him. The taller, more muscular kid was on his heels and reached for a beer eagerly.

As we sat waiting for Bill, I made a visual assessment. Toby, the blonde, had been a damned good-looking kid in the recent past, but drugs and booze were already taking their toll. His bloodshot blue eyes were sunken and deeply circled. His face was pasty, and his jowls sagged with fat. He had a good start on a beer gut.

John was not good-looking in any normal way, though he exuded sensuality. His nose had been broken and was slightly flat and askew. He had thick lips and a slack-jawed expression on his face. He did not carry an ounce of excess fat on his six-three frame, and he looked as strong as a bull. His most notable attribute, though, was his eyes, which were cold and vacuous. He gave the impression of having no feelings at all. I suspected he had very limited intelligence.

It did not take long to learn that Toby was the leader, quick-witted and sharp-tongued. He controlled John through superior intelligence and Charles through intimidation. Within minutes, he had Charles waiting on him like a servant, even making him light his cigarettes for him.

As soon as Bill came in, I cornered him in the kitchen. "These kids are trouble," I warned. "Let's get rid of them right away."

"I think the blonde is cute," he answered, and I knew that there was no way to persuade him that the blonde was also dangerous. In the presence of a "cute" kid, Bill lost all capacity for thought.

The kids had finished all of Bill's beer before I got there, and my six-pack was gone in nothing flat. "We need more beer," Toby said.

"I'm broke," I said, staring at Bill and praying that he would use his head.

Bill reached for his wallet. "I've got twenty dollars," he said. "Dave, why don't you go buy more?"

Toby grabbed the twenty. "I'll go with you, Dave. I know where they'll sell it to me," he said. "Come on, John."

As the three of us went outside, Toby turned to me. "Let me drive, okay?" he said.

"Uh-uh, I can't," I said.

"Come on, Dave," he wheedled. "I know how to drive. I got a license and everything. Let me drive."

"I can't," I repeated firmly.

"What's the matter?" he asked, an edge of belligerence in his voice. "You think I'm drunk or something?"

"No, I don't think you're drunk," I said, trying to be the diplomat. "It's just that my insurance doesn't cover anybody your age."

"Fuck it. You drive, then," he said.

He directed me to a run-down grocery with a gas pump on the outskirts of town. John and I waited in the car while Toby went in for beer.

"I sure am horny," John commented out of nowhere.

"That so?" I said, trying to convey more disinterest than I was feeling.

"Yeah, I got nine inches that needs some action tonight," he said, spreading his legs and rubbing his crotch. "You know Toby is going to be with Bill. Maybe you and me ought to get together, huh?"

"I'm broke, remember?" I said.

Toby returned with a twelve-pack before John could entice me any farther, and I drove back to Bill's, my sense of impending trouble losing out to the promise of nine inches in John's jeans.

Toby and John guzzled beer while we listened to a hard rock station and made inane conversation. John had been right about one thing. Toby launched a campaign to set Bill's groin afire, flirting and groping and teasing until he had Bill practically coming in his pants.

"Bill and I are going in his room," Toby announced finally. "John, you and Dave can take the spare room. Charles, you get the couch." He led Bill off to bed, his arm around Bill's waist.

John, Charles, and I sat for a few minutes finishing our beers, and then Charles grabbed sheets from a hall closet and opened up the hide-a-bed.

"You ready?" John asked me. Wordlessly, I followed him into the spare bedroom and closed the door behind us. He was already half undressed.

He did not have anything approaching his vaunted nine inch cock, and what he did have would not get fully hard, no matter how I teased and squeezed it. "I don't know what's wrong," he said. "Usually it's lots bigger than this."

Quickly losing interest in his nearly flaccid dick, I kneeled between his legs and raised them to my shoulders. When he did not object, I spit on my genuine nine-inch boner and slipped it up his ass. He did not even let out a groan as I sunk it all the way.

John Patrick

I slid his legs off my shoulders and lay down on his chest. He wrapped his legs loosely across my back, and I fucked him hard and fast. After awhile, he complained that I was hurting him, but I kept pounding away.

"Hurry up. I can't take much more," he said finally. His legs slid off my back and sank down on the mattress while I continued humping up his ass until I gave out a few grunts and shot my wad deep inside him.

I lay heavily against his chest for awhile, caressing his cheek and running my fingers through his hair. When I rolled off, he turned on his side and was snoring in minutes.

Although it had been a good fuck, not having his dick had left me only partially satisfied, and, after I washed off and dressed, I decided to see how lively Charles was.

"You awake?" I asked, sitting beside him on the hide-a-bed.

"Yeah," he muttered, rolling onto his back. "You leaving?"

"In a little bit," I said. "Too bad you have to ride the couch by yourself tonight. Toby sort of took over, didn't he?"

"He always does," he said, his voice laced with disgust." I shouldn't have ever told the bastard about Bill."

"You feeling horny?" I asked, dropping my hand on his upper thigh.

"Yeah, man!" he said, flipping the sheet off his body.

When I slid my hand up to the pouch of his briefs, I knew we would not have the problem John had had. Charles was practically bursting out of his underwear by the time I touched him.

"Bill will be pissed that I put the make on you," I said.

"Fuck Bill," he said. "He's in there getting screwed by Toby and not giving a shit about me. Come on and give me some head, and don't worry about Bill."

I slid his briefs off and went exploring. Charles did not have an exceptionally big cock, but it was cut and perfectly formed, the shaft the same thickness along its full length, the flared head broad and firm. I went down on it with relish and gave it my best moves. Charles squirmed and moaned and clutched at the mattress, occasionally lifting off the bed to shove more of his rod into my mouth. When I knew he was close, I took my mouth off and sat up.

"What can you do for me?" I asked, squeezing my hard-on.

"I don't give head or get fucked or nothing," he said.

"How about a hand job?" I asked, sliding my pants down my thighs.

"Well, maybe," he said. "Then you'll finish sucking me off?" He reached for my cock without waiting for an answer. "Man, that's a big dick," he said, stroking it gently.

I stretched out beside him and fingered his cock just enough to keep it hard. "Spit on it and tighten your grip," I instructed.

He worked away diligently, and in no time, I was spraying my second load of the night all up my abdomen and across his thigh. He reached for a corner of the sheet and wiped us both off.

"Now come on and suck me," he said, lying on his back and thrusting his stiff cock forward with his thumb.

I went back down on his rod, which was made for sucking. I teased and delayed his climax for a long time, enjoying it as much as he obviously was. Finally, he could hold off no longer. "It's coming! I'm gonna shoot!" he gasped. He grabbed both hands full of my hair and hunched frantically into my mouth, driving down my throat, as his dick throbbed and twitched and spewed into my mouth. He held on even after he sagged back onto the mattress, and I finally had to break his hold on my hair after he softened in my mouth.

"Man, you give better head than Bill," he said. "Why haven't we done this before?"

"It won't be the last time," I promised.

Just as he slipped his briefs back on and I was ready to leave, a loud commotion broke out in Bill's room. Toby yelled out, "I want my money, you faggot!" and something crashed against the wall. Bill burst out of the door, Toby right on his heels, both of them stark naked. Toby grabbed Bill's shoulder and spun him around. "Gimme my money, queer," he snapped.

"I don't owe you any money," Bill said, moving beside me.

"You sure as shit do," Toby said, turning back into the bedroom for his clothes. He slammed the door with a loud bang.

Bill pulled me aside. "I didn't promise him any money," he said. "He sucked my dick. I didn't even ask him to, but he went down on me for a little bit and then said he'd finish me for the change from the beer. I didn't promise to pay him."

Toby came back out, zipping up his jeans. "I'm gonna get my money," he threatened.

"I don't owe you any money," Bill stubbornly persisted.

"Just give him the money and I'll take them home," I said. The way they were yelling, I was afraid they'd wake the whole neighborhood.

"I'm not going to give it to him," Bill said. "He sucked my dick without me even asking him."

"You're a fucking liar. I don't suck nobody's dick," Toby snarled. He went in and shook John awake and then went back to finish dressing. He came back out wielding a small pocket knife. "Gimme my fucking money," he said, advancing on Bill.

"Just calm down," I said. "You'll get your money."

"I'm not going to pay him," Bill insisted.

"I want my money," Toby said, waving the knife.

John boiled out of the bedroom tugging on his jeans. "And I want my money," he said to me.

"You know I'm broke, John," I shrugged.

"You fucking shit packer, you better turn up my money," he threatened.

"Look, nobody promised anybody money," I said. "But there's–how much?–left from the twenty. Bill, give it to them, and I'll pay you back tomorrow. And come on, Toby, I'll drive you guys back to town."

Bill relented and gave Toby the money and then went to dress.

"What about mine?" John said.

"John, I told you I was broke in the beginning," I tried to reason with him. "You know I didn't say I'd give you any money." I reached into my pocket and pulled out maybe a dollar in change. "This is all I have."

"You fucking fruitcake," John snarled, snatching the change from me.

After everybody was dressed, I decided that I really did not want to be alone with Toby and John. I suggested that Bill and Charles ride with us.

"This time I'm driving," Toby said as we walked to the car. "I'll show you I can drive."

At that point, I just wanted to get rid of them before a neighbor called the cops. I knew resisting Toby would just lead to further trouble.

"Okay," I said, handing him the keys. "But I'll sit up front with you. Bill, you and Charles get in back with John."

It immediately became obvious that Toby was too pissed just to drive somewhere downtown and walk away from us. He had to preserve his image with John and Charles by trying to make Bill and me grovel. When he did not get the expected response to his threat to deliver us to the sheriff, he drove out a winding county road until we were several miles from town. When he turned off onto a narrow logging trail nearly overgrown with broom sedge, I suspected that he planned to beat Bill's and my ass and dump us out there. My mind raced with a rapidly developing plan. I would switch off the ignition, snatch the keys, and roll out of the car before it stopped. If I was lucky, I could find a stout tree limb or something to use as a weapon before Toby and John could react.

Toby killed that plan. "Take off your belt, John," he ordered. "Now loop it around this fucker's neck and choke the shit out of him if he tries anything."

He stopped the car and killed the engine and lights and then walked to the passenger side. He opened the door and grabbed the belt out of John's hands. "Get out," he ordered, tugging at the belt. "John, you bring Bill, and don't give him a chance to run."

Toby led me over to a small pine tree. "Charles, take off your tee shirt," he said. "Sit down and put your hands over your head around the tree," he told me, snatching on the belt until I dropped to my knees and then back onto my ass. He handed Charles the belt and twisted the tee shirt into a rope and tied my hands behind the tree. After he tugged on the knots to make sure they were secure, he took the belt off my neck. "Take the fucker's clothes off," he told Charles, moving over to Bill.

"I'm sorry. I've got to do it," Charles whispered as he undressed me.

"I know. It's not your fault," I said.

Toby and John made Bill strip, and Toby came back over to me. "Give me one of your shoe laces," he told Charles. When Charles handed it to him, he tied one end tight around my balls and the other end just under the rim of my cock head. He gave it a sharp, hard tug, sending shooting pains through my groin. "Don't give me no trouble, or I'll pull your fucking balls off," he threatened. He grabbed both my ankles and snatched my ass away from the tree, scraping my back against the rough bark, until I was lying flat on the ground, my arms stretched full length overhead.

"Now, let's have some fun," he said, moving back to Bill, who was cowering and quaking and shielding his crotch with his hands like a shy little girl.

They all three stripped naked, and Toby shoved Bill to his knees in front of them. He crammed his stiff cock in Bill's face and Bill started sucking it. Toby grabbed him by the hair and rammed it down his throat, purposely making him gag time after time. "Suck my dick! And you better not puke on it!" he said.

When he got close to coming, Toby stepped back and shoved John in front of Bill. In the pale moonlight, it looked like John was fully hard and closer to nine inches than he had been with me. He locked his fingers behind Bill's head and began pile driving his cock into his throat. Oblivious to the danger we were in, Bill actually was getting off on being dominated. He grabbed his own stiff cock and began stroking it while John fucked his face.

"Get on your knees, John," Toby said. John kneeled down, pulling Bill's head after him. "Come here and fuck his ass, Charles," Toby instructed.

"I don't want to," Charles said.

"Do it–or I'll fuck yours," Toby said.

Charles spat on his dick and stroked it a few times to get it hard and rammed it up Bill's ass. Toby kneeled and crammed his cock in beside John's and they fucked Bill's mouth together. Then Toby pulled out and forced John out. "That's enough, Charles. Come here and let him clean your dick off," Toby ordered. "I hope you got it good and shitty." He watched intently as Bill licked and sucked Charles' cock to his satisfaction.

Toby sat on Bill's back and grabbed him by the hair. "I want a pony ride," he said. "Giddy up, horsy." He raised his legs and began kicking Bill, bending his heels under his body until he was hitting him in the dick and balls. Bill started shuffling along on hands and knees, struggling to support Toby's full weight.

"Break some switches and get this horsy moving," he told John and Charles.

With the two of them swatting his ass with pine branches, Bill huffed and puffed around in a wide circle with Toby kicking him in the groin. When he was too tired to move, he collapsed onto his stomach.

"Get back on your hands and knees," Toby said, getting off his prone body. "Get one of John's tennis shoes, Charles."

When Charles brought the size twelve sneaker, Toby reached under Bill and tied the laces to his balls. "Now, find some rocks and fill it up," he told Charles. "John, you go check on the other fucker. Make sure he ain't trying to get loose."

John strolled over, his hard-on wagging before him, and kneeled beside me. He grabbed the shoelace tied to my dick and balls and tugged on it enough to make me groan. "I'm going to pack your shit and make you eat it off my dick later," he said with his slack-jawed grin, a sadistic glint in his eyes. He straddled my chest and poked his dick at my mouth. "But right now, just eat my dick down to my balls." He kept pushing forward until his abdomen covered my whole face and fed his cock right down my throat until my nose was pressed tight in his pubic hair. Then he started rocking back and forth, fucking my mouth.

About the time he was gasping and ready to spew out his load, Toby interrupted him. "Save it for later," he said. "We're ready for more fun."

As I struggled for breath, I noticed Bill grimacing from the downward pull of the rock-loaded sneaker on his balls. Toby had John play jockey this time, and as Bill struggled to move along on hands and knees, the big sneaker dangling awkwardly between his legs, Toby walked behind, kicking at it and occasionally yanking it down until Bill screamed with pain. When he wasn't tugging at the shoe, he swatted Bill's ass as hard as he could wield the belt that had been around my neck. Bill had lost all sense of manly dignity and was screeching and crying and begging like a child, not conscious of the fact that his emotional collapse fueled Toby's sadistic lust.

When Bill got so tired that he wouldn't budge even when Toby stretched his balls or swatted his ass, they would give him a rest while they took turns ramming into him and then making him lick them clean. Charles had to work up a hard-on every time, but Toby and John stayed hard, obviously fanning themselves into a sexual frenzy with their torture, maybe not for the first time.

During some of their rest periods, they would back up into Bill's face with their cheeks spread and make him tongue their asses, whipping him with the belt until he got his tongue far enough up one of them to suit Toby. When Charles announced that he had to piss, Toby made him spray a steady stream over Bill's hair and face and then finish up in his mouth.

I lay watching and straining against my bonds, which were so tight they threatened to cut off circulation in my hands. I knew Bill would catch the brunt of Toby's sadism in payment for announcing that Toby sucked cock. I also knew, though, that when they tired of torturing him, it would be my turn. This thought made me try even harder to free myself.

They kept forcing Bill to crawl around on hands and knees, supporting one or another of them on his back. He moved slower and slower, and, with John astraddle him, he suddenly collapsed face down. John put his feet on the ground and then hopped around frantically on one foot, grabbing at the sole of the other foot.

"Goddamn it, you dumped me in a patch of sandburs," he swore at Bill. He picked several out of his skin and then stood over Bill. "Get up and ride me out of here, queer," he ordered. When Bill did not move, John went crazy. He started kicking Bill in the ribs with his bare feet, yelling, "Get up, damn you!" at the top of his voice. When Bill did not respond, he bent over and started hitting him in the face and head with openhanded slaps and closed-fist blows, cursing him all the time.

Toby grabbed John roughly and spun him around. "Cut it out, John," he said, slapping him hard. "You can beat the piss out of him later, but I'm not through with him yet."

"But he dumped me right in them sandburs," John complained, calming down.

"Then let's show him what they feel like," Toby said. "Charles, break off a handful of them."

The burs were just at the stage where they were about to fall off their stems, and the slightest touch would disengage one or several from the stalk. Their dozens of tiny needle-sharp spikes stung like fire when they punctured the skin.

Toby took a stalk containing a dozen or more burs from Charles, spread Bill's ass cheeks, and laid the stalk in the crack. He popped Bill's buttocks together with the palms of his hands. Bill let out an agonized scream and tried to reach back to rip the spikes from his flesh, at the same time coming to his knees. Toby shoved him back down and got a knee in the small of his back. He stretched Bill's cheeks open and then squeezed them together several times, implanting all of the burs. He stood up and listened to Bill whimper as he reached back to try to remove the spikes, only to drive them into his fingers through his efforts.

Toby rolled Bill onto his back and the three of them took turns whipping him with the sandbur stalks, each lick embedding several burs on his face, neck, chest, and abdomen. After awhile, Bill quit screaming and just lay whimpering pitifully. Toby whipped the soles of both feet with them and made Bill stand up, forcing him to drive the spikes even deeper into his skin. When Bill collapsed again after a few agonizing steps, Toby took a tee shirt and roughly scrubbed the burs off his body.

"Come here, Charles," he said. "Since we're having so much fun, I think you ought to jack the faggot off to show our appreciation. Skin him back." Charles grabbed Bill's limp dick and pushed the foreskin back. Toby carefully circled a stalk of burs just under the rim of Bill's cock head. "Now, squeeze it tight and jack it," he ordered Charles.

When Charles drew the foreskin up over the burs, Bill let out a long tortured scream and tried to come up off the ground, but Toby threw his weight on Bill's chest. "Grab his legs and hold him, John," he said. "You keep jacking him," he instructed Charles.

Bill kept screaming as Charles' movements drove the burs deeper into his sensitive flesh. "He's bleeding," Charles said after a few strokes.

Toby let out a maniacal laugh. "That oughta work better'n spit," he said. "Keep jacking it. But I can't take his crybaby noise." He straddled Bill's chest and crammed his cock in his mouth. As he shoved it into Bill's throat, he leaned forward and held both his arms against the ground. Bill bucked and fought against the pain in his cock, but John and Toby held him down and all I could hear were his whimpers around Toby's pounding cock.

When Toby got close to coming, he crawled off Bill's chest and told Charles to quit torturing his bleeding cock. He walked over to a hawthorn shrub near me and broke off several three-inch long thorns with needle-sharp points.

"John, grab the fucker's arms, and Charles, you sit on his legs," Toby said. "I'm going to decorate his little girl titties." He laughed again insanely.

"Don't do that, you bastard!" I yelled out as he got ready to puncture one of Bill's nipples with a thorn.

"Oh, the smart ass feels left out," Toby said, sauntering over to me. "Don't worry, you're going to have all the fun you can handle, fucker. But until I'm ready for you, keep your mouth shut." He grabbed the cord around my cock and balls and pulled straight up, lifting my hips off the ground. The pain in my groin was excruciating, and I twisted and squirmed trying to escape. When he finally turned loose and let me drop back to the ground, I drew my knees into a fetal position and lay groaning in agony. Toby kicked at my balls and went back to Bill.

In the midst of my pain, though, I was elated. In my agonized struggle to free myself, I had felt the tee shirt binding my hands loosen. I kept pulling and tugging with growing hope that I would be free within seconds.

Toby kneeled beside Bill, squeezed one of his nipples between thumb and forefinger, and jabbed the sharp thorn through the nub. Bill let out only a little whimper and his body spasmed slightly. All the fight had gone out of him.

"Look at the fucker bleed," John laughed. "Let me do the other one." He and Toby changed places, and John gleefully jabbed a thorn through Bill's other nipple. Again, Bill's response was muted.

"You get the honor of puncturing his dick, Charles," Toby said. "We'll fix him so he won't ever butt-fuck another boy."

"I can't do it," Charles said.

Toby slapped him hard. "You damn well will do it, or we'll give you the same treatment. Now grab his dick and stick a thorn right through the head. I want it to come out the other side, hear?"

Sniffling, Charles squatted down and grabbed Bill's dick. While he was getting ready, I managed to free my right hand. As I opened and closed my fists to get circulation going, I reached for a piece of pine limb which I had already spotted beside me, hoping and praying that it was not rotten. When I got my hand on it, I knew it was solid. I placed it within easy reach and put my hands back over my head behind the tree.

"You fucking idiot," I yelled to Toby. "Why don't you leave him alone and fight me like a man?"

"I don't have to fight you," Toby sneered, walking over to me. "I got you right where I want you, and there ain't nothing you can do." He reached for the cord around my balls.

I quickly drew my leg up and kicked him right in the nuts. He doubled over and hit the ground with a yell. John saw what had happened and came running over. Just as he reached for me, I grabbed the pine limb and swatted him across his temple. He went down without a sound, all dead weight. I jumped up and hit him across the head again for good measure and then hit Toby so hard that the limb broke.

I grabbed my clothes off the ground and hurriedly searched pants pockets where the other guys had undressed until I found my car keys. Not even bothering to dress, I threw Bill's and my clothes into the car, anxiously watching for movement from John and Toby. They had not stirred.

"Come on, Bill," I urged, lifting him up. He was in complete shock and unresponsive. "It's over. Come on," I urged, but his feet would not move. Desperate, I hoisted him over my shoulder and dumped him in the passenger seat.

"Let's go, Charles," I called, starting the engine.

"I can't go," he said, walking up to the car.

"Come on, damn it," I insisted.

He looked at Toby and John and then back at me. "I can't," he said.

"What'll they do to you for not trying to stop us?" I asked.

"I don't know," he said with a note of resignation.

I got out of the car. "I hope you understand this, Charles," I said. "Maybe I'll see you around." I drew back and clipped him with a solid jab to his mouth. He collapsed to his knees and stayed there, spitting blood, as Bill and I drove off.

# A Real Handful

## *James Wilton*

It was a weekday afternoon and I went to the local watering hole. I have a circle of friends who meet for happy hour. The local hustlers, hoping for an early score, usually turn out at the same time. We are not usually shopping but it is always a joy to see all this young flesh and frequently watch a gent make a selection.

On this particular day I arrived early and was chatting with the bartendber. While we talked the crowd began to grow–both the suit group and young men. The boys covered a large range: the humpy swimmer type, the scruffy little tough boy, the prissy child with bleached hair and tight pants, the dirty boy with bad teeth, and the-kid-next-door-type in jeans and a red T-shirt in need of a wash. Some were regulars and some were part of that never-ending flow of new flesh working its way through town.

As the afternoon wore into evening, the crowd began to wane. Very few of the boys appeared to have made connections and they, too, left to prepare for their night activities. A toughy boy who had been trying very obviously to rent himself out approached me. Ken was about five foot four, stringy brown hair touching his collar, broad shoulders and a very narrow waist. His jeans weren't tight enough to show a basket but his buns bulged out like a pair of melons. He had a really hot aura about him.

For whatever reason, he had an immediate need for money and nearly begged me to hire him for an hour or so. I, on the other hand, wasn't desperate. I had no intention of cruising that afternoon so I was in the power position of taking or leaving the offer. Ken saw the chance of scoring with me and, knowing he had no other option in the rapidly emptying bar, he gave up that control hustlers protect and promised me "anything I want" at a good rate. I couldn't resist such a deal so we agreed on a price and headed out for the cheap "No Tell Motel" nearby.

We walked into the room and I led Ken in front of the full length mirror. I stood behind him and checked out what I had hired. I ran my hands across his shirt and felt his firm pecs. His nipples began to harden, telling me he had sensitive tits. I worked on them through the fabric while kissing his neck and watching the effects in the mirror. His dick began to harden and snake across his right thigh. I ran my hand down his hard stomach and cupped his basket. His cock stuck out the side of my grasp but I did get a nice big handful of balls. I rolled my hand across his hard-on and got him to moan. I found it a real turn-on to get this butch little toughy to weaken under my manipulation.

Meanwhile I was getting real hard and began to dry hump his tight buns. I got so hot that I grabbed his hips and gave him a good ride. However, I was

afraid of an early ejaculation and quit. It was time to get back to playing with my toy.

While my hands massaged his hard thighs I ran my lips and tongue along his strong neck. Again I had found a button to turn on this love machine. His eyes rolled back and then closed as he leaned his head onto my shoulder and sighed. The tent on the front of his jeans was clearly showing his pleasure. I decided to enjoy the rest of this body without touching his cock for a while. I wanted to get him so hot he needed release and I could hold off and make him suffer a little.

It was time to unwrap this delicious little package of sex. I began to unbutton his flannel shirt and feel that smooth hard chest. His skin was tight and nearly hairless. As I worked my way down to the bottom buttons I finally found some hair around his navel, arrowing down toward his love-center. His pants were loose enough that I could run my fingers under his belt and, to my pleasure, I found he was not wearing underwear. I explored as far down as the top of his thighs and his pubic nest but I didn't touch that throbbing phallus.

My light touch was driving him crazy and his moans had turned to groans and whistles. He finally couldn't take it any more and reached for his cock. I grabbed his wrist and yanked it away. This was my game and I wasn't going to let him set the pace. Instead I let him grab my throbbing cock as I pulled his hand down to my crotch. He felt his way around until he had the lay of the land. He lightly massaged my balls and then ran his hand along the length of my dick. As I moaned he slowly ran the ball of his hand up and down the fabric covering my tube.

I was tired of seeing a clothed boy. It was time to completely uncover the goods. I first took off the shirt and let my tongue enjoy his upper back and shoulders as my hands worked on his chest. I had him put his hands behind his neck. This had him in an even more exposed and vulnerable pose and gave me a view of his lightly haired young armpits. His upper arms had nice, hard muscles that looked natural, not sculpted. After some licking on his arms and feeling the fine hairs in the pits I moved to the center of attraction.

From my vantage point behind Ken I could see his bulging crotch clearly. I unbuckled his belt and opened his 501's one button at a time. As more of his lower belly came into view I could follow that line of hair down toward the pubes. When I exposed his bush and the base of his cock, his tube was bent over to the right and disappeared behind the denim. I ran my finger along the length of that column. It jumped to my touch and Ken tried to hump my hand but I rode with his hips. I touched the tip of his cock for the first time and felt the dampness which told me how much he was enjoying his job. Slowly I worked the pants over his butt and down his thighs, gradually uncovering more and more of his hard penis until it flipped up and slapped against his belly. His relief was obvious as he let out a loud sigh. I lightly ran my fingers along its underside and made him shudder.

I stepped back to look over my plaything from the rear as well as in the mirror. He was beautiful. His body was hard. His skin was smooth and almost hairless except for the trail down his lower belly, his crotch, his armpits, and a light dusting over his legs and forearms. I caressed his whole body, front and back. His naked buns were firm and high. His thighs were hard and muscular. His crack was hairless and steaming. His cock stood up at a 45-degree angle and must have been eight inches long. It was smooth and, fortunately, uncut with its purple head entirely out of its skin-collar.

I had Ken lie spread-eagle on his back with his hands behind his head while I undressed. He was a beautiful sight to behold. When I was naked I climbed onto the bed between his legs and took in the sight of this creature from the front. I leaned over and teased his nipples with my tongue. Before long Ken was humping his hard cock up against my chest, the gooey head gliding across my nips. I lowered myself down on him and ran my hands over his sides, armpits, and arms. I worked my mouth up his chest to his neck and ears. Again, I had him writhing. Meanwhile I was working my cock into his crotch and humping between his hard thighs.

Before things went too far I dropped my attention back to his dick. I wanted to play with his foreskin since I have been deprived of one. His cock was slimy with precum which was freely flowing from his slit. I began tonguing Ken's balls and the shaft of his dick. His smooth skin and strong man-scent were real turn-ons and his long, thick cock gave me plenty to enjoy. I pulled the sheath up over his glans and ran my tongue inside it. Everything was so lubricated that I had no trouble circling his cap. This drove him mad. Slowly I eased the casing back to expose its contents, then covering it up again pulled the wrapper tight over the cock head. Uncut men don't realize how lucky they are to have this extra toy.

While playing with his manhood with one hand, I tickled his ass crack with the other. This made him writhe even more. With some goo from his dickhead I lubed the hole and worked a finger in. As my rent boy rolled from side to side I found the button deep inside his rectum. The precum began dribbling down his shaft. His dick bobbed in my hand as I massaged its base from the inside.

I had the kid begging for release. My little friend was hot as fire and ready for a good strong ejaculation and I was ready to watch. I had him kneel, straddling my chest so his cock was right in front of my face for the best vantage. Starting with the root of his cock, behind the balls, I massaged his member with one hand as I finger fucked him with the other. I eased my hand up and kneaded his pole with the heel of my hand. Precum was flowing onto my neck. As soon as I grasped his whole hard-on he threw his head back, bellowed, and bucked into my hand, fucking my grip. He shot supercharged spurt after spurt into my shoulders, neck, and face. When it was over he collapsed onto his elbows, his belly just over my face, his softening dick lying down the side of my neck.

John Patrick

Now it was my turn. I was hard as I've ever been and ready to go but I wanted Ken to suffer one more little humiliation so I had him clean his cum off my body. He obviously didn't relish the idea but did as he was told. The sight of this little toughy licking up his own juice was as much of a turn-on as the feel of his tongue on my face and body. When he was finished I rolled us over so I was kneeling over Ken. I had him wet his hand and wrap it around my cock. I pumped into his grip like I was fucking a moist hole. It didn't take long before I was spewing myself onto this young thing's chest and face. I finished with the last of my strength and fell onto his hard torso. My spatterings made his sweaty chest even more slick. I lay still, catching my breath before slowly sliding off him, feeling as much of his body as I could before I had to give it up.

I dropped him back at the bar before going home to relive every detail of our hour together.

# Carnival Nights

## P. K. Warren

*Give me a boy whose face and hand
Are rough with dust and circus-sand
Whose ruddy flesh exhales the scent
Of health without embellishment;
Sweet to my sense is such a youth,
Whose charms have all the charm of truth.*
– Strato

Like many boys I ran away from home to join the circus. I never made it to The Greatest Show on Earth, but I did get to Sleeman's Traveling Carnival and Shows. Strictly second-rate, but I had to start somewhere. Besides, I liked the sleaziness of Sleeman's and I stayed with them for four years.

By the third week of October 1982, I'd been made a foreman and we were setting up the show on the outskirts of a small town in southern North Carolina. I was setting up the track for the kiddie roller coaster when I heard glass breaking behind me. Behind the game tents which faced the opposite midway a kid we'd hired from town as a temporary was setting up the equipment for one of the games which gave out stretched cola bottles filled with colored water as prizes. The kid had dropped a bunch of them and was bent over picking them up. My eyes became riveted on his small, hard ass threatening to split out the seam of his jeans.

As he stood up to toss the broken glass into a crate, the full view was impressive: shoulder length, straight-black hair, broad shoulders that tapered to a small waistline, a nice bulge at the crotch.

Suddenly the generators came on so I had to get back to work. I ran the coaster around its track a few times and then went out to make the proper adjustments for safety and function accuracy.

I had also noticed that the loud noise of the coaster while in motion had not so much as evoked a backward glance from the kid scrounging Coke bottles.

As I reached the extreme back of the ride, I was right on top of the kid. I stopped long enough to ask him if he would like a soda when I finished up with the coaster. He didn't respond, so I called to him a little louder. He still didn't respond.

Instead of yelling at him a third time I tossed a pebble at him, which struck his thigh. Well, I got the response I was seeking. But nothing could have prepared me for what came next.

John Patrick

He spun around, gave me a mean look, picked up a stone and threw it at me. I ducked as it traveled past my head and struck the track behind me with a loud clang. I was set on climbing over the fence to beat the tar out of the boy until I noticed him moving his hands around, pointing to his chest, his ears and then bringing his rough hands together in front of him, as if praying to me. I took it he was begging me to understand.

Now I wanted to kick myself for not realizing the logical reason for him not responding to the noise of the coaster, or my calling to him, because, he was a deaf mute.

The most I knew about sign was some rusty finger spelling from my days as a boy scout, but I did the best I could to convey that I was sorry, and had only wanted to ask him if he wanted a soda.

Walking up to the fence while rubbing his right fist over his chest and miming "Sorry," we shook hands. It was frustration from then on. I really wanted to talk with this kid in a normal tone of voice, but that was clearly impossible–to say the least. And he was becoming equally frustrated, because he was finger spelling too fast for me to keep up with him and had to slow down. Clearly, we were getting nowhere fast. I got my journal from on the deck of the coaster (by then I was in the practice of keeping it around to record my private thoughts). I wrote him a note, saying I wanted to buy him a soda. He nodded vigorously.

On my way to get sodas I warned myself against getting involved, yet he was such a beauty, I couldn't pass it up.

He looked to be Italian, with maybe some Indian thrown in, smooth clean features, hair parted in the middle, greenish-blue eyes. If it were not for the light dusting of hair over the upper lip and thick brows he would have made a beautiful girl. I was instantly in lust.

Returning with our sodas, I nearly dropped one when I saw him bent over the ovens used to heat the bottles and he stood up. He was shirtless. Except for a few strands poking out from under his arms and a thin line connecting his navel and the waist band of his jeans, he was hairless.

Giving him his soda, I pulled the journal from my back pocket and wrote that I had to get back to work and might see him later. He read it and nodded.

After a shower and joining the boss at the grub joint (food concession) for dinner, I went for a walk around the lot, checking on the security of the rides. My plans for the evening were to visit the hospitality tent for a few drinks. Now I wasn't sure what the evening held.

Walking up to the coaster I noticed someone sitting on the stairs in the dark. Drawing near, I saw it was the deaf kid. Finger spelling in the dark wasn't any easier than in daylight, but he had hung around waiting for me to show up so he could see me. His name was David. I told him mine–finger spelled it that is–and we shook hands.

I wrote another little note to him, asking him to follow me at a discreet distance. I would go into my trailer and, after waiting a few minutes, I would

let him in. He seemed to understand. He probably was not aware that the management did not permit the crew to fraternize with the locals we hired. It was done, of course, but you had to be careful. I had lost Jed, my trailer roommate, when they caught him screwing some slut while I was having dinner. He blamed me, of course, but it was the hysterical moans of the girl that brought on the attention. I would have been the last to turn him in. Just having him around got my juices flowing. I knew I could never let it be known I wanted him, but he knew and teased me, running around nearly naked in the trailer and sleeping in the nude. Truth was, I missed Jed more than I cared to admit.

On my way to my trailer, I squeezed my cock through the tight denim of my jeans. It wasn't just the sex, it was that I'd waited so long to be with someone, and I wanted so much to be with someone tonight. Tonight, for some reason, I felt more lonely than in a long while, and what made it worse was that I hated the idea that I did not know how to live with myself much longer. I might get fired for what I was about to do, but at that point I didn't care.

When I arrived at the trailer, I stripped off my clothes, lay down on the bed in the dark, and started masturbating. I worked up quite an erection before I heard a gentle rapping on the door of my trailer. David stepped inside. Seeing my erection, he smiled. He began pulling the shirttail from his jeans and I got up. I helped him undress and he stood before me nude, his cock gloriously arched to the ceiling. It was in perfect proportion to the rest of him: long, thick, with a large head.

I knew it was dangerous, but there was no turning back now. I took David in my arms. The first kiss was light, tentative, uncommitted. Then David arched his pelvis forward, and the pressure produced a sudden explosion of desire in me. I tightened my embrace and kissed fiercely, mashing my lips against David's, my tongue insistent, aggressive, leaving no room for ambiguity. David moaned under the attack, and he appeared to go limp. But I held him, supported him, kissed him again, and this time I dropped my hands to his cock and gripped it hard.

Nothing was rushed. No part of him was left unexplored. No sounds were made beyond sudden rushes of breath, though a million words were conveyed through sensual touch, caress and the movements of two bodies moving as one.

After a spirited sixty-nine, he went to the bathroom and I came behind him to stroke his buttocks. Then I bent and kissed them, licking into the groove, pulling the cheeks apart with my hands to get my tongue into the wet conch of his ass. I sucked him there, loving the smell of him, exciting myself as I pressed my nose against his asshole. My fingers found his cock, hard again, and I rubbed the swollen spike as my tongue foraged everywhere.

His head down, his feet almost off the floor, he started shuddering as he felt my cock slowly working into his wet ass.

I fucked him slow and easy for a few minutes before we moved to the bed. I hiked his legs over my shoulders as David lay on his back, and I dipped down to get my mouth on his sweet ass again. My cock had left his ass loose and warm, and I was able to get my tongue deep inside as he started moaning again.

I became wild with desire. Part of it was the danger of being caught. But mostly it was David, the way David looked, the way David turned me on. David's audacity and strength. The knowledge that with David there were no limits.

My moment of glory is to have a man shuddering, coming while I fuck him. I intended to get David so aroused, he would come without even touching his cock. I sucked some more on his asshole, my nose filled with the musky scent of my new lover. I sucked noisily, my tongue sinking deep into the tender crevice, darting like a pink lizard.

David sobbed, rubbing his thighs against the sides of my head, his legs bicycling in the air. I slid my hands up the front of the lad's body to grasp his glorious erection. I teased it, stroked it, as I entered him. He was so ready for it, my entire length went in him with one stroke. As I fucked I brought my mouth to his and we kissed each other all the way through it, through his orgasm and then mine.

This is all I want, I thought. There was no meaning to anything except this.

Finally we found sleep in each other's arms.

During the four remaining days the show was in town, we enjoyed each other using a language no one else could understand.

\* \* \* \* \*

I had written to David several times before returning home in late December. Waiting for me was a single letter from him. He wanted to let me know that after a big fight with his foster parents he had left town and was living with his real father in Florida. He wrote, "Dad say it ok you come here visit and stay for long time I go back to school and finish to reed right like my friend you come here soon. I love you. David."

Unfortunately, he neglected to put a return address on the envelope.

# All in a Night's Work

## *Jesse Monteagudo*

"Hibbert!" boomed a familiar voice that shocked me out of my reverie. Putting down my dog-eared copy of Blueboy magazine, I looked up to see my superior, Captain Floyd Bucket, literally fuming in front of my desk, with a folder in his hand and a cigar in his mouth. Before I could say anything, Bucket planted his fat ass on the chair across from my desk and grabbed my Blueboy.

"What are you doing reading this shit?"

"Hey, I'm just doing research!"

Bucket nodded; he seemed to believe me. After all, I was the man in charge of keeping the queers in line. Blueboy, like other gay mags, has informative articles about Fort Lauderdale's infamous "Boyzone" that could help me with my job.

"Jesus," muttered Bucket, leafing through the magazine. "Look, I need you to do more work and less reading! Mayor Hay's breathing down my neck for us to do something about the hustlers on the beach!"

I gave him a sidelong glance, a look of deep concern on my faintly handsome face, a ploy that worked back in college when dealing with straight guys whose girlfriends would not put out. I slid the magazine out of his hands and stuffed it in my desk drawer. "What else is new for Chris sakes?"

"Look, with all your fuckin' degrees in law enforcement, psychology and social work you were the ideal man to clean this up. At least that's what you said. Yeah, you said, 'Lay off the kids,' you said, 'let me do it my way.' So we laid off, and we let you try your new-age, nice-guy approach. Well, it's now 1977 and the boys are still coming down from all over, still hanging around the 'zone, doing drugs and selling their little perverted asses. In fact, there's more of 'em than ever! What the hell are you doin' about it?"

"Plenty," I said, as I leaned over the desk. The Captain had garlic for lunch, I coughed. "Things like this take time. If you go in there and arrest those boys, they are just going to lay low for a while and then go back on the streets. I deal with the kids on a one-to-one basis. I show them that there is more to life than drugs and hustling, and they get the message."

"Is that so? It didn't seem to work with David Shaw."

I cringed. David Shaw was a strapping teen, with a face and body reminiscent of Huck Finn on steroids. The 'zone's most notorious hustler, Shaw was the boy who was going to help me get his pals off the street. Shaw worked with me, but in more ways than I expected. Some of my best quality time was spent on my knees, sucking David's large, uncircumcised cock; or

on my back, receiving David's thick prick inside my firm, round ass. My rear twitched in its seat as I recalled such good times.

"I thought Shaw left town?"

"He did. But he didn't take the other kids with him, as you and he said he would. And now that the Mayor is trying to get re-elected on a family values platform, the last thing he wants to deal with is a bunch of boy whores on the beach! Either you do something about it or we send the vice squad in after them!"

"Don't do that! If you have the vice squad go in there like gangbusters, arresting every boy and john in the place, it would only make things worse. It would destroy all the goodwill and trust that I developed with those boys over the past six months. The kids like me and I like them, and I have the satisfaction of helping boys go straight." All except David Shaw. "Just give me some time and I assure you those boys will go home."

"That's all good and dandy," cried Bucket, as he spit tobacco juice in my direction. "But we don't have time. Mayor Hay won't allow it. Even worse, Reverend Johnson of Happiness Tabernacle is getting into the act. Have you seen Johnson's television show?"

"I don't watch television." Not with so many boys around.

"Well, you should. His show is called 'Reverend Johnson's Happiness Revival.' Though it's mainly a religious program, it has political overtones. Lately Johnson has started a crusade against homosexuality, with the 'zone as Exhibit Number One. In his words, 'we must destroy them before they destroy us.'"

That's all we need. It's bad enough that the mayor is trying to use the hustler issue to get re-elected. Now we have a publicity-seeking preacher to deal with. And Johnson is not alone. It's only a matter of time before the Baptists and the Catholics and the Mormons get wind of the matter, and join Johnson on a crusade similar to the one Anita Bryant started in Miami. "It looks bad, Chief."

"That's not the worst of it. As it turns out, some of your kids are not satisfied with selling drugs or turning tricks. They are forming gangs and attacking innocent civilians."

This was too much. I know those boys. Most of the time, they are too stoned to get up in the morning, much less join a gang and attack the natives. Besides, those kids wouldn't hurt a fly. If Bucket wanted to tackle youth gangs, he should lay off the hustlers, who are mostly gay or confused, and go after the straight dudes, who beat up queers or rob the banks downtown and the fancy homes up the boulevard. "This is serious. Do you have any proof?"

"I sure do. According to Mrs. Sheila Adams, she and her daughter were walking over from the Beach to their car when they were attacked by two boys, a Latino and an Oriental, who stole their purses and scared them to death. And they are not the only reported victims. Apparently these two kids are hustlers who rob people during the off hours, for kicks and for money."

"Do you know who they are?

"Yeah, I do," said Bucket, as he pulled two photos out of his folder. "Carlos Mendoza and Charley Lui. Both 18 and have worked together as a team since they dropped out of high school a couple of years ago. They live in the dump behind the 'zone in an apartment that's owned by a fag who gets to swing on their little dicks in return for room and board. Nice, eh?"

I looked at the photos. Nice indeed. Carlos and Charley were really cute. Though both boys had long, black hair that flowed down their shoulders, they were different enough to complement each other. Carlos had a powerful nose, sensuous lips and a slight, dark mustache. Charley, on the other hand, had soft features and was clean-shaven. These boys could get top dollar for their services, if their bodies are anything like their faces. Why would they need to steal purses? "What do you want me to do?"

"I want you to arrest these pieces of shit! This goes beyond your social work crap. I have a warrant for you." Bucket handed me the folder, in which I found an arrest warrant. "And I want you to use it."

I had no choice. Either I get Carlos and Charley off the streets or Bucket kicks my ass out of the force. But one thing was clear. I was going to do this my way. "I'll do it, Captain. But I'm going in there alone. No partner, backup or reinforcement."

"Now don't go risking your life. Those punks are dangerous! I think Officer Lara should go in with you."

"No way! Gil Lara hates queers, and his trigger finger is always itching to shoot one. The last thing I need is for an arrest to turn into a shootout. Just let me handle this by myself. I'll go in there, have a nice talk with them, and bring them over for questioning. You might be pleasantly surprised." I could tell the Captain was skeptical, but as usual he let me have my way.

"Very well, Hibbert. But I want you to go in uniform. And I order you to carry a gun and a nightstick. You might have to beat some sense into those boys!" Swell. That's all I needed. Bucket wanted me to show up in uniform, with gun and nightstick in hand, and march Carlos and Charley off to the pokey. But then, he is giving me plenty of leeway, so I had to compromise.

"Alright, you win! I'll take my uniform out of mothballs and wear it tonight. The same thing goes for my gun and my stick." I rolled my eyes, just to show my frustration.

"And take your walkie-talkie with you. In case anything happens, Lara will be right down the street. He will rush right in and get you out of trouble."

I gave him a doubtful look. "Anything else?"

"Just bring those two in! Even if they're not purse snatchers, I still want 'em off the streets. Enough of your nice guy approach."

"Yes, sir!", I said, standing in mock salute. "But now you must excuse me. I must get ready."

"Now don't forget what I told you, Hibbert," yelled Bucket, as I walked out the door. "You bring those boys back here no matter what. Or else." But it was too late, for I was already nearly out the door .

John Patrick
* * * * *

I arrived at the boys' apartment alone, having left Lara at the 'zone. There were plenty of boys around for him to do his tough guy routine on, which should keep him out of the way while I had a good talk with Carlos and Charley. The door was unlocked, so I let myself in. Bucket was right. The place was a dump.

I looked around. The apartment was barely functional, a one-room efficiency with a small card table, chairs, a dresser, a mirror, and an unkempt bed, with a closet and bathroom on the side. The bed was unmade, and there were clothes and junk all over the place. The air conditioner was broken, which explained both the heat and the pungent odor that surrounded the room. Brushing the sweat off my brow, I looked inside the closet, only to find more junk. I was so intent on my search that I did not hear the front door close behind me.

Suddenly, I was seized by a pair of muscular arms, which grabbed my hands and held them firmly behind my back. Though I struggled vigorously, I could not free myself. While my assailant held me in his grip, his partner went through my uniform pant pockets, removing my walkie-talkie, handcuffs, nightstick and gun. With one quick move he slipped the cuffs around my wrists, locking them securely in place. I was handcuffed, and helpless.

"You thought you would get us," said a voice behind me, as he turned me around. "Now we got you."

Expecting to see a pair of silly little boys, my mouth dropped at the sight of two magnificent specimens of young manhood. Carlos Mendoza and Charley Lui were both shirtless, with sweat dripping down their swarthy, muscular bodies and over tight, cutoff shorts that barely concealed their bulging baskets. Carlos, the one who grabbed me, was tall and husky, like a wrestler, and Charley was short and trim, with an Olympic gymnast's built. Each boy was a perfect embodiment of Latino or Asian youth at the height of his animal beauty and sex. Together, they were every queer's dream.

"You like what you see, uh?" smirked Carlos, as he caught me staring at his crotch.

I glared at him. Yes, I was interested. Yes, I liked it. But I wasn't ready to admit it.

Still, with a nod from Carlos, he and Charley took off their shorts, revealing two of the most perfect sets of genitals I'd ever seen. Both boys had big, uncircumcised cocks and full, low-hanging balls. The only difference was in the details: while Carlos's peter was thick and meaty, Charley's prick was long and lean. Both boy cocks stood up in full attention, pointing in my direction.

"You like cock, don't you, faggot?"

I said nothing. I wasn't ready even now to admit how tantalizing they were.

"Okay, let's see you do something about it."

- 198 -

"Hey Carlos, the fag likes it," laughed Charley, hearing my moans. "His pussy's all wet!" It was clear to me that Charley was not satisfied with holding me down, but wanted to take part in the act.

Before I knew it, he took my head in his strong hands and shoved his lengthy sausage inside my mouth, fucking my face with a force that matched his buddy's violent ass fucking. Carlos began to work my nipples through my shirt, driving me to a still-higher level of sexual bliss.

Time stood still for us, three young men in the throes of violent man sex. I ceased being a cop and became a sex object for two young savages. Sweat dripped down my shirt as my two studs drove their manhood inside me. The power of their cocks inside my mouth and ass, Carlos's rough tit play, and my own hard dick rubbing against the card table, drove me to an erotic state beyond my wildest dreams. We were three young animals, oblivious to all but the force of our maleness. It was only a matter of time before we would all reach the point of no return.

"I'm gonna cum, Man! Shiiiiit!", Carlos yelled, as he shot his cream deep inside my ass. At the same time, Charley grabbed my head with his hands and shoved his cock down my throat, feeding me gallons of his young man milk. As Charley pulled his dick out of my mouth, Carlos lifted me off of the card table and took hold of my own throbbing cock, pumping me to orgasm. I screamed as my sperm shot out of my restless prick. I collapsed into Carlos's arms, totally spent.

"Hey, Man, you were great!", said Carlos, as he and Charley unlocked my cuffs. "We've had some wild tricks in our time, but you were the best!" We smiled. It was the best sex I ever had. The only thing better than a hot teenager are two teenagers.

I finally had to admit to them they had been the best for me too. And to prove it, I told them I'd give them a chance. "Now here's what I want you to do," I said, as I pulled up my pants. "You're going to get out of here, and I am going to call Officer Lara and tell him that you knocked me out and ran away. You are going to have to lay low for awhile, at least till after the election. Okay?"

"Sure, man. Anything you say. But we want some more of this sometime." He squeezed my ass cheeks.

"Okay. We'll work it out." Little did they know that after what had just taken place, I wanted that even more than they did. "But for now, you'd better get the hell outta here."

"You know, you're not a bad guy–for a cop," said Charley, as he and Carlos walked out the door. "Are there any more like you?"

"Nah, I'm one of a kind. But that's why I enjoy my job. To me, this is all in a night's work."

# A Rocky Road

## *Edward Bangor*

I was doing the Time warp when I first met Chris. I'd just taken the "Jump To The Left" and was about to take a "Step To The Right" when I sent him staggering sideways with a squashed foot.

The Duke of York's Theatre in the back streets of London's West End was fairly packed for a Thursday. Not that I was surprised for it was the one day of the week on which half-price tickets were offered in the stalls. It was my fifth visit to "The Rocky Horror Show," and my third for this year's run starring the former Olympic Gold Medalist ice skater Robin Cousins as Frank N Furter. From the third row back from the five foot stage I was sure I would be able to answer the one question that had bugged my previous visits. Did Robin Cousins have something down the front of his knickers that shouldn't be there? For despite his athlete's legs showing more than one encounter with a razor sharp ice skate, Robin's black and extremely brief briefs jutted forward a more than impressive bulge that had to be more than his microphone battery pack.

I hadn't intended to go to the show alone. My sister had introduced me to Richard O'Brian's rocked-up musical when I was still an impressionable teenager and I had planned to do the same for Ben. Young Ben Philips, the apprentice steel erector on my building site, was a virgin. Unfortunately I only knew that to mean he hadn't been to this show before but, I reckoned, if I could lure the teen away from his studies of erecting I'd find out how much of a virgin he really was. After all I'd caught him watching me work shirtless often enough to have an idea where his interests lay. Now I only had to confirm it and his having expressed an interest in rock music and never having seen a London show I thought that this, the queerest of musicals would tell me what I wanted to know.

But, alas, the best laid plans of mice and queers don't always work and Ben returned to his home town of Bournemouth the previous Tuesday, having run out of steel–and a steel erector without steel is about as much use as a boy with no dick. At least Ben didn't have that trouble, as I knew from the time the father and son team of Neil and Reace with whom he worked de-bagged him and swung him naked from the crane as part of his Rights of Indenture! Not big, but terribly responsive, springing a stiffy when rubbed in grease before taking a 300 foot flight across London. Ben was perfectly formed in every place that mattered on a boy, especially at the back, with a perfect spanking bum that I'd love to lay my hands on, and I would, too. It was only a matter of time.

Anyway, so there I was, the aisle seat on the right hand end of row 'C' with a sorrowfully empty seat to my left and nothing but narrow passageway

and a wall to my right. Having decided to make the most of Ben's absence I went for it in the sort of fashion a gay man could only get away with at "The Rocky Horror Show": I shouted out the well-known ad-libs; called 'Brad' an arse-hole and 'Janet' a slag; had several exchanges with game-show host Nicholas Parsons, who played 'The Narrator' for a second year; squirted water, waved a lighter and wore a newspaper umbrella during "There's A Light"; and, naturally, was the first on my feet to Time warp, not that those around me were slow to follow. I was just the keenest. All my frustrated attempts to seduce Ben Philips poured into my pelvic trusts that I hoped would drive him insane. My hands clapped rapidly through Colombia's tap-dance interlude and then, during the following chorus it happened. My size ten industrial safety boot with its steel toe-cap and sole plate came down with a crunch on somebody's foot.

"Sorry mate!" I yelled over the music blasting from stage side speakers not six feet from my head without turning. Moments later, having only taken the slightest interest in the damage I'd done I was back clapping my hands to the recorded kick drum beat that signaled Frank N. Furter's impending appearance at the top of the on-stage balcony.

It wasn't until "Hot Patootie–Bless My Soul" that I finally checked no real damage had been done by my attending the theatre direct from work and, fuck me, wasn't I missing something! While I'd joined the old queens in the audience staring at the well-formed body of Tony What's-his-name (the former singer of BAD BOYS INC pop group playing the title role this year) I could have watched my own fantasy not more than a couple of feet away.

Unfortunately one of his feet appeared to be a little sore from the fourteen stone builder that had landed on it, but other than that he was a legal perfection. Mind you he looked to be about fifteen or sixteen but had to be over the newly reduced age of consent for he wore a shirt that proclaimed him as "Duke Of York: Staff." Shit if I hadn't stomped the foot of an usher employed to keep the likes of me from going completely over the top. Usually, these people are uglier than sin with a temper to match but this one sure wasn't. As tall as my five-foot-ten frame but roughly half my bulk he wore his thinness extremely well. His jeans were baggy down his legs and at the front but tight enough in the rear to cling to one of the nicest bums on the planet–barring that of young Ben Philips. Of course I didn't see his bum first, just his face but it was enough. As I said, hardly looking old enough to shave yet this boy had the one thing that was always my weak spot: a bum-fluff moustache. That did it, I had to get to know him better. A lot better.

Thankfully the half time interval stopped me from having to think up too difficult a plan. The gods must have been with me that night for after I stood from extracting my money from the torn denim jacket that had been my constant companion since my thirteenth birthday there he was, asking me if I wanted to "buy one."

"One what?" I asked looking for something at his groin and thinking I couldn't be that lucky. I wasn't.

He shoved a pile of thin full color magazines stuffed with photographs from the 1994 production under my nose, "Programme."

"Oh, right. I got one already." said I, slipping onto the folding seat so my size wouldn't intimidate him. Then I asked what has to have been one of the most stupidly obvious questions in history. "You work here then?"

"Yeah, for the summer."

"Then what?"

"University."

"A clever one, eh!" I laughed, knowing he had to be eighteen, even if he didn't look it. My favoured sort. Ben Philips could pass for twelve, believe it or not, assuming he was dressed right and kept his hairy chicken legs covered. Above the waist there wasn't a hair on him but for under his arms and that was as sparse as the bum-fluff under his nose.

"No," my programme seller joked back, "Lazy. Anything has to be better than working for a living."

I couldn't argue with that, so I didn't. Instead I turned the conversation back into a more interesting direction. Him. "Do you enjoy it here?" I asked, purposely nodding his attention towards two elderly queens busy tickling each other's tonsils in the front row.

My new friend stared for a couple of moments and then, to my delight, replied, "It has its moments."

"I bet."

"Still, I could do with a job for the daytime as well."

"Why, don't you get enough of a work out at night?"

He smiled somewhat shyly at my sarcastic sense of humour and looked around at the other attendants plying their wares amongst those who couldn't, or wouldn't, face the crush around the theatre's two bars. "I'd better get back to work."

"No rest for the wicked, eh?"

He blushed. "Something like that."

"See you later then ..."

"Chris," he offered.

"Eddie," I returned. "See you around, Chris?"

"Sure Eddie. I'll be back." Chris turned and returned to hawking his wares, bending over the seats to peer at the six- foot, shirtless and extremely camp, but straight, squadie who was showing his Rocky Horror tattoos to any one who'd look. That's when I saw Chris' back-side for the first time and decided Ben Philips could wait just a little while longer to sample my charms. This Chris had suddenly achieved pole position and a pole is just what that taut trim bum of his had given my jeans.

I couldn't concentrate on the show after that. During the various sex scenes between Frank & Brad, Frank & Janet, and Janet & Rocky, Chris and I constantly exchanged glances across the audience that showed good signs

for the future. Nicholas Parsons looked disappointingly at me several times because I was no longer shouting out his cues for his allegedly spontaneous put-downs. It was only during the encore that my natural fun-loving self came back on line. With Frank risen from the dead and the entire cast hovering on the stage parapet urging the balcony up onto their feet as we were down in the stalls Chris appeared, as if by magic, at my side. But as the reprised Time warp begun Chris remained strangely stationary.

"Come on!" I shouted as his foot withdraw from my jumping left. "If you danced I wouldn't hit you."

"I can't," he yelled.

"Nonsense. Anyone can do this and even if you can't, it don't matter none." I indicated those around us who clearly didn't know the movements but were trying their best and enjoying themselves for it.

He shook his mousy coloured bushy hair. "I mean I'm not allowed." He pointed to his shirt. "I'm staff."

"Soon fix that." I whispered purposely so he wouldn't be able to hear. Facing him I yanked the offending shirt up over his head and sent it on a short trip towards the stage where the peroxide blonde 'Rocky' caught it and used it to rub his crutch and crack much to the delight of the Queens–and one out-of-place teenage girl–who were all hungry for a taste of his pop-star cock. I wasn't one of them, for now I was faced with the sort of chest I'd happily die for. Shit, I'd even vote Tory for a bit of this. As flat as an ironing board and completely clear of hair, Chris's chest was everything Ben's also was. Perfect. From the duel rings of tight flesh that circumnavigate their belly buttons to the two pence pieces that were their nipples. An inch across, the colour of dirty copper plated coins, with a tiny raised central piece that stared right on back to me.

"STOP EYEING UP YOUR BOYFRIEND AND DANCE, MOTHER-FUCKER!"

Robin Cousin's words boomed out of the speakers directly at me. It was an opportunity I couldn't miss. Without turning from Chris's blushing face I raised my right arm as high as it would go, balled my fist and extended my middle finger which I pointed at the lighting rig above the stage. I winked suggestively at Chris while the crowd watched us laughed, and said "Want to make them jealous?"

Chris glanced about the auditorium nervously but nodded.

The Duke of York's was nearly completely silent as I kissed the delightful boy and Chris melted into my arms. The computer controlled music stuttered on the final chorus, then died. Hands started to clap. The assembled queens and Rocky Horror Fan Club members counting the seconds Chris and I stayed attached by the lips. This was soon joined by feet stamping the stage as the tempo increased. Nicholas Parsons made a joke about my being an out-of-work dentist checking for fillings but, for once, didn't get a laugh. It surprised me but Chris was quite an accomplished kisser and the less said about what his hands were doing in such a public

place the better. Needless to say, the hardest thing–sorry, better make that the second hardest thing–in that theatre was when I broke the embrace. Turning to the stage I caught the eye-line of the ex-sports star called a life-long bachelor by the London Evening Standard and yelled over the applause, "Hey, Frank!"

"Yes, darling." Robin Cousin answered in his impression of Tim Curry's voice as the original–and best–Frank N' Furter.

"It's just a jump to the left."

He replied automatically, "And then a step to the right."

"With your hands on your hips."

Robin's somewhat knobbly legs jerked together as he recited the next line, "You bring your knees in tight."

"But," I turned to Chris. "It's the pelvic thrust, that really drives them insane."

"Let's," Frank/Robin shouted.

"Do." I joined with him as he looked around for support.

"THE." shouted the cast.

"TIME WARP AGAIN!" yelled all, or nearly all, the capacity crowd. Somewhere up the back of the auditorium the Sound Engineer flicked a switch that triggered the music and we were off.

The unusual second encore of "The Rocky Horror Show" really is something that has to be experienced rather than written about. I hadn't seen the crowd and cast go for it like that night since the final show of the 1994 season when Richard O'Brian himself got up on stage and led us through the highlights of the show he wrote twenty-two years previously at the height of the seventies glam rock revolution. That show over-ran for nearly an hour, this for only half that but it really was something else. You really had to be there, you really did.

We continued to dance as the house lights came up and that night's fifties rock 'n' roll classic signaled the end of the show. Then, at the end of it Chris collapsed into my arms and we hugged and rubbed swollen crutches. My legs gave way a short while later, which wasn't surprising as I'd been up since five thirty that morning, landing us into my seat with Chris on my lap.

"You going home now?" he asked me as we became alone.

"No," I answered truthfully. His face fell. I patted his thin leg, almost able to close my hand all the way around his thigh. "But you can still come with me if you want."

He looked puzzled in a cute, little boy, sort of way with his head neatly cocked to one side and his nose wrinkled above that almost moustache of his. Quickly I explained how I would be returning to my building site and staying the night there in the caravan Neil, Reace and Ben used to prevent them having to travel up and down the M3 and across London every day.

"I've never slept in a caravan." Chris said, "What's it like?"

"Basic," I told him.

He squirmed on my lap moving my hardness into the gap between his buttocks." How many beds?"

"Just one." I lied I didn't think he'd mind given the way he teased my dick.

"That's okay then. I'll just get my shirt."

"Don't bother." I gave him my jacket, "Wear this."

He put it on and looked so erotic shirtless in my oversized denim jacket as we traveled on the Piccadilly tube line out of London it was all I could do not to fuck him between stations, but I didn't. Later we made the caravan rock and little Ben's sheets so sticky they became uncomfortable to sleep on. Not that we slept.

The following Monday Chris started on the site as 'General Labourer' under me, in more ways than one. From then on the plan was short and simple. Chris seduced the more than willing Ben and I 'caught' them naked and at it. It was after the punishment spanking had been administered to both sets of cute boy buns that I finally proved young Ben could erect more than steel, although what he did erect had many of the properties of steel. But that, as they say, is another story.

# Diamond Stud Puppy

## *Dan Veen*

"The worst kinds of one-night-stands," my buddy Max was telling me during Happy Hour at The Leather Rose, "are the ones that are more suck than fuck, and more sock than cock."

(The Leather Rose is what Max sarcastically calls a Meaningful Relationship Bar.)

Max went on, "Whatever happened to the good days when you hardly knew the guy fucking you unless you looked over your shoulder?"

I said, "Things change. I guess people are looking for more romance in their pants."

"Uh-huh," he snorted. "Go home with any of these guys and he'll expect breakfast in bed. And before you know it, you'll be watching his boxer shorts spin-dry at the Kwick Kleen. Talk about static cling. I tell you, all the mystery has gone."

Now I was fed up with Max: "Then what the fuck are you complaining for? Why don't you just put a revolving door in your bedroom and leave your phone number at the baths? Max, you're full of it. The only reason you're a faggot is so you can be a pain in the ass!"

I stomped out.

Outside, I was deciding which one of my former tricks I was still friends with when a man I didn't know from Adam came up and started coming on to me. He wore a chauffeur's uniform. He had on reflective sunglasses even though it was night. He said he'd eavesdropped on me in the bar. He said he liked my style. "Thanks, but I'm not into uniforms," I said. "It's not me."

He handed me a card.

"It's not me who is interested. My employer ..."

MUSCLES RESPLENDENT
AEROBICS/SPA/GYM/WEIGHT MACHINES

"Is this anything like free dance lessons?" I asked.

"Not in the least." The chauffeur didn't smile a crack. "Muscles Resplendent is his name. Legally changed for commercial purposes. It is the business he owns. I sense that 'M.R.' would enjoy meeting you. Are you free at 7:00 tomorrow?" I had so hoped for spear fishing in Bermuda with tall Grecian teenagers, but since that was unlikely, I played along and I told this chauffeur guy sure, I'd be free.

Next evening this honest-to-god limo picks me up in front of my duplex. I was ready for anything now. I had to be. Chauffeur kept mum. Not a word the entire ride down the back roads behind the Shrub Curtain of Suburbia. I

had told Max about my mysterious rendezvous with Muscles Resplendent. "Are you stupid?" Max sputtered, "What kind of name is that? They'll probably gang up on you and take all your clothes off and throw you in a hole and turn the hose on you and laugh at you and point." Max sneered. "Hey, don't be stupid! Are you stupid?" But something told me go. A hunch said take a chance. Risk it. For once.

So we arrive at this ... place. A palace. Actually it's an estate. A palatial estate place. Something right out of a ritzy TV mini-series: circular driveway, cascading fountain splashing Olympian statues, peacocks, real flamingos tiptoeing across a golf-course lawn, a mansion that'd make a Rockefeller green with envy and, finally–silhouetted in the portico–a figure with all the attributes of a sleek thoroughbred stallion. Only so very much a young man.

Believe me, this boy's physique is an estate in itself. It makes his name an understatement. Muscles not only Resplendent but Muscles downright Large, Abundant, Mountainous–a royal banquet of beefcake swelling super-tight black Faure corduroys. A gold chainlet glints beneath his Respecchi shirt. One small diamond stud earring flickers in his ear. Approaching, I see his nostrils flare a welcome–anticipant. In some nobler era this young man might've been a dashing count or a swashbuckling prince, but in 20th century U.S.A. he is your basic hunky Rich Kid.

Chauffeur makes intros. I say hello. MR smiles hi. Emerald eyes blink at me almost bashfully. With a claiming gesture MR glides me through the marbled hallway, past the drawing room into the parlor where we stand on a plush white fur rug before a fireplace.

"My chauffeur is a great judge of character," M.R. begins, looking me over. "He says you'll be perfect for my needs." We admire each other in the mirror over the mantelpiece. Gold ornaments and silence and incense envelope us. "Of course, he's never done this kind of thing before. And I haven't either." Here in the firelight I can see his face really good. He is exactly twenty. I can always tell. Poised between virginity and virility, twenty year-olds always have that fresh-from-puberty look, skin clearing, body ripening, hormones a pumping: on the threshold of the voluptuous decade.

"You can call me Mister," he dimples gently. "What friends I've got call me that." New black velvet stubbles his jaw, circles a wet red little mouth. His cheeks show blue blood beneath enamel white skin. But his body, of course, is Mister's overwhelming asset.

"It's good to meet you." Mister eyes me down and up gratefully. "I just hope all this ... stuff isn't too intimidating. I'm rich and, frankly, I don't know why I should hide it. My parents made a fortune in health clubs. I grew up smothered in developing muscle. Of course, I took advantage of all those free memberships."

I couldn't agree more. His body has to be the finest piece of human equipment I ever set eyes on–a masterpiece of genetic engineering and a

Nautilus bench press. My own body, however, feels uncomfortably inadequate in Mister's superior presence. (I'm your average, but only average, Adonis.)

"I've traveled all over the world, won what contests I could. Bought my own home. I've seen armies of narcissistic men strutting in their world of abs and pecs."

Maybe, I'm thinking, maybe an average Adonis guy like me looks kinda fresh–even exotic–to a kid who's spent his whole childhood surrounded by genetically-enhanced steroid supermen. He talks and my eyes caress his chest of sinuous perfection. His ass is prime sirloin. And his crotch–well, it has a life of its own. His crotch shows and roils with minute, flickering, optically tricky movements in the firelight. It breathes with individual yet collective electric busy-ness, like an ant-farm.

"Now I'm feeling like settling down to run the family business. If I can find someone with a good business sense. It's a fun, pleasant life but ... I ... get..shy." Shy? This cutie with an ass of two round squeezable sculpted muscles?–a tempting crease right down the middle with matching dimples on each side?–and this crotch, a handful–or mouthful–of hefty meat–shy? Impossible to keep my eyes off that black corduroy crotch of his. I want to tell him, Just lay back and let me take it, kid, you don't need to do a thing, just dribble my head like a basketball all over your big, fat kid-prick.

My own eight-incher gets hard to handle. Obvious as hell, too. I'm ready for anything this young stud has to offer.

Except for what he says next: "I don't know how to–what to–I mean," his shrug wins my heart, "This is my first time." He looks at me like a hungry puppy. His first time. I stand for a second stunned. This millionaire stud puppy is a virgin?

"I'm not sure just how." Mister pouts, stroking at my denim fly. "All I know is I want to do it. With a guy. I've got to get some fucking. With a man. Sure I've seen pictures and read stories. But it's always different from the way it is in those movies, isn't it?"

"Yes," I said. "Always."

"Will you show me what to do?" He checks out my crotch. "My dick is nine inches long. That's okay, isn't it?"

I chuckle. "Sure it's okay."

"I was afraid it might be too long, or something."

"No, it'll do." I assure him, my own cock and balls rearing up at the very Platonic ideal of nine-inches of perfect boy cock on this perfect boy male. "Why don't you let me see it? Take your cock out and let me see you play with it. Go ahead. It's okay."

Mister smiles shyly, but peels away his pants. Black corduroy gives way to firm white haunches. His pink and white cupcake bottom makes me hornier than ever. His cock is a luxuriant exotic fruit, succulent in its banana-creamy length. It looks new. He starts jerking his ample cock automatically

back and forth, as if that is the first thing to do with a cock hanging out of your pants–and looks to me for approval.

"Yeah, you're good and ready to use that meat of yours," I grunt. I shuck my own jeans. He stops frigging when he sees my meat fall out. I grab hard at my cock: "You like this, huh?" Open-mouthed, he starts frigging his cock meat like a fucking accordion. Oh, he likes it alright. He likes looking at another guy's real live cock. I tease him a little to heat him up. He wants to be talked dirty to. "You like jerking that tool of yours?" He groans. He jerks faster. "Do you? Do you like to beat your meat?"

"Ye-ah ..."

"Yeah? What do you think about when you jerk that cock of yours?"

"Guys." His balls are flying with his strokes. "Hot-looking guys like you."

"What about my cock?" I get into it. I get into teasing him. "What would you like to do with my cock?"

"I ..." he hesitates.

"Yeah?"

"I want to lick it. And suck on it."

"Then suck it, kid. Get down on your knees. That's it. Take it slow." He falls at my feet he's so anxious to get at an honest-to-god throbbing cum-drooling cock. "Choke on it," I watch him gobble. Slobber drools out his mouth. "Easy. We've got all night. Watch the teeth." His stubbly virgin mouth on my cock feels damn good, he smooches it up and down, tongues my sweet sweat off my balls, serenading me with his slurpings. "That's good. Real good. Move your tongue all around it, cocksucker. Play with it, kid. Lick it like a good little sucker." My dick pops its head full into his hot mouth hole. His tongue flicks my stiff-swollen cock shaft, slurping like he wants some more. I give him more, slam my balls smack up to his prickly chin.

"Now you've got a throatful of my cock–" I look down at his receptive penetrated face. "Just relax ... swallowing the whole thing, put me all the way down your throat."

He deep-throats the tip, eagerly savoring the flavor of his very first prick. His tickling tonsils open full out. His face is flush into my crotch.

"You're getting the hang of it. Work it up and down with your mouth."

That instinctive tongue slathers my rod good. His eyes widen when my cock hardens in the confines of his throat. But his head keeps bobbing my crotch while I hold his ears. He gargles my pre-cum with wet slurping noises and I flex my cock and plug it in still further. He gags for a second, but my hard hot cock is exactly where this rich bitch wants it. "You like the way that cock tastes? You like getting your face fucked, don't you?" The muddy sounds of his throat burble with pleasure. Since this virgin hunk doesn't know what to do, he tries everything–and then some. He discovers some quick eager strokes at the very tip of my meat that rockets me right out of my foreskin. I reach down, paw at his pinprick pecs and pinch both those hard

titty buttons till he moans. Good and loud. He tugs back at my ball sacs. His index finger scrapes that inseam of flesh between my cock and ass, then works its way up into my butt. He sticks it up me, and that does the trick. "Get a load of my cum you cum sucking cocksucker!" Bolts of my cream hose down this baby's throat. First cum he's ever tasted from another man's cock.

He gasps like he's getting scalded by my sizzling wads, as he samples my juice. My cum stuff fills his cheeks. He swallows the warm mouthful I shoot him like a real cock sucking pro.

"First time anybody's called me a cocksucker." He gasps, cum dripping from his chin.

I rub my stuff into his face with my rubbery dick. "Well, cocksucker, that's what you are now. You're going to be one helluva blowjob expert. You really make a guy cream. You're a natural, kid."

"Thanks!" Mister wipes his mouth over my balls. "I practice on myself."

But his lesson isn't over by a long shot. "Lean back and stick your cock in the air," I instruct him. "I'll show you the best way for a beginner to fuck ass."

"Like this?" He props himself back on his elbows. His randy cock waves high before me. I grab his metronoming prick. I arch over it. I lower my butt hole to meet his meat, fixing my ass to ride this buck. He has waited twenty years for this fuck. I ease down on it, stopping my ass halfway down his pole to squeeze it and let him get a feel of his very first piece of ass, my ass. He likes that so much he tries to push it up. But I'm not having any of that. This is my show. I'm initiating this virgin boy my way.

With a few extra pulsing squeezes I sink further down his cock, feel it hit bottom, his pubic hairs sponging my ass ring. His balls and the fur carpet tickle my stuffed ass crack. Ah! Nine full fucking inches of fresh virgin boy-dick just hits the spot. My own dick hardens up again, so I grab him tight and rub away, grinding our hips together like horny Siamese twins. More of my cum is reaching the boiling point fast. We both cook spunk. His dick flicks around inside my guts like a cat 'o nine tails, so I wrap my legs around and hang on.

"My dick's gonna bust your ass!" he gyrates and humps helplessly.

"No pain, no gain." I hump back. I ram down hard on his cock, determined to make this virile virgin cum like he's never cum before. This first fuck will be the fuck of a lifetime -

"I'm–I've never–I–gonna–" He was giving me the ol' Yankee yawn now, cracking ecstatic, "Cuu-uum!"

"Cum in me kid! Cum! Cum in my ass!" I hiss in his diamond-studded ear. My shooting cum smears across his rippling abs–all over the fucking place. "Bring it home! You've got one helluva dick! Use that cock on me!"

And for the first time he cums up someone's ass, right up my butt, bucking me up in the air. I ride that ass-ripping saddle till his cock pumps its last spurt. We both collapse. I sprawl on top. I listen to him breathe relief.

His heart beats. By midnight we've made it to his bedroom, and by that time he's gotten his hard-on up a half dozen times. It seems bigger than ever now that we've both given it a good stretching. His bedroom is lined with expensive gym equipment. Mirrors face both sides of his bed. "I like to watch myself work out." He explains while our tongues knot themselves.

"Me too," I say, biting his nape. "

I used to jerk-off by the gallon in here, working up a load just looking at myself in the mirrors. Sometimes I'd shoot all the way across the room." I pin him down, roll him over. I feel him excited again. It's a turn-on just watching me get ready to fuck this muscular young hunk in the mirrors. Mirrors are arranged so the reflections reflect reflections.

What you see in the mirrors are row after row of two guys fucking each other ad infinitum. Dozens of horny bodies seem to be screwing in unison. I picture my dick shoving his ass with a thousand other dicks in the mirrors shoving a thousand other hungry virgin assholes.

How many other eager innocents would be losing their cherries this very night?

When I hoist his legs over my shoulders, a thousand pairs of legs kick up in the mirrors like a chorus line. I grab a bottle of hair oil to lube up this juicy kid's chute to be sure this chicken feels loose and easy for his premier butt fucking. It's a squirt bottle, so I squirt him a dose of the stuff into his upturned slot, then squirm my finger into his butt hole, slowly sending it up to the knuckle as his anal passage loosens for my fucking.

Like a helpless animal, he looks down anxiously at what I'm doing to his invaded ass.

"It'll start feeling great in a minute or two," I lie, winking up at him. It's not like in the movies. It'll hurt for a day or two after. "This finger fuck I'm giving you is just a warm-up for my cock."

"Oh yeah," he mumbles.

I give his ass a poke or two to make sure he wasn't getting too comfortable.

"I don't think I can take it all in me!" He yelps and starts to whimper into his pillow. Gasping like a hooked fish, he looks down at my prick poised to fuck his ass.

"Sure you can," and with that I uncork my fingers from his gaping little asshole and plug it with my eight-incher before it has a chance to squeeze shut on me.

My cock head nudges between his buns. His surprised ass doesn't even know what hit it. Of course he bucks and screams a bit about how my prick is killing him, it's breaking him in two and he's screaming, "Please stop–no, don't stop! Push it in more–don't stop!" His ass makes tiny appreciative sucking noises like it's nibbling at the end of my cock. His spongy guts absorb me. His hot ass percolates and bristles, starts to welcome the all-out sensation of a fuck. His newly dicked ass fits all around my prick like a

corduroy glove. It takes some doing, but I stuff in a few more inches and, just like quicksand, the more he struggles, the more I sink into him.

"Put it all the way in! All of it!" He thrashes about, biting his pillow. The now ex-virgin feels no pain now. His legs kick uncontrollably over my shoulders. He's well into the Land of Fuck. I plow his pasty hole just like I'm doing push-ups with my cock wedged up his ass. That plush pucker of a rectum feels like a tightening cockring as I smear his backside into the box springs.

When I give him a good workout, and I'm ready to polish him off, I spread-eagle his legs and pound his pelvis. He whips about, cheering me on from below. My cum empties into his ass. His own whipped cream begins to spew. His cock lets fly a splatter of gumdrops. It splashes his face and the remainder paints his chest and fills his navel.

\* \* \* \* \*

Well, I kid you not, we got it up three more times that night. (Ah, twenty–the age of the perpetual hard-on!) Of course, I made it up his asshole again. He decided he liked it with him propped against the bedstead, and he liked to suck his own dick while I fucked his up-turned ass.

He had a real toilet tongue on him by the time I finished screwing all his holes. He was developing a truly filthy mind, and all those dirty words sure did sound hot coming out of his cutey-pie face. Hell, I had to cum all over him just to shut the fucker up.

Three o'clock the next afternoon we woke up. I half-expected this to all be gone, that maybe I would wake up into real life, life ungenerous with its love and mercenary in its friendships; that I would get paid for my boning services then sent packing back into the cynical lonesome world. But nobody showed me the door. Mister showed me his naughty-boy smile and put his hand in my cookie jar. Chauffeur served us eggs, toast and champagne in our cum-soaked bed. The whole thing felt funny and honeymoon-y. Like Mister, here was something true I wanted, but never thought I'd ever really get.

Mister eyed me with admiration and gratitude and leftover lust. Me, I could hardly believe my good fortune, wallowing in more bed sheets with a rich young stud. Oh, there was still lots Mister and me didn't know about each other, but he'd already mentioned a fishing expedition in Bermuda. I was sure we'd get to know each other better there–inside and out.

# Seeing Stars

## *Mark Anderson*

A horror feast, that's what they called it, at the Palace-Odeon, starting at noon and running up till midnight. The most terror ever assembled on film, all in one day! Well, that sure got the attention of me and my buddies, and we were there at noon. Popcorn and colas consumed by the container and gallon, soon had all eight of us hopping up, trekking to the washroom. Pee-shy, I waited till I was sure all had gone, at least for the first time, before I ventured to drain the snake, as we called it.

Alone at the porcelain altar, my first spurts started, when an older man, (all of twenty or so) entered the washroom, and stood beside me. Wasn't he the man who I saw earlier standing in the dimly lit lobby? Not wanting to, but helpless to do otherwise, I took a quick glance at his dick, to confirm what I suspected. Sure enough, he was uncut. That's a talent I had, and still do: Looking at someone and being able to tell if they are cut or uncut. Boggles the minds of some of my friends, even today. Well, that summer of 1957, I proved myself correct. The penalty for looking at him was that my dick stood hard in a flash, cutting off my stream of piss.

I could feel his eyes on me, and I knew my dick was not going to go down. What to do now stupid, I thought, as my face turned bright red, my mouth went dry. My heart was pounding so fast, I thought I was going to faint. When he started talking to me about "liking" what he saw, I could not answer him I was so excited.

My voice quivered and disappeared, for lack of breathing, and I knew I was shaking, but eventually I did manage a "Yes," to him.

Smiling at me, his arm moved, capturing my standing dick in his hands. Now I was shaking, petrified that our space was about to be invaded by someone really needing to piss.

"Not here," I was bright enough to squeak out.

He agreed, but first took my hand, and wrapped it around his hard cock. Wow, I wanted to scream with joy, finally a real man dick in my hand. Up to that point in my hidden gay life, all I had done was diddle with my buddies, as we explored puberty together. All young boys do. This was a first. About time I realized, having needed this all along, knowing I was not the only one out there who was different from all the other school chums of mine. His cock was thick and incredibly hard in my hand. Brushing his balls, the hair felt silky and luxurious. Just then the outer doors opened, signaling someone approaching.

"Outside," he said, as we both crammed our cocks back into our pants. I was so nervous and excited, I had zipped before putting it back into my underwear. There I was, pants closed, walking out of the washroom with my

dick rubbing between underwear and pants. Too late now, I thought, as I followed this stranger into the lobby.

"Got a pencil and paper?" he asked.

Sure, I thought, every kid carries around a pencil and paper when going to a show. But, desperate to be with him anywhere, anytime, I hustled to the food concession. Borrowing a pencil, I retrieved a candy wrapper from a waste bin to write on. I could hardly write my phone number down, I was shaking so, but did finally.

He told me he would call me the next day at seven o'clock, then turned away, but not before flashing me the greatest smile I had ever seen.

My buddies were so enthralled by the show they hadn't even realized I was missing for so long.

The next day was almost unendurable, especially dinner with my sister and my parents. Stationing myself by the phone in the laundry room in the basement, I waited. Again I could feel an aching desire coursing within my body. Shit, yes, I was as hard as a rock. Seven sharp, the phone rang. I grabbed it on the first ring. It was him, and I realized I didn't even know his name.

"Can we get together?"

"Hell, yes," I almost shouted into the phone.

Location and time fixed, I hung up the phone feeling drained, yet excited beyond belief. Now to make up an excuse to get out of the house, wash, and be on time. Done! I was at the corner, waiting, and on time.

The classic MG-A, British racing green, rounded the corner, slowed and stopped at the curb. Guilt seem to vaporize as lust pushed me into the car.

He was handsome all right, and smelling wonderfully masculine, his hand covered, grasped mine intimately.

"Where's a good place?" he asked,

"The lake," I managed.

He soon was rubbing my leg slowly and moving up to my groin. Smiling, he probed my crotch. Finding me as hard as before, he sighed. I ran my hand over the hairs on his thick wrist. How natural it all seemed, I thought, feeling suddenly comfortable, like never before. He drove while my hand explored his hairy arm, wanting more. I moved to his thigh, and he grabbed my hand, placing it over his crotch. I probed, finding the fat, semi-erect tube laying sideways in his loose pants. I clutched the prize, never wanting to let go, while it grew, pleased at my touch.

"Park here," I said, breathlessly.

Following the path from the driveway of the deserted summer cottage on the lake, we skirted the house, to the yard out back, down the cement steps to the deck and boat house. Finding our spot, we stood facing each other. Hands on each other's crotch, we began gently manipulating, teasing, till he took me in his massive arms and kissed me on the mouth. Stars, yes, I saw stars, and the moons, and planets, all at once. Intoxicated, I wanted

more, holding on, clutching at him like a live-preserver, my mouth going into overtime.

"Whoa, slow down," he said, pulling from me. "You really want it bad, kid, don't you?"

"God, yes!"

"Right! Just stand still for a moment," he told me, unbuttoning my shirt to the cool night air. Bending his tongue, he flicked at my nipples, causing me to gasp. He told me to be quiet. I didn't know why I should be quiet, there was no one within a mile, but obeyed.

Lower he went with his lips, while his fingers worked my beaded Indian belt open.

Zipper, pants and underwear down, a breeze sent my balls up hard against my arched cock. His searing mouth took my dripping dick all the way down his throat. His tongue wrapped, scraping me downward the second time, causing me to suddenly gasp, giving him my boiling, squirting cum, all too soon. Jerking, he clasped on to my ass, holding me till I calmed, became still at last.

Standing, he held me, soothed and stroked me, while I came back to earth. Gently kissing my forehead and cheeks, brushing my lips with his, his strong arms pulled me closer to him. Feeling his hardness pressed against me, I moved my hands up, over his chest. Opening his shirt, I found a forest of soft hair. My heart skipped a beat, finding nipples hard and standing to my touch, hidden amongst all that hair, protruding from palm size pectoral muscles. Hearing his sighs, I let my fingers slide over the nibs. Holding each, standing like little cocks, in my fingers, I rotated them, squeezed them, and gently pulled them, while his moaning grew deeper.

My dick soon was hard again like the one poking at me. Fumbling at his own belt, and zipper, he pulled his dick out over the waist band of his underwear.

Looking down, still playing with his tits, I heard first, then saw in the darkness, the wondrous foreskin slip, snapping back and forth over the glistening ripe knob in his fist.

Joining his hands with mine, I managed to retain sole possession of the bone like smooth-skinned cock. Arched like mine, but the head of it was twice the size.

Fascinated, I bent to look closer, only to feel his hands on my head encouraging me.

Automatically my mouth opened, and he was in me. Silky, warm, moist, and smelling like baby powder, I wanted it all. Deeper and deeper he worked it down my eager throat. Slick with my spit and his dribbling precum, my lips slid back and forth over the pole. Pulling his underwear down, I reached his testicles, which were about the same size as mine, but stretched lower because of the thin skinned sac. Teasing the opening of his piss slit, then the ridge below his cock, while jostling his balls, my hands and mouth were lost in a world of lusting delight.

"No," I heard him say, pushing me quickly from his cock. Pulling up, both our pants gathered at our feet, he turned me, wet his fingers, and probed my asshole.

Wanting it, I bent to allow further access for his fingers. Spitting, coating his cock and my ass with lubrication, he pushed forward. After the initial jab of pain, I welcomed his total penetration. Reaching around, and finding me hard, he groaned and placed his hands on my thighs, pulling me back. Encouragement I did not need, and I backed up, sucking all of his dick inside.

Clutching, feeling the thickness of him, I worked back and forth, enjoying the sensations as the knob bumped repeatedly over my prostate gland. His long sac swung upward, hitting against my balls pulled up high in their sac, sending tingling tremors of excitement rushing through me with each thrust.

Meeting him now half way, I drove back, impaling myself with a building frantic fever pitch. More, I wanted to yell, feeling him grow larger, expanding in my ass.

Without touching myself, I clenched down on his cock and ejaculated into the air. He stiffened, and I could feel his hot release flood, filling me.

Pulling me upward, his arms held me while he spasmed. Slowly he relaxed, softening, and with a pop, withdrew, leaving me with a terrible sensation of loss.

He nibbled my neck, and I turned for his full kisses. Smiling we bent to retrieve our crumpled pants. Satiated, we kissed tenderly and then walked back to the car.

Walking on clouds, I returned to my parents home. I didn't clean myself that night. I wanted to keep what he had left in me as long as possible.

I met the man, whose name I never knew, only three more times. The last time was by chance at the theatre were we had met. We went to the washroom and he sucked my cock, busting my testicles so badly that my toes curled.

# Private Dancer

## *John Patrick*

*"I'm your private dancer,*
*a dancer for money ...*
*I do what you want me to do,*
*and any old music will do."*
*– Mark Knopfler, Alamo Music Corp.*

He seemed to dance for himself, a private performance as if the men at the bar were peeking through a crack in the curtains. He slithered across the bar with a tremble designed to shake the money out of the most well-protected wallet. He melted into the music, appearing at times to be suspended from the ceiling, his head rolled back, his neck exposed as if ready for the executioner's blade.

His name was Tony and I imagined he had few illusions left, but he knew every corner of the erotic dreams of the men watching him. He gave them a rear view, bending over, taunting them with it. He wrapped his great long legs around one man's head and let him feel his body, firm, sensual, warm, burnt by the Florida sun. He bounced off the man and, stretching his arms above his head, smiling at no one, he went into his final moments, knowing to play to the gent at the bar who was showing the most interest. He bent his knees, then dipped, turned, and dropped in front of the man who held out a five-dollar bill: me. He leaned back and they all came forward, thrusting their tribute. He shivered delicately away from the sweaty hands trying to run fingers across the bulge in his g-string while sticking a dollar in.

Pausing at the far end of the bar for a moment he bent forward to run his hand across my shoulder. Jumping off the bar, he took a gulp of the Coke Jeff, the bartender, had set up for him, still shaking his ass to the rhythm.

I paused in the middle of a swallow, holding the vodka in my throat so it burned, wondering if the boy would come over to me, what we could say to each other. Behind my shades my eyes were fearless, setting myself for the inevitable encounter with Tony's incredible sexuality. Tony lit a cigarette and I liked the way his lips curled around it and his eyes narrowed against the smoke. He had a tumble of black curls surrounding a long, clean-shaven face, with a sensuous mouth and startling green eyes. Only the overlarge, slightly crooked nose kept him from beauty, but his was a striking face and my eyes were not the only eyes drawn to stare at it. Nor was it only his face that attracted. He had a physical presence as disturbing as some rare perfume.

He turned his head lazily toward me as if he'd felt, and liked, my touch. I moved my eyes back up his body to meet his eyes, and I didn't smile. He was the first to look away. Then I did smile, but only to myself.

Someone else, a man much older than I, in his sixties, approached him, cigarette in hand, and Tony gave him a light and responded to his conversation absently, his attention hooked by me. I could feel his senses straining in my direction even when his back was turned, his eyes fixed elsewhere, his ears assaulted by the blandishments of the other cigarette smoker–who eventually gave up and took his need to someone else. Which was when my prey turned around and looked at me again.

I had to hide a smile. For some odd reason, I found my ability to make a whore desire me reassuring, and his look sent a surge of well-being through me. As he straightened, flexing his shoulders and the muscles of his back before moving away from the bar with an easy, loose-jointed motion, I imagined his cock in my mouth and aroused and felt a tightening of my ass muscles.

I swallowed the last of my vodka and smacked the glass down on the bar. Jeff brought me another. I told Jeff to have Tony order whatever he liked. Jeff gave Tony another Coke and Tony saluted me, then made his way down the bar and stood behind me, his ass still swaying to the music. I turned around and smiled.

"You're very good," I said.

Tony smiled slightly. "You don't know the half of it."

I lifted my shades off his eyes. "But I have a wonderful imagination."

Tony's hand dropped to my thigh. Instinctively, I turned sideways on the stool to make room for Tony, who turned and dropped his ass right into my crotch. I took a deep breath, inhaling the sweaty, smoky essence of Tony.

Now Tony told me a story. That afternoon he passed a man jumping and jerking, hand out for spare change. Tony gave him what coins he had and the man blessed him. He said that was the way he felt about the men he entertained privately, as if he was somehow blessed by his ability to please these men. Sometimes Tony even enjoyed the encounter. He'd done many things, he said, but there were many things he'd never done.

"When you're so young, life is an adventure," I said.

Tony snuggled into me, bringing his lips to my ear. "You have a place?"

"No. I'm in town for a national sales meeting, staying at the Radisson with my boss." It was true. It was the first–and last–time I ever shared a room with someone. My boss was a nice guy but he snored and was a slob. Besides, he was so straight it hurt. He was now sleeping off dinner and I was working on some tasty dessert.

"I'm not cheap," Tony said, figuring if I had to share a room I must be a sales trainee, which I was.

"I didn't think so."

"It'll be fifty if we do it here."

"Okay," I said, handing him a fifty-dollar bill.

"It's getting late. Come with me."

We were in a long, dark corridor which ran behind the bar. This was where the dancers changed and I stepped over duffle bags and several pairs of sneakers. Tony put his arms around my neck while I squeezed his buttocks tightly. I bounced them playfully, rotating the fleshy mounds in widening circles. Moving him into the deepest shadows near the end of the corridor, I unzipped my jeans so our cocks could rub together between us, without any interference from the denim. Tony's cock was still encased in the elastic pouch of his g-string. We continued to sway to the music while I eased my hand down inside it. He enjoyed my right hand gently polishing the knob of his thick, swelling prick. With my left hand, I began to fondle his ass and soon my middle finger massaged his moist ass lips, gently at first, then more urgently. He bent to get a tube of lotion from his dance bag. He applied some to his hole.

"Have any poppers?" he asked hoarsely when my fingertip began to poke inside him.

I didn't. He left me standing there with my cock out while he went back to the bar. He swiftly returned, snorting from the bottle. We resumed our position. I poked the first knuckle of my middle finger into his ass and was amazed at how tight it was. I twisted my finger, popped it out, and spun him around. He just kept snorting, becoming dazed as I peeled away the G-string and took his buttocks in my hands.

I kissed first on cheek, then the other. Under normal circumstances I would have dwelled there for several minutes, eating it, but now I quickly brought my cock head to the opening. The large head of my cock slithered up and down in his sweaty, lubed crack a couple of times before I began jabbing against his opening. With a quick little shove, my cock head popped up inside him. He was virgin-tight, even after the preliminary finger-fucking I had given him. I clamped my hands around his hips and waited for the hole to loosen up a little.

"Don't you have a place? I usually don't do this here."

"What do you usually do?"

"A guy just blows me. This will cost you a lot, man."

I took a fifty from my wallet and dangled it before his eyes.

"Okay," he said.

I dropped the bill to the floor on top of the g-string and the rest of his cash and thrust my hips forward, stuffing the head of my cock and about two inches of my eight-inch cock into him.

"Oh, shit," he gasped as several more inches found their way up into his pretty butt. He continued to squirm restlessly while his asshole alternately fluttered and contracted, knowing precisely what to do.

I pushed more dick into him before easing out a little. With each careful jab, I stuffed it in deeper than before. By the time my thick cock was completely buried, Tony was perspiring heavily, pleading for mercy. I

pistoned slowly in and out a few more times, and he looked back over his shoulder at me, blinking back tears as he looked around to see if anyone had joined us. We were still alone. "God that feels good," he admitted, then took another hit off the bottle of poppers.

I ran my hands up and down his sweaty torso while I continued to pump steadily, slowly at first, then undulating my pelvis faster and faster until I was pounding deep, letting loose with my most intense orgasm in weeks.

I popped out my dick and turned him around to face me. He gasped for breath. The underside of my cock briefly tangled with his when I hugged him to me. My hands gripped his quivering buttocks. I pressed him back against the wall. He wrapped his arms tightly around my shoulders and held me close. Then, as if he feared my cock would get away, he brought his hands to it and began stroking it. "You sure you don't have a place to go?"

"No. How 'bout you?"

"No. I got an old lady."

I understood perfectly. I had been married myself once, briefly. I leaned into him to get what I'd paid the first fifty for, a go at his cock, now incredibly hard after his fuck. I bent down and began to move my lips slowly over his hairy, washboard stomach, licking his sweat. He moved towards me, shoving his cock, oozing precum, against my cheek. I knelt and began kissing the smooth inside of his sturdy thighs. His cock throbbed against my ear. "Oh, suck it," he moaned.

I feared he would come before I could get my money's worth so I moved my hand over his heavy balls, holding the cock steady at the base and began to suck. I'd had a hundred dollar piece of ass for fifty bucks so I wasn't about to complain if he came too soon.

I locked my lips around Tony's cock, pulling and kneading the mounds of his ass to make his slender organ lurch down my throat. I curled my tongue around the underside of his swollen cock. His big heavy balls dangled down beyond my chin and I went for them, sucking, licking, nipping on them. Then I returned to the cock head, and he began moaning, rocking his hips back and forth. As he fucked my mouth, I raked the tips of my fingers over his ass cheeks. When his cock began stiffening in my mouth, I parted his well-fucked ass cheeks and sent two fingers in deep.

I knew it wasn't in the contract that he had to come but I was determined I would see his load, even if it meant another fifty on the floor. Suddenly, he stopped fucking my mouth. I opened my eyes and realized we were being watched. Three men stood in the corridor, blocking out the light from the barroom.

Tony murmured, "Please, let's go to your place."

I let his cock plop from my mouth. "Dammit, I haven't got a place."

"Oh, shit," Tony cried, "just keep suckin' it."

I did as he commanded, but reluctantly. The private dance was not private anymore. The men were soon surrounding us. The light was now sufficient that I could see them. Jeff, the hunky bartender, was one of them.

The other two were dancers, Jeremy, a boyish, very slim blonde, and Mark, a short, hairy bodybuilder-type.

A voice called out, "Lock the back when you leave, won't you, Jeff?" It was the manager. The club had closed for the night.

"Yeah," Jeff answered. "We'll just be a minute."

A door slammed shut. It was suddenly still, except for the heavy breathing of the four youths surrounding me.

I continued sucking as g-strings were dropped. Two hard cocks were presented to me. I left Tony's cock for Mark's, cut, thick and stubby. Jeremy stuffed his little cock in my mouth alongside Mark's.

Jeff was out of his tight shorts and tank top in seconds, leaving him standing there in just a jock strap with his giant balls protruding out from the side.

Tony went down on his knees in front of Jeff and put his mouth over the bulge in the jockstrap. I sucked both cocks while I watched Tony squeezing his lips around the growing cock. Tony managed to get the jockstrap down around Jeff's ankles and everyone leaned back to take a look at this masterpiece.

Jeff's cock was magnificent, the perfect shape and size. He was completely shaved which made it look even bigger. His balls were smooth and pink and hung low in their silky smooth sack. His cock head was dribbling a small amount of precum.

Tony took the whole thing in one gulp. Jeff grabbed onto his head and started to slowly fuck his face. Jeremy watched hungrily while I sucked him alone, then took Mark back in my mouth.

Tony stood up and the four of them formed a circle around me. They started to jerk themselves off. Jeremy pulled on his own dick with one hand and rubbed and fingered his asshole with the other. He turned so that they could get a better view of what he was doing to himself. Jeremy's finger slid in and out of his asshole smoothly and he worked another one in, moving them both around in a circle.

Tony got his tube of lube and put some on his fingers. Jeremy let Tony grease him, watching intently as Jeff and Mark pulled and tugged on their own big dicks. Tony left Jeremy and brought his cock back to my mouth. Drops of precum fell onto my chest and stomach. Tony pumped his cock furiously into my mouth while he stared down at Jeremy finger-fucking himself.

Jeff, surprisingly, was the real show-off among these dancers, probably because he had so much more to show-off. He stood with his legs spread. Drops of sweat rolled down his stomach and along his bulky thighs. His balls were swinging with the swift movement of his hand on his cock. The vein that ran along the underside of his cock pulsed. Mark held his balls in one hand and worked the head of his dick with the other. Occasionally Mark would spit into his hand and use it for lube.

Jeremy faced the wall and spread his legs wide, showing them his puckered, lubed butt hole. He wanted all of them to take turns fucking him. He arched his back and pushed his butt up in the air.

Spitting into his hand again, Mark went first. He slathered the spit over the head of his dick. He got behind Jeremy and pushed his legs further apart. Jeff moved in closer to watch Mark enter Jeremy. Mark leaned forward and teased Jeremy's asshole with his cock head, pushing it in while keeping one hand wrapped around the base of it. Jeremy rose to meet Mark's thrusts, grunting as Mark plowed into him.

It seemed Tony was ready to explode after a few minutes of watching Mark fuck Jeremy. He pulled his cock from my mouth and moved around to take his turn.

I stayed on my knees, moving over to Jeff. He stopped jerking off and shoved his cock into my mouth.

Just then Mark withdrew and fired a big load onto Jeremy's back. Tony moved in quickly and before Jeremy's butt hole had the chance to close, he plunged his cock right in. He went in so deep that Jeremy squealed. Tony laughed and fucked him with incredible force, pumping him harder and harder.

Tony was sweating and every muscle in his body was working overtime. After a couple of minutes, Tony pulled out and came right at the entrance.

All the while, I had been preparing Jeff, who had one of the biggest cocks I'd ever had the honor of pleasuring. I knew that I would be returning to this bar every night of my stay.

Jeremy took his g-string and wiped the cum from his ass, then got on the floor on his back. We stood over him as Jeff got between his thighs, hoisted his legs over his shoulders and slid his cock up and inside Jeremy's by-now loose, wet hole.

Jeff built up speed, pumping back and forth. His balls were slapping up against Jeremy's ass cheeks. Jeremy's legs were bent and his feet were pointing up to the ceiling. Jeff pulled on Jeremy's nipples and rubbed his hands over his hairless stomach. Jeremy began jerking himself as Jeff fucked him wildly, and he brought himself off. The three of us stood around them, furiously stroking our cocks.

Suddenly, Jeff pulled out, stood up and let go a geyser of cum all over Jeremy's body. I didn't wait for Jeremy's permission, I swiftly got between his thighs and slid my cock into the slippery hole. Above me, Tony moaned and deep-throated Mark's dick.

As I entered Jeremy, Tony shoved his cock back in my mouth. I took in every inch, nearly gagging on the length of it. As Tony pumped my face, I pumped my cock very slowly into Jeremy, then with an increasing rhythm. I was amazed at how smoothly my cock slid in and out. On every stroke, I pulled my cock all the way out and then I would plunge back inside.

Jeremy bucked and I slammed it all the way in, making him squeal. Grunting, I came with four strong pushes.

I still had Tony's swollen cock in my mouth and rolled the big head around on my tongue. I hung on to his hips as he pulled me off of Jeremy and leaned back against the wall while I continued to blow him.

I was certainly getting my money's worth.

So lost was I in the adoration of Tony's perfect cock that I didn't notice the other dancers had left. Only Jeff remained, now wearing his shorts and tank top again.

"Hey, guys," he said, stepping over to us, "why don't you come over to my place and finish this?"

# Lies Boys Tell

## *John Patrick*

As I walked into the bar, he was shooting pool and my eyes became riveted on his black Spandex shorts, artfully shaping the crotch. He saw where I was staring and smiled. It was a small smile, a knowing smile, a smile he would turn on me several times after I got a beer and perched on a stool at one of the small round tables.

After the boy finally finished his game, he raised his eyes. I nodded. At that, he set his beer down on the table next to mine and went to the john.

In retreat, he moved so gracefully, so confidently, I thought he might be a performer, perhaps even a stripper. He seemed to be the kind of boy who could put on a good front, but I knew if he was in this bar there was something damaged inside of him. And that's what I needed that night: A boy who could use a little mending.

After a few minutes, he emerged. I held him steadily in my gaze as he made his way across the room. He had adjusted the bulge in the shorts so that it was even more provocative. Yes, a performer, I thought. I had to fight the urge to kneel down right there and do it, to slip what I knew had to be magnificent between my lips.

In one sweep of gusto, he grabbed his can of beer and plopped himself down on the stool next to mine.

"Hi! My name's Michael," he said, holding out his hand.

We shook hands and began chatting amicably. Indeed, he was a stripper. But presently unemployed. "The joints that pay $30 plus tips don't have dancers every night," he explained. "The others, it's just tips. In season, it's good. I can make $200 a night. Now, I can make more going out with guys than dancing." He pushed the long wave of blonde hair away from his eyes.

"I see," I said. "What's bad for them is good for me, right?"

He nodded and smiled. Now all we had to do was agree on the proper compensation.

"Yeah, I'm really desperate. See, I'm just outta jail. My boyfriend turned me in. He told 'em where I was. Fucker just wanted company in jail. We were together a couple of times. I blew him. I even blew a guy in the holding tank. Yeah, he said he was goin' up for a long stretch and I wanted to give him somethin' to remember."

"I'll bet he's still thinking about it."

"Yeah, I've gotta tell ya, I'm good."

"I could tell, just by your choice of shorts."

"Think these are tight, man, you shoulda seen the ones I used to wear goin' into Rounds in New York! Talk about tight, I could barely walk. And I

had blue contacts, a deep tan, with my hair almost white, and a little tank top–"

"A real killer."

"Yeah."

Eventually we got around to the matter of a place. "I'm just here for the night," I said. "I'm staying out by the interstate."

"Too far for me to go, man. But I can't go back to my apartment. There's a warrant out for my arrest. I've been violated again; I didn't report. So, anyhow, I got this room at the Lauderdale, just up the street."

"I know it. In fact, I always stay there but this time, for some reason."

I'd lost him now. He started looking around the room, as if assessing if there were any other possibilities, if perhaps there was someone who might offer more.

The impression he gave was one of transition, flux. Satisfied that perhaps I'd do the trick, he returned his eyes to mine and said, "Well, you want to go to my hotel?"

"I'm not sure. You see, I'm not a rich man. I–"

"I never go for less than seventy."

"That's okay then."

\* \* \* \* \*

On the way to the hotel, he talked more about his time in jail, his boyfriend and the troubles they'd had. Finally, he said, "I've never told anybody this much about me before."

"I've been known to be a good listener."

"You good at everything?" he snickered, kneading my crotch.

"That's up to you."

\* \* \* \* \*

Only one of the double beds in the room appeared to have been slept in. He tossed the bedspread away and explained, "You're my second one today. The first guy rented me this room. He's writing a play. He told me he had a part that would be perfect for me in this play but the producers will only use real actors. He bought a joint for me and we smoked it and then he sucked my balls while I jacked off. That was it. I never even had to touch him."

I sat on the edge of the bed with him before me. I nuzzled the crotch. He smelled of soap. Slowly I peeled the Spandex down and his luscious, nicely cut eight-incher popped out. It was even nicer than I had hoped it would be. I didn't ever want to stop sucking it.

But I had to. The phone was ringing.

He talked a bit, then hung up. "That was my dealer. He'll be here in five minutes."

"But …"

"Don't worry. I'll be right back."

While he was gone, I removed my clothes and got into bed.

He came back into the room with a rock of crack and a can of pop. He emptied the Mountain Dew into the toilet and crushed the can, then punched holes in it and put some ashes from his cigarette on the holes. He laid a bit of the coke on it, then lit it. He inhaled the drug through the hole in the lid.

"We can get about five hits from this," he said, offering me a hit.

"I'm afraid I don't do drugs anymore."

"I don't do 'em very often. When I do, I usually just do Ecstasy. That's really my drug. It turns me into a real whore. One night when I was on it, I did seven guys."

He began to put on a little strip show for me, shedding his clothes in time to the rock tune blaring from the tinny speaker of the radio encased in the TV. I had to admit he was talented. I especially liked the deep bends he did. I could imagine him doing them over me, with my cock sliding into his ass.

When he was done he climbed over me and brought his cock to my eager mouth.

"You want to get fucked?" he asked as I brought the beautiful thing back to hardness.

I looked up and nodded, still not wanting to remove it from my mouth.

"You got a rubber?"

I shook my head.

"Hell, I should supply the goddam rubber!" He climbed away and reached for the phone. "They must sell 'em downstairs."

He dialed the front desk. Yes, they sold them in the bar. Back on went the Spandex shorts and he was gone again.

\* \* \* \* \*

He took me on my back, my legs slung over his shoulders. Jerking my cock, he said, "I've only been fucked seven times. After thirty beers maybe I could take yours. Shit, your cock's so damn big it'd kill somebody."

After doing the drugs, he couldn't get his cock fully hard but he was able to get it in and keep it in. Just the sight of his lithe, nearly hairless body steadily invading me brought me to the brink in a hurry. Sensing I was close, he increased his tempo, both in his fucking and his jerking. The intensity of my orgasm stunned him.

"God, you were horny," he said, wiping the cum off his fingers onto the sheets.

He pulled out without coming himself, slipped the rubber off, and went to the bathroom.

When he returned, he went back to smoking on the makeshift pipe. Soon he was in a somber mood. "I've gotta find something legit to do, you know? I'm 25."

"You could easily pass for twenty," I said, wiping the remaining cum from my cock with the sheet.

"Yeah, but I'm 25 and into chicken." He shook his head disgustedly. "Yeah, I gotta get my shit together."

I examined his face closely for the first time. It was a fine face, to be sure, but there were many miles on it for a boy so young. "Hey," he said, his face brightening. "Maybe I could go back to Sarasota with you. Just to take a rest for a while. Get my shit together."

"No, I don't think my wife would like it."

I was now out of bed and tugging on my pants.

"Oh, yeah, your wife."

As he slipped back into his Spandex shorts, I counted out the seven tens and handed them to him.

He shoved the cash into his wallet and said, "Let's go."

"Go?"

"Yeah, we'll go out and get a kid off the street. The ones near the Copa are the best; the ones further up on Federal are real trash. It costs sixty or seventy near the Copa, twenty or thirty up on Federal."

"You get what you pay for, but, well, I don't know. I really haven't got much left and I've got to get started early tomorrow ..."

"Hey, my treat."

"Well—"

"C'mon, you and me in that convertible, with some crack–shit, man, we'll have the pick of the litter."

\* \* \* \* \*

The cute little French-Canadian kid said he was straight, was just on the street looking for someone who had a place he could crash for the night. I had to agree with Michael that he was indeed the "pick of the litter" that night.

Michael told him all about the room he had for the weekend at the Lauderdale, with a pool "and everything." And how "everything" included the fresh shipment of crack and a bar full of pretty young girls.

The boy seemed delighted. "Cool," he said as he got comfortable in the back seat.

"Yeah, there's nothin' I like better than a little crack and a little pussy and a good blowjob."

"Me, too," the kid said.

Michael's hand slid into my crotch and he groped me. "And speakin' of blowjobs, wait'll you see the weapon my man here has inside these pants."

"Oh?" the kid said.

"Oh, yeah," Michael snickered, glancing at the kid. "Just you wait."

\* \* \* \* \*

I showered while they did their drugs. The kid said he would rather have some grass so Michael willingly obliged. He was prepared for any eventuality. When I came back into the room with a towel wrapped around my waist, Michael was on the bed with the kid's ample uncut cock in his mouth. Michael still had all his clothes on, but the boy was naked, appearing tiny, almost lost on the huge bed with Michael stretched out between his thighs going at it.

I kneeled on the bed and Michael stripped my towel away. While he had discussed his "blowing" of his boyfriend and another inmate at jail, he had not expressed any oral interest in my cock. Now he began alternately sucking me and the kid. He handled both of us expertly. Before long, I was fully erect and ready to go to work.

"Hey, how would you like that?" he asked the kid.

The kid didn't answer, just stared. The grass seemed to have done its thing.

"Good," Michael said, standing and stripping off his shorts. He took the kid by his shoulders and turned him around so that he was on his knees in the center of the bed. There were no signs of protest. Then Michael got into position so that the kid's balls were in his mouth and the boy could lean across his body and suck Michael's dick.

I unwrapped the second condom Michael had purchased from the machine downstairs and slid it on. The two boys sucked each other as I prepared the puckering pinkish-purple hole of the French-Canadian with my saliva. Luxuriating in the tightness of it, I took my time entering him. I was glad the condom was lubricated. The kid groaned as I shoved and shoved. And shoved some more. When it was all the way in, he gasped.

I began in earnest and soon he was coming. Michael sucked his balls as the kid ejaculated all over his hard, tanned belly.

When I returned to the bedroom after washing myself, Michael was smoking more crack. "Straight shit," he laughed. "You stayed hard all the time and you came."

"Doesn't mean a thing," the boy said, puffing away on the last of his joint.

"Hey, man, hard-ons don't lie."

I winked at Michael. "But boys do."

# The Good Hustler

## *Keith Davis*

"I'll give you $20. No more," the man says.

"But look at it," I reach inside my 501s and pull out my thick, veiny nine-inch prick, "Come on. A piece of meat like this is worth at least a hundred."

He grabs my cock, copping a free feel. He shakes his head.

I pop my big bull balls out for his inspection. "Just think what fun you could have with these nuts." I thrust my pelvis forward so the man can get a good look at my fuck set.

After carefully weighing my balls he says, "I'm sorry, kid, but thirty dollars is as high as I could go."

"Forget it," I say. The man leaves the bathroom and heads back to the bar. He knows I'll have to follow him. What choice do I have? I'm hungry, homeless and out of smokes. I'd been hustling ever since I ran away from Indiana and my parents' farm three years ago. Now I'm considered past my prime. Every day, bus loads of fresh-faced, big-dicked runaways arrive at the Port Authority. How can I possibly compete?

I look in the mirror and I still look damn good. Handsome boy-next-door face, the kind guys love to smack around with their big cocks. Big blue eyes. Dark brown hair. Great build–fantastic pecs with nipples aching for attention. I'd been really popular when I arrived. Too popular. Now I'm shopworn.

The man is sitting at the bar waiting for me. I bum a cigarette.

"Thought it over?" he asks.

"Fifty and you can finger fuck my ass." Everyone knew I'd always been strict about keeping my backdoor off limits to Johns. Now, I'm forced to sell my cherry hole to survive.

The man cups my bubble butt in his hand. "Any objection to film?" he asks.

"Give me a hundred and you can film me." I offer.

The man massages my basket, thinks for a moment and says, "Let's go."

When we arrive at his apartment two men are already waiting for us. One is older, and balding. With him is a cute young blonde. The kid looks scared.

The man with me speaks. "Carl, you've out done yourself. He's exquisite." He walks over to the lad and caresses his cheek. "Oh, yes. Very nice. Stand up, son." The boy rises while the man's hands fondles him like a piece of goods. "Oh this is nice."

The man tugs on the boy's cock. The kid's embarrassed to be another man's piece of property. The man gives his ass a couple of swats. "Lovely. Nice and firm."

"Thank you, Timothy. I see you went for an old but reliable choice."

I remember Carl. I tricked with him a couple years ago. He dressed me in a sailor's suit and had me dance on a table with my cock and balls hanging out.

"You boys get to know each other and I'll set up the video equipment."

I ask the boy his name.

"Tyler."

"You new to the City?" I ask. Of course he is. He's one of the cadre of farm-fresh chicken taking work away from me. The bastard. He's a naive 18-year-old from South Carolina. He whines that his parents threw him out when they discovered a copy of Jock in his bedroom.

I feel guilty for resenting him. A sweet kid like Tyler should be working at the mall and dating a boy from The Gap, not living on the streets of New York. And definitely not hustling. His parents really fucked up. They hate his being gay so they force him to sell his hole to any old troll who wants to stick it in him. I decide to take him under my wing. "Don't worry. I'll take care of you."

We strip off our clothes. I'm not wearing any underwear. A piece of meat like mine can't be constricted in a pair of shorts. I love the obscene bulge my unconstricted dick makes in my Levi's. Tyler's little boy Fruit-of-the-Looms are already damp with pre-cum. Tyler is a skinny young lad. His small arms and bird chest are more like a boy's than a man's. His teen cock is about seven inches and skinny like the rest of him. He's already rock hard and dripping pre-cum. His gentle eagerness make me pop a boner right away, too.

I catch Tyler drooling over my meat. Little fucker's probably only seen equipment like mine in the pages of Jock. Now he's face to face with object of all his jack-off fantasies. I wag my cock for him and give it a few strokes.

"Like what you see?"

The lad is so impressed he can barely speak. He just nods "Uh-huh."

I reach over and grab his dick. "You've got a pretty nice set of equipment yourself." He didn't. At least not compared to me. But I didn't want him to feel self conscious. "Bet you can't wait to have my big dick down your throat or up your ass."

The boy nods. He's about to cum just from the excitement of anticipation. Tentatively he reaches his hand forward and wraps it around my cock.

"Oh, God. It's so beautiful," Tyler whimpers.

With the video equipment in place, Carl comes over to us. "Looks hot, boys," he says, snapping a Polaroid. Then he addresses me directly, "I hear we're going to get to take a crack at that ass of yours."

Now it's my turn to blush. I'd forgotten my promise to let their fingers do some walking up my old dirt road. I'd been acting like a butch top with Tyler and found it humiliating to admit that I'd turn my ass into a boy pussy for a few dollars.

"Bend over. I want to get some picture of that pucker, boy."

Reluctantly I bend over. I'm embarrassed, but I'm a pro. They bought the rights to my backdoor for the evening and I'm going to oblige them. Word gets out fast if you're uncooperative or renege on a promise. I lean over the couch and spread my legs as far as possible. I reach behind and open my ass cheeks up wide, shedding light on my tight little bung hole.

"Just beautiful," the men gasp.

"You like that. You like that hot hole?" I ask, "That hole belongs to you now. You can do what ever you want with it. You guys own my fucking asshole." I flex, winking my pucker at them. I here the click of the camera as Carl takes a couple close ups of my shitter.

"You want to touch it?" Timothy asks Tyler.

Great. They're gonna let the biggest bottom in the world diddle with my hole. "Go on man," I say, "You want to mess with my hole. You want to get inside me. Come on man. My ass is waiting for you."

Tyler sucks on his index finger and hesitantly slips it up my shit chute. I moan like he's tearing me apart.

"Go on. Make it two fingers. He loves it," Carl urges.

"Oh yeah. Another finger, stick another finger up my butt, man."

Tyler obliges, adding his middle finger to his exploration expedition up my nether chute.

"Guys, you're going to scorch the film, you're so hot." Timothy says. "Now let's get started."

Tyler removes his fingers from my ass. I catch him smelling them.

"You can taste them if you want," I say, "I'm clean."

Tyler smiles and sucks my remnants off his dirty fingers.

Carl hands me a razor and shaving cream. "I want you to shave baby here. Make him nice and smooth."

I start to object, but Tyler stops me. "I don't mind. As long as I have a place to stay tonight, I don't mind."

Carl sets a scenario up for us: We're brothers. I catch Tyler masturbating and give him hell for it. Timothy gives us our marks and yells "Action:"

Tyler lies on the bed and beats his young dick. Automatically, one finger, the same one that he'd probed me with, starts knocking around his own little fuck hole. I walk into the room and with all the sincerity I can mange I say, "Little brother, what in the hell do you think you're doing?"

He stops mid-stroke–finger up to the second knuckle inside his butt. "Please don't tell Mom and Dad I was playing with myself," he pleads.

"I think you need to be taught a lesson."

"Please, I'll do anything. Just don't tell Mom and Dad."

I yank Tyler up by his hair. "Yes, sir, boy. I think you need to be taught a real lesson." I throw the kid across my lap. His hairless, white butt cheeks quiver.

SLAP! I bring my hand down hard across the runaway's young ass.

"Ouch! Fuck that hurts!"

"It would hurt more if Dad did it!"

SMACK! SLAP! WHACK!

I really thrash Tyler's ass. He screams and squirms, grinding his hard little pecker against my pole. I spread the little fucker's cheeks. Tyler's got a cute pink rosebud. I spit a lugey on it before aiming a couple hard slaps right on his shitter.

"Fucking son-of-a-bitch, I'll teach you to play with yourself."

I see Carl, behind the camera signaling me to start the shaving. I order Tyler to stand up. He's still rock hard. I see a few tears in his eyes. The spanking and humiliation got to him. Good. Better he learn the underside to hustling from me than someone who would really hurt him.

"What's this?" I demand, smacking his puny hard-on, "You like being spanked? It turns you on?"

"No."

SLAP! I deliver another blow to his manhood.

"No what?"

"No, Sir!"

"That's better." I grab a fistful of his light brown bush and yank it. Tyler winces in pain, "Seems to me you don't deserve this. Only men are allowed to have hairy bushes."

"Please, Sir. I'm a man."

"No you're just a little boy. A little boy who likes playing games with his pee-pee."

WHAP! I make the underside of his shaft sting.

"OUCH! That hurts, Sir."

"Good. It's supposed to. Now lie down while I decide what to do about that bush."

Tyler still has a few tears in his eyes so I decide to be gentle now. I want to reassure him. I lovingly lather his bush up. I smile at him and wink. He knows I am just playing a part. The kid doesn't have much hair. A few quick swipes with the razor and his pubes are completely bald. He really looks like a little boy now.

I order Tyler to lay on the bed, spread-eagle. Now it's my turn to probe HIS butt. I spread those pink cheeks (they still glows red hot from their recent thrashing) and look at his pussy. There really was no other word for the hole between Tyler's legs. It's a pussy. A pussy that would see lots of dick in his lifetime. I shove an unlubricated digit inside him. Tight. At least for now.

"Little Bro," I say, continuing the scenario, "Seems like you're not as tight as you should be. Have you been sticking things up your asshole?"

"N ... n ... no!"

SMACK!

"Don't lie to me!"

"Well, maybe I've stuck a couple fingers up my butt. That's all."

SLAP!

"That's all! That's all? Finger fucking is something you do to a pussy, not an asshole."

"I'm sorry."

"Makes me think maybe you got a pussy between your legs."

"No. I have an asshole."

"I don't know." I say, wiggling my finger inside his chute, "Feels nice and hot like a pussy. You like havin' that finger inside you, don't you?

"Yes!" Tyler confesses.

"You know, I LOVE eating pussy. I wish there was some pussy around here that I could start lapping."

"You can eat my pussy," Tyler says, shaking with excitement.

WHAP!

"What pussy? I thought you were a man. I thought you had an asshole."

"No. I'm not a man. I'm a faggot. Please eat my pussy."

"Okay, that's better," I say. I bury my nose in his hairless crack and inhale deeply. The musky scent of boy sweat fills my nostrils. My tongue takes a long swipe up the entire length of the runaway's ass crack. The kid moans in pleasure, arching his ass, grinding his hot spanked bottom into my face.

"Oh, God. This feels so good! Eat my asshole."

I stop and give his pucker a sharp blow. "I'm no fag. I don't eat asshole. I only eat pussy."

"Please eat me!" he bawls, begging me to get my tongue back inside his pulsing posterior.

"Yeah, I'll eat your little boy pussy. I need to make it nice and wet so I can fuck it long and hard."

I nuzzle back in to Tyler's warm, moist crack. I flick my tongue lightly around the boy's sensitive pucker before actually penetrating his shitter. The familiar taste of a young asshole is a rush. I shove my tongue as far in as it will reach, French kissing the teenager's bung hole. Rooting around inside the young boy's shithole.

"Oh, Jesus, man, it feels so good."

I tear my mouth away from his pucker long enough to say, "As soon as I get a fuckin' rubber on, I'm gonna plow that hot pussy good."

Carl shakes his head. He doesn't want me to use a condom.

"You don't have anything, do you?" Tyler asks.

I don't, but I say, "That doesn't matter."

"It's okay," says Tyler, "You can fuck me without a condom."

John Patrick

I see he needs looking after more than I though. After a few minutes of negotiations, Timothy produces a Trojan. I toss it on the dresser. I'm glad to know it's handy.

I stand up and straddle the prone kid. My big dick is at full mast. "Okay you worthless faggot. Show me how bad you want this dick up your stinking pussy hole. Get your mother- fucking, cock-sucking lips wrapped around this dick NOW!"

The eager kid doesn't need to be told twice. His hot adolescent mouth is gagging on my fuck stick in no time. I glance over and see Carl zooming in for a close up with camera. I decide to put on a good show. I grab a mass of blonde curls and force his face all the way onto my gargantuan meat. The boy gags and squirms trying to pull himself off my massive flesh pole. The kid's not an experienced cock-sucker. I can see tears welling up in his eyes as he chokes on my big dick.

"What's the matter? I thought you wanted this. I though you wanted to worship my big dick with your mouth."

The kid is really struggling now. He can't breath with his gullet stuffed with my fat nine inches. I feel sorry for him and pull out. Tyler gasps sucking in air. I start to abuse his face with my dick. "What's the matter, fag? Don't you like sucking a grown man's dick? Too much for your puny faggot mouth to handle?"

SLAP! WHAP! My spit-slick tool pounds his face.

"I'm sorry, Sir. I loved sucking it. I really did."

"Yeah fuck that shit. I'm going to have to punish you."

Tyler looks scared. Already tonight he's been shaved, spanked and face-fucked. I can see he's having second thoughts about hustling. I turn around. "Okay, faggot. Clean my shit hole."

Tyler breathes a sigh of relief as he raises his head to my hard globes. He's wanted to eat my ass ever since he first got a good look at my tight wrinkle. "Yeah you're going to have to use that sissy tongue of yours to clean my asshole out good," I taunt. I feel kid's warm, wet mouth press up against my backdoor. Unlike the tongue rape I gave his shitter, Tyler tenderly, lovingly kisses my hole, making love to it.

The boy pulls his mouth away long enough to murmur, "It's the most beautiful thing I've ever seen."

Timothy moves the camera in for an extreme close-up of my brown eye. Again I flex and wink it.

"Okay," Carl whispers, "Now I want you to stick your tongue in as far as you can."

"Beautiful. You look just beautiful tongue-fuckin' his ass." Timothy says.

"Do you like it?" Carl asks.

"I love it," the boy replies before shoving his taster back inside me.

"Yeah that's it. Lick that butt hole. Lick it good."

God!" I groan as my balls unload a full twelve spurts into the reservoir tip of the rubber. "Oh you're the best!" I collapse on top of him, panting.

I kiss Tyler as my shrinking member slides out of his hole. I sit up and stare in amazement at the boys asshole. His tight pink asshole is now big, dilated and pulsating. Slowly I bring my finger to it. Tyler spasms. "Wow. You really do have a pussy now," I say, leaning down and kissing his greasy hole. He spasms.

"It hurts," he says.

"I know it does," I say, taking off the condom, "But look what you made me do." I empty my hot man spunk onto his skinny chest. "Look how hot you got me," I say.

We lie in bed holding each other until Timothy interrupts our serenity. "Okay boys, that was real hot. But it's getting late, so take your money and let's go."

"But you said I could spend the night?" Tyler says.

"Did I?" asks Carl, "Well, I've changed my mind. You'd better go."

"But you promised ..." Tyler whines.

Foolish boy, I thought, as I start to dress, "Look, Tyler, you can spend the night with me." I take the money and we leave for a cheap hotel on St. Marks. I fuck him once more that night before we fall asleep in each other's arms.

Our lives change after that night. I do a photo shoot for a major fuck book and land a job dancing at a Times Square theater. I make a ton of money and quickly have my own tiny apartment. Tyler hooks up with a generous sugar daddy and moves into an Upper East Side co-op.

We still see each other from time to time and remain friends.

Then, about six months later, as I'm leaving the theater I see Tyler. I'm in a good mood. I'll be leaving New York soon on a national stripping tour ending in Los Angeles where I'm promised an audition with a major adult video company. All this and Tyler was still the only person to get inside my rear entrance. I wave to him. He looks like shit.

"What's the matter?" I ask.

"I'm in deep shit," he says, "I'm in real trouble and I don't know what to do." The poor boy breaks down in tears before confessing that his sugar daddy was a coke dealer who frequently turned abusive. He'd thrown Tyler out and the boy was hustling by the West Side Highway for drugs when he'd hooked up with another dealer, a bad-assed mother-fucker named Jose.

"What do you want me to do about it?" I'd seen so many guys like him. You get mixed up with Jose and you end up dead.

"I want to go home. I want to go back to South Carolina."

"Yeah."

"I need $600. $500 for Jose and $100 for the bus ticket."

"Can't you earn it yourself?" I ask a little exasperated.

"No, man, Jose got guys everywhere."

For the first time I see how truly terrified he is. My heart melts. I don't have that kind of money. But I'll get it for him. I deposit Tyler in my apartment and head to the bar. I see Carl and Timothy at the bar, scoping out their next film star. Immediately I walk over to them.

"I need six hundred dollars."

"Who doesn't?" laughs Carl.

"I'll do anything to get it."

"You'd have to let us film you being fist-fucked for that kind of money," he jokes.

"Done," I say. I knew I'd been saving my cherry for something special. Helping Tyler was it.

"You ... you mean it?" they ask. Good-looking hustlers generally don't let you fist-fuck them, let alone film it.

"You give me the money up front and it's yours," I say.

Timothy starts to bargain but Carl stops him. "We'll give you half now, half when you've finished.."

"Fair enough." It's what I expected.

The two men quickly whisk me to their apartment. They seem nervous, worried that I'll change my mind.

"Can we put you in a sling?" Timothy asks.

"If you like. You're the director."

Carl emerges from the bedroom dressed in full leather. I'm surprised how hot he looks in his leather harness and chaps. A leather cap hides his bald spot. His chest is covered with tufts of grey hair leading down to a bulging codpiece. In spite of myself and my apprehension about being fisted, my dick starts to grow.

"Are we ready to start filming?" Carl barks, a complete change from the grand queen I'd known before. He marches me into the bedroom. The video camera is set up in one corner of the room. In another corner, bolted to the ceiling, hangs a sling.

"You know why you're here, boy?" Carl demands.

"Yes. Yes, Sir," I answer.

"I want you to look into that camera," Carl says pointing, "And tell me why you're here."

"I'm here to be fisted, Sir."

"You have much experience, boy?"

"No, Sir. Shit, I've never even been fucked."

"Then what makes you want to take my fist up that tight little virgin ass of yours?"

I hesitate. I can't very well say that I'm only doing it to help a friend in trouble. Besides, the pulsing in my groin tells me that can't be the only reason.

"Answer me, boy."

"Well, Sir. I want to be fisted because you want to do it to me. I'm here for you pleasure. Mine doesn't matter, Sir."

"Get on your knees, boy, and crawl over here."

I obey immediately.

"You think it gives me pleasure to waste my time on your punk hustler ass?" he bellows, "Do you? I'll tell you what, I want you to make me want that worthless hole of yours. I want you to beg me to rip you wide open. I want you fucking pleading to be my fucking fisting slave, you hear me?"

"Yes, Sir."

"Then get to work. Prove to me that sluttly little hole of yours is worth my time."

Having played the dominant role so long, I find Carl's rough talk refreshing and the image of the sling hanging suggestively in the corner incredibly arousing. I make him want my ass.

I peel off my T-shirt and flex my hard pecs for him. Slowly I slide my black denim jeans down the white globes of my perfectly shaped ass. I am now completely nude in the presence of a leather master. I'm a piece of goods. Naked. Trying to convince a man that I'm worth his time. I start showing off my assets.

I caress my chest. Pinching and squeezing my nipples. "Yeah. Look at these babies. Nice and tender. Tasty too. You could really chow down on a pair of nipples like these."

Carl reaches over and pinches my right nipple like a vise. I drop to my knees in pain as he pulls and twits it.

"Owwwww! Shit, that hurts," I gasp.

SMACK! Carl backhands me across the face.

"Thank you, Sir. May I have another?"

SLAP! SMACK! Two more blows land on my cheek of tan.

"Thank you, Sir," I say eager to move attention away from my face, please don't forget my other cheeks. I turn around and wag my bad boy bottom for the man in charge. A swift kick from a leather boot sends me sprawling across the floor.

"You aren't doing a good job of convincing me, boy."

Lying on the floor I reach back and spread my cheeks. "You're telling me that's not convincing you. That's a fucking cherry hole I'm offering you. You want it? You want to rape my ass with your hand? You want to steal my cherry? Do you?"

"Stand up!" Carl orders.

I do. Surprisingly my cock is still hard. I've never guessed that submitting to the abuse of another man is so erotic. Carl's focus turns to my dick. I've always been so proud of my family jewels. I'm lucky to have such a big, beautiful dick and well proportioned balls and a thick hairy bush. I am definitely centerfold material and I know it. But now I'm anxious to surrender these assets to the man in charge. Eager to see what he'll do with them.

Carl starts by delivering a stinging slap to the underside of my shaft. I wince in pain, but find the sensation oddly pleasurable.

"This," Carl says grabbing my fuck set and twisting it–HARD. "This is going to need a lot of work. Too long you've been a slave to your cock and balls. Snotty bastard. Thinking you're something special cause you lucked into a big box of tools. You're nothing. You're a worthless whore. I'll show you who's in charge. WHAP! BAP! Two more blows to my manhood before he leads me over to the sling.

Neatly laid out on a table beside the sling are a six-pack of Bud, box of tissues, a jar of Elbow Grease and a box of surgical gloves. It's really happening. Carl really is going to try and fist me. Carl lays me back in the sling, shackling my arms and legs. I am completely at his mercy. He pops open a beer, pours it down my throat. The cold brew comes too fast; I gasp and choke as it runs down my chin. As I try and catch my breath I feel alligator clamps bite into my nipples. I feel sexy.

Roughly, Carl seizes my most valuable possessions. He amuses himself by batting them around. I am powerless to stop him. I have to take his abuse and thank him for it. From the black box on the table he takes a leather string and binds my balls up TIGHT! Carl crisscrosses the string up the length of my shaft, the rawhide biting into my fuck flesh. Just below the corona he ties a knot. My mushroom shaped head swells purple from my excitement and the leather bondage.

The man in charge takes a handful of clothes pins, smaller than normal size, and clips them at the two at the base of my dick head. The rest chomp into my aching nuts, I've never seen anything as beautiful as the sight of my own big cock bound and clipped, being slapped around by a leather daddy. I'm afraid the excitement of it all will make me shoot without permission. Carl lights a joint and shoves it into my mouth. With my hands constrained, I have no choice but to smoke the entire thing, letting the hot ashes fall onto my chest.

"You ever seen your asshole, boy?" Carl barks.

I shake my head no. I've seen many fuck puckers before, but never my own. Carl holds a mirror at an angle so I get a clear view of my long, hairy ass crack, with my confined boyhood drooling precum above it and my tight, virgin shitter smack in the middle. Carl makes a fist and holds it next to my hole to give me an appreciation of what I've agreed to let inside me. It seems impossibly large. I see my butt hole involuntarily quiver. Carl rubs his index finger around the outer lips of my opening. He's spreads my tight little pucker opening letting me see the velvety inner walls of my chute.

Carl sucks a finger and I watch transfixed as it slowly disappears inside the crevice. The wrinkled pucker of my ass lips grip the man's digit, holding it tightly in an obscene embrace of faggot lust. I moan in ecstasy as the invader locates my prostate. Suddenly Carl pulls his finger out, leaving my hungry ass vacant and throbbing. I swallow the joint roach and, now completely stoned, watch as Carl slides a latex glove over his massive hand.

With a sharp blow right to my opening, he slathers the lubricant on my quivering entrance. Since Carl has set the mirror down I close my eyes and concentrate on the sensation.

"Look at me, boy," Carl snaps. "I want to see the look on your face as I remove the last bit of your manhood. You can't take a fist up you fucking ass hole and still call yourself a man. You do realize that don't you, you stupid whore?"

"Yes, Sir," I answer, opening my eyes.

"How's your ass feel boy."

"It hurts a little, Sir."

"I've only got two fingers in you, boy. You've got a hell of a long way to go."

"Make it three," I beg, "Make it three and I'll be over half- way there."

Another finger squeezes past my ass ring. I will myself to relax as Carl's fingers pump in and out of my hole. It feels so good being finger-fucked that I regret all the years I kept my cherry intact. I grind my ass forward pushing my slut butt onto Carl's hand.

"Fuck, yeah, man. Fucking open up my hole. Make it four fingers inside my fucking pussy hole."

"Yeah, that's the stuff. Open up that hole for my fucking fist, whore. Ride up and down on my hand."

I can feel four fingers inside me I whimper in ecstasy, "Yeah, man. I should of let you do this a long time ago. Should've let you fist my fucking punk ass!"

Carl slaps my face. "Yeah, slut, I'm gonna fuck that ass of yours."

"Yeah, do it. Do whatever the fuck you want," I say. I never dreamed being completely subjugated by another man could be such a rush. Carl's thumb assaults my ass ring, stretching it even wider. I have five fingers inside my asshole!

"Oh God, you're fist fucking me, aren't you?" I moan.

Carl holds up the mirror so I can see my formerly virgin hole grasping tightly around his fingers. "I'm not fisting you yet. I'm going to get inside that slit of yours up to my wrist."

I groaned. I was so proud to take five fingers up my old dirt road that I'd forgotten that when men talk about fisting they mean the whole fist! I'm scared. I don't think I'm relaxed enough to take his whole hand.

I'm wondering if I can stop it and still get all the money, when Timothy asks me if I have any words for the viewers at home. I think for a moment and say, "I'm a fist-fucking slut and I'm going to take that entire hand up my ass!" With that I push down on Carl's fist My ass is clenched around the widest part of his hand. I can't go any further.

Then Carl holds up the mirror again, "Look at that, boy, look at that fucking hand going deep inside you." I stare at my asshole stretched wide open over his hand. Without realizing it I watch as it disappears. As my ass hole opens up and swallows the rest of Carl's hand. God!

"You did, boy. You did," Carl says, "How do you feel?"

"It feels so good. But I'm scared. It's such an intense feeling."

"Stroke your dick boy. I want you to come while I'm fisting you."

My prick is incredibly hard and it moments it explodes without my touching it. The feelings and sensations are so intense that I start to sob. Slowly I feel Carl's fist gently slide out of my hole. He holds the mirror up so I can get a good look at myself. My ass has become a huge, pulsating pussy and I don't care. I loved it. I look into the camera and say, "Shit, that's what I've needed for a long time."

\* \* \* \* \*

Tyler got back to South Carolina. He sent me a postcard from Myrtle Beach. He's working in a T-shirt shop–and living with a boy his own age.

# Dreams in the Night

## *Bert McKenzie*

"Bob, I've known you for years. You're as healthy as a horse despite your diet. But you didn't really come here just for a physical. What's eating you?"

Bob looked at his friend for a long minute, then dropped his gaze and began to rebutton his shirt. "Gail and I are trying to have a baby," he said uncomfortably.

Jerry's face of concern broke into a wide grin. "A baby? Well, that's great! It's about time you two settled down and concentrated on a family." Bob continued to look down at the tiled floor and squirmed nervously on the edge of the examination table. "Okay," Jerry said, again frowning in worry. "So what seems to be the problem."

Bob raised his head and finally looked his doctor in the eyes. Jerry noted the sense of panic that slowly etched his face. "Jer ... do you think I could be ... gay?"

For a moment the doctor thought he misheard his friend. Then he let out a belly laugh. "Gay? You?! Bob, how many times did I make a pass at you back in the dorm at ESU when we were undergrads? No, I hardly think you're gay."

"Jer, I'm serious. Are you sure?" Bob's voice held the sharp edge of hysteria as he reached out and grabbed his friend's arm.

"Okay, okay, sit down over here and let's talk about this," the doctor said, leading his friend to a comfortable chair opposite a small desk. "Now what makes you ask if you're gay?"

Bob took a couple of deep breaths to calm himself, then began to talk. He told his friend about how he and Gail had decided to have a baby, and about how they had been actively trying for quite some time now without much success. He took another deep breath and began to tell about the dream.

At first it was only an occasional occurrence, but now it seemed to happen almost every night. The dream always started the same way. Bob is in bed with his wife, tossing and turning. He awakes to find himself stifling under the covers, as if he can't breathe. There is no oxygen in the hot, stuffy room. Bob throws the covers back and gets out of bed, fighting for air. Somehow Gail always manages to sleep through this.

Drenched in sweat, Bob stumbles across the room, ripping off his pajamas, trying to find a cool breeze to comfort his overheated body. Fearing that he might wake his wife, Bob pulls the door open and steps into the living room. Here too, it is stifling, and Bob moves to the sliding glass doors that open onto a small balcony. He jerks the door open and is suddenly

greeted by refreshing, cool air as it rushed over his nude body, bringing welcome relief.

Despite the fact the moon is brightly gleaming, lighting up the balcony almost as bright as day, Bob steps out into the cool night air. There is a rush of adrenaline as he realizes he is still naked, and now in full view of anyone who might chance to look up at their apartment. Experiencing a bizarre, exhibitionistic thrill, Bob leans against the wrought iron rail, his hips thrust forward, reveling in the feel of the cool night breeze circling his cock and his balls, cooling the sweat-soaked pubic hair.

Only then does Bob realize he is being watched. He looks down to see a pale face gazing back up at him. Surprised and a little frightened, he steps back from the rail, slipping into the shadowy doorway, standing still and holding his breath to quiet the racing of his heart. Then a hand reaches up to the rail. It is the stranger who was watching. The young man climbs up the railing and then lightly leaps onto the balcony. Ghostly pale in the moonlight, his angular face is framed by long dark curls. His thin body seems covered in black, a dark t-shirt, dark jeans and boots which make his face, arms and hands appear that much paler. He appears young, little more than a boy, perhaps a teenager, maybe as old as eighteen.

Bob feels torn in two. He feels a sense of outrage and wants to ask what the hell this young man is doing on his balcony, but he feels a strange paralysis in his voice and muscles, a condition that isn't unusual in a dream environment.

The stranger takes a step forward and Bob recoils further into the shadows of the living room. The kid follows him into the apartment, then drops down, kneeling before Bob, his arms outstretched. An odd feeling of power seems to rush through Bob, power and control over this young man who has followed him into the room.

Bob steps forward, his hips thrust out, his dick in the boy's face. He watches with an unusual sense of detachment as the young man leans forward and kisses his cock head. His prick begins to stir, slowly coming to life as the stranger sticks out his tongue, lapping at the clear precum that oozes from the opening. He then opens his mouth a bit more and sucks Bob's hardening cock inside, swirling his tongue around the shaft and darting his head forward to swallow the full length.

Bob can feel his dick stabbing into the back of the stranger's throat. He begins to groan with pleasure as his legs start to tingle.

Bob throws his head back and allows his body to enjoy the physical pleasure. But it isn't just physical. There is a psychological pleasure too. He smiles as he watches the virginal young stranger, kneeling in submission and worshipping his body. He begins to pump forward, humping the boy's face. He reaches down, twining his fingers into the dark curls, and bucks his ass as he drives his eight-inch cock in ever faster rhythm. He is now thoroughly lost in his fucking.

Then, just as he is approaching climax, the strange boy pulls back, letting Bob's dick slide from his mouth. He reaches forward and lifts the throbbing man meat, ducking his head beneath it and opening his mouth, his tongue lapping at Bob's tight balls, drawn up against the shaft in their sack of flesh. The youth places his lips over Bob's nuts, sucking and biting, and then Bob begins to shudder.

His orgasm is more violent and satisfying than anything Bob has ever experienced. It puts his lovemaking with Gail to shame. The violence of his cumming always wakes him, and Bob finds himself in bed, next to his sleeping wife. He is nude and still has an erection, and his body is shaking from the after- effects of the climax, his chest covered with a clear, sticky liquid. He is surprised that it isn't thick blotches of creamy white cum.

"So how about it?" Bob asked uncomfortably. "You think maybe I really am gay?"

Jerry thought for a long moment, sucking on the end of his pencil, before responding. The story had really gotten to him and he had to cross his legs to avoid showing a deepening wet spot in the front of his slacks where his own prick was leaking its supply of precum. "You know, Bob, the mind is a tricky thing," he said, pulling the pencil slowly from his mouth as if it were a tiny dick he had been sucking. "As far as you being gay, well, no one is 100 percent straight or 100 percent gay. We all fall along a continuum. Most people are definitely way out there on the ends, mostly one way or the other, which accounts for straights and gays. I'm very close to the gay end.

"Some people fall close to the middle, which accounts for bisexuals. In the past I would have said you were on the other end of the continuum, close to the straight end of the graph. "But almost anyone, given the proper conditions, can have an experience, and even enjoy it, which he might never do under ordinary circumstances. If this dream fantasy really excites you, you might have some buried homosexual desires that you need to deal with." Jerry mentally slapped himself for making such an obvious psychological pass at his friend. He was ready to volunteer to be Bob's test case for a gay experience.

"But Jer, this isn't an isolated incident. I've been having this same dream almost every night for several months now." The hysteria was creeping back into Bob's voice.

"The exact same dream?"

"Well, practically. Sometimes it varies a little."

"How ... how does it vary?" the doctor asked, his own body temperature escalating as he reached down to rearrange his cock which was already uncomfortably hard in his tight slacks.

"Well, sometimes he ... does it to me on the balcony in full view of anyone who might walk by."

"He sucks you off, outside?" Jerry responded, running his tongue over his dry lips.

"Yeah, and sometimes he strips himself naked before he does it to me."

"What does he look like?"

"I don't know," Bob responded with the typical disinterest of a straight man. "Just like any skinny, pale, naked kid. Once, he did it to me right in the bedroom while Gail slept beside me."

"He just climbed into bed with the two of you and sucked your cock?"

"Yeah, he gave me a blow job right there next to my wife. What upsets me is, he was a whole lot better than she could ever hope to be. Crazy, isn't it?"

Jerry swallowed slowly, nodding in what he hoped would look like a professional manner. Then he pulled his thoughts together and tried to focus on the problem, purely as a physician. "Bob, you said you were trying to conceive a baby without much luck."

"Yeah."

Jerry began writing on a small pad on the desk. "This is probably nothing more than an anxiety-provoked dream. It's your subconscious trying to deal with the pressure to perform, and the lack of success. I'm prescribing you a mind tranquilizer which should help with the anxiety, and I'm referring you to Dr. Goldfarb. He runs a fertility clinic. I want you to have him check you over, and if he doesn't find any problems, then that will take the pressure off and solve your dreams. And if he doesn't find anything wrong with you, then we need to get Gail in to see him."

"Thanks, Jer," Bob said, his eyes tearing up in gratitude.

* * * * *

Two weeks later Bob was sitting in yet another office. Dr. Goldfarb was not at all what he had expected. He thought he would be meeting some stodgy old man with white Albert Einstein hair. Instead, the doctor appeared to be a young man in his late twenties dressed in a conservative, Republican style. The doctor shuffled through some reports on his desk, then looked up.

"I think we've determined the cause of the difficulty," the doctor said as he picked up a piece of paper and scanned it while he spoke. "You have one of the lowest sperm counts I have ever seen."

"Why?" Bob asked. He always thought of himself as a normal, virile man, and this young preppy doctor seemed to be challenging that image.

"Well, we would have to run some further tests to determine the actual cause." He blinked his eyes in surprise as if he never expected Bob to ask such a preposterous question.

"And what can be done about correcting the problem?" the patient pressed.

"Well that all depends on the root cause. Assuming there is no physiological damage, we may be able to try some hormone therapies or other techniques to raise your sperm count." The doctor again shuffled the papers on his desk. "Let me ask you some very personal questions. How often do you and your wife have sex?"

Bob blushed a bright red and focused on the floor when he answered. "We used to do it just all the time, but lately I'd say once every two weeks or so. Sometimes even less."

"And do you have any other sex partners?"

An image of the young man from his dream flashed into Bob's mind. Then suddenly his brain played a trick on him. He looked up at the young doctor sitting across from him, and for a moment, the man appeared to be naked. Bob shook his head to dislodge the image and the doctor appeared clothed again. "No!" Bob responded a bit too enthusiastically.

"What about masturbation? How often ..."

"I don't."

"Mr. Rusk, there's no need to be embarrassed. It's perfectly natural to ..."

"I don't!" Bob again blushed. How could he talk about beating off to this preppy snob. "I don't need to. I ... I've been having this dream."

The doctor's eyebrows raised slightly. "You've been having nocturnal emissions?"

"Well, I have this erotic dream, and I guess it satisfies me. I don't think I actually cum. I mean, when I wake up I'm only covered in what looks like precum. There isn't any ..." He couldn't really go on. It was too personal. "Well, it seems to take care of things."

"And how often do you have these erotic dreams?"

"It's only one dream. I have the same dream almost every night."

Dr. Goldfarb stood up and stepped to a side door, opening it and revealing a small examining room. "Mr. Rusk, would you step in here, please?"

"Why? What are you going to do?" Bob asked, his stomach suddenly cramping with nerves.

"I just want to give you a simple examination. If you'd please undress and put on this gown, I'll be right with you." Bob stripped out of his clothes, slipped the paper gown on, and then sat nervously on the edge of the padded exam table. In a few moments the doctor returned and pulled on some disposable plastic gloves from a drawer. "Stand up, please." The doctor squatted down, lifting the gown and reached out to examine the patient's cock. Bob had to grit his teeth and look at the ceiling, counting the holes in the acoustic tile. There was something in the doctor's position that reminded him of the strange young man in his dream, kneeling before him. Again he had a mental picture of the doctor naked, and he suddenly felt himself begin to get aroused.

"Mr. Rusk, when did you injure yourself?"

Bob quickly glanced down. "What do you mean? I haven't ... ah!"

Dr. Goldfarb was holding his prick out of the way and examining what appeared to be small puncture wounds on his balls. When the doctor touched the area, expecting it to be tender, it provoked an entirely different and unexpected reaction. Bob, already becoming aroused, suddenly grew rock

hard, his dick shooting up to its full length, jerking itself out of the doctor's hand and curving up toward his belly. It throbbed and precum began to ooze from the opening. Bob's body showing all the signs of imminent orgasm. The physician reached out to take hold of the pulsing penis. "What caused this?" he asked, his brow wrinkling in confused concern.

All Bob knew was that he had to get out of there before he embarrassed himself by shooting his load all over the young doctor's face. He jerked back, pulling his throbbing prick from the doctor's grasp and grabbed for his clothes. Despite the doctor's protests, he quickly dressed and ran out the door, out of the office and out of the building, his dick still making an obvious tent in his pants.

Back at home Bob locked himself in the bathroom and stripped his slacks off to examine himself. Once again he gently lifted his now flaccid dick and studied the small red marks on his ball sac. He reached down and gently touched them, and he again instantly grew hard as a rock. Bob pressed against the marks and felt his body begin to tremble and tingle, then he suddenly felt moisture: A thick secretion of white mucous was oozing from the red marks while he felt the cresting waves of an orgasm. He groaned with pleasure and jerked, trying hard not to fall over, however, nothing came from his penis but thin stream of clear fluid. His cum, usually thick and gooey, was replaced by what looked like a cascading supply of natural lube. As Bob caught his breath, he sat back on the edge of the bathtub. "It's real," he muttered. "It isn't just a dream. It's really happening and that weird kid did this to me. No wonder we can't have a baby. No wonder I have a low sperm count. He's taking it. He's taking all my cum!"

That evening, Bob sat in the living room, ready and waiting, determined to stop this insanity once and for all. Gail was already sleeping soundly in their bed as Bob sat in the dark. He relaxed outwardly, but his body tensed inside with anticipation, a small caliber pistol resting in his lap. Around one in the morning Bob jerked awake. He must have dozed off. Everything seemed just as it was before, only it seemed overly warm. He stood up and stretched, then realized that he was drenched with sweat. Ignoring the closeness of the room, Bob began to pace nervously, but that only made things worse. His body began to itch, and then to burn. It was as if his clothes had been treated with acid. Putting the gun down on the end table, he quickly began ripping off his shirt, pants and underwear. In a matter of seconds he was standing in the center of the room, totally bare-ass naked. Bob turned to the balcony door, feeling the call, only this time he wasn't asleep and he wasn't dreaming. This time he knew his experiences were really happening.

Bob opened the sliding glass door and stepped back. A moment later his pale visitor quietly vaulted the balcony rail and stepped into the room. Despite his revulsion, Bob's body began to respond, his thick rod slowly growing and raising up to meet its expected lover. The young visitor quickly

peeled off his shirt, kicked off his boots and dropped his jeans. Now naked too, he stepped toward his victim.

"No," Bob managed to say.

The visitor froze, a look of surprise on his thin, angular face. "So," a soft voice issued from him, warm and comforting. The voice seemed weighted with age, an age that was belied by his youthful appearance. "The change has come already."

"Change?" Bob suppressed a shudder.

"Yes. You are no longer in a hypnotic state. You are fully aware. I am no longer in control of you."

The words made an impact, causing his heart to beat more rapidly. Bob was now in control of his own actions, and yet, he felt a nagging worry eating at the back of his consciousness. "What did you do to me?" he demanded.

"I fed," the boy answered simply. "Just as you will now feed. Here." The kid reached down and cupped his own balls, pulling them forward. They were full, round and low hanging, a man's nuts, not a child's. "You know the hunger ... now."

And he did. Bob tried to resist. His logical mind said he was a normal, healthy, straight man. But this wasn't about sex. It was about hunger. He now had a burning desire, a desire to drop to his knees and worship the young visitor in the same manner he had been worshipped. His thoughts of revenge, and the gun lying on the end table were gone. His thoughts of Gail and the baby they wanted were just dim shadows in the recesses of his mind. All that mattered was the need, the hunger and the need to worship, to kiss and caress those nuts in their skin sack. The need was on him to reach up and take that rising tube of flesh between his lips and suck it into his mouth. He wanted to taste the cum issuing from his young night visitor.

Bob fell to his knees, opening his mouth. The boy stepped forward and pushed his prick up against Bob's mouth. The lips parted and it slid smoothly into the hot, wet cavity, pressing down into Bob's throat and making him gag for a moment on the unaccustomed fullness. "Such fools," the soft voice said in the darkness above him. "They thought it was the blood we came for."

A startled gasp broke the silence, and the young visitor looked up to see the wife standing in the bedroom doorway. He grinned, then began the chuckle, the sound swelling to a full, throaty laugh. "Behold," he said softly. "Behold your husband, feeding as one of us." He gestured down to where Bob was working furiously. His head was darting as he sucked and lapped at the boy's cock, fingers reaching around to the naked ass and forcing the young man deeper into his mouth, fucking himself on that hard shaft.

The quiet was shattered with the loud, staccato report of the revolver. The noise seemed to break the trance, and Bob looked up in horror at his wife as the visitor collapsed before him. In a last reflex, Bob swallowed the thick cream which had only moments before shot out of that now dead body

John Patrick

and into his throat. Gail held the smoking gun at arms length, still pointing to where the succubus had stood.

\* \* \* \* \*

She knew her nightmare was not over. In fact it seemed to be only beginning. Although he appeared to be the attentive husband, there was now a vast difference in Bob. His doctor had told her that her husband was sterile, and that knowledge may have affected how Gail viewed him. But that wasn't what really bothered her the most.

Bob didn't know that his wife frequently awoke in the middle of the night when he was gone. Once or twice she had seen him slip out of the bedroom and leave their apartment. He slipped off his pajamas and then naked, climbed off the balcony to prowl into the darkness beyond. At first he returned in a few hours, waking her almost nightly to mad, passionate love-making. It was almost as if he had to give her his cum as quickly as possible.

Then Gail became pregnant! Once he realized this, Bob again changed, still slipping off naked into the darkness, but he never returned to fuck her. He had done his duty. Now his nightly travels seemed only destined to satisfy his own physical urges. She knew what he did. There was often a telltale streak of cum at the sides of his mouth, or flaky patches of dried jism in his chest hair. Although the doctor said he was sterile he was the only man to make love to her, and she still got pregnant. Gail often wondered about that. She would sometimes sit up, waiting for him to climb back onto their balcony, his lust satisfied. Then she would ask him, "Who is the father? Who is the real father of my baby?"

Bob would only look at her with a distant stare, smiling as he licked the taste of man from his lips.

# Pokey

## *Greg Bowden*

It was dusk and I had about given up on picking up a hitchhiker when I saw him, standing by the guard rail, holding out his thumb: five-foot-ten or-eleven inches of slim young beauty, with short, curly reddish-brown hair and the sort of smile they use to sell toothpaste. I slammed on the brakes and pulled onto the gravel shoulder. Lowering the passenger side window, I asked, "Where're you headed?"

He came over to the car and bent down. Looking in, he said, "Atascadero. You know, down the road?"

"I know. Hop in."

He picked up his backpack, swung open the door.

"Toss it there in the back seat."

We drove along for a few miles in silence. Finally, he reached for the knob on the radio. "Mind?" he asked.

"Sorry. It just gave out. I guess I'll have to replace it."

He shrugged and leaned back, stretching his legs. I gazed at the admirable bulge at his crotch. I lingered over it, making sure he saw where my eyes were glued.

He didn't say anything, but shifted around in the seat, making the bulge even more enticing. His stomach was growling.

"Hungry?" I asked.

"Yeah. I haven't had anything to eat all day."

"Tell you what, if you provide the entertainment I'll give you enough to buy a big steak dinner."

"What do you mean 'entertainment'?"

"Well, I'll tell you. What you have to do is take your shirt off, push your pants down and play with yourself while we go. And you have to come at least once before we get there."

"And what're you going to be doing all this time, feeling me up? No way, man."

"I keep my hands to myself. No touching, no fooling around. I just want to watch you get off. What do you say?"

"Well! That's all I have to do? Just play with my dick while you watch? I don't have to touch you or anything?"

"Just play with your dick. But you do have to come at least once, don't forget that."

"You get off on that? Watching a guy fooling around with himself? That's weird, man, really weird."

I laughed. "Don't knock it until you've tried it, I always say."

"I don't know."

"Come on. It'll be dark soon and I want to see it without having to turn the lights on."

"Well, I am hungry." He shrugged out of his T-shirt, threw it on top of his backpack in the back seat.

I liked what I saw but wanted more. "You going to take your pants down?"

"Yea, yeah, just wait a minute. This is kind of embarrassing, you know? I never did anything like this before! In front of someone I mean. I guess I jacked off a million times before but ... ! Well, it's weird, that's all." He fingered the buttons on his jeans for a moment and then suddenly pulled them open, shoving them and his shorts down to the floor. "Okay, there. That what you want to see?"

"That's what I want to see. It's a handsome one, too. You're lucky. Your folks left you natural."

"Natural? I don't think I ever saw an unnatural one. Did you?"

"No, I mean they didn't have you circumcised. I like that. Most guys don't have any skin."

He turned and looked directly at me for the first time since he'd gotten in the car. "You seen a lot of guys? I mean, do you do this a lot?"

"When I can. Is that beginning to feel good, your dick being out in the air like that? Looks to me like it's beginning to grow."

He looked down at himself. "You want me to jack off now?"

"Suit yourself. But remember, you have to play with it all the way to Atascadero. Maybe you want to hold off for a bit!"

"Maybe. It's beginning to feel awful good though." He took his cock in his hand and fondled it for a couple of minutes. Then he raised his hands, like a hold-up victim. "Look at that. It'll stand up all by itself."

"It's a strong one, all right. Pretty big, too. Skin it back, will you? I want to see what the head looks like."

He pulled the skin back, holding it at the base. "Like this? Makes it looked clipped doesn't it, like the other guys." He held on to the base, watching me look at him. "You like that? I thought you liked them! What'd you call it? Natural?"

"I do. Natural ones are the best but I like to see it that way, too."

"It won't stay like this. Look, see how the skin just slides up? It wants to stay covered up."

"Can I see that again?"

"This?" He pulled the skin back again and then let it go, watching it slowly slip up to cover the head of his cock.

"Yes. That's nice."

He did it again, still looking at his cock. "Can't let it do that too much. It feels too good." He let go of his cock and moved lower, hefting his scrotum.

"You like that, playing with your balls?"

"Yea. Sometimes. Lets my dick cool down some." He was silent for a bit, kneading his balls and taking quick glances at me. "You're really getting off on this, aren't you? Watching me? You watch a lot of guys?"

"Some. When I can. You ever play with your tits when you jack off?"

"Why? You get off on that too?"

"Not especially. Unless you do. I like seeing whatever you like doing."

His hand slowly drifted up to his chest. "They get hard, sometimes, just like my dick, if I play with them." He licked his middle finger and lightly touched his nipples. "See? Just like tiny little dicks sticking out of my chest." He closed his eyes for a few minutes, giving himself up to his nipples. "Aw, man, I can't keep doing this too long, you know?"

"I can see. Your dick is beginning to shake."

"It does that. When it's aching to let go. It just wants to unload all that stuff my balls are pushing up to it." He stroked his dick a few times, slipping his fist over it and slowly pushing down until his cock head pushed out through the circle of his thumb and forefinger. "Man, I think I just gotta get it off. It's too much!"

"Skin it back. I want to see the cum shoot out."

"Sure? I mean, I shoot a lot." He pushed his fist down one more time and sucked in his breath. "Okay. Okay, here it comes, man. It's on the way. Really. Here!" He took his hands away and let the first few shots go wild, his dick jerking and spitting where it pleased. After that he took it back in his hand, making it last.

"That was beautiful. There's some Kleenex there if you want. Under the seat."

He found the tissues and dabbed at himself. "Oh, man, it's always so sensitive after I come, you know? I can hardly touch it, even with the skin up." He wiped his belly and chest and then glanced around. "Sorry, I guess I got it on the console, too, didn't I? I told you I shoot a lot. Here! Shit, I got you, too. You want a Kleenex?"

"No, I'm okay. And it's not yours, it's mine."

"It is! You mean you shot off in your pants? Watching me get off?"

"It happens once in a while. When it's very exciting."

"I can't believe it. I got you off. Just by sitting here jacking off." He looked out the window for a few moments, thinking. "You do that when you watch other guys?"

"I told you, it has to be very exciting for it to happen. And let's not talk about other guys. Let's talk about you."

"What do you mean? Talk about what?"

"Whatever you want to talk about. How did it feel when you came just now?"

He shrugged. "I don't know. Good, I guess. You know?"

"No, I don't know. I wouldn't ask if I knew."

"It's hard to say." He was quiet for minute, actually thinking about it. "Kind of cold, all through me, but hot, too, you know? Like it's these waves

or something, like when you sneeze only a million times better." He shook his head." "What can I say? It's like coming."

"Can you do it again? Before we get to Atascadero?"

"If we keep talking about it." He looked out the window again, his hand tracing a slow path down his chest. "My record is eight times. In one day, I mean. I probably could've done one or two more, only it got kind of raw, you know? From all the friction. One day in school, in physics class? we were learning about friction and Mr. Dodge, he's the teacher, he asked us for examples of what we couldn't have if we didn't have friction. I said 'orgasms' and everyone just cracked up. Except ol' Mr. Dodge. He got all embarrassed." He abandoned the passing scenery and looked at me. "You think he does it too? Mr. Dodge?"

"I never met a man who didn't."

"Yeah, I guess." His hands drifted back to his crotch and he began touching himself very lightly. "Look, it's starting to come up again." He shot me a quick glance. "You really like looking at it?"

"I really like that, yes. It's a very handsome dick."

"Why do they call it a dick when it's really a penis?"

"Why do you think?"

"I don't know. Maybe some guy named Richard called his that and it stuck. You know, like a pet name."

"That could be. Do you have a pet name for yours?"

"No!" He looked down, studying at himself. "You'd laugh."

"No, I wouldn't. Try me."

"Well! Okay. Pokey. I call him–it–Pokey sometimes."

"Why Pokey?"

"I don't know. Because he pokes out in front of me all the time, I guess."

"Yes, and it pokes a lot of pussy, I'll bet."

He shrugged. "Some."

"Yeah, Pokey. The pussy poker. That's very good. I like it."

He looked up at me again. "What do you call yours?"

"I never thought about it. I guess it doesn't have a name."

He grinned at me. "I know what I'd call him. I'd call him Shooter. 'Cause he shoots off in your pants all the time."

"Not all the time. But thanks, maybe I will name it Shooter."

"Would he be Big Shooter or Little Shooter?"

"Well, compared to you, if they were just lying there asleep, I guess it'd have to be Big Shooter. But up and ready for action, like Pokey is now, well, maybe Shooter Junior would be about right."

"No kidding. Can I see?"

"You like to look at other guy's dicks?"

He looked away. "No, but! Well, I guess everybody does, right? I mean, just to compare. See how you stack up and all."

"How do you think you stack up? In the locker room, say."

He shrugged and looked down at himself again. "Okay, I guess. But like you said, Pokey's not all that impressive when he's! asleep. There's lots of guys bigger than him."

"Too bad you can't show him off when he's up hard. I'll bet that'd give them something to be envious about."

"You think so? Like now?" He sounded excited.

"Especially like now, when he's half way to shooting and feeling so good. Haven't you ever seen any of the other guys when they're hard?"

"No." He played with himself for a while, thinking. "Well, maybe a couple. There's this one guy, Billy, who gets hard all the time in the showers. At first he tried to hide it but we all kidded him so much now he just lets it stick out and acts like he's proud of it."

"Should he be proud?"

"I guess. I mean, it's not as big as Pokey or anything but it's nice. He's clipped, too, so it's kind of different looking, you know, with no skin on the head or anything."

"Lots of natural guys don't have any skin on the head when it's hard. The skin just naturally slips back and you'd never know they had any. That's one reason I like yours so much, the skin stays up unless you pull it back."

"I never thought about that. I thought all uncut guys were like me."

"Didn't you ever see another guy with skin get hard?"

"Once. But he was like me. More. None of the head showed and when he shot off he held the skin closed and kept it all inside. I can't do that, I mean, it always overflows and runs out. Or shoots out all over the place if the skin is pulled back like it was, well, you know."

"You watched him jack off?"

"Uh, well, yeah, sort of. I mean, he was just finishing up when I came in the locker room and I think maybe he couldn't stop, you know? Like he was already there and even if he let go he'd still shoot off. It only took a couple of minutes and he didn't see me or anything." He went back to staring at his dick. "Anyway, it was interesting watching another guy like me do it."

"Skin it back and hold it for a minute, will you? I want to see how you'd look if you were clipped."

He slid his hand down the shaft, gathering and holding the skin at the base. "Like this? Shit, that really feels good, the air blowing all over it." He contemplated himself for a long moment. "You think it's okay? I mean, would I look okay if I was clipped?"

"Yes, I think you would. But I like it better the way you are. Let go and let the skin slip back up."

"I once wanted to see what it'd be like, being clipped, so I tried to go all day with the skin pulled back. I couldn't though, because it kept slipping back up, so I got me a rubber band–not a tight one, I heard if you put a tight one on your dick it might fall off–anyway, I put this rubber band around it, to hold the skin down."

"Did you like it, feeling like a circumcised boy?"

John Patrick

"I never found out. I couldn't stand it, feeling the head rubbing in my pants and it was hard all the time so I had to take it off."

"You should have used a condom."

"A rubber? What would that do?"

"Hold the skin back. And if you put on two you'd feel pretty much what a clipped guy feels because you wouldn't be so sensitive."

His cheeks colored just a little. "I ... I guess I never tried a rubber."

"There's some in the glove compartment there if you want to try one now."

He jumped at the chance. "Shit, you buy these things by the case? You must use a lot of them."

"Sometimes guys like to fool around with them. Go ahead, tear it open. Now, skin yourself back and just roll it on."

He positioned the condom on the head of his cock and noticed the reservoir tip. "What's this for?"

"That's for guys like you who shoot off with about a cup of stuff. It holds your cum."

"Neat idea. Man, that feels good, rolling down my dick. Hey look, it's keeping the skin down." He ran his fingers experimentally over the latex covered head of his dick. "But still, I'd have a hard-on all the time with the head out like that, rubbing around in my pants."

"That's why you need two. Or in your case maybe three. Go ahead, stick a few in your pocket and take them with you. You can experiment with them later."

"Okay, thanks." He pulled at the base of the condom, pulling it down tight and then letting it slip up just a bit. "It's really weird, you know? Wearing this thing? Like Pokey is in someone's fist, not even mine, and getting squeezed. And everything moves doesn't it, all along it. Man, I can't take much of this or I'm going to blow off again."

"You going to do that? Shoot off in the rubber? Or take it off and let loose in the air the way you did before?"

"Which way do you want?"

"Take it off. I like the way you smell when you come."

He nodded. "Yeah, I kind of get off on that too sometimes. After I come I rub it all over me, you know, just for the smell. And then I have to jack off again because, I don't know why, I just always do." He busied himself taking the condom off. "You ever taste it, your cum?"

"Do you?"

"Sometimes. Just lick my finger, you know? Just to see how it tastes."

"How does it taste?"

"Like it smells. Almost exactly like it smells except it's kind of salty, too." His voice was getting ragged and he seemed to be losing track of what he was saying. "I'm about ready to shoot, man. Shall I peal it back like last time?"

"Do what you always do, how it feels best to you."

"Oh, man, I think! Yea, it's coming, fast now. Get ready. Oh, shit, here it comes. Go, go, go ..." He did it again, dropping his cock at the last minute so it thrashed around and the first shots came out wild. Then he took hold of it again and stroked it hard and fast, squirting more of his stuff around the car.

"If you ever do that with a condom on you'd better be careful. I don't think the condom's been built that could hold it all." He reached for the window switch but I stopped him. "No, don't put it down yet. Let's keep the smell in the car for a while."

He dug under the seat and pulled out the last of the tissues to mop up his chest and the dash board. "You're running out of Kleenex, you know?" He glanced out the window. "Hey, this is my exit comin' up. Can I put my pants back on now?"

"Yes, and you can let the window down, too. I think I've got you memorized."

"What, my smell? You going to stop somewhere later and jack off, thinking about me and how I smell when I come?"

"I'll probably wait until I'm home in bed but yes, I'm going to jack off thinking about you and Pokey and how you both smell when you come. You mind?"

"I guess not. I mean, I'll be doing the same thing, thinking about you, you know? About jacking off for you and how much you got off on me doing it. So I guess we're even, huh?"

"I guess maybe we are. Now, where shall I drop you?"

"Right here is okay. It's only a couple of blocks and I think I need the walk. You know, to kind of cool off. See ya."

"Have a nice dinner," I said, giving him a twenty.

"Thanks," he said as he hopped out of the car and retrieved his backpack.

"Thank you," I said.

"Sure," he said, grinning.

And then he went off down the street, disappearing into the night without even a backward glance.

# Sex on a Summer's Night

## *John Patrick*

Florida is not its best in the summer. With each day a carbon copy of the last, temperatures hovering in the 90s, it's too uncomfortable to leave the house during the day and claustrophobia sets in. One lives for the nights. On a steamy night in '84, I was at the Carousel Club where, amid chaos and ugliness, there always seemed to be a modicum of beauty. I was following my usual practice of taking in the entirety of it and, within that, disregarding the things that disgusted me and concentrating on the things that seemed to grow more lovely with every drink. Suddenly, at the opposite end of the bar, I saw a new face, a fine face, one that inspired me to rise and take a closer look. I stood behind him and drank in the sight of the young, lean, beautifully-tanned torso and, when he turned to see who was staring at him, the sly smile. He wore no shirt and I admired the highly developed pectorals. The jeans were filthy and he showed no basket but his face was divine, his dishwater-blonde hair falling over it because of an unflattering cut. Considering the totality of it, I knew with a bit of scrubbing, a bit of polish, this could be a diamond.

At first, he was paying unusual attention to the balding, 50-ish man sitting at the bar to his left. I observed the interplay for a while until finally the man got up to go to the john. My desire for the boy was so great that I threw caution completely to the wind and approached him. "Whatever he's paying, I'll double it."

The boy blinked, shook his head incredulously, then smiled. "Okay." Saying nothing more, he reached up and yanked his T-shirt from a rafter above the bar and began moving towards the exit. As we approached my Mercedes roadster, he chuckled, "Oh, yeah."

"I like it," I said, unlocking my door and hitting the button to open his.

As he slid into the leather bucket seat, he asked, "Where do you live?"

"At the beach," I replied.

"All right," he said emphatically, then introduced himself as "Tracy."

During the 45-minute ride to the beach, he laid his history on me: he was from Texas, had only been in town a short time, had a job at Intertel fixing phone lines and his car had broken down so he had no way to get there. I vowed if I had anything to do with it, he wouldn't have to return to that job.

After a drink at my bar, we retreated to the bedroom and I went to relieve myself. When I returned to the bedroom, he was sitting on the edge of the bed nude. He wrapped his arms around my torso and hugged me, then proceeded to devour my cock. In my heightened state of sexual hunger, I came very quickly, but not without appreciating the quality of his efforts. He

seemed to have no desire for me to reciprocate so I joined him under the covers and he fell asleep in my arms. The next morning, he repeated the process, this time jacking off to climax as he sucked. At the height of our passion, I asked him to stay a few days. This involved picking up his things, which were, to use his phrase, "stored" at a man's apartment in Tampa. He told me he'd lied about the car, he didn't own one, and had lost his job at Intertel. He reminded me of Jean Genet's line, "For a time I lived by theft, but prostitution was better suited to my indolence."

Later that day, we went to the man's apartment and I witnessed my new lover's ability to open a door by sliding a credit card between the lock and the jam. I knew then I would never be safe from him. Still, he was quite methodical about taking only those things that he said were his and leaving a note for the man. On the way home, we stopped at a department store and I bought him a few new items of wardrobe, then got his hair cut and highlighted. That night, dressed for dinner, he was absolutely stunning. We celebrated our good fortune with a bottle of champagne.

When we returned home, he hurriedly undressed me and began blowing me. When I was hard, he undressed himself, lay face down on the bed and moved his hips seductively, offering up the prize he had not shared with me to that point. I kissed the ass cheeks, then invaded the space between them, first with my tongue, then with fingers coated with lube. Before long, I was charging my swollen flesh deep into his anus and he was bucking to meet every stroke. I wanted it to continue long into the evening but I came quickly, so excited was I at finding such a perfect sexual match. I crushed him with my spent body and he kissed me lasciviously on the face and lips. Before he drifted off to sleep, he thanked me for "everything."

The next night, after a late supper, we lay beside each other on the chaise on the deck, a salty gulf breeze blowing. I entered him gently and soon his cum was gleaming in the moonlight, splattered against his thigh. Palm tree shadows skittering across my tanned skin, he let me finish inside of him and I went crazy with it. Later, he said he wanted to watch a movie on TV so I went to bed. I switched off the light and the moon was like a lamp outside, illuminating the ripples of the Gulf. I closed my eyes and fell asleep at once, like the falling of a shutter in a camera which ends a time exposure. I slept peacefully and, if I dreamt, I didn't remember it the next morning.

Around noon, Tracy got up and, as he was coming down the stairs, still nude, I sat at the table eating a Swiss cheese sandwich on pale crusty bread, slathered with mayo. I felt like Isak Dinesen, who only ate white food. The beautiful blonde boy dropped to the cushion of one of the bar stools, just staring at me, a look in his eyes that was at once hopeful and desperate. I smiled, almost as if saying to myself: Take it easy. This too shall pass. But I knew it wouldn't pass quickly, not this time. It had been two days of bliss. The monotony, the ennui of the summer, had been erased in a single, decisive stroke. I knew what I was doing.

As he approached me, I held out my arms. He kissed me as he lowered himself into my lap. In a matter of moments, he was on his knees between my legs, fellating me with an eagerness that shocked me. I closed my eyes, sighed deeply and prayed that this one not pass quickly.

In order to keep Tracy, I knew I had to invent something for him to do. He was enamored of my computer so I had him take over the fulfillment operations of the real estate magazine I published. Like everything else he took up, he became immediately proficient at coding the subscriptions and processing the labels. A routine developed. In the morning, he would work at the computer, then take my second car, a Corvette, to the bank and post office. Our lunch consisted of wine, sandwiches and sex, usually him simply blowing me. But sometimes he would treat me to a full-blown fuck, depending on his whim. Then he would run on the beach and go swimming in the Gulf while I worked. Dinner was a fancy affair at a fine restaurant. I loved to watch him eat; his appetite was enormous. Afterward, we'd bar hop, see a movie, go shopping or just go home. The affection seemed to flow out of him. He could never ride with me without holding my hand; I could never stop spending money on him.

Evening always ended with his payment to me, namely the sex, usually with him on his stomach, moaning in ecstasy with my every thrust as I fucked him to orgasm. After I drifted off in a satisfied slumber, he would lie on the floor at the foot of our bed and jack off to pictures in Penthouse. At first I was shocked, but then I decided if that was what made him happy, so be it.

As summer turned into fall, we flew off to Key West for Fantasy Fest, California for Thanksgiving, and New York for Christmas shopping. It seemed I had found the tonic for my boredom in the person of a loving 20-year-old.

One day in early March I was on my way to a meeting when the car phone rang.

"Please come," Tracy cried. He had been to the bank and on the way home he had run a light.

When I arrived at the intersection where the accident occurred, I found the Corvette was totaled but he was not harmed. "It's a miracle," I said when we were in my car following the tow-truck. He was numb. His pride was hurt. He had hurt me. "I'm so sorry," he kept saying over and over.

"But you're all right, that's what matters."

"But the car."

"Really, you've done me a favor. I couldn't afford it anyway. Now the lease is paid off."

But our routine was broken. Tracy lost his license for six months. My young lover was deeply depressed. He moped around the condo for days. One day, I returned from the bank to find him gone. Minutes dragged into hours. Finally he showed, stoned out of his mind. He sat at the bar while I

fixed drinks. Before I had a chance to vent my frustration with him, he fell backward, narrowly missing a glass topped table. I put him to bed.

The next morning, he was still passed out when there was a knock on the door. It was Brett, a former prostitute with whom I had maintained a monthly assignation. Brett was always short of money and I was always eager to help him out. But I had begged off every call he had made to me since Tracy moved in. Now, however, my anger with Tracy was such that I wanted to attack someone, something, and the short, dark-haired bottom boy Brett provided the perfect outlet. But before I let things go too far, I wanted to show off my prize. We went quietly to the bedroom and I opened the door. Seeing Tracy was still out cold, I let Brett have a peek. When we returned to the living room, he said, "God, he's gorgeous. You'll have to have me over sometime for a three-way."

"Tracy's not that kind. Strange as it may sound, he's very jealous of me."

Brett groped me. "Yeah, I know why."

We went to the garage and I locked the door behind me. As I leaned back on the hood of the Mercedes and began massaging my hard-on, Brett dropped his shorts and backed over me. His hand steadying my erection, he lowered himself onto it, then pushed.

"God," he sighed, "I'd love to watch this big fuckin' dick going into Tracy."

"Maybe someday, but I doubt it."

"Oh, god, I love it," he moaned as he jacked off as he bounced up and down in my lap. We came simultaneously, but I was still in the mood to harm. I turned him around and made him lie across the hood while I continued to blast my flesh into him. I always let him come first and then showed no mercy in my final thrusts. For the first time this prostitute admitted he would come over for this even if I never paid him.

Later that afternoon, Tracy finally awakened. Part of me wanted to listen, the other part couldn't afford the hassle. He had become expendable.

Eager to make amends, he wanted sex. He caressed my arm, my thigh. As always, I bloomed under his magic touch and, as he eagerly took my cock in his mouth, I knew I was beginning to think too much.

He lay face down across my knees and I played for a time with his incredible bubble butt. I stroked it, pinched it all over, rubbed my hands up and down the division, then pulled the cheeks apart. I put my lips there and slathered the area with my saliva. He was always clean. I never feared touching any part of him. I reached under him and played with his erection as I worked my tongue into him. When he was close to coming, I worked two of my fingers in. After he came, I rolled him over. I mounted him and slid into him. Holding his cock tightly, I made love to him in earnest; heaving his bottom up to meet my plunges, he came again, this time more intensely than I had ever remembered. I followed suit, and, after a final

wriggle of my cock in his ass, we lay in each other's arms, breathing heavily. I decided to try to work things out.

But, as the days went by, his afternoon disappearances grew more frequent and prolonged. Occasionally he would return home after running on the beach and mention he'd met a girl and they had talked, but I reacted so negatively to such information that he stopped providing it. When he didn't show until after dinner, I would be furious with him and we would fight, only to make up and have sex, but I realized he had begun to feel trapped. I could sense he was psyching himself into enjoying the sex, pretending that it mattered. Early on, he had maintained he was basically straight, showing a peculiar lack of interest in passive sucking or active fucking. Those things, he led me to believe, he did with girls. I began to sense just having a place to stay became a sorry excuse for his sticking around. It had become a difficult, complex relationship of dependence and attachment, one that often arises between victim and victimizer, abuser and abused. We each had our own idiosyncratic moral vision and it became a thing of knots and complications, often sending me into despair but without somehow ever becoming truly hopeless. With each argument, it seemed it was an appalling revisiting of the past upon the present. Finally, I suggested we both seek psychiatric help. Tracy agreed but went only once, to take the test and to have a short chat with the doctor.

A week later, the doctor confronted me. "If you stay in this relationship, eventually one of you will be harmed. Terribly harmed, perhaps physically, indeed mentally." In a few moments, he told me everything I knew about my lover. I was amazed that a test and a simple chat could reveal so much about someone. "Oh, there's no mystery to it," the doctor said. "We study sociopaths like him all the time."

I wanted an answer to the question that might give focus to my dilemma: why? But this was the very answer the experts couldn't provide.

"We have few definitive answers," he said. "These people have had troubles from their earliest days. We have studied heredity, looking for a genetic explanation and there has been some evidence that it plays a role."

"Yet Tracy's parents aren't criminals. His father works for the phone company in Texas."

The doctor shrugged, as if the answer was beyond reason. "He may be lying to you. These people learn to become good liars, effective manipulators, as you've seen by his taking you on sexually, effectively learning to assert control over his world. But no matter how much in control they think they are, these people are completely unable to sustain meaningful relationships with anyone. If you know what's good for you, you'll end this."

Tracy was strangely silent when I returned from my visit to the doctor. He had told me he would not return. To him, it was so much "idiosyncratic bullshit." He seemed to sense from my quiet demeanor that I was deeply

troubled. He did what he always did in these moments, cajole me into sex, knowing that at the height of orgasm, all is forgiven.

We went to Tampa to dinner. I had too much wine and, mixed with the coke I had done earlier, I became unreasonable. We argued about the psychiatrist. I wanted him to see him again. He refused. He left the table and called a cab. I followed him. I knew he would go to the Carousel, to return to the place where we had met, to remind me of what a treasure I had found there amid the sleaze. As he was paying the cab driver, I parked the Mercedes and ran to him. Under the influence of drugs or booze or both, my wayward intelligence guttered like a candle. I grabbed at him, tearing his shirt. He swung and connected with my eye. I saw black and fell to the ground on the street in front of the bar, blood spurting from my eye.

The bouncer witnessed the scene and came to my rescue, whisking me to the hospital where an eye surgeon happened to be on duty. After stitching my eye, the officials asked me to stay overnight. When I refused, they ordered me a cab. I had the driver take me to where I had parked the Mercedes. The bar had closed; the lot was empty. I paid the driver $40 to lead the way while I slowly drove my car to the beach. On the way home, I recalled the trauma connected with my father's beatings. Fear. Pain. Hurt. Embarrassment. Degradation. Humiliation. Anger. Resentment. Powerlessness. Helplessness. Revenge. When he'd been drinking, I knew to keep my distance. The worst time was Friday nights, when he would watch boxing. The slugfests would put him in such a state that once they were over, he would seek me out, berate me for being such a sissy and throttle me as I lay helpless in my bed. If Mother had not intervened, I'm sure I would have been killed. One of the consequences of corporal punishment is that it sets the stage for the child to try out the behavior he has experienced.

In my case, I nearly killed several of my pets. When I tried this, I was scolded and often spanked. Very confusing. So I learned that I needed to grow bigger before I had the right to be violent. I learned that Dad's rules don't have to be consistent. I learned to mistrust dad. Dad's love was painful. I looked forward to growing up so I could be just like Dad. Mean. Tough. Big. And, maybe, just maybe, I would be big enough to kill him.

As I grew older, I sought out people I could dominate so if they disobeyed, I could discipline them. Power coursed through my body as I would lash out at the girl I dated in college and who eventually became my wife. My violence worked on her. I had earned my privilege of power. The cycle of violence was complete except for one thing, I didn't need to kill my father. I saw he was slowly killing himself with drink. And my wife couldn't take it. Most of the time she spent locked in our bedroom. But Tracy was not so easily disposed of. My violence did not work on him. He fought back and his rage was greater than mine.

When I arrived at the beach, Tracy had packed his things and the two suitcases were sitting by the front door. He sat on one of the bar stools.

"I'm sorry," he said.

"So am I." It could have been much worse, I realized. It was as much my fault as his. More really. If I hadn't been drinking, hadn't been doing coke ... but, still, it had been boiling up for weeks.

"I'll call a cab," he said, reaching for the phone.

I let him make the call. He could always tell the cab he'd called in error.

"I wish you wouldn't go–" I muttered, finally, as I lay down on the couch in the living room.

"Does it hurt?" he asked, standing over me nervously.

"No, it's numb. But I'm sure it'll hurt tomorrow and then when they take the stitches out in a week or so. But what hurts more than anything is what I've done. What I've done to us."

"It was my fault. All my fault. I haven't been right since the accident. I thought you'd take me back to Tampa right then but you didn't."

"No. I couldn't. I love you. I love you but we can't live together."

"I know. I've been all messed up. I really want to date girls."

"Perhaps this was just something you had to try out. Now you have to put it behind you. And it won't worry you anymore."

I rented a car for him for two weeks and gave him enough money to rent a room and keep himself together until he found work. He called every day and finally I agreed to see him. For lunch.

He didn't bother to knock, just walked in. I was opening a bottle of wine and when I looked up my anger with him, with myself, returned. He was so beautiful I wanted to smother him with kisses but I stood where I was, waiting for him.

"Hi," he said sheepishly, sliding onto one of the bar stools.

"Hi." As I poured the wine, a chill descended upon me. I handed him his glass and he sipped it.

"Tastes good," he said, half-smiling.

I came around the bar and sat next to him. He took my hand and squeezed it. I shook my hand free, like a young boy confronted with an over-ardent admirer.

He shrugged his shoulders and brought both hands to his glass of wine. He said he'd gotten a job at a gas station in Tampa and he was dating the owner's daughter, who was only 17.

"Nice pussy?"

"Shit, I haven't got that far yet."

"That's right. Take it easy. When they're that young they need to be broken in slowly." My denial of his power was coming at a cost of sentimentality. I remembered what my psychiatrist said, that such repression is unhealthy. Sooner or later the hate turns up. In my case, it was the fine line between love and hate. I could only hate something I loved so much. I wanted to cry but instead I smiled and kept listening as he chattered on.

We sat at the bar and ate chicken salad sandwiches and then I cleared the dishes away. When I returned to the dining room, he was still sitting on the bar stool but now he was nude. "I've missed you," he said, stretching his

John Patrick

arms wide, "soooo much!" I stepped close to him, letting his arms envelop me, press me tightly against his smooth, hard body. We kissed. It was a harder, more urgent kiss than any I had remembered with him.

His hand groped me. Feeling the bulge in my shorts, he whispered, "Yeah, you missed me, too."

The removal of my shirt and shorts was swift and he was on his knees, sliding my prick between his lips, down his throat. Before long, he was on his back on the carpet, his legs spread wide, and I was between them, entering him. As I lowered myself on top of him fully, his arms held me again and we kissed. My cock buried in him, I began fucking madly, and it was as if nothing had changed. Yet everything had changed. As I climaxed, I thought about offering him a hundred a week just to visit me on Fridays for lunch, but by the time I had withdrawn my dripping prick and was lifting myself from the floor, I came to my senses. He seemed to sense I was remorseful. As he pulled on his shorts, he said, "It's just not right, is it?"

"No, I'm sorry. This will have to be the end. I can't go through this. Neither can you. I love you more than you'll ever know but it's just no good."

"No, it's me. I'm no good," he muttered and raced out the door.

I slipped into my shorts and ran after him but by the time I reached the driveway, he had driven away.

Three days later, I found the little rental car in the drive, the keys in an envelope on the front seat. There was no note of explanation.

# Warm Nights on Tobacco Road

## *Edmund Miller*

*With no particular apologies to Erskine Caldwell.*

I 'member my first time like yesterday, well, it wasn't my first first time, seein' as how I was marr'd already. But I mean my first time with another fella.

He come through our little town o' Hick'ryville sort of by accident since there was a detour on out to the highway where the colored chain gang was a-workin'. And then the Hollow was all tore up count of the work that was being done them days on the big dam. My third cousin Hank threw his back out real bad workin' on that dang dam. Still feels poorly when a storm's a-brewin'. 'Course this was a couple o' year back. Afty that there dam went up, they done flooded out that whole area.

My first fella, he was one o' them travelin' salesmen. But we wouldn'ta o' had much use for any o' his 'lectrical appliances in them days seein' as we didn't have no 'lectricity till the dam came in. He was all suited up like a city fella, but he didn't look soft like most of them city boys. It was like to late, and he was like to lost, and we didn't have no phone, o' course. So I just invited him in to set a spell and maybe spend the night. Maryanne got him some victuals, and, I must say, for a big fella he et like a bird, barely pickin' at his food.

When Maryanne excused herself to put the little'ns to bed, naturally I invited him out to the still to have a nip or two. I handed him one jug and picked up another for myself. I took a big swig and just had time to grab his arm to keep him from doing the same thing. "Strangers 'round these parts usually find this stuff a might strong at first." He took it slow then t' begin. He mite not've et nothing, but with his likker he kep' up with me. He was game all right; I'll say that for him.

So we got to puttin' it back pretty good, and I was felling real nice 'n' cozy. And he must o' been feelin' mighty like to nearways the same 'cause he pullt out his makin's and started in to roll hisself one o' them cigarettes. Well, naturally I pullt out my cob and was just along to light up to be neighborly like when he put his hand on my arm and said, "No, try one of these."

Well, I don't hold much with smokin' on them cigarette things. All that rollin' and lickin' seems like a might bit o' get-go for all the howdy-do in the end, but he said as these was extry special. Well, I just had to be neighborly, so's I done went and lit the thing up. It was kind of hard at first gettin' the knack o' hanging the little thing from my lip and then pullin' it back away all the time t' take a good big gulp o' air. But I got the hang of it soon

enough. And danged if he warn't right: they was extry fine! For it warn't more'n the time it takes a cat to drop a kindle o' kittens afore I was feelin' all easy and loose like floatin' up in the sky.

He asked if I liked that cigarette he'd done give me, and o' course I did. So he made me up another. And while I was smoking that'n, I commenced to noticin' he was takin' off his shirt, sort of grad'al like as if the whole world was moving real slow. He had big arms bigger'n my upper legs. And his chest was big too. His things there, they looked like boobies to me just at first so naturally I reached out to touch 'em. I felt around real good kind o' caught up in the new idey that a man might could have somethin' up there that was just as interestin' as a girlie's but real different. Then I reckoned I was takin' a sort of liberty and started to pull my hand aback, only somehow slower than I thought I was gonna.

But he took a hold of the hand and held it right up ag'in' him, real gentle like. He was standing there just in his store-boughten undies by this time, and I was rubbin' his chest and a-rubbin' and a-rubbin', and it was just the most nat'al thing in the world. His boobies was all hard like rocks, but all smooth and slick too, and the edge was real clear t'round each of 'em on three sides. It was like a-falling off'n a cliff just to touch 'em. Though they was round sort o' like a girlie's and the skin was so smooth and purty, they didn't feel nothin' a-tall like Maryanne's, no siree, 'cause he had these little bitty ridges all t'along in between there 'stead of a great valley of flesh you could lose yourself in. Oh, he was real purty!

I took a few more puffs of that there cigarette he give me, then went back to examinin' these real interestin' new things. But then suddenly they just jumped right into my hands. Well, you can know I pullt back off real quick like and was about to near fall all the way back on my bottom. When I looked up ag'in I could o' sworn they was dancin'Chis boobies I mean, if you can beat that!. I knelt up in front o' him and slowly brought my hand back up to touch. And sure enough, danged if they warn't dancing, first the one and then t'other: they was bouncin' and jumpin' to beat all. I put my both hands up to get a feel o' this 'mazing sight.

Whiles I was a-doin' this, he must o' reached his hands back a-rears o' me and pullt me up real close right into that there hard valley o' his. Danged if it didn't a-turned out you could might get all lost in there afty all. I opened up my mouth to say somethin', but I mustn't o' couldn't o' seemed to think o' nothin' quite to the right. And whiles I had my tongue a-sort o' all a-hanging out anyways, I kind of went and pushed it 'round a bit and started lickin' away. I really must o' could o' liked it 'cause he tasted real sweet, not girlie sweet but maybe sort o' store-boughten sweet. He'd kind of let up on holding me all close by then, but then he done pushed my head over on to one o' his man-titties, and it was near t' leap into my mouth. It liked to fill up my mouth, if that don't beat all! I never seed something so big on no man afore and only oncet on no girlie t'either, as I re-call: that was my Aunt

Violie, the fourth wife o' my Uncle Seth the one what runned off with that travelin' preacher man.

Whiles I was a-lapping away at this man-titty o' hisn and it was a-bobbin' and -weavin' 'round my tongue, he must o' could o' reached over a-rear o' me and grabbed a hold of my shirt tail 'cause all of t' sudden I was a-tangled up in my shirt all inside out. I got kind o' mixed up at first and must of been a-fighting my way out, but he stayed perfectly calm and grabbed a hold o' my arms real firm like to quieten them, and then he just slipped the thing off over my head. Well, naturally the strap of my overalls was all undone by this time the good strap; the broken one was hangin' loose the whole time, o' course. And so the overalls just sort of slipped right down 'round my ankles too. I thought this was all kind of funny, me just standing there in my birthday suit, so I kind of got the giggles. But he was just calm as calm could be. He reached down and pullt the overalls away from by my bare feet, and there I was naked as a jay bird and twice as skinny, leastwise compared to him.

Next thing I knewed he was grabbing a hold o' my jewels, and when I pullt back a little 'cause it seemed to me just at first that that wasn't hardly right, why, I just fell over and near to pullt him down on top of me. Just near squooze me to death! But he must o' seen this a-coming 'cause he managed to hold hisself up off'n me. O' course he was laying right over on me all right; he just warn't touchin'. But then he did commence to touchin' and rubbin' hisself ag'in' me and then pullin' back and then rubbin' ag'in. And I noticed that his thing was about to pop out o' them tiny little store-boughts he was a-wearing, and it calculated to be just about the size o' my arm. He put the cigarette back in my mouth, and while I was a-puffin' away at this a few more times, dang if he didn't shimmy them store-boughts right off'n o' him, flappin' that big thing back down against my belly.

Well, by this time it seemed like a really good idey to give it a couple o' squeezes just to see if it was real, like. And sure enough it was, and it really truly was bigger'n my arm! As I was commencin' to contemplate that there point, I put the cigarette down and kind o' went at feelin' up his thing with both hands. There was a kind of big bone all down the front end o' his thing as it was a-swingin' and -swayin' up at me. I could might feel it in there with my own two hand, but I just couldn't scarce believe it. I ran my thumbs all along this bone inside there and I still couldn't hardly believe it. I never knewed a man have a bone inside o' his dickie afore. I had done seen one fella this big afore, of course, my cousin Zeke, but for all he used to like to pull his thing out and wave it 'round, I know for a fact he never could get it hard: his first two wives bein' sisters of mine and all.

Well, this fella did not seem t' have that problem, and whiles I was a-staring and -touchin' and -dreamin', he up and surprised me again-t'fore. I might must o' had my mouth hangin' open kind of just amazin' away and all, when didn't he just go and lean forward ever so itty bit, tucking the head o' his big thing hich was just about the size o' my Aunt Lucretia's prize

turnip from two years afore right dang into my open mouth. Well, right off I naturally gagged a little with the surprise sneakin' up on me and all. But then it did seem like a purty good idey oncet I had got to a-doin' it. So's I tried all t' swallow, and by openin' up real wide I could near t' get the whole thing a-goin' in countin' side t' side, I mean: I was only just able to get the head part in countin' top t' bottom, although he surely tried to get me to do some more, thrustin' and pushin' and changin' position like a house t' fire.

After we was goin' at this for some time, and I was kind o' workin' up a sweat the kind you get from hoein' a field for a whole day, why didn't he up and pull out all of t' sudden and turn 'round as he was about t' take a shit on my face or leastwise t' smother me! And didn't he just set down right on my face. Well, naturally, I opened my mouth to let out a holler, and then I discovered that his shitter was right there over my face. He was a-holdin' hisself open real wide like. And maybe you won't believe this, but somehow it seemed like a good idey at the time to be a-lickin' and -suckin' and -pokin' my tongue right in there. He tasted real fine. And I was all hot 'n' sweaty just at the idey o' having' that big mountain of a man settin' over my face near t' crush me flatter'n a field just ploughed under. Just thinkin' 'bout it was makin' my own dickie flap in the night breeze. I reached 'round and felt up his big thing ag'in, and sure enough there it was springin' up in the cool o' the night same as mine. I wrapped my fingers 'round it and gave it some strokes, still feelin' that amazin' bone all up the front side there. As I was a-lickin' away and a-strokin' away, he commenced to let fly with his jism all down over my hands and, truth to tell, all over my belly and legs and feet too. I even got me all sticky between my toes. And he just kep' spewin' and spewin', and I wasn't about t' stop him.

Well, naturally, my own thingy was gettin' all hot and bothered by this time, so when he was done a-spewin' and naturally just fell forward over me sort o' half-sleepin' the way you do, my dickie was a-takin' a rest there buried in between that big valley on his chest. And just feelin' those hard ridges there next to it, it just sort of got the idey of spewin' all by its lonesome. So it was a-spewin' off big, and I could near to feel it hittin' 'gainst his chin and then runnin' off down my legs kind o' slow and easy.

Well, he sort of woke up a bit a that. He even laughed hisself. Then he rolled off o' me, only he pullt me t'long with him so's I was atop o' him. And since he was a-laughin', he started ticklin' me to get me a laughin' right along to him. And whiles we was a-laughing and a-gigglin', he reached 'round in his duds setting there next to by us and pullt out some little bitty store package o' something. He tore it right open. And it turned out to be some little bit of inner tube no bigger'n that ugly ol' wart on Great Aunt Beulah. But he went and stuck this little bit o' inner tube up on top o' his thing, which was reposin' there takin' a little nap.

Well, much to my surprise, he commenced to pulling this bit o' inner tube down over his thing, and don't you know: it act'ally stretched and pullt all the way down or near 'nough to so's you couldn't hardly tell the

difference. Well, what with his pullin' and pushin' and me gettin' back in there and rubbin' and rubbin' and lookin' for the bone and all, it warn't long afore his thing was a-standin' up aga'n standin' high as my nevy Tall Luke with his hat on.

I thought I might kind o' try to hide the turnip ag'in, so's I got up on my hands and knees and was just leanin' over t' commence t' try when he up and slipped to his knees kind of lettin' me fall forward on my elbows sudden like. Well, then he did something even more surprising: he put one of his big hands between my shoulder blades keeping my head down there in the grass, and he put that bone o' his right up against my shit hole. Well, naturally I bucked a little, but then his thing was cool and slick from somethin' like molasses all over that bit o' inner tube. So before I quite knew what was happenin', he had his thing half way up inside me! I thought for a minute I was like to ex-plode. But it felt real good too, fillin' me up and puffin' me out. It was like discoverin' sex for the first time all over. And truth to tell, my own thingy was kind o' likin' it too. Leastwise it started in to grow. And then too I reckoned I had a real itchy feelin' back there behind. The more he did it, the more I liked it. And I just had to get him all the way inside o' me. So's I reached back 'round best I could kneelin' there with my head in the grass and sort o' pullt back on my ass cheeks, and all o' t' sudden there was a great whoosh and he shot forward into me like a tractor ploughin' a field on a big tobaccy spread. And it hurt somethin' fierce. But it hurt something' good.

But whiles I was a-screamin' but lovin' it all the same somehow, somethin' else happened. There was a terrible loud bang, and then there was a light flash like it was mornin' already. I think the cock crowed in there too. Anyway soon enough all the animals got to yappin'.

It seems that just when things was gettin' interestin', the dang still had gone and blowed itself up. I calculate it might o' had somethin' to do with that little cigarette I'd been a-puffin'. It looked mighty like it might could have caught on fire in the grass. There warn't very much grass around, I reckon, but there was some of that likker we'd might just have spilled in the grass. And I guess one thing led to t'other. And anyway, boom, up went the still.

Well, naturally all the noise brought Maryanne and the little'ns a-runnin' out of the shack to see what all the fuss was about. And there I was with my face in the dirt getting plugged like a bitch in heat. The traveling man just pullt out as calm as could be (there was a little poppin' noise). Then didn't he smile at Maryanne a-standin' there with the baby in her arms, pick up his duds, and walk off slow like to his car, his big thing still bobbin' in the air in front o' everybody (Maryanne, she covered the eyes o' little Pearl). He lit out of there purty quick once he got to the car, howsomever.

Maryanne didn't say nothin'. She just turned and walked back into the house with the little'ns. She took 'em and the baby and went back to her pap that very night. And Maryanne didn't never say word one to nobody

afterwards about what happened the night the still blew up neither. I got me a new still now. I got me a new wife too, though I keep a look out for travelin' men. But I don't allow no smokin' 'round no still no more.

# Boys of the Night Confess

## *A Stripper's Fantasy*

When I start dancing a surge of power rushes through my body and I feel high. I love that feeling; I live for the nights at Angels. I undulate to the music, pretend not to notice the men staring up at me; I keep my eyes discreetly lowered, at least at first. But I notice who's looking and who isn't, and when I have an audience, I make small gestures to further entice them.

My first night here, I realized this was the place for me–it made me feel alive.

I was supposed to circulate, even after my dance. I collected my tips and dates for later. At first I didn't let the men feel me up, let some of them see my cock, but now I push the limits; I know I should be more careful, but it makes me hot to see how much power I have. Being rebellious always gets me in trouble, but I don't intend to change–at least not yet.

When I came to Tampa, I was a typical boy from a respectable family. I had graduated from high school, and since I did well in my studies it wasn't hard for me to get a job. But here the pay is much better than what I was getting at the burger joint or the quicky printer where I was working. The dancing was easy; it was the tricking that was difficult. Frankly, I was uneasy the first time–actually, a little scared–because you never know if they're just going to be a little pushy, or if they might actually force you. After all, they figure you're fair game if you're flaunting yourself at the bar.

I love how it feels to mix with the men, all the time pretending to be this innocent kid from Nebraska. Now that I've had many tricks, I know what to do and how to act to make them crazy for me.

To get ready I take a long bath and then I oil my skin. I stand naked in front of the mirror and admire myself while I dress. I pinch my nipples several times to make them stand out and rub against the fabric of my shirt. Then I put on my bikini underwear. Sometimes I get so excited I have to jack-off before I can get my jeans on and go to Angels.

If I don't get a trick I lie in bed in the dark and remember the night, watching the scene as if it was a movie in which I star. My favorite fantasy takes place at Angels. I am on the stage dancing. I am wearing only my G-string. I look directly at each man, my eyes hard, my mouth in a sultry pout, as I move my hips in rhythm with the music. I sensuously pull on my nipples. My hands follow the contours of my body down my hips, I rub my crotch. I slowly look from man to man, pulling my G-string down, showing them I am getting it hard for them.

I slip my fingers inside while my other hand plays with my nipples, and I arch my back, my face toward the ceiling, so they can see how good it feels

to have my fingers playing with my prick, how hot and horny I am getting. I bring my fingers to my mouth and slowly suck them, all the time staring blatantly at the men's crotches. They are all growing very hard. Good. That is just what I want. I ease my G-string off and look through the audience and see my bosses standing there, shocked and amazed looks on their faces. Then I see the cute guy who paid me $200 just to squat over him and shit in his face. And the guy who paid me $300 to keep me all night and couldn't get it up. Still, I came for him–twice. And the other dancer, Aaron, who let me fuck him in the ladies' john that passes for our dressing room.

They are all there, and they all admire my total control. They are mesmerized. And, too, they are very aroused. Aroused in the way that our genitals tingle when we are repulsed by but also drawn to something truly scandalous. The way I felt when I saw a picture of a little boy sucking an old man's cock.

I am heady with power. I say to my audience, "Show me what you have that I might want," and they all comply, unbuckling belts, unzipping flies. Their dicks are hard and moist. I study each one carefully. "Come up on stage with me." Then I kneel down to look at each beautiful prick. I suck each one, one at a time. The men are going wild, stroking themselves, eyes glued to the spectacle. After I suck each beautiful prick, I choose one man, a man whose handsome face I have never seen before. And he is very big, the biggest cock of the bunch. He follows me with his hard cock leading his body. There is a bed now on stage too; the other dancers have brought it there, and they flank it on both sides. I lead the stud to one side and he removes his clothes for everyone to see. The other dancers take me in their hands and lay me on the bed, spread my legs open, and caress and lick me all over. The man I have chosen and those standing around us ache so badly they can hardly bear it.

The other dancers stroke me and lick me until I am so hot I must have the stranger to ease the throbbing inside. Two dancers lead him to me, and another two hold my legs open. He enters me hard, thrusting into me again and again until I come very hard and I scream. Sometimes I allow him to come, other times, I don't. It is my choice, after all, my pleasure, my fantasy.

The other dancers are now free to have whomever they choose from the men standing around jacking their dicks.

The music returns, loud, and I grab my handsome stranger's hand and we flee the club, to his car, to his apartment, to fuck the night away. That is my fantasy.

– Adapted by the editor.

# A Hustler's Confession

"I got picked up eventually," Dewar said. "For hustling a cop."

"Hustling is a lot like hitchin'," he said. "A lot of standin' around in the middle of nowhere with your thumb out tryin' to look casual and harmless instead of like some kind of perv. After a while, you learn to read people from a far distance. You know who's cruisin' by how fast they're goin', how straight they're drivin', even what they're drivin'. You can just tell whether they're goin' to slow down for a closer look or speed on by like you're not even there. Sometimes a ride'll stop a ways off, make you walk a little 'cause they haven't quite decided to pick you up yet. They've still got the doors locked, and you can see by the brake lights that their minds are goin' back and forth, off and on as you come closer. You know a woman'll never stop; with men you can never be sure. They might peel out just as your hand reaches the door.

"I was always on the lookout for police, and sometimes that meant leavin' the streets. I was too young to get into the bars," he grinned. "Not the kind of joints you managed to get into at half my age, Charlie!"

"What can I say?" I played along. "I was mature for my age."

He splashed me with a face full of water. I sprayed him back with a hard shake of my hair in his face. "Oh, shit!" he screamed, "It's a bird! Its a bird!" and he ducked under the water, out of sight. When he surfaced, he wiped the clowning from his face with the water that he rubbed away with both hands. "I knew without even tryin' to know that the toilets could be a hustlin' place and not just the bus station, Charlie. Almost any of 'em, anywhere.

"If I couldn't pick up cash, I'd settle for a ride across town or a joint or beer, maybe a drive-in hamburger or just a single night in a real house. It was like barterin' what I had for what I could get.

"Well, what it finally got me was busted for solicitation. You know that fancy word, Charlie? I know it from my official record. It means a fuckin' lyin' cop.

"But, since I was a minor and a runaway and my folks refused custody. I was sent here to the Home until they change their minds or until I'm eighteen or until I die of boredom."

"I don't think you can die of boredom, Dewar. I'm living proof."

"I ain't planning on it," he said, his body levitating to the surface of the water in front of him, his head sinking back until his ears were buried and he fanned his arms in a backstroke toward the clay shore. I followed him in a weighted trudge until we had returned to our spot beneath the elm. We began peeling off our sopping clothes. "I feel like I'm skinnin' a rabbit," Dewar complained with his pants inside out around his knees. I couldn't help laughing at the sight of him struggling with the drenched denim. He sat, grunting and cursing under his breath, his underwear grass-stained where his butt rocked against the ground.

"These will never dry out by morning," I laughed, stooping down to pull the rolled socks off his feet. He leaned back on his elbows, kicking out one leg at a time until I'd inched the jeans off of him. I hung them over a low limb next to my own, picked up his shirt from the grass and hooked it on a twig of the same limb. Before I could turn around, Dewar's shorts hit me in the back with a cold wet smack. I spun around and stepped on them with my bare foot. There he was, flat out on the grass, one hand behind his head, ankles casually crossed, a hoodlum's smirk on his face, an erection not too well covered by the hand that loosely cupped it. Defying my shyness and mustering a grin to approximate Dewar's, I stepped awkwardly out of my own wet shorts, twisted and wrung them out for a few nervous seconds and finally just tossed them onto the grass. "Those are gonna be swarmin' with ants if you don't hang 'em up somewhere," he smiled.

"I don't think I'll be putting them back on," I answered.

"There was another place, too, where I wound up a lot," he said. "My first stop in Tulsa was the bus station. That was just the end of my ride. I went into the bathroom there to take a leak and wash up and was followed in by a Coast Guardsman stuck between buses on leave from Galveston. He walked off from a duffel on a bench to follow me, came up to a pisser beside me, and started talkin' like he hadn't spoke in so long he had things stored up to say–about how many buses he'd rode, some game he had a bet on, a girl he was dyin' to see. "The whole time not pissin' a drop but his pants wide open, pullin' and squeezin' his dick, stretchin' it out like taffy, like there was some problem with it or maybe he was tryin' to wring the pee out of it.

"It was weird the way he kept on talkin' while messin' with his dick like that–about how much he hated his whites and his clipped hair, how he'd joined the Guard at eighteen and wasn't even twenty yet, but all the places he'd been.

"I hadn't said nothin' to the guy, had just been listenin', eyein' him head-on, him bein' a sailor and all. I tucked myself in and went over to the sink. The perv turned around so I could see him full-out in the grimy mirror. Still waggin' it back and forth in his hand, says, 'Be a pal, man–help me out here ... I looked back at him, said, 'I don't know what your problem is, man. I'm just washin' up.' And he came a little closer, says, 'There ain't no problem, man. It'll feel good, I promise. Just take it out. Let me do you. You don't have to do nothin'. Here,' he says, layin' a ten next to the sink and diddlin' some more. 'Over here,' he says, backin' into one of the stalls. "I took the money and thought a minute about just walkin' out. What was he gonna do about it? But, I didn't know shit about Tulsa or where I even was, where else there was to go.

"'What the hell,' I thought–I'd fooled around some before. At least this guy was beggin' for it, even payin' for it. I let the faggot blow me. No problem."

I took a few strides toward him, my hand modestly hiding what swung freely between my legs with each naked step and sat down beside him. I removed my grandfather's retirement watch from my wrist, studied its watertight face in the moonlight, and placed it in the heel of my nearby shoe. "Two-thirty-five," I announced, reclining next to him.

"I used to come here all the time a few summers ago for the privacy," I told him. "It's easy to feel like you're the only one in the whole world here, isn't it?"

"I don't much care for that feeling," Dewar sleepily responded.

His head was next to my feet, and we each stared overhead. ... My eyes were fixed to a particular star, one of the smallest and dimmest among hundreds of brighter, more obvious and sparkling points. I couldn't see Dewar at all, not even peripherally, yet I felt him looking up the length of me, sensed it somehow through my skin as if his eyesight had a weight that my entire skin prickled beneath. My dick swelled against my hand the instant he touched me.

His hand came down, soothingly cool, on my leg just above my knee. "You don't have to do nothin," he said. "Just this once only, I promise, Charlie. You can pretend you're drunk, so passed out drunk you won't even have to remember. Just this once, I promise. It'll feel good. Say it's all right."

A couple of syllables of sound tumbled out of me. Dewar's hand remained motionless. "Go on," I said hoarsely, cleared my throat. "It's all right." With my tentative permission, my life shifted forward with an energy much greater than my will and with a motion that made me dizzy, meek, and confounded as if born again. Dewar's hands defined my body, sculpted its vague boyish matter into an adult form that was surprisingly masculine and joyous in its manhood. His hands touched me with liberty, unsatisfied to rest in any one place concerned with a mission that eventually became my own. He touched me with his soft lips from my chest to my knees, leaving moist marks that ached in the air that wasn't his breath when his mouth lifted and moved away. I deliberately contained my pleasure while Dewar expelled his in loud moans and sighs. My closed eyes became the only barrier between our mirrored figures meshed in their sliding and pressing efforts until Dewar's face fell heavily into mine and his mouth pried my lips apart. It felt as if the seal of the noisy self inside me was broken and a great energy rushed up to meet his tongue in the melding caverns of our mouths. The lids of my eyes rose up, Dewar's jaw rose in a taut point upward, his shoulders pulled back, my groin rose up against his, straining the ropy ligaments that bound its pleasure within me as the warm, fast spasms of our coming glued us at the stomach, face to face but for a breathless frozen moment that seemed, surely, to have been a second of God's eternity. As my blood gradually retreated to its normal course, leaving my extremities unengorged and listless against the rested weight of Dewar, the whole environment appeared softened at its edges and throbbed like Dewar's heart, which I

could feel through his ribs, now heavy and inanimate against me. The invisible crickets seemed to be applauding the transformation of their lakewoods with their rhythmic leg music. His weight upon me was the most alive sensation I'd ever held until my rational thoughts returned from their blood journey of my body's unmapped wilderness. Then I felt compelled to speak, to use words as a bridge back to reality from this strange ethereal glow of thoughtlessness, back to the comfort of my own discomfort.

Dewar ungently lifted and rolled off me.

"Sorry," he said, tossing the apology haphazardly from the side of his mouth while turning his face slightly away.

"It's all right," I said, sitting up, scouting the grass for the cigarettes. "I mean, don't be sorry." My false assurances belied my own creeping panic, the taste of guilt rising in my throat and my near-frantic search for the cigarettes. I was desperate to occupy my hands.

Dewar handed me the half-crushed pack, dropping it to the ground between us before I had a hold on it. "Sorry," he said again.

"It's all right," I repeated, irritated with his tone. I dug into the pack and salvaged the last bent and flattened cigarette. I stroked and straightened it between my fingers and lit it, luckily, with the only remaining match, inhaled as deeply as my lungs would accommodate, smothering my hurt feelings with the smoke.

"I never kissed no one before," Dewar confessed. "I didn't mean to do that."

It seemed the toll of what we'd done weighed as heavily on him as it did on me. But I chose not to be pinned down by it just then. I didn't want to talk about it yet. I smiled conspiratorially. I broadened my mouth and bared my teeth at him. "I was so drunk, Dewar, I don't really remember," I said.

"Don't do that," he commanded seriously. "I got to tell you something. I've never kissed nobody before, not a guy, I never did nothing before with a guy. And I ain't never been to Tulsa, either, or nowhere else really. I've been raised in foster homes my whole life, one after another. I've always been the new kid or the foster son or the orphan boy. I never knew my folks at all, and if I have any family, they've never stepped forward to stake a claim on me. I feel like an asshole right now." He was almost mumbling, rocking a little, speaking as much to himself as to me. I wanted to gather my own wits together and escape before the same devil of confession possessed me.

"Dewar," I interrupted calmly, "it's all right. Truth is, I wanted this to happen. I'm not sorry about it."

My hair was windblown and tangled, my complexion still flushed from the hike. My eyes were as clear as prized marbles. My prominent nose appealed to my sense of handsomeness, and I turned my head in both directions to study my profile from objective angles. And as I untied and shrugged the robe off my shoulders to the floor, I was surprised by the sense of uprightness and outwardly presence that emanated from my body.

This particular vanity impressed me, not with any vainglorious pride, but with the confidence that I was at least attractive enough to be memorable. I was impressed finally that I was not invisible. I closed my eyes and was able to see the mirror image of my own face, which I held in my head for a moment while my hands wandered down the front of me, recalling the touch of Dewar's hands, and I thought of his face grinning on the verge of telling before it vanished. I opened my eyes to the overhead bulb shining on the bathroom tile, the bathwater rocking near the rim of the tub, and I let go of my body to, once more, submerge, soak, and cleanse it of any queer traces of love.

As I stewed and stirred up food like a wife in the kitchen, Dewar sat like the idea of a daddy in the living room, his feet propped up on an ottoman, a textbook uselessly open across his lap, mesmerized by the television, smoking sensuously, often dozing off for short naps that added up to hours of wakefulness at the end of the night as we slipped into bed. He'd start babbling then. He talked a lot about the routine of the Home. "Half of the boys jerk the other half off under the sheets, all night long. In a room of a dozen bunked boys, if you can't hear what's going on, man alive, you can sure smell it."

I laughed quietly in the dark. "What's it smell like, Dewar?"

"You should know by now," he said.

I laughed again. "What do I smell like?"

"Eggnog," he said.

"Well, you smell like flat beer," I countered. Then we started an exchange of such examples. "The Home boys smell like hot wax," Dewar declared. "The younger ones, anyway. Little beaded drops of wax. The older ones are full of sulfur."

Once we had cracked the safe of our sexual attraction, we were surprisingly conservative in the divvying up and doling out of its illicit fortune.

Given the vigor of our youth and the uncensored privacy of the house where we hid out, we were not gluttonous lovers. As we stripped down and climbed into bed each night at our disposal, sex was an awkward kind of chore, difficult to initiate. Each time was wobbly and clumsy, slightly embarrassing but respectful and never regretted.

Our queerness was quite contained to the weekends, to the house, to what we sometimes did in bed, when not sleeping soundly side by side. There was a kind of domesticity to our days and nights in the house. It evolved a weekend at a time. Dewar liked the house itself, the shelter of its drawn window shades, the quiet of its multiple rooms.

"Pryor boys smell like molasses, except the redheads. They're maple syrup."

Dewar snickered. "They ain't that sweet." He thought for a moment. "A room of Purley boys smells like a bushel of stewed turnips." I laughed harder. "No," Dewar changed his mind, "a pot of beets."

"I hate beets!" I rasped.

"Yea," he agreed. The spontaneity seemed to evaporate with the laughter.

In the quiet, I asked, "Do they really all smell so different?"

"You think I'd know?" he immediately responded.

"I thought you'd lie if you didn't."

"You're the only one. I told you," he said, as if ashamed to confess it again.

"How come?" I pried. "If everybody at the Home does it all the time, how come you never did it with any of them?"

"How come you didn't?" he asked, rolling over to face me, wadding the pillow beneath his cheek. "I'm not the first orphan they ever let out, you know."

I thought about it, quietly piecing together Dewar's form in the shadows of the bed. "I first knew a long time ago," I told him. "Fay Rose's nephew or something. She showed me his picture. He was older, about your age now, I guess. I fell in love with him, with the way he looked, I mean. And I just knew that that's how it was."

"He's a grown man, now," I said as an afterthought. "Hunter. Married, I would reckon, without the slightest thought ever of what he meant."

I let my thoughts drop like loose reins to the ground. Dewar picked them up gently and said, "I had this one foster daddy when I was littler. He wasn't really so bad. He didn't ignore me like some or treat me like a new dog that needed trainin'. But I didn't feel nothin' for him. I didn't feel too much for any of 'em, to tell the truth.

"I wasn't a baby, but still too little to know anything about sex. I don't even remember that house or his wife. I don't think they kept me very long. There were so many when I was little. But I remember one night in a room, my room, I guess. The light from the other side of the closed door woke me when the door opened.

"And I remember the man comin' in, closing the door, just standing next to the bed. This tall man next to the bed. I just laid there, lookin' up at him. I couldn't see his face, so I knew he couldn't see me lookin' back at him.

"Then, finally, he knelt down like he was goin' to say bedtime prayers or somethin' and he started touchin' me. He just kinda patted and stroked me. But I just laid there like I was still asleep and waited for what he was goin' to do.

"He got around to it—you know—my peter, down there, through my pajamas. Through the covers even. It seemed weird, but I didn't really mind it. It felt nice. Not sexy or anything. It just felt good. It didn't scare me.

"I don't know. It was dark. He was kneeled down. He was quiet and it was all real slow and careful, even his risin' up and walkin' out the door.

"It was just that one time and nothin' was different after that." Dewar rose and recrushed the pillow, then fell back into it.

... I reached out for him under the covers, hooked my fingers in the waistband of his underwear. "What did he smell like?"

"Like wood polish on a church pew," he said with a grin.

– *Excerpted from "Pryor Rendering," by Gary Reed, available from STARbooks Press.*

# Another Hustler's Confession

*"In the dark corners of even darker streets exists a world that too many see–too many potential-thirsty youths, too many repressed and lonely children, too many sons and brothers and neighborhood kids. Too many walk those boulevards of social disconnection under a thin blanket woven from the bleak threads of frosted evenings and frozen despair."*
– Alan W. Mills, In Touch magazine,
 reviewing the book "Male Order"

I remember when I was just twelve, I was watching television and there was a prostitute in it. It was about a brothel. I thought to myself that was what I wanted to do. I got butterflies and thought, my god, I want to do that. Not for the money, I would have done it for nothing. It just really appealed to me. Having sex with all the men really appealed to me. I didn't even know what sex really was.

When I was young, my cousins used to call me a bastard, saying I hadn't got a dad. It wasn't really a big thing, but by the time I was twelve I started thinking a lot about it. I knew I wanted a dad. I knew I liked men. I was very mixed up. I really didn't know what was going on. I remember hearing my mum talk about Auntie Meg when she turned lesbian after having her kid. She said it made her feel sick, she was really anti-gay. Then she used to tell me when I got older that men are only good for money and sex. I really thought a lot about that comment. I did like the idea of sex with men. That's when I started thinking about wanting to have a man to buy me things; this is what it meant to have a dad. I was very confused inside. I felt such a freak. I phoned up Childline but in the end I actually told them I wanted to go back and live with my nan; they couldn't help me.

I was arguing constantly with my mum. I felt like some kind of pervert. I thought I was sick in the head. I thought I was the one and only male who felt like this about other men. I wanted to stop liking them. My mum didn't know how to handle me. I tried to hang myself a couple of times. I threw a rope over a branch and tried to do it. The other time, I tried to strangle myself with some string from my hood. I felt no one understood me, and I didn't understand myself.

*– Excerpted from the book "Male Order," available from STARbooks Press.*

# A Night Cruiser's Confession

"When in Philadelphia, I recommend cruising Seger Park, 11th and Pine Streets. It's a small, local park with paths in weeded areas for quickies. It's cruisy only in the early morning hours–3 a.m. It is frequented by closeted local married, bisexuals, straights, and fraternity guys–lots of horny, straight-acting Italian guys who want to be serviced. Beware of homeless people. One tip: don't talk to these strangers, just do them! Talking scares them.

"Also, Schuykill River Park, 27th & Spruce Streets. It is called 'Judy Garland Park' by locals. It's located at the west end of Spruce Street. Is three blocks long, and is busy from dusk onwards every night. Be aware: park closes at 1 a.m. Police occasionally cruise through in their squad car. Just lay low and they'll be gone soon. All areas near the fence separating park from the railroad tracks. It is dangerous to cruise near the railroad side, due to railroad employees cruising for trespassers. Hot, anonymous sex abounds here. I've had four-ways often. Lots of willing cock suckers and hard tools. I was fucked by the largest cock ever–a young Univ. of Penn. student, drunk, at 5 a.m. fucked me with an incredible arm-width, twelve inch cock for over an hour!"

*– Informant for Steam magazine*

# A Club Kid's Confession

*"Kids ... Why Can't they be like we were, perfect in every way?"*
*– Lyrics from the musical "Bye Bye Birdie"*

Wallace McCay reports from Manhattan:

I'm researching a story on the club scene, comparing today's with those of the '70s and '80s. I really have all the background I need but I have yet to do an in-depth interview. No one attracted my attention until tonight, when I saw Travis again. I knew that was his name because I had seen him almost everywhere I went and a week ago I had heard someone calling his name as he was leaving one club, presumably to go to another–club kids never seem to sleep.

"Yeah, it was fucking cool. I was walking home at five a.m. last Tuesday from Egg when I passed this little bar playing jungle. A lot of kids were there. I went downstairs to the bar and some people were like 'Do you want a drink?' but I had no money, so they said 'Have a line of coke instead.' But I said, 'I'll pass. I'm already flying on a line of K, thank you very much."

Travis, a 19-year old platinum blonde, waifishly thin sophomore-to-be at NYU, given to wearing potato sack-sized denim and Fred Perry tennis togs, seems to be taking the drug's effect in stride.

Far removed from the protective trappings of his native Texas, the soft-spoken, gentle dreamer has been a fervent devotee of the animal tranquilizer since he acclimated himself to the vibrant club scene of the city last year.

"Clubs are kind of addictive. In the course of a single night you run into tons of cool people. Plus, the music is playing loud as fuck, and you get to dance in wide spaces."

Events like Egg (an "IT" night held at the Cooler, a former meat warehouse), Friday at the Roxy, and special events like "Purple," provide despondent, wayward teens with a sense of communal, spiritual fulfillment.

"I have found answers to questions I hadn't even thought of yet while dancing at the club," says Travis. "Sometimes it's the music the DJ may be spinning. Sometimes it's the way I'm feeling, and sometimes it's because of the amount of drugs I've taken."

What makes the '90s rave scene different from its predecessors like disco and sock-hopping? The elements which constitute the structure and backbone of the scene each mean something different which, collectively, make for a singular experience.

"It's kind of like floating outside your body. You're on the sidelines taking notes," explains Travis. "Now you've got to imagine several hundred, sometimes thousands of people feeling like this and then you'll really understand the power of clubs."

- 291 -

Let's break down the power of clubs. For starters, you've got a cornucopia of drugs to choose from. Right now, special K, a powder originally intended for horses, serves as the high of favor. It's cheap and powerful. Other favorites include crystal meth, coke, and that old stand-by, acid.

"Drugs are important to me," says Travis, "because a club can be pretentious sometimes, but if I'm high or whatever, it helps me deal with all the people even though I find that a lot of the time, I can't talk. So I'll be like 'Bleh-bleh-bleh'–just have mush mouth."

Equally important in the equation, if not more so, is the music. Whether it be jungle (a hyperkinetic, phantasmic cauldron of noise, bubbling with overlapping, virulent strains of hip-hop, ragga-dub and next millennium-derived "tech-know" insinuations), techno, trance, ambient, dub, trip-hop or whatever some demented schizoid has concocted in a suburban basement somewhere, the genre effortlessly meshes a future primitive spew of Paleolithic, tribal rhythms and otherworldly, space blanket syncopation washes.

This is the warped, apocalyptic music that our technological advances has spawned. It is the soundtrack for the next century. Music for the jilted generation. In the clubs or at home in the headphones, it is pre-recorded, electronically derived and manipulated sound. There is no live performance.

Thus, when at a live club, it is the DJ who serves as performer. It is how he spins and cuts and builds from one song to the next that determines the outcome and the evening.

As Travis says, "DJs kind of fuel where the action will be that night. The music is what makes the space. The DJs have a ridiculous amount of clout and power."

Just as crazy is the laissez-faire manner in which Travis explains the sexual behavior of clubland constituents.

"Sometimes I'll go to a club and see people fucking each other in a corner or something. The bathrooms are even worse. I'm afraid to go in them. I'll be passing one stall and a girl will be sucking like ten dicks at once.

"People are very conscious of AIDS, but they kind of toss their brains away sometimes."

Sex comes easy. Hook-ups are inevitable at the end of a long night that often stretches into the mid-morning.

Travis is a club kid.

He does drugs, listens to music that is considered passé after three weeks, and is constantly on the cutting edge of defining his look to society and his peers.

Says he, "Fashion, dress and style serve as a lifestyle and personality marker for me. I change and remake myself as I feel the trends moving and changing. I don't stay the same person for very long.

"At clubs, you will definitely stand out in a bad way if you're some weirdo or tourist who doesn't look cool. People will go up to you and tell you that you're a nerd or whatever. Right now, there's so many fashion cliques that define who you are in the eyes of the other kids at the clubs. You've got Polo kids, thrift shop kids, all types. I've begun to see people wearing, like, country and western clothes with combat boots and stuff."

All things must come to an end someday. Although the scene is still fresh and vital today, so too will it be usurped by an even more daring thrill ride.

Travis knows this and does not lament such an occurrence.

"I like it now," he says, "but I know it can't last. I guess I'll be having fun for a couple of more years or so. School is important to me. Right now, I can go out every night and have fun. But I, unfortunately, can't make a career out of it. Who remembers the bartenders at Studio 54 from 1979? What the fuck are they doing now?"

While Travis may have his head screwed on–somewhat–there exist vast legions of young adults and kids who have already burned out. They are the drugs and music clubs' casualties.

"It's sad," laments Travis. "I know so many smart kids from NYU who just got too fucked-up on the drugs and going out every night. They got kicked out of school, lost a lot of their friends because they got to be mistrustful, and now they aren't even speaking to their parents. And the fucked-up thing is that the kids this (is happening to) are getting younger and younger. I see thirteen and fourteen year old babies fucked up on K staying out for nights at a time. The future doesn't look good. I can't imagine what they'll be doing when they reach my age. That's if they're still alive."

# Rendezvous

*Antler*

The two boys embracing in the thunderstorm
Don't care if they get drenched,
Don't care if as they strip each other
their clothes drop in lightninglight
into puddles
and are kicked laughingly into the mud.
It's the first time they've kissed each other,
The first time either of them ever kissed
a boy
And neither has ever kissed
a girl
And neither ever kissed before
with his tongue.
They had no idea
how passionate
passion could be–
they can hardly believe it,
That merely putting their lips together
could be so ...
ah.
For a moment they stand apart
silently gazing at each other
in the flashes and thunder,
Centuries of Boyhood, Aeons of BoyLove
proud in their playful smiles,
Knowing just what they're going to do,
even though they never did it before,
Knowing that before long
each of them is going to jack off
the first boy he ever jacked off
besides himself,
Knowing both of them can come
and giving in, giving themselves
to boyfriendship's topsecret gesture,
Knowing they both know
how to jack off real good
and aren't going to stop frenching
while they whimper toward the brink.
Sure, it's beautiful

John Patrick

to see a boy you love
ejaculate in the lightning in the rain,
Crying with pleasure while the thunder thunders
and the sky ejaculates millions of raindrops
As you squirm in rapture
on the muddy grass
under the tossing trees.

# One Leg, The Hustler

## *Ken Anderson*

One leg,
you have lost your footing. Without crutches,
your classic symmetry topples
from its base.

Your cute face baited the old park queers,
but a bullet cracked your stance.

Now what is it like
in the grave
to the thigh–the false sensation?

You reach
to scratch the anti-heel.

And what
do you tell your love's sure-footed surrogate
and when–a plastic part, the vacuous shin?

Do you dream yourself
the park's new Captain Hook?

Since fate has snapped you off
at the crotch, are you more now, less, whole
at last, wanting?

The Louvre's polished marble bares
all that there is
of antique gods
once lithe.

You are 1 now–or 7.

You must fuck
from the side
or fall.

# The Hustler's Ball

## *James S. Arthurs*

It's cold and dark as they hustle around,
Shuffling feet on stony ground.
Projecting contours
In efforts to find
Sometone to take them.
Hope they're kind.

Hispanic smiles and greasy skins,
Blacks and whites,
They're tall and thin,
Short and chubby,
Lovers all,
Just rent by the hour
The hustler's Ball.

Men in blue stroll down the street,
Knowing looks as eyes they meet.
They pass on by,
It's safe again,
Bubbles of chatter
Avoid the pain.
Murmurs and mumbles as strollers pass
"Loose joints", they say and eye your ass.
Bulging pants, some wistful looks,
You don't read this in story books.
Pockets with hankies hanging out,
Blue right, left red;
Signs and signals
Telling what it's all about,
The scene in bed,
Like drums and cymbals.

C'mon boy, take your pick,
Look us over, find your trick.
We'll treat you nice,
No bugs, no lice,
Pay your money,
Call you honey.
Get your car,

John Patrick
>
> Drive not too far,
> Take a chance,
> Let's dance.
> The hustler's Ball.

# The Real Thing – A Novella

## By Frank Brooks

"I prefer to be a top, but my ex-boyfriend really liked to be a top, so one of us had to give it up, and he fucked good. So I guess I have to say I'd be willing to go versatile with the right person."
– *Porn star Gianfranco, of "Sex Hunt" fame*

# 1

"How are you hung?"

"I guess. Eight, maybe eight and a half," I said.

"Well, which is it?"

"It depends on how excited I am. Right now, talking to you, eight and a half. It would probably swell to nine if we meet."

"Hmm," said the boyish voice on the other end of the line. It was the voice I knew so well, from his films, from my dreams. "Is it cut or uncut?"

"Uncut," I said. "But when it's really hard the skin pulls back tight enough that it's hard to tell if it's cut or uncut by just looking at it. Right now it's pulled back like that."

"Sounds yummy," said the boy.

I still imagined him a boy, maybe 18 or 19, though younger looking, whom I'd seen in so many films. But time had passed since he'd made his last film and Caley Anders could be 20, even 21 by now–possibly over the hill. I'd seen boys in the porn film business go to hell overnight, and Caley, who had given his all for the cameras, with no holds barred, could easily be one of them, now burned out, his youth and beauty spent in a few short years. But his voice hadn't changed–he still sounded sweet sixteen, and so seductive that I nearly came at the sound of him–so maybe he was still the boy of his films.

"How are you hung?" I asked.

He laughed. "You don't know? I thought you were my number one fan, that you'd seen all my movies."

"Fifty times over," I said, hardly exaggerating. I was nuts about the kid. I'd had a lot of favorite young porn stars over the years, but Caley was at the top of the list. "I mean, I know it's big, but exactly how big?"

"How big do you think?" he asked.

"Seven, seven and a half."

"Good guess. Seven and a quarter. It's not a monster, but it's always hard, which is more than you can say for a lot of the monsters around."

"You can say that again." I'd seen Caley tied with his arms above his head while being gangbanged by a dozen men, his young cock standing acutely erect throughout the hour-long assault. I'd seen him with a fist up his ass, with half a man's foot reaming out his insatiable little butt, and he hadn't lost a millimeter of hard-on. "You know, I don't think I've never seen you soft."

"In the last ten years, I hardly have either," Caley said with a chuckle. "I'm hard right now. You can probably sense that. I've been rubbing my stiff pecker all the while we've been talking. You sound like a real stud. Are you muscular?"

"I'm not Mr. America, but I'm defined. Square pecs. Washboard abs."

"Mmm, hot daddy!" breathed the boy. "How old are you?"

I could have said 35 and got away with it, but I told the truth. "Forty-five."

"You sound better all the time! I like older guys, especially men over 40."

"I guessed that. You seemed to really get off on the older guys in your films."

"I sure did. Give me those hot daddies." He laughed. "What you saw in the films is the real me. I never did anything in a film that I didn't really want to, and I mean anything. I mean, it was supposed to be a gross-out when I sucked off that grandpa cock that time–you remember that one?–the guy was really over 60–and I was supposedly being forced–but I did it because I wanted to–I was hungry for that hot Daddy cum–and a lot of people said it was one of the hottest scenes they'd ever seen. I mean, the guy was more than 50 years older than me. He could've been my grandpa! But I really got off on it, man, and that grandpa nearly had a stroke. He said he hadn't felt that good in 50 years. Does that shock you?"

"Nothing shocks me," I said. "I got off on that scene myself. I can't say I understand what your attraction to older men, though, since I've never gone for them myself. If they're much over 18, I lose interest."

"I'm not 18 anymore," Caley said. "How do you know you'd go for me anymore?"

"I'll take that chance."

Caley laughed. "Brave man. But remember, I get paid for the interview, whatever happens. If you decide you want to enjoy my body–and I decide I'll let you–then you also pay me a big fat tip on top of the interview fee."

"Agreed," I said. "Just don't jack off too much before I get there. I expect you to shoot quarts, like in your films."

"Then you'd better hurry, daddy, 'cause I'm a fucking horny boy!"

# 2

Caley Anders (neither his legal name nor the name he used in films) became one of my major obsessions the moment I first saw him on the video screen. It happened at my friend Ed's, where I'd gone for an evening of beer and video porn with the guys. At our weekly meetings, I supplied the homemade beer, Ed supplied the video (his latest acquisitions), while other guys supplied snacks, lubricants, and whatever else we used during our evenings of naked, laid-back fun. Occasionally we'd all chip in for a young hustler–it was my job to pick him up–who acted as the evening's pet and plaything and who helped get us off as we watched the films. Usually, six to ten of us made it to the meetings, and it never took long–after we'd stripped down in Ed's rec room and sprawled on vinyl couches or on exercise mats on the floor–before the room reeked of sweat, beer, and freshly shot cum. Most guys got off several times during the evening. I was seated on the couch, my dick up the wiggling ass of our young hustler of the evening, who was bouncing on my lap, when I got my first glimpse of Caley. I'd been licking the nape of the hustler's neck and playing with his stiff cock as I fucked him–not paying any attention to the film–when two guys said, simultaneously, "Look at that baby squirt!" and I glanced back at the screen.

And there was Caley's flushed, boyish, ecstatic face as he shot streams of spunk across his perfectly smooth stomach and chest. He was on his back on a couch, his spread legs waving in the air, his toes clutching as a hairy brute with one of the biggest cocks in the porn universe rammed his clutching little asshole. I'd rarely seen such an expressive mind-blowing ecstasy on a kid's face, nor such powerful, profuse ejaculations, and in two seconds I was exploding with him, my cum shooting up the hustler's asshole. Caley must have turned on the hustler, too, because suddenly his cock bucked in my hand and he was squirting teenaged spunk all over. And we weren't the only ones coming. Three of the other guys got off with us.

"Gorgeous kid!" one guy muttered.

"Sexy little bitch stud!" said another.

"Who's the new star?" I asked Ed, still flexing my cock inside the hustler's asshole. The moaning kid had wilted in my arms, knocked half-unconscious by his orgasm.

"Caley something," Ed said. "He's in a lot of the new films lately. Hot little fucker, ain't he! Real active prostate. Hell, watching him gets me off just like that, and I ain't even into chicken. He must shoot a cupful every time he comes, which is about every five minutes."

Ed wasn't exaggerating much. By the end of the video Caley had copiously ejected his young juices eight times, and I'd come with him half that many. He was one of those boys who have a devastating effect on me.

After that evening, I wouldn't let one of our meetings go by without cajoling Ed into showing us at least one Caley film, and the effect the boy

had on me was always the same. I swear, I could literally feel what he was feeling as he displayed himself performing a myriad of sexual acts.

For me, he was real-est boy in the porn universe–because I knew he wasn't acting, I could tell he was just being himself.

# 3

Caley had given me directions to a ranch in the costal mountains south of San Francisco. I got lost a few times after I turned off the coast highway and I was starting to wonder if I wasn't on a wild goose chase. Caley wasn't the first porn-film heart-throb I'd sought out to interview, but he'd proved the most elusive, and other stars, less elusive, had played games and stood me up, so why not Caley? The boy hadn't made a film in almost two years, directors he'd worked for had either disappeared or were of no help, and other actors he'd worked with either couldn't or wouldn't give me information about him. I'd almost given up trying to locate him when I'd stumbled across an old ad in an old skin magazine.

The ad pictured Caley naked to his shaved groin and said that he was working his way through college by selling hot pictures of himself. It also implied that, for a price, one could buy more than his pictures. The address was a San Francisco post office box and, on a long shot, I wrote to it. Two months later, after I'd given up hope of hearing anything, a postcard arrived.

One side of the oversized, European postcard was a photograph by the Baron von Gloeden of three naked Sicilian boys photographed at the turn of the century, their large, fat, uncut cocks dangling sausage-like between their thighs. I was surprised that such a postcard could make it through the U.S. postal system without causing a full-scale FBI investigation or national riot, but, since the photograph had been taken nearly a century ago by a German in Italy, I guess it was considered "art," not pornography. On the other side of the card was a note, printed in blue felt-tip, that surprised me even more than the picture:

YES I'M STILL ALIVE AND IT'S GOOD TO KNOW THAT THERE ARE STILL FANS OF MY MOVIES OUT THERE. THE POST OFFICE HAD TO FORWARD YOUR LETTER A FEW TIMES BEFORE I GOT IT, SO THAT'S WHY IT TOOK ME SO LONG TO ANSWER BACK. I REALLY "GOT OFF" ON WHAT YOU SAID ABOUT ME, SO, FOR THE RIGHT PRICE I MIGHT GIVE YOU AN "INTERVIEW." I'M NOT CHEAP. BUT, IF YOU HAVE SOMETHING "BIG" TO THROW INTO THE DEAL, I MIGHT GIVE YOU A DISCOUNT. HERE'S MY PHONE NUMBER. CALL AND WE'LL TALK ABOUT IT. IF AN OLDER MAN ANSWERS, PLEASE BE DISCREET. LOVE AND LUST, CALEY.

Luckily, I hadn't forgotten to bring the phone number along with me on my drive to the ranch and, lost for a third time, I called Caley from a strip mall.

"Where are you?" he asked. "You were supposed to be here a half hour ago. I'm so horny I'm almost having convulsions."

My right hand shook as I copied down revised directions. My left hand squeezed my cock through the denim of my jeans. I could feel Caley's breath in my ear as he spoke. He was so close now that I swore I could smell him.

John Patrick

After turning off a paved road flanked at quarter-mile intervals with mock Spanish villas, I followed a dusty, unpaved drive marked PRIVATE ROAD, NO ENTRANCE, NO TRESPASSING, LOCKED GATE AHEAD, and drove toward hills ripening gold under the afternoon California sun. The landscape itself would have set my heart pounding and my loins throbbing, even if Caley hadn't been waiting for me somewhere in the hills up ahead. After a half mile I came to the gate, a break in a high, chainlink fence that apparently surrounded much of the property. As Caley had instructed me, I pressed an intercom button in a box mounted on a post in the middle of the driveway.

"Who's there?" said Caley over the intercom.

I waved at the surveillance cameras mounted on top of the fence. "Your interviewer."

"Finally!"

"Can I come in?"

"Step out of the car so I can get a look at you. Take off your shirt and pull out your schlong so I can see it."

My cock was so hard and distended that I had to undo my jeans and lower them to set it free. The naked, half-peeled head shined in the sunshine. I clasped my hands behind my head like a posing bodybuilder and flexed all my muscles, including my cock, making it wiggle up and down.

Caley whooped. "Come on in!"

# 4

The gate hummed open. Without bothering to refasten my jeans and with my cock still sticking out, I slid back behind the wheel and drove on as the gate swung shut in a dust cloud behind me. Soon I was passing grazing horses. Topping a rise, I spotted ranch buildings in the distance. The main house was architecturally complex, sprawling and built on at least five interwoven levels. Then, Caley appeared.

He was riding a palomino stallion, its mane flowing in the warm breeze as it cantered toward me. I stopped the car to watch them approach. The boy was nude except for a cowboy hat and a halter of sorts, and he was riding bareback, his blonde forelock flopping in his eyes, a devilish expression on his face. The halter he wore was fashioned of two leather straps that came over his shoulders and down his torso and passed between his legs on either side of his balls. His stiff cock whacked up and down with the stallion's movements. He reined the stallion next to my car and shoved a naked foot in through the open car window and tweaked my nose with his toes. His big toe slid between my lips and I sucked it.

"That drives me crazy!" he said, grabbing his cock. "If you keep that up, I'll shoot off right here. You're hotter than I expected."

I spit out his toe and kissed his instep. "So are you." My voice was shaky with excitement. In person, the kid was even sexier than on screen and, if anything, he looked younger now than in his first film. He still had freckles on his nose.

He let go of his cock and it flexed up and down as if about to ejaculate. A few drops of pre-cum oozed out and dripped. He let his tongue hang out. "Fuck, I'm horny! Can you ride a horse?"

"Not as well as I can ride young ass, but I've done some riding."

"Then get up behind me. But first get out of those clothes. All of 'em. No clothes allowed around this place."

He watched me strip and toss my clothes into the car.

"You're leaking goo as bad as I am," he said. "You're gonna get my ass all slippery. Come on up." He reached down to assist me and, after several attempts, I managed to scramble up behind him astride the stallion. His skin was like hot silk as I hugged him. A leather strap passed up his ass crack and back, then split into the two straps that went up over his shoulders and down his front. My cock slid against the leather.

"Wanna fuck me?"

"Christ!" I said, clinging to him and grinding against him.

"Does that mean you do?" Before I could answer he shook the reins and drove his heels into the stallion's flanks and we took off at a gallop. "Wheeee!"

If I hadn't been clinging to Caley I'd have been thrown off. He laughed as we shot across the pasture.

John Patrick

"Slow down!" I shouted.

He slowed the stallion to a trot, then a walk.

I pinched his nipples. "Are you trying to get us killed?"

"Maybe. Hey, that drives me crazy!"

"I think everything drives you crazy."

"Just about. I'm a sensitive boy." He rubbed his bare feet up and down my shins and insteps and I tickled his soles with my toes.

"Hold on," he said, nudging the stallion's flanks, and the animal resummed trotting. "Too fast?"

"Just right." I slid a hand down the boy's smooth, muscled stomach and closed it around his cock, which was red hot and hard as steel. "How'd you like to get fucked while we ride?"

"I am getting fucked while we ride. What do you think these straps are for–besides making me look sexy? They keep a nine-inch dildo anchored up my butt. Daddy says I have to wear it around the house to keep my asshole in shape. It's like getting screwed all day long, especially when I'm out riding. Makes my asshole tighten up every time it moves inside me. By now I've probably got the most muscular asshole in California. You oughta feel it! If we ride long enough, I'll come just from the bouncing."

"Who is Daddy?" I asked.

"My sugar daddy, of course!"

"Where's he now?"

"Don't worry, he's gone on business. He's gone on business almost all the time. This time it's Europe, I think, or Hong Kong. I forget. How do you think he affords this Ponderosa–or me?"

"Does he know that you give bareback rides to naked men while he's away?"

"He knows I mess around a little behind his back, he just doesn't know how much. If he knew how much, I don't know what he'd do--probably lock me in a cage. You know, if I don't make it with a man at least once a day I go bonkers. I mean, I've been 'out' and doing it for a long, long time. The first time daddy found out I'd been playing around behind his back he locked a chastity belt on me, if you can believe it. I thought it was a joke, until he took off on one of his trips and took the key along with him."

"I thought they only made chastity belts for women, back in the Middle Ages."

"I don't know anything about them. I think he had this one custom-made. I wore the thing for nearly a day after he left, and it actually felt sexy at first. But then, when I had to get off and realized I couldn't even do myself, I about went nuts. I mean, I've been coming at least five times a day since the first day I could cream, usually more than that. Luckily, I got hold of a gay locksmith in San Francisco–at daddy's expense, believe me–and he came down here and got me out of the damned contraption. Then we had a great time–me and the locksmith. He had eight incredibly thick inches and

loved to fuck young ass. I made sure that we made up double for my prison time in the belt."

"Lucky locksmith."

"By the time he left he could hardly walk," said Caley, giving me a sexy smirk over his shoulder. I licked his nose.

"And then, when daddy got home, I told him that if he ever put me in that torture device again that our arrangement was off, that he could kiss my sweet little ass goodbye, that I'd be finding myself another daddy."

"If you ever decide to change sugar daddies, keep me in mind," I said.

"Do you have a ranch?" asked Caley.

"No."

"Do you make lots and lots of money?"

I laughed. "I'm afraid not."

"There's more to being a sugar daddy than providing stud service," Caley said.

# 5

Caley's leather halter, sexy as it looked on him, was, in its own way, another variety of chastity belt. If a leather strap hadn't been covering his ass crack and a dildo stuffing his asshole, I'd have slipped my cock inside him within seconds of getting up behind him and I'd surely have shot off in him before we'd reached the ranch house. As it was, I nearly creamed against his ass more than once as we rode, so it turned out that the halter was a blessing in disguise. I'd spent a lot of time and effort hunting the boy down, and blowing my pent-up load within minutes of meeting him would have been too much, too fast. I needed to prolong my time with him, to slow down and make things last.

In the stables, I watched Caley put the stallion in its stall. Every ripple of muscle in the kid's body sent a thrill through me, making my cock jerk. I only dared give my cock a few strokes now and then, just barely sliding the foreskin, or I'd have shot off onto the straw on the floor and against the slatted walls of the stall. The boy had the sexiest-looking erection I'd seen in ages, and one that never quit. To top things off, the stallion itself suddenly sported a hard-on about two feet long, as if he shared our excitement.

"Now that's a big one!" Caley said, feeling up the stallion's cock. "Wanna suck it?"

"I'd rather suck yours," I said.

"Have you ever sucked a stallion?"

"Possibly," I said. "Once we get to know each other better, maybe I'll tell you. Have you?"

"Maybe, maybe not," Caley said, smiling mischievously. "Once we know each other better I'll tell you."

"I'll bet you have. I think you'd try anything." I imagined the blonde kid on his knees, the golden stallion's enormous cock head stuffing his cute face, horse spunk running out of his mouth and down his hairless chest. I was hoping he'd get down on his knees right now and go to work on that magnificent equine prong, but instead he locked the stallion in its stall, wrapped his arms around me, and shoved his tongue in my mouth.

My knees shook as I sucked the boy's squirming tongue and drank his warm, sweet saliva. He had the silky-soft skin of a boy many years younger and as he rubbed against me I felt my nuts swell to the verge of unloading. I had to push him away to keep from creaming against his stomach.

"What's the matter, you don't like me?"

"I like you too much," I said. "All we've gotta do is touch and I'm ready to unload."

"Don't do that. I want your cock in my mouth when that happens." He lifted his right arm, showing me his hairless armpit. A trickle of sweat moved down his flank. "Want a lick?" I caught the trickle of sweat moving down his flank with my tongue, then lapped up into his armpit. He sighed

and fed me his other armpit, then went for my nipples with his lips, tongue, and teeth. I was panting so hard I was nearly hyperventilating.

He slid to his knees and started licking my balls. I lifted my right foot and played with his cock and balls with my toes.

"I can get off that way," Caley said. "I've had guys jack me off with their feet." He slid down, crouched, and held my right foot in his hand, kissing the instep. "I love a man's muscular feet." He licked all over and between my toes, then sucked on the big one, his eyes turned up at me.

The sensations of his toe-sucking went straight to my cock, which I let throb untouched, fearing an accident if I took hold of it. It jerked with each suck of the kid's lips, dripping lube.

He released my foot. "That turns you on, huh."

"That's putting it mildly."

"Turns me on too," he said. "Both ways. Giving and getting." He picked up my left foot and gave it the same treatment.

He stood up and gripped the shaft of my cock. "Come on, I'll show you the house."

"Careful," I said, holding my breath.

He let go of my cock and I followed him down the straw-covered central aisle of the stable. He wiggled his ass as he walked in a way that made me dizzy with lust. If he'd paused even for a second, I'd have fallen on my knees and kissed his ass all over, then gnawed apart the leather strap hiding his crack, pulled out the dildo with my teeth, and buried my face between his spread cheeks–or that's what I imagined myself doing.

"I love being naked around this place," Caley said. "I'm naked all the time. Doesn't being naked around here make you feel sexy?"

"Sexy" was too mild a word for what I was feeling.

# 6

The ranch house–sprawling, airy, and bright, with few doors between rooms and none between the various levels of the house–gave me as much of a sense of freedom indoors as I'd had outside. The outer walls were made up mostly of large, curtain less windows that looked out on woods and pastures to the east and on the hills to the west. Skylights made up much of the roof space, and diagonal rays of late-afternoon sunshine poured in through both the windows and overhead skylights.

As Caley moved through the shafts of sunlight, his stiff dick bouncing and wagging, it was as if he were performing on stage or in front of cameras. Even his simplest movements, so sexy were they, seemed as if they'd been calculated and rehearsed, as if Caley thought of himself permanently on display in front of an audience of men whom he had to keep stimulated. I think, though, that his seductiveness was either natural to him–inborn–or that by now he had practiced and perfected his seductiveness to such an extent that it had become him and that he moved as he did unconsciously. I'd never encountered a boy who could turn me on so much by simply walking.

"I never, ever wear clothes when I don't absolutely have to," Caley said, stretching to show off his nakedness. "I'm naked 24 hours a day around here, sometimes for days on end–except for this thing." He tugged on one of the leather straps of his harness. "When I leave the ranch and have to put on shorts I feel like I'm wearing that damned chastity belt again or something. Clothes are unhealthy. That's a fact. I do everything naked around here, indoors or outdoors, and it keeps me feeling so sexy that this thing's always sticking up in the air." He pushed his cock downward with the tip of his finger and twanged it.

I licked my lips, watching his cock flex up and down. I was seated on a long white couch in the main living room. Licking his lips as well, Caley unbuckled his harness and let it drop to the floor. Then he reached back, catching the dildo as it popped out of his asshole and he tossed it to me. It hit my chest with a wet thud as I caught it. Though shiny and clean, the flesh-colored rubber had the mild, musky scent of young ass, and it felt warm, as if it had just popped out of a toaster. I couldn't resist rubbing it all over my cheeks and even licking it, then sucking on it.

Caley watched, smiling. "Guess whose monster that one is." The dildo was a replica of a real cock, complete with veins and wrinkles. Next to the living cock it had been cast from, it would have been hard to tell it from the real thing.

"Rick Donovan," I said, whose cock was the first "monster" cock that came to mind.

"No. Rick's doesn't curve that way. I know, man."

"Jeff Stryker."

"Jeff's is prettier than this, man. I oughta know!"

My, had he had them all? I plunged on, making a few more guesses before Caley gave in and named a porn star who had fucked him on film more than once. "I've had the real thing up my ass at least ten times," Caley bragged. "And man, let me tell you, that dude knows how to use it."

My mind replayed film scenes of Caley getting rammed so hard and fast by that real monster cock that the kid's eyes nearly popped out and his skin sex-flushed from ears to toes. In my mind, jets of teen cum sloshed across the boy's heaving chest as the muscular stud hammered him and Caley's face contorted with such pained ecstasy that just the memory of it made me want to jerk off instantly.

"I've got a big dildo collection," Caley said. "Almost 200 so far. All custom-made replicas of the real ones made from casts of the real ones. There's a guy who makes them for me free of charge. Some boys collect baseball cards, I collect cocks. But only ones that have fucked me or that I've sucked."

"You can have a replica made of mine."

"We'll see," Caley said. "It depends on how good you are. I'd have to call the dildo man and make an appointment and you'd have to come back another time."

"I'll come back as many times as you want."

"We'll see," Caley repeated, looking at my standing cock as it throbbed against my abdomen. "It's certainly big enough for my collection. I wonder how it tastes."

I slumped further down on the couch, clasped my hands behind my head, and spread my legs. "Why don't you find out?"

My cock strained upward, so hard and swollen that my foreskin stretched down all but free of the knob, which gleamed maroon in the sunlight. Caley dropped down on all fours and crawled toward me, his pecker sticking forward under his belly and wagging. The sight of his willowy little figure on all fours made me pant. He mashed his freckled nose against my nuts.

"I love sweaty balls," he said. "The smell of a stud's sweaty balls gets me high." He inhaled deeply and rolled his eyes. They were hazel eyes, tending toward brown. "You haven't washed these big hairy gonads in a week, I can tell. Mmm, I love 'em!" His tongue began to probe and slither, up and down and all around my nuts. He nuzzled down under my balls, which looked huge draped over his nose, and he sucked my crotch.

I had to resist grabbing my cock and jacking off in two seconds. My toes spread and clutched as I squirmed under the boy's nibble tongue and hot lips.

He grasped my cock at the base of the shaft and lifted it away from my belly, testing its hardness, inspecting it, sliding the foreskin. Pre-cum leaked out and ran down the shaft. He rubbed his nose up and down the belly of the shaft, sliding it in the slick fluid. "I love cock!" he growled, licking the lubricant off my cock shaft. "Big sweet cock!" He bent my cock down and engulfed the knob. It looked as if he'd swallowed a rattlesnake.

"Sweetheart!" I moaned, caressing his sandy-blonde head. "Sweet baby!" My loins strained upward, forcing my cock deeper into his mouth, stuffing my apple-sized cock head down his throat. He was able to swallow nearly every millimeter of thick man-cock.

His eyes turned up at me, watching my reactions to his cock sucking, turning me on with their seductive expression. A trickle of his warm spit ran down my balls. Very slowly, he began to move his head up and down, to slide his lips around my cock-shaft, as if he were savoring the taste of it and enjoying the feel of it stuffing his face.

His tongue churned, thrilling the most sensitive parts of my cock as his lips rippled over the veins of the shaft. Saliva filled his mouth, little streams of it escaping now and then to tickle my balls. His eyes continued their upward gaze as he sucked. My fingers slid in his silky hair, kneading his warm scalp. I moaned, my loins rocking. In another few seconds I was going to blow his head off.

"Easy, baby! Easy!"

He released my cock at the last possible moment, then sat back on his heels and wiped his mouth. He gave me an impish grin. "You're gonna have the worst case of blue balls you ever had when I get done with you."

I groaned, half with pleasure, half with frustrated pain. I wanted to come, needed to come before I blew a gasket, but then, I wanted to make my virgin excitement of being with Caley to last for as long as I could possibly hold out.

"Daddy wants to get off, but daddy doesn't want to get off yet," Caley said, reading me perfectly. He leaned forward again, now licking and kissing my abdominal muscles. He slid up and bit my nipples. With each electric nip of his teeth I gasped. He had me raise my arms again so he could lick out my armpits, growling like a hungry puppy as he sucked my armpit hairs.

"I'm glad you don't use deodorant," he said. "I hate that stuff. I like men who taste like men, not like perfume." He kneeled up on the couch between my thighs, his stiff cock jabbing my chest, and shoved his hairless armpits in my face. "Taste me again. I don't use that crap either."

He raised his arms and I licked out his armpits, savoring their salty-sweet, boyish flavor and scent. Then I sucked and chewed his nipples, making him gasp and wince.

"You're getting me hot, Daddy. God I'm horny!" He braced his hands on my shoulders and stood up, his toes under my balls, his stiff cock throbbing in my face. The tip of it smeared pre-cum on my nose. He rubbed the sizzling, silk-skinned knob back and forth along my lips, which felt as itchy-sensitive as my cock head. My lips parted and his young cock entered my mouth.

"Oh Daddy, suck it!" he crooned.

I had the feeling that I was either dreaming or hallucinating. I'd watched Caley make these same moves and use these same words on film. In the past I'd identified with his co-stars on film, pretending to be making it with him.

Now I'd become that co-star. I no longer had to imagine the taste and feel of Caley's cock now. Now it was real. The seven inches of young dick throbbing in my mouth were the realest thing in the world. I pressed my nose to his perfectly smooth, stubble-free groin, loving the silky feel of it.

"You like my smooth pubes?" Caley asked. Again, it was as if he could read my mind. "Electrolysis. Daddy had every hair on my body permanently removed, except for my eyebrows and eyelashes, of course. I'm smoother all over now than I was the day I was born. I had a hard on all during every electrolysis treatment. Being so smooth all over makes me feel so fucking sexy!" He flexed his cock in my mouth.

I tightened my lips around the throbbing young cock and began to bob my head. His dick-lube ran down my throat like warm sap. The extreme hardness of his cock thrilled me, as did its velvety skin and its sexy veins. Each flick of my tongue made his cock quiver and throb.

"I love a good blowjob!" Caley purred. "You suck good, daddy. I'm gonna cream real quick." His hands cradled my head and his loins thrust, sliding his cock in my mouth faster. "Yeah!" He churned his hips, screwing his cock in and out as I sucked rhythmically. "Man, I love this feeling!"

From Caley's films I knew that he had a short fuse, but also that he could come repeatedly. My lips smacked as I sucked for his load.

Caley raised his right foot and stroked up and down the belly of my cock with his toes, getting them greasy with my lubricant. "Yeah!" he breathed. "Big sexy cock! Daddy, I'm so fucking close!"

I growled, sucking hard, Caley's cock plunging in my mouth, his balls slapping my chin. Spit trickled down his balls and dripped on my chest. His toes masturbated my cock, tickling it in exactly the right spots. I rubbed my ass against the couch, going wild, fucking his wiggling toes. My balls would literally explode if I didn't get off soon.

"Daddy, I'm coming! Oh, suck it!"

Caley's cock flexed and his cum burst from his piss hole and filled my throat. I gulped to keep from choking. Caley gasped, hugging my head, grinding against my face, reaming out my throat as he filled it with spurt after hot spurt.

"Yeahhh!" he moaned. "Drink it!"

Although his body convulsed with spasms, he managed to keep his right foot moving between my legs. As his cock shot spunk, his toes shot electricity into my cock and I saw stars. Suddenly my nuts were contracting and the jism was hurtling through my piss tube. Cum splashed against Caley's shin, creamed his moving foot and toes. Cum shot against my belly, fell on my thighs, splashed in sticky gobs onto Caley's other foot.

Caley was moaning. "Do it, man, shoot it!" His cock pulsed in my mouth and a few last cum gobs oozed out.

As our orgasms subsided, I slumped back, my head whirling inside. Caley lifted his dripping right foot to my mouth, grinning wickedly as I licked my cum off his instep and toes. Then he fed me the other one.

"Kinky!" Caley said. "That was fun."
He jumped off the couch and left the room.

# 7

As I sat there recovering, I expected to see Caley return with a bucket of soapy water and some cloths for cleaning the cum off the expensive couch before it left permanent stains. I imagined his sugar daddy discovering them and throwing a royal fit. Instead, Caley returned with two bottles of an expensive German beer. His cock was still sticking up in the air. "Sex always makes me thirsty," he said, handing me one of the beers and plopping himself down next to me.

"What about this?" I pointed down at the mess between my thighs on the couch seat.

He reached over and wiped up the cum with his hand, then rubbed it onto his belly and chest. "Cum makes excellent skin lotion. I saw it in some movie about Caligula or somebody. This queen had these big muscular stud slaves jack off into a cup, then she rubbed the cum on her tits like fresh, warm skin lotion. Great scene!"

"What about these stains on the couch?"

"Don't worry, the house cleaners will take care of it. In fact, they'll be thrilled. A couple of young boys from San Jose who still get turned on by cum stains. They come in to clean whenever I call them. Cuties. You'd go for them."

I thought of one of Caley's films in which some young studs come in to clean house while Caley's sugar daddy is away on a trip and Caley seduces them both.

"Do you go for them yourself?"

"Of course. I don't go just for older men."

I mentioned the film that had come to mind.

"Life's like that," he said. "Full of coincidences. Besides, 'truth is the same as fiction,' isn't that the saying?"

"Stranger," I said, tasting the beer, which was full-bodied, strong-flavored, and had even more of a kick than I expected. "Truth is stranger than fiction."

"Well, in my life they're the same," Caley said. He dribbled some cold beer on the tip of his cock and watched it run down the shaft and over his balls.

"I'm surprised the beer doesn't steam," I said. "Be honest now: Do you ever get soft?"

"Not much," Caley said. "I mean, how else could I have been a porn star? We were supposed to stay hard all day. That was our job. Nobody wants to see a limp dick in a porno movie. Of course, that doesn't mean that some guys didn't have problems keeping it up. I could name names. Big names, some of them. They were in the wrong business, if you ask me."

He grabbed my cock, made a cup of the foreskin, and poured some beer into it. Then he bent over and sucked the beer out of the cup. Finally, he

sucked my knob clean. Suddenly I was hard as bone and ready to come again.

"Taste good?" I asked.

"Foreskin adds flavor to the beer," he said, and repeated the procedure.

"You were saying that some guys you worked with had trouble keeping it up. That you could name names?"

"I could, but I don't know if I will," Caley said. "Actually, not many guys can keep a dick hard all day. It helps to be young–the younger the better. A lot of the big studs don't have much stamina. They come once or twice and then they can hardly get it up again. Hell, I pop two or three loads before I'm warmed up. One day I shot off eight times on the set and nobody could believe it. I offered to shoot a few more loads for extra pay, but they just shook their heads and told me to save it and go home. Cheap bastards!"

"You should be in the record books," I said.

"I won all the circle jerks when I was younger," Caley said. "Fastest, farthest, most."

"Most what? Most cum shot, or most times got off?"

"Both."

"I wish I could've been there," I said, trying to imagine Caley and a half-dozen other boys beating their throbbing young cocks in a frantic attempt to come fastest or farthest or most.

"For me, making porn films was just like a continuation of our circle jerks. It just came naturally."

"You came out pretty young."

"I've always been out," he said. "I've never been 'in.' I don't know what coming out means. I mean, I can't remember any time in my life when I was not thinking about cocks and sex and getting off and all that. I've been shooting five loads a day for as long as I can remember. I can't remember ever not being horny and trying to see or get hold of some other guy's dick. And I can't understand these guys who can't keep it up. I mean, mine just stands up and throbs all the time. I can't keep it down."

Looking down at his cock, he made it flex and wiggle without touching it. He dumped some beer on it and I leaned over to lick it off. He surprised me by pushing me away before I could go down on him.

"We'd have cock-wiggling contests during our circle jerks," he said. "We'd all stand with our hands on our hips, making our cocks jump around without touching them. We'd all be laughing, flexing our cocks up and down until they were all dripping. Then we'd jerk them off."

"Who instigated these circle jerks?" I asked.

"Me, mostly. Sometimes one of the older boys"

"Did you get into anything wilder than jacking off?"

"What do you think? Sucking, fucking, peeing contests, peeing on each other. Over time, we did everything. Boys will be boys, you know."

"You all took it up the ass?"

"We all took it at least between the legs. Some boys wouldn't have a cock up the ass, but they'd all take it between the thighs. Everybody liked me because I never refused a cock up the butt." He fingered the mouth of the beer bottle. "I'd had lots of hard dick up the ass before I ever got into porn films."

We finished off our beers.

"Your sugar daddy is a lucky man," I said. "I'll bet he fucks you silly when he's home."

"Not as much as I'd like. He's more into sucking young cock than fucking young ass. He claims that drinking young jizz keeps him younger than the youth drugs he gets in Europe."

"How old is he?"

"Fifty-five, sixty-five–I don't know. He won't say. Not that I care, as long as he stays hard and keeps me in style. So he doesn't satisfy my ass as well as I'd like! What does it matter? I've got more men than I'll ever be able to handle who are dying to do that. All I've gotta do is turn up my ass and the men go nuts–even so-called straight men."

He got off the couch and bent over, then arched his lower back and turned up his ass. I swallowed. Reaching back, he spread his cheeks to show me in the flesh the young asshole I'd seen so shamelessly displayed so many times in films and porn magazines. I wondered how many men had shot their loads gazing it, hungry for it.

"I'm so fuckin' horny!" Caley said. He took his empty beer bottle and worked the neck of it up his ass.

"Careful," I said. "You don't want the whole thing disappearing inside you."

He gave me his patented, mischievous-little-boy grin. "Why not? Then somebody would have to reach in and fish it out. That could be a turn-on."

He fucked himself a while, rotating his ass and sighing, then pulled the bottle out and twitched his pucker at me. "Come on, daddy, get up on me. I need a real fuck."

A container of Lube sat on one of the end tables–Caley, like a good Boy Scout, apparently was always prepared for a fuck–and, after finishing my beer, I picked it up and greased my cock, my eyes focused on Caley's twitching anus.

He gyrated his butt. "Come on, man, hurry up!"

As he bent over, one hand braced on his knee, the other pounding his cock, I mounted him. Grabbing his hips, I pressed my cock head to his pucker, which opened as soon as I applied pressure, and my cock sank up him to the hilt, as if being sucked inside by a hungry mouth. Despite the ease of penetration, I'd never sunk my cock up a hotter, tighter young ass, and the fuck sensation pulsed all the way to my toes.

"Oh baby!" I moaned, clinging to him, my belly grinding against his ass, my cock churning inside him. He had one of the most incredible asses I'd ever fucked. "Hot baby!"

"Do it!" he grunted, gyrating his butt. "Give it to me!" As he squirmed in my embrace, he contracted his asshole, making it suck. "Fuck me, daddy!"

Licking his back, biting his shoulders and the back of his neck, I humped, plunging my cock, my muscular lower belly smacking his butt. His asshole tightened with each thrust of my cock. I straightened up, gripping his hips, watching my huge, veiny, gleaming fuck-snake plunge in and out of him. I'd never fucked a hotter, tighter, sexier-looking ass. Each thrust sent me to the edge of climax.

"Feels good!" Caley moaned, shimmying his legs together and wiggling his ass in a way that excited me even more. "Ooh, daddy, I want you to come quick!"

Why not, I thought. Why fight it? He squealed as I let go, ramming as fast and hard as I could, trying to literally fuck the shit out of him. After a few dozen wild thrusts it was all over.

"I'm coming, baby!"

"Yes!" Caley gasped, then squirmed out of my grip and turned in time to catch my flexing cock before its second ejaculation. Kneeling in front of me, pumping my spasming cock with two hands, he smiled as my cum shot all over his face and chest. He got his mouth over my cock head and continued pumping the shaft, gulping my spurts as they splashed against his tonsils. His mouth sank farther down on my cock and he sucked vigorously, torturing me, making me whimper and jerk.

As he sucked, he smeared his right hand in the cum I'd shot on his chest, dropped the dripping hand to his cock, and started jerking, using my cum as a lubricant. After a dozen rapid strokes his eyes rolled back and he went off against my shins.

Pulling out of his mouth, I dropped down on all fours and caught his hot spurts on my tongue. As his spasms eased, I sucked the head of his cock as his hand milked out the last thick wads.

"Whew!" Caley said, sitting back on his heels to catch his breath and wipe my cum off his face. "We're a pair of fucking animals, ain't we? Ain't it great?"

# 8

After running back to the car for my portable tape recorder, I had Caley sit across the living room from me, out of temptation's reach, so we could do some serious interviewing. After two successive orgasms, I was in need of a break and ready to do some interviewing. I was, after all, paying him well to talk to me.

Caley slumped in a plush white easy chair, his legs apart, his feet propped up on a footstool. As we talked, he massaged his balls, stroked his cock, wiggled his toes, and otherwise squirmed. It was hard to keep my mind on the job at hand and I was thankful for the tape recorder. The interview material that follows is a lightly edited transcription of Caley's taped words.

CALEY: I was born and grew up in Modesto, California, one of the major redneck towns of the Central Valley. My grandparents on both sides were Okies who came to California during the Dust Bowl and never saw life as anything but back-breaking labor and praisin' the Lord. My parents preached God, Country, and Nose-to-the-Grindstone to both me and my younger sister from the cradle onwards, with church twice on Sunday and twice more during the week. Virtue was anything painful, sin anything pleasurable.

Despite nonstop brainwashing, I discovered the pleasures of my cock very early, got caught playing with it, and was punished repeatedly with spankings and threats, then with being sent to ministers and therapists for "help." By the second grade I was madly in love with almost every boy in my school class and knew exactly what I wanted to do with them, even though nobody had ever showed me what I could do with them. By the fifth grade I was lusting not only after most of the boys in school, but after older men as well, and I starting flirting with men shamelessly. Finally, after years of sex on the sly, and tired of parents, teachers, ministers, therapists, and other fools meddling in my life, I ran away to San Francisco and I knew from my first day there that I'd never have trouble surviving. All I had to do was to sell what I'd been giving away for so long, my always-horny young body.

I tried to get into commercial porn films right away, but the producers wouldn't accept my fake IDs. I acted in a bunch of private films for individuals who filmed me and other boys with their home movie cameras, but if those films still exist, they're probably locked up in vaults somewhere. I've never got to see them, although I'd love to now. I think they were probably hotter than anything I've made commercially because there was no director to interfere with the spontaneous, natural action of horny boys going at it, no holds barred.

Anyway, the day I turned 18 I walked into a commercial studio in Los Angeles and during my first day on the set I shot seven loads, astounding the

director, crew, and other actors. I'll never forget that day. I was gang banged by six men and I left the studio with the feel of phantom cocks sliding in and out of me for hours afterward. I couldn't sleep all night, reliving the scene in my head. I'd been ordered not to jack off at home, to save my cum for the next day's filming, but I was so horny I jacked off twice during the night reliving that gangbang.

ME: How did the shooting (pun intended) go the next day?

CALEY: Fantastic! I was so horny with the anticipation of what was in store for me that day that in the first scene we filmed I shot off while Rod– the actor who was supposed to suck me off through a glory hole–was just licking my dick. His tongue hit my magic button once too often and I started gasping and shooting cum all over his face. "What the fuck!" the director says, then shouts for the cameras to focus in on my jerking, spurting cock.

After I came, Rod did give me the blowjob and I came again, this time in his mouth. Rod gulped half my load before backing off my cock and jacking the rest of it onto his face for the cameras. The director had a fit because Rod had swallowed spurts that were supposed to have been caught on film.

In porn films, every spurt counts. Cum shots are the money shots, the payoff. Viewers don't like it when they don't see the cum fly. That director knew this and he wanted three or four cameras filming every cum shot, filming it from different angles. Then, in the finished film, he'd show the cum shot over and over, from all those angles and at various speeds, including stop action and slow motion. I thought it was a little too much. I mean, after five minutes even a cum shot can get boring.

ME: I love seeing cum shots, but I also like to see an actor's face while he's coming, as long as his facial expressions are for real and he's not faking them. I know that directors will sometimes film faked facial expressions when the actor isn't even having sex, let alone an orgasm. I can always tell the faked crap, and it turns me off.

CALEY: I've never faked anything in a film. Whatever you see me do, whatever expression you see on my face, is for real. Sometimes, usually, in fact, I come so hard that I almost faint. You'd think I was being whipped. And my toes go wild.

ME: Your toes go wild when you're getting fucked, too. I've caught glimpses of them on film. Unfortunately, film makers mostly focus on close-ups of a cock sliding in and out of a mouth or ass and ignore almost everything else that's happening. It makes me grind my teeth sometimes.

Do you consider yourself an exhibitionist?

CALEY: Me, an exhibitionist? Whatever would give you an idea like that?

[He clasps his hands behind his head, squirms in his chair, and flexes his cock. I have to resist pouncing on him.]

When I was a tot they couldn't keep clothes on me. My parents would have guests over, their church friends, and I'd come out of the bedroom without a stitch on and parade around in front of them as they stared in shock. I was thrashed every time, but that didn't stop me from doing it again. Almost 30 years later I'm still getting naked in front of people. I don't think you can be a successful porn star without wanting to show it off. I like being stared at and lusted over.

[He squirms into a position so I can view his ass and he parts his buttocks, letting me glimpse his anus.]

I love to see the expression on a man's face when I show him my most-delectable parts.

ME: Some people would call you a shameless whore.

CALEY: I hope I am, it's what pays my rent.

ME: How many men have fucked you in films?

CALEY: Good question. A few hundred, I suppose. I don't keep track of these things like some guys do, keeping a diary and all that of tricks. I'm too busy enjoying today's fuck to keep track of yesterday's. Of course, not every fuck I got in front of a camera made it into a finished film, not even the best fucks. I'd love to see some of those out-takes. I always wondered why they chose to print what they did or cut what they did. Some of the best stuff gets cut out, if you ask me.

ME: I think those choices are just a matter of taste, which there's no accounting for, or stupidity. Were you ever propositioned by directors or crew?

CALEY: What do you think? A lot of those guys were on me like flies on shit. I've got an irresistible ass, in case you hadn't noticed. Besides, after filming all that sex, wouldn't you be horny too? I've been gang banged by entire film crews. I've had a producer's cock up my ass and his director's cock down my throat at the same time. Some actors won't put up with that, they're untouchable except for pay. Not me. I've given away as much ass as I've been paid for, slut that I am.

ME: Which are your favorites of the films you've been in?

John Patrick

CALEY: You won't believe this, but those couple of low-budget, amateurish jobs I helped write and produce myself. I don't know if they're my best films, but they're my favorites. Ten of us actors got together and thought we could make some good movies, not to mention a lot of money. We used borrowed and rented equipment and filmed where we could, including in our own apartments, some park johns, and a bathhouse. The results look more like home movies than professionally made porn. The picture and sound are fuzzy and the acting is a joke. We couldn't distribute them big time and, after paying our bills, we actually lost money. They were disasters businesswise, but they're my favorite films because they're raunchy and real.

The actors all got into the action in a big way. All of us were really turned on, all of us doing what we wanted to do, and when, without some director telling us what we should be doing. We more or less forgot the cameras and just fucked. Eight-man orgy at the end of the one movie is just ten horny guys with big cocks getting carried away with each other. The only ones who missed out in that last scene were the two guys behind the cameras. The cum really flew in that scene and my mouth and ass got a workout. I mean, all seven guys had me.

ME: How many times in your life have you been screwed?

CALEY: How many times in my life! God, how would I know! A thousand? That's just a wild guess. I started very early. The man who took my cherry got some very fresh young ass, to say the least, and I've been addicted ever since. I need a big cock up me, though, to really blow my mind. I mean, the bigger the better. Huge, hard, fast, and deep–that's how I like it.

ME: Why is it often the skinny, willowy boys who dig getting their asses rammed by pile-driver's big enough to split them in half, while so many of the big hunky guys are afraid of anything larger than a middle finger?

CALEY: Maybe us skinny, willowy boys are smarter than the big guys. Or maybe we've got hungrier and more-elastic asses.

ME: Tell me more about losing your cherry.

CALEY: Am I allowed to talk about it?
Like I said, I was pretty young. One of the ministers I got sent to who was supposed to counsel me and cure me of my "self-abuse problem" had me pull down my pants so I could show him exactly how I "abused" myself. He watched closely as I demonstrated. I'd probably have popped off in his face if he hadn't suddenly turned me around and pushed me face-down over

- 328 -

his office desk. When I heard him unbuckle his belt, I thought he was going to whip me with it. But when I heard him unzip and heard other strange noises, I dared to look back, and there stood his monster cock, throbbing away as he greased it with Vaseline. Then he was on me, jabbing at my ass until he found the hole, then clapping his hand over my mouth as he skewered me and I let out a yelp. The pain was unbearable for about ten seconds, and then suddenly it dissolved into a wonderful throbbing warmth and I started squirming under him with pleasure rather than pain, my wiggling butt urging him to fuck. He grunted and labored for several minutes before he lost control and shot his load. I can still feel his cock jerking inside me and him groaning with pleasure.

After he'd had his fun, he made me pull up my pants before I could jack off, then scolded me severely for having "enticed him." He said I'd brought the devil with me into his office and had sent the devil from myself into him. Then he wailed and shouted and prayed over me, his big hairy paw squeezing my head as he ordered the devil, now back inside me, to depart. Then he begged "Almighty Gawd" for forgiveness for me and for himself.

I knew it was all a crock. I mean, the devil hadn't brought that half-used jar of Vaseline into the office and I guessed that I wasn't the first boy he'd fucked. After that I voluntarily presented myself in his office for counseling a few days each week and he soon used up that jar of Vaseline and bought an economy-sized one, and soon he'd used up that one too. I was addicted to getting fucked from that first fuck on. He always carried on with his scolding and wailing and praying afterwards, but I learned to close my ears to it until it was over and to hardly even hear it. To this day, I don't know if he was serious about the sin and forgiveness shit. All I know for sure is that he loved to fuck young ass. He fucked me until the day I left Modesto.

ME: Was he the only man who fucked you there?

CALEY: God no, there were dozens. Once I learned what some men liked, and where to go to find those men, I offered my boy-pussy regularly. Talk about being a slut! I could never get enough stiff man-cock.

ME: And after all those years of reaming and plowing, you're still as tight as a virgin. How come?

CALEY: For one thing, I exercise my hole for hours everyday. I can clamp it so tight that you couldn't get your little-finger up it.

ME: Plus, you're still young and elastic. That certainly helps. Why don't you age? You look younger now than you did in your films. Is your sugar daddy giving you youth drugs from Europe? What's your secret?

John Patrick

CALEY: I use the same youth drug he does–cum–and lots of it. I drink it and rub it all over me and shoot lots of it. Maybe, though, drinking and squirting all that cum doesn't matter. Maybe though, like the minister said, I've made a pact with the devil–and it's the devil who's keeping me looking like jailbait.

# 9

Before long Caley had had enough interviewing for a while and said he wanted to show me more of the house. He led me straight to the master bedroom, a huge space that spanned the width of the house, allowing views of the mountains on one side and the pastures and woods on the other. Mirrors covered what wall and ceiling space wasn't either window or skylight. A plush red carpet covered the floor. Ten people could have stretched out on the sprawling bed, which was equipped with leather straps anchored to the frame at both the head and foot of the mattress.

"Daddy likes to tie me down like I'm his slave boy," Caley said. "Nothing heavy up here in the bedroom, though–just light bondage. The torture chamber is in the basement."

"Torture chamber?"

"You'd be surprised what can go on in this house," Caley said, a glint in his eyes. "Daddy can be a real mean dude sometimes. He can get me screaming like a hysterical girl. He enjoys that."

"You allow him to torture you?"

"I don't have a choice when I'm his slave boy–or the slave boy of any man who can handle me."

The look Caley gave me sent a powerful surge through my cock. I picked him up like a sack and he laughed as I flung him onto the mattress. He squirmed as I bound him at the wrists and ankles with the leather straps attached to the bed frame and spread-eagling his boyish figure face-up.

"What're you doing to me?" he said, lying there helpless and panting, his excited cock flopping against his belly like a fish out of water. "Daddy, what're you gonna do?"

"You'll see," I said, although I hadn't the faintest idea. I got up on the mattress and I stood over him, stroking my rigid cock, dripping pre-cum on his tanned skin. My right foot rested on his chest, my toes tweaking his nipples. Then my foot slid up farther, the big toe stroking his lips until his mouth opened and his lips closed around it and he began to suck like a baby at a bottle.

"Nice," I said, pumping my throbbing fucker. Each suck sent a thrill through my toe and cock. I wiggled my big toe and began to slide it in and out, fucking his mouth. After a minute I pulled my toe out and lowered myself, straddling his chest, shoving my dripping cock into his mouth, forcing it down his throat, burying all eight-plus inches into his cute face.

As many times as I'd seen Caley on the screen swallow cocks that dwarfed my own, it surprised me that he was able to swallow every inch of mine without gagging and that I was able to fuck his throat without choking him. His eyes crossed as he watched my veiny fucker sliding in and out of his face. My hairy balls slapped against his chin. I glanced back at his cock and saw it wiggle and flex, as if responding with a throb of its own to my

every thrust into his mouth. When I felt myself getting close, I gave his mouth a few more pokes, then pulled out. His spit was dripping from my prong and trickling down my swollen balls.

I lay on him then and kissed him, tasting my cock on his lips and tongue. He moaned, grinding up against me and sucking my tongue. With his arms stretched over his head, his armpits were exposed, and I went to work on them, nuzzling and licking the moist, satin-smooth flesh. The taste and scent of his boyish musk drove me wild. When I'd finished with his armpits, I moved to his nipples, sucking and chewing them until his eyes nearly popped out. Then I nuzzled and kissed up his throat and kissed his face all over. Our mouths locked and he gazed into my eyes with lust bordering on pain, writhing against me, grinding his hard cock against mine. Suddenly he started to grunt and jerk and his spunk burst between us like hot milk.

"Ahhh yeahhhh!" he moaned, pumping out his load, greasing our bellies until I nearly slipped off him.

As his orgasm subsided, I lifted up off him and crouched over him on all fours, lapping up his warm, spicy boy-cum. After cleaning his belly, I sucked the oozing tip of his cock, then swallowed his entire cock and sucked it dry.

"Stop!" he gasped, nearly jumping out of his skin. "It's too much!"

I let his wet cock slide out of my mouth and licked the sweat off his balls, then sucked his perineum. His cock did flip flops and he started moaning, working his loins up and down.

"Suck my crotch, Daddy."

I continued sucking and licking under his balls and I darted my tongue down into his ass crack, tickling his pucker with the tip of it. As he moaned and squirmed, I licked his silky inner thighs and moved down farther, kissing and licking his knees and shins. Finally, I pressed his feet together, then forced my mouth down over them, swallowing all ten of his toes at once. His cock flexed wildly.

"Cut my hands loose," he begged. "I gotta jerk off. Toe sucking drives me nuts."

I ignored his request, gnawing and sucking on his toes and enjoying the sight of his cock jumping against his stomach as if it would shoot off at any second. His balls squirmed and throbbed in their hairless sac. When I feared that his eyes would roll permanently back into his brain from the stimulation to his sensitive toes, I released his feet and slid up to crouch over him and to work on his nipples, pinching and tugging on them, sucking and licking and biting.

"Please, Daddy!" he whimpered, arching up, trying to thrust his cock against me. "You're giving me fucking blue balls!"

I'd seen Caley on film get fucked a hundred times, but I'd seen him fuck other guys only a few times, usually boys his own age, whose eyes had nearly popped out from Caley's rapid and intense rutting. Although Caley was a natural bottom, there was no doubt that he enjoyed screwing and could

fuck like a pro when the occasion demanded it. Snatching the container of Lube off the bedside table, I dipped my hand into it and rubbed a generous gob of the fuck-grease all over Caley's cock.

Caley moaned, his eyes closed, his head rolling from side to side. "Jack me off, man!"

I released his cock and reached back to grease between my buttocks.

"Cut me loose," he begged. "I'll jerk it myself."

"I like you tied down," I said. I straddled his loins and bent his cock up, guiding the red-hot head of it between my ass cheeks. When his cock touched my asshole, I rotated my butt and began to screw myself down on his cock.

"Yeahhh!" he said, when he realized what I was doing.

"Yeah!" I said, feeling his stiff rod sliding up my ass. His young cock was so hard that you'd have thought it hadn't shot off in weeks. Once it was entirely inside me, I sat there a while, just enjoying the feel of it pulsing and flexing in my ass.

"Tight ass!" Caley groaned, straining upward. "Feels fucking hot!"

Without touching my cock, I began to ride him, to slide my ass sheath up and down his stiff fuck pole, gasping as his sizzling pecker rubbed and jabbed my prostate. As our fucking established a rhythm, I gyrated my ass, screwing my asshole up and down his rod, my own cock whacking up and down and from side to side, still untouched, but nearly going into spasms from his electric prodding deep inside me.

"Fuck me, baby, fuck me!" I moaned, watching our fucking in the wall and ceiling mirrors.

As I bounced over his loins, Caley bounced his ass against the mattress and drove upward, thrusting his cock into the pit of my bowels. I was sweating, and so was he, our bodies taking on a sheen. I imagined us as oiled dancers, performing a sexual dance on stage. We fucked with such beautifully synchronized movements that it was as if we'd been lovers for 20 years and had practiced this naturally choreographed routine five thousand times. Caley's glazed eyes told me that his orgasm was near, so I grabbed my cock and jerked it, trying to synchronize my orgasm with his. After a few dozen jerks my asshole and cock were contracting in unison and I was ready to unload. "Baby!" I moaned. "I'm gonna come!"

"Do it!" Caley grunted, ramming upward. "Shoot it!"

I started to jerk as if I were being flogged and my cum splattered all over Caley's chest and face, some of it falling on his extended tongue and flying into his open mouth. As he tasted my spunk, his cock started to flex and shudder inside me. He whined, his loins jerking, his jism drilling my asshole.

In my excitement I lost control of my movements and slipped off Caley's spurting cock and felt his hot cum splash onto my back and ass. He groaned, thrusting his cock at air and fucking out his load. I watched him in the mirrors.

"Damn!" he moaned. "It slipped out."

Sliding forward, I shoved my cock into his mouth and let him suck my piss tube dry. Then I slid backward and crouched over him, licking my cum off his face, chest, and belly.

"You did that on purpose," Caley said. "I'll get you for that."

"I did not," I said. "I just lost control."

"Sure," he said. "Untie me, I need a fuckin' drink."

# 10

We relaxed on chaise lounges next to the swimming pool, sipping a punch of fruit juice and rum. Caley's cock lay hard against his belly, the tip of it near his navel. I wondered if even he had ever seen it soft. I'd lost count of how many orgasms he'd had since my arrival.

He bent his cock down and dipped the head into his glass and, as it snapped back against his belly, punch ran down its shaft and over his balls. I resisted the temptation to suck the punch off his cock. I wanted to ask him more questions. "Who maintains this estate?"

"Who do you think?" Caley said. "Not me. I'm daddy's sex slave, not his work slave. Daddy's got an army of boy-slaves to do the work–not that he doesn't treat them like sex slaves as well, the old pig. He can never get enough young cock."

"Who can!" I said. "Where are these young cocks today, these work-slaves?"

"I gave them the afternoon off. When I entertain men, I don't want distractions around, not to mention competition."

"Do you ever make it with these boys?"

He smiled and licked his lips. "They're young and cute and always hard. What do you think?"

"In one of your films you played a boy whose sugar daddy leaves town, and as soon as he's gone you're seducing two young gardeners or cleaning boys. When you made that film, did you ever imagine that some day you'd literally be living that scenario?"

"I knew it before I'd been in San Francisco a week. One day on Polk Street I got picked up by a chauffer in a limo half a block long. He took me home to his millionaire boss, who proposed marriage after one taste of my ass. I mean, this guy was nuts for teenage butt. He'd bury his nose in my crack for hours, sniffing and sucking, licking me out. While I was laying there getting rimmed, I knew I'd never have to work another day and could live like a prince if I just stayed with him and fed him my ass all day long."

"Why didn't you?"

"I wasn't ready to be kept. I'd just escaped from parents, school, church, wacko therapists, and all that bullshit. I wanted freedom. So I turned him down, knowing that I could have my pick of sugar daddies when I was ready for one."

"I'm glad you did. Otherwise you'd never have gone into porn films and I wouldn't be sitting here right now. You were a rising star. Why did you quit?"

Caley laughed. "A rising star to chicken-hawks like you maybe, but most guys who watch porn idolize the muscular studs with big dicks, not the skinny boys who suck their cocks and get fucked by them. The big stars are

tops, not bottoms. Boys like me are just cannon fodder for ten-inch cocks. It's the big-dicked stud that the main audience focuses on, not the reamed-out chicken. Name the big stars and they're all muscular brutes with cocks like stallions."

"So you quit because you didn't think you'd ever become a major star."

"That's part of it. Also because I was working hard and making peanuts while the big stars–a lot of them lazy bastards who couldn't even get it up half the time–were making more for one scene than I made for a hundred. Here I was, sucking and fucking myself goofy month after month so the producers and directors and big stars could live in mansions and drive big cars while I had less than nothing in the bank. Don't get me wrong, I loved the work, but I was being used, and after a while I decided I'd had enough. If I was going to sell my body, I was going to be paid for it, and paid well."

"So you quit when you realized you were being used."

"To tell the truth, I realized after only a month in the business that I was being ripped off, but it took me a dozen films before I threw in the towel, before the novelty and excitement of fucking for the cameras were no longer enough. I mean, I was addicted to the studio scene. I really got off on being dirty in front of an audience, pay or no pay. I wanted to show the world that I'm a total slut, out to get my boy-pussy fucked by every big cock around. But finally I decided that I needed to be paid what I was worth."

"Were you ever afraid that nonstop sex day after day would leave you jaded? That you'd burn out?"

"Me, burn out? Never! My problem is that I'm always horny. I shoot a load and a minute later I'm itching to shoot another one. I don't see how guys who aren't as horny as I am can work in porn films very long. I mean, I've worked with guys who had to flog their meat to get it up for the cameras. Why bother? They should go into computer programming or something. And some of these guys are big names. If their fans could only see them behind the scenes! I would love to see that! These so-called stars would manage to shoot one load for every twenty of mine and they'd get paid fifty times more per load than me. Unreal!"

"So all the big stars aren't real studs?"

"Are you kidding me! Without camera tricks and slick editing, a lot of these 'stars' would be finished. I mean, they're boring to watch even with all the editing. That's because they're fakes. I don't care how handsome or pretty or muscular or hung they are, if they aren't really horny, they can't get it up and it takes hours and hours. Eight hours once for a ten-minute sequence! But the fans don't have a clue. Not a fuckin' clue, man. They believe what's on the screen! They're into watching a cool, muscular stud, a fantasy doll, even if he performs like a robot. They can't sense that he hasn't had a genuine hard on in months. If I were making films, I wouldn't use anybody who wasn't for real, big name or not."

"Maybe you should go into film-making."

"Someday, maybe. Right now I'm just a horny boy being lazy and enjoying life, and finally being paid for it. I was horny every second that I spent on the set, and gave my fans more genuine sweat and cum and feeling than any other porn actor, as far as I'm concerned, but one morning I woke up and realized I was tired of working for almost free, and that was it. I gave notice."

"How did they take your resignation?"

"They acted like they didn't care, because they figured I'd be back. I mean, actors quit often enough, then came back a month later, cock in hand, begging for a job, even for lower pay, if they could just work again. When I didn't return after a few months, they started calling me, telling me about all the hot new dicks they had lined up to fuck me, saying they might even consider upping my wage. I was tempted more by the thought of the hot new dicks than by the pay increase, which I knew they'd never raise high enough to be even remotely fair. I was surprised by how much they actually offered me before they gave up and stopped calling. (I apparently had a small army of fans out there who were hungry to see more of me and were pestering the producer.) By that time, though, I was kicking my legs up in the air every morning, noon, and evening for a handsome Italian sugar daddy who was the spitting image of the hairy actor whose monster cock had fucked me out of my mind in one of my favorite films. Here I was, living in luxury, sucking and being fucked by a gorgeous man three or more times a day, and otherwise just lazying around and enjoying myself, and the idea of going back to the set for anything less than the big stars was out of the question."

"Was your first sugar daddy one of your fans?"

"Of course. All my sugar daddies have been fans of my films. One guy has every one of 'em, even one that was never released because it was so bad! How he got it he wouldn't say, but he got it. God knows what he had to pay for it! More than the real thing cost him, probably!"

"Do you miss making films?"

"I miss being a whore for the cameras and getting to make it with dozens of new hunks every month, most of them blind dates. I mean, a lot of them you don't even meet until you get to work and you're supposed to fuck them on the spot. Slut that I am, I miss being a piece of hired meat in that way, but don't miss being a wage slave.

"Sometimes I'll be watching an old film of mine and I'll relive the experience–I mean, actually feel the sensations and emotions–and I'll be dying to go back and make just one more film.

"Or I'll be watching some new film just out and get steamed up over some hunky new actor and I'll imagine myself calling the studio and begging to make a film with him.

"But then I remind myself that it's silly to go to all that trouble just to get my rocks off when I'm enjoying as much hot dick now as I did then. In fact sometimes, through connections, I can get literally hold of that hunky new star and get him to come out here.

John Patrick

"Shit, man, I'll even pay for a fuck sometimes–if I have to. It kind of turns me on."

# 11

As the recording tape rolled, Caley grew restless. He was a boy who couldn't easily sit still, a boy of action, not words, and I could see that the interview was becoming tedious for him. He squirmed continuously, wiggling his toes and rubbing his feet and legs together, playing with his cock and pinching his ball-sac. He was bursting with both nervous and sexual energy, and watching him got me restless and horny and, as we talked, I worked the foreskin up and down my cock, from time to time wiping off the gob of lubricant that oozed from my piss-hole. Whenever Caley looked ready to pounce on me, I ordered him to stay put, until finally I realized that his patience was running out and I suggested that we take a swim to cool off.

Caley dove into the pool with the froglike form of a farm boy at a swimming hole, his legs kicking up behind him as he broke the surface, his stiff cock, like his body, torpedoing into the water. As he swam, his ass broke the surface, smooth and gleaming, looking lusciously edible. When he flipped over to backstroke, his erection jutted up into the sunlight and his swollen nut-sac resembled a golden-brown peach glistening with water.

"What're you waiting for?" he called, flipping over again. "I bet you can't catch me."

I dove in and caught him before he'd swum five strokes. As he struggled in my arms, laughing, I hauled him into shallower water and kissed him, grinding against him until I almost shot. He squirted saliva into my mouth and I drank it.

"Blow me," he growled, pushing down on my head and forcing me under water.

Even in the cool water, his cock head was sizzling. I managed to get his cock into my mouth without drowning and, keeping my lips closed around it, I bobbed my head, sucking the succulent knob and ivory-smooth shaft. He probably would have popped his load in another few seconds if I hadn't had to surface for air.

"Great head!" he said. "Now it's my turn."

His blonde hair waved upward like golden seaweed as he slid beneath the surface and went down on me. His tongue wiggled between my knob and foreskin and slid around and around, driving me nuts. He gripped my cock-shaft and jerked it as he worked his mouth up and down, sucking and tonguing. I moaned, cradling his head in my hands, working my cock deeper down his throat. He had me humping in a pleasure-crazed daze by the time he came up for air.

"Quick!" he panted, pulling down on my head. "Suck it!"

As I sank beneath the surface again I saw his right hand pumping his cock. His piss hole was open and leaking a cloudy fluid. From inches away, I watched a rope of cum snake from his piss hole in slow motion. Another

spurt escaped his cock before I got the pulsing cylinder of young meat into my mouth and felt the burst of hot cream into my throat. I sucked until he stopped shooting and I swallowed every drop.

When I came up gasping for air, Caley was floating away on his back as if unconscious. "Thanks," he sighed. "I needed that."

# 12

After the sunshine and breeze had licked us dry, we went to the TV room to watch some of Caley's video flicks. I felt as if I had entered lotus-land, and doing any more interviewing this afternoon was the farthest thing from my mind.

The TV room was furnished with a bed almost as large as the one in the bedroom, and we lounged on it, leaning back against thick pillows. A projection screen in front of us covered most of the wall. On the screen, Caley was struggling to suck the python-sized cock of a hairy Italian-looking stud.

"Eleven inches," Caley said before I could ask how big the stud's cock was. "Measured it myself. One of the biggest cocks I ever sucked. I almost choked to death on it. God, it was great!" He stroked his hard on, watching himself sucking cock on screen.

At home I had a magazine containing stills from this very film. The cover shot showed Caley looking more boyish than ever, his jaws dislocating as his mouth stretched around the nearly foot-long cock, his eyes turned up in blissful ecstasy, cum squirting from his own cock, which he was jerking.

"He's the one who looks just like my first sugar daddy," Caley said. "Except he's got a few more inches. I'd have married him in two seconds, if he'd asked me. Watch this now."

On the screen Caley started shooting cum against the stud's hairy legs. The man hauled his cock out of Caley's mouth and pumped thick wads all over Caley's pleasure-contorted face and into his open mouth. Caley's tongue dangled, catching every stray drop.

"Feed me, Daddy, " Caley said, laughing as on screen he licked the tip of the man's dripping cock. "Yummy!"

On screen, the scene switched from living room to bedroom. Now Caley was up on all fours on a bed, his ass turned up, the hairy daddy humping him from behind, all eleven inches of man-cock slicing in and out of his young hole. It didn't seem possible that a cock so thick could enter such a slim-hipped, small-assed boy without splitting him into equal halves.

"That had to hurt," I said.

"Yeah," Caley said. "It hurt real good."

On screen Caley said, "Oh, Daddy, fuck me! Fuck me hard!" Beside me on the bed Caley got up on all fours and wiggled his ass in my face. "Oh, Daddy, fuck me! Fuck me hard!"

Using Lube, I greased my cock and kneeled up behind the boy. Gripping his hips, I rammed my aching eight-and-a-half inches straight up his ass. He moaned deliriously as I scoured his butt with my muscular lower belly, his asshole tightening around my plunging cock like a rhythmically squeezing hand. Both on the screen and in the flesh, Caley's cock stood straight out under his belly, ramrod stiff, flexing with each thrust of man-cock up his ass.

"Oooh, fuck me!" Caley moaned in unison with himself on screen.

The Italian stud started slapping Caley's ass on screen, so I did the same to his real ass.

"Oh, Daddy, spank me!" gasped both Caleys.

Each slap caused the boy's asshole to grip, to suck, which sent a jolt of pleasure through my cock and balls, spurring me to fuck him faster and to slap his ass harder. We both shuddered as my muscular loins collided with his butt.

"Oh, Daddy!" Caley moaned. "Give it to me!"

On screen the Italian stud flipped Caley onto his back and began fucking him face to face, his hairy shoulders pressing against the backs of Caley's smooth legs and forcing his knees to his chest. Caley had his arms up over his head, as if his wrists were tied to the headboard, and his untouched cock jumped all over his belly as eleven inches of rock-hard stud-cock rammed him.

Following the film script, I flipped Caley onto his back and fucked him face to face. As he threw his arms back, showing me his armpits, I lapped at the succulent smooth flesh there, drinking his sweat as I fucked him. Our energetic fucking had us both dripping sweat.

On screen Caley's eyes rolled back, only their whites showing. His body began to jerk, his toes clutching, his teeth gnawing his lips. Then his mouth gaped in a silent scream and jism streamed from his cock, splashing across his chest, onto his face, into his open mouth. The silent cry turned to an audible, ecstatic wail as the cum continue squirting from him.

Under me, Caley whined in unison with himself on screen. His eyes rolled back and spunk shot from his cock, landing on his chest and nipples, pelting his chin. His asshole chewed up my cock and I saw stars. As my spasms hit, I grunted like a bull and exploded into him, expecting to see my cum burst from his gaping mouth.

On screen the Italian stud pulled out of Caley's asshole and shot cum onto Caley's squirming body. Caley laughed, smearing the slick man-juice all over himself as it landed. At last, a close-up of his face showed him licking his fingers clean and smiling for the camera.

Under me, as his gripping asshole sucked the last orgasmic twinges through my cock, Caley was smiling too.

# 13

The torture chamber was more than just a basement room, it was an actual underground cave, entered through a hidden door in the basement wall. It was a large chamber, equipped with as many S&M pleasure devices as Vic Tanny's was equipped with workout machines. The room was almost dark, lit only by isolated spotlights over the machines and by spotlights that illuminated the dozens of photographs, drawings, and paintings that adorned the walls. The chamber had an art-museum feel, as if the torture devices were sculptures in the middle of a picture gallery. Despite being underground, the chamber felt toasty-warm.

I perused the pictures on the walls, most of which depicted naked boys being punished–on the rack, hanging by their arms and being whipped, hanging in slings while being gang raped, etc. The photographs looked both vintage and contemporary and in some of them I recognized other porn stars besides Caley. The paintings and drawings included works by well-known contemporary artists and by old masters, none of whom were known for depicting erotic subjects.

"Where does he get hold of these?" I asked.

"Daddy buys new ones all the time on his trips," Caley said. "He sells them too. These are only a few of his pictures. He has ten times this many in his vault."

"I'd like to get into that vault," I said.

"Me too, but he won't give even me the combination."

Caley led me over to a large, floor-to-ceiling display cabinet in the corner and switched on the cabinet lights. Through the display windows I saw shelves packed with dildoes, all of them as lifelike as real cocks, most of them huge, although a few looked almost pre-adolescent.

"My collection," Caley said. "I have nearly 200. All of them were made from casts of real cocks that I've sucked or fucked. Now I want this one in there." He squeezed my cock and slid the foreskin.

"No problem," I said, grabbing his cock, "as long as I can have a replica of this one."

"That can be arranged," he said, flexing his cock in my hand. "Now let's play."

He led me by the cock over to a sling that was hanging from the ceiling and had me strap him into it. His legs were spread wide, his hands restrained above his head, his balls and asshole fully exposed and vulnerable. There was a photograph on the wall of him suspended in this very sling, a muscular naked giant in a black cowl standing between his legs and fucking him. A dozen other naked, cowled, sweat-shiny men with large erect cocks were standing in line, waiting for a turn between Caley's legs. Two men, one stationed at each foot, were biting his toes. Two other men were pinching his nipples.

"Now get some cocks from the cabinet and fuck me with them," Caley said.

I came back from the cabinet hugging a few dozen rubber dildoes in my arms. As I greased them with Lube, Caley squirmed in his sling, watching.

"Hurry up!" he begged. "Before I go crazy!"

I started with one of the smaller cocks, a mere eight-incher, and Caley's asshole sucked it up. It would have disappeared completely inside him if not for the set of fat balls at its base. I wondered who owned the original of this one.

"Poke me hard! Give it to me!" Caley was panting, wriggling as I dildo-fucked him.

After a minute, I pulled the first dildo out and replaced it with a larger one, a nine-incher, marveling at the elasticity of the boy's asshole as I slid the thick rubber cylinder in and out. He purred with pleasure and begged for more. I fucked him soundly and poked him with a ten-incher next.

It didn't seem possible that something so long and thick could fit completely inside a canal so small and tight, but Caley didn't flinch as I cranked the dildo inside him.

"Oh, Daddy!" he sighed. "Do it!" His toes worked to the rhythm of my fucking.

The next dildo I picked up had to be eleven inches long, as large as the cock of the Italian stud in the film we'd just watched together. In fact, with its set of lifelike, hairy balls, it could easily have been a replica of that very stud's cock.

"Stick it in!" Caley begged. "Fuck the shit outta me, man!"

His toes clutched as the massive cock stuffed him, and he squirmed, his cock flip-flopping against his belly. The bigger the dildoes got, the more excited Caley became and, as I fucked him with one dildo after another, the more excited I became myself. Each thrust of a dildo up Caley's ass sent a thrill through my own cock, and the more excited I became, the faster I screwed the boy and the more impatient I became to stuff a fresh dildo inside him.

All the dildoes I'd chosen were huge and beautiful, their various curves and veins and heads thrilling me, and thrilling me most as they disappeared up Caley's insatiable young ass. I got so excited that I began yanking one cock out of Caley and stuffing a fresh one inside him before his asshole could close.

"I can't stand it!" he gasped. "I'm going nuts! Don't stop!"

By the time I'd fucked him with nearly two-dozen different dildoes, I couldn't stand it anymore myself. Not only was I sweat-drenched and breathless, but my balls were aching and my cock was so steel-hard that I feared it would split down the middle. In a dizzy frenzy, I picked up the largest dildo of the bunch, which I'd saved for last, the one that had to be over a foot long and as big around as my fist, and I forced it into his body.

His mouth gaped and he started to shake. I twisted the rubber monster inside him. He twisted his head from side to side, his eyes rolled back. In and out I screwed the monster cock. His body started to jerk and, with a whimper, he shot a torrent of spunk from his cock, a few drops of hot juice flying up over his head.

"Yeahhh!" he moaned, jerking and spurting. "Oh God!"

I released the dildo, watching his spasming asshole chew it up. I had my cock in my hand and was pounding it. When the dildo slipped out of his asshole and hit the floor with a wet thud, I drove my splitting-hard cock up the still-open fuck-chute and went off after two thrusts. His asshole gripped my churning, jizz-spewing cock, gnawing it until I wanted to scream. I clamped my mouth over his and inhaled his very soul.

## 14

A month after our interview Caley called and asked me to come back to the ranch to have a replica made of my cock. I was surprised, as he hadn't returned my call of a few weeks earlier and I'd given up on hearing from him again. I reminded him of our agreement, that I was to receive a replica of his cock in exchange for his getting one of mine.

"Of course," he said. "Now get down here."

It was another idyllic, sunny afternoon when I got to the ranch. Mike, the dildo maker, had arrived before me and had already set up his equipment in the tool shed. It didn't surprise me to find Mike as naked as Caley when I arrived, nor to see that his erection was shiny with spit. From the impish expression on Caley's face I knew without doubt that he'd been working on Mike's eight inches with his lips and tongue.

Mike was a chubby, balding, daddy-type of about 55 with tons of body hair. His beard had as much gray in it as black. When he saw my erect cock he rhapsodized, saying it would make a "beautiful sculpture."

"You consider yourself a sculptor," I said.

"But of course," said Mike. "I make the most beautiful sculptures in the world." He had his arm around Caley and was caressing him as Caley stroked the man's hairy back and nuzzled his beard. They kissed, tongues churning in each other's mouth.

I suspected that Caley was making out with the man for my benefit, maybe to make me jealous, but as his young cock throbbed and jumped, excited by their kissing, I couldn't resist going down on it. It felt like hot bone in my mouth and tasted sweaty and sweet. I could have sucked it for hours, but Mike started complaining.

"Hey, stud, I could use some head too."

"Suck Daddy's cock," Caley said, pushing my head away from his cock and forcing me down on Mike's. "Choke on it!"

I almost did. Compared to Caley's honey-flavored cock, Mike's cock tasted like salty leather.

"Yummy!" Caley said, jabbing his hot dickhead against my cheek and smearing it with cock-lube as he jerked my head up and down. "Eat Daddy's fat sweaty cock!"

"Yeahhh!" Mike growled. "Eat that beautiful piece of meat!"

"Suck!" Caley hissed. "Suck!"

With Caley guiding my head up and down and ordering me to suck, I got more and more turned on and found myself sucking in earnest.

Before long Mike started to tremble. "Oh, shit, yeah, here it comes!"

As the thick man-spunk burst into my mouth, Caley jerked my head back and suddenly Mike's cock was spewing cum in my face. Caley grabbed the hairy, flexing daddy-cock and went down on it, growling as he sucked

out the rest of Mike's load. The boy was beating off as he gulped the man's spunk.

"Christ, baby, eat it!" Mike grunted, fucking Caley's mouth. "Drink it all, you filthy boy-slut!"

When Caley had finished with Mike's cock, he licked Mike's jizz off my face. Then he kissed me and I spit the wad of Mike's cum I'd received into Caley's mouth. As he swallowed it, he rose to his feet, his right hand pumping, and suddenly he was shooting off in my face. Mouth open, I swallowed his cock head, then the rest of his bucking young cock, sucking until I'd drained him of every sweet, slimy drop.

"Caley, darling," Mike said, "you little bugger! You weren't supposed to come until after I made the cast. I wanted your cock as big and hard as possible."

"Sorry, Daddy," Caley said. "I got carried away. But don't worry, I'm still almost as hard as before."

"I want your cock so hard that it's ready to jump out of its skin," Mike said.

"Give me half a minute," Caley said, playing with his balls and stroking his cock. "I'm getting horny again."

As he prepared the casting medium, Mike mentioned that Tom of Finland had worked totally nude when he made his drawings, and with a roaring hard on to boot. "And that's how I work too," Mike said. "I'm a sculptor, but I'm also a great fan of Tom's work."

"Daddy just got some new Tom of Finland originals," Caley said. "If you want to see them."

"Bring them out," Mike said. "This is my day."

Caley performed a seductive dance as he left the shed, wiggling his butt, pointing his toes, and finally pulling apart his ass cheeks to give us a glimpse of his pucker before he blew us a kiss and disappeared.

Mike's cock, which had fallen to half mast after his orgasm, rose again to full. "What an ass!" he said, stroking himself. "What a boy! I come up here all the way from L.A., at a moment's notice, and work for free, whenever he calls me. I have to cancel other appointments, for Christ sake, and sometimes I lose customers. I must be crazy. The kid has me eating out of his hand. I've seen all his films ten times over."

"Me too," I said, stroking my own cock, the after-image of Caley's naked ass, buttocks parted, still in my mind's eye.

"What is it about him?" Mike asked. "I mean, I've seen cuter boys, boys with bigger dicks–but nobody does it for me–turns me on–like Caley. Know what I mean?"

"I know what you mean," I said.

"But why is he so special? Sure, he never gets soft, but I know other boys who never get soft, either. What's so extra-special about Caley? I've been trying to figure it out. Why does he have this effect on me?"

"He's the real thing," I said.

Mike nodded. "He's the real thing, all right."
"Yeah," I said, "and he knows it."

.

# Love for Sale – A Memoir

## By William Cozad

What follows is the continuation of Mr. Cozad's memoirs, which began with "Lover Boys" in the anthology of the same name.

*A boy on the corner stands so still*
*Idling there, staring at traffic.*
*Making eyes at passers-by,*
*Do they know why?*
*Blonde and tanned, he always smiles*
*Or winks and grins as he*
*Catches a glance,*
*Does he have a chance?*
*Exposing flesh as if it's meat*
*On sale to others. His body*
*curves so neat and round*
*He hopes he's found*
*Another trick. That's it.*

*Someone's stopped,*
*he's old and gray,*
*A chat, a nod,*
*He'll have to pay*
*To satisfy that hidden urge.*
*It's love for sale.*

*A little cash brings happiness.*
*The boy to live,*
*The man can give.*
*They help each other*
*With love for sale.*

*A moment's joy,*
*The boy's a toy.*
*Pleasure money,*
*Money pleasure.*
*Take me home*
*I've love for sale.*

*The boy survives another day.*

John Patrick

> *He met his match and took his pay.*
> *He'll make the rent,*
> *It's pleasure spent.*
> *He'll grow on up to be a man*
> *And when he is*
> *Will he then look*
> *For love?*
> *For sale?*

> *– James S. Arthurs*

"The basic problem with being a male prostitute is your own and other people's perceptions of the occupation, not the reality of it. It can be difficult to overcome the internalized interpretation that only people with low self-esteem would sell themselves to a stranger. Forget it. Laugh all the way to the bank and, if your self-image is in bad shape, remember that someone else thought you were hot enough that he was willing to pay for the privilege of sucking your cock."
– John Preston

# *Prologue*

On Market Street I started to notice the hustlers, the boys for rent. Some were teenagers and cute, runaways trying to survive. Others were looking for scores to get money to buy drugs and stay high. The meat rack moved down from Powell to Sixth and Market, although some boys worked out of Union Square.

Tricks never asked me for "a date" before because I was young myself. Some assumed that I was in the business like them but queer and not trade, as many fancied themselves. But, as they say, today's trade was tomorrow's competition.

I picked up Gene, 19, short, muscular and hairy, brunet with green eyes–and truly handsome.

He wanted ten dollars for which you could suck his dick or he'd screw you. I'd been with boys who'd hustled but had never paid them. Ten dollars at that time seemed like a lot of money for what I'd always gotten for free. I didn't like to haggle but other boys solicited for only five bucks.

"I can give you seven,"' I offered.

"Okay, let's go."

Inexperienced with hustlers who had a reputation for being thieves, I took Gene to my apartment.

"Here's your money so you won't think you'll get burned."

I gave him seven singles.

He tucked the money into his pocket, then undressed. He was stunningly beautiful naked. He had a big, fat, uncut dick.

I shed my clothes and got on the bed with him. I kissed and tweaked his small nipples. His body was covered with brown fuzz like a teddy bear. Scooting between his legs, I held his soft dick and sucked it. It took a while but it got hard and was easily a seven-incher. It took him even longer to come but I nursed his cock till it was hard as a rock and it blasted, flooding my mouth.

Gene lit up a cigarette, staying nude.

I asked him about himself. He said he was from southern California. His father was in San Quentin. Gene admitted that he asked for ten bucks because he used heroin.

"Got a nice dick on you," I said.

He smiled.

I liked him, his looks and his casual manner. I played with his cock and it got hard faster the second time around.

Suddenly I got the urge to sit on it. I wanted to feel that big thing inside me. I hadn't gotten fucked since Larry. After spitting on my palm and lubing my crack, I reached back and guided Gene's stiff cock up my hole. It hurt but I got used to it fast. He held my waist and thrust inside me. I bounced up and down on his dick and he came inside me.

I wasn't into getting fucked but sometimes real macho numbers like Gene made my asshole twitch.

I saw Gene downtown on the meat rack and picked him up several more times. I took him home and sucked his cock and he'd stick me. There was never any hassle over money. I'd feed him and give him a few dollars, depending on what I had in my pocket. He never complained.

I thought about making Gene a steady boyfriend. He was hot stuff. But the hard drug use put me off and, seeing him on the meat rack meant that anybody with a few dollars in their pocket could swing on him.

When Al, the big merchant sailor, was in port he came over to my place. This time, I'd just finished sucking off Gene.

I knew Al's taste: young with a hard dick and big balls, the boy-next-door type.

Gene was still in his briefs. I'd tugged on my britches. I could tell that Al liked him. Al bought some beer and whiskey at the corner Chinese grocery. We drank boilermakers.

"You can have Gene if you want, Al. I usually give him five to seven bucks."

Suddenly I felt like a pimp, but Gene didn't seem to object.

"Oh, he's your boy," Al said.

"No problem. He hustles."

In no time Al had Gene sitting on his lap and was feeling him up. I watched while Al slid down Gene's briefs, and seconds later he was honking away on him.

I was surprised when Al gave Gene a crisp twenty-dollar bill.

Gene wanted to go. I knew that he wanted to get some junk, not booze it.

I suppose I should have showed more respect for Gene, but the bottom line was that he was a hustler, not my boyfriend. The incident with Al, passing Gene around like a herring at a Jewish picnic, changed my relationship with the boy. He was pleasant but not real friendly like before.

Eventually Gene got involved with a pretty young drag queen who was on welfare. I didn't mind because at last he had a place to stay and someone to shoot up and tweak with. Still, I thought I should have treated him better.

After some heavy drinking bouts and talking with Al, he was surprised that I was picking up hustlers at my age when guys would offer me money to go with them. No doubt he remembered that I'd been paid by his old friend Harold, at whose house I'd met Al so long ago. He cautioned me to be careful with street boys because they could be dangerous. I guess Al had some rough trade in his day. He was seven years older than me and had been around the world on ships so I respected his advice.

I started hanging out with Jake, who'd once worked for the Captain. Jake was a retired Army sergeant, and he picked up a lot of young hustlers. He gave them only five dollars but he also fed them. I was amazed at some

of the hunks he'd find, while others were bad news. Jake was short and pushing seventy. He wore shades, even at night. He liked young, tall guys, and spent all day and half the night cruising the streets. He worked weekends in a bookstore on Powell Street which hustled simulated porno films to Japanese tourists who hid them in their dirty laundry to get them past Customs.

Jake knew the score on a lot of the street hustlers. He introduced me to Michael, a tall Italian boy. Jake wasn't jealous. He invited us to his place, a dumpy apartment on O'Farrell Street in the Tenderloin where he lived with his dog.

Jake told me it was okay to go with Michael, give him only a fiver. I sucked Michael off while Jake fed his bowser. Michael had a nice circumcised prick. Later Jake told me that Michael sucked dick as well. I said he looked so macho I assumed he was strictly trade. (You never can tell.)

Through Jake I met Hugh, an Englishman who was a merchant seaman, a steward aboard ship. Hugh was a good cruiser: around forty, with thinning black hair, with a fancy blue Oldsmobile. He liked to cruise pool halls in areas where there were a lot of teenagers.

After my experience with Larry I steered clear of anybody who was even a day under eighteen. I'd learned my lesson.

Hugh had a line of shit that wouldn't quit. I was shocked when he told guys that he was a ship's captain or a movie director. He took boys to expensive restaurants, then beat the check. He was a booster who stole stuff out of the big stores downtown. I couldn't believe it.

But I must say he had good taste in boys. I kept my friendship with him because he'd pick up super cute sailor boys sometimes and didn't mind passing them along. He confessed that no matter how beautiful a guy was he always saw somebody the next day that he liked better.

I guess Hugh lived a charmed life because he was never arrested for picking up minors or for shoplifting. He had a heart attack aboard the next ship he was on and died in port in the Orient. Jake said that he died broke, but at least he enjoyed himself while he was living. And I intended to follow his example.

# 1. The Storyteller

While I was deciding what to do with the rest of my life, I started writing short stories based on what I'd done so far.

Back in high school I'd written essays and placed in some contests for thrift, highway safety and temperance organizations, but I liked fiction best. There was a writer in town named Henry Gregor Nelsen who wrote novels about hot- rod teenagers and their problems. He subbed for some high school English classes, where he played calypso music and read from the novel he was working on, Crash Club. I thought he was brilliant. He came into the department store where I worked and we chatted. Later I re-read his books and wrote him, getting a nice letter in response.

I took a couple of writing classes in college. One professor gave me an A because of the volume of stories that I wrote, not because they were particularly good. He was head of the department. I took an international literature course where Bay Boyle was one of the teachers. She was famous as a writer who'd lived in Paris in the '20s with Hemingway and others. Her stories were beautifully written and I was really impressed by them.

My writing career didn't take off. I wrote more than seventy stories; all came back with printed rejection slips, but a few had encouraging notes scrawled on them.

I read magazines directed at writers, and studied the markets, but I still didn't score. Then, after many months, out of the blue, I got a letter with a check for $100 from Road King, a magazine by Union 76 Oil Company for truckers. The story was a fantasy piece about a cat who was on the road with a trucker. I'd sold a story and was now a published writer!

But despite that success, my stories kept bouncing back with rejection slips. Eventually I sold a couple of confession stories to True Love and Secrets, with no byline.

After that I was on a roll, selling stories to New England Senior Citizen, Lighted Pathway and even Billy Graham's Decision magazine.

I checked out the few gay male magazines on the stands. I wrote a story about a couple of merchant seamen in port in San Francisco and sent it to Blueboy. A year later the phone rang and Rick told me it was the editor of Blueboy. They wanted "San Francisco Liberty" for an issue they were doing on San Francisco. And they'd pay me $250.

It was a story about the relationship between an older and a younger sailor. They said they'd write a sex scene and add it to the story, which they did.

I wrote more stories for Blueboy and Numbers that were accepted and printed, and I found I liked writing erotica best. As Dean Drury, the editor of Blueboy told me, "Select an unusual setting and get into the guys' heads."

I sent a manuscript of a short novel to Greenleaf, which published Adonis Classics in San Diego. They paid well, and I wrote seventeen more

short novels for them which were all published under the byline of Wes Cranston, a name Ralph Vaughan, the straight editor, selected, coded to my initials. Eventually Greenleaf dropped their gay line because it didn't sell as well as their straight porno books.

I wrote a half dozen books for Surrey but they kept dropping the price, from $600 all the way down to $170 for 150 pages, when they changed editors. I was used to getting $200 or more for ten to fifteen pages.

I sold the Mavety Group in New York City stories for $100. They have several magazines and have bought many stories over the years and are terrific editors to work with.

I was not only a word merchant, I was dealing in gay men's fantasies about truckers, cops, coaches, jocks, punks and, my favorite, military men. Military men are my favorite. Also stories about men from different races, Asian, black and Latin men.

I dealt with editors who really helped me improve my craft. Editors like the late Stan Leventhal, Aaron Travis, Ralph Cobar, Diana Sheridan and Gerry Kroll. And editors who anthologized my stories like Winston Leyland and the late John Preston.

My best stories I think are those based on real people and incidents, bits and pieces of experience and the gay lifestyle as I see it, or my own structured vision of reality.

On the home front, Rick became the love of my life and a real encouragement with my writing career. I found I could make a meager living writing erotica–but only meager.

# 2. At the Racetrack

During the summer Rick and I took some getaway trips to Reno. I liked the drive through the Sierra mountains. We'd stop and drink beer, even get it on, sucking and fucking when we were horny.

We enjoyed playing the slots and had some luck with them. Going in to see the comedian Don Rickles's live show, Rick dropped a couple dollars worth of quarters into a machine while standing in line. Three swamis came up, bells rang, lights went on, and he collected $250.

The Rickles show was a hoot with his insults. The crowd loved it, even though he made fun of people and their ethnic backgrounds.

Upon leaving the show, feeling salubrious after several drinks, Rick dropped a few quarters into a yet another slot and won a $150 jackpot.

I was amazed at the boy's luck. At that point, I wasn't into casino gambling, I didn't like the odds. The only even-money shot was the come out roll in craps. I knew that the odds on slots were against you. The other games were just as bad. And if you won on a trip, you could expect to lose the next nine times.

Driving back to San Francisco, we stopped at the State Fair at Cal Expo in Sacramento. We went to the races, but I didn't know anything about the sport and lost fifty bucks betting.

Later we went to the Bay Meadows racetrack a couple times during the season and cashed a few tickets.

By the time the Golden Gate season opened I was hooked. Rick wasn't excited, but went along.

All I knew about the track was the stories you heard about losers. I knew a guy named John from the arcades who was a heavy gambler. He got a bank loan for three grand to pay off his debts. Instead he took the money to the track and lost it in a few weeks. Sometimes when you talked to him about tricks he'd have flashbacks and say that the horse he bet on came in last.

Another guy from the streets, a friend of Jake's, was a man named Carl who looked both Jewish and queer but wasn't either. What he was was a horseplayer. Once when he was on a winning streak at the track he showed Jake his money stash at the bank vault, fifteen grand in cash. I was impressed because I knew Jake was telling the truth. But by the end of the season, Carl was flat broke and eventually he split town because some bookie enforcers were looking for him.

Opening day at Golden Gate Fields it was raining. Rick and I were making small bets and were breaking even.

In the ninth race exacta there was a filly, Betty Taz, against male horses in the mud at a route. The favorite was Chief Piawatha.

On a hunch I decided to bet the filly. Rick liked the favorite and he combined the two horses in an exacta box.

The horses were off and running. In the stretch, where the real running begins, Chief Hiawatha was clear. At the sixteenth pole from out of the clouds came Betty Kaz the filly. At the wire it was a photo finish.

When the results were made official on the tote board in the infield it was Betty Kaz the 4 horse at 30-1 odds on top of Chief Piawatha the 10 horse at 5-2 odds. The five dollar exacta paid a whopping $1200. That win gave us a bankroll to bet horses. And it also got us hooked.

Like all gambling we got on some winning streaks but had some losing streaks as well. For me it was the juice, the action. I didn't care so much whether I won or lost, only that I could play.

Rick landed a job at the Hyatt Regency, starting out as a busboy, and soon he was a waiter and making good tips. At night I pounded the typewriter, writing stories.

I started going to the racetrack in the daytime while Rick was working, but I wasn't doing very well. I could pick enough horses and good betting spots but I was poor at money management. That was what Rick was good at, handling the money. Together as a team we cashed plenty of tickets and won enough to keep at it. He'd joke that we needed to break even this time at the track because we needed the money. Winning you were on top of the world. Losing you were lost at sea.

One day at the track by myself I spotted a good-looking young guy. Usually I had horses on the brain, not tricks. And I was loyal to Rick. I mean, I wasn't looking for a fling. Especially since I had deep feelings for Rick and never saw anyone who I thought was better. Besides, Rick had a big heart and cared about me.

The races were boring that day, mostly maidens who had never won a race and cheap claimers who had all beaten each other at the bottom of the barrel price at which they ran. I couldn't pick my nose, let alone pick a winner.

Curious, I followed the good-looking guy into the john. He had frizzy brown hair, brown eyes and a muscular body. He was in his early twenties, a hot number.

He went into the end stall. I went into the stall across from it. The announcer's voice on the speaker said it was post time. But I didn't really care. I was interested in what he was doing in the stall.

Since the toilet was empty with the race on I went over to his stall and peeked in the door crack.

The stud had a huge kosher cock. Over eight thick inches. He stood up and masturbated at the door for me to see.

I was on the verge of being unfaithful. I'd like to jack that big cock, even kiss it. But it was too dangerous to do anything in the john.

Splat! He shot his wad onto the door and it dripped onto the floor.

Someone came into the toilet to take a leak.

The jack-off artist bolted out of his stall. I was going to follow him. Instead I went into the stall and smelled his musky aroma and looked at his creamy cum dripping down the gray metal door.

I looked around for the guy but he was long gone, lost in the crowd of bettors.

That night when I crawled into bed with Rick I was still thinking of the jack-off boy at the track and I sucked my lover with gusto, fantasizing about the guy in the stall.

\* \* \* \* \*

When Al was in port he started going to the racetrack with me. He had older buddies from the union hall who played the horses and I was driving them to the track. They put out their cigarettes on the floor and upholstery and never offered to buy gas, despite hints. Screw that. So I told Al that I'd take only him with me. He understood.

We never bet together like Rick and me. He'd play his hunches or tip sheets; I'd bet horses I'd observed and thought were ready to win. He did as well as me. Luck was the bottom line.

On the days we won we would go out to eat afterwards–but usually we lost.

Rick wasn't jealous of Al because he knew we were just buddies, and they liked each other as well.

One day at the track I saw a cute kid who turned me on. He was standing around looking at his racing program. He was short and brunet, boyish looking.

"Getting any winners?" I asked.

"You kidding?"

The favorites had all stiffed that day.

"Want a beer?" I asked.

"I'm tapped out."

"It's okay, I'm buying."

I was supposed to be getting a beer for Al and me but I got sidetracked by the cute boy. Besides I was tired of losing money that day; betting long shots but not getting any winners. I bought three beers and took the young man to meet Al, whose blue eyes lit up and sparkled like polished gems.

After losing the last race, I invited the young man, who said his name was Ronnie, to go with us to drink beer. I had the feeling that I was going to cheat on my lover for the first time.

We went to the Grand Southern Hotel on Mission Street near Seventh where Al was ensconced. I carried reserve money in the trunk in case of car trouble. I never gambled with it so far.

I bought us sandwiches and beer and we went to Al's hotel room. After a couple brews Ronnie spilled the beans that he was an AWOL soldier. Of course, finding out he was military meat made me horny as hell.

Feeling high off the beer, I groped Ronnie–and he didn't stop me. In a flash I had his dick out and was sucking on it. It was stubby but hard and juicy.

Al sat in the chair beside the bed and watched me gobble up the soldier. Ronnie gushed a big creamy load in my mouth. His cock stayed stiff.

I don't know what got into me. I stripped off the soldier's clothes until he was wearing only silver dog tags on a chain around his neck, then I shed my clothes.

His body was smooth and compact. He was so butch and his cock was so hard. I took a couple of slides on it. And then I sat on it. It made my asshole burn. He thrust upwards. I wrapped my fingers around my cock and beat off, splashing slimy goo onto his smooth torso, which I rubbed into his skin till it glistened.

Climbing off the young soldier boy, I cleaned up the gunk on his cock with my tongue.

Checking my watch, I realized how late it was getting. Rick would be wondering what happened, and I felt guilty about cheating on him. I left Ronnie with Al, knowing he'd have him too, which was okay.

The next day Al told me that he borrowed some money from another seaman who was staying in the hotel, and bought Ronnie some new clothes at one of the stores on Market Street that stays open late. Then he sucked Ronnie off and put him on a bus to Sacramento.

That Saturday Al got aboard another ship and I didn't see him for several months. He was on the S.S. Raphael Simms which shuttled between Manila, Hong Kong and Tokyo.

I was back at the track by myself, winning and losing. There was no consistency in betting horses. Sure, you knew the result of your investment in under two minutes. Horse sense was a matter of stable thinking. Sometimes they just exercised horses and didn't even try until they found a spot and bet it themselves with the barn's money. That was the business when stables didn't have stakes horses to win big purses with.

Rick and I started to quarrel more. I was more interested in betting horses than having sex. Gambling had become a stronger passion. Plus I'd been unfaithful to Rick–with the teenaged soldier–and he seemed to sense it.

Rick started going to the dive bars at daybreak on his days off when they opened at six, since he was used to getting up at five to go to work.

I kept going to the track but he'd lost interest along the way. The time had just gone by so fast.

I was shocked and felt desperate when my foster mother Hazel suddenly dropped dead from a heart attack. She was a heavy smoker. Before she died she sent me several checks for a thousand dollars each. I didn't understand

why. She wrote me telling me to be sure to cash them right away. Within a month she was dead. I was devastated. But I had Rick and knew I'd survive.

In her will everything went to her husband. She'd always told me that I was the beneficiary of her annuity retirement fund.

No one told me that she'd died until after she was buried. I spoke to her husband who said that there was no record of the fund in my name: it was small and went to pay off the bills of her estate. I knew that was a blatant lie but couldn't prove it.

Suddenly all the money she sent me made sense because she had doubts that her wishes would be followed, what with greedy relatives and sleazy lawyers.

But I loved her like a mother, not her money. She'd stood by my side when I was in heavy trouble with the law and believed in me as a person and loved me like the son she never had.

I never spoke to her husband Bill again, not ever. He lived for another thirteen years but I knew that he hated my guts because I was queer and didn't care whether I lived or died.

I kept going to the track. Rick tried to comfort me when Hazel died. But he was drinking heavily and I knew that our relationship was on the rocks. I went to the track and he went to the bars.

He was getting into fights at dive bars. I was afraid he'd get hurt bad or killed. But he wouldn't stop, wouldn't listen to me.

I don't know how he kept his job. He'd get only a couple hours of sleep sometimes. He became violent and abusive toward me. Our sex life was over; there was too much bitterness and resentment between us.

One time he stayed away for almost a week. I was frantic, checking the jails and hospitals. Nothing. I looked into the restaurant where he worked, no sign of him. The employees were not allowed personal calls and I didn't want to cause him problems on his job but I was worried sick.

He showed up at home and said that he was leaving. He'd met a thin man with money at the bar he frequented. I couldn't believe it. It was over. The love of my life was gone. And I knew he wasn't coming back.

I stopped going to the racetrack. I'd lost interest. My bankroll was gone. I'd have to use the money I made off my stories to pay for necessities. I had no savings. For the first time in my life I felt totally alone and abandoned.

# 3. The Bookstore

Being on my own again, I didn't know what to do with all the time and freedom. All the years spent in the relationship with Rick seemed like a waste, with nothing at the end.

No doubt about it, I was rusty at cruising. I didn't fit in with the Castro clones with their 'staches and bomber jackets and interchangeable partners.

Seemingly overnight, it seemed to me, the gay world had changed. Videos were in. Better and clearer than porno films, cassettes played in VCRs. Adult bookstores had arcades with booths; the booths had peepholes and glory holes.

The Tenderloin, the downtown red light district, had four arcades in close proximity. And the meat rack with hustlers had moved to enchanted Polk Street with the construction of the BART fast transit system on Market Street.

Cruising the arcades, I was surprised to see boys of different races. Before, I rarely saw blacks, Latinos and Filipinos, and now they were everywhere. This wasn't a problem: I was an equal opportunity cocksucker. With inflation, boys wanted ten bucks, although you could still get some of the wetbacks for a fiver.

And I saw some beauties. Cute young Mexican boys who were passing through the city to go north to work the campos, the fields in Oregon and Washington.

I was in lust if not in love many a time.

There was a gorgeous Filipino boy who played the video games like Pac Man and hung around. He was very young, not real friendly but I managed to lure him into a booth to watch the porno videos. I never knew his name but I came to know his dick. It was six inches, fat, cut, hard as a crowbar and real juicy. He wore blue bikini briefs and shoes without socks. He was slim, which made his dick look even bigger jutting out from his frame. He had short black hair and brown eyes. And he shot a big load every time. I tossed him a fiver, sometimes a couple bucks bonus when I was flush. I blew him on and off for a month. It was a silent routine, eye contact, into a booth, the suck job and he'd split. Sweet loads of Filipino boy cream. But as suddenly as he appeared he disappeared from sight without a trace.

One day I spotted a short Mexican teenager. He was in front of the bar at the corner. He was such a guapo, cute boy, I smiled at him. He smiled back. "Wanna go watch a porno movie?"

"Como?"

Uh-oh. No English.

I dredged up my high school Spanish and the street language I'd learned from Johnny before.

Seems like his tios, uncles, were in the bar drinking cerveza. He wasn't old enough.

John Patrick

His name was Jose. I managed to lure him into the arcade next door. He wasn't sure what to expect. Watching a porno flick, I groped him. He hesitated. But I could see his dick was hard. I unzipped his fly and freed his fat little dick. Only five inches but it was hard and juicy. I slurped on it and he stood on tiptoes and blew down my throat. I gave him three dollars. He didn't seem to understand but took the money. Guess I made a whore out of him.

"Manana," I said.

His cum tasted kind of bitter. Maybe he smoked mota or it was his diet. Like drinking the water in Tijuana, I got the runs and hightailed it to the toilet at the big department store on Market Street.

I went to the Tenderloin every day. There would be Jose, who swore he was eighteen, waiting in front of the cantina for his tios.

I led him into the arcade and took down his pants and sucked his plump balls and fat little pecker. He gushed in my mouth but I spit out the bitter tasting loads that were like Montezuma's revenge.

Still I liked Jose. He was a nice muchacho and cute as a bug's ear.

The last time I sucked him off he said he and his uncles were going to Los Angeles. "Adios," I said.

\* \* \* \* \*

Wandering around the four arcades I saw plenty of young guys.

When I went to the piss trough in the arcade on Taylor Street a cute Chinese boy put his dick in my hand and I jacked him off on the spot.

In the arcade there were some nude girl dancers, who made a lot of straight guys hot. Then they'd beat off in the booths.

A hairy Hindu boy who wore a blue shirt with a roofing company logo left his booth door unlatched. I horned in. His long, thin, dark cock was stiff. I sucked it off. I tried to be friendly, asking him his name but he said it didn't matter.

Hanging around the arcade on Turk Street, I met a tall teenager named Brian. He was handsome and reminded me of a swarthy basketball player from my high school days. He wanted ten dollars but it was worth it because he had a thick eight incher which shot big juicy wads.

There was a Latino boy who was tall and thin with long, curly hair. He went into the booths with many different guys, and I was curious about him.

Inside a booth he unbuttoned his shirt. He said his name was Juan. He had a smooth, bronzed body and a big, fat, cut dick. I gave him an Alexander Hamilton and sucked on his dick. He fingered my butt hole and slid down my pants. He put on a condom and boffed me, to my surprise. I hadn't expected that. His best buddy was a big twenty-year-old black stud named Antoine. I later checked him out. He had a whopper nine-inch dick. We jacked each other off, shooting at the same time. He didn't ask for any

amount of money so I tossed him a fiver and he was happy. I saw Antoine several times later, always friendly. He said he had found a white sugar daddy and that Juan went back to Acapulco.

I liked some of the arcade boys but I wasn't really into hustlers. Nothing against them, because everybody's gotta make a living. But I found some scam artists and dopers who wanted ten bucks but their dick couldn't get hard and if it could they couldn't cum no matter how much you jacked or sucked it.

At the bus stop near the arcade on the corner of Turk and Taylor I saw a really hot looking Latino. Trying to strike up a conversation before the bus came, I asked him if he knew Juan. He didn't but he smiled. He had a trim 'stache.

"You like porno movies?"

"Sure," he said.

He was from Guadalajara. His name was Fernando.

When I saw the bus coming I urged him to go with me into the arcade. He smiled but said he was going to visit some amigos to smoke grass.

"I'll give you ten bucks so you can buy some."

He hesitated, but agreed.

Inside the booth, Fernando watched the fuck flick. I took out his dick. It was over eight inches and fat with a mushroom head. He had big low-hangers. I laved his big stiffer in spit. It was a beauty. I sucked on his balls. He shot a big sweet creamy load.

I was so horny I just whipped out my dick and jacked it. He watched. His dick got hard again and we jacked off while watching each other and shot off at the same time.

"Meet me here tomorrow, same time," I said.

The next day I showed up but Fernando didn't.

A few days later I saw him at the same bus stop. He apologized but he was working and couldn't make it.

I took him into an arcade booth and sucked his fat chorizo again. He jacked off while I did. I liked to watch him beat that monster with the taste of his leche in my mouth.

I offered to take him out to eat. He agreed, so I didn't give him any money. Instead I insisted he eat a big prime beef dinner with spuds and gravy at the cafeteria on Mason Street.

Fernando and I hit it off. He liked me and I liked him. He liked to dance, he said, so I took him to Buzzby's, a gay disco on Polk Street.

He liked brandy so we drank that. He coaxed me out onto the dance floor of metal squares with the sound of Madonna's "Crazy for Love" blasting in our ears.

Fernando was quite drunk by the time I drove him to the place he was staying with his friends.

Later I saw him downtown with his buddy, Jesus. Jesus was a few years older but macho and handsome in a rugged way. He was nice, so I took them both to the disco and we danced the night away.

Eventually Fernando decided to go back to Guadalajara because he couldn't find steady work. Besides, he said he had a wife and a son there.

I started going around with Jesus. He was older and smarter. But I didn't have sex with him yet.

I took him out to the beach to party. A beach bum asked us for a beer. I gave it to him.

Jesus stripped to his briefs to take a dip in the ocean. I was stunned by his body. Because of the loose clothes he wore, I had no idea he was built so beautifully.

The beach bum tried to steal Jesus' wallet, and Jesus flipped out. I thought he was going to kill the guy. I managed to separate them and the beach bum took off running with a bloody nose and bruises.

Jesus calmed down. I could see the outline of his fat prick in his briefs.

"When it was dark we built a bonfire with driftwood and stayed the night, drinking Corona beer.

"You want me to fuck you, don't you?" he asked.

"I want that big dick I know that. Oh, Jesus!" I blurted out.

"Everybody says that when they see my big dick."

I sucked off Jesus and he shot a big salty load.

Jesus said he wanted to be my boyfriend.

# 4. Jorge, the Aztec Indian

I thought I might get something going with Jesus. He teased me by telling me how big his dick was, which I already knew, of course, and by saying that he could fuck me all night long. The idea was exciting.

But a part of his past experience he revealed with gay men put me off. Seems he was living with these two rich queens. He was giving them both stud service but they just let him crash there and didn't feed him. After one of them dumped Jesus' clothes in the garbage Jesus set fire to their expensive Austrian drapes before he split.

Jesus liked to go to the cheap movies at the Embassy which he said helped him with his English. I'd pick him up around midnight and buy him a hamburger at Carl's Jr.

One night he was with another Mexican boy when he approached the car. He said adios to his amigo.

"Invite your friend to go with us, it's okay," I said.

He hesitated but yelled to Jorge, who came back to the car.

Well, Jorge was about the most beautiful Mexican boy I'd ever seen. He had straight jet black hair, almond-shaped, coffee-colored eyes, luscious full lips and perfect teeth.

He was quiet but friendly and smiled.

I think Jesus was kind of jealous of all the attention I gave Jorge. I simply couldn't take my eyes off him. Jesus was in his late twenties; Jorge was only nineteen. I took them to Carl's Jr. and bought them burgers and Cokes. We talked, then said goodnight. I told Jesus to bring Jorge with him the next night. They showed up after the movie. They said they weren't hungry so I drove them out to the beach and stopped to buy some Corona beer along the way.

"Okay if I smoke?" Jorge asked.

"Sure."

Damned if he didn't light up a joint. I politely refused but he shared it with Jesus. Jorge was from Mexico City, Jesus from Acapulco, but they'd met at the border in Tijuana.

It seemed that Jesus got into a brawl in a bar and it took four cops to subdue him. Jorge watched as Jesus struggled and was impressed.

The next night I took them to the disco and danced my ass off.

Jorge wore loose jeans and shirt but I realized that this youngster had a solid, muscular body.

One night they didn't show up after the movie. I figured maybe they were smoking mota and didn't watch the time.

I looked around downtown for them but there was no sign. I was worried that perhaps immigration picked them up since they didn't have papers.

I went home disappointed. I liked both of them but I had the hots for Jorge, no denying it. I think Jorge sensed it. Maybe that's why they didn't show up.

Since I wasn't tired I got out my typewriter and worked on the raunchy erotic novel that I was writing for Greenleaf.

By dawn I decided to go downtown and see if I could find Jesus and Jorge in Civic Center where the Mexican boys hung out.

I wasn't sure where they were staying. Sometimes with some Mexicans who they worked day labor construction jobs with. Sometimes they slept in abandoned cars out in the Mission district.

Outside Carl's Jr. I spotted Jorge with two other mojados, wetbacks. He left them and came over to me.

"Where's Jesus?" I asked.

"Haven't seen him."

"Wanna go with me?" I brazenly asked.

"Sure."

I drove Jorge down to the Embarcadero waterfront and parked. Soon people would be coming to work.

He was sleepy. He leaned against me and closed his eyes. He went out cold. He was so cuddly that I didn't have the heart to wake him.

I could fall in love with a boy who looked like Jorge and was so sweet and eager to please. All I know is that my heart skipped a beat whenever I saw him. I knew I'd have him eventually.

Several minutes later he stirred and rubbed his eyes. He took a joint out of his Marlboro box and lit up. The burnt rope smell of mota filled the car.

He placed the marijuana cigarette in my mouth. I pretended to take a toke but I didn't really.

"I feel crazy now," Jorge said.

I wondered if he felt crazy enough to go along with what I wanted.

"You make me hot, Jorge."

He smiled.

"You know what I'm saying? You know what I want?"

"Yes," he said.

"Is it okay?"

He nodded.

I thought about blowing him in the car. I was horny enough, but people were starting to arrive for work. I thought about taking him home with me but nixed the idea. I didn't want to take any boys home. Besides, Rick still had the keys and might show up at any time.

I drove Jorge out to Golden Gate Park. Stopping near the soccer field, we got out of the car. I led him into the bushes where there was a clearing.

Kneeling in the grass, I pressed my face against his crotch. I grabbed his legs, which were muscular and hard.

Anxious to get at him, I tugged down his britches. He wore white cotton briefs.

Looking up at him, he flexed his biceps which were bulging. He grinned.

I peeled down his shorts. His crotch hair was straight jet black like that on his head. He was circumcised, which surprised me. His cock was around seven inches and fat. It pointed upwards. His balls were hefty.

Gobbling up his Aztec prick, I managed to deep-throat it. He sighed.

I bobbed my head up and down on his dick. Suddenly it was hard as a rock and I knew it would shoot. Shoot it did, blasting gobs of thick sweet Mexican jizz into my mouth. I swallowed every delicious drop.

"Okay, let's get outta here," Jorge said.

I guess he was nervous about somebody seeing us. We'd passed some joggers on the way.

I drove him back downtown and gave him a few bucks to get something to eat.

"See you around midnight with Jesus."

"Esta bien," he said.

I went home with visions of Jorge dancing in my head. I jacked off, reliving every delicious moment of our encounter. I had to get Jorge before someone else did. A Mexican boy who looked and acted like him was primo stuff. So he smoked weed, I drank beer.

The next night Jesus and Jorge showed up at my car parked on Jones Street near Market.

I guess Jesus knew that I'd sucked off Jorge. Whether Jorge actually told him I don't know.

"I met some guys who are going north to work in the fields. I'm going with them," Jesus said.

My heart sank.

"What about Jorge?"

"I'm no going," Jorge said.

"It's okay, I know you like Jorge. Hasta luego."

Jesus was gone and Jorge stayed with me.

I felt sorry about Jesus. But I didn't dump him, it was his decision to go up north. He'd mentioned it before. I was relieved that Jorge wasn't going with him.

Jorge smoked grass as we drove around and talked for hours. I wanted to take him home with me. Instead I dropped him off out in the Mission district but he'd meet me the next night.

I started to see Jorge every other day so that I could work on my writing and make money.

In my heart I still loved Rick. I guess I always would, no matter how mad I got or how betrayed I felt. But I had Jorge now and he was something special.

John Patrick

I took Jorge home with me, but only to visit. I told him that I lived with my brother. It was a lie but that made things easier and let him know why he couldn't live with me because he hinted that he wanted to.

I met him at seven o'clock out in the Mission District every other night. We spent hours together, talking, parking at Twin Peaks or Coit Tower and looking at the spectacular views. I drank beer and he smoked weed. He got some day work painting houses.

What I came to discover was that Jorge's body was all solid muscle, from his work with his father in a slaughter house in Mexico City, carrying carcasses, to playing soccer and doing calisthenics all the time.

Some mornings when he was bored and not working he came over to my place.

He'd strip to his shorts and exercise. He knew that made me hot, watching his hard, smooth, perfectly shaped body. He knew I couldn't keep my hands off him and that was okay with him. He liked all the attention.

Afterwards he'd take a bath. I'd go into the bathroom and wash him with soap and water like you would a baby. I loved the look of the suds on his bronze body and his cock got hard as a rock just by touching it.

Sometimes when I met him he'd be with his amigos. They were always macho and cute. I particularly liked Hector, who was his best friend. But I never messed around with his buddies because I didn't want to risk losing Jorge. Besides he was better looking than all of them anyway. They all smoked marijuana but that never bothered me. I took them to taquerias in the Mission district and bought them burritos. They were young and always hungry.

I settled into a routine with Jorge. When I had free time I took him to Lake Berryessa. I loved to watch him swim nude. I always sucked him off afterwards. I took him in the mountains and to Reno.

The pain of loss over the relationship with Rick became easier to handle. But it was different with Jorge. He was like a son, and I was his queer daddy.

Girls liked Jorge and he was a flirt, but he was loyal to me. I figured I'd enjoy him while it lasted, while he was around.

One day when he popped up uninvited at my place he woke me out of a sound sleep. But I was always glad to see him. He was happy in his heart and he made me happy.

He went into his exercise routine, which made me horny. Like putting on a show for me in his briefs.

I loved sucking his dick. I could have died happy doing it. But I got the urge to taste his butt.

Lying on the bed naked with him, I spread his legs. I'm sure he thought I'd blow him and beat off while I did it.

But to his great surprise, I spread his sinewy thighs and dove into his ass. I licked his crack. It was tangy and sweaty from the exercise.

I had a boner that wouldn't be denied. I'd never rape Jorge because I cared about him and didn't want to lose him. But I rubbed my cock in his crack.

I was amazed that he didn't stop me. Maybe he was curious. I spit on my dick and eased it into his hole. It was tight but I pushed past the mass of muscle to his ass.

There was a grimace on his face but I forged ahead. When I figured he could take it I pumped his cherry Aztec butt hole.

I was startled when his asshole spasmed. He had a boner but he didn't even touch it. His cock spurted all over his belly like a busted hose. The sight of the cum on his bronze body brought me off. I lunged in to the hilt and sprayed his asshole with my gringo jism.

His eyes sparkled but his face looked sad.

"It was bound to happen, Jorge. I want you so much, all of you. Comprende?"

He smiled. His cock was still hard. He rolled me over on my side and lube my hole with the jism on his belly, then he rammed his stiff prick up my chute and started to assault me.

It felt good knowing it was Jorge. His creamy load squirted deep into my ass. When he pulled out I felt his jizz trickle down my thigh. I loved giving him tongue baths, licking his pits and sucking on his nipples. He even sucked on my dick once just because he wanted to please me.

His dick was hard all the time. I massaged his beautiful hard body and sometimes sucked his dick a second time. I liked to jack-off and cum on his cock and crotch as well.

It went on for a couple years this way. He was romantic, said sweet nothings and liked to please me. He said Mexican men were hot. He told me that I'd never find another boy like him. But I already knew that.

Then Jorge started to change. I didn't notice it at first. He practically begged me for us to live together. His life was hard.

But I didn't listen. Maybe I thought Rick would come back. But with the passage of time I knew that wasn't going to happen.

Just nineteen, Jorge was in his prime–and he knew it. He started sprinkling his marijuana cigarettes with white powder which I learned was cocaine. I never thought smoking weed was a big deal. I knew older guys who'd smoked it all their lives and they were still functioning.

It wasn't the cocaine so much as it was the cost of it. I was forking over forty bucks for him to buy a dash of the powder. That was way out of my league.

Jorge would toot. I wasn't interested in trying it, although I'd heard that it made you feel like a god. I already felt like a god when I had Jorge naked in bed with me.

He started acting funny. I still didn't get the big picture until I saw him with a thirtyish guy from Spain who told me that Jorge was his lover. I couldn't believe it.

Hector told me that this Spanish guy was a drug dealer and had Jorge hooked. He took out the cost of the drugs in trade.

I got a bizarre phone call from Jorge saying that he never wanted to see me again. He called back later and told me the Spanish guy made him say that. He was now living with him.

How could I compete with this Spanish guy and his cocaine? I knew I was losing Jorge. I was crushed.

Jorge's brother showed up at my place. He was a couple years older but he looked like Jorge. He'd come to take Jorge back to Mexico City.

I told Jose where his brother was living; I'd gotten the address from Jorge.

Jorge called me. He wanted me to meet him and Jose. They were going back to Mexico City pronto.

I met Jorge. He was nervous. He was wearing expensive clothes and a black leather jacket. He looked like a million bucks. From the gist of his conversation he'd ripped off the drug dealer from Spain who'd told him that he was a millionaire. He and Jose were going back to Mexico City. He said he was sorry and that he really liked me. Jose didn't understand English.

I was sad that Jorge left because I knew he wasn't coming back. He called me like he said he would for almost six months.

I got all these crazy calls from the guy from Spain who said he'd gotten my phone number out of Jorge's wallet. He was convinced that Jorge was staying with me. But I told him that Jorge went back to Mexico. The crazy calls continued for a long time and I'd just hang up when I recognized the voice.

# 5. More Mexican Boys

After Jorge was gone and I felt certain he wouldn't be back, I developed a real appetite for Mexican boys, the wetbacks who came to the norte for a better life: All those boys that were available but I'd passed on because I didn't want to lose Jorge.

For openers I started with Hector, who was Jorge's best friend. I'd always liked him. He was a chilango like Jorge, from Mexico City, and a couple years older. He was a sweet kid. People thought Jorge and he were brothers. Hector had sad brown eyes and luscious bee-stung lips.

I picked him up on Market Street near Jones by St. Anthony's Church, which some called the Avenida de la Reforma because there were so many Mexican boys hanging out.

It was dusk and I got us a couple of six-packs of Budweiser and drove out to Twin Peaks. A clear night with a beautiful view. It was like a lover's lane with people parked and necking.

After a couple beers Hector shocked me when he just unbuttoned the Pendleton shirt he was wearing and pulled his jeans and shorts down below his knees. His cock was long, fat and uncut.

No words were spoken. I just went down on that fat chorizo. He encouraged me by rubbing my head. When I deep-throated his cock he blew, spewing salty jizz into my mouth.

The next week Hector came to my place to see me. He let me know that he was available now that Jorge was gone. But I still had feelings for Jorge and didn't want another boyfriend. There was a long shot chance that Jorge would come back. How could I explain that I'd switched to his best amigo? (Tragically, a few years later Hector became a heroin addict.)

There was another teenage Mexican hailing from a tongue-twister state I couldn't pronounce. He had long, shiny black hair and was cute and slim. His name was Jose. He didn't speak English but I was able to communicate with him with my broken Spanish. Jose and an older fellow from Guatemala were rateros, they broke car windows and stole stuff, especially leather jackets which they sold in cantinas in the Mission district.

Jose explained how they did it. They took broken pieces of porcelain from the white of spark plugs, tossed it at windows and shattered them. If the car alarm went off sometimes they stole that too.

I liked Jose and bought him hamburgers or burritos when I saw him and he was hungry.

One time I just came out with it. I figured he knew the score with Jorge and me. Besides the more I looked at Jose the better I liked him. I invited him to go see a porno movie in an arcade on Turk Street. He must have been horny because he agreed to go.

While he watched the porno flick I groped him. His cock was hard. When I took it out I was surprised at how big it was, seven-plus inches, fat and throbbing. I sucked up a storm and he gushed jizz in my mouth.

I later ran into him out in the Mission district. He took me up to his room. He teased me by showing me his big dick. I was about to swing on him when his ratero amigo from Guatemala showed up. Later I heard the older guy later went to jail and Jose went back to Mexico.

After Jose I hit a dry spell. There were plenty of Mexican boys around. But I avoided the hardcore hustlers who wanted only money. I liked the innocent, macho looking types who played around because they were horny. They were hot sex and shot big loads.

I hit a bonanza when I ran into another Jose in an adult bookstore. He had a big hard-on from looking at the porno magazines. It stuck out horizontally from his pants pocket.

I approached him and told him about the porno movies in the arcade in the back. He had thick black hair and big brown eyes. He went along with me.

Under the eyes of other cruisers I got Jose into a booth and dumped quarters into the machine.

I groped his boner and unzipped the fly of his tan chinos. His cock was huge and like a steel pipe. In the flickering light from the movie I saw that it was a beauty, uncut with thick folds of foreskin, and he had big low-hangers. I gobbled up his dick and he gushed a big juicy load into my mouth.

Jose had been in a fight and had a couple of teeth knocked out. Other than that he was a macho twenty-one year old with silky bronze skin.

He told me that he was from Mexicali, a border town. He'd some north looking for work with a couple buddies.

All this conversation took place while he wolfed down two hamburgers at Carl's Jr. -

"Wanna watch more movies?" he asked.

That surprised me but I took him back to the arcade and sucked him off again and he blasted what seemed an even bigger load.

Walking on Market Street we ran right smack into his buddies from Mexicali. He introduced me. Ricardo was a doll, only eighteen. Antonio was twenty and macho-looking.

A few days later I saw Jose again. I took him into the same arcade as before, only I rented a hetero movie he selected. The prevue booth was larger and I got him buck naked. God, his cock was perfect. I swear I sucked him off three times and he jacked off a fourth. I couldn't remember the last time I'd seen such a horny youngster.

I found that Jose was a sex machine. I got some big ideas about him. But I saw him on the street with a tacky drag queen and sort of lost interest, figuring he was fucking him.

When my birthday rolled around I was going to see Al the merchant seaman and have a few drinks to celebrate. Al was told by the union croaker that he couldn't sail anymore and he took it pretty hard. He was used to jumping on ships and running away to sea.

On Market Street I ran into Jose's buddy, Ricardo. He gave me a big smile. I wasn't sure if he knew the score with me. I invited him for a cheap steak dinner at Tad's on Powell.

He didn't speak English but we managed to communicate a bit. He was a living doll with his hair cut like a roquero, short on top, long in back. I couldn't take my eyes off him.

He told me that they were splitting up, Jose went to Reno to get a job, he wanted to go to his brother's place in Los Angeles, and Antonio was going back to Mexicali.

I invited Ricardo to go with Al and me for a couple drinks. He accepted. I made a further proposition: I'd buy him the bus ticket to Los Angeles.

Big Al was kind of cool about my passion for Latinos. He liked big blonde white boys with big dicks and balls. When he saw Ricardo he kept raving that he'd never seen such a good-looking young wetback. But he'd liked Jorge.

I got the big idea to drive across the bay and rent a hotel room in Vallejo and party. Al drank most of the case of beer.

Ricardo took a shower and came out bare-ass naked. Nice smooth, slim body. He had a big uncut dick.

He lay on the bed and I went to work with my tongue. I licked him from head to toe. Spreading his legs, I ate out his ass.

Al drank beer and pretended to watch the music videos on MTV but I could tell he was watching us.

I sucked and rimmed Ricardo for hours. He dug it. When he was ready to get his rocks he pumped his prick and I swooped down on it and drank every delicious drop of his sweet boy juice. Then I sucked and rimmed him some more. I beat off and splashed my load on him, then I licked it off his smooth, tender bronze skin. He was a macho kid. I think I could have fucked that bubble butt if Al wasn't around.

The next day I put Ricardo on the Greyhound for Los Angeles.

A few days later Al and I were walking around. He'd lost interest in boys temporarily because of his not going to sea and the big loss in income. He'd applied for disability and got it besides his meager union retirement. But that wasn't the big bucks he was used to spending.

It was Sunday night late and I took Al into the Greyhound depot. I liked to check out the Mexican boys getting the last bus to Los Angeles. There I spotted Antonio with a couple of Mexican boys I'd never seen before. I didn't say anything but he caught my eye and he smiled. He was leaving town, I told Al. Not so. He was only saying goodbye to his friends.

When the bus left I waved at Antonio and he came over to us. He spoke some English.

I invited him for a burger and Coke at Carl's Jr. He was hungry and ate two burgers.

We walked around downtown and I steered Antanio into the arcade where I'd met his pal Jose.

He was horny. Al stood as lookout and I left the booth door open for him to check out Antonio.

Antonio was short and hairy. From our earlier conversation I learned he was twenty and married with two kids.

While he watched the porno movie I pulled down his pants. His body was hairy and macho. His dick was stubby but real stiff.

I sucked on it but he reached down and grabbed my ass. He wanted to screw me. What could I do? I carried rubbers so I sheathed his prick in latex. He humped me until he shot up my butt.

I think Al was surprised since he sort of thought I was a boy fucker, not fuckee. But there were exceptions. I thought Antonio was a hot little stud. I envied his wife. When he was finished I pulled off the rubber and drank his jizz, which left Al with an open mouth.

Later Antonio was on Jones Street selling mota. He flashed me a fistful of greenbacks. Never saw him again.

With the three amigos gone I hit another dry spell.

One night I was cruising Market Street when I saw a tall, baby-faced wetback with long black hair. He was a real looker.

I stopped and talked. He spoke English. He was from Tijuana. His name was Marco.

"So what's up?" I asked.

"Will you pay for me one burrito?"

"Sure."

I was getting used to Mexican boys; I had some damn good experiences with them.

Marco ate a couple of burritos at Taco Bell.

"You like to watch fuck movies?"

He grinned and nodded.

I whisked him away to the arcade on Turk Street. He was a hunk and we got lots of stares from cruisers.

Marco had a fat, eight-inch, uncut, drooling prick. I chomped on it till it gushed its salty load in my mouth.

I was kind of lonely so I invited Marco to spend the night and drink some beer.

"No more sexo," he said.

"Hey, it's okay."

I figured he might change his mind after he relaxed.

I hesitated, I don't know why. I never took boys home, not hustlers or strangers anyway. I opted for the motel in Vallejo.

Marco was quiet but I figured he was just shy. He watched MTV and the Spanish station. I drank several beers.

I just passed out. Usually I'm a light sleeper, more like an insomniac.

When I awoke it was still dark outside. I looked over at the next bed. Marco wasn't there. I figured he was in the toilet since the light was on and the door closed.

I got a funny feeling that something was wrong. I opened the door, the bathroom was empty. Marco was gone. That was okay, if that's what he wanted to do.

I put on my clothes. That's when I realized that my wallet and car keys were gone. Uh-oh, I'd been careless and fallen asleep. I was so used to boys I could trust.

Looking outside I saw that, sure enough, my white Ford was gone. I kind of panicked. But I knew I had to report it to the cops in case there was an accident or tickets on it.

I called the Vallejo police and they sent a cop out, a big black man.

The cop wrote up the report. I tried to explain what had happened but he thought it was a woman.

"It was a boy. Name was Marco, eighteen, from Tijuana."

He gave me the once-over.

"You're lucky he didn't cut your throat. That happens."

He wasn't uptight about it when he realized it was a queer scene but he made me aware of the violence that exists.

I lost my wallet and car. And the expensive Omega watch that Al had given me years ago that was like a good luck piece.

The cop drove me to the BART shuttle connection. I had enough change to get home.

I'd been a fool. Marco looked so innocent. True, he could have done me in. I felt lucky to be alive considering everything.

Luckily I didn't lose my car. I was sure he'd take it to Tijuana and that was that. But the police found the car on private property in Sacramento and it was towed away.

I took the bus to Sacramento and got my car. It cost a couple hundred dollars in fees. The car ran okay and I drove it back home, vowing never again would I be so trusting, especially to a complete stranger. Like the pictures of innocent looking boys on TV and in the papers who murdered gay men, I could have been dead meat.

# 6. The Black Soldier

I checked out the gay porno movie theater in the Tenderloin with the live male dancers, the jack-off studs. Between videos on the large screen a dancer came out and stripped to the buff, showing his jewels.

The first dancer was a thirtyish muscle-bound man who was short and swarthy. All oiled up, he posed and strutted his stuff. His cock wasn't big but when he pounded it furiously it sprinkled a few cum drops on the floor.

Out came a theater worker, an older Puerto Rican, who wiped up the sticky goo with a rag.

Another video featured two buffed blonde surfer boys at the beach cavorting and sucking each other's dick. The taller one boffed his buddy in the sand.

The next dancer was a twentyish skinny blonde punk with an average-sized dick which got only semi hard, no matter how much he stroked it. He wandered among the small crowd of patrons, shoving his dick in their faces for dollar tips. Back on stage, he worked his meat but his batteries were dead, no juice in him.

Ho-hum, the live show was boring. So were the videos.

I was about to split when I decided to take a quick leak.

In the john in the rear there was a black guy around twenty-five with his shirt off. He had a magnificent torso. Standing at the urinal, he was pumping his fat, cut ebony cock with the pink prick head.

He was much hotter-looking than the dancers in the live show.

"Wanna see it shoot?" he smiled.

"Oh yeah, get it off!"

He grinned, with his fist flying over his prick. Grunting, he blasted big gobs of syrupy jizz all over the urinal.

"That was fucking hot," I commented.

My own cock was straining in my pants.

The black stud left the john and I whizzed with a half hard-on.

I was about to exit the sleazy theater when I spotted the black man alone in the row in the back with his shirt still off.

I brazenly sat down beside him.

"Shoot a mean load," I whispered.

"Plenty more where that came from. I just got out of the fucking Army and I'm really horny."

He was a soldier, which explained the hard muscular body. But I'd always thought blacks had the best bodies. Harrison, the black stud I played football with in junior high, I'd secretly admired his build. He was hung big too, like most of the brothers. A Navy corpsman who'd looked at cocks for twenty years said that black ones were on the average two inches bigger. I remembered the young black on the bus who spread a newspaper over his

- 381 -

lap. He groped me and, under the Chronicle, we jacked each other off with people in nearby seats. He had a long, fat rod.

The black soldier in the theater made me horny. I hoped he'd take out his cock and jack it some more, maybe let me jack it, maybe let me suck it.

From under the seat he took out what looked like an empty baby food jar with a straw in it. And he smoked it. Dawned on me that it was crack. I'd only recently heard of cheap rock cocaine.

"Want me to go home with you?" he asked.

"I'd like that but I got company, my brother's staying with me," I fibbed.

I'd have liked to go somewhere with him and swing on that big black dick. Only jacking off was allowed in the theater. But I was still gun-shy after the ordeal of having my car stolen.

When the soldier went to the john again I was tempted to follow him, but I sneaked out of the theater instead.

I thought about the crack-smoking soldier with his ripped body and big dick and beat off like mad that night. Like they say, he who hesitates masturbates.

# 7. On Polk Street

I was looking but not touching, until I walked up Polk Street one night. Enchanted Polk Street was now the meat rack in San Francisco, where the hustlers hung out. It was also a street with drug dealers and violence. There was a lot of competition among the hustlers for johns, probably because the economy was bad. I'd heard through the grapevine that hustlers that wanted forty bucks were going for twenty, even for ten as the night wore on. Some settled for just a place to crash. The boys on the street with the big bucks in their jeans didn't get them from prostitution but from selling drugs.

I saw a vaguely familiar face when I crossed Pine Street. A guy in his late twenties, tall, brunet and handsome.

"Hi, remember me? I'm Grady."

"Uh, yeah."

I still couldn't place him.

"Used to see you on Market Street. I've been away, spent six years in the Army. The city's really changed."

Suddenly I remembered Grady. He had a big dick. Yeah, he was drinking. He was such a cute kid. I gave him a lift. He wanted a half pint of whiskey. I bought it for him. He indicated that I could suck his dick. Adventuresome but cautious, I parked and followed him through the tradesman's entrance of an old apartment building and through a maze to a storage room with a narrow bed and a stereo which he turned on real loud.

It was late, and Grady stretched out on the bed and sipped the whiskey. I pulled down his pants. He had a beautiful circumcised prick and a set of big balls. I sucked on his dick. It took a while to get hard because of the drinking.

While I was bobbing up and down on his dick I heard footsteps. A skinny black man wearing a caftan and a nightcap, like on the Hill Brothers coffee can, sashayed over and turned down the stereo, then wandered out without a word. I went back to blowing Grady and he got his nut, shooting his wad into my mouth. Yes, I remembered Grady–fondly.

The only difference between Grady then and now was that his tender skin was leathery. He was still handsome.

"You living in the city now?" I asked.

"Just passin' through. Goin' back up north to work on my father's ranch near Santa Rosa."

Our eyes locked. His gray eyes were glazed.

"We could get it on for old times' sake," I teased.

He smiled.

I took him to the arcade nearby. His cock was as huge as I remembered it, and I sucked him off. The big surprise was that after I'd finished I stood up, and he kneeled on the piss-and cum-stained floor and gave me a

marvelous blowjob that drained my balls. I invited him out for a drink but he said he had a bus to catch.

A few nights later I went back up Polk Street. At a phone booth on Geary I saw a big butch blonde kid. I lingered nearby as if I was waiting to use the phone.

Finally the kid hung up. "Damn, no answer and it took my money anyway."

I quickly pulled out some change. "Here, try again."

"No use. Nobody answers."

He had big baby blue eyes. I wondered if he was a hustler. I could sail for him if he didn't want big bucks.

"From the city?" I asked.

"No, Vallejo. Been working on a job here. My truck's about out of gas. Trying to borrow some money from a guy I work with but he's not home."

I nodded. "Maybe I could help you."

"Why should you?"

"I was your age once. And horny."

He got the idea. "I gotta get back home tonight somehow."

"What's your name?"

"Maurice." He looked away, then back at me again.

"Interested?"

He shrugged. "Yeah, I guess so."

He motioned for me to get into his battered red Ford pickup.

At a gas station on Van Ness I bought him ten dollars of gas. I figured he might kick me out of his truck and take off. He didn't. I was thinking maybe we could park in a dark alley and I'd honk on him.

"Where to?" I asked.

"We can go to the flat I was painting out on the avenues. I got the keys. No one's there."

I was leery, but Maurice was friendly and smiled. He parked near a pizza place.

He opened the door nearby and I followed him up the stairs, smelling the fresh paint.

With music coming upstairs from the pizza restaurant he sprawled out on the rug.

I rubbed his crotch bulge. He lay back and watched me minister to his dick. I didn't know what his experience had been with guys, if any. What I did know was that he had a huge, thick, cut dick and large cum-filled nuts. I sucked up a storm and he moaned. He liked getting head.

"Gonna cum, man. Gonna shoot in your mouth!"

That he did. His cum tasted sweet and delicious. With the exception of Grady it had been awhile since I had white meat, I'd gone with so many Mexican boys.

"You're gorgeous," I gushed.

"Ready to roll?" He said, pulling on his pants.

He drove me back to Polk Street.

"I'd like to see you again," I said.

"I'm going into the Marines. Just signed up. I don't wanna be a painter for the rest of my life."

A Marine, I thought. Jesus, maybe I could have fucked him!

He shook my hand and thanked me for the gas. I thanked him for "everything."

# 8. Joey, the Filipino

Sitting in my car on Leavenworth Street near Market, I watched the rain pour down. It was early evening. I didn't want to get soaked but I didn't want to call it a night either. I was in terrible heat.

Soon the rain stopped. Looking out the car window, I saw a cute guy climbing the slight hill. He was Asian, Filipino I guessed. I got out of the car. Instead of going downtown I walked in the direction of the boy. I wasn't following him exactly but I was curious about where he was going.

There'd been a recent movie that was popular called "Macho Dancer." It was about boys in Manila. The scene where one boy soaped up the other one was hot and it made me curious about boys of the Pacific Rim. Rim indeed.

I flashed back on an encounter I'd had with a twenty-five- year-old Filipino named Roberto. I met him in a downtown arcade. He wasn't hustling, just looking to get his rocks off. In a booth, I felt him up. I liked his smooth, tawny body and took him to a cheap hotel room. Naked, he was affectionate and horny. His dick wasn't big but it was stiff. We had a hot sixty-nine.

Walking down Geary, the Filipino boy went into a store that sold records and cassettes. I got a good look at him inside the store. He had short black hair and big brown eyes. Even cuter than I'd thought. He looked to be in his late teens. But Asians were often ten years older than they looked to me.

I hung around for awhile and then decided to kiss him off. I figured he was probably totally straight and didn't speak English. Nearby Daly City was called the New Manila because it was the biggest settlement of Filipinos in the country, and he probably lived there.

After I walked a couple blocks I backtracked, thinking I'd go back to my car. It started to rain lightly.

Crossing the street, I spotted the Filipino boy again. He walked down Leavenworth and turned at Golden Gate. Instead of getting into my car, I walked down Golden Gate. Maybe I'd get a coffee. Actually I figured the Filipino boy would go south of Market, but, no, he went into the cheap porno theater on the corner.

I'd been inside the theater before, checking it out. It was bad news. In the upstairs toilet behind the screen there were guys shooting up drugs, and homeless people slept across the seats.

Inside the theater, I felt like a stalker, hardly my usual modus operandi. The Filipino had no idea I was even interested in him. It was just a hunch. Maybe he'd pull out his dick and jack-off. Maybe I'd get lucky and he'd let me suck it.

When my eyes adjusted to the darkness I spotted the Filipino. He was sitting in a row with vacant seats around him. I sat a couple seats away.

While he watched the woman give the man in the movie a blowjob, I watched him. He rubbed his crotch.

I don't know where I got the nerve, I'm not usually so brazen, but I had a hard-on from looking at him. I scooted over and I groped him.

He jumped, a bit startled. But he didn't push me away.

"I suck better than that bitch in the flick. Want me to show you?"

"Uh, can't do that here."

That didn't sound like a total no. At least he spoke English. True, there were other people around, some even snoring. But I'd seen dicks get sucked in this sleazy theater before. It was a dark corner.

"Go with me," he said. "You won't be disappointed. Meet me outside."

It was a line like in the phone sex ads where guys said you wouldn't be disappointed if you called them.

I went outside. Dumb, I told myself. He's not coming. I wasted money and I was getting wet.

Suddenly he came out of the theater. We walked down Golden Gate. I think his dick was still hard.

In a cheap hotel on Sixth Street the clerk, an older Mexican man, asked me for fifteen dollars for the room. I was about to shell it out because I wanted the Filipino boy so bad I could taste it.

"How about five dollars? We're only staying for an hour," the Filipino said.

That surprised me.

"Okay," the Mexican man said.

We had to walk the stairs because the elevator wasn't working. The place was a real dump.

Soon after I shut the door there was a knock. Uh-oh. This was a setup, I thought.

"Don't say nothing to the Hindu when you leave," the Mexican said.

"Gotcha."

It dawned on me that he was putting the fiver in his pocket since we never registered.

Inside the room was a mess. Peeling paint. Cold. Bedspread with cigarette burns. Outside it was pouring down rain.

"You from Manila?" I asked.

"Yeah." He spoke with a slight accent.

"What's your name?"

"Joey."

I told him mine. I wanted to get right to the meat of things, and I groped him.

"God, you're a good-looking kid."

He sat on the bed and I kneeled on the floor. I pulled down his jeans and shorts. He had a nice fat cut dick which looked really big on his slim frame.

It was chilly in the room but I wanted to see him naked.

"Let me see your body."

He obliged. Tawny skin, smooth as silk. Muscular thighs.

I went right to work on his stiff prick. I was able to take the whole thing in my mouth and even tongue at his nuts at the same time. His dick got steely hard right away and he shot a big load of frothy jizz down my throat.

I was so horny from looking at his naked boyish body and from the taste of his sweet cum I lay beside him on the bed and pulled my prick until I shot a puddle onto my belly. I rubbed the slimy goo into my skin.

Poor Joey was shivering from the cold and hurriedly pulled on his clothes. He never mentioned money. Neither did I. He said he worked in a restaurant.

I wanted to see him again. I was tempted to give him my phone number, but I hesitated.

"You ever had a guy give you a blowjob before?" I asked.

"No. I've only been with girls.'

"You're a handsome kid."

"I'm just eighteen," he said.

"Still a baby to me."

He smiled, and we left. The hotel was the Anglo and it was destroyed after the big quake of '89. Later when I drove past it; it was a pile of rubble but, why I'll never know, it was eventually resurrected.

I thought a lot about Joey. I really thought he was hot stuff. Cute, sweet and innocent.

A couple weeks later I saw him on Market Street.

"I've been looking for you," I said.

"Why?" he smiled.

"Because I think you're a living doll and I gotta have you again."

It was a line of shit but it worked.

"Follow me, don't walk with me. My brother's around here somewhere, I just saw him."

I guess maybe he didn't want to be seen with a white guy,

and older one. Jorge once told me that whenever Latinos saw an older gringo with a boy they thought puto and said shit.

With Joey looking back periodically, I followed him south of Market into the Filipino area. I wondered if this was smart. Maybe he belonged to a gang. But I'd met him on the street by chance. Besides my brains were in my dick. I was hot for him.

He crossed a parking lot to the back of some three-story frame houses. It was dark. I closed the gap behind him.

On the landing under the stairs he unzipped his fly and pulled out his dick. It got hard as soon as I put my lips around it.

Without warning there were footsteps on the stairs. Holy shit! I hightailed it across the parking lot. Looking back, I saw Joey following me. He motioned me back. The man who came down the stairs was walking up the alley.

John Patrick

I went back and Joey moved up to the second landing where it was dark. He pulled his dick out. Soon I was sucking like crazy. He was getting into the blowjob because he was thrusting his dick down my throat. I clasped my hands around his bubble butt and he blasted his sweet load down my throat. I was so horny that I creamed my drawers without even touching my dick.

I walked away with my belly full of delicious Filipino boy juice.

I looked around for Joey on Market Street after that but no sign of him. But there were plenty of gangs of Filipino boys wearing loose clothes with turned-around baseball caps on their heads like homeboys.

One day Joey walked into Jack-in-the-Box where I was drinking coffee. He had a girl with him who was hanging onto him. I stared at him and he gave me a slight smile of recognition.

The next time I saw him on the street he was alone and stopped to talk. He'd changed jobs and was now working as a carpet layer. He said it was hard on his knees. I sympathized because I spent a lot of time on my knees, not praying, and they were like a camel's. He was friendly but in a hurry because he was going to a rock concert at the Warfield. It was the last time I saw him.

# 9. Sami the Arab

One night I was cruising the arcade on Taylor Street. Nothing was happening. They'd taken out the live girlie show which had attracted a lot of trade. Now the arcade was being used as a shooting gallery besides a sex place. I was careful, afraid I might sit on a needle left on the bench in a booth.

About to leave, I saw a short young guy with a thin stache. I thought he was a Latino. I looked him over and he looked back and smiled.

"You wanna see a movie?" I asked.

He nodded.

Opening the door to a booth at the end, I dropped quarters into the slot. He stepped into the booth and sat down on the bench beside me.

While he watched the movie on the monitor I groped him. He had a big crotch bulge. I ripped open the metal button fly of his jeans and took out his hardening cock. It was long and fat with a bulbous head. He had big balls that were hairy.

Leaning over, I circled my lips around his cock and started blowing him. I bobbed my head up and down. His cock was rubbery, a big joint for a little guy.

When I took my mouth off his cock he started jacking it. I squatted between his legs and licked his jumbo egg-sized balls in their hairy sac and sucked on them. Looking up, I watched him spit on his palm and fist his dick. It was incredibly hard and he was breathing heavy. I figured he was ready to blow so I deep-throated his cock down to the balls basted with spit and he gushed a salty load into my mouth.

He smiled and buttoned up his fly. I figured he might ask for money since he was twentyish and well-hung but he didn't.

"What's your name?" I asked.

"Sami."

I later learned that it was spelled with an I. He had a thick guttural accent that definitely wasn't Spanish.

"Where are you from?"

"Jordan."

Arabs were short and brown like Latinos, but they usually had money. I was fascinated.

"Wanna go for a beer?" I invited.

He accepted. I took him into a dive bar on Turk and we sat at a table and talked.

"What kind of work do you do?" I asked.

"Mechanic. But my family has stores, grocery stores." "Different this country, from Jordan, huh?"

"Things are cheaper here."

That was a surprise since I considered inflation was rampant.

"A Jordan dollar is worth three American dollars."

We sipped bottles of Bud. I had a little trouble understanding Sami because of his accent. My ear was used to hearing Spanish. He had some difficulty with speaking English.

"Lot of crime in this country," I said, since we'd passed a car at the curb with a shattered window which someone had obviously broken into.

"In Jordan you can leave the windows down on your car."

"You have a car?"

"I got a BMW like I had in Jordan."

That was a real expensive car for someone his age.

"You live with your family?"

"Yes. With my father and cousins."

We finished our beers. Sami was looking at his watch.

"Well, see you around," I said.

I left the bar. I don't even remember the last trick I had who had money. I liked Sami but I was disappointed that he wasn't a Latino, like he had a choice, for goodness sake.

A few days later I ran into Al the sailor on the street. He was flush. I think he got retroactive pay on his disability claim or something. He wanted to go drinking but I just wasn't into the bar scene.

Approaching my car on Ellis Street where I'd parked, we ran into Sami. He was friendly and gave me a big hello. I introduced him to Al. Al seemed to like him.

"Why don't we go somewhere and party?" I suggested.

That's what Al had in mind.

"Can you go with us, Sami?"

"Sure."

It was dusk. I didn't want to have the party at my place. I never let tricks know where I lived. And it was a hassle taking guests to Al's hotel room.

"Let's get a motel room," I suggested.

Since Al was well-heeled, I knew he'd help with the expenses.

We drove across the Bay Bridge on I-80. I passed the cheap Vallejo motel because of my bad experience. There was another Big 6 motel near Fairfield so we went there.

Stopping at a big Raley's supermarket, we loaded up with beer and snacks. In the motel room Al and I drank beer. Sami wanted coffee, so we got it out of the vending machine. He drank it all night long.

Al and I talked, trying to include Sami. He didn't much get of the drift of the conversation, but he smiled a lot.

In the wee hours, it was time to crash. Al was sprawled out on one double bed. Sami and I shared the other one.

When Sami undressed I was surprised at how hairy his body was. He was like a little teddy bear.

In bed he snuggled up to me. That led to me feeling his dick which was hard and ready. Light was flickering from the television screen which was playing MTV videos.

Sami had such a nice body that I spent much time licking it all over, spitting out hair occasionally.

Al was watching us. I thought he might join in with Sami but he just watched. At the Health Club baths I'd suck a trick's tits while Al blew him, then we'd change places, going back and forth. If it was a hustler I'd let Al take the load but often as not he let it splash all over the number's body. One time Al and his longtime friend Jim, when they were in the Navy together, were at the baths when I brought a trick there named Chuckie. We were all pretty swacked on vodka. I lay on my back with a big boner. They positioned Chuckie, who was brunet, thin and boyish, on top of me and guided my dick up Chuckie's butt hole, like they did a stallion in a breeding shack. I think it was rough on Chuckie's ass but he didn't protest too much.

Another time I brought a teenage AWOL marine I'd met on Market Street named Danny to the baths. He was tall and thin with a small cock. But he had a beautiful butt. Al, Jim and I were in the cubicle drinking vodka with Danny, who was lying on his belly. I slipped off the loincloth. Mounting Danny, I fucked him. After I shot up his ass, Danny grabbed Al's boner. Al boffed him with his big dick. Jim was watching and jacking off his big boner. When Al was finished Jim fucked Danny. Danny was from Kentucky, with a delightful southern accent. I'd never seen a young guy who liked getting fucked so much. I saw Danny many years later. He was a cross country trucker with a beard and was married with teenaged children.

Maybe Al hesitated with Sami, who I regarded as just a trick, because I was real jealous and protective of Jorge, who was my steady boyfriend. Once we went to Al's hotel room and Jorge took a shower. Al handed him a towel, getting a glance at Jorge's gorgeous body and fat dick, but I was right there making sure nothing else happened.

Al was moody. Sometimes we shared tricks, other times he preferred to watch, even when the trick wanted three-way action with a dick in his butt and a dick in his mouth at the same time, like a blonde surfer boy named Carl who I fucked while he was wearing a jockstrap.

Sami wasn't a hustler used to the wild gay orgy scene. He was modest and tried to pull the sheet over himself.

But when I started sucking his dick he was thrashing around on the bed. I nearly brought him off, stopped, then started the buildup again. He wanted to get his rocks off and began pulling his pud. While he was occupied with that I spread his legs and dove into his hairy crack. That surprised him. What surprised me was how bristly the hair was, like a Brillo pad. While I tongued his hole he spurted cum drops all over his hairy chest, and I licked it off, eating the Arab jism.

Sami and I snoozed awhile. I think Al stayed up guzzling beer because he was awake when I opened my eyes.

Sami's dick was hard so I woke him with my tongue. I swooped down on his meat and it blasted. I drank his salty load.

It was a fun party.

I gave Sami my phone number and began calling occasionally, usually late at night, and I'd meet him downtown in an arcade and feast on his tasty Arab cock. This went on for a few months, then he stopped calling.

I ran into him downtown with an older woman. I thought it might be his mother, she was old enough. She rattled on but I didn't make much sense of the conversation. She was pawing all over Sami and kissing him, so I realized that she must be his girlfriend–or whatever.

He told me that he was going to Los Angeles to work in his cousin's gas station there. And the floozy was going with him. So I shook his hand goodbye. That was the end of my romance with him. I was kind of jealous because the old woman was getting a nice rich Arab boy with a big dick. I should be so lucky.

# 10. Ricardo from Guadalajara

Cruising a bookstore arcade on Polk Street, I spotted a hunky young Latino. He was short with curly black hair. He was a tapitio, with bright brown eyes, from Guadalajara, different- looking from the Aztec Indians from Mexico City, and he was lighter skinned.

I lured him into a booth and checked out his big fat uncut dick, like I'd imagined. And giant balls. I chomped on his chorizo until he blew. It was one of the sweetest loads I've ever tasted. His body wasn't muscular but it was smooth and real sensuous.

As much as I liked the hairy Arab boy, I was back in my element with a hot Mexican stud. He said his name was Ricardo. I liked his accent–and that big juicy piece of meat that swung between his legs. He left the arcade afterwards. He was friendly with a nice smile, perfect teeth. I should have invited him out for a drink or something, but I thought he was just trade, probably another wetback just passing through. I could spot them by now.

I kept thinking about Ricardo. I'd had encounters with two other Ricardos; both were stunning-looking hombres. There was the Ricardo that I took to the motel on my birthday. And there was another Ricardo I'd followed around the arcades in the Tenderloin. He was handsome, real macho. He didn't seem interested but I was persistent, hanging around.

I finally caught his eye. Talking to him, I got him into a booth. He had one of the biggest, juiciest uncut dicks I ever sucked. I took him for a drive to the Coit Tower parking area and drank beer. He was in his early twenties, married and totally faithful to his wife, but he conceded that letting me suck him off wasn't like he'd gone with another woman. He squirted like a fountain, one of the biggest loads I ever swallowed. I gave him my phone number but he never called. He was planning to go back to Mexico soon.

I started looking for Ricardo from Guadalajara on Polk Street. It was several days before I spotted him. He was standing on the meat rack near Geary where cars stopped to pick up hustlers. I was disappointed but figured he probably needed the money, if indeed he was hustling. A bus also stopped at that corner.

"Como estas?" I said.

"Bien, bien."

I could tell that he remembered me. He spoke English better than I spoke Spanish, which wasn't saying much.

"Tiene hambre?"

He said he was hungry so I took him to the Burger King for a Whopper. He was willing so I took him back to the arcade and sucked his big dick. This time I gave him a few bucks so he could get something to eat later since he wasn't working.

That weekend I took him to the Vallejo motel for the night, and confronted my fear, which vanished. He was very intelligent and educated, although I must admit that I liked them young and dumb and full of cum.

In the motel it was a night of passion. Jesus, I was falling for this guy. I tongue-bathed his body and sucked his dick all night long but he wouldn't let me stick him.

Later he said, "I'm going back to Guadalajara. Gringos don't like me. I can't get a job without papers."

He told me that he'd worked in restaurants and as a carpenter but with the fines employers got now for hiring illegals they weren't taking chances on employees without green cards.

In the back of my mind I'd been thinking about a getaway trip to Reno. A change of scenery and getting away from the typewriter for awhile. I could see my old friend Jimmy who worked at the Hilton there. He had connections to get me all the free drink coupons I could use.

Ricardo said he'd been to Las Vegas but not Reno, and he agreed to go with me. But then my car broke down and needed major repair. We went on the Greyhound. I'd driven to Reno many times but hadn't taken the bus for years.

Ricardo fell asleep and snuggled up next to me on the bus at night. I was going to miss this guy. I thought about persuading him to stay but he'd made his plans and his best friend was expecting him.

My mind harked back to two other trips I'd taken alone to Reno.

I'd scored both times. I wasn't gambling because I lost my bankroll within hours and had set limits.

Walking around downtown Reno, I ran into a young blonde guy who was visiting Reno. I don't remember his name but I remember his face and slender body. I'd been drinking and was high. The car was in a lot and I didn't have a motel room. He was with his family, but he was gay and interested in fooling around. He took me to a spot near the Truckee River which runs through downtown Reno. Under the wooden pillars that held up a restaurant that was closed, we felt each other up.

He dropped his pants and bent over. I fucked him hard while he moaned and begged for more until I shot a big pent-up load up his tight ass.

During my other trip to Reno, I came out of Harold's Club. On a big streak with blackjack, and I was several hundred dollars ahead when they changed dealers. This guy dealt himself almost all twenties. In no time I was in the dumper but I'd been gambling with money I'd won.

Outside on Virginia Street I ran into a hunky black-haired stud in his early twenties. He had been drinking.

I offered to buy him another drink, whatever.

His name was Tom and he said he worked as a cook and was out drinking on his night off. He invited me back to his rooming house in the downtown area. I picked up a six-pack at a corner grocery store.

Inside his small room at the rear of the house we sipped beer.

Although I think he was basically straight, he knew what I wanted and he was horny.

Lying down on his narrow bed, he rubbed his crotch.

I swooped down on him like a vulture. Hungry for dick, I pulled down his jeans and shorts. He had a big, rosy, cut cock. His body was hirsute.

He groaned, "Suck my dick, man."

I gobbled up his pecker. It was a fat eight-plus inches and hard as a rock.

"Lick my nuts."

I tongued his hairy balls.

"Suck those motherfuckers."

I sucked his balls into my mouth.

"Get down on my dick. Oh fuck yeah. Let me shoot in your mouth and you can do anything you want to me."

He held my head to his crotch and mouth-fucked me, spurting his load down my throat.

My dick was hard. I whipped it out, thinking he'd blow me, but no.

"Suck me off again," he said.

His cock was soft but I nursed it and it was hard before long. While I sucked him off the second time I jacked off.

I swallowed another load of his salty goo and left my pecker tracks on his bed. He didn't notice or care.

He passed out cold and I split in the night.


The Greyhound bus was now at the Donner Summit and descending into the Reno valley. The snow was piled high and it was cold. In Reno I got us a room at the Ramada Inn on Lake Street.

Ricardo took a shower, then came out to get dressed. I got so horny just looking at him with that fat piece between his legs that I gently shoved him down on the bed naked and gobbled up his dick.

He was horny and rubbed my hair while I sucked him to a gut-wrenching orgasm that sprayed my throat with wads of sweet Mexican leche.

At the Hilton's casino I looked up my friend Jimmy. He took a shine to Ricardo. On Jimmy's break we had dinner.

Ricardo and I hit the casinos, the green felt jungle. I didn't gamble, just drank beer and watched him. Instead of throwing away my money gambling I'd decided to buy him a bus ticket to San Diego and give him enough money to get back to Guadalajara.

We had fun and hit several jackpots. That night in the room I celebrated by sucking him off three or four times.

I didn't want to lose him, but he was taking the bus to San Diego when we got back to San Francisco.

Luckily he'd actually won enough money for his trip but I gave him an extra C-note to make sure. He was worth it.

In San Francisco I made it a quick farewell. I didn't want him to go. He was something special.

John Patrick

I thought I'd never see him again, like all the other Mexican boys after they went back to their country. But I was wrong. I would see Ricardo again.

# 11. Tony from Puebia

I was eating at a cheap Chinese restaurant on Market Street, chow mien with rice and beef, when I saw the new busboy/dishwasher. He just blew me away. He was a big hunky Latino boy with coal black hair and brown eyes. He wore a red apron but I could still detect a crotch bulge. The apron was open at the back with dangling strings, and I saw he had a round, muscular butt inside those jeans.

I watched him clear the tables while I poured too much soy sauce onto the food.

His name was Tony. I heard the Chinese owner call him that. But he made motions to the boy what he wanted, like holding up a plate. The boy didn't speak English.

I played with the fork. I wasn't interested in the food but I was really interested in Tony.

The next night I went back to the restaurant, and the next. I didn't really like Chinese food, but I sure liked the Mexican boy working there.

Tony began to recognize me and nodded. I spoke enough of his language to eventually engage him in conversation.

I learned that he was from Puebla, and he'd just turned twenty. The Chinese paid him three dollars an hour, ten hours a day, seven days a week.

I thought about tipping him to show my interest. Instead I bought him a lottery scratcher ticket which they sold in a booth at the entrance, and left it under the plate.

A few days later he showed me a fifty-dollar-winner ticket. I knew that was like thirteen hundred to one odds. He was really excited.

When he wasn't too busy he'd linger at my table and talk. He'd sort of bunch his crotch on the edge of the table. That made me nervous. It's hard to concentrate when I got a woody. I don't think Tony was really a prick teaser but he had to know that I liked him by the way I ogled him. He liked boxing but didn't have much time to go to the gym with his work schedule. I told him that I'd like to see him in his shorts and he smiled.

This cat-and-mouse game went on for nearly three months. I was losing weight with all the Chinese food I was eating every day.

And I wasn't getting any, not that I couldn't. But I preferred to fantasize about Tony and beat off.

One day when I saw Tony he was sad and quiet, not his usual friendly self. I knew something was wrong. I wanted to ask but I decided to wait and maybe he'd tell me.

The place was nearly empty. I usually went in the last hour before the eight o'clock closing time when it wasn't busy. That way I could just sit and watch Tony sweep up.

He sat down across from me at the table, something he'd never done before.

John Patrick

"My brother was hurt bad in a car accident," he said in Spanish.

"Lo silent, I'm sorry."

He was worried, thinking maybe he should go back to Mexico because his family wanted him to, although he'd come to the United States with his married uncle and lived with him.

"Meet me when you get off work. We can talk. I'll wait at Jack-in-the-Box on the corner."

He nodded and pushed the cart full of dirty dishes into the back.

At Jack-in-the-Box I drank a coffee and waited. It was fifteen after eight, and I guessed he changed his mind. Maybe he didn't want to be alone with me. By now he had to know the way I was interested in him.

Looking outside, I saw Tony. He had his bicycle. He waved and I practically ran out the door.

I thought about taking him home. I knew he was okay. Instead I opted for a cheap hotel room. That way I could leave if it went badly and he wouldn't know where I lived.

"Let's get something to drink," I said.

I stopped at a grocery store that sold liquor on Sixth Street, the skid row area. Tony liked whiskey and beer, boilermakers. That was fine with me.

He accompanied me to a cheap Hindu fleabag, the Alder. He was on his bike, with me walking along beside him. The elevator didn't stop on the ground floor, just the second floor where the office was. Tony carried his bike up the stairs.

I got some weird looks from the Hindu, what with young Tony and his bike, but I paid the room rent and got a key.

Inside the dreary room Tony and I sat on the bed drinking boilermakers. He was getting high.

"Your brother will heal fast, he's young. You're sending your family money. Try not to worry. You can call them tomorrow."

He relaxed and smiled. I could tell he trusted me. I didn't want to take advantage of him but I wanted him so bad I couldn't stand it. He'd come to a hotel room with me, he had to know the score. He didn't have time to date and look for girls when he worked seven days a week. He had to be horny at his age and tired of jacking off.

"You know, I really like you, Tony."

"I know."

"I meant what I said about wanting to see you box. But I'd really rather just see you nude."

By this time he'd had enough to drink that his inhibitions were gone. He said nothing, just began stripping. My heart skipped a beat. He was everything I'd expected and more.

He was wearing blue bikini briefs with his fat verga in a horizontal position and hard. His body was smooth and muscular.

He was standing by the bed, and I pulled him down on the bed. I was all over him. Nuzzling his nylon briefs, licking them, nibbling, smelling his musky body.

He was excited and breathing heavy. I peeled off his briefs. His cock was a beautiful uncut slab of meat. His big balls heavy.

"God, so guapo."

He smiled.

No experience with jotos (gays), he later told me, he didn't know what to do. He lay there and I feasted on his body, slurping it with my tongue, arousing him to a fever pitch.

His cock was at full mast, throbbing and drooling.

I sucked on his balls. He moaned.

I took his big dick in one fell swoop all the way down my throat. I worked it with my throat muscles.

Suddenly he shoved me back. Uh-oh. What was wrong? I hadn't bitten him. He couldn't have changed his mind at this stage.

"Miar," he grinned.

He had to piss.

"Do it in the sink."

I didn't want him to dress and go down the hall to the pisser, for fear he'd change his mind and leave.

As he ran the water and peed in the sink, disturbing only the cockroaches, I got a good look at his bronze, muscular butt cheeks. I'd love to lick them and dive into his crack, but he was macho and I didn't want him to freak.

I lay on the bed and he climbed on top of me. He must have pissed with a hard-on, because his cock was stiff and throbbing in my face.

He held it and rubbed it against my cheeks and painted my lips with his clear pre-cum. My own cock was pulsing in my pants, leaking like a sieve.

Macho Tony parted my lips with his dick and shoved it down my throat.

I clasped his butt cheeks and held on while he mouth-fucked me.

There's nothing quite so nice as a macho guy mouth-fucking you rough, like they're teaching you a lesson for being queer. Like that Guardian Angel boy that an older cruiser I knew named Hank pursued. He gave me all the sordid details. When he got the Guardian Angel into an arcade booth the stud pumped his prick down Hank's throat until he practically choked him.

Like Tony was doing to me now. His spit-soaked balls were slapping against my chin. He was fucking my face like it had never been fucked before. His cock reamed my throat until it was raw.

Just when I thought I'd be choked to death by the huge Mexican dick that was steely hard I heard Tony grunt and his cock gushed, flooding my mouth with nutty-tasting sperm. It trickled out of the corners of my mouth.

Just from feeling Tony's muscular butt cheeks, touching his steamy crack and tasting his spunk my cock gushed in my pants like a broken pipe. I hadn't even touched myself.

Tony lay spread-eagled on the bed.

I decided to clean the goo off his cock head and maybe catch any remnant of cock cheese before his meat softened and retracted into the foreskin.

When I licked his dick it throbbed and stayed stiff.

Tony's brown eyes were glassy.

Suddenly I realized that there was more cum in his big balls.

I started out sucking him slowly. I pinched his foreskin while I did a butterfly flick on his shaft. I jacked his dick while I lapped at his balls and sucked on them.

His cock was at full mast. I deep-throated it and bobbed my head up and down on it.

Tony was breathing heavy again. It took longer the second time around but I was in control. I tongued the sensitive ridge below the crimson crown where his foreskin gathered. I held his veiny shaft at the base and darted my tongue into his piss hole.

"Chupa," he moaned.

And I did. I sucked with gusto. He thrust his pelvis upwards and crammed every inch of his dick down to the short curlies down my throat and blasted.

The second load was even bigger than the first. Salvo after salvo of nutty ball juice flooded my mouth. This time I was ready, sealing my lips around his cock. I drank every delicious drop.

"Nectar for the gods," I cried, and I didn't bother to translate.

Tony and I drank the rest of the booze. He was higher than a kite. So was I but I was high off him. I never thought I'd ever get my hands on him. The long wait had been worth it.

Tony was tipsy and running into parking meters with his bike on the street. He was skylarking but I was concerned for his safety.

I took him to Carl's Jr. near Hallidie Plaza where the cable car turnaround is and I fed him a big cheeseburger and coffee.

He was sober enough to ride his bike home.

"See you manana, Tony."

"Adios, amigo."

Tony was just as friendly as ever when I saw him in the Chinese restaurant the next night. He'd called Puebla again and his brother was going to make it. I had big plans for Tony, but I decided to take it slow and easy.

# 12. The Tearooms

In all my years of cruising I'd never had sex in public toilets. I even thought it was all a joke with those holes in toilet stalls with "Show Hard–Get Sucked" written beside them.

And I'd seen guys sucking dick in the balcony of a Market Street movie theater, but I'd never participated. Usually they were trolls. I'd watch a movie and split. I·heard that the vice squad told the management to install bright lights, which they did, but that didn't stop the action.

Big Al's longtime buddy Jim was an aficionado of this theater. I think he clocked in more time than most of the employees. He never watched the movies, never had any idea of what was playing on the silver screen. He told me that he once jacked off a lad when suddenly all the theater lights came on as the boy shot his wad because the movies were over. He didn't know what to do with the cummy load in his hand so he finally wiped it on a seat cushion.

The new management of the theater soon 86'd the regular cruisers and didn't allow them into the theater. So the same group of guys started going out to Land's End, a wooded area by the Cliff House at the ocean, and continued carrying on. Jim said it was like an animal dragging fresh meat off into the bushes.

Then the theater management changed again and all the regular cruisers gravitated back to the downtown theater balcony and it has been just like old times ever since.

I'd stopped in the rest rooms in the big downtown department stores to relieve myself. I never stayed long enough to see what went on. Oh, I'd seen guys with their dick hanging out at the urinals but they were ugly men and I wasn't interested.

But then one day I stopped in to piss at a store. The downstairs toilet was closed for cleaning so I went up to the fourth floor where the sign directed.

It was a small toilet in the rear with only two urinals, separated by a metal shield, and only one stall.

Standing at the urinal was a good-looking tall blonde guy in his mid-twenties wearing an Army field jacket. I figured he'd piss and go.

He stood back and flashed me his peter. A thick, hard seven-incher, plus he was real butch looking. Knowing that I was checking out his meat, he started to stroke it. My dick got stiff from watching him. By now he was jacking off to beat the band when suddenly he shot off, spewing pearly cum drops all over the place.

He grinned, stuffed his pecker back in his jeans and left the men's room. I was so horny I was tempted to jack-off myself but I split. That night I had a leisurely jack-off session remembering every little detail of the blonde stud's performance.

John Patrick

That incident whet my appetite. I began lingering in public toilets to see if I could get any quickies.

I remembered back in college when my best buddy Keith once drew me a map of the outdoor toilets in Golden Gate Park. I didn't think it was for real at the time. Once Keith pulled off the freeway when we were out for a ride. It was a place where truckers shut down to take a break. Keith brazenly knocked on a trucker's cab and the guy let him in. He told me afterwards how he blew the hairy bear of a man who was wearing a wedding ring. He also said he'd sucked dick in the bus station john.

Now I was sitting on the throne in a store toilet waiting for something to happen. There was a guy in the next stall, but I didn't get a look at him. I had a boner.

Soon he handed me a note on a piece of toilet paper wrapped around a felt pen. The note asked, "What do you like to do?"

I wrote "Everything," and passed the note and pen back under the gray metal partition.

I wasn't sure if this guy was serious.

When the urinal flushed and the inner door creaked open, then the outer door closed, I knew there were just the two of us in the rest room because no other shoes were in sight.

Since I was horny I figured I'd let the guy take a few slides on my dick. I kneeled on the floor and showed him my boner in an upright position.

Immediately I felt a warm mouth on it, coating my cock with spit. It felt so good that I came right off.

Suddenly the outer door opened and I jumped back onto the commode with cum still bubbling out of my piss hole.

The urinal flushed and the man left.

I figured I'd better hightail it out of there before the security guard or janitor came in. I hiked up my britches.

Curiosity got the best of me. I decided to peek at my cocksucker in the stall. Probably an old coot, I thought, but he was a cute young Filipino boy stroking his fat little pecker. He was licking his chops and gave me a big smile.

The outside door opened and I heard voices so I left the room.

I was back the next day. The stalls were occupied and two guys were washing their hands. When I glanced into the stalls I saw four guys, two were stroking their prick. The guys outside made me as queer so they peeked into the stall, where the two guys were masturbating.

In the end stall against the wall was the Filipino boy. He recognized me and smiled.

The two guys jacking off in the stalls unlatched the doors and I watched the two other guys go down on them. The guy in the first stall was down on the floor, watching.

I took out my dick which was hard from the heated atmosphere of the toilet and flashed the Filipino boy. He opened the stall door and I stepped

inside and fed him my dick. He sucked like a champ, beating off while he did me. I came off in a flash.

Good thing because the outer door whooshed open and the activity stopped. Three straight guys pissed and washed up. They took their sweet time about it and all the other cruisers left the toilet, except the Filipino boy and me.

I went into the stall next to him. He must have recognized my shoes. No sooner had I sat down on the throne then he presented me with his stiff, drooling prick.

Kneeling down, I fattened my lips around it and he shot right off, coating my tonsils with hot sweet Filipino boy cream.

Outside the stalls we both washed our hands at the sinks.

"I'm Brian," he smiled.

"Bill."

He had a maroon knapsack.

"Student?"

"Yeah, I go to City College."

Someone came in to take a leak.

"See you later," I said.

"Until we meet again," he said.

I saw Brian several more times.

When the toilet was too busy with traffic he tapped his shoe in the adjoining stall and whispered "Gimme your hand."

I thought he wanted to squeeze it. No way. He rained hot cum drops on it, then he split.

No use letting it go to waste, I licked it off.

But Brian stopped coming into the toilet. Maybe he met somebody special or got a job.

I checked out the toilet in the big adjacent store. It was located next to a glassed-in security office so I was sure it was a blank, with no action, but I was wrong. Peeking into the only occupied stall, I saw a tall cute brunet, around nineteen. He had a long, thin dick which was hard.

I went into the stall next to him. The room was empty except for us.

"Want it sucked, baby?" I asked.

He answered by kneeling on the tile floor and presenting me with his boner.

I took less than a dozen slides on it when it spurted a big load of hot, salty jizz down my throat.

It was a good thing he was a fast comer because as soon as I licked up the last drop I heard the door open.

The brunet bolted out of the stall.

No problem. Not the security guards. Only an old geezer wanting to whiz.

Back in the other store, I sat in the end stall. The toilet was empty.

Someone came in and sat down in the stall next to me.

John Patrick

He wore white L.A. Gear running shoes so I figured it was a youngster. He stretched out his feet and was rocking his heels. I figured he was pulling his pud.

Curiosity got the best of me. I leaned down and took a look-see. Lo and behold if he wasn't one of the cutest young guys I'd ever seen. Another Filipino. Jet black crew cut. Soft brown eyes. His shirt was open. Smooth, tawny skin and bee-stung nipples.

His dick was hard, six inches and fat. The cock head was rosy but turned purplish the more he stroked it.

He pumped it awhile. My mouth was watering and my dick was hard.

Without a word he kneeled down and presented me his throbber. I held the shaft and laved the cock head with spit. I licked his big balls.

"Suck me."

I swallowed his cock, working it with my throat muscles, tonguing the ridge below the crown. He thrust it down my throat a couple times and soon it whitewashed my tonsils with sweet, creamy jizz.

I held my dick under the partition. He was hiking up his jeans. I fisted my prick and spewed a puddle of sperm on the tile floor.

He looked into the door crack and smiled before he left.

I wiped up the gooey mess with toilet paper.

Even cruising the toilets I hit a dry spell. There were plenty of guys, but no one struck my fancy.

Until one day I was sitting on the commode with a random hard-on. Standing by the sink outside the door was a Chinese boy with wire-framed glasses.

I stood up and jacked my dick. I motioned for him to go into the next stall. He did. No one else was in the room.

I was expecting a blowjob from the way he was ogling my dick. Instead he kneeled on the floor and flashed me a big, thick, uncut dick which surprised me because of his skinny frame.

I licked the cock head, then the balls. He gasped when I sucked on his nuts. Fastening my lips around his cock, I bobbed up and down on it. He held my head and roughly pumped his prick down my throat. I almost choked. Suddenly he squirted, flooding my mouth with Chinese cum that was like rice water.

The next time I saw the Chinese boy was in the basement of the store. He stared at me but continued walking away. I trailed him to a small toilet. Inside he latched the door. I didn't even know about this room.

He unzipped. His cock was soft and hooded. Kneeling, I licked it. It ballooned into the fat seven-incher it was. He moaned while I ministered to his dick. I jacked it, admiring its hardness while I lapped at his nuts. He rammed his prick down my throat and pumped with his balls flapping against my chin until he filled my mouth with his jizz.

When I looked up his glasses were all steamed. He grinned.

He left first and I followed him outside.

"You're hot stuff," I said.

He smiled.

His name was Tim, from Malaysia, and he had just gotten off work, but was going to a night class to study English.

Another time I met a young, long-haired, macho Latino who was cruising in the basement store. He got the message when I rubbed my crotch. I led him to the secluded toilet and latched the door. I took out my dick. He dry humped me while he jacked me off and I shot all over the floor.

He said he was nineteen, from Columbia; his name was Juan. The door handle rattled, startling us. I flew out of the room while he washed his hands at the sink. Outside was a man with a small boy who had to tinkle.

My encounters in the store toilets came to an abrupt end when the big department store toilet was closed for repairs. And the heat was on in the other store where the security cops threatened cruisers they caught red-handed with arrest or had them sign an agreement to stay out of their stores for two years. I decided to cool it. The quickie sex with hot guys was fun but I was ready for a real boyfriend.

## 13. *The Return of Ricardo*

While drinking a hot coffee at Jack-in-the-Box at Seventh and Market I saw Ricardo walking past. He was with another Mexican man. I had no idea he was back from Guadalajara. He'd sent a note with some picture postcards with scenes from his city but never mentioned he was coming back. I'd assumed that I'd never see him again, like all the other Mexican boys I'd known who returned to their country.

He said that he'd tried to call me. He looked a little thinner but his eyes were bright like his smile and he seemed glad to see me.

His friend Nicolas was a few years older than Ricardo but had a green card and was sure he could get a job, although he didn't speak English.

They were hungry and I popped for a couple of cheap Big Deal meals: hamburger, taco and fries.

The more I looked at Ricardo the more I liked what I saw. At the same time, unbeknownst to him, I still had the hots for Tony from the Chinese restaurant but I wasn't making any further progress with him.

They had a room at a Hindu fleabag hotel on Mission Street.

After they ate, they were tired from their long bus ride, so I agreed to meet them the next night at the same time and place.

I went home and tried to work on a story I was writing but I couldn't stop thinking about Ricardo. So I tossed the story in the trash and wrote a fantasy story based on Ricardo. It must have been hot because it sold right away.

Meanwhile, I was meeting Ricardo and his amigo every night and feeding them, but it wasn't expensive.

Ricardo knew from the way I gawked at him that I was still hot for him. He must have been horny too, because Nicolas was only an amigo.

While Nicolas was drinking his coffee I invited Ricardo to go to an arcade down the street. He told Nicolas in Spanish that he'd meet him back at the hotel.

In the sleazy arcade above a bookstore I got Ricardo into a booth. I was incredibly hungry for him. I got his big fat prick out of his jeans and kissed it, licked it, then swallowed it up. I worked my tongue on the sensitive spot below the bulbous crown where his foreskin gathered.

With his spit-soaked dick bobbing up and down I sucked on his plump balls.

He shoved my head back onto his dick just in time. His cock was hard as a rock and throbbing, gushing ball juice into my mouth. I swallowed it all.

The next night I met the two Mexican boys again. There was no jealousy because Nicolas wasn't my type, and I don't think he liked me much. They couldn't find jobs and Ricardo told me that they were going to be put out of the hotel.

John Patrick

I'm not cold-blooded but I was paranoid enough that I didn't want two guys staying at my place. It could be dangerous with two guys. Although I trusted Ricardo to a point I really didn't know anything about his buddy. Together they could pull something on me if I tried to be a Good Samaritan. Besides it wasn't my problem. There were shelters but I knew they were full.

In my whole life I'd taken two guys together for a sex party only one time. But I was younger and more trusting. Oh, I'd picked up two sailors in my convertible many times but one was usually a bow-wow. And I took the beauty and gave the beast to Frank the Italian. I think he preferred ugly guys anyhow; he wasn't that particular who fucked him.

By sheer luck I'd picked up two teenaged merchant marines who'd just gotten out of the academy at Piney Point, Maryland, and were picking up a ship on the West Coast. I got them at the Greyhound station. One was blonde and slim, the other ruggedly handsome and dark.

It was my twenty-something birthday and I wanted to party.

They were to stay at the Apostleship of the Sea, a dormitory for seamen, but I convinced them to go to the baths with me. They were adventuresome and agreed. I snuck in a bottle of vodka. I had to fight off other cruisers who were like vultures. I tipped Eric the attendant a fiver and he gave us one of the special rooms with a real bed and mirrors, up on the top floor of the bath.

I had the two young merchant seamen all to myself. The three of us wore just loincloths. We were drinking vodka-7s and having a ball. They were randy and knew that I wanted to suck their dicks.

I started out with the blonde. Baby-faced and gorgeous. I gobbled up his dick, which was only average-sized but really stiff. I'd sucked on it only for a moment when it spurted a creamy load into my mouth.

The swarthy sailor had a hard-on from watching me blow his buddy. When I turned my attention to him I was surprised at how muscular his body was. His cock was an eight-inch-plus whopper, and he really got into getting it sucked. He rubbed my body and pulled my hair. I'm sure he'd have given me a hand job or more if his buddy wasn't with him. When he came off he rammed his bone down my throat and practically drowned me with his juicy load.

The three of us polished off the fifth of vodka. Then I jacked on both of their dicks at the same time. Then I sucked on both of them, going back and forth, like a trained seal tooting horns. Then I sucked them together. I jacked off while they poked my mouth. I shot off all over my belly. When they got their guns at about the same time they rained cum drops all over my naked body. I rubbed the sticky goo into my skin.

I drove them to the Apostleship of the Sea. They couldn't have been nicer to me. It was a real wingding. I'd been so hot for the blonde but the swarthy one had turned out to be better. It was a wet dream come true. I wondered if they ever later did each other aboard ship when they were horny. I doubted it, but they shared a secret with the party they had with me.

I figured I had a fighting chance with one trick. With two guys they could get the jump on you, rob you, kill you. It happens.

With that knowledge in mind I no longer took guys home, not even nice kids like Ricardo.

The rainy season was coming. Both Ricardo and his amigo were in the streets. I began to think I didn't have a heart, that I was callused. Eventually Nicolas found an old queen who took a liking to him and let him stay in his room. But Ricardo was outside if he didn't find a shelter. With his looks and big dick he surely could have found somebody to help him.

Then it started to rain. A deluge. I didn't have extra money to give him for a hotel room. It was crazy. I genuinely liked Ricardo. But I knew if I took him home that would change our relationship. It did. He became my boyfriend. Ricardo was passionate in bed, and I was sucking him off twice at night and twice in the morning. The pace of my new May-December romance was killing me! And not only was he hot sex, Ricardo was a good cook, having worked in restaurants in Mexico.

For some reason I didn't want to get involved. Still, I wanted him to stay with me.

When he finally went out and got a job in restaurant and brought home a paycheck I felt blessed.

He was full of surprises. I'd mostly sucked his big burrito and beat off. Of course, he was macho and wanted to fuck me. He'd fucked women but admitted that he liked men better. My kind of guy.

All my life I'd been mostly a top, and I'd had my eye on Ricardo's macho butt since day numero uno. But he never let me do more than finger his crack.

Once I managed to diddle him things changed. He became a bottom. When his butt became attuned to my dick it was paradise.

He became more affectionate, with light kissing. We even fell asleep in each other's arms.

This went on for several months at fever pitch. Although he never said the words, never told me that he loved me, his actions said plenty.

But the hot romance simmered down when he lost his job. A new Filipino manager at the restaurant got rid of all the help and hired Asians.

With local experience and the reputation that he was a hard worker and dependable, it seemed only a matter of time before he connected with something else. But he didn't. After he filled out dozens of applications, he found there were just no jobs. Employers just weren't taking chances with undocumented workers.

I was selling enough stories to keep body and soul together but it was getting rough. The quarrels were getting worse. I didn't have money to fix my car after it was stripped and vandalized. Then the landlord tried to evict me.

The anger and resentment between us spilled over in bed. Some days we barely talked.

Eventually I found myself secretly hoping he'd leave. I'd been a fool. There was too much difference in our ages and cultures. The radio was always on the Spanish station. The same with television.

He'd changed me. Suddenly I knew more Latino singers than American ones, from Luis Miguel and Magneto to La Loca. I was eating a lot of Mexican food.

I tried to get a handle on our relationship. He was slipping through my fingers like quicksilver. I was afraid of losing him. I had mixed feelings, I wanted him and I didn't.

He talked about going back to Mexico but Luciano, his best friend there, had recently died. Ricardo's family turned on him because he was gay. His buddy Nicolas had already gone back to Mexico, abandoning the dream of the norte.

\* \* \* \* \*

After six years Ricardo split. He'd started staying out all night, with no explanations. He had found someone else, a bigger dick, whatever. I was lost. At first I was worried that he had been in an accident, maybe in jail. I called the hospital and city jail. Nothing.

I couldn't sleep at night. I'd pass out for an hour, exhausted, then lie in bed for a couple more hours unable to sleep, then get up. I was crazy with worry. I left the TV on and listened to the religious crazies rant and rave, drifting in and out of their religious rap, much of which consisted of asking for money.

In the morning I went to my typewriter. I knew that I had to go on. I had to keep writing. Editors were starting to buy my stories again. At times I wondered if what I wrote made any sense at all.

Two weeks later I got a note in my mailbox on the back of a receipt from Burger King down the alley that stated simply: I'm going to Los Angeles. Don't look for me. You'll hear from me again some day.

At least he was still alive. Toward the end we didn't speak much, drifting apart, living around each other, not with each other.

I wasn't sure whether to believe him. I got the feeling that he was still in the city. Where else would he go? He didn't have money. Maybe he found a sugar daddy, another boyfriend.

I walked the streets, alone all the time. I wandered around the Mission district, the Latino barrio. I saw a lot of cute, bronze-skinned boys, but no Ricardo.

One Sunday night, three weeks later, I ran into Ricardo on Market Street. He was with an older guy. He ran off but I chased him down. He said he was going to come back, that he was working. He'd call me at 11:30 that night. I didn't believe him.

He didn't call. He wasn't coming back.

The next day I went to see my lifelong friend Al, the retired merchant seaman, in his fleabag hotel room in the Tenderloin, where people roamed the halls on speed at night and two people had recently jumped off the roof, thinking they could fly or something.

We talked and reminisced. I remembered a tall, young oiler on the ship he'd sucked off after the boy came out of the shower in their cabin with a boner. Al liked the Greek boys. He stayed in his hotel room most of the time now. He had a big video library and watched movies like Howard Hughes, a recluse.

A week later, I was drinking coffee in Carl's Jr. on Market Street. Ricardo came in. He looked beat and hadn't shaved in several days, looked more ethnic. He sat down with me and we talked. He'd been in San Jose.

I invited him to come home with me, to eat, clean up and wash his clothes.

He said he didn't want a sex relationship with me. He just wanted to be friends. I figured he was just tired.

He was still working part-time for the janitorial service. He needed a place to crash. So I gave in.

When he started to stay out late, didn't call or anything, we had a big row. He told me that his sex life was none of my business. Okay, fine. But it wasn't my party so why should I pick up the tab?

He contributed some when he had money. Then he lost his job. I felt sorry for him. I knew he was broke. I didn't have the heart to throw him out.

When he saw he got his way again he didn't bother to look too hard for another job. I figured he had some tricks or johns, whatever. He was gone for long periods of time. He was secretive and not about to level with me.

I kept busy working at my typewriter, trying to keep things going. I calmed down. I'd helped other friends in the past. I'd treat him just like another friend. If he thought he was such hot stuff, Mr. All That, and had it going on, he could do it his way. Eventually I lost sexual interest in him. He slept on his side of the bed under all the covers to avoid any physical contact and kept his body covered like a puritan.

That wasn't the way the world was. I wasn't a sugar daddy. He could pay his way, at least keep the place clean and cook, which he agreed to do. Sometimes it felt like living in a cold war zone. But it was less hassle not to quarrel. It became routine. He had a place to lay his head and I had the pleasure of his company sans sex. We salvaged a half-ass friendship out of the deal, like a Mexican standoff. He changed from stud to houseboy.

Since he thought he was God's gift and wanted to trick around with anybody and everybody he wanted to, I no longer fought it. But I wanted a life too. I was as alive as he was. If he didn't want me someone else might.

He got into playing the California lottery. He'd been lucky a few times but the odds suck. And I hate to see a young guy chasing a score, even if there are no sure things in life.

John Patrick
* * * * *

My birth mother passed away on the morning of February 1, 1996. My sister Mary wrote me a note telling me. Nellie was 74 and was in the hospital with pneumonia. She had been in and out of institutions, slipping in and out of reality and composing religious songs of praise. She was the common-law wife of an old alcoholic coal miner named Charlie King who'd passed away twenty years ago. His sons by a previous marriage put Nellie out of the house, which they inherited. She did get his pension and spent her last days in a convalescent home in Des Moines. I hadn't seen her in nearly four decades. But I felt the sting of her death because of the biological connection. I never blamed her for the breakup of our family. She was a kindly woman–with problems.

* * * * *

At Cala Grocery Store one night the fat man behind me in line looked somewhat familiar. He recognized me and told me his name was George. He used to work for the Captain and his partner, like me. He told me that the Captain, his wife and all the old gang were dead now. I didn't know that but they were like, thirty years our senior. I remembered that George had been busted for the heist of a coin store, with a tough guy named Bernie, who looked just like Mickey Cohen the gangster. Bernie used to think everybody was a piece of shit. Word was, guys were scared of him because he'd threatened their families. He was a scary guy. He liked young Chinese boys he told me, and had a contact to get them.

* * * * *

My landlord tried to evict me since I paid lower than market- rate rent under the city rent-control law. I decided to fight back and won the court case. He had to pay me $1,225 for my car, which was vandalized and he'd towed off illegally. The eviction effort was declared wrong and unjust by the court and I was given a big rent reduction for the loss of the garage space. I'd been at the same address for over twenty years. The owner has since sold the building, which they do after they get the depreciation out of them.

* * * * *

All in all, I have been blessed. Besides boyfriends, I've had two great cats, Puss and Otis, who both lived long lives and were a real joy.
So I might let a cat take advantage of me, then ignore me, but not a boyfriend.
I trust people. Even if most try to use you, not everyone will, because I don't want to become a bitter and lonely person. And I don't worry about the

small stuff, because everything's small stuff. I've learned the sun outlasts the storm.

# *Epilogue*

Since I no longer had a lover in my life, I decided to explore what was out there and available in the gay scene in San Francisco. I was determined not to become a bitter, lonely person. I kept a cruising journal, which I never showed to anyone before. Following are the entries from the last half of 1995, an account of some pretty lewd conduct. What they demonstrate is that even these days, there are still plenty of hot guys out there, but you gotta play it safe.

### June 14: In Frenchy's Video Arcade

A mid-twenties Hispanic with bad acne approached me, inviting me to watch a movie. But I knew he was looking for money. I'd seen him before. It wasn't just the money, I wanted something hot, not mechanical. I wanted fresh meat, not a pro interested in money and in a big rush.

Checking out the arcade on Market Street, I wandered around for an hour. The place was dead, at least nothing that interested me, no young trade, only older meat beaters. As I was about to call it quits I walked past a cute Hispanic teenager with the grunge drag, baggy pants and shirt and a baseball cap turned around on his head. He was definitely my type.

When he asked me for a cigarette, I told him I didn't smoke, but would he like to watch a movie? He said he really needed a smoke. I told him I'd buy him a pack afterwards. He agreed and followed me. Then he suddenly got cold feet.

Another cruising wetback queen was on the make: cute and macho, short, around eighteen, with sparkling dark eyes. The vibes were right. He knew he'd get his chorizo sucked. I wondered if he was hard with anticipation. "Better not now. Someone might see me. I used to work here," he said. It was no problem, I tried to persuade him. I'd leave the booth first and check to see that the coast was clear.

It was too late. He'd changed his mind. I know it was because the queen had gawked at us. And I'd led him to a booth at the back. He might have ducked into a front booth with me, without incident. He was nice, said thanks anyway.

If we hadn't been eyeballed by the jealous cruiser, I'm sure I'd have had a mouthful of his creamy mecos. Alas, I didn't.

### June 15: Through A Peephole Darkly

In the Market Street straight arcade with all the videos, I noticed a short, stout man, well-dressed, sport coat and checked trousers. He was eyeballing the few customers who totally ignored him, heading into booths and locking the door. A slim, thirty something blonde went into a booth, left the door unlocked. The stout man opened the door and entered the booth. I went into

the adjoining booth with a peephole. I watched the stout man kneel and obviously mouth the guy's exposed prick, while the guy getting sucked fed a quarter at a time into the coin slot. I couldn't see well because of the angle and the flickering movie. Mostly I saw the suckee's denim jeans from the rear.

The man getting sucked off was moaning louder than the soundtrack of the video. He paused to feed another quarter at a time. In quick time he blew his wad, because of the groan. The stout man stood up and made a hasty exit out of the store. The suckee left a moment later.


June 21: Mexican Hustler

On Geary Street, where the young Latino drug dealers hang out, I spotted this young boy. He was standing alone by a grocery store. I smiled at him. I figured he was a drug dealer. The hustlers were on the meat rack over on Polk Street. I struck up a conversation with him. His name was George. He was eighteen. From Mexico. He came to the U.S. with his older brother. George didn't have a job. "Sell mota, marijuana?" I asked. "I want to buy some but got no dinero. How much?"

"Ten dollars."

"I might spot you, if I can suck your dick," I brazenly said.

"I can get twenty dollars for that. But I don't like. I got a girlfriend."

"Up to you."

"Got a place?" he asked.

I was leery. Considered an arcade but they all had big glory holes. I liked privacy. "Some other time maybe," I said.

"Uh, we can go to my place. My brother is at work. It's on Sutter Street."

Risking danger, I tagged along. In the apartment, the lights weren't turned on yet. They'd just moved in. He lit a candle.

On the couch where he slept, I groped him. He leaned back and pulled down his jeans and shorts. He had a fat, uncut dick, around seven inches. I licked it. He was skinny and hairless. I wanted to fuck him, thinking the closer to the bone the sweeter the meat. Surprised me when he didn't object. I took a condom out of my jacket pocket, threaded up. Screwed him. Came off pronto in the rubber in his tight butt.

"My turn," he said.

I took the position, spread and lifted up my legs, gave him a rubber. He jacked his rubbered dick and poked it in me. It took just a few seconds before he shot. I sucked his sweet cum out of the rubber.

I gave him the agreed-on ten bucks and walked back to Geary Street with him. I split and assumed he bought his weed.


June 25: Cinco de Mayo

I listened to a street band in Hallidie Plaza playing "La Bamba."

A young, thin Mexican standing by me at the brass railing around the BART station asked me the time.

"Eight-thirty," I said.

In English, he told me that he had to be at the shelter at Fifth and Harrison by the freeway before nine. His name was Raul, he was 21, from Durango.

I walked with him, plotting how to get some dick. I'd have to take him home, but I nixed the idea with a stranger.

He talked about how he'd fucked a young Latin girl by the freeway, three times with the same rubber.

"Do you like blowjobs?" I asked.

"Oh, si."

I was tempted to get a cheap hotel room but didn't have enough money on me. We stood across from the shelter and talked. He'd been doing day work as a painter, but was getting his pay and going back to Los Angeles tomorrow. I followed him down an alley. He stopped, pulled out his dick and pissed. He had a fat five inches of soft, uncut dick. It made my mouth water. He shook it to tease me. It hardened. I dropped to my knees and started sucking him. He came quickly. I took it all, wiped my mouth and held his cock in my mouth while I jacked myself off.

I wished him a safe trip and went on my way.


June 26: Asian Boy

In Frenchy's, I checked out the video boxes of gay male porn.

Along came a young Asian boy wearing wire-framed glasses. He eyeballed my crotch.

I was horny so I followed him into the arcade into a booth.

"I've been partying for two days," he said.

He kissed me right on the mouth. I could smell the booze.

He grabbed my crotch. I grabbed his. He had a small dick.

I was considering jacking him off.

"Can you give me a tip, like five bucks for a cab?"

I didn't have any extra money on me, so I left.


May 8: Tearoom Game

I stopped in the men's room of a department store downtown. A hot looking guy was in one of the stalls. A Latino. He nodded. I went into the next stall.

Peeking through the crack in my stall door, I noticed a middle-aged black man eyeballing the Latino. The black man was masturbating but I couldn't see his dick, only the movement of his hand. I peeked under the stall. The Latino had a smooth body and a fat, uncut dick and big nuts tucked between his legs. I reached up and felt his thigh. That startled him and he glared at me. The Latino came out of the stall. He washed his hands. The older black man stood at the urinal, jacking off for him. I still didn't see the

black dick. But the Latino was fascinated by it and not interested in me. He gave me a dirty look and left. The black man turned his back and his hand stroked his dick, with the vision blocked. He stayed at the urinal, waiting for another horny guy to play with.

July 15: Voyeur Delight

It was an unusually hot day in more ways than one. Record temperature in the mid-nineties. I checked out the crowd at Frenchy's.

The Latino janitor was mopping the place and had one side blocked off. It was stuffy inside, so I sat in a plastic chair in a booth and waited awhile. The door opened to the next booth and someone came in. I peeked through the large and obvious glory hole in the partition. The man dropped his pants and inserted a few tokens. He had smooth, muscular ebony thighs. His cock was average-sized, circumcised and black as midnight. He started jacking it fast right away. Clear pre-cum lubed the crown. I peeked up through the hole. He was a black man in his mid- twenties with long, wavy hair and a handsome face. He was oblivious to the fact or didn't care that I watched him. He was busy beating his meat to the obvious the video. He inserted a couple more tokens and whacked away at his bloated dick with a blurry hand. He came quickly, matter of just a few minutes. His nuts belched cum all over his cock. I watched while he scooped it off his corona and shaft and flung it on the opposite partition wall. Then he hiked his briefs and britches. I went outside the booth to get a closer look at him when he left. He gave me a passing glance and left the arcade right away.

Hanging around the arcade, I went into another booth, where I noticed a man in a white T-shirt was kneeling and sucking a dick through the partition on the opposite side while he jacked off. The man stood up and fed the guy in the opposite booth his dick. I could see his small, hairy butt cheeks. He kneeled and sucked the other guy some more. I stood around in the stuffy arcade, wiping the sweat off my brow. Inside came an Asian in his early twenties. Small 'stache, kind of butch looking.

Soon there entered a short Filipino around the same age with handsome features. He wore a white T-shirt and red shorts. I noticed the Asian with the 'stache enter a booth. The Filipino followed him inside, whether by pre-arrangement or chance, I was not sure. I entered the booth next to them. There was a big glory hole. Both of them stripped off their shirts and dropped their pants. Both had smooth, hard, tawny bodies. They jacked off while they felt each other's body. The mustachioed one sat down on the plastic chair and jacked his cock. It was a fat six inches. I didn't see the Filipino's dick. When the Asian stood up he leaned against the partition, with his bare butt in my face; I had to refrain from touching it–or taking a lick.

The Asian sat back down and jacked off furiously. I didn't see the cum shoot. They both hiked their pants. The taller Asian left the booth and the arcade. The Filipino cruised the arcade, looking for more dick. I don't think

he got his rocks off. The arcade was too hot, even with the fans, and I decided to take a hike.

### July 17: Glory Hole Trade

I stopped in at Frenchy's arcade. I didn't expect much but I hung around awhile. There was a lot of booth action, traffic in and out. Then a guy entered the arcade and I was awestruck. But I kept cool. He was my macho fantasy in the flesh. He checked out the wall display of videos playing on the machines while I checked him out. He was about twenty-five, medium height, muscular. He looked like a construction worker. He wore jeans and a white T-shirt. He had black hair and sparkling brown eyes. And facial hair, 'stache and goatee.

He was brazenly cruised but he didn't seem interested or pick up on the signals. I think the other cruisers took it for attitude. To me he spelled trade as clear as if it were written on his T-shirt.

I discreetly eyeballed him. He stayed nearby. I think he knew he had a cocksucker on the line. I moved around the corner by a wall of booths and waited, playing the game. Several minutes later he went into the booth across from where I was standing. Lucky for me the cruiser came out of the next booth, unaware of who'd just gone in. Inside the booth, I covertly watched him through the ample glory hole. The wall was solid on the opposite side of both our booths. He dropped several quarters into the slot, and sat in the blue plastic chair. When he unzipped his jeans, I noticed his blue briefs. He fingered his cock through the cotton. Soon, when his dick was stiff, he slid down his jeans and shorts. He had a nice fat, six-inch, cut dick. A drop of silver pre-cum hung from the piss slit. He slowly stroked his cock. I figured he was just going to beat off, unaware of or not caring if someone was watching him. But I was pretty sure he picked up on my vibes and knew I was the one in the next booth. I was going to say something, but I didn't want to scare him off in case he wasn't interested in a blowjob. I opted for sticking my finger through the hole.

He stood up. But he didn't leave. Instead he stuck his dick through the hole. It was a beauty. I licked it and it throbbed. I engulfed it in my mouth, all the way down to the hairy root, with my lips against the crude wooden hole. Kneeling on the floor and bracing my hands on the wall, I sucked his cock. I could hear the heterosexual video track, a bitch was moaning while she was getting her box banged. I was so hungry, but I decided to tease his dick. I took my mouth off and licked the shaft, below the crown, even tonguing his piss hole. His meat just throbbed. I know it sounds far-out but I didn't even remember the last dick I sucked at a glory hole, it had been so long ago, I sort of bounced on my legs like a pogo stick as I sucked away. His cock got harder and harder. And I knew I had him close to blowing his nuts. I kept the pressure on, devouring his dick. The bitch in the vid was screaming that she was cumming. He gushed, a big wad of creamy sperm, and I nursed his cock until it softened.

John Patrick

I didn't swallow the load but I savored the essence in my mouth. I watched while he stuffed his soft dick back into his blue shorts and hoisted his jeans. I glanced up at him, not sure if he noticed. He didn't say anything but left the booth and the arcade. He was a tasty treat that I had denied myself too long. But he was worth the wait.

## July 20: Big-dicked Asian

Frenchy's was very busy in the late afternoon. I noticed an Asian, who looked around thirty, but they always look much younger to me than they really are. Not that it matters, long as they're not jailbait. He was wearing a black leather jacket.

He stood near me for awhile and I eyeballed him. He walked around while I stayed still, holding up the wall, leaning against it.

Soon he went into a booth and I went into the one next to him, with glory holes on both sides.

I looked into his booth. He was standing close to the monitor. His jeans and shorts were down and he was beating his stiffer. My mouth watered: It was a fat eight inches and circumcised.

He spotted me when I looked up at him through the hole. He waited a moment, then he shoved his hard dick through the glory hole. It took up the whole width of the circle.

I examined it closely. It was superb. I jacked it and squeezed the base. Engorged, it was dark and throbbing. I played with it awhile, jerking it and blowing air on it. He took his dick back. I figured he might be interested in my meat since it was hard. So I shoved my dick through the hole. He jacked it awhile, squeezing it, making it feel good. When I withdrew, looking through the hole, I invited him into my booth. I figured I might suck his big balls. But he didn't seem to understand me. I waited with the door unlocked. Another cruiser opened it but I kept him at bay. I heard the Asian leave the booth next door. I walked around the square of booths and spotted him again. He went into another booth, and I went into the booth on the opposite side. Whether it was by mistake or not, I watched him drop his pants and jack his dick and get it stiff. It was a nice piece of meat, real suckable. To my dismay, he poked his boner through the hole on the other side. I don't know whether he was confused or the man in that booth just had his mouth at the hole. Whatever, the Asian was holding onto the mesh wire on top of the booth while he humped the hole, ramming his dick into the cock sucker's mouth. I noticed the small birthmark on the Asian's nice bubble butt.

I missed the boat. I went outside the booth and stood within viewing distance to see who the lucky cocksucker was. Soon the Asian came out. He didn't look back at me but left the arcade right away. I knew he'd blown his nuts. I hung around awhile. Eventually the cocksucker came out of the booth opposite the Asian. It was a black man I'd noticed earlier. He was the cat who got the cream. The lesson was not to change horses (or horse dicks) in the middle of the stream (or arcade booths).

Aug. 4: Arcade Watcher

It was mid-afternoon when I wandered into Frenchy's. The janitor was mopping up the piss and cum in the booths and wiping them down. He was a twenty something Hispanic with long hair, kind of chubby, likely an illegal. Half of the arcade square of booths was blocked off, so that half a dozen guys stood against the wall, waiting for a booth, while the other dozen guys were inside. Only a few red "occupied" lights were on outside, so there was hanky panky going on inside with all the glory holes between the partitions.

A Filipino in his early twenties was cruising a thirtyish Latino who wore short pants. The Latino wasn't interested in him, but he seemed interested in me, going into a booth and leaving the door ajar. But I wasn't really interested in the older Latino, who I figured just wanted to be serviced, with no reciprocation. Soon the janitor had the other side all swabbed down and open. I went over there to check it out. I noticed a balding blonde in his late thirties go into a booth. A Latino in his late twenties went into the next booth. So I went into the booth opposite the blonde. The blonde plunked some quarters into the machine and watched the video. He dropped his pants and sat down. He had a fat seven-inch dick. Through the hole, I watched him stroke it. I could see the Latino on the opposite side through the large hole rapidly beat his meat. The blonde stood up and shoved his dick through the hole and the Latino began sucking it. The blonde had a nice, smooth, fuckable butt but he wasn't really my type. I watched his pear-shaped ass undulate while he rammed his dick through the hole into the Latino's hungry mouth. He pressed his body against the partition, and he must have shot his wad. Soon he sat down in the chair and wiped the goo and slobber off his pecker.

I went outside the booth, having witnessed the suck job from the rear. The Latino came out and hungrily went into booth after booth looking for more dick to suck. The blonde looked disheveled and leaned up against the wall to take a breather. It was time for me to go. I didn't want to just get my rocks off like some guys do. I wanted a hot adventure.

Aug. 7: All-day Sucker

At Frenchy's I saw this big, macho Latino in his mid- twenties, wearing gray sweats, enter the arcade. Right away some short queen beat me to the punch in the booth next to him at the end. Going into the next booth, I watched through the glory hole. In no time flat the queen was down on his haunches sucking away on the Latino's boner. Suddenly the queen stopped and went into the Latino's booth with him. I hustled over to the booth next to them. Jeez, the Latino had a big, fat dick. He was watching a het video on the monitor, with a bitch moaning and groaning. Through the glory hole, I watched the queen grab that big Latino dick, which was oozing, and swoop down on it.

After a few minutes, the queen stood up and said something. Then the Latino sat down on the plastic chair and the fem queen sat down on the Latino's dick. The Latino thrust upwards. I watched the queen bounce around on that big dick. He was so delirious with joy that I couldn't tell if the moans were coming from the video or the live action. While humping that huge prick the queen jacked his small, uncut pecker, not a pretty sight. I guess I was jealous because I didn't get a shot at the macho stud. Eventually the Latino must have come because the fem queen hopped off his prick.

I went outside to get a better look at the Latino when he left. He was hot stuff, no doubt about it. Guess he just wanted to get his dick sucked and got to poke somebody in the bargain.

Soon I spotted a short Asian wearing a white T-shirt and short pants. His black hair was buzz cut. He had almond-shaped brown eyes, and was real cute. He was twenty- three or so. A blonde guy in his late twenties went into the booth beside the Asian. I went into the booth on the other side of the Asian. I think he was Filipino but could have been Chinese, not sure.

From the opposite booth I watched him hump the blonde's mouth. The Asian had a nice, smooth, tawny butt, eatable. The blonde sucked awhile, then left. I wondered why. Then the Asian left. A while later I noticed the Asian enter a booth. He was watching a het video so must have been trade. I went into the booth opposite him.

He dropped his short pants and briefs. He had a nice fat, cut dick, six-plus inches, truly suckable. I bent down at the hole and watched him. He stuck his hand out at the hole. Looking at his trim, tawny body, silky bush and hard dick made me horny, but there was no response from him. Suddenly it dawned on me that he wanted quarters. So I gave him several. That was the key. As long as you paid for the video time, his dick was yours. Okay, fine. He poked his dick through the hole. Now I noticed the rubber on his pecker, the ring at the base. I chomped away on his throbbing dick. Rubber or no rubber, it was a lovely, lively piece of meat. He pumped it down my throat, accelerating when he got turned on by the video action with the bitch moaning.

All too soon the video dipped to black. His hand was at the hole again. I ducked out and bought a few dollars worth of tokens. I returned to the glory hole, gave him some tokens. He fed me his dick again. For a moment I thought about the blonde cocksucker who preceded me. He must have run out of tokens or patience. Certain it was the same rubber on the Asian's dick, it was like French-kissing the blonde by proxy. The Asian's dick got stiff but he never got his rocks off. He was an all-day sucker. The rubber was thin and not too yucky tasting, and it was a joy to chomp on his prick, but I was running out of time and was short on cash. I did lick his naked nuts, but the problem was the glory hole. Although it was big, it was rough around the edges and my face was rubbed raw. Not only that, I was probably getting some of the blonde's slobbers around the hole as well. Anyway, I decided to

go. Maybe I'd see the Asian again and rent a video for him to watch while I played the skin flute accompaniment.

### Aug. 8: Arcade Dance

I was beginning to recognize some of the regular afternoon cruisers at Frenchy's. Some real cock hounds, like myself.

For instance, the thirtyish balding blonde with a slim build and fat cock, which I'd seen him play with and feed a cocksucker on the opposite side of the booth the other day. The same blonde talked to a short black man in his early twenties. He led him to a booth. I went into the booth next to them. The black man was watching a het video. The blonde took out the black man's dick, which was like a polished ebony shaft, around seven inches, jutting out from kinky pubes. The blonde jacked the dick, then sat on the chair, giving me a bird's-eye view. He slowly began sucking the black dick, but something happened, the black man hoisted his jeans. Whether it was to get money or tokens for the machine, the blonde left the booth before getting the black off. The black sat down on the chair and fondled his dick in his pants. When he noticed me watching, he stuffed his sweat shirt into the hole. I left the booth. A good-looking Latino entered the booth I'd been in. I heard the black yell at him for poking the sweat shirt out of the hole, and the Latino left. Going on the other side of the arcade, I spotted a sharp-looking blonde around twenty-five. Dressed nicely, macho; I figured him for trade. He went into a booth. I went into the booth next to him.

Standing up, the blonde dropped his slacks and shorts. He had a nice fat seven-inch, cut dick. He jacked it and got it hard. Noticing me watching him, he poked his dick through the hole. I fondled it. He took it out and poked his fingers into the hole. I had a boner, so shoved it through the hole. He stroked it and took a couple wet slides on it. Then he stopped. I watched while he arranged his clothes and left. Maybe he was mad because I hadn't sucked on his dick.

Wandering around the arcade, I noticed the blonde on the other side. I went into a booth. He went into the booth next to me, but his slacks were against the hole in the wall, showing his shapely butt. When I saw light, I noticed there was another guy in the booth with him, a real troll. But the blonde was sucking the old man's stubby dick and the old man sucked on the blonde's dick. I don't know if the blonde got his nut but he left the booth. Leaving my booth, I noticed the blonde exit the arcade. The troll came out of the booth and eyeballed the other passersby. I decided to call it a day.

### Aug. 15: Big Black Stud

In the arcade I watched a tall, thin man with beard stubble, in his late twenties, go into a booth. He left the door open for a hot-looking short Latino with a leather vest who was standing across the aisle.

From the next booth, I watched the action through the hole. Actually the view was from between the legs of the suckee, while the Latino kneeled

down and chomped on the other man's meat. The Latino had his own pants down but his shorts covered the view of his meat. His steel-toed boots were visible so I knew he was the cocksucker, with the limited view. If he was bare-butt I could have smelled his ass and watched his butt cheeks flex as he humped the cocksucker on his knees. Eventually the Latino discovered that his performance was being watched so he stuffed something in the hole to block the view. I left the booth but a tall, thin Chinese entered and stayed in the booth, with no red light outside when the video played. Maybe he could see around the hole stopper. Wandering around, I noticed an elderly man enter a booth. He had to be way over seventy. I figured he could be straight and just watching a video. He looked too old to get it up. But old-timers can fool you sometimes, I'd heard. He left the door ajar. Maybe he forgot to close it. A while later I saw a thin black man in his late twenties stop at the old-timer's booth. He stepped inside, by invitation I heard.

So I went into the next booth to watch through the hole. The black dropped his pants. He had a big cut dick, with a studded cockring around the base. The old-timer wasted no time going to town. He sucked on the black dick like it was a stick of licorice. Neither was aware that they were being watched, or cared. The old-timer sucked away for several minutes but the black dick didn't get really hard or shoot off. The black left the booth and walked around. A moment later he went into a booth with another white man. The booth was next to a preview booth, without a hole to watch through. The old-timer left the arcade. The black man came out several minutes later and stood around, looking for another cocksucker. I'd clocked in over an hour and decided it was time to go. All I got was eye candy.

### Aug. 24: Marathon Suck

Stopping in Frenchy's arcade, I noticed among the cruisers a guy who looked like Lyle Menendez from the murder trial, wearing short pants. I stood around, holding up the wall. Later, by chance, I went into a booth. I gazed through the glory hole. There was the twenty something Lyle look-alike, and boy, was he busy.

Stretched out on a plastic chair with his pants down and his shirt off was a dark, hairy man in his mid-twenties wearing wire-framed eyeglasses. His body was not buffed but not bad. His dick was only average size, cut and hard. The Lyle double was jacking the dick and twisting his hand on the shaft while he sucked on the knob. He stopped sucking. I bent over and looked through the hole. The two guys were sucking face like mad. Then the Lyle double went back to jacking and sucking the hairy man's meat. I watched them go at it, the blowjob and the sloppy kissing. It was hot in the booth, so I went out into the arcade where there were a couple overhead fans stirring up the piss-and-cum-smelly air. Later I went into the booth on the opposite side, with the glory hole. The Lyle look-alike and the hairy guy were still going at it. From the other side, I got a bird's-eye view. The hairy man stood up and the Lyle double chowed down on his meat. Then the Lyle

look-alike sucked on the hairy man's tits. The hairy man rubbed his cock sucker's chest under his shirt. Then they sucked face some more.

I'd never seen two guys kissing in a booth before. These two were having a ball, oblivious to whoever was watching. I could see a black man looking through the hole on the other side, watching the action. Better than anything I saw on the vids. Alas, I had some errands to attend to before the places closed, so I gave up my seat for the live show. Besides, I didn't think the hairy guy was ever going to get his rocks off.

### Aug. 25: Latino Stud

After stalking the arcade in Frenchy's for three months in the afternoon, I found what I'd been looking for, my type of macho Latino in his mid-twenties. He was checking out the videos. I watched him from afar. I didn't really think I had a shot at him. Figured he was looking for a booth without glory holes, like some straight guys do, so they can beat their meat without being watched and are not interested in sex with another man, even getting head through a glory hole. In the arcade shuffle, I lost track of the Latino. Just when I was about to lose interest in the chase, I spotted him in a booth with the door slightly ajar. Some guys didn't latch the doors.

Certain it was the Latino, I cracked open the door. He didn't say anything. The video wasn't playing, he either didn't have time to do it or was out of coins. Staring at his basket, I stepped inside. He didn't make any attempt to stop me. Brazenly, I groped his blue denim jeans. He was a looker. Trim 'stashe. Short black hair in a military cut and round brown eyes. Smooth olive skin. He didn't flinch or protest. His cock was like a crowbar. I unbuckled his jeans and zipped open his fly. He let me. His cock was hard, fat, uncut, a solid seven inches. Squatting on my knees, I began the suck job. I started with his hairy balls. They were sweaty. The scent and taste of them drove me wild. I stuffed them into my mouth and sucked on them. Looking up, I noticed he was watching me. I didn't even think about dumping coins into the video machine for him. I was so busy, lost in servicing his beautiful dick. I gobbled him up and he moaned. It was juicy and rock-hard. Succulent, to say the least. He got into action and rubbed his fingers through my hair. Clasping his hands on my head, he bobbed my head up and down on his dick. I didn't want him to blow right away, so I backed off. I swabbed the spongy, pink crown. He clasped his dick and smeared the pre-goo on my lips and cheeks.

I tugged down his jeans and squeezed his smooth, muscular bubble butt while I serviced him. That gave me a roaring hard-on. He was lost in lust and didn't stop me. His balls were heaving, full of cum I was sure. He began to mouth-fuck me. I swallowed his cock down to the base. He fucked my face. Suddenly his cock was steely-hard and I knew it would blow. He was panting and crammed his cock down my throat and blasted off, flooding my mouth with his thick, sweet cream. He held back his foreskin. After he got his rocks off, I let go of his dick. The cock head was sensitive and he jumped

when I swabbed it and sucked on it. Standing up, with my own cock stiff, I realized that he was straight, with no reciprocation, and that was okay. I could whack off later, savoring the delicious details. Looking into his coffee-colored eyes, he was friendly, and I wanted to know something about him. His English was broken but I knew enough Spanish to talk to him. His name was Jose and he was saving up to go back to Mexico where his girlfriend was waiting for him. He was a hunk and I told him he was guapo and he smiled.

I told him that I'd like to see him again, that I came to the arcade in the afternoons. He nodded. Looking at his watch, he told me that he had to go to work. Guess he'd just stopped in the arcade to watch a vid and get some quick relief, which I had gladly provided.

Aug. 26: Homeless Boy Jack-off

The cruisers at Frenchy's were going in and out of booths, some were looking for quarters or tokens in coin return slots instead of looking through the glory holes.

Coming into the arcade was a young Latino wearing sun- glasses. He looked kind of scroungy. Showered and with clean clothes, he'd have been a good-looking kid.

He went into a booth without glory holes in the sides. So I went into the booth next to him, knowing there was a small, unnoticeable peephole. Staring through the tiny hole, I had a bird's-eye view of the young Latino. He dumped several coins into the slot and sat down in the plastic chair. He was totally oblivious to me I was sure.

In no time he tugged down his jeans and shorts and fondled his soft dick. I could hear the moaning of the woman in the video getting poked. When the Latino's dick got hard, I got a perfect view of it in the light from the monitor. Fat, six inches with a foreskin and pink crown. Nice stiff prick, the kind I could do wonders for. Whether he was turned on or afraid he'd run out of coins and time on the machine before he got his nut, he really pumped his prick fast and hard. Watching him stroke that randy fucker made my balls tingle and my own dick stiffen. It wasn't long before he was ready to blow. I wanted to see that young dick shoot off. However, he stood up for the cum shot and was out of view except for his hand pumping away at an angle. Suddenly it was all over, and he was stuffing his dick back into his jeans. I left the booth so I could get into his booth before somebody else did. Entering the booth, the scene of the young Latino's jack off session, I inhaled his sex, the manly aroma of sweat and cum. On the floor were the clear drops of cum from his dick. I was tempted to scoop it up and sniff it but I didn't because the floor was so filthy.

I left the arcade after him. At the corner, I spotted him at the homeless shelter, waiting to get inside to crash. Sad story. Such a young, macho stud deserved better than to be homeless.

## Aug. 29: Latino Jackeroo

In Frenchy's arcade, I saw a tall Latino walk in. I'd seen him before. He went into a booth and the red light came on. I went into the booth next to him. No glory hole but a tiny peephole at just the right spot. The tall Latino dropped coins into the slot. He took off his baseball cap and jacket, wearing only a white T-shirt. He settled down in the plastic chair and unbuttoned his jeans. He fondled his cock and in no time he had a full-fledged hard-on. His cock had a thin cowl of foreskin. It was long and fat, a solid eight inches. Kneeling to get a better view, I watched the tall Latino abuse and amuse himself. He jacked with his left hand, jerked it fast at times, at other times merely rubbed it over the crown slowly. All the while he fondled his big balls. He continued to slowly masturbate, then beat it fast at the good spots in the video, no doubt. He stopped only to get more coins out of his jacket pocket. He'd switch hands and jack-off with his right hand, jerking it real hard. Then he switched back to his left paw, which he favored. Peeking upwards, I got a good look at his face, contorted and intense. He was smooth-faced and bronze-skinned. His hair was thick, jet black and disheveled. But my attention was soon riveted back to his dick and watching him beat his meat. At one point I thought he spotted me watching him through the peephole because he suddenly stood up. Standing at an angle, he whipped his dick wildly, but I didn't get to see the shoot because the angle wasn't right. All I could see was his hand pumping away. Then he buttoned up his fly.

I wanted to go into the booth and smell his essence. Standing up, my knees and legs were stiff, so was my dick. Outside I waited for him to leave. He did, but another man made a beeline inside the booth to check out the evidence of the jack-off session.

## Nov. 10: Meat beater

In the downtown arcade on Market Street I spotted a Latino around nineteen, macho looking, black hair and brown eyes, short but muscular build. He went into a booth. I was hot on his tail. He gave me a glance but locked the door. What a waste. Some guys prefer to just beat it. Trade often doesn't pick up on the vibes and signals of a cruiser. When the Latino left, and, around ten minutes later, I checked out the booth. Gooey cum drops on the floor and a Kleenex. The booth reeked of sex, musky. I'd heard of guys who lapped cum off the floor but that was too dirty for my style. Boy, I'd sure have liked to drink his load from the fountain, which I imagined was a fat, juicy, uncut Latino dick. Later I noticed a booth door open. A thirtyish guy with hairy thighs and a six-inch fat prick at attention. He stroked it slowly, trying to attract a cocksucker. But he looked kind of scroungy and I have to like the face as well as the dick to get aroused. But I watched him stroke it for a few seconds. Other guys passed the open door but they were not interested, just straight guys looking for a booth.

In a while the attendant, who checked the coin return slots for quarters, saw the man and told him to drop a quarter. When he didn't, the old man screamed for the security, a fortyish black, and they gave the man the bum's rush.

No one interesting around, so I split.

### Nov. 11: Grunge Blowjob

I checked out Frenchy's, with the glory holes on each side of the booth walls. Watched a guy around twenty-three in grunge drag with a baseball cap turned around on his head. He sucked off a thirtyish man wearing a white shirt and tie. I'd seen them going to the adjoining booths, and I watched from the end booth. The grunge-drag guy sucked the other guy and jacked his own fat dick at the same time. He left, and his jaws must have been tired after several minutes of sucking. The suckee watched a video and threaded a condom on his cock to catch his load. Soon the arcade was humming with cruisers, some faces I knew, guys on the prowl, real hungry for dick.

I ventured downtown to the big arcade on Market Street with the live girlie booths with a ten-dollar minimum to enter and signs in English and Spanish to not touch the women. A tall number was standing outside a booth watching a video someone left playing time on. I cruised him. He was around twenty-five, wearing gray sweats and fondling himself through them. I brazenly looked on. On the other side of the arcade I watched a guy with a knapsack, early twenties. He went into a booth where there was a tiny, unnoticeable peephole, at the exact level of the plastic chair, in the wall between the booths. He was brunet and blue-eyed, macho-looking. His cock was a fat eight-incher. I ogled it through the tiny hole while he worked it, stopping only to feed more quarters one at a time, probably on a tight budget. His cock was cut and hard. He finally blew his wad and wiped it with a white paper napkin.

### Dec. 6: Latino Bodybuilder Hustler

In Frenchy's the temperature was in the 80's. All those blowers around, and the place was still hot. I noticed a Latino stud in his mid-twenties. He wore a blue athletic shirt and his muscles bulged. He disappeared into a booth and I lost track of him. Later, I noticed the same Latino come in again. Soon I got a peek at him coming out of a booth pronto. There was an older man in the booth with him, a Latino. So I figured he might prefer to go with only his race. I eyeballed him. His trim stache was sexy. He was good looking in a rugged way, nice bulge in his jeans. He entered a booth next to me. Another cruiser cut me off, but the Latino gave him the take a hike sign. He nodded when I stood at his door.

I entered the booth. I groped him. There was a het vid playing on the monitor. I dumped in some coins to keep it going. I was a bit surprised when he asked me for some money. Hell, I thought, I could spare a few bucks. When I offered him a ten-spot, he chuckled, said that wasn't much. Well,

that was all I was willing to invest. I knew that was the going rate for arcade hustlers, even in the '90s. There was plenty of free head, whatever, available with all the glory holes. The Latino said it was okay. He liked to jack-off, just touch. I felt his arms, like steel. I hiked up his shirt over his head. His body was to die for, smooth and bronze, solid muscle. He wasn't so big in the dick department, and he was cut. His dick was thick but only average length, but it was steely, like his body. While he beat off I watched. His dick was dark and oozed lots of clear pre-cum. I got the stats on him. Name was Jose. To my surprise, he was twenty-eight, from Mexico, Guanaiuato. His English was broken but he understood my broken Spanish. I slipped him the Alexander Hamilton and he put it in his jeans. He wore black bikini briefs.

He invited me to take out my dick, saying it was for me, I was paying. I jacked his dick, then he jacked it. I asked him to jack mine but he said that's not macho. Okay, no big deal. I got off more on touching the sheen of sweat on his bronze chest than I did on his dick. I should have licked it. He wasn't going to shoot a load. Neither was I, I decided. Although my balls were cum-laden. He mentioned that he'd cum earlier. That made me glad that I didn't empty my pockets for his spent prick, hard, but no cum to spill. I copped a last feel. He poked his pecker back in his pants. I told him he could stay in the booth and watch the rest of the video if he liked. Then I split.

Dec. 15: The Cum Shot

I prowled around Frenchy's for three hours. I saw several cruisers, even got scoped out myself, but I didn't see anybody to my liking. Setting an eight o'clock deadline to go, I took a final look-see. Some of the regular cruisers I saw there all the time had sucked their fill and left. I was still hanging out, with a case of blue balls. Just before I left I checked out a booth at the rear. The red light was on outside the last booth. I didn't see the occupant enter. The arcade was nearly empty.

Sitting down in the chair, I looked through the hole in the wall to the other side. I heard a het video playing, with a gal moaning. What I saw was one of the hottest looking twentyish Latino studs ever, and he had his pants down and his dick in hand, slowly stroking. His dick was only about six inches but hard, jutting out from his black bush. It was circumcised. His thighs were hairy and sexy.

Suddenly his cock just gushed, spurting four or five volleys of hot cum that landed on the floor. I was caught totally by surprise. He looked at me as he shot, his dark Spanish eyes cloudy. He had a handsome, masculine face, with just a little stubble, which added to his sexy look. I'd have sucked his dick gladly, but he was finished and ready to go. He hiked up his boxer shorts and jeans and split. I was so shook up that I'd missed the chance to service him that I didn't even go into the booth to smell his essence and look at his spilled seed. Alas, it was not meant to be. But the image wouldn't go to waste. Later, I would remember him in my fantasies.

John Patrick

Dec. 18: Reno Getaway

The peep show scene at Frenchy's can be boring, standing around for hours, same shit, different day. When a wacko poured acid on a couple hard dicks sticking through glory holes it was time to give it a rest. Besides they closed down most of the arcade for renovation.

My old friend Jimmy came from Reno for a visit. It was his birthday, a perennial 39 like Jack Benny. He was born in San Francisco but moved to Reno nineteen years ago. His passion for poker kept him at the Cal-Neva Lodge for days on end and he finally stayed. It worked out well, however: He got a gig in a casino and met a Chinese boyfriend who can handle his ass.

Celebrating with a big steak dinner and wine at Original Joe's we ventured to a theater to see a live meatpacker show with boys jacking off.

There was a tall, muscular kid wearing a cowboy hat, boots and jockstrap. He gyrated to the music tape and stripped off the jockstrap. He looked more like frontier sissy but he tried to please the small crowd, wandering among them and waving his fat, uncut wang, letting dirty old men cop feels and stuff dollar bills into his boots. He jerked his prick a lot but didn't shoot off.

Next up was a thirty something bodybuilder, short and swarthy, who oiled up and posed on stage. He had a stubby pecker which he jacked while the music played. He flexed his biceps and tugged on his love muscle. Craning my neck, I watched his face contort while he pumped away. Eventually he squirted but there were only a few drops. When the lights went out an old black man wearing a bandana ambled onto the stage and wiped up the slime so another jackeroo wouldn't take a spill I guess.

The third set was worth waiting for. A twentyish baby faced Filipino wearing orange nylon running shorts came onto the stage. He had buzz cut black hair, almond-shaped brown eyes and a natural, smooth, tawny body which aroused me. "Mony Mony" blasted through the speakers and he danced around. Alas, a silver-haired gent in the front row by the stage began tucking dead presidents into the boy's running shorts. No dummy, the boy strutted his stuff in the man's face. Like a private show, he ignored the crowd and gave his admirer his money's worth. He even pulled down his flimsy shorts and flashed the man his plump weenie as the spotlight faded.

Jimmy and I stopped at a quiet Polk Street bar for a nightcap. We reminisced. He had a hot flashback about the young soldier coming back from Korea (my brother-in-law's cousin) who'd been down on him all night long. We talked about old times and the baths. He informed me that the baths were still open in Reno.

I was surprised. After all, Snoopy Silverman, the health director in San Francisco, had closed them all down with the AIDS crisis. With his encouragement, I decided to go see for myself. I could get away for an overnighter. I hadn't been to Reno for nearly six years.

The next day I took the bus to Reno with Jimmy. The trip itself was a good change. Crossing the majestic Sierra Mountains, which were a winter

wonderland with snow falling, the bus descended from the Donner summit into the Reno valley. The skyline had changed with the MGM Grand and the new Silver Legacy casino. Garish neon lights lit up the sky.

Jimmy went back to his cashier gig at the Hilton and I checked into the Reno tubs, located near West Virginia Street downtown where the neon arc across the street proclaims "The Biggest Little City in the World."

There were small cubbyhole rooms upstairs. Downstairs there was a wet steam room, sauna and small pool.

I wandered into the empty wet steam room and sat down on the bleachers. The steam rose. A bald man entered the room and sat below me. He reached up and groped me. I got a boner. I was hoping for some head but he just jacked my dick. The gray haze was thick and made me sweat profusely. When the steam subsided, the bald man had disappeared.

I went into the sauna. There were two guys in their thirties who were copping feels. I scooted over by them and dropped my towel but they were interested only in each other and left the room together, to continue their party in a more private place.

Strolling into the showers, I noticed a hairy older man was standing under the spray of water and lustily eyeballing me. He wasn't my type but I was pretty horny. While the water cascaded down my body, he grabbed a bar of soap and lathered me up, spending a lot of time washing my genitals. I got a roaring hard-on and rinsed off. The man bent over and took a couple of slides.

"Let's go to my room, baby," he said huskily.

I dried off and cinched the towel around my waist as did the older man. I trailed him upstairs to his room. I figured he'd give me a blowjob.

He sprawled out on the thin mattress on the wooden rack and pulled me on top of him. He stuck his fingers in my crack and poked my shitter. But I didn't want him to fuck me. He was pretty old and his dick was withered, although he had big balls. I wanted some head. I waved my dick in his face and smeared the oozing goo onto his lips.

"Do it, baby. Dump on me. Shit on my chest!"

"Oh wow, man. Ain't my scene. Can't do that."

"I bet your shit tastes like peanut butter. Give it up, baby." Realizing that he was serious, I knew it was time to go. In my whole life no one had ever wanted my waste.

"Gotta go, man."

I went to my room and closed the door, in case he followed me. I listened to the loud rock music blasting on the stereo speakers, since there was no top on the rooms, like the Tijuana jail.

Later, I opened the door and watched the few passersby. A twenty something short blonde stopped to take a gander inside. He looked like fresh meat. I motioned him inside and he entered. He pulled off his towel and I saw his dick, which was average size but suckable.

But it got only semi-hard. He grabbed my dick and examined it, then slid a rubber on it. Before I knew it he straddled my legs, reached back and guided my stiff prick right up his butt hole. He rode the peg, bouncing up and down on my dick, rolling his head from side to side and moaning.

I pinched his pointy tits and he sighed, I thrust up into his guts and blasted my hot load into the condom embedded in him. He hopped off my dick and left without saying a word.

Listening to the music, I snoozed awhile.

I met Jimmy when he got off work and we ate breakfast in the casino restaurant. He listened to the blow-by-blow account I gave him of my trip to the tubs. When I mentioned the scat man he laughed like a hyena. I didn't think it was so funny.

The next afternoon I checked into the baths again. The place was practically deserted. I splashed around in the small pool. I took a steam bath, sat in the sauna, then took a shower.

I figured it was the down time for the baths, like the wee hours in casinos, just the grinder gamblers. But no one was interested in my charms. I went to my room, thinking that I could always take advantage of myself before leaving. I lay on the rack on my belly with my butt exposed.

An old-timer passed by and gawked, then kept going. If anyone was alive he was my type. I was in terrible heat.

A short, muscular, mustached Latino in his late twenties peeked into my room. Ah, he was exactly my cup of tea. I motioned him inside. No, I snared him in like a spider gets a fly in his web. I stripped off his towel. He was perfect. Nice, fat, uncut cock. I gobbled it up. He rubbed my hair. He grabbed my butt cheeks.

"Wanna fuck me, hombre?" I asked.

He gave me the answer when he poked his finger into my bunghole. I found a condom and suited up his seven-inch drooling dick.

He crawled between my legs and I held them up. Looking into his smoldering eyes in the dark room, my butt hole twitched.

He shoved his hard pecker up my ass and I let out a scream. He went right to town humping my butt, with his balls slapping wildly against my cheeks.

"Yeah, chinga mi culo, stud."

He jackhammered my ass. Hot, sweaty and breathing heavy.

"Do it, bastardo. Tu mecos!"

His cock was incredibly hard, and he stroked my hole lustily.

Suddenly and without warning, I let out a cry which startled him. The deep prostate massage made me flush my nuts and I sprayed my wad all over the place. That excited him and he plowed my butt faster, gushing his hot load deep inside me. He collapsed on top of me until his cock softened and fell out.

I slid the condom off his softening dick. While he watched bug-eyed, I turned it upside down and drank his spicy ball juice. I kissed his soft prick with the head in the hood. He had a shit-eating grin on his face when he left.

I got dressed and checked out. It was time to catch my bus back to the city by the bay. I'd lost my ass in Reno but not in the casinos.

On the trip back across the Sierras, with snowflakes falling and the spectacular flocked trees, the vision of the blonde boy and the Latino stud danced in my head and put me in the holiday spirit.

Well, you get the idea. My journal continues, of course, and will, as long as I am able. For me, the thrill of the chase is heightened by the knowledge that I can record it all and enjoy it again and again, making it last.

As the poet Bernard Noel said, "Eroticism is the art of making last in the body that which merely made it tremble."

"I'm a father, lover, doctor. I'm all that. I'm going out every goddamn night, hustlin', suckin' dick. All I asked of them was complete loyalty and trust ... I have set times of the day you eat breakfast, you eat lunch, you eat dinner. How hard is that? You eat at those times, or you don't eat at all."
- Alex, a pimp in the Montrose section of Houston, as reported by Rolling Stone

\* \* \* \* \*

"I'm bisexual–you buy me, I'm sexual."
– Streetboy found in the Montrose section of Houston,
quoted in Rolling Stone

# Contributors

(Other than the Editor, John Patrick)

*"Wait Until Dark" and "One Leg"*
Ken Anderson
The Intense Lover, a book of Ken's poetry, was published by STARbooks earlier this year. The author lives in Georgia and is currently finishing a novel.

*"Seeing Stars"*
Mark Anderson
Retired from Ford Motor Co., the author is active with Toronto's Suicide Hot Line, and vacations often in Palm Springs, where he is occasionally inspired to write erotica for STARbooks.

*"Rendezvous"*
Antler
The poet lives in Milwaukee when not traveling to perform his poems or wildernessing. His epic poem Factory was published by City Lights. His collection of poems Last Words was published by Ballantine. Winner of the Whitman Award from the Walt Whitman Society of Camden, New Jersey, and the Witter Bynner prize from the Academy and Institute of Arts & Letters in New York, his poetry has appeared in many periodicals (including Utne Reader, Whole Earth Review and American Poetry Review) and anthologies (including Gay Roots, Erotic by Nature, and Gay and Lesbian Poetry of Our Time).

*"Love for Sale" and "The Hustler's Ball"*
James S. Arthurs
The poet lives in Fairfield, Connecticut. These poems originally appeared in the New York-based literary journal, Our Lives.

*"A Rocky Road"*
Edward Bangor
The author, an Englishman, is a frequent contributor to the anthologies of Acolyte Press. Under the name of Head banger, he contributed a piece for the fourth issue of the American gay comic book Cherubino.

*"Angel of Mercy"*
Kevin Bantan
The author lives in Ohio.

John Patrick
"*Barrio Boy*"
*Michael Bates*
The author, who lives in Seattle, has had numerous stories published in erotic magazines and a half dozen in Leyland Publications' True Gay Encounters series.

"*Pokey*"
*Greg Bowden*
The author, who lives in California, has contributed many stories to gay magazines.

"*The Real Thing*"
*Frank Brooks*
The author is a regular contributor to gay magazines. In addition to boys and writing, his passions are figure drawing from the live model and mountain hiking.

"*Runaways*"
*Leo Cardini*
Author of the best-selling book, Mineshaft Nights, Mr. Cardini's stories and theater-related articles have appeared in a variety of magazines. He is the co-author of a musical now being fine-tuned for Broadway.

"*Love for Sale*" and "*Mouting Mikey*"
*William Cozad*
The author is a regular contributor to gay magazines. His memoirs began in Lover Boys and conclude in this volume.

"*The Good Hustler*"
*Keith Davis*
The author resides in New York and has contributed many stories to gay sex magazines.

"*The Ski Bum*"
*Jarred Goodall*
When he is not accepting sabbatical appointments abroad, the author teaches English in a Midwestern university. Born in Wisconsin, he loves back-packing, mountain-climbing, chess and Victorian literature. His favorite color: blue-green; favorite pop-star: Leonard Bernstein; favorite car: WWII Jeep; favorite drink: water, preferably recycled; favorite actor: River Phoenix (alas); favorite hobby: "If you want to know that, read my stories."

*"A Hard Night in Georgia"*
*Thomas C. Humphrey*
The author, who resides in Florida, is working on his first novel, All the Difference, and has contributed stories to First Hand publications.

*"Dreams in the Night"*
*Bert McKenzie*
A free lance writer and drama critic, the Kansan writes a column for a major Midwestern newspaper and has contributed erotic fiction to magazines such as Torso, Mandate, and Playguy. He is a frequent contributor to STARbooks' anthologies and an anthology of his work was published by Badboy, Fringe Benefits.

*"Warm Nights on Tobacco Road"*
*Edmund Miller*
Dr. Miller, a professor of English, is author of numerous stories in gay male magazines and of the legendary poetry book, Fucking Animals. He is at work on a new collection of his poems.

*"All in a Night's Work"*
*Jesse Monteagudo*
The author is a regular columnist for The Weekly News in Miami and is noted for his non-fiction writing, including a passage in John Preston's highly-acclaimed Hometowns.

*"Street Scene"*
*Thom Nickels*
The Cliffs of Aries, the author's first novel, was published in 1988 by Aegina Press. His second book, Two Novellas: Walking Water & After All This, was published in 1989 by Banned Books.
A collection of his work, The Boy on the Bicycle, was published to great acclaim by STARbooks.

*"Diamond Stud Puppy"*
*Dan Veen*
The author's first stories were based on his experiences as a hustler in San Francisco and New Orleans. He has written erotic fiction for Honcho, Mandate, Playguy, Torso, Inches, and First Hand magazines. He writes regular film articles and erotic video reviews for Honcho under the name of V.C. Rand. He has a PhD. in English Literature and Germanic Languages.

John Patrick
  *"Carnival Nights"*
  *P. K. Warren*
  The writer is currently "on retreat," courtesy of the State of New York. A graphic story about what goes on where he is now living will be in an upcoming STARbooks anthology.

  *"A Real Handful"*
  *James Wilton*
  The author, who resides in Connecticut, has contributed stories to various gay magazines. The stories in this collection were written especially for STARbooks Press.

  *"Just Another Night in Finsbury Park"*
  *Ian Young*
  The famed writer and critic's latest book is The Stonewall Experiment, an utterly politically incorrect take on how we got from Stonewall to AIDS in just 12 years. He is also finishing a third volume in his Male Muse gay poetry series. He lives in Toronto and writes a regular book review column for Torso magazine.

# About the Editor

JOHN PATRICK was a prolific, prize-winning author of fiction and non-fiction. One of his short stories, "The Well," was honored by PEN American Center as one of the best of 1987. With writing and editing over 60 novels and anthologies, his over-the-top style continues to gain him new fans every day. One of his most famous short stories appears in the Badboy collection Southern Comfort and another appears in the collection The Mammoth Book of Gay Short Stories.

A divorced father of two, the author was a longtime member of the American Booksellers Association, the Publishing Triangle, the Florida Publishers' Association, American Civil Liberties Union, and the Adult Video Association. He lived in Florida, where he passed away on October 31, 2001.

# Books by John Patrick

## Non-Fiction

A Charmed Life: Vince Cobretti
Lowe Down: Tim Lowe
The Best of the Superstars 1990
The Best of the Superstars 1991
The Best of the Superstars 1992
The Best of the Superstars 1993
The Best of the Superstars 1994
The Best of the Superstars 1995
The Best of the Superstars 1996
The Best of the Superstars 1997
The Best of the Superstars 1998
The Best of the Superstars 1999
The Best of the Superstars 2000
The Best of the Superstars 2001
The Best of the Superstars 2002
What Went Wrong?
When Boys Are Bad
& Sex Goes Wrong
Legends: The World's Sexiest
Men, Vols. 1 & 2
Legends (Third Edition)
Tarnished Angels (Ed.)

## Fiction

Billy & David: A Deadly Minuet
The Bigger They Are...
The Younger They Are...
The Harder They Are...
Angel: The Complete Trilogy
Angel II: Stacy's Story
Angel: The Complete Quintet
A Natural Beauty (Editor)
The Kid (with Joe Leslie)
HUGE (Editor)
Strip: He Danced Alone
The Boys of Spring
Big Boys/Little Lies (Editor)
Boy Toy
Seduced (Editor)
Insatiable/Unforgettable (Editor)
Heartthrobs
Runaways/Kid Stuff (Editor)
Dangerous Boys/Rent Boys (Editor)
Barely Legal (Editor)
Country Boys/City Boys (Editor)
My Three Boys (Editor)
Mad About the Boys (Editor)
Lover Boys (Editor)
In the BOY ZONE (Editor)
Boys of the Night (Editor)
Secret Passions (Editor)
Beautiful Boys (Editor)
Juniors (Editor)
Come Again (Editor)
Smooth 'N' Sassy (Editor)
Intimate Strangers (Editor)
Naughty By Nature (Editor)
Dreamboys (Editor)
Raw Recruits (Editor)
Play Hard, Score Big (Editor)
Sweet Temptations (Editor)
Pleasures of the Flesh (Editor)
Juniors 2 (Editor)
Fresh 'N' Frisky (Editor)
Taboo! (Editor)
Heatwave (Editor)
Boys on the Prowl (Editor)
Huge 2 (Editor)
Fever! (Editor)
Any Boy Can (Editor)
Virgins No More (Editor)
Seduced 2 (Co-Editor)
Wild 'N' Willing (Co-Editor)

the park. He was wearing these really tight jeans, so tight you c
ng any underwear. "Excuse me," I said, having a hard time lookir
ed by that bulge in his crotch, "but don't I know you?" "Maybe,"
of te ⋯ bout a r
Ra⋯ ⋯od, yo
er? ⋯ in?" he
"⋯ stronge
ody ⋯ e on Gre
he ⋯ I ever s
to t ⋯ ny idea
ing ⋯ e same
oul ⋯ ery long
rac ⋯ ne swel
with ⋯ e in stor
go ⋯ behind
ee ⋯ in publ
he ⋯ vent to t
cy. ⋯ grabbed
I. I ⋯
aci ⋯ fir
, ha ⋯
m ⋯ dic
g, ⋯ cock,
und of unzipping ruled the small space. I don't know who's hat
before I knew it, I had his rod in my hand, and mine was in his.